CODE EZRA

GAY COURTER

CODE EZRA

1986
HOUGHTON MIFFLIN COMPANY BOSTON

Library of Congress Cataloging in Publication Data

Courter, Gay.
Code Ezra.
I. Title.
PS3553.086185C63   1986   813'.54   85-27339
ISBN 0-395-36438-8

Printed in the United States of America

P 10 9 8 7 6 5 4 3 2 1

The quotation on page 271 is from *Madeline* by Ludwig Bemelmans. Copyright 1939 by
Ludwig Bemelmans. Copyright renewed © 1967 by Madeleine Bemelmans and Barbara
Bemelmans Marciano. Reprinted by permission of Viking Penguin, Inc. The passages from
Allison's thesis on pages 545–549 are based on material contained in pages 236–238 of the
Diagnostic and Statistical Manual of Mental Disorders (Third Edition). Washington, D.C.:
American Psychiatric Association, 1980. Used by permission.

For those who have taken
such good care of me:

Philip, Blake, and Joshua Courter
Elsie and Leonard Weisman
Donald Cutler
and
Raphael Elan

EZRA = HELP

AUTHOR'S NOTE

Make no mistake, this is a work of fiction. Interlaced among the actual events and historical figures are my imaginary characters. Although I am devoted to maintaining authenticity of mood, detail, time, and place, in several instances I have been willing — for the story's sake — to manipulate facts to suit plot considerations.

Curiously, while diligently attempting to establish a date or definitive interpretation of an event, I was often faced with conflicting data in works of nonfiction by highly placed journalists and authorities. Frustrated by the inability to be accurate, I made choices based on the exigencies of the novel.

Then, while working in Israel, I was taken to the home of a former head of the Mossad, Israel's secret service, and it was here I was able to reconcile my tamperings with history.

I had asked him whether, in light of his experiences, he would consider certain actions by my characters outlandish or unreasonable.

"Not really," he said. "If I believed an idea might be viable, I could try it — I could try *anything*. The possibilities had no boundaries. You see, I had the second most creative job in the world." He paused dramatically. "But you, *you* have the first most creative job."

ACKNOWLEDGMENTS

Books of this complexity are not written in a vacuum. Instead of merely listing those accomplished and generous people who have assisted me on this project, I would like to credit them with the specialties they shared.

Aircraft and Flying: Captain Tom Davis, flight instructor; Luis Evans, Piper Cub instructor; Paul Guay, mechanics; Gudrun Lashbrook, flight instructor; Jerry Renov, Israeli pilot; Virginia M. Thomas, Springfield, Ohio.

Airlines and Travel: Bill Atwell, Ann's Travel; Tina Pogach and Bruce Haxchausen, Air France; Ron Wilson and Deborah Bernstein, British Airways; Mr. E. Swinglehurst, Thomas Cook Ltd., London Archives; Caroline Cohen and Richard Davis, Dukes Hotel.

Antiquities: Irving "Guv" Driman.

Art: Sandra Branch, Rita Baragona Sullivan.

Editorial Consultants: Beverly Crane, Caroline Dawnay, Nancy Eckert, Sarah Flynn, Gerry Morse, Nan Talese, Elsie Weisman.

France: Annette and Gérard Pesty; Anita McClellan, Quai Voltaire.

Historical Guide: Gil Elan.

Horses: Valerie Blethen.

Israeli Experts: Tamar Avidar, Netiva Ben-Yehuda, Daniella Boukstein, Yaacov Caroz, Aharon and Aviva Donagi, Raphael Elan, Yuval Elizur, Carmit Gattmon, Ashsa and Zvi Geyra, Lou Kedar, Paul Kedar, Matti Peled, Sinai Rome, Raisa and Yoash Sidon, Lillian and Ron Sivan, Raquel and Yehuda Taggar, Carmela Zabin, and Zvi Zamir.

Libraries: Nina Myatt, Curator, Antioch College Antiochian Archives; Crystal River Public Library; Edward N. MacConomy, Chief, National Referral Center, Library of Congress; *Ma'ariv* Newspaper Archives, Tel Aviv; Scott Sullivan, *Newsweek* Archives, Paris; Ocala Public Library; Robert Singerman, Curator, Isser and Rae Price Judaica Library; Valerie A. Walker, Liaison Assistant, UNWRA; University of Florida–Interlibrary Loan; Katherine Shimabukuro, USIA Library; Dina Abramowicz, YIVO Institute.

Mountaineering: Fred Jacobson.

Psychologists: Peggy Drake, Robin Weisman.

Researchers: Ed Becker, Mary Ann Boline, Kathleen Cossey, Jacqueline Fontaine, Kathleen Fusick, Nova Haun, Dalia Lipkin, Daniel Starer.

Religion: Donald Cutler, Yael Romer.

Switzerland: Irma and Hansjorg Dütsch-Grandjean, Hotel Fletschhorn; Walter, Nininhya, and Anna Illi.

With special thanks for the kind assistance of: Robert Drake, Dan Drooz, Esty Elan, Guy and Hila Elan, Libbie Elan, Gay Gold, Donald Gregory, Jac Jaeger, Ralph Keyes, Krista E. Leone, Barbara Norris, Clara and Eitan Porat, Colleen Rand, Gail Ross, Margaret Schmidt, Ruthanne Sutor.

CONTENTS

THE INCIDENT

The Messiah will not come to the sound of high explosives.
                                    Chaim Weizmann (1874–1952)
                                    First President of Israel

TOULON, FRANCE: APRIL 6, 1979

"How soon?" she asked.

"There is still time to rest."

"But not to sleep?"

Eli lifted his binoculars. "Yes, sleep if you can."

Charlotte closed her eyes and turned away from Eli.

Each was listening for the explosions that would come before dawn. The conspirators sharing the hotel room were but two of the dozen awaiting the tremors and ensuing chaos. Only one of them, Eli Katzar, knew the precise moment.

An erratic wind blew the diaphanous side panels of the draperies into the hotel room, partially blocking Eli's view of the port. The Frantel, situated just below the cable car station on Mont Faron, was well positioned for his observations. He pushed aside the curtains to get a better look at the quadrant of Toulon that most concerned him. From his months of studying maps of the area, Eli recognized the location of many of the coruscating lights in the panorama below. Just slightly to the west was the Arsenal Maritime; to the east, the commercial port in the old city; and beyond that the Arsenal du Mourillon. Best of all, there was a clear line of sight across the bay to the focus of so many months of elaborate planning: the port of La Seyne-sur-Mer and the CNIM warehouses. Nothing extraordinary appeared on the scene. There was no unusual military or civilian activity.

Eli turned over and stared at Charlotte in the twin bed on his right. Her body curled away from his as she slept. That she could relax at such a moment seemed incredible, but then, she had been through far worse during her years in the Israeli secret service. This was the first time in more than ten years that they shared a mission. It was unlikely to happen again, but for the moment, it seemed curiously right to be Mr. and Mrs. Roland Woodrow, a couple traveling in France on a long-anticipated gourmets' holiday. They had used South African passports, but had made it clear that Charlotte was an American.

After dinner Eli had informed the desk clerk of their early departure and had asked to settle the bill. "Prenez-vous le petit déjeuner?" the clerk had asked.

"No, we have a schedule." Eli smiled and pointed to Charlotte's complex itinerary. "My wife's very organized. I am more, how do you say . . . spontané?"

The clerk nodded knowingly. "Oui, les Américaines!"

Eli stared at the guidebooks on the bedside table. "Americans adore guidebooks," Charlotte had explained when he questioned the necessity for both a Michelin and a Gault-Millau. Now he could see that her extra touch of a folder containing clippings of articles on dining in France from the *New York Times* and *Gourmet* had been inspired, since only the most dedicated tourist would have planned so meticulously. Charlotte's thoroughness had won over those early doubters who not only did not want women among the ranks of espionage agents but had balked at the idea of an American girl. Eli was proud of her. More than anyone else, Charlotte Green MacDonald had far exceeded his expectations.

Charlotte stirred. Eli stared affectionately at the outline of her rounded buttocks under the bedclothes. The two had known each other for more than thirty years; they had been lovers for only a few weeks, a long time ago. Immediately afterward, he had regretted breaking the professionalism of their association, especially when Charlotte had confided how long she had desired him. Had he been as surprised as he had feigned? No. From the first he had sensed her attraction to him. All these years she had remained in the game of her own volition — even after he blatantly discouraged her romantic illusions — so he felt no guilt and only a modicum of remorse as he contemplated her silky skin, her butter-soft thighs, and recalled her total abandon with him. The only promise she had extracted — when they both knew they could not stay together — was that he would never ask her to make love to him again. And he had not.

Charlotte coughed and turned over onto her stomach. The curve of her back was as appealing as ever. He glanced at his watch, the Baume et Mercier Lily had bought him in Geneva years ago. Less than two hours, then the sound of splintering wood crates and vibrating metal . . . the raucous sirens of the police, and, if Aviva had done her job thoroughly, no ambulance.

He sat on the edge of the bed and tried to memorize the scene below. His eyes focused on the lights of the Concorde apartment tower. Very few were lit. The professor would be waiting. He rubbed the crystal of his watch nervously.

"You plan for all that can be imagined" is what Reuven Shiloah, his first mentor in tactics, had taught him. "Then you pray that the unimaginable — the human elements that can never be predicted — will not surface."

Over the years, analytical minds in the Mossad studied the degree to which they could predict how people would react. There was even a statistical table to factor in accidents and untoward events, yet there were always last-minute complications; individuals had to make crucial decisions without consulting desk-bound analysts and computer spread sheets. For that reason this crucial assignment was being handled by Eli, as head of operations, and his most seasoned troupe. All had received training in the latest techniques and counterespionage trends. From the men who had set the explosive charges during the night, to the scientist who had calculated which crates held the elements to be destroyed, to the group who handled the early surveillance — all were top operatives with long records of successful missions in hostile environments. Eli had left nothing to luck — down to personally placing fresh batteries in the watch of each agent as well as double-checking his own last night. Once again he studied his watch.

"Charlotte," he said gently. "It is time."

❖ ❖ ❖

Aviva Tabor left Marseille just after midnight, driving west on the autoroute. The sign ahead read: NICE, 188 km; CANNES, 163 km; AUBAGNE, 17 km; TOULON, 64 km.

She had driven the same road a dozen times the past few weeks, mostly at night. On a clipboard beside her she had noted the times between certain points, the traffic conditions, and when and where she saw military or civilian police. But this was secondary to her primary responsibility: monitoring the departures and arrivals of nuclear equipment division employees of the Constructions Navales et Industrielles de la Méditerranée. With the help of French compatriots, Aviva had acquired a list of the vulnerable workers, denoting their work schedules, home addresses, make and model of their automobiles. After several weeks of fastidious data collection, she had determined when the fewest personnel would be in the vicinity and knew the best hour to set as well as to detonate the explosives. Later, would any of the workers comprehend that it was not just good fortune that, unless someone deviated from his routine drastically, not one of them would be injured?

The French factory was the site of the construction of two nuclear research reactor cores for Iraq. Israeli intelligence reports indicated that the major components were ready for shipment. While the Arabs claimed the reactor was designed for the peaceful use of atomic energy only, it was known that the contract for the controversial project involved the eventual delivery of enough 93 percent enriched uranium to make about ten Hiroshima-sized atomic bombs.

Aviva had been told only what was essential to her role in the operation, even though she surmised far more — as might have been expected of someone who had three decades of secret service experience. Without being briefed specifically, she understood the limits of her decision-making responsibilities. She could alter; she could question; she could do whatever was justified to get the job done, but only if necessary. Up to this point, she had been following orders. Aviva Ben-Zion Tabor had built her reputation on precision, devotion, and accuracy. Because she coordinated the men who would arrive and depart by ship, as well as the back-up emergency land arrangements, Eli had based the crucial timing of the explosion on her information.

Although Aviva's tasks in Toulon were quite routine — counting cars, listing license plates, collecting the most ordinary statistical data — she knew she was at the hub of a team that would, if they performed their tasks flawlessly, be ensuring the survival of millions. How many other women would know the satisfaction she would feel that night? Or had felt on several other nights, interspersed by years of ordinariness. Even those times: raising her children, running her modest travel agency, had seemed more significant, more intense, because of the secrets she carried. And now, at the culmination of a major mission, she was infused with the sense of purpose she had felt during those early years of Israel's struggle when she had been an adolescent radio operator training a new recruit fresh from the British army: Eli Katzar.

Eli. Where was he now? Probably quite close by, even if she had not seen him since a brief rendezvous in Marseille more than a week earlier. He never led a task force without being at its center. She wondered if Charlotte and Lily might also be involved. The three women had not been assigned to the same mission since Cherbourg, but it was possible her old friends were nearby. A pity she would not know for certain who the other operatives were until much later, if ever. For security, a cell had to be small. Information was doled out strictly on a need-to-know basis. After all these years, Aviva had almost lost her curiosity about the grand scale of a plan — almost, but not quite. Months after a mission, she sometimes pieced together the more complete story from what she read in the press. Usually she discovered her own role had been an essential yet puzzling part of a larger process. At other times, a sudden trip, a transfer of papers or funds, a quick surveillance posting or code transmission, had remained a mystery. No matter. The system was efficient. Israel had survived.

As she approached Toulon, Aviva contemplated the last time she had been active in a French seaport. It was during the brilliant Cherbourg missile boat coup, which had raised Israel's esteem in the eyes of the world. She wondered how today's incident would be perceived by the press. The recent difficulties with the nuclear power plant near Harrisburg, Pennsylvania, might place sympathies in their camp. The fact that their French compatriots' cover was that of a group of antinuclear environmentalists meant Israeli involvement might never be suggested.

She took a long, deep breath of the dank sea air. Her part was almost over. Executing this plan had been a simple matter compared to the years she had spent in deep cover in Iraq. In a few minutes she would rendezvous with André and Michel near Toulon and continue on to Cannes. In a few weeks she might see Eli at a Tel Aviv gathering. They had run in the same social circles for years. Of course, hardly anyone knew that they worked together. The secret she shared with Eli was delicious, even after so long. Maybe that is what made it all worthwhile — and always had.

More vehicles were on the road now. A slow-moving dairy truck pulled out in front of her. As Aviva passed it, her hands gripped the wheel too tightly. The road ahead was clear and she was tempted to accelerate, but she could not jeopardize security by breaking the law. That is why Eli had selected only seasoned professionals for this operation. How much longer the secret service would employ her was questionable. Maturity aside, a Jewish grandmother-to-be was an unconventional spy. This may very well be my final chance, Aviva guessed. So, if it is, I shall remember every moment. Even this one, sitting here in the dark blue Renault with the Avis sticker, the light breaking in the eastern sky, here on this quiet morning in southern France, waiting . . . waiting for the silence to be shattered.

Lily was exhausted. The noise of motorcycle engines and hysterical laughter from the area around the quay was especially vexing at that early morning hour. Although Lily would have preferred a small inn away from the waterfront, she had been told to stay at the large Hotel Liautaud so she would be as anonymous as possible. How could the inhabitants of the seaside village of Cassis tolerate the inconsiderate revelry of the young tourists? She supposed the town would collapse without the transients' revenue; nevertheless, if ever a place could survive on charm alone, this was it. The calanques of Cassis, long creeks between rugged white cliffs, were the most celebrated in the Mediterranean. The town itself seemed an incarnation of a seaside village by Dufy, complete with bowls players posing under spreading plane trees.

"Quiet!" Lily wanted to shout, for she was completely drained. She recognized the stress-induced heaviness in her face and limbs that began as a numbing and tingling. She would give anything for sleep that would overcome the shouts of the boys, the giggles and coy screams of the girls. Lily *had* to sleep or she would lose the alertness she needed for the last phase of the mission.

Sleep. The increasing anxiety over whether she would get enough made it even more difficult to relax. The longer she craved it, the further she came from having what she wanted most. Years ago she could sleep through anything. The only way to get through the long days in hiding had been to force herself to sleep away the dull hours.

Hunger helped. Deprived of energy, she found it easier to slip into the numbness of a slumber that was actually a type of dormancy sustaining her in her weakened state. Nightmares became a serious problem. Dreams of her parents, friends from school — everyone who had disappeared — caused her to wake up screaming. She wore a scarf around her mouth to muffle the first cries and prayed one of the other children would wake her quickly. Later, after they were captured, sleep was solace once again, for the nightmares that began upon awakening were far worse than the ones her subconscious could devise.

Annoyed that she could not settle down, Lily stumbled out of bed and went to the window. She opened the wooden shutters and looked out at the cliffs of Cassis, which in the moonlight resembled the distorted faces of giants leering down menacingly. Lily preferred last night's hotel on the Côte d'Azur and she wished she had not been ordered to move. Last month she had arrived in St.-Tropez and posed as a tourist. A location worthy of James Bond, she had thought when she saw the tickets that routed her from Frankfurt to Cannes. Twenty years ago, she might have expected this to be another of Eli's attempts to indulge her. But no, St.-Tropez had been all business. Briefed in both the surveillance and documentation components of the mission, she also had been equipped with a transmitter to relay her findings at exactly one o'clock each morning. The planning had paid off and the mission progressed uneventfully. She had met up with André and Michel at the Pizzeria Romana on time and delivered them to Toulon. Officially, she was not supposed to know the actual identities of these operatives, but she had worked with them in Cherbourg.

Another facet of Lily's current assignment included gathering information about waterfront conditions: weather, tides, nautical charts, tourist activities. In her guise as an artist, she had hired boats from various small marinas and made excursions to the Corniche du Mourillon, the Arsenal Maritime, the piers of La Seyne, the Pointe de l'Aiguillette and its naval museum, and finally around the Corniche des Tamaris to the Pointe de Balaguier, where Fort Balaguier made a likely subject for an artist's sketch as well as an ideal site for a secret, nighttime rendezvous. During the past fortnight she had anchored offshore at more than a dozen crucial locations and worked on the banal watercolors of a tourist-artist, all the while making the strategic observations that were the purpose of the venture.

Her "brilliant eye for detail" was why Eli had proposed Lily for the assignment. When she resisted volunteering, he had argued convincingly. "We cannot afford to trust someone with less experience — not in France, where one slip could cost us dearly in world and European relations."

France was Lily Jaeger's territory. She had spent more years in Paris than in Tel Aviv, although Switzerland was her favorite place and she secretly hoped for a "retirement" position in Zürich or Geneva, in a building large enough for her to set up a studio for les vitraux — stained glass, the medium in which she had been concentrating lately. Maybe this would be the last assignment; maybe she could finally get the rest she deserved.

After a refresher course in Israel — where she had impressed even the experts in the documents section with her scrupulous forging of anything from a passport to a driver's license — she had returned to her home in Paris and let her friends know she was taking an extended painting holiday in the south of France. She had found rooms alternately in St.-Tropez, Marseille, Martigues, Bandol, Salon, St.-Raphaël, and, last, Cassis — not following a logical itinerary, never staying more than two nights in any location, changing her clothing and hairstyles so she could not be traced easily, and generally being so quiet and drab that no hotelier would remember her. Tomorrow she would return to the Riviera for one night to be available to the six people code-listed in her notes in case any documents needed reworking or exchanging. If all went well, the prearranged documents would suffice; if there were complications, she had the expertise and equipment to establish an identity that would hold up for at least forty-eight hours. At the moment, she fully expected to keep her booking on the Blue Train to Paris.

A motorcycle revved up and sped away. Lily sighed and climbed back onto the lumpy mattress on which countless others had slept, made love, been ill . . . or died. For that very reason, she hated hotels and longed for her own white linens with the eyelet edges, the cotton blankets that were washed weekly. Her mind raced ahead, imagining the sweaty youngsters satisfying their every urge: normal urges, yet ones she had never had — or been permitted to have — at their age, since sexual needs had been far overshadowed by those for food, warmth . . . even sleep.

At last, all she could hear was the faint hum of a boat slipping into the dock. Their own boats should have left La Seyne by now. Lily drew her knees to her chest and placed her hands between her thighs. Her heartbeat settled. Her breathing slowed as she wondered where Eli was at this very moment. She sensed he was quite nearby. And Charlotte. Maybe even Aviva. Sending her transmissions out into the great trembling void, Lily found it easier to imagine that one of the original Ezra group was on the receiving end than some faceless, nameless functionary. Electronics was a technology with a subtle yet detectable human component. Lily felt she could tune into the respirations of the airways and, based on the rhythm of the pauses, the pace of the responses, decide whether she was communicating with a man or a woman, a friend or a stranger.

Images of Charlotte, Eli, and Aviva swam in her mind. She sat up and checked her watch. The explosion would come within the hour. Well, it is done, she told herself as she fell into a blank, dreamless sleep.

❖   ❖   ❖

The nuclear equipment section of the French shipbuilding company was in an isolated area of the waterfront shipyard. Of the fifty-six hundred CNIM employees in the Toulon area, fewer than a hundred highly specialized technicians and engineers were permitted in the huge unmarked structure surrounded by electrified barbed wire and metal fences, security posts, and intruder detection devices. Since there had never been a hint of a security problem here, only three night watchmen protected the valuable construction equipment inside the compound. Israeli intelligence knew they took turns visiting a neighborhood café.

The twenty-five-meter-high hangar itself was maintained at a constant temperature because the computers and calibration equipment used in precision engineering could be made inaccurate by the humidity and climate fluctuations so common in a seaside location. Those who worked inside wore white uniforms and gloves in order to minimize dust and contamination of sensitive electronic components. As long as employees arrived properly dressed, they were usually waved through the gate.

In several crates, marked only with code numbers and letters, were the crucial parts for an atomic reactor, including the concrete, beehive-shaped pressure vessel for atomic fuel rods. In only a few days, these components for a plant designed to produce seventy megawatts of power would fulfill the deal originally negotiated in 1976 by France's Prime Minister Jacques Chirac and Iraqi leader Saddam Hussein.

During the day shift, one team of "temporary" workers had

marked the crates in question; a second group had come along during the night to place efficient military-type explosives in special lead-lined boxes to minimize both noise and damage to the structure or other equipment and materials stored nearby but increase the destruction in the targeted area. Finally, highly accurate timing devices had been set by remote control. If someone had passed by, looking for something suspicious, he would have been disappointed. All the evidence was meticulously hidden from view.

In the surrounding waterfront village the night was unusually balmy. Windows were opened to a light sea breeze that hinted of summer and tourists and days at the beach and ripening vines. The families of La Seyne breathed in and out peacefully. A few trucks passed along the Quai Saturnin Fabre. A cathedral clock chimed twice. The wind rattled the masts on the sailboats at the town marina. The night watchmen patroling the perimeter passed each other in the empty parking lot while almost everyone else dreamed the dreams of the happy, the depressed, the lonely, the lovers, the newborn, the dying.

⁙   ⁙   ⁙

Eli drove down the steep, winding streets that led to the center of Toulon. In the distance he could see the Concorde, one of the largest apartment buildings in the city. It had been chosen not only for the anonymity it afforded but also for its superb location and the three entrances that made it excellent for security. The flat itself was on one of the lowest floors so that the stairs could be used instead of the elevator in case of emergency.

He slowed the car at the side entrance in front of the Alfa Romeo showroom. He turned off the motor and said to Charlotte, "Wait here. I'll return in a few moments."

"But —"

Charlotte caught herself. She knew better than to expect an explanation. During the last few weeks she had acted the part of the passive Mrs. Woodrow. As Eli went about his work she remained behind in the sequence of hotel rooms from Marseille to Nice to Aix-en-Provence, and, last, Toulon. Twice a day she reconstructed the miniature radio receiver from parts hidden in her hair-curling unit, contact lens disinfecter, and travel iron. At specific intervals, she changed frequencies, listened for signals, transcribed and decoded the traffic. She marveled at how far the technology had progressed from the days of her Zamir radio in Egypt. The simplistic codes of the 1950s, the shadow broadcasts of the 1960s, seemed primitive by comparison. Last month at the military communications center near Herzliya, she had been retrained in spectrum transmission technology. With the instruments doing all the hopping across the wavelengths automatically, the short messages she was receiving every day were virtually undetectable, giving far greater security to this operation than others she had been involved in.

Even with the decoded messages in hand, Charlotte did not fully understand what was going on. Until last night, Eli had told her as little as possible about the goals of the assignment. On one hand, Charlotte understood that she was kept ignorant for self-protection. If you knew nothing, you could reveal nothing. On the other, Charlotte resented his lack of faith in her. It was the same decades-old feeling that she was still being penalized for the aftermath of the Egyptian operation. Eli would deny it, of course. He would remind her that if there had been the slightest question of her integrity she never would have been selected for this assignment. Finally, he had explained they could expect an explosion, yet she had no idea what was being blown up — or why. She could not ask questions, but she knew that France was supplying the Arabs with nuclear technology and this put Israel in danger.

In 1959, when Iraq was accepted into the International Atomic Energy Agency, Israel decided a potential nuclear threat had been posed. The following year, Iraq signed an agreement with the USSR for the building of a research reactor, and three years later the Soviets helped break ground on the project in Tuwaitha, outside Baghdad. The thermal power reactor was completed in 1968, and in 1978, the Soviets agreed to change the fuel from 10 percent enriched U-235 to 80 percent enriched uranium. This raised the reactor's power to five megawatts. But the Soviets kept such close inspection on the plant, the Iraqis could never store enough military-grade uranium or plutonium to produce a bomb. Recently, though, Iraq had convinced the French to help them develop an Osiris research reactor, which operated on enriched uranium and would give them nuclear warfare capabilities.

Charlotte rested her head on the seat back and closed her eyes. This explosion was likely to create a major incident with international consequences. Eli could be secure in the knowledge that she was one agent who would never talk, hint, brag. That was the hardest in the end, knowing you had been there, been a part of a mission that had received worldwide press attention — like Cherbourg, a

successful job renewing esteem for the Israeli intelligence service —
and never, ever be able to receive even a modicum of personal credit
or glory. Not then, not decades later. To be an unsung heroine took a
special sort, the sort she had proved to be over and over.

.⋮. .⋮. .⋮.

The last detail of the Toulon operation was to escort an Israeli scientist, cover-named Freddie Dütsch, to safety. Eli had a key to the
Concorde's lobby door, a key he was planning to discard as they
drove north. But the door was open slightly and this tiny variation in
a set of crucial final maneuvers was what alerted Eli. His mind raced
with the possibilities. Doctor Z, as he affectionately called the professor, might have left the downstairs door ajar in his anxiety for a
quick departure. More than likely he was ready, his briefcase and
baggage packed, anxious to be gone. Brought along because of his
expert knowledge of nuclear reactors, the scientist had been given
only limited training. He lacked the experience to handle these final
tense moments as easily as a seasoned veteran, but there was no logical alternative. The professor's presence made it possible to pinpoint
the placement of the charges to guarantee the complete destruction
of the critical components of the reactor while minimizing the
chance of killing anyone.

The Concorde had been an excellent choice for a safe house. In a
building that large, the neighbors were rarely a problem. Many cor-
porations maintained apartments for executives who had business
dealings with the nearby naval departments, and the elevators were
filled with gentlemen from all over the world who traded with the
French military establishment. Dr. Asher Ze'evi had looked the part
of a distinguished businessman, especially after the London trip to
exchange his Negev desert cottons for Jermyn Street shirts and
ready-made, yet impeccably tailored, suits. The only unexpected
concern had been over a Mme Odent, the widow across the hall,
who had taken an interest in the "Swiss" gentleman, inviting him to
meals and inquiring after his health for the first week or so. Eli had
instructed Freddie to be cordial, even to accept a few drinks, but to
insist that he was a faithful, happily married man with grandchildren of his own. As far as Eli knew, this had worked. The doctor reported that her interest had dwindled rapidly.

Cautiously, Eli made his way up the stairs. The elevator made
noise and could attract attention in the eerie predawn hours. As he
cracked open the door to the hall marked "quatrième étage" a

sound startled him, but it was only the mewing of Mme Odent's cat. It sounded as though it was coming from inside the professor's flat — which was odd, because Doctor Z was not at all fond of the large orange and white cat.

"It's a sneaky one, always tries to rush in whenever I open the door," the professor had complained. "I would tolerate it better if he didn't shed his hair and spray in the corners."

The night before last, when they had finished the final details of their collaboration, the professor had shooed the cat out into the hall and said, "Won't miss that damn beast!"

"Freddie?" Eli tapped on the apartment door. It swung open at his touch. A light from the kitchen spilled out into the vestibule. The cat appeared and rubbed against Eli's leg, then dashed into the corridor, leaving footprints on the terra cotta floor. Eli flicked on the light by the front door, kneeled down, and touched a wet print. It was blood.

Eli held his breath. He listened.

Had he surprised someone?

"Meow . . . meow . . ." The cat's noises were gratingly loud.

Eli inched forward along the hallway, his back flat against the wall so he could look in both directions. When he reached the bedroom, the light was bright enough for Eli to see that someone — no, something — was on the bed. The utter stillness, the unmoving black shape, the absence of moving air, were obvious. It wasn't a person, it wasn't Dr. Ze'evi — it was a body.

Eli lifted his handkerchief to flick on the light switch. He blinked, then turned to the bed.

It had been more than a murder.

Eli reeled backward and stumbled over the cat, which had crept back into the room. It shrieked and jumped onto the bed. Blood that had pooled on the coverlet spattered the stucco wall.

Eli gagged.

Dr. Ze'evi's throat had been sliced by a sharp blade. His head was tilted as far back as the severed sinews and muscles would allow. His mouth — his gentle, sweet mouth, which had never said an unkind word about anyone — had been forced open and stuffed with what appeared to be a red, pulpy mass. Even without close inspection, Eli knew all too well what it was. Mutilated genitals in a victim's mouth were the calling card of a vicious Arab bent on revenge.

"Why, Asher, why?" Eli moaned. His hands began to shake uncontrollably. His mind strained to master the situation. He could not call the police; he could not move the body; he could not even notify the next of kin, his own cousin Esty. Somehow he would have to see that the body got home, but not now. He had already been in the building far too long. He looked around for the professor's briefcase. It was missing, but Dr. Ze'evi's suitcase was at the foot of the bed. Eli decided he had better take it. He started to lift it and stopped. Although he was trying to avoid looking at the upper part of the body, something caught his eye. The professor's hands had been laid across his chest and folded together. Between them was a slip of paper rolled into a cone. Gently, Eli lifted it, and as he did, one of the dead man's hands flopped to the side and fell in a warm scarlet pool.

"Bloody fucking hell!" he shouted. "I can't leave him like this," he said more softly.

Eli ran into the bathroom and grabbed a towel. With it he gingerly removed the flesh from the mouth. Retching, he rushed to flush the organs down the toilet. Blood had dripped on the gray tile floors. With another towel, he removed fingerprints from light switches and door frames and wiped up the blood spots on all the floors. Then he stuffed both towels into the suitcase and washed himself well. As soon as he was certain he had left no further traces, he lifted the suitcase, locked up the apartment, rushed down the stairs, got into the car, and started it.

Charlotte opened her eyes. "You took so long. Everything all right?"

"Not exactly." Eli tried to swallow the saliva that threatened to choke him. "Did you see anyone?"

"No," Charlotte said.

Eli glanced at her. Why had he been so unreasonably confident? Why hadn't he told her to stay on guard?

She caught his displeasure instantly. "I'm sorry . . . I . . ."

Eli forgot to hold down the clutch, so the car lurched forward, banging the truck parked in front of it. "Bloody hell!" He rammed the clutch to the floor, cranked the engine again, backed up, and pulled out without worrying about the truck or his grille.

The streets of Toulon were quiet. At the end of the Avenue d'Estienne-d'Orves, he did not slow to read three direction signs: AIX-EN-P. PÉAGE for the left lane, LA SEYNE for the center, and MARSEILLE PAR R.N. 8" on the right.

"My God!" He swerved to avoid missing the left lane turn. "Fucking signs!" He swore so vehemently, Charlotte jumped.

"Eli, are you all right?"

He didn't answer.

"Do you want me to drive?"

"No, just turn on the dome light for a moment."

He took the rolled piece of paper he had removed from the professor's hands out of his pocket so he could read it. Pasted on a stiff piece of a typical Riviera postcard was a torn Bible verse. Eli recognized it at once.

So that the people could not discern the noise of the shout of joy from the noise of the weeping of the people: for the people shouted with a loud shout, and the noise was heard afar off.

It was from one of the first chapters of the Book of Ezra, referring to the time the foundations for the second Temple were laid in Jerusalem. He shoved the paper deep into his pocket as the meaning began to sink in. The joy of the temple . . . the joy of Jerusalem . . . the weeping of the people . . . Ezra . . . the name of his group . . . the basis for the code they had used during their early missions when their radio equipment had been far less sophisticated. An enemy knew about Ezra and was flaunting his knowledge now.

He had been betrayed. Yet if that were so, why wasn't he the victim? Was this a warning that he was going to be next, or had the killer made a mistake? Whatever the answer, there was an enemy, an enemy who knew about his group's involvement in the mission. Eli's superiors were at Mossad headquarters in Tel Aviv. Who could have known enough about the mission to have followed them to France? He had European back-ups who could expect to hear from him if he used a password, but they had no briefing on this assignment. All the other operatives had worked through Aviva, Lily, and Charlotte. All three could be trusted implicitly, yet one of them might have been followed. He had had direct contact with each during various points in the mission, which could have led someone to him. And he, inadvertently, could have led the killer to Dr. Ze'evi. But when? How?

Eli glanced over at Charlotte, who was sitting stiffly in the bucket seat, staring at the roadway ahead. She seemed tense, watchful, even shaky — just the way he would expect an operative to behave at this crucial moment. Could someone have been following her? Or *him*? Eli scanned the cars and trucks around them on the road. None looked to be a likely tracking vehicle. But a bug in the car could be so miniature it would take an expert to strip the car and locate it. It was impossible. He thought his security inviolable. But the impossible had happened.

As soon as he was on the outskirts of Toulon, he allowed several trucks to pass him, swerved off to the side, jumped out, and asked Charlotte to take the wheel. Without a word, she got out and moved around to the driver's seat. Soon they were continuing on the toll road in the direction of Aix-en-Provence.

Betrayal. The ugly thought surrounded him, choked him with its presence. Eli's mouth tasted of chalk. For money, for love, for God only knows what reason, someone, somewhere, had given out enough information to lead them to him and from him to the professor.

Asher, dear Asher . . .

Father of three daughters, husband to one of Eli's Rehovot cousins, brilliant physicist who had so much more to contribute to Israeli and world science. What had they gained compared to what they had just lost?

Boom!

Eli's tortured thoughts were blunted by the jolt of the first fully expected, yet still surprising, explosion.

"What . . . ?" Charlotte's voice was thin. Her fingers clutched the steering wheel tighter and she slowed down. "What was that?"

". . . and the noise was heard afar off . . ." Eli mumbled.

"What did you say?"

Boom!

"That was the second one."

And then three more. Boom! Boom! Boom! It sounded like faraway fireworks — festive and heartening. They turned in the direction of the noise in time to see a bright flash in the sky to the southeast.

"So, we did it!" Charlotte was elated.

He waited for more shocks. How many had there been? Four? Five? There should be at least seven. "I do not delight in destruction . . . of anything," he said somberly.

Boom! Boom! The sixth and seventh heaving rumbles pummeled the sky. The destruction was complete. But there was no satisfaction, no glory. The price for the crumpled wreckage was too high; the result — a year or two of delay in the inevitable nuclearization of an enemy — was too minimal. The final volleys echoed in their wake as the two of them — one confused, one shattered — sped away from the absurdly lovely pastel sky dawning behind them and into the bleakness of the unlit road ahead.

PART ONE

VETTING AND TRAINING

1

In wartime, truth is always so precious that she should be attended by a bodyguard of lies.

Sir Winston Churchill (1874–1965)

BLETCHLEY, ENGLAND: 1939–1945

There had been a time when Eli Katzar had not been an intelligence agent. He was born Elliot Short, the child of an unlikely union, yet one that had endured against tremendous odds. His father, Hugo Short, had been an officer in the First World War and then served in Palestine with General Allenby. As a young captain stationed in Jerusalem, he fell in love with a blue-eyed, black-haired beauty, Ruth Epstein, the daughter of a distinguished family of early Jewish pioneers. Her shy smile combined with a prodigious will were so captivating and unsettling, he could not bear to live without her at his side. While he was afraid her family would never welcome him, it turned out Hugo had more difficulties with his regiment accepting the union than Ruth had with her family, who were just liberal enough to grudgingly agree to the unorthodox match.

Despite their differences, Ruth and Hugo were more compatible and found more happiness than most of the other couples of their acquaintance. Ruth's sunny moods, her fascination with every word Hugo said, her sheer pleasure in his company, fulfilled Hugo. To Ruth, her handsome husband was the most kindly, gentlemanly person she had met. Ruth wanted to remain in Palestine. She believed in her family's Zionist vision for a Jewish homeland, even though none of the Epsteins practiced their religion with great fervor. Hugo had promised that he would do everything in his power to remain there. And he had. In time, Ruth came to realize Hugo's refusal to accept transfers abroad, combined with his "Jewish associations," had limited his military career severely. Eventually he resigned and joined the Palestine Police, where he rose to the position of district superintendent.

"The worst time your father and I had was naming you," his mother said fondly. "I wanted a Hebrew name; he insisted on an English one."

Ruth selected her favorite name, Eli, meaning "the highest, or Jehovah is God," then translated Short to Katzar in Hebrew. Hugo thought his son should have a typical Christian name and suggested Edward or James because he had despised the "Hugo" he had been saddled with. Ruth had asked that the name be as close to Eli as possible to "help the child adjust to a situation that is already complicated enough." In the end, they settled on Elliot quite amicably when Hugo remembered it had been the maiden name of his Welsh grandmother.

Both had doted on their only child. Eli had inherited his mother's dark-rimmed sapphire eyes and easy smile. From his father, he received dimpled cheeks and chin, sandy straight hair, a slim build, and a perfect ear for music.

"He would make an angelic choirboy," Hugo teased Ruth.

"But never stand still long enough," she retorted. Eli was so physically active he left both parents exhausted in his wake.

Police Superintendent Short had a simplistic view of his son's dual identity. "When he's in Palestine, he will be a Jew; when in England, he will be British."

As Eli Katzar he attended primary school at St. George's, where Arabs, Britons, diplomats, and Jews who planned to someday send their children to school abroad enrolled their children. On the High Holidays he joined his Epstein grandparents at the synagogue; on Christmas and Easter he attended chapel with his father. He spoke Hebrew with his cousins, Arabic with the neighborhood children, English at home and at school. As Eli Katzar he spent two years in secondary school at the Rehavia Gymnasium; as Elliot Short he attended the Perse School in Cambridge, as had his father.

"It's the best place for the boy," Hugo had said to calm his wife when she did not want her only child sent so far away at twelve.

"He will never be comfortable in that environment," Ruth worried. "Besides, his mixed parentage might place him at a disadvantage."

"People will know only what he tells them. Eventually, he will have to make his own way in the world and sort all this out." Hugo had hugged Ruth to him for reassurance. "We haven't done such a bad job of it. You'll see."

At last Ruth had capitulated, even agreeing that Elliot should live at West House and participate in all required church services, instead of Hillel House with the other Jewish boys. For twelve years he had been exposed primarily to a Jewish way of life. He was scheduled to be bar mitzvahed during his first holidays at home. What harm could he come to in England? After all, Hugo had kept his word and remained in Palestine at the expense of his career, so now it was Ruth's turn to keep her side of the bargain that their son would know both sides of his heritage. In the end, she took consolation in the fact that nothing they had done sealed their son's fate. Because she was Jewish, the child, by Biblical law, was considered Jewish; because his father was British, he could always have claim to a British passport and identity. In her heart Ruth believed Eli would choose the ways of her family because the ties of infancy were the ones to which a man eventually reverts. This was her secret, for she knew Hugo trusted just as fervently that a boy was most influenced by his school years.

Superintendent Short was rewarded by Elliot's exemplary progress in school. Never an athlete, he willingly participated in enough sports to satisfy his requirements and developed an interest in individual endurance activities, especially long-distance running and mountain climbing. Upon being graduated in 1938, he won a Higher Certificate in mathematics, which led to a coveted scholarship at King's College in Cambridge.

Elliot had finished only one year at the university before the war began. After his mother implored her husband to keep Elliot from combat duty, Hugo's brother, Brigadier General Harvey Short, arranged for Elliot to be assigned to the Government Code and Cipher School, which insiders irreverently referred to as the Golf, Cheese, and Chess Society. "The perfect place for a boy with his logical mind," the brigadier wrote his brother, satisfied that he had kept his only nephew far away from the bloodshed.

Elliot wanted to resist the family's arranging his life, but didn't because the work suited him perfectly. Besides, he was in excellent company. Gordon Welchman, his lecturer in mathematics at Cambridge, was there, as were a dozen others from his college, most of whom were noted for their ability at crosswords, calculations, linguistics, word and number puzzles of all sorts. Within a few months, they were all evacuated from their quarters near Victoria Station in London to a red brick monstrosity of a house in Buckinghamshire called Bletchley Park.

When one of the gray-flannel types complained about the location, he was told it was chosen for security. "You see, Bletchley is the place in England where one is farthest from the sea — at least sixty miles from the nearest invasion beach."

Safety was also a consideration for the next wave of newcomers to the quiet market town. Soon after Elliot arrived, thousands of children were sent from London to the Bletchley area, and along with the children came women to care for them. The mothers of Buckinghamshire could not be expected to handle the more than seventeen thousand young visitors, so nurses and nannies from all over the British Isles were recruited to tend the charges. One of them was Maura Doyle.

At the beginning of his second year at the GCCS, Elliot was on the train platform when a little boy ran up to him and called loudly, "Could I read your secret writing, mister?"

Elliot tried to retain a stony face and ignore the boy, but his complete lack of guile about what everyone presumed was quite clandestine forced him to smile.

The woman who had been tending the boy caught up to him. "Tony, don't bother the gentleman," she chastised with a distinctive Irish lilt. Then, catching Elliot's grin, she laughed along.

"That's all right," Elliot replied. "At least he didn't ask why an able-bodied man was not doing his bit."

"As I tell the children, each man serves in his own way." The pretty woman with sea-green eyes stared at him for a couple of seconds.

"Yes, well, I thank you for your confidence." He turned away slowly, wondering how he might prolong the conversation.

The woman tucked some loose wisps of auburn hair under a frayed scarf and waited a few beats. She looked for Tony, but he had disappeared around the corner. "That child!" she groaned and ran after him.

Elliot followed.

"Tony, wait!" he heard her call. The boy paused at the curb. She grabbed him so he could not cross the street alone and held one of his hands firmly while reaching down to pull up her stockings. Elliot caught up with the two of them easily.

She spoke first. "You're billeted at Shenley Brook End, aren't you?"

"Why, yes, I am." He smiled as winsomely as he could. "I just hope you're working for our side. Your intelligence work is very professional."

"It's just that the mother of one of the other nurses in our group is your landlady and I thought I had seen you at her house."

"At Mrs. Henshaw's?"

"That's right. My name is Maura Doyle. I share a room in town with Tillie Henshaw."

Elliot had not known what to say next, but he need not have worried. By the time they walked to the turnoff for the Park, she had arranged to meet him at the Crown Inn the following Sunday.

From the start they were completely at ease together.

"Compatible" was how Maura put it. "You're so comfortable to be with, Elliot. It's as if we've known each other forever."

Elliot agreed entirely. It was simple to plan a day together because what she wanted to do was invariably what he wanted as well. On days off they would go into London and eagerly take standing room in order to see a matinee of the latest Shaw revival. He had gotten permission to invite her to the grounds of the Park, where they played a complementary game of doubles tennis, often winning against Alan Turing and his friend Joan Clarke. They both loved movies and sat through several twice so they could hold hands and kiss in the dark. They took long walks, shared copies of Arthur Koestler's *Darkness at Noon*, Emlyn Williams's *The Corn Is Green*, and Hemingway's *For Whom the Bell Tolls*. They both admitted their enthusiasm for American music. She began to appreciate his scratchy recordings of American blues singers with the unlikely names of Blind Lemon Jefferson and Mississippi John Hurt. They spent a few weeks sneaking off on their bicycles and meeting on the outskirts of town, but almost everyone knew they were seeing each other, and they finally decided it was ludicrous to meet in secret. Soon Maura and Elliot walked openly arm in arm.

Although Elliot knew when to grumble aloud about "missing out on the war," privately he was perfectly content at Bletchley Park. Here he was, side by side with Dillwyn Knox, the classical scholar and Fellow of King's who had been far more elusive at Keynesian

Cambridge; Alan Turing, the odd but brilliant cryptanalyst; and the more genial college dons Frank Wilkinson and Frank Lucas. An added benefit was the influx of clever, if not comely, young women from Newnham College who demonstrated an intense tolerance for the assembling, ordering, and understanding of the great mass of superficially trivial snippets of paper — then, hour after hour, winnowing them into piles of related material so they could be decoded more effectively.

In the years that followed, he often wondered what had become of the best of them: Jenny, with her untidy knee socks . . . Rebecca, with her intuitive game of chess . . . Olivia, with her lovely long braids . . . Blanche, with her mouth pursed prettily as she studied a problem. They had been stalwart girls with strong, vibrant minds and sensitive souls. Perhaps it was those admirable Newnham girls who first gave him the idea that women could do anything. When the cipher groups were bogged down and discouraged by their lack of progress, it was as often as not one of the "big room girls," as they were called, who rescued them with the next clue, the pattern that led to a major breakthrough. They could be so damned competent, so clever, so utterly resourceful! Even now he would not have minded a long chat with one of them, especially Rebecca, who could be so practical, so trustworthy, so optimistic despite the air raids, the death tolls, the gloom-sayers all about them.

Some people thought there was no glamour in ciphers — even after the war when it was known how much they had contributed. Instead of finding the work dull and monotonous, Elliot undertook every assignment as a personal quest and accepted every solution as a personal victory. At the time, the ciphers did not yet rely on any great mathematical sophistication, but on the simple principles of substitution and addition. A further refinement of the day led to the development of "one-time pads," which required the key to be written out explicitly, twice over, with one copy given to the sender, one to the receiver of the transmission. The security of the system was in having the key constructed by a random process so there could be nothing for the enemy decoder to go on.

Fortunately, Elliot had always been good at meticulous work, just the kind he was required to slave at day after day. In the mornings he would get his numbers, subtract from the groups corresponding to the one-time pad, and look up what the resultant groups signified in the code book. Any mistake in the groups or subtractions threw out the whole series of calculations. While other clerks got in terrible muddles transcribing their wireless telegraph messages, Elliot won the reputation for the fastest work. He would have remained at those tasks he excelled at for the rest of the war had he not made a stunning breakthrough, shortly after the move to Bletchley, that brought him to the attention of the highest levels of the secret service.

Once in a while, when he was in a reflective mood, he would think nostalgically about that particular week and wonder what elements had aligned to give *him* the definitive clue. Had it been pure chance? Destiny? Merely coincidence or a hunch? At the time all he knew was that something had been irking him. He had refused to give in to the lateness of the night or the soreness in his throat until he solved the riddle. Then, all of a sudden, the numbers leapt from the page and saluted. He had had moments like this before: the name of a solid-fuel propellant might ring a bell, and searching for the word in the files, he might find an earlier reference that would help break the code. But this time the connections were most amazing.

Just when he was not certain if he had found it or was hallucinating, Alan Turing knocked on the door of the drafty, wooden Hut Six.

"My God, Short, in seven days you must have put in more than a hundred hours. Are you trying to fight Hitler single-handed?"

Elliot wheezed and coughed. "Can't sleep with this damn cold anyway."

"Must I send someone to order you out or will you wise up and take care of yourself?"

"There's a pattern here and I mean to pin the elusive bastard down."

"Listen, we've enough casualties at the front. How about taking another crack at it tomorrow?"

"Just a few more minutes. I'm on to something."

Turing bent over and studied Elliot's calculations. "Show me what you've come up with."

"I hesitate to explain it before I have all the proofs, but . . ."

"Yes?"

Elliot hesitated. His analysis was as irrefutable as it was Machiavellian, yet he wondered how it could possibly be true. "Look here, are we the lunatics? Or are they?"

Turing came to agree with his theory. It was a revelation that roared through Bletchley Park and came to the attention of the head of British intelligence as well as the Prime Minister. The praise Elliot won was welcome, but the horror that dawned as the numerical forms revealed the sinister derivation of the code changed the course of his life.

His discovery would come to be known as the Dachau Example.

"You see," he later explained to Israeli students of cryptology, "the basic problem, as we've discussed, was to establish pure randomness in numbers. Only today with the most sophisticated computer techniques are we beginning to achieve this, but even now, as in the past, we must be ever watchful for the personality of the creator of the cipher."

"Machines don't have personalities!" a student commented in the long pause Eli deliberately left.

"Certainly they do, because every machine is operated by a human being. If you can find out who that person is, you have your first clue."

"Are you suggesting a psychological test on an unknown person?" someone else inquired.

"Indeed. Behind every number, there's a person with a family, a culture, a language, a history. I've seen patterns to Iraqi codes that would never be the same for Egyptian ones. You must search for differences in syntax, reasoning, habits. When I was working on the Enigma project" — another pause, admittedly an egotistical one, because Eli knew the word "Enigma" brought instant respect from the few doubters in the group — "we were deciphering *German* codes. Apparently, the technicians responsible for deriving random settings thought they'd hit on a bright solution. Every day the concentration camps rendered returns giving the numbers of prisoners who had been delivered to the camp, the number who had died or been killed, and the number of surviving inmates. These were truly random figures, which were reported in a medium-grade cipher. The recipients of these messages passed them on to their Enigma colleagues, who used them in determining the settings of a particular cipher. Because I was reading the messages that used the same medium-grade cipher as well as looking at Enigma ciphers, I wondered if the Germans, who so meticulously kept their ghoulish concentration camp figures, were applying their body counts for another, or from their distorted point of view, higher purpose. When I compared the numbers, I found they often matched."

It was the best lesson Eli ever taught. The permutations and implications of the discussions that inevitably followed inspired many a student to remain in the service of Israel for many years. His personal victory at Bletchley Park won him a place directly under Turing, where he was put to work on the machines that were being invented to break the German electronic codes.

It was during this time that British intelligence at Bletchley Park started a file on Maura Doyle because of her association with Elliot. At first Elliot had been angry, but she stared at him with her hypnotic green eyes and said, "I'm a security risk. I know that."

He was confident that she would never betray a trust, but he had never told her about anything — not even the concentration camp discovery. When she met his associates, work was never discussed. Even the simplest or silliest message was top secret. A few times he almost slipped with some anecdote that might have amused Maura and would have been of little import, but he always caught himself. Eventually, reticence became routine.

Although he talked about his admiration for her beauty, thanked her for the joy she gave him, and recounted the usual comical tidbits about his school days, Elliot preferred to ask questions about her family rather than tell stories about his own childhood. Maura obliged him with long descriptions of her three overbearing older sisters, who were always trying to make her over into someone she did not want to be; her stern Irish father, whom none of them had ever found a way to please; and her English mother, who was more fond of whiskey than keeping a home. But mostly their pasts didn't concern them; their futures were tied to the uncertainty of the war. All that mattered was that day, that night, and the morning to come.

When Elliot and Maura were alone together, life was an idyllic interlude from the cares of the war and the rest of the world. At first there was the usual erotic tension that eased only after fervent embraces — a necessity that suppressed more mundane matters of food or sleep. Then, as with most mergings, they passed into a period of equanimity. Their lives and interests fused. Their conversations were stimulating, but differences — and there were many — were put aside when lips touched, arms entwined.

However, as much as they might have wished, two cannot live alone in the midst of a world at war. Elliot had friends in Bletchley, as did Maura. Foursomes and larger groups would gather at pubs or billets to dissect the headlines of the day.

The two were an eye-catching couple: Maura petite with her mag-

nificent swirls of auburn hair; Elliot tall, at least by comparison, with
the physical presence of a natural athlete. Despite the fact he was
basically cerebral in nature he was always asked to join in every
game organized at the Park because he radiated such boundless energy in his purposeful gait. Maura found herself taking two steps for
his every one. A glance from his startlingly blue eyes could be riveting or affectionate at will. His hair was cropped short in the military
fashion, but nothing had been done to diminish his thick eyebrows
that were several shades darker than any of the streaks in his sandy
hair.

Maura would wet her finger and attempt to groom the unruly
brows, chiding as she did, "There, now you don't look so *intense*, darling."

When they greeted each other with a quick kiss, she always aimed
for the dimples on either side of his mouth. "Bet your mother adored
those."

"Not half as much as you," Eli replied as he brushed aside a cascade of her luscious hair and returned the kiss at the nape of her
creamy neck before working up to the richness of her sensuous mouth.

In public, Elliot was fairly reticent about his opinions; Maura was
not. Her vituperative statements about the competence of the world
leaders and the inanity of military decisions often stunned the Cambridge intelligentsia, mostly because of her simplistic analyses of
events. Eventually, when Maura was present, the conversations
veered to more neutral subjects or someone produced a pack of
playing cards.

"Maura, darling, the world is not black or white, but shades of
gray," Elliot would remind her when they were alone.

"No, you're wrong," she countered affably. "All can be cate-
gorized quite simply. There is either good or evil; there's no such
beast as 'partially wrong' or 'almost right.' People either lie or tell
the truth. If you can find me any virtue in Hitler, though, I'll recon-
sider my position."

He had deferred to her then to keep the peace. Only later would
the full force of her opinionated personality affect him.

When she was off duty, Maura slept at his quarters. Nobody questioned her absence from the children's hall because few of the adults
could sleep properly with half a dozen sleepwalkers, bed-wetters, and
other understandable disturbances from children wrenched away
from their homes.

"Maura, my Rose of Tralee," he would whisper into her sweet

hair when they awakened entwined in each other's arms. He had taken an interest in things Irish, including reading aloud from a volume of Irish poetry. A favorite was Mulchinock's "The Rose of Tralee."

> "Yet 'twas not her beauty alone that won me,
> Oh, no, 'twas the truth in her eyes ever beaming
> That made me love Maura, the Rose of Tralee."

He always changed Mary to Maura and kissed her at the end of each stanza.

"Truth in her eyes!" How could he ever have been so young, so blindly in love? How could he have brought so much perception to his work and such vast ignorance to his own life? When he was in a mood to forgive himself, he would admit that his twelve-hour shifts requiring intense concentration had blunted whatever practical sense he might have had. And what young man of twenty-one could have resisted the wide embrace of her smooth white arms, her taut, fragrant thighs, her willing, petal-soft mouth, her endless hunger for him?

In another time, their affair might have been openly criticized, but at the height of the war, the unspoken feeling was to let the young people take as much from life as possible. Privately, however, they were cautious, because Maura was concerned about avoiding a pregnancy. On what seemed to Elliot a goodly number of the days of the month, she would insist on "alternate shenanigans," which he labeled "Shannongins" because his proper Irish lass resisted mechanical birth control. Although their "everything but" sexual encounters became quite inventive as time wore on, he prevailed on a questionable day of the month that arrived in June 1944 during the celebrations following the Normandy invasion.

By mid-July Maura was almost frantic. "I don't know what I shall do if . . ."

"You can't be certain yet." He tried to be reassuring, but convinced neither her nor himself. She was at least three weeks late. They sat together in a clearing in the forest near Shenley, their chins upraised to the warming sun. The children under Maura's charge who hadn't yet been claimed by their parents were playing nearby, and all were in unusually high-spirited moods in anticipation of finally going home. Filled with vibrant energy, they ran between the glittering pools of light, pretending the bright circles were puddles in some inspired game. A soft wind whistled above, the children's laughter echoed in the treetops, and everything seemed so right in the world that Elliot was determined to be optimistic.

"I've never been this late before and you weren't careful, Elliot, you know you weren't."

In the dappled light, her face pink and chapped with tears, her eyes the color of the sparkling canopy above, Maura had never looked more appealing.

"I would love you to have my baby."

A fresh waterfall of tears spilled down Maura's cheeks. "Do you —?"

Just as she started to speak a little girl came rushing past, her long braids flying behind her. "Bobby Collier," she cried like a sweet calling bird. "Bobby Collier, wait for me!" Looking at the child in the grimy plaid apron and drooping stockings, Elliot wondered if they would have a girl like her and, if they did, what she might be called.

"What's her name?"

"Who?" Maura hadn't seemed to notice the little girl.

"The child with the long braids."

"Oh, Elizabeth Petrie. Sad little thing. Misses her parents terribly."

"She's happy today."

Maura nodded glumly. Elliot reached for her hand. "Come now, let's not be so miserable."

"All our plans . . . You wanted to return to Cambridge when all this is settled and —"

"I don't have to plunge right back into academic life. I want to take you to Palestine to meet my parents. We might even consider staying there until the baby comes."

"I don't know if I'd want to have a child in that difficult climate."

"You would be surprised how cool and pleasant it can be in Jerusalem, even in summer."

They heard the children's voices far ahead in the forest. "We'd better catch up to them." Maura stood up. They followed the shouts down the path to a small stream. Under a wooden bridge several boys were lifting rocks, looking for lizards. "Don't get wet," Maura instructed. Then she leaned against the rail of the bridge and smiled at Elliot hesitantly.

He took her hand in his and spoke sincerely. "I hope you are pregnant, I truly do. And if you're not, I vow to make you so within the next month. Then we won't have any excuse to postpone our life together."

"We haven't postponed very much, have we?" She pouted.

"Every night we're apart is a waste."

"Do you really want to . . . to go on with it?"

"What's 'it'?" Elliot grinned.

"Me . . . us . . . the . . . the wee one." She looked down at her belly and stroked it hesitantly.

"Yes, I *honestly* do."

"Well, we had better make plans and a few decisions," she replied, brightening.

"They won't be difficult. We'll make a list and solve our problems one by one."

"First, there's the matter of religion."

"A technicality." Maura's father was Irish, so Elliot had supposed her to be a Roman Catholic and expected she would want her child to be brought up in that church.

Elliot thought for a moment about the religious aspects of his upbringing and wondered, for the first time, how his mother had reconciled her marriage. Suddenly he realized he had never explained about his mother's faith.

"Weren't you raised in the . . . Roman Catholic . . . Church?" he asked haltingly.

"Yes, I was." She was almost whispering. "Would you object to raising the child as a Catholic?"

"Maura, I am not a religious man."

"I know that, but we need a place to be married and a faith for our child. Besides, it all comes down to a belief in basic Christian principles, doesn't it?"

"Don't make this more difficult for me . . ." He was stammering. "I haven't tried to keep this from you, but it has never come up, I don't know quite why . . ."

She clasped his hand in hers. "Elliot, what's wrong?"

"My father's Anglican, of course, but my mother, well, she is Jewish and so . . ."

Maura dropped his hand and stepped backward.

He rushed on with his explanation. ". . . By Jewish law I am Jewish, but in England I am a British subject and at school I worshiped in my father's church. I know it all sounds quite confusing, but it's never been a problem for me and so it shouldn't be one for our child . . ." His voice drifted off.

Maura was no longer listening. She was calling to the children under her care. "Bobby, Michael Bakersfield and Michael Stubbs, Evan, Willy — boys — get away from the water and come here immediately!"

"Maura!" Elliot ran to catch up with her. She would not look at him. Nor would she speak to him all the way back to Bletchley, and she refused to see him for several days thereafter.

One evening he planted himself outside her door until she had consented to a short discussion in the corridor. She accused him of deliberately deceiving her. He protested to no avail.

Finally, she spoke in a low, mean voice. "I've requested a discharge. Most of my children will be returned to their families next week. I'll escort them and then go home to mine."

"If there's a child?"

"This is probably just some kind of female disturbance. Many women have them, particularly during times of crisis, I'm told. I expect that as soon as I'm home everything will right itself. After all, I feel perfectly fine!"

"All our plans —"

"It's impossible!"

"Why, because I'm —"

She cut him off. "It's because you lied to me with your silence."

"It never seemed to —"

"That's where you were so wrong. What sort of husband would you make? Marriage is based on openness, not disguises. How I *hate* disguises." She spoke furiously about principles and truth, but Elliot noticed the nervous twists of her hands and felt that she was not being entirely truthful with him — or with herself — about her anti-Semitic feelings.

"How could this have happened to us?"

"Ask yourself — after I'm gone."

"You won't be coming back?"

"Never."

"If there's a baby —"

"There will not be one," she said fiercely, as though conviction would make it so.

"I cannot give you up, Maura. All we had . . ." His voice cracked. "Don't you love me?"

"No. I don't." Her voice was clipped. "Perhaps I never did. In any case, I could never marry a Jew."

Her words were like a vise crushing his heart. All the blood drained from his face. "I'm sorry then" was what he said, but somewhere deep inside, someplace where the sharp pains had not penetrated completely yet, he was thinking he had done well to discover her true character now, before it was too late. "If you need me, or my help —" he whispered.

"I shan't!" she screamed and shut the door.

Maura left Bletchley the next day.

If that had been the end, Elliot would have been relieved. It was not to be so simple.

Three months later, Jocelyn Sedgewick, a friend of Maura's, met him on the street.

"I suppose you've been wondering about Maura."

"Has she written from home?"

"Yes, she's been in touch, but she never went home. She couldn't, under the circumstances."

"Is she having a child?"

Jocelyn sighed loudly. "That was never in doubt, my dear boy."

"She said —"

"She didn't want you to know. That was foolish on her part. Why shouldn't you be made to suffer? You got off too easy as it is, but most men do," she finished bitterly.

"For heaven's sake, Jocelyn, you know how much I wanted to marry her!"

Jocelyn, who undoubtedly knew everything, simply said, "She's done what she had to, but it's a pity so much joy is being lost."

"You know where she is, don't you?"

"She's going to do quite well without you." Jocelyn started to walk away from him.

Elliot pursued her. "She'll need money. She's alone."

"She will not be alone."

"You said her family doesn't know."

"I said she didn't go home to her family."

"Is this some sort of sanity test? My God, Jocelyn, you are talking about a woman I loved who is having my baby."

Jocelyn sighed. "You might as well hear all of it. If I didn't know Maura as well as I do, I'd think she was off ruining her life, but she's the type who will always come out on top. She found herself another bloke and married him right off."

"Married him! In so short a time?"

"She went to London for just that purpose, volunteered in a hospital ward, and got herself assigned to some recuperating officers. She checked them out and picked herself a young major with a wooden leg."

"You make it sound as easy as picking fruit in an orchard. Did she say, 'I'll take that one there and he'll marry me and we'll all live happily ever after'? Pray then, Jocelyn, what did she tell the one-legged major about my baby?"

"She told him that the baby's father had disappeared in action. He's perfectly delighted to bring it up as his own."

"So that's her idea of honesty, is it? I haven't bloody well disappeared, have I? She's the one who's vanished."

Jocelyn wilted a bit. "There's no way to know exactly what's right or wrong in these matters. She has to protect the baby, too."

"Who is he?"

"I cannot tell you that, Elliot. You owe her some peace and happiness."

"He will be my child's father!"

"That's right! Aren't you fortunate that you're free of any responsibility?" Jocelyn's voice was too cruel and she caught herself. "I'm sorry, Elliot, I don't mean to be so rough on you. I know you loved Maura, or at least believed you did. Put her out of your mind and get on with your life. If you show up, you'll ruin everything. Can't you see that? I met her husband last time I went to London. He's a good man. He'll always have a pension and their families will help out as much as they can. The child won't starve."

Elliot had not tried to contact Maura immediately, but later, he used all the intelligence sources at his disposal to track her. He had known the date and time of his son's birth and where the boy had lived every day since. He had photographs from the distance, but in them, the boy's features were blurred. Yet Elliot kept them in a book and pulled them out regularly to stare at the infant's unformed features and wonder what he might be like. Someday he would meet his son, he vowed, though he wished never to see Maura again.

JERUSALEM, PALESTINE: 1946

Had it not been for his dual identity, Elliot/Eli might not have come to the attention of the Political Department of the Jewish Agency. Had it not been for Maura, Elliot might not have been so receptive to their advances. They had been following his career since Bletchley Park. In early 1946 they knew his military term was about to expire.

Discreet inquiries through his family revealed that Elliot's fellowship could not be resumed before autumn and so he had signed up for an additional tour of duty as a movement control officer with the Allied Control Commission in occupied Germany.

After three boring months in the documents office in London, Elliot was posted to the port of Bremen, checking credentials of travelers immigrating or returning to the West. Before leaving for West Germany, Elliot was permitted a short leave. In the years he had lived abroad, there had been a dramatic increase in the level of hostilities between the British and Jews in Palestine. He had been away at school and at war for almost thirteen years, and in that time the British had broken their mandated promise to maintain Palestine as the national Jewish homeland. Furthermore, they had denied their obligation to uphold the Balfour Declaration at the moment in history when the Jewish people's plight was most critical. No more than seventy-five thousand Jews were to be permitted into Palestine over the next five years, after which the gates of the Holy Land would be closed forever. While fifteen thousand people a year, twelve hundred fifty a month, might have sounded generous to the authors of the immigration act, its effect was to throw millions of Jews to the Nazis and relegate those already in Palestine to the position of a permanent minority. A more poignant example of what these numbers meant was that for the more than two hundred thousand Austrian Jews trapped in Nazi-occupied Vienna, only sixteen certificates for Palestine were made available.

It had pained Elliot to confront the conflict because one side of him understood the British point of view, the other the Jewish. If it had not been for Hitler, he might have found it difficult to take a stance, but the results of the Final Solution cleared away all vacillation. To anyone in England who would listen, Elliot would launch into a tirade against the British policies. "How can we deny Jews their homeland now when it is most needed?" he asked, only to hear specious rebuttals about "a Mandate to keep the peace," "oil interests," and "our Arab friends must be considered as well." His father agreed wholeheartedly with Elliot. After the British White Paper of 1939, he had almost resigned his police post in protest.

During this time, Ruth's brother, Jonathan Epstein, had become an official with the Palestine government secretariat and risen to the position of economic adviser to the chief secretary. Torn between his loyalty to the Jewish Agency position and his responsibilities at the British secretariat, he handed in his resignation, but was persuaded to remain at his post by his friends and family, who knew that he was an excellent intermediary, having influential friends on both sides.

In Cambridge just before the war, Elliot had lunched with Uncle Jonathan when he was on a business trip to England.

"What was the logic behind the White Paper?" Elliot had asked.

"The British think that it will guarantee the support, or at least the neutrality, of the Arabs in Palestine and neighboring countries in case war breaks out with Germany."

"Do *you* think it will have that effect?"

"The Arabs consider it a minimal concession at this point. To them it's only a beginning. For years they've expected a revision of the Balfour Declaration, which they felt was a terrible injustice to their side."

Just a month after that lunch, Britain was at war with Germany. Ben-Gurion ordered Palestine's Jews to "fight Hitler as if there were no White Paper, and fight the White Paper as if there were no Hitler." The Jews obeyed. Many enlisted in the British army; others joined forces underground to bring in illegal immigrants. Officially, Uncle Jonathan had worked on the side of legal immigration, but he had won painfully few battles in that arena, making him a pariah among old associates who espoused a more direct approach to the conflict. Elliot was convinced his uncle unofficially had aided the Mossad le Aliya-Bet, the Institute of Illegal Immigration.

In the summer of 1946 the war in Europe was over, but a new one was erupting in Eli's homeland. The enemy was the British. The oppressed were the Jews. And he was both.

During his brief holiday at home, Eli felt out of sorts and out of place. His friends were widely scattered; his parents were quarrelsome. The strain of the last few years was evident. The police superintendent's usual nip or two of his favorite Scotch before dinner, and possibly another at bedtime, had increased to the point where he was never without a half-filled glass close by. If Ruth mentioned his drinking habits, Hugo would fume, make a great show of pouring his glass down the sink, and spend several hours sulking in the bathroom.

His mother was opposed to Eli's re-enlistment. "If you're not going back to the university," she argued, "remain in Palestine. All your friends are serving in the Haganah. This is where a man with your background can make a contribution."

But Eli felt unable to make the commitment. At the end of the month he would be posted to Bremen. Once there, he might more clearly decide the direction of his life. So far his choices had never been his own; his parents had picked his schools; his uncle had placed him in wartime service; Maura had made the decision to leave him and give his child to another man to raise; the re-enlistment had been offered at a time he had had no better option. Maybe in Germany he would be able to make one logical, deliberate, unemotional move about where he would live, what he would do, how he would get on in the world.

❖   ❖   ❖

It was Monday, the twenty-second of July, in the year 1946: a date all Jerusalem would never forget. That morning, with only a week to go before his leave ended, Eli made every attempt to be the dutiful son, but his father had begun to drink early in the day and had been unusually surly, his mother had gone back to bed, and he had needed to get out on his own. He headed for the YMCA.

"Here is a place where atmosphere is peace, where political and religious jealousies can be fogotten and international unity be fostered and developed." These were the words on the plaque outside the Y's stone gate. The quotation was from Lord Allenby's dedication address in April 1933.

Completed the year he was sent off to the Perse School, the YMCA had been a haven during visits home: a place he could relax with other boys, Jewish and British, Arab and foreigner, where both his identities were accepted completely.

"Hello!" someone rushing down the outside stairs called to Eli. The face was familiar, but Eli could not recall the name.

"Hello," he returned anyway.

At the doorway, he paused and looked across the street to the King David Hotel, which was as busy as ever with people arriving for lunch. As he crossed the entranceway, Eli stared at one of his favorite floors: the mosaic copy of the Madeba map of Jerusalem from which scholars have learned much about Roman and Byzantine Jerusalem.

"Eli, how are you?" a voice called from the end of one of the long, arcaded galleries.

"Hello, Paul!" Eli looked up and greeted a boy with whom he had attended St. George's School for several years. Paul also served in His Majesty's Forces and now was posted at the Allenby Barracks. They had renewed their friendship during the past few weeks, but it was restricted to the Y and did not extend to each other's residences, even though the families touched in numerous ways. Paul's father, Dr. William Tallman, was a military dentist who had recently filled two of Eli's teeth; his mother, Marjorie, worked across the street in the King David Hotel as a secretary in the same office as Eli's Uncle Jonathan.

"Still as 'short' as ever!" Eli quipped. It had always amused them both that he, named Short, was almost a head taller than Paul Tallman.

"Are you coming to eat or to swim?"

"Both." Eli looked at his watch. It was a few minutes before noon. "I think I'll swim first. Fifty laps before lunch. Want to join me?"

"Sure, I was just heading to the pool. I think I saw Kenny Bell going down there. Remember him?"

"Ding Dong Bell!" Eli laughed, then stopped himself. "Didn't somebody tell me he was badly wounded?"

"He's a sapper . . . lost an arm. He swims for therapy. Amazing how good he is at it."

"Swimming, or defusing bombs?"

"Both. The guy's fearless, even after what happened. He's teaching an explosives course at the barracks."

The air in the room was dank and warm. Eli dove gracefully into the pool. The water was deliciously cool. After thirteen years, the pool still impressed Eli as the most beautiful in the world. Its deep midnight blue tile contrasted with the lighter gilded tile on the walls. He almost felt as if he were swimming outside on a moonlit night instead of in a basement in Jerusalem at midday. To begin, he took long, graceful strokes, aware of every breath and sensation. As he reached one side and started his third lap, he caught Paul's competitive glance and reflexively picked up speed. In a moment he regretted being jarred from his own rhythmic stroke and into an unwanted contest. He automatically was determined to win.

Eli stopped in midstroke. A weird tightness gripped his head and neck. His body was massaged by an unusual vibration in the pool. All at once the noise poured from the stone walls and thundered through the tiled room. In the series of aftershocks, the windows under the eaves shattered, glass sheets and shards fell inward. Eli ducked under the water and tried to make his way to the side. When he emerged, the room was spinning.

Someone was shouting, "Where's Bell? Get Bell!"

It took a few seconds before he could see someone under the

churning surface. Paul, who had somehow gotten out of the water, jumped back in and dragged the stunned swimmer to the side. Eli helped to lift the limp man onto the deck. Blood oozed from cuts on Ken's neck. Eli splashed water from the pool on Ken's back to see how deep they were.

"His color . . ." Paul pointed out the strange blueness around Ken's lips.

Eli tipped Ken's head sideways, pushed on his chest, and a gush of water spewed forth. Ken started choking and spitting.

"Thank God . . . thank God," Paul groaned. Ken was going to be all right.

"What the hell was that?" Eli finally asked. "An earthquake?"

They could hear shouting and screaming. Everyone ran up the stairs; Ken brought up the rear.

"There's a bloody great hole in the King David Hotel!" someone shouted.

"My mother!" Paul ran past Eli.

Two women who had been in the courtyard rushed inside, blocking the door. "There are bodies — everywhere!" one of them screamed.

"Get him off the wall," the other pleaded, but nobody could figure out what she meant until they saw a head plastered to the wall of the Y. Its body had slipped down to the pavement, leaving a scarlet silhouette. The head was too high to be easily removed. Concerned with who might be alive and helped, everybody ran to the hotel to offer assistance.

As he crossed the street, Eli cut his foot on some rubble. "Damn it! Paul, we've got to get dressed." But Paul was already asking people if they had seen his mother.

Eli ran back to get their shoes. Once in the dressing room, he decided to put on his uniform. It turned out to be a good move, because less than thirty minutes after the blast, the secretariat had been cordoned off. The police were turning back the crowd. "The gathering place for information will be in the YMCA courtyard," they announced. However, Eli's uniform took him past the barricades and into the hellish aftermath of the disaster.

"There'd been a warning. They called a warning, but the place wasn't evacuated!" a man yelled. Others were rushing around asking if anyone had seen their friends and relatives. Eli knew dozens of people who worked in the secretariat, but his prayers were for his uncle's safety.

He caught up with Paul. "Any word?"

"No." Paul trembled uncontrollably. Eli made him put on his shoes.

"She might not have been in the building," Eli suggested gently. "It's still lunch hour. She might have been anywhere —"

"She rarely goes out," Paul responded frantically. "Likes to work straight through . . ."

Everywhere Eli turned, the sights were grisly. One body was hanging in the branches of a cypress tree; another was draped over a nearby coil of barbed wire.

A dignified gentleman pointed to the head on the wall of the YMCA. "Good God! Could that be Postmaster Kennedy?" he shouted.

Frantic calls pierced the air: "Has anybody seen George Farley?" "Have you seen my father?" "Have you seen John Gutch?" "Grace Baramki?" "Hilda Azzam?" In only a few cases was anyone rewarded with hopeful news.

Paul approached an army chaplain who was passing out glasses of lemonade. "Have you seen Marjorie Tallman?"

"I can't say, son, but have some lemonade."

"I don't want lemonade. I want my mother!"

"Captain Tallman." A policeman came running in their direction, shouting. "I think they may have found your mother!"

"She's all right?"

"Don't know, sir."

Eli followed. Since Marjorie Tallman worked with Uncle Jonathan, she might know whether he had been in the building or not. They walked over piles of fragmented glass. Ambulance sirens played endlessly. They had to stop twice to permit parades of stretcher-bearers to pass. Eli stared intently at every face that was not covered with a handkerchief, indicating a fatality. A few minutes later he berated himself for not looking at the dead ones too.

Arab workmen burrowed into the rubble with picks and jackhammers. Steel rods and metal furniture were being broken up with acetylene torches. Just to one side a doctor jumped into a crevice created by huge concrete slabs and shot morphine into a man trapped below who writhed in agony. A medic lowered a tin cup of water tied on a string to someone who reached through a hole in the debris.

Marjorie Tallman came limping toward her son. They embraced. "I had just returned to the office with a missing file for Mr. Epstein when . . ." she explained in a faraway voice.

"My uncle. Have they found him yet?"

"He was in a meeting next door. Then the blast threw me across the room. Dust was everywhere. When it settled I was standing on the edge of a precipice. Sir John Shaw pulled me back in and helped me to safety. Your uncle . . . Where he was collapsed."

By evening, Jonathan Epstein had been reported among the missing. Sixty hours after the explosion, army doctors announced there was no possibility that anyone trapped remained alive. In the end, Eli's uncle was identified only by his gold cuff links.

The family sat shiva, the ritual seven days of mourning, at the Epstein house in the Rehavia quarter. Many of those who came to pay their respects to his Aunt Julia had also been in the King David at the hour of the explosion. Their tales of miraculous survival contrasted grimly with those less fortunate.

"Did you know that they took Rashid Sbeitan to the mortuary and informed his family that he was dead? Hours later, one of the attendants saw him move! A doctor revived him and they say he'll recover."

"Lubah Wahbeh is fine, but her sister died. It was God's will to spare one, don't you think?"

"Did you hear about Rose, the clerk from the French consul's office? She was standing on a fifth-floor balcony and landed on top of the rubble without so much as a scratch!"

The stories were endless. Harry Beilin, one of Uncle Jonathan's best friends, came every day. "I myself would have been killed if I had gone to my weekly visit with Jonathan," he said over and over again. At the last minute, Golda Myerson, his boss, had arranged for him to attend a meeting that day with Major Ernest Quinn, the officer in charge of intelligence.

Noticeably absent from that parlor was Uncle Jonathan's daughter, Dorit. Recently married to a member of the underground terrorist organization the Irgun, she might have had an indirect responsibility in her father's death. She appeared only briefly at the funeral.

One of Jonathan Epstein's closest friends from the Jewish Agency's Political Department, Reuven Shiloah, offered to be among the ten men needed to make up the minyan for the prayers held each morning and afternoon. For several hours each day, Shiloah sat quietly in a chair with his eyelids half-closed behind his rimless glasses. Most assumed him to be resting, but Eli noticed that the man was following every word being said in the room. Often

Shiloah would ask gentle questions about Eli's work at Bletchley Park and what was in store for him in Bremen.

Reuven Shiloah had been the first person who sensed the fury building up inside Eli. He listened as the young man raged alternately against the Irgun for the senseless bombing and the British for their blind policies.

"Anger changes the world faster than any other force," Shiloah began with a half-smile on his tightly closed lips. "Human nature, being what it is, has each of us striving for ourselves first. But if a whole group can be made furious at the same time, they will band together and create a revolution." His words were so well modulated, his ideas so organized, Eli could not help but admire the soft-spoken man.

Born in Jerusalem, the son of a rabbi, Shiloah won the attention of friends in the Jewish Worker's Federation when he was a student. It was suggested he study the Arab question firsthand. Sent to Baghdad, he worked officially as a journalist for the *Palestine Bulletin*. All the while, he traveled throughout Iraq and learned to speak each of its dialects, including Kurdish.

"Three years later, when I was twenty-six," he told Eli, "I was appointed by the Jewish leadership here in Jerusalem as a liaison officer with the British. In 1939, I was chosen to be one of the counselors to Ben-Gurion and Chaim Weizmann at the Round Table Conference in St. James's Palace. Then the war broke out."

Eli had heard rumors about what Shiloah had done next. They said that he led special operations behind enemy lines for the Jewish Agency and had been involved in the formation of a Jewish commando corps to carry out acts of sabotage in occupied Europe. Although Shiloah supposedly had a desk job now, Eli surmised that man's undercover activities had never ceased.

On the last day of mourning, Shiloah had taken Eli aside. "We have an office in London. Someday perhaps we will meet there," he said cryptically. "If not, I hope you will call on me when you return home again."

"I most certainly will," Eli had responded politely, not fully comprehending the meaning of the man's offer.

BREMEN, WEST GERMANY: 1946

By accepting the military assignment outside England after the war, Eli felt that he was participating in the real world at last. While his efforts at Bletchley Park had probably saved more lives than any one man's combat experience, there was no tangible proof that he had accomplished anything.

After leaving Jerusalem, Eli was to spend two weeks in London before beginning his West German assignment. He stayed with his father's elderly Aunt Harriet in Camden Town. The Sunday morning of the second week, a man came to his aunt's flat inquiring for him.

Aunt Harriet showed him into her modest parlor and, with a trembling hand, poured the visitor a glass of sherry. "I expect you two boys would like to be alone." She lifted her huge Siamese cat from the sofa and padded off to her room. The man identified himself only as "Saul" and said he was a friend of his late Uncle Jonathan's. Eli suspected Reuven Shiloah had something to do with the visit.

Saul was an easygoing man with a pleasant lilt to his speech. "First I want to offer my condolences. Your uncle was a great man. He will be missed by us all."

"Thank you," Eli replied.

"We would like to ask you to do us a favor," Saul began softly.

"How can I help?" Eli responded evenly, just barely controlling his enthusiasm.

"We have word that a man will pass through Bremen in a few weeks. His papers will be irregular, but he must get through without any delay."

"You must be aware that I will be under the jurisdiction of the British military government," Eli whispered uneasily.

"This matter should not be of interest to your superiors. We only wish to facilitate a man's journey along the route to his final destination."

"You must know better than I how few visas for Palestine are available. There is nothing I can do once he leaves the port."

"He will get on the list," Saul said emphatically. "He's receiving priority as a teacher. Your uncle would have approved of this request. After all, we're not asking for so very much."

Momentarily, Eli wondered if he was being disloyal to his job, if not the government that employed him, but the doubts quickly vanished. Since the King David disaster, Eli's sympathies were with the Jews. The British limitation on immigration to Palestine, which had been severe enough during the war, was now indefensible. Stateless Jews from all over Europe required a homeland. It was a moral issue, not a political one. Besides, Saul would not ask him, in the name of his uncle, to jeopardize his career. Eli had no twinges when he replied, "It is the least I can do."

The British checkpoint in the port of Bremen was an especially crucial spot after the war. Thousands en route from East to West had used every known ruse to create new identities, and even true stories were difficult to verify at a time when so many records had been lost. It was the perfect opportunity for war criminals, Nazi sympathizers, collaborators, and petty thieves to hide their origins.

The first weeks at Bremen were uneventful except for the ten continuous days of rain. Eli's desk job was surprisingly interesting: every face, every passport, seemed to hold a story. Deciding what questions to ask, which facts to explore further, was always a challenge. Eli impressed his superiors with the many inaccuracies and false passports he uncovered. Even when all was in order, he watched the paperwork lest it was too perfect. Eventually, most travelers, other than the stateless Jews, were given clearance to depart. Fewer than 10 percent were detained — mainly with good cause.

His successes included a KGB agent disguised as a refugee and a Russian officer posing as a civilian. These were dealt with by higher-level authorities. When he uncovered inconsistencies in the background of a man named Horst Fasser, who claimed to be a mechanic from Prenzlau on his way to visit relatives in Chicago, Eli was certain the man was a Nazi war criminal. But there was no proof, nobody available to interrogate him at the moment.

"A small fish, at best," his immediate officer had decided. "Throw him back in the sea."

Eli had no alternative but to follow orders. Nevertheless, his resentment festered.

While the routine of the job was fairly comfortable, the deep distrust and fear Eli felt among the German populace seemed to increase as time passed. He hated every syllable of the guttural language. He choked on the greasy sausages. And though he spent a few obligatory evenings in the tavern-studded Schnoor district and once made a trip to the Ratskeller, where the Faust legend was said to have originated centuries earlier, his grudge against the Germans extended as far as disliking their beer.

Before long, Eli looked forward to making his connection with Saul's friend, speculating he might be a secret agent carrying papers to the Haganah, a courier with illegal currency, or a Nazi-hunter knowing the whereabouts of Mengele or Eichmann.

At the expected date and time, Saul's man passed his documents through the barrier at the port of departure. Eli studied the man's face. Monsieur Bille, whose occupation was listed as laboratory technician, seemed younger, more urbane than he had expected. He had a short mustache, which he stroked with his forefinger in a thoughtful rather than nervous fashion. His physique was strong and muscular; wherever he had spent the war, he had been given enough to eat. Immediately, Eli liked the bright, brown eyes that stared at him steadily but uncritically. Every flicker and minute gesture seemed to be a subliminal message to Eli; there was unspoken friendship, camaraderie, gratitude — all expressed wordlessly.

His Swiss passport, in the name of Raymond Bille, revealed no obvious discrepancies. Eli asked a few questions in halting French. The sequence of responses was perfect.

"Everything is in order," he said in English. To himself he murmured the ancient prayer, "Next year in Jerusalem."

KIBBUTZ HAZOREA, PALESTINE: 1947

The next time Eli met Saul was in London at the end of his tour of duty in Bremen.

"I understand you have volunteered to help the Jewish Agency further," Saul said. Once again they were in Aunt Harriet's Camden Town parlor, sipping sherry.

Eli pretended to be surprised. "Word travels fast."

"We want you to come to Palestine."

Though he was curious about who "we" referred to, he knew he had best only answer questions, not ask them. "Whenever you like" was his simple reply.

Within two days of arriving in Palestine, he was contacted and taken to a warehouse along the banks of the Yarkon River in Tel Aviv. There was a black curtain at the end of a long, bare room and on a table lay a Beretta and a Bible. After a few preliminary questions he was asked whether he was willing to take the oath to commit himself to the cause. When he agreed, a voice behind the curtain called out, "Please take the gun in one hand, the Bible in the other."

From the table draped with the blue and white Zionist flag, Eli lifted the 7.5 mm automatic pistol with the initials "PB" scrolled on it prettily. The cold metal in his left hand contrasted oddly with the warm, leather-bound volume in his right.

"Now recite after me," the disembodied voice ordered. "With this weapon . . . "

"With this weapon . . . which has been entrusted to me by the

Haganah, in the Land of Israel . . ." The word "Israel" made Eli's
heart leap with anticipation.

"I shall fight against the enemies of my people . . ."

"I shall fight against the enemies of my people . . ."

"For my country . . ."

"For *my* country . . ." His emphasis was deliberate.

"Without surrendering . . ."

"Without surrendering, without flinching, and with complete
dedication," he finished emotionally. For the first time in his life, Eli
sensed he had willingly joined a group where his participation would
make a difference.

Two weeks later he was in a secret Palmach training camp in the
Jezreel Valley, being ordered about by teenagers, young men and
women ten years his junior. "The Old Man," they called him good-
naturedly.

The Palmach, which derived its name from the Hebrew Plugot
Mahatz, or striking units, of the Haganah, had been established in
1941 with the encouragement and help of the British army in anticipation of the Nazis' invasion of Palestine across North Africa and
Egypt. At that time, the Palmach was to provide rear-guard action
to enable the British forces to withdraw eastward. Survival for the
Jewish population, not sovereignty, was the issue for the Jewish leaders; yet its founding was a decisive step toward the birth of a professional Jewish defense force.

The first days of Eli's training were punishing. Knowing that his
ultimate placement was to be in some area of intelligence work, he
wondered at the necessity of such rigorous indoctrination in the use
of armaments. Besides conventional guns, he was expected to master
explosives, truncheons, and knives, as well as prove his mettle at daily
lessons in hand-to-hand combat. Dressed for farm work, in case the
British came searching for illegal military installations, he labored
in the melon fields alongside the other kibbutzniks until called upon to
take apart and reassemble sten guns while blindfolded. In the heat
of the day, when it was unlikely they would be bothered, the rigorous
drilling began. They hiked in and around the newly planted orchards,
carrying impossible loads on their backs. His years in Bletchley
Park decoding lists of numbers in drafty huts had taken their toll.
Eli was humiliated whenever he staggered in as one of the last.

A final endurance test, a cross-country trek to Megiddo at night
carrying more than fifty kilos on his back, almost convinced Eli he
did not belong anywhere except in study rooms beside the river

Cam. The small town on the skyline seemed farther and farther away as he staggered closer and closer. Several of the girls in the group and one of the boys chose not to go on. Determined not to fail, Eli plunged ever forward, the memory of an old Perse School sermon on Armageddon floating in his mind. In the Bible, the very sound of the name Megiddo was a trumpet call to war.

"Har Megiddo," he said under his breath. Mount Megiddo, which some believe St. John made into one thundering, cataclysmic word — "Armageddon," the ultimate battlefield. Was that why they were being tormented? Was their destination then and later to be some ultimate battlefield? Was Armageddon actually Megiddo, or could it be in the heart of Jerusalem at Mount Zion, as some scholars argued?

Armageddon. A myth or a prophecy? Eli heaved and groaned. His legs shook with exhaustion. His arms strained to lift the weight from his back and ease his burning shoulders. These youngsters, with their Biblical names and faces, their tense determination, their heroic songs — where were they leading themselves? To Megiddo? It all made about as much sense as the great red dragon with seven heads and ten horns and other satanic monsters of the Bible. Eli fumed and snorted. His rage at primitive images and two-thousand-year-old connections engulfed him and at the same time prodded and sustained him as he stepped one foot at a time ever onward into the starry night.

Eli survived the trek and passed the fitness part of the course. The longest period of training, which was reserved for radio communications, required stamina of a different sort. Drills in Morse code began each morning in a small room beside the barn and continued for more than twelve hours a day. Proficiency could be developed only by brutal, dogged repetition. Some members of Eli's class were reduced to tears, shakes, violent headaches, under the pressure to build up speed.

"There are no short cuts," their instructor, an intense seventeen-year-old girl, conceded.

If someone made it through the first three weeks, he was graduated to the second phase, during which one was expected to attain the level of fifteen to twenty-five words per minute within the next month. Eli knew the code fairly well because of his work at Bletchley Park, but he sweated with the rest. His arm trembled after about six hours; his neck developed a chilling numbness at the end of each exhausting day.

By the time he went on to coding, maintenance, repair, and electronic theory, he had spent almost seven hundred hours at the Morse key and claimed he was "sending his dreams in his sleep."

After learning the corresponding codes in both English and Hebrew, the trainees had been shown how to translate between the two.

"Remember that the English alphabet has more letters than our Hebrew one. The letters we do not have an equivalent for are 'J,' 'Q,' 'W,' 'X,' and 'Y.' Therefore we use these as punctuation signs and spread them as statistically evenly as possible throughout." Aviva Ben-Zion spoke in so soft a voice that Eli had to strain to follow her. "Why are we doing that?" she asked the class.

"To make the code more complex?" someone asked.

"Yes, but there is another, more important reason."

Eli spoke up. "If you omitted those letters — which, while not occurring very frequently in English, are bound to appear at certain logical rates throughout a text — someone listening in would know that the code was not in English."

"That is right," Aviva responded flatly and went right on with her lecture. There would be no pats on the back, no coaxing along. The material was either mastered or not. One was either accepted or removed. "The code is always broken down into two groups of five letters. Each letter is given a numerical value. The key, the number of which is always transmitted in the opening of the message, will be ten letters long. When you find those numerical values and determine whether they should be added or subtracted, it is a simple matter to do rapid self-crypting without machines or aids."

At this point Aviva had lost most of the class, but Eli's background made it easy for him to follow what was basically a very simple system. With lightning speed, she next demonstrated the rate they were expected to achieve: twenty groups per minute received and deciphered simultaneously.

"Whew!" Eli called out, impressed at her skill. "Are *we* supposed to be that good at the end of six weeks?"

"It is possible," she replied sullenly.

"How many years have you been studying?" he asked.

"More than three."

"But that was before you learned to talk," he kidded.

Her steady stare indicated that she did not appreciate jokes about her youth.

As they walked to supper in the communal dining hall that evening, Eli slowed to wait for Aviva. "Slikha, I'm sorry, I didn't mean to insult you," he said in Hebrew. "It's only that such talent in one so young is bound to make an old man like me feel . . . how shall I say it? . . . insecure." He beamed charmingly.

When Aviva did not respond, he understood that her tiny voice and insistent businesslike manner were only indications of shyness. He was determined to put her at ease.

"You're very good, you know, as a teacher as well as a radio operator. Not many people could break such a technical subject down into small, easily understood bits."

"Do you think so?" she asked in a whisper.

"What I was wondering was, in your experience, do you find men or women better as wireless operators?"

"In training, the answer is definitely women. Whether or not the men catch up in the field, I cannot say."

"Do women get the feel of it faster?"

"Yes, but also they are more willing to accept that it takes hours and hours of practice."

"Was it very difficult for you at first?"

Aviva paused and pursed her lips thoughtfully. "In the old days we had more time. They gave us six months to achieve twenty-two words a minute. Now, we need to train as many as possible, and fast. You have seen for yourself how exhausting it is. Most of the group cannot tolerate the pressure, not because they are weak. Most would be superb soldiers, but something happens in the mind when you work so intensely with tiny dots and dashes over and over. Ori vomits; Meir has migraines. The strain is terrible and I sympathize. My job is to weed out those who cannot achieve proficiency under pressure and push those who can to their limits."

"What do men excel at, if anything?" He laughed easily, but her lips only twitched slightly.

"They get into the complex codes faster. The women seem to fear the work when there are too many numbers all jumbled up. The men are more willing to take stabs at all kinds of patterns until one makes sense."

"From my own experiences during the war I found that to be true as well."

"What did you do?" Aviva asked curiously.

"I was in codes and ciphers, actually."

Aviva nodded respectfully. "Then you could teach me a trick or two."

That night the kibbutz held a kumsitz, a get-together around the bonfire. An old battered brass finjan, an Arab-style beaked coffee-pot, was being passed around. The Palmachniks sang their songs of unity and hope, beginning with the theme song of the Palmach.

"Misaveev yehom hasa'ar
Ach roshainu lo yeeshach
Leefkuda tameed; anachnu tameed
Anu, anu, hapalmach."

All around us blows the storm
But our heads are raised on high
For an order — always; we are ready — always
We are, we are, the Palmach.

As they sang, Eli watched the earnest faces of the teenage boys and girls who were mobilizing themselves. Most had gone into the underground army after a few years in the scouts. At the tender ages of fourteen, fifteen, and sixteen they had taken the oath, pledging their lives and futures to their country. All of them were children who deserved a more carefree life, for at least a few more years. If you asked any one of them if he or she regretted the loss of their youth, the answer would probably be a shrug and the Palmach's motto: ein breira . . . no alternative.

Almost a third of the group were female. From the start, girls were taken into the Palmach for active duty and given the same commando training as Eli had received. When he had suggested that the hike was too strenuous for some of them, his leader had replied, "Just try to suggest that to the girls. They will jump on your back and say that Palestine is being built by a new society that will not restrict women to domestic chores. So far, they have proven themselves competent sappers and marksmen."

Eli questioned whether it might not have been wiser to place the young women in units of their own so that they would not have to compete physically with men. At least half the women had not completed the hike, but perhaps they were not expected to. To him it made more sense to use women for defensive warfare — especially as nurses, scouts, or quartermasters, and in jobs such as wireless operators, where they clearly surpassed the average man. If a full-scale war was ever to break out in Palestine against the British or the Arabs, the women captured at the front lines might be raped and tortured by their enemies. It was a terrible thought — and one he did not wish to contemplate for too long.

Eli sat next to Aviva. In this group of sturdy young men and women she seemed one of the most vulnerable. Passing her on the street, one would not sense anything extraordinary about her. She was short and muscular, lacking the soft curves and delicate features most men appreciate. But here, in the primitive light of the flames, her eyes blazed as brightly, her voice was as rich and lusty and her dedication as firm, as any. While other girls might be considered more sensual, there was something about Aviva that drew Eli to her. In the classroom she spoke authoritatively so long as she was discussing her specialty, but she was too unsophisticated to handle the unruly jokes and banter of the students. Instead of chiding them, she would stand in front of the room quietly, eyes straight ahead, and embarrass them into attention. Here, in the fireside group, she was still remote, and this fascinated him.

Because they were all training under cover names, Aviva was called Daniella at the kibbutz, but once he had heard a girl friend slip and call her Aviva. From then on she was Aviva in his mind. He was curious about where she was from, who her parents were, how she had come to Palestine. Her face had the Semitic look of a Sephardic Jew, yet her accent, her cultural tendencies, seemed far more European. At that moment, as they listened to tales of the Palmach commander who had trained under Orde Wingate and had been a member of his famed night raiders squad, Eli glanced over at Aviva now and then.

He was captivated by her hands.

At first glance they appeared extraordinary because they were so very large. In class, Eli had observed her gestures as she spoke and the way she held her hands together thoughtfully while she listened. On closer inspection, he noticed they were quite fine-boned. Each broad finger tapered to a perfectly proportioned tip. Close up, they appeared smooth, flexible, almost erotic, because they intimately revealed the sensitivity of the person locked away in an ordinary shell. Functional, muscular, with calloused fingertips, they were the opposite of Maura's lotioned-smooth, manicured, and pampered pale hands. And yet, when Aviva turned them upward, the palms were whiter than the rest and seemed softer, more tender and yielding, than Maura's had been. Clenched, the fist was a powerful, threatening force; concentrated on the keys of a radio transmitter, the fingers were dexterous and worthy.

The time had come for the last song of the evening: "The Finjan," an ode to the ubiquitous coffeepot.

"Haruach noshevet Kreera
Noseef od kaisam lamdura . . .
Sovev lo sovev hafinjan."

The wind blows lightly,
We'll put more kindling on the fire . . .
Pass around the coffeepot.

Aviva caught Eli's stare. Their eyes locked. What was she feeling? He suspected that despite all the bravado about equality in the camp, she was quite inexperienced with men. Did he want her? Yes, he admitted to himself. He would love to see her fawn-colored flesh stretched out on a cot. He wondered at the shape and feel of her breasts. He yearned to kiss her tense little mouth until it sighed with pleasure. But he would not. A liaison with a teacher would not be politic. Besides, women were treacherous. Lust, he had promised himself, would never again control his judgment. Aviva was interesting, but not overwhelming. There would be hundreds of Avivas.

LONDON, ENGLAND: 1947

Over the next months Eli had to complete a long series of tasks, proving himself again and again. During a brief respite he attended his cousin Esty's engagement celebration in Rehovot. The party was attended by scientists from the Weizmann Institute, local dignitaries, including Israel's new President, Chaim Weizmann, and his wife, Vera. It was not until he was introduced to Esty's fiancé by his beaming Aunt Sarah that he realized his "Monsieur Bille" was about to marry into the family.

"Eli, I'd like you to meet Dr. Asher Ze'evi," his aunt said proudly.

Not wanting to acknowledge their previous encounter, Eli bowed stiffly. "Very pleased to make your acquaintance."

"What do you think of my cousin-to-be?" Eli asked Reuven Shiloah a few moments later.

After Eli's success in Bremen, Shiloah himself had formally asked Eli to join the Sherut Yediot, the intelligence information service of the Haganah. For many years, the Shai (as the service came to be called) had penetrated deep into the Mandate's administration of Palestine, infiltrated the Arab population, even studied dissident Jewish organizations. Shiloah had followed Katzar's progress with the GCCS and approached him when he had been emotionally susceptible to their advances. He had supervised as Eli's background —

and intentions — had been scrutinized, examined, tested, vetted thoroughly. Today Shiloah was more than a mere friend of Eli's family. He was Eli's boss.

"This is the first time you have met him?" Shiloah inquired.

"In our country, yes," Eli replied circumspectly.

Shiloah grinned, then spoke softly. "The professor's visa was sponsored by Chaim Weizmann himself."

"Why? What made him so important?"

"Weizmann had heard of Ze'evi's scientific work through his brother-in-law, Joseph Blumenfeld."

"The geochemist?"

Shiloah seemed pleased by Eli's knowledge. "When Blumenfeld visited the Soviet Union in 1935, he visited the Leningrad Physico-Technical Institute. There he met a young scientist called Asher Shapiro, who was pursuing the possibility of creating nuclear energy from radium. Shapiro also told him that there were many Jews in the laboratories who wished to leave the country. Blumenfeld was able to smuggle two of them to France before 1942, but their defections made it impossible to get Shapiro out for four more years."

Before Eli could state the obvious — that Asher Shapiro had chosen the Israeli name of Ze'evi — Shiloah deftly turned away and began socializing with other guests. Eli stood amongst the shouts and mazel tovs, pleased with the revelation that his first assignment for a Jewish secret service had been to aid the passage of one of the great minds in nuclear physics from Russia to Palestine.

A few weeks later he was unexpectedly transferred into an armaments unit. He was responsible for security during the movement of arms from Kibbutz Yagur, not far north of Hazorea, to sliks, or caches, in Tel Aviv and Jerusalem. Eli was amazed at how far Ta'as, the Haganah's weapons industry, had advanced. Their workshops were producing a deadly grenade modeled after the British Mills bomb; a version of the sten gun made by removing, cutting, reboring, and refitting rusty old Enfield and Winchester barrels from the 1870s; shells for two- and three-inch mortars; and, finally, the mortars themselves. At Eilon, a kibbutz even farther north than Yagur, on the Lebanese border, a bullet-making factory had been built seven meters under a laundry building. The remote kibbutz was further protected from intrusion by a large quarantine sign, which warned that hoof-and-mouth disease had infected the farm's cattle.

After two months of visiting these workers who, when they began to appear too pallid, were given ultraviolet skin treatments, Eli came to respect the young men and women working under such dangerous and harsh physical conditions. A sudden raid by the British would mean death or, at the least, a trial for treason. Once the weapons were in Eli's unit's hands, he was to transport them to the Lavkov leather factory in Tel Aviv, where the weapons were hidden in the vats of the tannery. The stinking tannery made a superb location because nobody ever wanted to search there.

Saul, the man Eli had first met in his aunt's London flat, reappeared to inspect the changes Eli made in the tannery's security. To the secret doors and tunnels under the building he had added warning devices with lights and bells that could be activated by pressing on certain places on the walls and floor without attracting attention. Saul had not taken the time to compliment him. All he said was, "We have decided that your identity and passport are too valuable to waste in the underground. We would like you to travel."

In two days, Eli was in London. He had been told to take an inexpensive room at the Russell Hotel and wait at a certain restaurant near Victoria Station every day from eleven to noon until he was contacted. The rest of the time he concentrated on tracking down his son.

By the end of the first week, Eli had become intimately familiar with the area surrounding the Warwick Avenue tube station. He knew all the possible routes to 44 Lanark Road. The short cut on Warrington Crescent was undesirable because of the large barking bulldog that might have frightened a two-year-old boy. Late in the afternoons he strolled by the shops on Clifton Road, past the post office and bakery — all the places a mother might go each day — and turned left on Lanark Road, crossing in front of number forty-four only at dusk to see if a child might be spotted behind the lighted windows.

Once he heard a high, boyish laugh. Several times there had been the cry of a baby — most likely the new child who was Colin's sister. Another evening he had heard a man shouting, "No, damn it! I told you not to do that!" It was probably Randolph Stewart, Maura's disabled husband. He sounded unkind. Eli was tempted to walk down Clifton Road, march into The Eagle, the pub Stewart managed, order a pint of Watney's, and confront the man who was raising his child. But he could not risk it — not that he cared about what Maura might think or say. There were other, more far-sighted reasons. It would be stupid to let emotions ruin the plans he was making.

For now the boy was safe in the house in Maida Vale. Eli liked the area, which included the lovely canal homes in London's Little Venice, but he thought it peculiar that Maura had chosen a neighborhood occupied by so many Jews. At least it was considered a safe place to raise a child.

"Colin." He said the name under his breath. He did not care for it — Colin Drew Stewart — but it was not the sort of name that would ever give a child trouble at school. It should never have happened this way, Eli reflected. Looking back, one could almost see flags as markers for moments when a life takes an irreversible twist down an unexpected path. As Eli reminisced, he saw two bright standards: the day he had met Maura, and the day she had left him. If she had not been so — there was nothing else to call it — anti-Semitic, he would have a wife, a son, other children perhaps. And what of Israel? Yes, he thought ruefully, it all could have gone another way because of his need — his pathetic need of a woman.

On the tube back to the Russell Hotel he noticed the man who sat beside him had a walking stick. A false leg, Eli guessed, like Randolph Stewart's. Randolph Stewart, the man Colin called Dad or Papa or whatever they used in that house, received a modest pension because of his war disability and managed The Eagle. And Eli had learned that up until her recent confinement, Maura worked evenings as a nurse at the Maida Vale Hospital for Neurological Diseases, within walking distance of their home. There was no doubt that the family was struggling. If they did not do much better through an inheritance or great luck, Eli's scheme for Colin's education and his own subsequent intervention in the boy's life was sure to succeed. But there was nothing he could do to influence or help the child for at least ten more years.

Eli was having a cup of tea at the appointed restaurant at eleven-thirty in the morning.

"Hello, Tom!" an unfamiliar voice called from behind.

Eli turned.

A short man with spectacles said amiably, "Forgive me for being late, but I missed the train from Ashtead."

"Ashtead" was the code word.

"Would you like something to drink?" Eli used the sequence of words to verify he was the contact.

"Thanks, but our meeting's in fifteen minutes. We'd better be on our way."

In the noisy underground he spoke again. "You may call me Leon."

Eli nodded.

Leon handed him a list of three telephone numbers. "Memorize these while we're riding. The first number is to make contact with me, the second is my superior if I cannot be reached, the third is for dire emergency."

When they reached Covent Garden they walked through the market to a small flower shop. The proprietor greeted Leon with a warm smile and unlocked the door to a back room. Two other men, much older than Eli or Leon, were waiting. One was bald, one bearded.

"Sit down, son," the bald man behind the desk said softly.

"What does he know?" the bearded one asked Leon.

"Only the phone numbers. What are they?"

Eli reeled off the three numbers effortlessly.

Leon smiled paternally. "Good. Now give me the paper."

"You have a British military uniform, don't you?" the bearded one asked.

"Yes, sir."

"And it fits?"

"I'd expect so."

"Is it with you?'

"Yes, I was told to pack it."

"So, we are getting organized at last!" He winked at Leon. "On Sunday you are to wear the uniform to the airport. You are returning home. Is that all right with you?"

"I said I would do anything necessary."

"How much are you willing to risk? After all, you have a British passport, a policeman father, you are very privileged. Why should you get involved in our cause?"

"It is mine as well," he replied firmly.

The bald man stood and walked around the desk. He scowled like a master about to deal with an unruly student. "Now let us be clear about this. We want you to commit an illegal act."

What did he mean by that? Eli tried to imagine what violent deed they had in mind, which made it impossible for him to focus on the explanation. Then he heard snatches: " . . . currency laws, more than a hundred thousand pounds sterling . . . Our struggle must be funded and there are no loans available for this sort of . . . So you see how important this assignment is."

A relieved Eli nodded. "I am confident I can handle this matter to your satisfaction."

The bald man folded his arms across his chest. "We would not think less of you if you refused us. Are you aware of the consequences should you be caught?"

"I am at your disposal, gentlemen."

The bearded man took off his glasses and wiped them fastidiously. "The second matter?" he asked his associates.

"Yes, why not?" the bald man responded.

"Excuse me?" Eli asked.

"There is the matter of another small package . . ."

For the next hour they briefed Eli. The heart of the plan involved his smuggling a hundred thousand pounds sterling into Palestine for the Haganah. Unless he was detained — a prospect made less likely by his impeccable credentials and uniform — it hardly seemed a risk. Tomorrow he would meet Leon again and go over the fine points. At the end of the meeting each of the three men, who he suspected were representatives of the Jewish Agency, slapped him on the back appreciatively. He left by himself.

It was almost four in the afternoon. Soon it would be dusk in Maida Vale. In a few days he would be leaving London. He might not return for months — years. If he were caught he would be jailed. Without thinking, he changed trains at King's Cross, then again at Paddington. By quarter to five he was at Warwick Avenue, briskly walking up Clifton Road to The Eagle.

He paused. A slate beside the front door advertised the evening's specials: JACKET POTATO, JUMBO SAUSAGE, STEAK AND KIDNEY PIE. The door opened with a jingle, so he ducked around the corner. A woman wearing a green cape stepped down to the street.

"Come along, Colin," she said loudly.

"No!" was the definitive response from inside.

The woman stepped up once again. "Colin, are you coming by yourself or am I going to have to come after you?"

"No!"

Eli rooted for Colin. That's my boy, don't let Mummy push you around!

"Colin . . ." The voice was completely exasperated. The woman

and child disappeared inside momentarily. Eli could hear sounds of
a scuffle. Little heels pounded the floor.

"I want to stay! I want to . . ." The boy's protests became weaker.

"Here you are, love." A man with ruddy arms lifted the bulky
child dressed in a warm coat, leggings, and cap out onto the pavement and set him down firmly. The door to the pub closed with a
bang.

"Mummy!" Little pudgy arms went up in the air. "Carry me!"

"You're not a baby like Edie. Mummies don't carry big boys. Big
boys hold Mummy's hand."

Now Eli could see the child's face. A fringe of hair peeked out from
under the cap. His cheeks were round and reddened by the wind. It
was too dark to tell the color of his eyes. Although he was not certain
how big two-year-olds were supposed to be, this one seemed a bit tall
for his age and wonderfully formed. The nose was small, the features
alert, and he spoke without a trace of babyishness. For a moment Eli
was afraid they were headed his way — but once Colin took his
mother's hand, they marched off in the opposite direction.

For a long while Eli stayed with his back to the building, thinking
about the boy's face, the sound of his voice, how tough and defiant
he had been. It was not until he was halfway to the hotel that he
thought about having seen Maura. Funny, except for the color of her
cape, he could not recall anything about her.

According to the plan, Eli arrived at Northolt Aerodrome two hours
early, so that he could select an unwitting accomplice from among
the waiting passengers. Leon had warned him to expect passengers
embarking for Palestine to be under surveillance. The CID was
especially vigilant because the Stern Gang and the Irgun, two Jewish
groups that advocated violent rebellion against British policies, were
becoming increasingly active. Eli studied several possibilities — a
white-haired man traveling alone, a mother and child, and a nun —
before noticing the sleeping girl. Her slim, silk-stockinged legs
peeked out from under the raincoat that covered her; her head rested
on a bulky leather handbag propped up by John Hersey's *Hiroshima*.
He moved close enough to read the luggage tag on her flight bag:
C. Green, 311 Hawthorne Terrace, Scarsdale, New York. An American. Even under these uncomfortable circumstances, she looked as relaxed and lovely as a child resting in her mother's arms. Who would
suspect such a sweet face? Wouldn't every inspector be just as fasci-

nated as he was with the charming upturn of her lower lip, her long graceful neck, the sleek shoulder-length pageboy hairdo? Nobody else in the room had so good a chance of eluding suspicion.

He signaled Sadie and Moses Goldfarb, the elderly couple Leon had introduced him to only yesterday.

Sadie tripped and bumped into Miss Green's bench. "Oh, I'm so sorry, my dear!"

The girl's eyes blinked open. "Did you hurt yourself?" She sat up and made room for the older woman to sit down.

Sadie rubbed her elbow. "I'll be fine. It just hit on that strange spot."

"We call it the 'funny bone' in the States."

Sadie smiled. "You're American, aren't you?"

"Yes. My name is Charlotte Green. And you?"

"I'm Sadie Goldfarb; that's my husband, Moses. We live outside London. Are you all alone?"

"Yes. I'm on my way from New York to Jerusalem."

"Such difficult times to be on your own."

Charlotte pursed her lips reflectively. "I'm rather enjoying myself. Are you traveling to Palestine today? Or Cairo? The plane stops there first, doesn't it?"

"I wouldn't know. I'm not flying with you." She dabbed her eyes with her hanky. "Oh, how I wish I were!"

With his back against a nearby post, Eli was thinking that Sadie was hamming it up too much, but there was no way he could interfere.

Moses stroked his wife's shoulder. "Next year we'll try to make the trip."

"If Shimon lasts that long . . ."

"Your brother is like an ox!"

"Without his medicine, the doctors say . . ."

"Mr. Baker said he would be here, don't worry."

The girl was sufficiently curious to ask, "Is something the matter?"

Moses explained that arrangements had been made for a business acquaintance to carry some medicine to Sadie's ailing brother in Jerusalem, but he was terribly late.

"He could have missed the train from Brighton." Sadie wrung her hands. "The next flight isn't for three days."

Then Charlotte, as if reading from a script, volunteered to be the messenger. She never suspected that detonator caps were floating in the medicine bottles.

For both their protection, Eli avoided Charlotte during the long flight to the Middle East. Besides seeing that the detonator caps were transported, he had his own courier assignment to perform. At first his mission seemed modest compared to placing bombs or carrying explosives, so it shocked him to discover what an intense fear a briefcase solidly packed with twenty thousand thin, white five-pound notes could induce. All it would take would be some diligent clerk, as he himself had been at Bremen, to ask him to "kindly open your briefcase, sir." What could he say? One hundred thousand pounds sterling on its way to Palestine was not destined to buy pita bread and olive oil. He would be detained and questioned — no, *interrogated* — then jailed. His silence would infuriate. His lack of cooperation would increase the harshness of his sentence.

As Palestine loomed closer, his watchfulness increased. For amusement he kept his eye on Charlotte. She was seated beside a mother and child and was making paper toys to delight the little girl. The American has a good heart, he decided. At first, he had rationalized using an innocent carrier because she could always tell the truth — that she knew nothing about what was inside the package. She could decribe the Goldfarbs and be done with the matter. But what if she was not believed? He knew he had placed her in jeopardy.

❖   ❖   ❖

The plane arrived at Lydda Airport only two hours late. Eli cleared passport control uneventfully. The first hurdle was over. He placed himself in a position to speak with Charlotte.

He bumped her accidentally. "Excuse me, miss. I'm terribly sorry." He stopped to pick up her flight bag and let the package she had been given in England slip out. "Let me help you with that —"

"Be careful, it's medicine."

He lifted the box and rattled it gingerly. "Don't think anything's been broken."

"That's a relief." She reached for the box.

Reluctant to relinquish it, Eli smiled winsomely. "Where are you going?"

Tucking the box back into her flight bag, she said, "I'm staying at the Salvia Hotel, in Jerusalem."

"I know where that is. I was born here." He grinned so broadly that his dimples showed.

Charlotte was warming to him. "Aren't you British?"

"My father's with the Palestine Police Force." He hoped this would instill a feeling of confidence. "I say, do you have a ride to Jerusalem? There's a curfew, you know."

"Isn't there a bus or something?"

"Probably. But the Salvia isn't far from where we're going. One of my friends is waiting and we have plenty of room."

"Well . . ."

"Would you like to see my passport, my military papers? Or perhaps I could get that officer over there to vouch for me."

"That's not necessary . . ." Her voice wavered for a second. She made up her mind. "I'm happy to accept your gracious offer."

Outside the arrivals area a uniformed Saul, sporting a mustache and military haircut, was waiting in a jeep. On the rutted road to Jerusalem, Charlotte became lively and talkative. She told them about the "nice old couple" who had asked her to take some medicine to their sick relative.

"Do you know where Narkiss Road is, Captain Short?"

Eli laughed gently. "Not 'Nar-KISS.' It's pronounced 'Nar-KEES' in Hebrew. But yes, it's on my way home, actually. Why?"

"That's where the medicine must be delivered. There is an old man who needs it desperately."

"I would be pleased to drop it by for you, unless you want to do it yourself."

"I don't know the gentleman or my way around, so if it isn't too much trouble . . ."

"Not at all," Eli responded nonchalantly.

Before they arrived at the Salvia Hotel, Charlotte bubbled on about her plans to attend Hebrew University. She told them about her father's request for her to spend a year in Palestine, her boy friend at Yale, her studies at Vassar. By the time they saw her to her hotel, Eli and Saul knew more than they ever expected to about their temporary charge.

"Not exactly reticent." Eli laughed when they pulled away.

"How did you find *her*?" Saul asked. "She was perfect. Did anyone bother her?"

Eli shook his head. "She could flirt her way through Gestapo headquarters if she had to."

"She didn't even know what she was doing."

"No, but can you imagine how terrific she'd be if she was *trying*?"

"Eli, what are you thinking? An American girl! She'd be about as loyal as a butterfly."

"I think we should keep our eye on her and some of the other foreign students as well. Now more than ever, we need friends with safe passports."

"I can't imagine headquarters approving, but if you're looking for an excuse to see her again, that's quite different, my good friend." Saul patted the suitcase between them. "Besides, once we get this baby to bed, you'll have earned the right to pursue your own interests . . . for a while."

CYPRUS: 1947–1948

In the late summer of 1947, Eli was sent by the Haganah to Cyprus. A veteran of movement control in Bremen and by now a highly trained and trusted documents specialist, he would be answerable only to the Haganah commander in the detention camps the British had set up to hold the thousands of Jews who, despite the stiff immigration laws, had tried to reach Palestine — and failed.

There were far more ways to get the Palmach operatives into Cyprus than out. Most began their journey as crew members to bring "illegal" immigrants to the Promised Land. When the ships were rerouted by the British navy, the Palmachniks were indistinguishable from the other refugees. In Cyprus they were then put to work organizing and training the refugees. Later, if their skills were needed outside the camps again, the Palmach agents escaped through the tunnels to a certain "Greek fishing trawler" and were back in Palestine or Europe in a matter of days.

Eli, however, was one Haganah operative who did not have IJI — for Illegal Jewish Immigrant — stamped after his name. Officially, he had been sent by Joint — the Joint Distribution Committee, an arm of the United Palestine Appeal. In the detention camps of Cyprus, Joint provided teachers and medical personnel to attend to the tens of thousands of prisoners. While Eli's papers listed him as a mathematics teacher, a posture well-documented by his King's College transcripts, he had been sent to verify identities of Jews coming to Palestine. It was his responsibility to weed out criminals, former Nazis, and other undesirables. As a trained radio operator, he kept in daily contact with Israel and the trawler via a transmitter hidden in a tunnel under his tent in Summer Camp number 55 in Caraolas.

When Eli first arrived, he found Jews were being held behind barbed wire, guarded by the British. Having survived death camps and the brutality of the war, they were now condemned by British policy to more wasted years. At the same moment, the United Nations Special Committee on Palestine (UNSCOP) was drafting proposals to partition the vital sliver of land into Arab and Jewish states. As Eli surveyed the condition of the Cyprus camps, he could not help but think there had to be a more humane way to care for these destitute souls. Jewish babies were being born behind barbed wire in appallingly unsanitary huts and tents, Jewish men and women were dying stateless, and thousands of lives were suspended until the world's diplomats had, with great pomp and civility, determined their ultimate fate.

Nearby, in Camp 62, was the secret Palmach headquarters, which governed the Jews, providing leadership, demolition experts, military instructors, escape leaders, peace keepers, dispute arbitrators — whatever was required. The autonomy inside the camp was so complete that Palmach workers under stress were permitted "escape leave." Eli was amazed to discover they had even braved the tunnels and crawled through holes cut under the barbed wire fences to see *Gone with the Wind* in Nicosia.

Fortunately, the British did not dare enter the camps to keep an accurate count of their prisoners. From the beginning, the Jewish camp commanders would permit the British entry only with escorts, although it was eminently clear who was in charge. At any moment the British could have cut off supplies of food and water to bend the refugees' wills, but given the world's interest in the plight of the Jews, they could not afford to have people starving or being shot for not following orders. So, as long as the camps ran smoothly, the British remained on the outside.

During the crucial days of the UNSCOP talks at Lake Success, Eli spent more and more time at his radio receiver to provide information for the word-of-mouth news delivery system, which was so well organized, an item was "broadcast" to forty thousand people in only a few hours' time. Cheering went out the morning of September 1 when it was learned that the members of UNSCOP, just five minutes before the deadline, had signed their names to the report to be presented to the General Assembly in November. Eli took a special interest in the news from then on, since Saul, assisted by a select team of multilingual Haganah members, was sent to New York to lobby for the Jewish cause. And one of Saul's star helpers on Moshe Shertok's staff was Eli's recruit: Charlotte Green.

It was the twenty-ninth of November in New York — but the early hours of the next day in Cyprus. Short-wave radios were brought out into the open and tuned to the announcements from Flushing Meadow as the United Nations delegates convened to determine the future of Palestine. The fate of all imprisoned there hinged on the outcome. From the first votes, Eli was pessimistic. When the Soviet bloc and many of the Latin American countries (whose delegates Charlotte had been assigned to befriend) voted in favor, the crowd in Caraolas became excited. Then, Great Britain abstained. Eli felt soiled by association. He walked to the edge of the crowd and spit in the sand.

Over the crackling Philips radio came yet another vote: "Venezuela: Yes." A scream rose up from a woman with a pencil and paper. It was taken up by the others as they realized the two-thirds majority had been achieved. "We've won! We've won!"

And then the final tally: thirty-three in favor; thirteen, including all the Arab states, opposed; ten, including Great Britain, abstained. As in Jerusalem, Tel Aviv, and Jewish communities the world over, there was jubilation. For Eli, who knew the conflicts were only just beginning, the victory was bittersweet. Nothing on Cyprus improved in the slightest. Even after the celebration, the noise, the rousing choruses of "Hatikvah," the immigrants were not free to leave. And the ships kept coming. Not to Eretz Israel, but to Cyprus.

It was in February 1948 that Eli first saw Lily Jaeger, standing at the opening of his tent, shivering in the damp evening air. Her blond hair had curled in the humidity, and with the twilight behind her, it appeared to frame her face like a Renaissance halo. Her eyes were pale and watery, her nose reddened by a bad cold.

A month earlier two huge troop carriers, the *Pan Crescent* and *Pan York,* had been escorted into Famagusta harbor by the British with sixteen thousand refugees, whom the camps were expected to absorb overnight. Working day and night, Eli and his team of identity verifiers had processed only a quarter of the families in four weeks.

"What is your name?" he asked the next one in line.

"Lily Jaeger," she answered hoarsely.

Checking his list, he found the number the British had assigned her along with her most recent addresses: the displaced persons camp in Belgium, a hospital in Munich, Theresienstadt, Bergen-Belsen, Westerbork, Amsterdam. She had been through some of the worst camps and had somehow survived. Her body was slender, but not emaciated. Many of the refugees had gorged themselves on the starchy foods they had been offered and tended to puff out with a queer, distended fatty layer — like a hasty renovation masking a defective structure. At closer inspection, however, they had a sickly tone, mottled skin, gaping holes between blackened teeth — all badges of suffering. This girl's cheeks were pink, her arms slender but well-formed, and despite her obvious head cold, she appeared more robust and healthy than most.

"Come in and have a seat, please," he said politely in English.

When she did not respond he tried Hebrew, then Yiddish. She nodded that she understood. "Ich spreche Holländisch und Deutsch," she said in terse German.

Eli stopped long enough to call in a translator because this was an official interview. "The names of your parents, please."

"Anna und Jacob Jaeger."

"Do you know where they are now?"

"Nein."

"Any other living relatives?"

"Nein. Ich weiss nichts davon."

"Did you have brothers or sisters?"

"Zwei Brüder."

"Their names, please."

"David und Peter."

"Last known whereabouts?"

"Die sind tot."

"They are dead," the translator repeated.

"Are you certain?"

"Ja."

Eli's antennae were raised. Something was wrong here. The flat, unemotional responses were atypical. Most people came to their appointments with him carrying lists of relatives and friends for whom they were searching. Queries about this family or that person were posted throughout the camps. Stories of people given up for dead but reunited right there in Cyprus were circulated daily. "Why are you so certain?"

She spoke slowly so the translator could follow her. "Peter died when we were in hiding in Amsterdam. David was with me in Theresienstadt. Two days before liberation the guards were panicking. They set several blocks of huts on fire. He burned to death."

The story was horrible, but Eli was almost inured after listening to pathetic tales fifty times a day. He sensed something was wrong here, and reminded himself it would not have been difficult for her to invent that past by combining any number of stories circulating in the camps.

He studied her more closely. Her features were not typically Jewish. The nose was small, the chin protuberant and pointed, the cheekbones broad and Nordic. Her height was taller than most, especially those who had been nutritionally deprived during their formative years. Her arms were long, white, and hairless. She kept her hands folded in her lap, clenched together tightly and twisting perceptibly. Her legs were especially lovely: long, slim, but well-rounded — feminine, without the angles caused by rickets, parasites, and other long-term effects of malnutrition and imprisonment. Where had she gotten the food to sustain her? Had she a Nazi lover? Was she a collaborator? Was she even Jewish? While he had seen some disturbed, withdrawn people before, this one's cold, flat, almost diffident attitude was especially queer. Furthermore, she would not look at him when she spoke. This was often the first sign of a prevaricator.

"Now is a perfect time for people to reinvent themselves," he had been told during his briefing for this mission. "It will be impossible to demand authentic documents for verifications of identities, so it will take skill to weed out those who have changed their stories to hide from misdeeds in the past. The dead and missing have provided a vast and tragic reservoir of identities of people with untraceable pasts. The more data you can gather the better, for we expect to put the backgrounds of these unfortunates to good use."

The skills Eli had learned from the Haganah operatives, combined with those he had gained under British intelligence, served him well, especially with certain complicated cases. In the concentration camps, the Germans chose Jews to be block captains to mete out food, as well as select those who would work and those who would die. Refusal to cooperate meant a swifter death. It was said that some of these Jewish captains were so good at their jobs, they were worse than their captors. When a refugee was accused of being a block captain, Eli would join a special investigative team to interview the accuser as well as the suspect. The decisions were a tricky business. The emotionally distraught victims demanded retribution. Many felt the collaborators should have the same fate as the Nazis themselves. Others, with more tolerance, felt that every Jew had been persecuted in some way and deserved a fresh start. Worse, it was sometimes difficult to mediate these cases, especially where there were few witnesses to speak against an alleged criminal. Also, Eli knew these tales were sometimes told for the sake of revenge in marital or financial disputes. It took a Solomon to know what to do.

The responsibility was enormous. He had constructed a system whereby he would act on a case only if it was verified by a significant number of witnesses. Then he would turn the case over to Noah, the Palmach discipline commander. He knew that Noah, as tough and methodical as he was reputed to be, would never harm another Jew. What exactly was done with these questionable people, he did not know, but he heard rumors that they were among those taken through the tunnels and given demanding, dangerous positions, either in Palestine or on the high seas, in order to redeem themselves.

For the moment he was concerned with this elusive girl who called herself Lily. Nobody had suggested she had been a block captain. But what the hell was she? Jewish or Gentile? Lily Jaeger or somebody else entirely?

"Is there anyone here who can substantiate your story?"

"Nein."

"Haven't you met anyone from Bergen-Belsen or Theresienstadt?"

"No. I keep to myself."

"I will give you some forms to fill out. Please give me as much detail as you can remember: names, addresses, dates, names of others who were in the same places at the same times."

She accepted the papers and fled from the tent without another word. For more than a week she did not return. Curious, he found out where she lived and questioned a few of her neighbors.

"Rarely visits with others . . . Sleeps poorly . . . Keeps her few possessions tidy . . . Fastidious . . . Avoids children . . ." were some comments he noted in her file.

In his mind Eli conjured a dozen ways to challenge Lily's story, then discarded them. She was in his thoughts constantly. Soon he was looking for her every time he went over to Camp 71. All right, he admitted, you are slightly obsessed with her. She is attractive compared to most of the sad cases around, but you must be awfully hard up to lust after so cold a fish.

Or was he being unfair?

What horrible brutalities had she endured? The idea that she had been some Nazi's sex slave crossed his mind. He was appalled at the idea of someone pinning down her graceful arms, forcing himself into her tender, rosy body.

The arms . . .

There were no tattoos on those arms! If she had been in Bergen-

Belsen, she would have been marked with the despised concentration camp number. He determined to find out who she really was.

It was not long before a middle-aged man who called himself Felix Jaeger appeared. It was seven in the evening and Eli thought he was finally through for the night. The man was the last in line for the day.

"Where were you from?" he asked distractedly.

"Amsterdam."

Eli filled out another identity form. "Profession?"

"Baker. I owned a small sweet shop on Prinsen Gracht."

He abbreviated the additional information in the allotted space. "The names of your parents, please."

"Marta and Paul Jaeger."

"Do you know where they are now?"

"They were both deceased before the war."

"Any other living relatives?"

"Not that I know."

"Did you have brothers or sisters?"

"Two brothers."

"Their names, please."

"Daniel and Jacob."

"Last known whereabouts?"

"They are also dead."

"Are you certain?"

"No. But they were sent to Auschwitz over two years ago, so it is unlikely that —"

Eli sat up suddenly. "Your brother was Jacob Jaeger?"

"Yes."

"Did you have any children?"

"No. I never married."

"Did your brothers?"

"Yes. My brother Daniel had one son who went to Auschwitz with him. Jacob had a daughter and two sons. The younger one died in hiding."

"What was his name?"

"Peter."

"The other? What happened to him?"

"David went to Bergen-Belsen with his sister. Both perished, I'm told."

Eli kept on writing. "The sister's name?"

"Lily ..." He broke down in tears. "She was my favorite, my flower."

Eli lifted his pen and stared at the man. A few months ago he might have felt some enthusiasm for an impending reunion, but after everything he had seen and heard he was calm and detached; Amsterdam was a big city; there had been numerous Jews; both Jaeger and Jacob were common names. So was Lily, for that matter. The odds narrowed when one considered her two brothers were also named Peter and David. Here was the verification he needed and yet he was hesitating. Why? Why wasn't he accepting this girl's identity? Why did he continue to feel something was terribly wrong?

After a few more minutes of questions, Eli told the man, "Everything seems in order. If you can come back tomorrow afternoon, I can issue temporary papers."

The balding man wiped his eyes and pumped Eli's hand. "Thank you! Thank you!"

That same evening Eli went to the tent where Lily lived.

"A man is here for you, Lily!" shouted the woman lying on the cot nearest the doorway.

"Lily's got a boy friend," a barefoot little girl called in a singsong voice.

Lily appeared with a comb in her hand. She tucked it into the pocket of her remarkably spotless dress. "You have come for the papers?" she asked tensely.

"No. I want to talk with you. Could you come outside?"

"Here, take my sweater," the woman on the cot said.

Lily nodded somberly. "Thank you, Raisa." Placing it loosely around her shoulders, she joined Eli. Without speaking for a few minutes, they strolled between the rows of tents. In the open air, families were preparing their evening meals on Primus stoves. Children bundled in coats too small or too big screeched and frolicked, while mothers warned them to stay away from the flames. As Eli passed his secret "radio headquarters" he did not greet Ephraim, the operator on duty, but noticed that the makeshift aerial wire spliced inside a piece of rope and stretched out between two tents was making do as a laundry line.

When they reached the end of a tent row, he decided to break his news. "I think I have something good to tell you." He spoke slowly in German.

"Ja?"

"We've found another member of your family."

"That is not possible —"

"Felix Jaeger, your father's brother."

"I never had an uncle by that name."

"Are you certain? He said Lily was his favorite niece."

"My name is not uncommon. There has been a mistake."

"He said you had two brothers: Peter and David. Aren't those the names you gave me?"

Lily began shivering uncontrollably. Eli had known something was wrong with her story. Somehow she had discovered rudimentary information about this family and had taken Lily Jaeger's identity. She had been clever, but not in the face of coincidence.

"Now will you tell me the truth?" he asked as gently as possible.

"The truth? You would not know the truth if it was served to you for your supper!" Her voice rose hysterically. "Who is this man? Who dares use my brothers' names? Who?"

"He's a man about half a head shorter than I am. He's fairly stout, bald except for the back of his head and a bit on the sides. He's from Amsterdam and says he owned a bakery there."

"My father owned a bakery, but he was quite tall and had a full head of hair. Besides, he was taken away in '42. The chance he would be alive is zero."

"Then we have a mystery to solve, don't we?"

"Take me to him. Let *me* question him!"

"That is not how we do it here. You will have to give me the facts and I'll see if he can corroborate them."

"Where is he?"

"Not in this camp. He's over in thirty-two or fifty-five. I'll have to check to be certain. I believe he's connected with one of the children's houses. That's why I'm inclined to trust him. How many men would take such an interest in orphans?"

"My God. You fool!" Lily began to scream so uncontrollably some friends from her tent came running to see what had happened.

Raisa was the first at Lily's side. "What have you done to her?"

"I . . . I thought I had found an uncle of hers. She went crazy."

"Do you know what she has been through? She probably does not believe . . ."

Lily's screams drowned Raisa out. "The children! For the love of God, get him away from the children!" Her arms flailed wildly. It seemed as if she was having some sort of a seizure. Eli and Raisa steered Lily into his tent. Raisa brought tea and insisted she drink it.

When she was quieter, the facts emerged slowly. The man claiming to be her uncle was Hans de Vries, a Gentile employee of her father's who took over running the bakery in his absence. After Lily's mother was taken away, he sheltered her and her brothers in his mother's home, where they joined several other children whose parents also had been apprehended. One day de Vries's mother, fearing for her life, told her son to turn in the children, which he pretended to do. Instead, he led them to a subcellar under the bakery where flour and supplies had been stored. For more than three years the children lived in the dankness of the cellar. Eventually, there were fifteen children who shared the sackcloth mats and meager rations provided by the baker. Lily was the eldest.

But de Vries was not what he seemed. The children were not hidden for humanitarian reasons, but to provide a ready supply of prepubescent bodies to satisfy the pedophile's sexual appetites. Raisa and Eli stared at each other in shock as Lily detailed the man's perversions. Despite the fact she knew they were horrified by them, she reeled off detail after detail of how the children suffered.

"Sometimes I wanted to run out on the street and beg the Nazis to take us away. But at least the children were well fed, if only mostly with sweets and water. I could not condemn them to death!"

"How were you discovered?" Eli asked.

"I am not certain. De Vries left us alone for days at a time. He said he was visiting his mother, who had gone out to the country to live with friends. Sometimes he would return with a few eggs or even some milk. He was increasingly nervous and more violent with the children — especially the youngest boys. I tended their sores and tried to keep them from him as much as possible. My brother Peter became ill — de Vries was too rough on him, there was too much bleeding, then he ran a fever. De Vries went to summon a doctor. After a secret signal, I was to let the doctor in. I did. The doctor was the Gestapo. We were taken away with the last roundup of Dutch Jews. It was the eighteenth of August, 1944, just four days after my eighteenth birthday. Peter died the next day."

Lily had not mentioned what this evil man had done to her personally, but Eli could well imagine. He asked Raisa to remain with Lily in his tent while he sent for Noah and asked him to detain "Felix Jaeger" immediately. The rest of the night was spent crouched by Lily's side, stroking her hand and listening as the tale of her wartime odyssey gushed out. Perhaps it was not any more hideous than those of all the other concentration camp survivors, but to him it seemed the most pitiful he had ever heard.

All the while, Eli berated himself for his disbelief. He had taken Lily's pain and disorientation for something sinister. The reason she seemed healthier than most was twofold. First, she had not been deported until close to the end of the war. Second, when she arrived in Bergen-Belsen, she had been selected out of the Star Camp — where most of the Dutch Jews had been sent and where they had worn the Star of David on their clothes — to be part of the Kastner group. Supposedly, these children were to be traded for Swiss francs, army trucks, and weapons in a deal struck by a Hungarian Jew, Rezsö Kastner, with Eichmann. That was why she had not been tattooed. The Kastner group was supposed to be left unmarked so the world would never know what was happening inside the camps. In the end, only a few children were actually saved in this manner because Eichmann recanted. Most, like Lily, were transported along the death camp trail.

Lily had been lucky all along — through the years in hiding, through the camps of Westerbork and Bergen-Belsen, through the forced march to Theresienstadt. Once there, she had avoided being sent to the family camp at Auschwitz by befriending a Danish Jewish boy who, to protect her, claimed they were married.

"I was not actually his wife," Lily maintained haughtily, as if it would make a difference to Eli.

Did she think he would despise her if she had slept with a man for food or other life-giving favors? Did she wonder if he would believe that even with so much horror surrounding her, somebody would care for her out of goodness, not lust? After the baker, how often had her body been her currency for survival?

Lily continued with her story. "You see, the Danes of Theresienstadt received special favors because their king kept up a barrage of inquiries to the Germans to see how 'his Jews' were being treated. The Danish group were the only ones to receive a steady delivery of food parcels. You can imagine the power they had! Everybody wanted a Danish friend."

She went on to say that when Theresienstadt was liberated by the Russians on May 11, 1945, she was suffering from typhus, which by that time was epidemic in the camp. "Immediately, I was taken to a quarantine center in the Sudeten barracks and treated by the Red Army doctors. For some reason, that particular outbreak of the

disease was especially virulent. Forty-five doctors, nurses, and order-
lies died while many of my hospital mates survived, even in our
weakened condition. The Danish boy succumbed three days after
liberation."

"You must be very strong," Eli said to fill in the silence.

"I had come so far," she explained, "I was not about to be killed
by an illness. I believed I was invincible. I pretended I was a bird
who could take to wing whenever evil spirits threatened. When I was
starving or in pain, I would just fly away from it. In some ways *I*
was never there; it never happened to *me*. Can you understand
that?"

As Eli stared into her liquid gray eyes, he saw an icy hell entrap-
ping her. If he could only warm her, melt her, bring her back fully to
the world. During the night his tentative German and her fragmented English melded into a totally comprehensible language. At
dawn, as she rested in his arms, Eli knew something remarkable had
occurred.

She sat up on the cot and brushed back her unruly hair. "I have
said too much. There are things which should never be spoken of."

"No. It was necessary, but . . ." He stood, pulled back the tent
flap, and stared out at the faint horizon of the sea as he deliberated
how to proceed. "I have a problem. You must help me."

"How?"

"The baker — you must identify him."

"No."

"You only have to see him once."

"No!" She doubled over as if convulsed by a stomach pain.

"It doesn't have to be face to face," he pressed.

She looked up coldly. "Face to face," she repeated slowly.

"It could be from a distance. Just as long as there are witnesses."

"Yes. Face to face. It will be awful for me, but so much worse for
him." She laughed, and the laugh seemed deranged.

Eli watched her turn from a frightened victim into a predatory animal. Her voice became guttural. "Yes. I will do it. For the children."
In the violet shadows, he could see her coming toward him. She
stood in front of him, her arms crossed against her chest. "I am so
afraid."

"I will stay with you."

"Thank you," she said simply. In English.

❖   ❖   ❖

Lily confronted Hans de Vries on March 15, 1948, while a provisional government for a Jewish state was being formed in Tel Aviv. The baker was under guard at the far end of Camp 32. He had been belligerent, alternately demanding his "rights" and weeping that a mistake had been made. Nothing was explained to him.

When Lily was ready, she walked to the tin-roofed shed where he had been isolated. She leaned against Eli as Noah ordered de Vries to step outside.

De Vries was astonished to see her. "Lily, my dearest little Lily! By the grace of God you have survived!"

Lily was motionless.

"Your brothers? Your mother?"

Silence.

"Lily, my pet. They have mistaken me for some kind of criminal. Tell them how I saved your life. All those years I kept you, fed you." His voice became shrill. "Tell them about the other children, how I risked my life for all of you."

Lily hardly took a breath.

"Lily, how was I to know the doctor would turn you in? I paid him well — in advance. How was I to know? I had to go into hiding myself afterward. I was on all the lists as a Jew-lover. I cannot return home again. Lily . . ." He raised his arms out to her in supplication. "Tell me you forgive me." He fell to his knees.

Lily stared at Eli and Noah.

Noah indicated she could leave if she wanted.

She turned back to the baker. She walked forward slowly. When she was beside de Vries she rasped, "Have you touched a child here?"

"What do you mean?"

She swung around to confront Noah. "Has he?" Her voice was slow and harsh.

"We are not certain —"

"Have you?" she shrieked in the baker's ear.

"Me?" His voice was weak.

"He has." She pronounced her verdict.

"Well," Noah admitted, "we are talking to the children. They will recover."

With her toe, Lily poked the baker's groveling cheek. As he stared up at her, she spit on him. "May you rot in hell."

"Lily . . ." He prostrated himself completely. "I . . . saved . . . your . . . life."

"For what?" she said so softly only Eli heard. "For what?" she muttered again as he led her away.

Perhaps Eli could have discovered how the Palmach commander had disposed of the baker, perhaps not. He did not want to know. From the expression on Lily's face in the days that immediately followed, he knew that she had been delivered of a terrible burden.

After that, Lily rarely left his side. Each morning she arrived at his tent, made his coffee, and asked how she could assist him. He had her bring him the names of families with unusual needs or reasons to get off Cyprus sooner than scheduled. The camp commander was in charge of compiling the names of the seven hundred fifty people a month who could legally leave Cyprus for Palestine. The first to arrive were the first to depart unless there were special circumstances. Lily discovered surgeons who were being wasted in the camp, as well as people needing special medical attention who should have priority for certificates. There were orphaned children under eighteen who were to join relatives. For them she located generous souls who gave up their places at the head of the list.

It was soon evident that Lily had extraordinary gifts. Her memory was astounding. She recalled names and their spellings when told them only once. If she transcribed a file, she could repeat details, including dates and other data, almost verbatim. When there was doubt about an identity, she had a knack for matching pre-war photographs with the actual individuals, despite the horrendous physical changes they had undergone.

Awed, Eli asked, "How do you do it?"

"It is in the eyebrows," she explained. "The eyes sink in and change, the bones of the face protrude and shift, the hair loses color and texture, but that one line above the eyes remains unique to that individual."

"Where did you learn that?"

"I discovered it for myself in Bergen-Belsen. I would stare at the half-starved, wild-eyed victims and imagine, from the shape of their brows, what they might have looked like when they were real people — when they were whole."

"When they were whole." The phrase echoed in Eli's mind. Children brought into this world, fed, educated, loved and nurtured by families, grew into whole human beings. War, deprivation, dehumanization, violence, disease, destroyed them piece by piece. Camps like Bergen-Belsen were expert at this process. There was no need for the efficiency of a gas chamber. Rather, they were killed by planned starvation and deliberately encouraged epidemics. The survivors were left to rebuild their minds and bodies, but how many could ever become integrated again? As he watched Lily transform herself from a vacant and angry woman to a motivated and dedicated worker, he felt renewed with hope for them all.

When Lily's own name moved closer to the top of the certificate list, she voluntarily withdrew it. "I am needed here" was her terse reason.

Impressed with her spirit, Noah gave his permission for her to receive Haganah training within the camp, where she excelled at her courses. Noah also assigned her to regular battery duty.

The Ambassador radio transmitter they had acquired had been set up to operate on household current, one of the many luxuries the tents lacked. One of the Palmachniks, who was a wizard with electronics, modified it to work from pocket batteries. A single battery gave only 4.5 volts and they needed a minimum of 250 volts, which meant the batteries had to be replaced by the spares the Joint nurses brought back from Nicosia. To further complicate matters, the radio required a car battery for the filaments in the tubes. Eli had been given one truck battery for the job, but it ran out of juice in seven days of transmitting to Palestine. Lily was in charge of selecting the water truck that would provide a fresh battery to "harvest" each week.

To avoid suspicion, she picked one in a different segment of the camp every time. The day before the battery was needed, she organized a group waiting in line to provide a distraction. A frequent ploy was for one of the young girls to flirt with the driver. In the meantime, the battery, which in those lorries was on the right side of the step below the driver's set, was "exchanged" for the dead one and swiftly covered with sand to make it seem like the old one. The British military drivers were so accustomed to pushing the trucks to get them to start, they never caught on to the switched battery trick.

But the time Lily proved her mettle was when a woman was needed to help destroy a British prison ship. Actions against boats were frequent, but usually unsuccessful. Everyone in the camps had a grudge against the ships, which had blocked their way to freedom in Palestine. Eli, for whom the prison ships symbolized all that he hated about the British in Palestine, wanted to destroy one before leaving Cyprus.

"An active blow!" he told Noah. "To make up for the paper-work." Noah had understood.

Eli and Lily left the camp through the tunnels under the barbed wire and were met by a cooperative (and well-paid) Greek driver. Pretending to be lovers, they hired a small boat, but the motor would not start. Together they had rowed out to the area where the British ships were anchored. Lily kept the boat stable on the waves while Eli prepared the small limpet mine. It had been made from a British helmet, the edges of which had been filed off. Magnets had been glued to its rim and five kilos of gelignite lined its metal shell.

Every so often their rowboat would be rocked by the depth charges being tossed off the sides of the prison ship to foil terrorist frogmen. "You will be killed," Lily had groaned when one hit especially close. Many men had lost their lives just that way.

"They won't bother me unless my head is under the water when it strikes. The body just gets a good massage; but a head is rigid and could be crushed."

"But ..."

"It's late. They've been tossing their charges out for several hours. I'm told they ration them. By the time I'm ready, they won't have many left."

Once in the water, Eli had worked as swiftly as possible. Lily handed him a paint scraper. As gently as possible, he prepared the surface of the hull. Noah had warned him that the last bomb had failed to adhere to the slippery, algae-covered hull. That Palmach team had been caught and were in prison in Famagusta. The sound of the scraper reverberating under water was a hideous *klugh* ... *klugh* ... *klugh*. Eli hoped the noise was not audible on deck. He had to breathe. When he popped up he spit out water and croaked, "Did you hear anything?"

"No, why?"

Just then a depth charge hit the water. He was thrown away from the prison ship's hull.

"Eli ..." Lily's voice was tinny in the wind.

Without answering, he dove down and finished the last few scrapes. When he surfaced, he reached for the mine and put it in place. Once he was back in the boat, Lily rowed with all her might as a light from the deck swooped down on the position they had just been in. It was almost seven kilometers to the dark corner of Famagusta harbor where they were to be met. Just as they landed, the sky was lit with their glorious explosion.

After Cyprus, Lily had distinguished herself in the War for Independence as a battalion welfare officer in the Negev Foxes unit on the march to Eilat. Next, she had been welcomed into intelligence training. Eli, among others, felt her potential was limitless.

CANDIDATE DOSSIER

Volume number: 2166
File name: Yoel Raphael
Date opened: 1 August 1946

I. Personal File
Name: Eli Katzar
Age: 25
Residence: Jerusalem, Palestine
Sex: Male
Birth date: 11 February 1921
Religion: Jew
Birthplace: Jerusalem
Height: 1.80 meters
Weight: 70 kilos
Eyes: Blue
Hair: Dark blond
Marks: Large birthmark on lower back, spider nevus on abdomen, scars left ankle from childhood bicycle accident

II. Sponsor   Reuven Shiloah

III. Education
Primary: St. George's School, Jerusalem
Secondary: Rehavia Gymnasium, Jerusalem
                    Perse School, Cambridge
Advanced: King's College, Cambridge University,
                    1938–1939
Languages: English, Hebrew, Arabic, German (weak),
                    French

IV. Financial
Employer:	British Army
Income:	£90 per month
Assets:	£350
Debts:	None

V. Marital Status   Single

VI. Medical History
Diseases:	Measles, chicken pox, whooping cough, mumps
Injuries:	Bicycle accident at age 12: broken ankle, scarring, full use of foot
Allergies:	None
Defects:	None

VII. Legal
Driver's License:	British Military No. 378018U
Issued:	1940
Vehicles:	Automobile, four-wheel drive, truck
Accidents:	None

VIII. Military
British Army:
OTC:	Candidate, 1936
Entry rank:	2nd lieutenant cipher school, 1939
Unit:	GCCS, Bletchley Park
Discharge rank:	Captain
Haganah:	Took the oath in 1947
Special training:	Kibbutz Hazorea, 1947
Advanced training:	1947–1948, Cyprus camps
Assignment:	Document verification; 1948 War of Independence, Unit 121

IX. Family History
Father:	Hugo William Short
Born:	Brighton, England, 1897
Residence:	Jerusalem
Occupation:	Palestine Police District Superintendent
Mother:	Ruth Epstein
Born:	Rehovot, 1901
Siblings:	None

X. Mission Assignments
Position: Section head, Political Dept., Foreign Ministry
Code name: Aster
Cover: Charles Ivy, tour guide/climbing instructor

XI. Notes
1949:   Special section appointment by T.G.

2

And if the avenger of blood pursue after him, then they shall not deliver up the manslayer into his hand; because he smote his neighbor unawares, and hated him not before-time.

Joshua 20:5

Dr. Ze'evi's murder did not alter Eli's original escape plan. His documents, as well as those of Charlotte and the other team members, had been prepared with enough care to withstand scrutiny after the explosion. Even if someone had seen them parked in front of the Concorde for a few minutes, the car, with its barely dented grille, had been returned to the Avis lot at the Marseille airport. Second passports and airline tickets had been picked up for both Charlotte and Eli from a contact at the Air Inter desk. There he briefed her on an alternate course of action.

"You are not accompanying me to London."

"I'm to visit Aunt Miriam, then?"

"Right, we're going to the Hur variation of the Caleb Plan." Hur was Caleb's son and Miriam's husband. Since the naming of the Ezra group, Eli had used Biblical references for all his plans and codes because of the infinite variety they offered, as well as the international availability of the source. "You'll be flying to Rome on this passport."

"Then to New York?"

Eli nodded. "Everything else remains the same. You know where to go at Leonardo da Vinci?"

"Yes. The ladies' loo nearest British Airways."

"Your contact will be waiting. Any questions?"

Charlotte looked at him searchingly. Something had gone terribly wrong since he had left the Concorde. Unexpectedly, he pulled her to him. "Have a good trip, my darling." He kissed her on both cheeks. "Give my best to Aunt Miriam," he called after her and turned for his gate.

His contact at Heathrow, whom he had known for many years as Albert Conrad, had three passports ready for exchange. Eli took his own brusquely. The worn navy blue hard cover with the partially rubbed off gold letters felt wonderfully solid. Once again he was Elliot Short.

Conrad waited until they were outside the terminal. "Nobody else is with you?"

"No." Eli slid into a kelly green Ford Escort that pulled up at the curb. "I have to file a report." Protocol demanded debriefing with someone more senior than Conrad. "Take me to Naor." Officially, Alex Naor was cultural attaché at the Israeli Embassy, but actually he was the European Division chief of the Mossad. In the past he had been peripherally involved with several of Eli's missions, and it was no secret that they had disagreed over the development of the Ezra group.

"Naor isn't available today," Conrad said. "Uri Ben-Yehuda could speak with you."

"That will be satisfactory," Eli said with a sigh of relief. Ben-Yehuda, the consummate dispassionate agent, was preferable to an opinionated and volatile Alex.

When they reached central London, the bearded driver braked the Ford at the corner of Wigmore and Wimpole streets and Conrad jumped out to make a call at a phone box. Young women attending the Royal College of Nursing down the block rushed in different directions. Two walked by the car in animated discussion, and as they approached, Eli winced. The one closest to his window had a long cascade of auburn hair and firm, high buttocks that reminded him of Maura. Even to this day, it irked him when he recalled how he had misunderstood Maura. Her legacy to him was a perpetual distrust of women, which led him to analyze their motives so thoroughly that from that time on, he had never permitted a woman to perplex him again. That is why the whole Ezra system had worked so well. Maura's lesson had never been forgotten.

He sat staring at the back of the driver's head, trying not to think of the present, the past, or even the future until Conrad returned. "What's your real name, Conrad?" he wanted to ask. "Cohen? Kabinsky? Kleber? Surely not Conrad." But he did not. Never ask for, never give, any information that is not absolutely necessary to the job at hand. No actual identities, just an endless series of disguises, of deceits.

The Ford pulled up to the corner of Curzon and Half Moon streets. Conrad handed him a key. "Shepherd Market. The building with the door nearest the phone box. Fourth floor, Four-C. Give Ben-Yehuda about fifteen minutes. When the telephone rings three times, look out the kitchen window. You should see him in the phone box. Signal by opening the window a few inches from the bottom. He will come right up."

Eli found the apartment decorated with drab hotel room furnishings. The worn edges of the couch and mismatched chairs were comforting. The Mossad never spent money on frivolities. This was a safe house for insiders. On the other hand, if an apartment had to be furnished to impress someone or to set forth an elegant lifestyle as the cover for its occupants, no expense would have been spared.

The telephone rang. Eli stared out the window at the phone box, where Uri Ben-Yehuda looked the model agent: someone so ordinary he could not be described or remembered easily. Ben-Yehuda was short, skinny, and with a hairline that had receded past the center of his head. He wore inexpensive black glasses a bit too large for his face. When he removed them — as he did often in a nervous gesture — his eyes seemed strangely startled, like those of a cost accountant who had discovered a serious discrepancy.

Eli opened the window. A few minutes later a key turned in the lock.

"Eli!" Uri Ben-Yehuda clasped his arm warmly. He stared at Eli's drawn face for a few seconds. "You look exhausted. When did you last have something to eat?"

"On the plane, a few soft drinks . . ." Eli's voice trailed off.

"This place is usually well stocked." Ben-Yehuda opened the fridge and took out a large pizza, and without consulting Eli, put it in the oven. Next, he plopped ice into glasses and poured them each some apple juice. "Sorry, there's nothing stronger aboard. Children's food. That's what Naor likes us to have on hand. Usually whoever's here is tense and the stuff of the nursery keeps them calmer than anything too spicy or complex. There are oatmeal and tinned milk, chocolates, jellies, biscuits . . ."

When Eli did not fill the silence, he stared meaningfully. "I gather there's been some difficulty."

"One of our associates . . . killed in France."

"The man's passport or the woman's?"

"The man's."

"He might have missed the plane, been delayed —"

"I found the body."

Ben-Yehuda paused again. "Where is Mrs. Woodrow?"

"Gone to see Aunt Miriam. There should be a message in a few hours from her and the others."

"I'll check on it later."

Eli seated himself on the hard kitchen chair. He spoke slowly, enunciating every word. "I was the only one who knew where he was."

"We will have to analyze the whole mission before we can determine the weaknesses. The most likely guess is that you were followed. How often did you meet with him?"

"Twice daily during the active phase. I would bring him the information gathered from our other operatives. He was the one with the technical background who knew exactly where we should place our explosives for maximum damage to the reactor."

Ben-Yehuda's face registered a hint of a smile. "You have not seen the first news reports yet, have you?"

"No."

Ben-Yehuda opened his zippered case and took out the *Daily Telegraph*. The headline read: SABOTEURS BOMB FRENCH PLANT CONSTRUCTING 2 REACTORS FOR IRAQ.

Eli skimmed the article. His eye caught the phrases "heavily damaged early today when explosive charges were set off by unknown saboteurs . . . No one was hurt . . . Responsibility was claimed by an anonymous French ecology group which was prompted to act by the recent U.S. nuclear power plant accident near Harrisburg, Pennsylvania."

"Ecologists." Ben-Yehuda grinned. "Very clever."

Ben-Yehuda opened the oven door and poked at the pizza, then sat opposite Eli and took a sip of apple juice. The thick jelly glass appeared huge in his thin, mottled hands. "Before coming here I was notified that your password is 'The Tower of Babel.' If that is satisfactory to you, we can proceed on a full disclosure, since European Operations must deal with the aftermath." He cleared his throat. "The body, and all that."

Eli looked up at Ben-Yehuda. "I'm sorry. This is very difficult." Abruptly, he stood, walked to the other end of the narrow kitchen, and peered down into the service courtyard. Banged and twisted trash cans lined the far wall.

Ben-Yehuda placed a slice of pallid pizza on Eli's plate. "Come, sit . . . Eat something first."

Like an obedient child, Eli lifted a wedge and tasted it. The outside was too hot; the crust was frozen at the thickest parts. He chewed it anyway. The mild sauce and doughy texture were surprisingly satisfying.

Ben-Yehuda waited until he had finished one piece before questioning Eli. "Who was he?"

"Dr. Asher Ze'evi. He was our scientist-consultant on the project. He's also a cousin of mine by marriage," Eli began.

After Ben-Yehuda was briefed on the background of the mission, he spoke calmly. "In order to return the body to the family, one of our agents could pose as a relative and bring it back through West Germany and perhaps Italy. Of course, that would involve the French authorities."

"It has been less than twenty-four hours and it's unlikely anyone's been in the flat. Couldn't we . . . ?"

"Attempt an inside removal?" Ben-Yehuda finished for him. "Let us consider the difficulties. Who do you think is responsible for the crime?"

"There were certain" — Eli paused — "mutilations."

"PLO?"

"Possibly, but it is tied to the explosions, so I would suspect the Iraqis."

"The assassins might tip off the police to publicize their revenge."

"If we hurry —"

"There was no plan for this eventuality."

"Surely in Marseille" —

"Possibly. What is the location like?"

"Downstairs in the building there's an Alfa Romeo showroom, a pharmacy, and Levitan's, an Oriental carpet store."

"Levitan? A Jew?"

"Yes. We have the details on file. There's only one neighbor to concern yourself with, and I know her habits fairly well."

"I will put an operations officer on this immediately. The rest of the debriefing can wait, don't you agree?"

"Ken, ken. Yes, that is best."

"You should be quite comfortable here." Ben-Yehuda stood and prepared to leave. "Eli, one more item. There have been some messages for you sent through Russell and Sutton."

"Recently?"

"Yes, the last one was only a few days ago. Were you expecting anything special?"

"Is one of them from a Colin Stewart?"

"All of them, I believe. They were sent to Charles Ivy. Isn't that gentleman inactive?"

"Officially, but Stewart's a lad I befriended many years ago and he's the sort who keeps in touch."

Uri stared at Eli with the eyes of a wary falcon. "Are you planning to return the calls?"

"I would like to, unless you think it unwise."

"They should not be made from this flat."

"Of course."

"You mustn't leave for more than a short time . . . for your own protection."

"I understand."

"Tomorrow evening we will have a meeting at the embassy or some other secure place. One additional caution: do not permit anyone access to the flat unless you have verified their identity by the signal from the phone box. An authorized visitor will phone first. 'Tower' or 'Babel' will be mentioned."

Eli smiled slightly. All the old methods remained in use.

"You are feeling better?" Uri asked solicitously.

"The pizza, the juice . . . Very calming."

"Sleep is what you need now."

"Uri, I'm sorry to leave you with this mess to sort out."

Ben-Yehuda's eyes twinkled momentarily. He was the type of mild-mannered operative who blossomed when his tactical skills were challenged. "We've handled worse, eh?"

"Todah rabah. Thanks very much, Uri." Eli closed the door.

Eli checked his watch. It was just past six in the evening. Colin might still be in his office at the BBC's Wood Lane studios. Quickly, Eli washed his hands and face and changed into a fresh shirt. Using every precaution, he let himself out of the flat and walked out into Shepherd Market. The square was a popular place after working hours. The Ye Grapes pub crowd flowed out onto the street and patrons leaned against the display window of the neighboring brass shop. Eli crossed Curzon Street and found a row of phone boxes beside the post office.

"Television Centre," the operator answered crisply.

"Colin Stewart's line, please."

"Hello, editing room."

"Colin Stewart, please."

"Who shall I say is calling?" a feminine voice asked.

"Charles Ivy."

"Hello!" Bright and cheery. "So good of you to call! You're back in town, are you, sir?"

"For a short while."

"I would love to see you. I've some news."

"Splendid. What's your schedule?"

"Very hectic. The rough cut on this show's due on Friday and the producer keeps changing his mind."

"I see . . ."

"He can wait, sir. I know how busy you are. When would be best?"

"I'm uncertain until I have my appointments tomorrow. In fact, I might only be here a few days. You wouldn't be available tonight?"

"Emily's working late, so I'd planned to do the same. But I could take a break."

"Dinner at Wheeler's?"

"Where else, Charles?" Then the laugh — genuine, full of sparkle and life. Eli's heart soared at the remembrance of its development from high and sweet to cracked and froggy to its present rich masculine warmth.

"Could you get there by eight, or is that too early?"

"Eight's super. See you then!"

The connection severed. Eli replaced the receiver very gently.

After years of planning, Eli had finally made contact with his son in the spring of 1957.

"I represent a group of professional men who are interested in furthering the education of worthy boys," he had written to the head of St. Joseph's Primary School. "Our intent is to make a long-term investment in each candidate, from public school through university. To qualify, a boy must demonstrate the ability for advanced academic work, although his current performance levels might indicate he is not fulfilling his potential. We take pride in giving such a boy the extra considerations to aid the development of his self-confidence and place him in the school environment which will best meet his interest and needs. The boy who is already an achiever might not need our services quite as much as the one who requires an extra push or specialized training. Further, a candidate should come from a family which would be unable to provide any financial help for boarding school or university expenses, and preference is given to boys with an active interest in one or more team sports, and those whose father was either killed or disabled during the war."

Eli had labored over the educational jargon and tried to be as specific as possible. He knew that Colin's father had lost a leg and received a pension; he knew Colin was more of a sportsman than a student; he knew that the Stewarts had not progressed financially. The letter he received from Colin's school came as a shock. The headmaster had put up two boys and neither one was Colin. Undaunted, Eli asked for additional candidates to consider, specifying the boy must already have "attained the age of twelve years" (Colin had been that age for just a month, but the other two were only eleven) and preferably was an eldest son. He hoped he was not sounding too eccentric, but then decided that a "group of wealthy businessmen" were entitled to be as outlandish as they wished.

To his profound relief, Colin's name appeared in the next correspondence. Eli replied that he was delighted with the latest candidates and set the next phase of his very personal operation in motion.

The boy and his family were informed by the school of the opportunity being offered. If they were interested, the father was to contact Mr. Charles Ivy of the Threadneedle Street Society at his corporate address. With this very scheme in mind, Eli had set up Russell and Sutton Ltd. two years earlier through the Israeli Embassy. There was a mail drop, a phone line for messages, everything he needed. In fact, it had been used several times by operatives and had proved a very convenient front. Eli took enormous pride in the concept of the Threadneedle Street Society. It took its name from the street in the City that runs between the Bank of England and the Royal Exchange, so the very name conjured substantial gentlemen who might very well enjoy helping disadvantaged children. The dual concept of "threading the needle" with education was particularly charming and one he meant to discuss with the child's father if the moment arose.

As expected, Randolph Stewart had been most appreciative that his son was under consideration. "He's a good lad, helps his mum and me. He should have better," he told Eli over the phone.

"The way we work, Mr. Stewart, is that each boy has an individual representative. I would serve that function for your son. We are not a large, uncaring organization. Many of our boys have gone on to distinguish themselves, and we stay in touch with most of them, even help them along in their careers when possible. What I would like to do, with your permission of course, is meet young . . . Colin, is it? . . . and be certain this is something he wants."

"He does. He's very proud to have been considered."

"I am pleased to hear you say it. However, we want to evaluate his interest personally. It is a big step — leaving home, changing schools. Let us all be confident he is ready."

So the arrangements had been made. Colin was directed to meet Eli at Wheeler's restaurant the following week. The boy was to come alone, "to demonstrate self-assurance." Later, Eli would wonder whether he would have permitted his child to go off to meet a total stranger, but at the time the request did not seem so outlandish.

Eli arrived early and waited outside on Old Compton Street to spare the child any anxieties about going into a restaurant by himself, forgetting momentarily that Colin was a publican's son. He spotted the boy a block away, but allowed him to approach the restaurant on his own.

"Hello. You're Colin Stewart, aren't you?"

Colin looked up into his eyes and said, "Yes, sir. Are you Mr. Ivy?"

"Right! So kind of you to meet me this afternoon. Did you have any difficulty finding the place?"

"No, my mother drew me a map, but I didn't need it. I memorize most directions the first time."

"That is very clever!" Eli said, thinking, We could use you in the Mossad, my boy. "Shall we go inside?"

The waiter led them past the bar in the front dining room and up a narrow, curving stairway into one of the smaller rooms upstairs, with only six tables. Eli nodded his approval of the corner table and gestured for Colin to take the chair by the open window. The air was fresh and the bit of traffic noise from the busy Soho street below lent the room a friendly feeling. Everything was going perfectly, Eli decided. The restaurant was an apt choice. With only two other tables occupied, it was quiet — but not so posh or stuffy that a boy from a modest background would feel out of place. Hunting prints, mounted game fish, and giant lobster shells decorated the walls. The floors were slanted at jaunty angles and some of the pictures hung off center, but the lamps with the red fringed shades glowed warmly on each table and the waiters were never overly fastidious or ridiculously deferential. Even so, Colin sat stiffly as the menu was presented.

"Might I get you gentlemen something to drink?" the waiter asked.

"A shandy, Mr. Stewart?" Eli smiled.

"No, I'm usually not permitted, sir."

Immediately Eli regretted suggesting something containing alcohol. "What about a squash? Orange or lemon?"

"Lemon please, sir."

Eli nodded to the waiter and added, "And a Beefeater gin and tonic."

"Very good, sir."

Colin opened the long menu and seemed to be reading each line. Grateful for a moment to study the boy up close, Eli remained silent. While he had seen photographs taken from a distance, there was so much here he had not expected. The skin on his cheeks was still baby soft; the lips were full and a deep pink, with chapped edges. His eyes were wide set and more expressive than Eli had imagined. Their intense blue rimmed with a darker margin was unnerving at first, until Eli started with the shock of recognition. Colin's eyes were exactly like those of his own mother, the same eyes that had so captivated his father. For his age, the boy seemed a bit shorter and plumper than ideal, but he played football and cricket so was probably well muscled.

Without warning, Eli was seized with an urge to clasp the boy's face in his hands and tell him: I'm your father and I love you. Fortunately, the waiter returned with the drinks. Eli reached instead for the cool glass as if it were a life raft in a strong sea. After two swift swallows, the impulse passed. Who *was* his biological father? Not Charles Ivy. Not even Eli Katzar. Colin's father was Elliot Short of Bletchley Park — a man who no longer existed.

"Sir?" The voice was high and sweet; the lips were pursed like those of a patient altar boy.

"Yes, Colin?"

"Do they have anything on the menu besides fish?"

"You don't care for fish?"

"No, sir."

Eli swallowed hard. After all his planning, he had selected a restaurant serving nothing but seafood. "What about scampi or mussels?"

"I don't think so, sir. I'm not very hungry."

"I've made a mistake. Shall we go somewhere else?"

"Oh no, sir!" Colin blushed and blinked his eyes.

Eli hoped he would not cry, for the boy's own sake, but he could see Colin was perilously close to tears. Eli flipped open the menu and hurriedly checked the offerings for a chop or salad or anything the boy might prefer. Wheeler's was defiantly a fish restaurant. "Do you like fish and chips?"

"No, I'm afraid not."

"Have you ever had any other fish?"

"No, sir."

Eli let out a great sigh and leaned back in his chair. "Then I fully understand your aversion to fish. I myself cannot tolerate it fried. But look, there are more than a dozen Dover sole variations on this menu alone. If you will permit yourself to be a bit adventurous this evening, I would like you to taste another way of preparing fish. If it does not appeal, put your fork down, and we shan't say another word about it."

"I will be happy to try, sir."

"Shall we begin with the simplest manner of presentation or the most complex?"

"Would you decide for me, Mr. Ivy?"

The waiter returned and Eli ordered Dover sole Véronique for Colin, poached trout for himself, and an extra order of potatoes (just in case). With the food issue temporarily solved, he went on to explain his "organization" to Colin.

"Do you have any questions?"

"What school would I go to?"

"We don't usually have more than one boy at a given school at a time. Even if we did, you wouldn't know who he was. Our boys never carry the stigma of 'scholarship' or 'charity' cases. They start out on the same footing with everybody else. However, to answer your question, we feel you'd do quite well at the Perse School in

Cambridge. That way you would not be too far from home for holidays and weekends and it would not be a strain for your parents to visit you. Do you think you would want to go away to school?"

"I can't see why not, sir. It's a wonderful opportunity."

"You'd miss your parents, your sisters."

"Well, may I speak honestly, sir?"

"I certainly hope so."

"My dad's a hard man to live with these days — I never seem to be able to suit him — and my mum's rarely home. Sometimes she works two shifts at the hospital. And my sisters are always into my models and books. So, I wouldn't have much to miss, would I?"

"Many boys your age feel the same way. I know I did."

"Did you have pesty sisters too?"

"No, but my father was demanding and difficult. A military man, and you can guess how they are! No matter how hard I tried, he always believed I could do better. Ah, here's our meal."

The platters were served on hunt scene place mats. With a worried expression, Colin peered down at the sole. It had been lightly poached and was served in a Sauterne sauce and studded with grape halves. Tentatively, he lifted his fork and poked at the white flesh. Eli reached over to demonstrate how to bone it. As he lifted the skeleton out in one piece, he could tell the feat impressed Colin. So the boy would not be self-conscious, he busied himself with his trout. Without raising his eyes, he was able to see Colin's empty fork return to the platter, stab a grape, and move upward — then return again for a second piece of sole.

"Fish and grapes! Who'd have thought they'd go so well together?"

Eli looked up and saw the boy aggressively devouring the meal. He'll do well, he decided. The boy takes risks; he plunges in; he admits fears, but moves beyond them. "I believe you'll take to your new school just as easily, Colin, as — if you'll permit me to use a tired expression — a fish to water."

"I hope I won't disappoint you or the other gentlemen, sir. I'm not the world's best student, you know."

"We do not expect you to achieve top marks. Just try to do your best. Everybody has ups and downs. We are interested in the long haul. Our only request is that you stay in touch with us. A letter to my office each month will meet that requirement. Plus, we want to meet with you a minimum of twice a year, more often if you desire or have a special need or difficulty."

"Do I have to meet anyone else or write any more applications?"

"No. You are accepted as of this moment. I travel a great deal, so I might not get back to you right away, but I'll be your contact person from now on."

"Will you meet my parents? My mother is quite anxious to learn more about all this."

I'll bet she is, Eli reflected. "No. We deal directly with the candidate who has been selected. Permitting a boy to manage his own arrangements is all part of the maturing process. Your parents will receive an official acceptance letter, of course. Tuition and boarding payments will be sent to the school. However, everything else is between the two of us. Is that satisfactory with you?"

Colin's pink cheeks glowed. "Yes, very, sir."

So it began. Twice a year — once during the Christmas holidays, once during the summer — father and son met at Wheeler's and worked their way from Dover sole bonne femme (steamed, with sliced mushrooms) to Dover sole Walewska (with slices of lobster and grated cheese). By the time Colin entered Oxford, he had graduated to Scotch lobsters, smoked eel and trout, even Wheeler's fish paté maison.

During this time Eli had watched his son grow half a head taller than himself, have his teeth straightened (courtesy of the Threadneedle Street Society), mend a broken leg (a jump from a dormitory roof — just why he was on the roof had never been made entirely clear), agonize over whether to do a continental study term in France or Spain. (France won out because of a girl friend who had selected the same country — a choice Eli, but not his mother, encouraged. The girl fell in love with a French boy and broke Colin's heart — temporarily.) As he looked back, Eli was aware that he *had* shared in his son's life. Not as a father, perhaps, but as a concerned adult whom Colin had trusted from the first.

In fact, searching for impartial advice, the boy had come to him with many secrets he had kept from his parents. Hardly ever again did Eli feel the temptation to tell Colin who he was. The more he grew to understand his son, the more he comprehended how painful such a revelation would be for everyone, especially when Colin himself confessed he knew that Randolph Stewart was not his biological father.

The boy had been seventeen. It was July and they were at Wheeler's, of course, but in a different dining room. Colin had been sitting under a painting titled *The Start of the Grand Prix* and eating Dover sole Capri (with sliced bananas and chutney sauce). The big news was the final results of the school cricket matches.

"The first part of the season was awfully wet," Colin began earnestly. "The Newport Grammar School match was drawn, but we won St. Edmund's by two wickets. Then we lost to Chigwell and Marylebone. After that, we were on a winning streak, capturing Culford, Ipswich, Kimbolton, Cowley, and, best of all, the Leys School, our arch rivals in Cambridge!"

"To what do you attribute this sudden turnabout?" Eli asked politely.

"Not my sterling performance!" Colin laughed good-naturedly. "Ralph Stenner made a total of twenty-nine wickets and Barry Feinstein was consistently aggressive and made over twenty. He has magnificent off-spinners, you know. Also, he's frightfully good in science, says he wants to go into medicine. What a waste of athletic talent, don't you think?"

"One can't be a sportsman forever, can one?"

"It would be lovely . . ." Then Colin's eyes took on a faraway look and he replaced his fork. "Feinstein's a Jewish boy."

"Yes?" Every muscle in Eli's body tensed. Had his mother poisoned *him* against Jews?

Colin poked at a boiled potato. "My father was Jewish. Did I ever tell you that?"

"I don't recall, actually," Eli said hoarsely.

"Well, I've known for some time that Randy is not my real father. But I didn't know when I was twelve — that is, when I was selected by your society. My mother was afraid that I might not get the scholarship, since I was selected because my father — I mean Randy — lost his leg and all that, so —"

"I see your point, but it wouldn't have made a difference in the end. You were qualified on other counts."

"I know that now. Anyway, I'm glad this has come out. My mother finally told me a year later. She was explaining about how when Jewish boys are thirteen they come of age, so she decided I might be old enough to know the truth about my father."

What in heaven's name had Maura been up to? Why couldn't she leave well enough alone?

"Mother said I might find out myself when I was older and she didn't want me to hear about it from anyone else. Mum is very sensible and I'm certain she was right."

"Wasn't it a shock?"

"Funnily enough, it was more of a relief. My two sisters *look* so much more like my father — I mean Randy. They have his brown eyes and thin nose, even the same crooked toe. You see, my mother had fallen in love with my natural father during the war. They were to have married, but he went off to the front and never returned. He never knew about me. Shortly after he was killed, she met Randolph. They were already married when I was born, you see."

"That's nothing to be ashamed about."

"I know. During the war everything was different. You couldn't make plans, live by ordinary rules. Nevertheless, Mum refused to tell me who my father was — his name, where he lived, and all that."

"Your mother must have had her reasons."

"That's how I found out he was Jewish. She said that his family never knew about her and would have been upset to know she'd had his baby and they'd never been informed. Also, she wondered if they'd think she was making something up to get some money from them — although Mum would never do anything like that."

"I am certain she wouldn't."

"Mum explained that Jewish people are frightfully protective of their own and would want me to be Jewish, but how could she raise a Jewish child? At the time, I was confused by so much of what she said, I didn't know what to think."

"And now?"

"I believe I have sorted it out since I've become friends with Barry Feinstein and some of the other boys at Hillel House — that's where the Jewish boys live. I get on with them very well and I've visited the Feinsteins in London several times. Sometimes I wonder if my father was like Mr. Feinstein — he's a barrister and was in the RAF. He even gave me a gift for Chanukah last year and told me about some of their other holidays. I find their customs quite fascinating. Do you know about them?"

"A bit. What does your mother say about all this?"

Colin shrugged. "I don't tell her much because it might hurt her feelings. It must have been horrid for her to have her fiancé die without even knowing she was having his baby."

"Yes, but she had you, and that must be a comfort."

Maura's logic was questionable. Why in the world had she opened the boy to so many searching problems? Hadn't she married Stewart to avoid this? What was she afraid of? Somebody like Jocelyn slipping in her dotage? As Eli seethed silently, he wondered what Maura would think if she could see him sitting across from their son at this very moment.

Colin's plate was clear except for the fish skeleton and a few pieces of parsley. His own remained almost untouched.

"You're not hungry tonight, sir?"

"No, not especially, but you have done quite well. Remember when you were afraid you didn't like fish?"

As Colin nodded his head, his reddish brown hair fell back against his face in an amusing, lopsided way. Eli reached across the table to fix it for him. As he did so, he reflected on how few opportunities there had been to touch Colin. His fingers lingered an extra second as he smoothed the boy's bangs.

"You look like one of those Beagles."

"You mean Beatles?"

"The singers, the boys with the long hair."

"Right. The Beatles. Edith is madly in love with them. Mum is worried she'll run off after them someday. She might, you know. She cried for days when they went off to play in New York." He drifted away for a second. When he spoke again it was with a different voice. "One more thing, about my father . . . When I was first offered the chance to go to Perse, my mother let something slip. She said she'd recalled my father also went there. Isn't that a coincidence?"

"Quite."

"Well, in the Assembly Hall there's a plaque on the wall which reads, 1939 TO 1945, IN HONOUR OF THE FALLEN, and then there is a list of names."

"Yes?"

"There are only two Jewish-sounding names: Tattenbaum and Cohen. I've looked up the records. Cohen was married to someone else and Tattenbaum died before I could have been conceived . . ."

Eli shook his head sadly. "I can see your mother's confession, while it may have helped her own conscience, has not been helpful for you. First of all, there are many Jewish men whose names have been changed from their original to Jones or Smith or Brown or any other ordinary name. Secondly, from the sound of it, your mother didn't know the man for a terribly long time. Perse School may or may not have been the one he attended. Perhaps it was something similar, like Purcell or Rossall, for instance. Both are fine public schools. Most important, your *real* father is the man who raised you from the moment you were born. No father is perfect; you would have quar-

reled with whoever had been the man in the house. Just be thankful
you have two parents who love you and are doing their best for you.
Think of the many others who care for you: your masters, your
coaches, your friends and their parents — and don't forget, I'll be
around to help you out — even after you've completed your education."

Colin was contemplative. Eli was grateful for the moment to
gather his thoughts. What if he wasn't around always? What if something happened to him even before Colin finished his schooling?
Why, he would just disappear from the boy's life without a trace. If
he came searching for the Threadneedle Street Society or Russell
and Sutton, he would come up against a blank wall. Eli wondered if
there was a way he could make provisions for the boy financially.
Some sort of secret trust perhaps? He laughed at himself. Who did
he think he was? All he earned was a government salary. By living
simply, he had saved enough for Perse, but Colin was his only luxury. Fortunately, he did not have a wife and family to support as
well. The best he could do was to hope no bombs exploded in his car
and his heart kept ticking away.

"The raspberries," the waiter said, setting two bowls of moist ber-
ries in front of them.

"Ah, this is just what we needed to cheer us up!" Eli passed Colin
an earthenware crock filled with thick cream and urged the boy to
ladle it out. Colin adored raspberries, and as he gobbled them intently, the subject of his long-lost Jewish father was dropped.

❖   ❖   ❖

Seventeen years later, they occupied a table in the very same dining
room they had first eaten in. Colin had recognized it the moment
they were seated and had pointed to where he had sat. "You can't
imagine how frightened I was that day. Randy had said that if I lost
this opportunity, there would never be another like it. My mother
fussed over my jacket and sewed the buttons on extra tight so one
wouldn't pop off, and gave me three handkerchiefs, one for each
pocket."

As the waiter brought dessert, Eli recalled his own emotions at
that first meeting. It was too early in the season for their traditional
raspberries, so tiny wild strawberries were set before them. Colin was
very frugal with the cream ladle. During the meal (Colin had ordered curried lobster, Eli grilled plaice), Colin had rambled on
about the film he was editing for the BBC — something about com-

puters for the handicapped. Eli, however, was too distracted by his own problems to give Colin his full attention.

". . . The point is, it's all a great lie."

Eli leaned forward attentively. What was a lie? "In what way?"

"Every film is a fabrication, even the so-called cinéma verité, because all the images, sounds, perceptions are filtered through a person's mind — a person with a cause or a slant or some position to uphold. Even if the cameraman turns on the camera and keeps it running during a complete unstaged action, he makes hundreds of minor decisions as the film rolls past the lens: where to aim the camera, whether to include only the main person in the shot or the others in the same milieu, the selection of a tight, pore-revealing close-up or a more flattering medium shot. From then on, the truth gets distorted at every pass through the filmmaking process. By the time it reaches my editing table, I'm God. I rearrange time; I juxtapose images which never would be together in daily life; I cut out contradictory statements; I can make a hero or an ass out of the same interview subject."

"How is that?"

"By removing their grammatical mistakes and ignorant-sounding 'you knows,' 'ahs,' and 'ums,' I can make most anyone sound literate. Listen, if Nixon had me on his staff, he would still be President!"

Eli beamed at Colin. The boy was amusing, talented, a remarkable person. Over the years he had come to Eli for all sorts of advice: which courses to take, which college to apply to, where to go for the holidays, how to tell a girl it was over. "What would my father know about the difference between Clare College and Trinity? How could he advise me about dating and all that?" Colin had asked when he was in his final year at Perse.

"He may not have been to a university, but he surely has had a few experiences with women."

"I don't think so. After all, he married my mother out of pity, not love. What sort of a man would do that?"

Calmly Eli had stared into his son's familiar eyes and said forcefully, "A kind one. A man of great strength. A man who raised you as his own and did his very best for you. All boys turn against their parents for a while. It's a natural part of growing up. Eventually, you will understand."

Colin had sulked a bit, yet he had never rebelled against his mentor. Eli came to believe he had had the best of his child and was grateful it had all worked out as he'd planned.

Eli was already late getting back to the safe house. He was beginning to feel edgy. A few minutes earlier, a short, swarthy man had
entered the dining room, apparently looking for someone who wasn't
there. Eli had caught the man's eye momentarily and the man had
scurried out. Something so inconsequential should not have concerned him, but his stomach had contracted. The events of the last
twenty-four hours were catching up with him. Ben-Yehuda was
right: he needed to rest.

As the coffee was served, Eli said, "I'm always pleased to see you,
Colin, but you have not yet told me your reason for contacting me."

"I've been saving it, actually. Emily and I are expecting a baby.
It's due in about a month."

"Congratulations. How many years have you been married now?"
Eli asked, though he knew exactly. Years ago, when Colin had confided that he was having a love affair with Emily Applebaum, he
had seen this as a reflection of the boy's curiosity about his Jewish-
ness. He had expected the girl's charms would fade and Colin would
settle down with someone who would suit Maura's preferences better.

"Three officially, but we've been together for almost five. So it's
time, wouldn't you agree?"

"You don't need my approval for this one and even if you did, it's
a bit late to ask."

"Well, I'm thirty-four and she's thirty, so we felt it was now or
never. And the Applebaums are desperate to be grandparents."

Grandparents! Of course, this meant Eli would be a grandfather.

Colin babbled on about classes from the Childbirth Trust:
breathing exercises, carrying pillows on the tube, midwives versus
doctors. Eli's attention, however, was diverted by the same dark-
skinned man with close-cropped, curly hair. This time he appeared
in the hallway between the two dining rooms. What was there about
him that made Eli's skin prickle?

He looked at his watch. "I'm so sorry, Colin, but I have to meet a
gentleman on business quite soon . . ."

"Oh, I have been going on and on. I never expected I'd get so excited about something as simple and ordinary as having a baby. But
as they say, when it's your own . . ."

Eli paid the bill. Colin stood at the signal and followed Eli into the
narrow corridor. A waiter carrying a tray of drinks pressed himself
against the wall to permit them to pass. Side by side, Colin was a
head taller than his father and stockier. Eli straightened his shoulders

and looked over at Colin proudly. Just then, the man who had worried Eli came out of the men's toilet on the upper landing. Was it his imagination or had the man quickly averted his face from Eli and hurried downstairs?

"I'll just be a minute, Charles." Colin was on his way up to the landing, and the door to the bathroom was opening.

"No!" Eli ran after him. He pushed the door in before Colin could close it fully, then shoved a startled man, who was zipping his fly, out the door. Crazed, as if an instinctive warning hormone was coursing through his blood stream, he pushed open each of the three stalls and scanned them from floor to ceiling. The Marks and Spencer shopping bag beside the bowl appeared innocent enough to anyone but a Mossad agent.

Instead of a window, the rest room had a door on the far side that opened onto the roof. Colin had discovered it years ago and they both had walked out and looked at the stars. Eli remembered placing his hands on the boy's shoulders. Colin had leaned into him and asked, "Do you think we'll get in trouble for being out here?" Eli had assured him they would not. Now Eli raced for the bolt and yanked it once, twice. It was stuck! He kicked the door violently and the milky glass window shattered but held between a sandwich of wire mesh. On the next try, the bolt loosened and the door flew open. Colin stood behind him, but Eli yanked the collar of his tweed jacket and shoved him out first.

"What is —?" was all Colin had time to ask before Eli pulled him down a ladder that led to the lower rooftop of the next building over.

He was thrown on top of Colin as the blast blew a hole in Wheeler's roof. As soon as the violent shock was replaced by sirens and screams, as soon as Eli knew Colin was unhurt, they made their way over two more rooftops and down to Dean Street.

"Where are we going?" Colin asked in a daze. "Shouldn't we go back?"

"We'd only be in the way, my boy. There are probably injuries. Look, there's a fire!"

From half a block away, they could see the commotion: fire trucks, ambulances, half-dressed strippers rushing out from the Sans Souci bar across the street, the wreck of a Mercedes that had swerved to avoid hitting a porcelain sink lying in the middle of Old Compton Street.

"But, we're witnesses, aren't we?" Colin asked naïvely.

"They've plenty of others to interview. We'd be stuck here for hours, and with my schedule, I can't afford to be involved right now," Eli ventured quickly.

Colin was breathing rapidly. His round cheeks were bright red, except for a few filthy spots where he had pressed against the asphalt of the roof. "I can't believe we escaped." He coughed and panted. "What do you think happened?"

"The loo is just above the kitchen. They must have had a gas explosion near the stove."

"How did you know we had to get out of there? You were running away even before it happened."

"I thought I smelled something. Must've been the gas."

"What if something had happened to me? What would Emily have done? And the baby — oh, God . . ." Colin leaned against the building and began to shake.

"Let's get you to a taxi." He steered Colin to Greek Street and hailed a cab. "You'll be fine. I'll call in a few days, if I can. Now wipe off your face before you get home. I'm sorry, I've got to run. Here's another taxi." He waved for it to stop. "Give my best to Emily." He slammed the door of Colin's taxi and ran to his own.

"Dukes Hotel," he told the driver, then leaned back, closed his eyes tightly, and fought the plummeting feeling that was threatening to overtake him.

3

And o'er the hills and far away
Beyond their utmost purple rim,
Beyond the night, across the day,
Through all the world she followed him.

Alfred, Lord Tennyson (1809–1892)
"The Day Dream"

ZERMATT, SWITZERLAND: JULY 1950

"No matter how well you believe you are prepared, there are bound to be surprises," Aviva's trainer had said on the last evening before she departed on her first assignment away from Israel. "How you cope will determine whether you pass this testing period."

Except for the pangs she felt each time she handed her false passport to an official, the trip had been uneventful so far. The flight on El Al's Douglas DC-4 to Rome had been her first experience on an airplane. From there she had flown on British European Airways to London. When she handed over her turquoise-blue Israeli passport to her contact there, she had to stifle the urge to grab her identity back, but she accepted the replacement wordlessly. Suddenly she was Jasmine Gregory, with an Egyptian mother, a British father, and a passport of a much darker hue of blue.

Going through passport control the next morning was another tense moment, but her papers had not caused a second glance. By the time Swissair's Convairliner landed in Zürich, Aviva was more confident.

She had found the train in Zürich without difficulty, and during the journey south across the Bernese Alps, through the long railroad tunnel from Kandersteg to Goppenstein, and down to the transfer point in Brig, she had been riveted to the wondrous Alpine scenery. But she had expected to find beauty in the Alps. What astonished her was discovering that Switzerland that July was unbearably hot.

All the way from Israel, Aviva had been anticipating crisp mountain breezes. Instead, waiting on the Brig railroad platform, she was covered with a thin patina of perspiration. Her wardrobe had been selected to make her look as unassuming as possible. Although she had never owned fancy clothing — for most of her life she had worn the practical, collectively owned farm clothing of the kibbutz — she knew this outfit was particularly unflattering. The long-sleeved blouse had a floppy collar that made her bosom appear too large, while the shapeless olive skirt had wrinkled during travel.

Aviva checked her watch to determine whether there was time to change into a lighter-weight outfit. Five minutes, if the schedule was correct. She had been told that the Swiss trains were the most precise in the world, so she could not chance it. She lifted her rucksack to one shoulder as the bright red train came into view. But it was not pulling up to the platform where she was waiting. All the other passengers were on what appeared to be the correct platform for the incoming train. The sign on the station wall read: "Zermatt — Gleis 1." Above her the sign clearly read, "1." No matter what it said, Aviva knew she was in the wrong place.

"Zermatt?" she called to a man just about to climb onto the train.

"Ja."

Aviva grabbed her suitcase and looked for a way across the tracks, but they were fenced off from each other for safety.

"I am coming," she shouted in English and ran down the stairway that led to the tunnel under the tracks, up to the correct platform, and toward the front of the train. Just as she leapt aboard, the train began creeping forward.

She found a seat, but her pulse continued to race. Her face was flushed. All at once she felt queer.

"Are you all right?" Someone slipped beside her on the seat. Aviva saw only a pleated white skirt, polished white shoes, elegantly manicured hands. Aviva took a few deep breaths and looked up.

"You speak English, don't you? That's what I heard you call out," the girl said.

"Yes, a little," Aviva replied warily.

"You almost missed the train. Apparently there are two platforms with the same number. I was warned when I transferred from St.-Moritz that the larger trains run on a different gauge track. This is a smaller line specially designed for going up steep mountains."

"I see . . ." She wondered if she should be speaking with the girl.

She felt better when the cool air blew through the window as the train began to climb away from the Rhône Valley toward the Valaisanne Alps.

"Have you ever been to Zermatt before?" the girl beside her asked.

Aviva knew the time had come to play the role for which she had prepared. "No," she answered tentatively. "Have you?"

"It's my first time as well. I'm American, by the way, and you?"

"Excuse me?"

"Where are you from? What country?"

"England." The deliberate lie was effortless. Aviva turned back to the view as a flash of the rushing Vispa River, the color of liquid granite, caught her eye.

The first stop was at Stalden, rimmed with mulberry trees and capped with a white church. To the left of the train tracks a road forked to the left into the Saas Valley. As they continued onward, graceful stone bridges arched across the jagged span between two brilliant green hills. In the distance Aviva caught her first glimpse of an immense snowy peak commanding the valley from above, while below, the Vispa churned itself into a milky foam as it poured through the Kipfen Gorge.

The train slowed at another mountain station: St. Niklaus. Its church had a surprising onion-shaped dome that glistened in the sunlight. Two dark-eyed children walked the length of the platform, selling strawberries from baskets.

"Aren't the wooden houses — I mean chalets — beautiful!" the American cried out. Then, more softly, "Have you ever seen so many roses?"

Aviva looked where she was pointing. There were geraniums, but no roses. "Where?" she asked, then caught herself. Roses! All the recruits were to have flower passwords. Hers was Violet. She had not been expecting any other women, though, and certainly not an American. How had the American known to make contact with her? Did she appear as raw as she felt?

The American was silent. Perhaps she was worrying that her comment about roses had been aimed at the wrong target.

"The fields are filled with flowers." Aviva spoke in a whisper. "I am planning on taking long walks to gather big bouquets. Violets are my favorites."

"Mine too!" the American said with a rush of relief. "My name's Carla Christopher, but everyone calls me Chris."

"I am Jasmine Gregory. Very pleased to meet you . . . Chris."

Chris? What an odd name for a new recruit in the Israeli secret service. Most everyone in the training course at Tel Hashomer had come from her own sort of background. They all had been born and bred in Palestine, had grown up with rifles in their hands, and had joined Palmach commando units from the scout movement. Before she was fifteen, Aviva defended her kibbutz, Negba, from the Arab bands that harassed the settlement. Too young to be considered seriously for intensive combat training, she received instruction as a wireless operator. Eventually she tutored men being sent on special overseas assignments. After the war, she herself was selected for intelligence work, much to her surprise.

The American had closed her eyes and rested her head on the beige antimacassar embroidered with the initials of the railroad: BVZ, for Brig-Visp-Zermatt. Her face was a lovely oval, her features regular, but Aviva was most captivated by her long, luxurious eyelashes and her wonderfully formed lips, which seemed, even as she relaxed, upturned in a pleasant smile. Afraid the American might open her eyes and notice she was staring, Aviva turned and studied the other passengers in the car: a mother and three children, four climbers with ruddy cheeks, two middle-aged women with matching luggage, and an elderly man. All were just as unlikely Israeli undercover agents as the girl beside her.

As the train struggled up the final stages of the journey, the American asked, "Almost there?"

"It seems so."

The train jerked to a stop. "I think we'd better get off separately," the American suggested.

"I suppose you are right."

She let the American collect her aluminum suitcase and small canvas duffel. After the American got off the train, she organized her rucksack on her back, adjusted the straps, pushed back a few wisps of unruly hair, and reached for her battered suitcase.

Some passengers were greeted by their climbing guides. Others set off for the town on foot. Ahead of her, the American was walking down the platform purposefully. Aviva was unsure of her next step.

A man stepped from between a line of horse-drawn carts. "Grüss Gott, God's greetings," he said as he handed Aviva a bouquet of flowers wrapped in a paper lace cone. The center was filled with purple violets, then rimmed in tiny pink roses, with white daisies as a border.

"Danke schön," she managed. He pointed to a bright blue carriage pulled by two horses. Aviva could see that the American was already sitting in the back seat. She also carried a bouquet. The driver helped her with her bag. Violets, roses . . . and daisies.

Aviva turned back to the train. Standing quite close to the engine was a young woman much taller than either she or the American. Her silvery blond hair was braided and looped on either side of her head. She was dressed in beige corduroy climbing pants and matching ribbed knee-high stockings. On her back was a deep green daypack; she carried no other luggage. This veteran climber was no recent arrival to the Alps. Their driver approached her with another bouquet. Intently, Aviva and the American watched as the newcomer made her way in their direction. They studied her loping walk, her haughty expression.

"Guten Tag," the blonde said perfunctorily.

When all three were settled, the driver maneuvered the cart into the long, narrow street where no automobiles were permitted. As it moved up into the town, the three young women caught their first glimpse of the mountain. Standing apart from the other peaks, it rose in a stark pyramid from the midst of the meadows. A few wisps of clouds floated near the peak, modestly guarding the summit.

"Mont Cervin, Monte Cervino, das Matterhorn," the driver announced in three languages.

Aviva was captivated. She could not turn her eyes from its eerie escarpment, its compelling presence so close to civilization. She twisted the bouquet in her hands as she wondered anew at all that had led to her, a sabra, coming to such a place at her government's expense.

The carriage slowed in front of the Grand Hotel Zermatterhof. Aviva was not surprised to be staying in the largest hotel in the village. "The smaller the establishment, the more they observe the comings and goings of the residents," she had been warned.

In the lobby, Aviva tried to muster the same confidence as the American as she filled out her guest registration form, but it was the third girl who did it with the most nonchalance. The blonde spoke fluent German and her attitude was almost surly, as if she had great distaste for all such procedures. Aviva noticed it was to her the clerk was most deferential.

There was space in the tiny elevator for only the porter, the baggage, and one other person. Aviva and the American each gestured for the blonde to go first. She complied without a courteous word.

As soon as the elevator light moved upward, the American muttered, "How could — ?"

Aviva whispered, "She does not even look Jewish."

"None of us is supposed to, but she is *amazing.*"

Aviva looked at her key. "What room are you in?"

"Five-zero-four, the same as you."

"And her?"

"I think we are all together."

"Will there be any men?"

"No. Weren't you told?"

"What?"

"This is a . . . climbing group just for women. We're all on the same level that way, not competing with men."

"How many of us?"

"Don't know for sure. Maybe just us three."

The elevator returned and took them upstairs. On the fifth floor the door to their room was ajar. The porter demonstrated how the draperies opened and closed and pointed out the mealtimes on a card. The American was quick with a modest tip, then closed the heavy door firmly behind the departing man.

Just then the blond girl stepped from a side room. "I have taken the small alcove here," she said in heavily accented but accurate English. "It was meant for a child, I think." Her "think" sounded like "tink."

The American shrugged and asked, "Which bed would you prefer, Jasmine?"

"Either," Aviva demurred. Both beds, capped with fluffy white comforters and two large square pillows, looked luxurious. Beside each bed there was even a small embroidered linen mat on which to wipe one's bare feet before turning in.

"Okay, I'll take the side nearest the bathroom. I always get up in the middle of the night. By the way, I'm Carla Christopher," she said to the newcomer. "Everybody calls me Chris."

"I am very pleased to make your acquaintance, Chris." The blonde stiffly offered her hand. "I am called Nicole Schmidt."

"Pleased to meet you, Nicole," the American said. "This is Jasmine Gregory. We met on the train."

The blonde extended her hand to Aviva, but she unexpectedly dropped it, reached out, and kissed her on both cheeks. "Shalom," she said brightly.

For a second, Aviva was startled. Then it was as if a great weight had been lifted. "Shalom!" she answered and hugged her back. The American was pulled into the group and the three sat down on the mound of soft, lemon-scented comforters and laughed together.

A knock on the door silenced them. "Probably just the porter again," the American said softly. "He has the hots for Nicole."

Aviva looked puzzled. "The 'hots'?"

"You know, he *likes* her."

"No, *you*!" The blonde's laugh sounded like spilling water.

Aviva called through the door. "Ja?"

"Mr. Ivy, from the climbing school," the man replied in a British accent.

Aviva recognized it at once. She opened the door. Standing in the entrance, looking every bit a climber in his navy breeches with drawstrings below the knees, plaid shirt, and well-scuffed climbing boots, was Eli Katzar. She had heard rumors he had moved into the upper levels of the intelligence network since his days at Kibbutz Hazorea, but had not expected to see him here. Before she could voice her surprise, the American called, "Eli!" and ran across the room to him.

He kicked the door shut and spoke severely. "Charles Ivy to you, my dear."

Aviva glanced at the blonde to see if she also recognized the visitor. The wry smile on her lips completed the puzzle. They all knew Eli. He had probably been involved in their selection, had known or perhaps arranged their courses, and had brought them here for the final phase of training.

Eli straddled the desk chair backward. "You have introduced yourselves?"

The American's mouth formed a sexy pucker. "Jasmine and I met on the train quite accidentally, and we are just getting to know Nicole."

"How did you identify each other on the train?" Eli asked.

"I was sitting next to Jasmine and just had a feeling, so I casually mentioned roses and she responded with violets."

Eli cleared his throat and addressed the young women who sat at attention across the bottom of the beds. "Each of you knows me by my true identity. It would be most helpful if you would make every effort to forget it." He paused to see if he had their complete attention. "Tomorrow we will meet our guide, Bernie Petrig. He is a local mountaineer who knows only that I am an amateur climber who wants to establish a regular summer climbing school for young ladies. He is the link who will help us establish our covers, as well as the place and date you three were together for the first time. Beyond that, the skills you will learn will be invaluable. But do not expect a luxurious holiday."

The American looked around the room. "This isn't exactly the Negev, however."

The other two girls laughed in unison.

"Jasmine, you know what 'gibbush' means, don't you?" Eli asked.

"In Hebrew it is working together, unification. In the army it is a time you live together as a group and learn to trust each other."

"Exactly. This week is designed to provide you with a similar experience. Do you have any questions?"

"Then Charles Ivy is your cover name?" the American asked.

"That is correct."

New recruits were inevitably entranced by how many names they were given. There were four altogether. Two never varied: their birth name and their bureaucratic nom de guerre. Two changed with every mission.

Once they were officially accepted in the Mossad, they were given their nom de guerre — the name under which their original reports would be filed and the name by which they would be known within the intelligence agency itself. This was to protect their identity from circulating within a bureaucracy that paid their salary, transcribed their reports, and kept their personnel files. Eli Katzar's nom de guerre was Yoel Raphael.

In the field, another code name — or password — was assigned for each mission. It was used as a buffer to prevent too many people from learning the official cover. A courier, for example, might know an agent only as Rose or Lion and, by using that name, could identify himself as the appropriate liaison.

"May we know your password as well?" Aviva asked timidly.

Eli stood up and replaced the chair beside the desk. "Yes. Staying with the floral motif, I'm Aster, for the alpine aster which blooms this time of year. Not that these passwords will have much meaning on this assignment."

The third and most essential identity was the actual cover under which the agent operated openly. This cover had to be precisely established with background information, passports, credit cards — all the paraphernalia of human existence — and had to be solid enough to withstand a check by a foreign security agency.

"Our cover names will be used from here on," Eli continued. "You will be Chris, Nicole, and Jasmine at all times. But I also want you to know each other's file names as well."

"Are you deliberately trying to confuse us?" the American challenged.

"Perhaps." Eli's face was immobile. "Tell us yours."

"Tova Namir."

Aviva was next in the line-up on the bed. "Daniella Kedar."

"I'm Rachel Yariv," the blonde concluded.

"And the fourth name?"

"Excuse me?" The blonde easily avoided his trap and did not divulge her identity.

"Good," Eli answered. "You three are to dine together in the hotel this evening. Get to bed early. Tomorrow will be a very long day."

He stood, and left the room without another word.

CANDIDATE DOSSIER

Volume number:	457921
File name:	Daniella Kedar
File opened:	22 February 1950

I. Personal File

Name:	Aviva Ben-Zion
Age:	19
Residence:	Kibbutz Negba
Sex:	Female
Birth date:	15 May 1930
Religion:	Jew
Birthplace:	Haifa, Palestine
Height:	1.57 meters
Weight:	52 kilos

Eyes:	Brown
Hair:	Black
Marks:	Moles on left wrist, right hip; scar above left eyebrow; burns on left thigh

II. Sponsor   Eli Katzar

III. Education

Primary:	Hebrew Reali School, Haifa
Secondary:	Kibbutz Negba
Advanced:	None
Special:	Palmach radio communications
Languages:	Hebrew, Arabic, English (weak)

IV. Financial

Employer:	None
Income:	None
Assets:	None
Debts:	None

V. Marital Status   Single

VI. Medical History

Diseases:	Chicken pox, measles, whooping cough, anemia
Injuries:	Broken arm after fall from tractor, 1944; multiple injuries, Latrun, 1948
Allergies:	Penicillin
Defects:	None

VII. Legal

Driver's License:	Class A No. 605987
Issued:	1946 (under British Mandate)
Vehicles:	Automobile, tractor
Accidents:	Turned over tractor at age 14

VIII. Military

| Palmach: | Took the oath in 1945. June–September 1945: Trained at Bet Oren; took part in Athlit camp escape mission under Yitzhak Rabin. At Kibbutz Hazorea: Radio |

| | communications instructor; injured in second battle for Latrun, 1948; Discharge rank: 2nd lieutenant. Returned to Kibbutz Negba. |
Foreign Ministry: Began intelligence training at Tel Hashomer, February 1950.

IX. Family History
Father: Mordecai Ben-Zion
Born: Plonsk, Poland, 1901
Residence: Kibbutz Negba; moved to Palestine at age 7; his father (Nahum Benkovitz) was a member of Hashomer-Hatzair movement. He helped found Negba in late 1930s. Entire family were pioneers there.
Occupation: Farmer
Mother: Raquela Arazi
Born: Beirut, Lebanon, 1905
Died: 1948, killed when as a surgical patient she was being transported in the Mount Scopus Hadassah convoy massacre
Siblings: (1) Dan Ben-Zion
Born: 8 March 1926
Died: 17 April 1946. Lehi member. Shot by British for placing bombs near police stations.
(2) Elana Ben-Zion Levy
Born: 15 December 1928
Married: Arik Levy, intelligence officer of the Palmach 6th Battalion, later company commander in the Har-el Brigade; currently chief instructor at 10th Regiment Infantry School

X. Mission Assignments
Code name: Violet
Cover: Jasmine Gregory: British Passport No. 77790; Egyptian mother, British father. Born Alexandria, Egypt. Schooled in Leeds, England, after mother and father died in airplane crash. Lived with British grandmother, who died during war. Now, with some money of her own, is traveling and deciding what she will do. Remaining family members are in Egypt, but she does not know if, having a British education, she wishes to subject

herself to the stringent rules Arab women must follow. During war helped as hospital volunteer, is considering nursing career, but likes to travel and may be suited to airline or related position.

XI. Notes   Admitted to Phase 1 training, 2/50. Distinguished record in communications, talent for cryptanalysis, excellent attitude under stress, good physical condition, nondescript appearance an asset, unmarried status and relative youth could be problematic. (R.S.) Admitted to Phase 2 training 5/50. Completed all assignments well; lack of experience outside Israel; must be closely supervised. English is not up to standard required to substantiate cover. Suggest additional intensive training in languages. (T.Y.) Approved for Phase 3 under Y.R.
Orientation: 6/50
Departure: 7/7/50

❖ ❖ ❖

Charlotte was not surprised to find Eli at Zermatt. He suggested she work with the Shai originally. He had recommended that she be sent to the United Nations Special Committee on Palestine meetings at Lake Success, and from the moment of the partition vote on, she had felt more Israeli than American. After that, her work during the War of Independence as a liaison officer with the United Nations delegation further cemented her beliefs. While she had seen Eli only briefly during the 1948 war, he had always taken an interest in her and inquired about her plans and intentions. When the conflict was over, they both worked for Reuven Shiloah — Charlotte as a clerical assistant, Eli as his right-hand man. When he suggested additional training, she leapt at the opportunity.

From the moment she had begun her official intelligence course at the Sarafand army base, the antagonism to an American girl had been overt. She had been pushed harder in the physical training, graded more severely on the tests, and badgered to perfect her Hebrew. To prove herself, to please Eli, she was willing to suffer almost anything.

The first morning in Zermatt she watched intently as Eli helped himself to a large bowl of oatmeal from the buffet, sprinkled it with brown sugar, and poured generously from the cream pitcher. Charlotte permitted herself only one cup of hot chocolate and an unbuttered roll.

"Chris, is that all you're having?" Eli asked as he reached the table where the three young women were sitting.

She looked up at once to prove she responded quickly to her cover name. "I always eat lightly in the morning."

"We are going to have a strenuous day. You must have cereal, or at least an egg."

Charlotte complied by serving herself a bowl of oatmeal.

"By the way, I have some curious information about our hotel," Eli said, then lowered his voice. "It is, more or less, a kibbutz."

"How could that be?" Charlotte asked.

"It is a continuation of one of the oldest orders of European society: the bourgeoisie of a commune. In these Alpine villages the bourgeoisie is composed entirely of the descendants of the original inhabitants; almost no one else, no matter how influential they are, may be admitted — so that part is different, but in other matters there are many similarities. All that is not strictly private belongs to the bourgeoisie. Here that includes the streams, the glaciers, the forests, even the mountains."

"Including the Matterhorn?" Charlotte asked.

"Yes, even that, at least on the Swiss side. All profits from the dairy products, the ski lifts, the utilities, the hotels — like this one — are divided among the families. Further, each citizen is entitled to free wood, grazing, and irrigation of his fields. When we are out in the hills, I will show you their system. Mountain streams are diverted to each family's land for a part of the day. I understand that there are but twenty-two families on the roll of the Zermatt bourgeoisie, with only one family being added in three hundred years."

Two couples walked into the dining room and took a seat at the table next to theirs. Eli changed the subject. "Our guide will be here at eight. So as soon as you have finished, meet in the courtyard with your hiking boots on. You will require a sweater and water bottle in your rucksack, nothing else."

Back in the room, Charlotte slipped two chocolate bars and a small zippered bag with tissues and sanitary napkins in her pack. She turned and saw that the blonde was watching. "I don't think he considered that women have certain necessities," she explained.

"Some women . . ."

Charlotte mistook her tone for condescension. "Are you so perfect you don't bleed every month?" Charlotte said, then immediately regretted her retort. This was no way to begin a formal unification. A gibbush? Nevertheless, this Nicole was so immaculate, so disciplined, so . . . *Gentile*. Her golden hair was brushed back into the most elegantly simple knot; her clothes were so absolutely right for Zermatt that she looked as if she had lived in the mountains all her life. Beside her, Charlotte felt awkward and useless.

The blonde continued to stare at her. Her dark gray eyes seemed almost like camera lenses mechanically capturing all they saw on permanent film. Aviva, who opened the bathroom door, sensed the tension and stood perfectly still.

"I have not had my period since 1944," the blonde said flatly. "The doctors say that it probably will return. It has for many of the women. I could take some medicines to bring it on, but what is the point? Who needs the bother?"

"Were you in a camp?" Aviva asked.

The blonde nodded.

"Which one?"

"Bergen-Belsen, then Theresienstadt."

Charlotte wished she could have disappeared.

Aviva slipped her rucksack on her back and handed Charlotte hers. She opened the door. "Time to go . . ."

"I will not tell Charles about the chocolates," the blonde said under her breath.

Charlotte spun around. The blonde had a wisp of a smile on her lips. Charlotte could not remember ever feeling more grateful.

CANDIDATE DOSSIER

Volume number:	523987
File name:	Tova Namir
File opened:	22 March 1950

I. Personal File

Name:	Charlotte Green
Age:	22
Residence:	Scarsdale, New York
Sex:	Female
Birth date:	1 October 1927
Religion:	Jew

Birthplace:	Bronx, New York, U.S.A.
Height:	1.65 meters
Weight:	55.8 kilos
Eyes:	Hazel
Hair:	Brown
Marks:	Moles on right cheek, strawberry birthmark on back, appendectomy scar

II. Sponsor   Eli Katzar

III. Education

Primary:	Fox Meadows School
Secondary:	Scarsdale High School
Advanced:	Vassar College, 1944–1946
	Hebrew University, 1946–1948
Languages:	English, French, Yiddish, Hebrew

IV: Financial

Employer:	None
Income:	None
Assets:	American bank accounts worth about $10,000
Debts:	None

V. Marital Status   Single

VI. Medical History

Diseases:	Chicken pox, mumps, appendicitis
Injuries:	None
Allergies:	None
Defects:	None

VII. Legal

Driver's License:	N.Y. State No. 21349876500W
Issued:	1944
Vehicles:	Automobile
Accidents:	Parking lot collision in White Plains, New York

VIII. Military

Haganah:	Took the oath in 1947. Assigned to the Shai. October–November 1947, worked in NYC and

	Lake Success with Moshe Shertok as a courier during partition meetings.
Shai:	Continued liaison work with U.N. observers during 1948 war.
Foreign Ministry:	Assistant to Reuven Shiloah, 1949. Army training at Sarafand begun March 1950.

IX. Family History

Father:	Harry Green (Hershel Greenblatt)
Born:	New York, New York, 1899
Residence:	Scarsdale, New York
Occupation:	Textile manufacturing
Mother:	Sarah Marcus
Born:	Kiev, Russia, 1904
	Immigrated to U.S. in 1906
Siblings:	(1) Evelyn Green
Born:	19 August 1928
	(2) Grace Green
Born:	11 July 1930

X. Mission Assignments

Code name:	Rose
Cover:	Carla (Chris) Christopher: U.S. Passport No. 902622. Born in Xenia, Ohio. Daughter of farmer with small crop-dusting business on the side. Father joined Air Force and was killed in war. Mother remarried and is living in California, but is not in touch with Carla, who cannot accept second husband. Mother will die before field operation is assigned. Carla was briefly a student at Antioch College, Yellow Springs, Ohio. Engaged to soldier who was killed during Normandy invasion. Came to Europe to visit his grave in France. On an extended tour.

| *XI. Notes* | Admitted to Phase 1 training, 3/50. U.S. passport, retains nationality. Proven reliable. Excellent at assignments involving travel, connections with individuals, concealment. Patient, trusted. U.S. citizenship may be problematic. (D.G.) Admitted to Phase 2 training, 5/50. Completed all assignments well; especially good at organization, developing plans for operations. Physical fitness borderline. (O.B.) |

Approved for Phase 3 under Y.R.
Orientation: 6/50
Departure: 1/7/50

          ⁜   ⁜   ⁜

Just as the women met Eli beside the fountain in the square in front
of the hotel, a herd of shaggy goats, their neckbells clanging, surrounded them. Young men with sticks poked and whistled them
back on the path to their grazing field above Zermatt. After the last
of the animals cleared the area, Bernie Petrig stepped forward and
introduced himself. He bowed slightly as he shook each hand. Immediately, Lily liked the stocky man with the powerful arms and firm
but friendly grip.

"I apologize for not meeting you yesterday, but I had a party to
escort up the Matterhorn."

Lily stared up at the granite presence guarding Zermatt. "It was
my father's dream to climb it someday."

"Your father was a climber?" Eli asked.

"He wished to be. Now it is too late."

"Perhaps not. I have taken up men in their fifties." The guide
stopped when he saw the expression on Lily's face.

"My father died during the war."

"I am sorry," Bernie replied simply. "So now you will have to
climb it for him."

"The Matterhorn?" Charlotte blurted.

"Why not? I have taken ladies before."

"I don't think I could ever —"

Bernie put his finger to his mouth. "Let me be the judge of that."
He headed away from the hotel. Lily walked along one side of Bernie, Eli the other.

Charlotte scrambled forward to keep up with the guide. "I heard
that just a few years before the war two women climbed it successfully — without a guide."

Bernie Petrig smiled benevolently, but kept on walking as he replied. "Yes, in fact, one was an American named Miriam O'Brien. It
required two seasons to complete the challenge because it seemed the
mountain and its changeable weather were determined to defeat her
party. Sometimes Le Cervin has a mind of its own. Do you know
what they say? 'Le Cervin n'est pas quelque chose, c'est quelqu'un.' "

"The Matterhorn is not something, it is someone," Lily translated
immediately.

The guide's eyes glinted with satisfaction. "Shall we proceed?" He led them farther up the narrow winding street to a small shop. Lily followed on his heels, but Charlotte and Aviva fell behind.

"Grüss Gott!" called the storekeeper, whose leathery face and slim waistline identified him as another mountain man.

"Grüss Gott!" Lily replied. Already she was enjoying the friendly sound of the ancient Alpine salutation.

Bernie inspected their equipment. Only Lily's knickers, the ones she had bought during her layover in Geneva, met with Bernie's favor. Charlotte and Aviva were made to change from their slacks into corduroys that tied at the knees.

"Their boots will not do either," Bernie decided.

Eli grimaced. Lily assumed the three pairs of boots would be a strain on his budget, but he did not object. Next they were fitted for crampons, iron spikes that strap onto boots to make it possible to climb over ice and hard snow. Finally, after each one was outfitted with glacier goggles and an ice ax, Bernie approved. They stepped outside while Eli settled the account.

Charlotte examined her new ax. "We'll be climbing on ice?"

"Not today, but it is also used for balance," Bernie explained. "Later, I will show you how to chop steps in ice, to probe for crevasses, and to stop yourself in case of a slip on steep snow. I want you to accustom yourself to carrying it at all times." He slung a heavy length of rope over his shoulder and handed a second coil to Eli. "You have climbed in Switzerland before?"

"Yes. I belonged to a Combined Cadet Force when I was at school in Cambridge. We trained in Wales and the Cotswolds; then I did the Breithorn the summer before I entered the university."

"You have been to four thousand meters. Congratulations," Bernie acknowledged kindly.

Bernie maintained a steady pace on a road that sloped slightly upward at all times. Lily, who was almost the guide's height, kept up easily. Sensing her presence, he stepped sideways so she could walk beside him. Eli slipped behind to keep an eye on Aviva and Charlotte.

"Do you like to hike?" the guide asked Lily.

"I do not have much experience."

"What is the longest walk you have ever taken?"

"Over one hundred kilometers." Lily turned for his response. Silently he stared with dark, almost black, piercing eyes. "It was a forced march, during the war. You went on, or you died."

Immediately Lily regretted the outburst. Her cover did not include any concentration camp experiences.

"Emotions are what will trip you up every time. Joy, sadness, fear, anger — all demand rapid responses from our nervous systems," her instructor at Ramat David had insisted. "With training you will learn to *think* before you permit yourself to *feel*."

Already she had made an unforgivable slip. How would she answer his questions? She *could* have gone on a forced march after France was occupied. Lily waited expectantly for him to speak.

Fortunately, Bernie did not press her. He ran his broad hand through his thick, blond hair, then responded indirectly with a story about his own wartime experiences. "After Italy surrendered to the Allies in September 1943, escaping prisoners of war attempted to cross through the mountain passes. From the patrol station on the Gorner Glacier we would watch with telescopes. If they encountered difficulties among the crevasses, we would escort them to the safety of the Bétemps Hut on Monte Rosa. Even so, many were lost in . . ."

As Lily nodded sympathetically, she reminded herself to be much more circumspect in the future.

A few steps ahead, Bernie paused at a crossroads. Two miniature signs pointed out the routes for hikers. ZMUTT, 2 km, SCHÖN-BÜHLHÜTTE, 11 km.

"We are going to walk to the hut and back again today. It is a long but not difficult hike. It will help prepare you for the days ahead. Begin at a steady pace, but do not overexert. Remember, we are starting out at just over sixteen hundred meters. You can lose your breath easily. We will be ascending an additional thousand meters during the climb. As an incentive, let me say that the views along this trail are some of the finest in Switzerland, and you will be seeing the Matterhorn from several unique vantage points."

As he spoke, Lily felt her skin prickle with excitement. Up until now she had been rather calm about the trip. Mostly she saw it as an interference, blocking the forward movement of her life. From the moment she had accepted the commitment to join the Foreign Ministry, she had been anxious to take on meaningful work. Already she had served unofficially in the British detention camps in Cyprus and she had fought in the Negev during the '48 war, but there was so much more to do. Israel's enemies were as determined to destroy her fledgling homeland as she was to protect it. Eli's excursion into the mountains had seemed a gross indulgence. For the present, she decided not to worry about how practical this training would be. The day sparkled with promise and she was exhilarated by every word Bernie, the consummate mountaineer, spoke. Standing there, with his head framed by the edges of the Matterhorn, her guide seemed the mythic hero.

The morning air was fine and cool. As she walked, she was acutely conscious of breathing: the inhaling sharp, the exhaling familiar. At the top of the field, stone farm buildings were perched on a knoll. From a distance they appeared to be rickety and leaning on stilts. Up close they seemed sturdy enough to have weathered centuries. The sweeping view across the green valleys filled her with nostalgia for her family. If only her brothers could have seen this.

Charlotte caught up with her and Bernie and asked, "Why are the houses sitting on rocks?"

"Those are 'mazots' — storehouses. The wide, slippery stone disks prevent the rodents from reaching the grain."

Taking advantage of the break, Charlotte removed her rucksack and pulled out her water bottle. Bernie watched her take a sip, then shook his head. "Save it. You must toughen yourself against thirst."

Quickly, Charlotte did as she was told.

Lily was the first to move forward along the path again, then waited for the others to catch up at an outdoor altar that displayed a hand-carved wooden Virgin Mary. Bernie stopped for a moment and crossed himself. Since her cover, Nicole, was Catholic, Lily mimicked his gestures.

Soon the trail wound past a small reservoir across from a complex of water conduits. She and Bernie were the first to arrive at a ledge overlooking a river of rubble that had careened down a long valley and turned into a crevice of ice. "The Tiefmatten Glacier," Bernie explained. "Why don't you go ahead and wait for me under the overhang of the cliff."

Lily admiringly observed the easy strides Bernie took as he went back to check on the less athletic members of the group. Aviva caught up to Lily first and sat down in the middle of the path.

"My feet!" She untied her right boot. "Ow! Look at this. Already my heel is bleeding," she groaned. "How are yours?"

"Tough. I did not wear shoes for two years." Lily took off her rucksack and pulled out a pair of socks. "These were sold to me at the store in Geneva where I bought my mountain clothes. They are made of silk and you wear them under your heavier socks. The clerk swore they would prevent soreness. Try them?"

Aviva took them gratefully. By the time Charlotte, holding on to Eli's arm, had caught up with them, Aviva was ready to move on.

"A stitch in my side . . ." Charlotte explained.

Stitch in side? Lily did not understand. "I will carry your ruck-sack," she offered.

"No," Eli insisted. "Chris will be fine."

All at once the views expanded dramatically. Bernie quickly reeled off the names of prominent ridges as if he were introducing old friends. "Dent d'Herens, Dent Blanche, Zinalrothorn." Towering above all was the closest — the Matterhorn. While it was not the highest, nor the steepest, Lily clearly felt its compelling stature.

"Matterhorn." She said the word aloud with the same Dutch pronunciation her father always gave it. He had read books on mountains and their conquerors as bedtime stories. It was his way of giving confidence to the little girl who had had a pathetic fear of the dark — a fear soon to be replaced by others far worse.

Here she was, the sole survivor of her family, walking so close to the base of the Matterhorn she had to crane her head back to glimpse the summit. It rose above her, cliff upon cliff, ridge upon ridge, until the curving wedge of its peak seemed to pierce the sky. "Oh, Papa," she murmured. "Do you know I am here?"

Bernie paused to drink from his bottle, a welcome signal to all the rest. Lily noticed Aviva took only a few sips. She must be accustomed to heat and lack of water. Even Charlotte did not gulp. We might all make it, Lily surmised, at least through today.

The final part of the climb became steeper as the trail passed under a glacier that literally hung on the side of the Pointe de Zinal outcropping. Then the path switched back up and stretched to a hut in the distance.

Bernie explained about glaciers to the others, who were breathing much too hard to hold up their end of a conversation. "A firn is the basin in which snow accumulates and turns into ice. That is succeeded by a tongue of ice, or Gletscher in German, which is crossed by those networks of crevasses to carry the overflow. Over to the east, those moraines are piles of debris brought down by the glacier and . . ."

Bernie's voice droned on as Lily left the others far behind. In less than ten minutes she arrived, panting, at the Swiss Alpine Club hut. Staring out at the panorama of mountains on one side and the splendid view of the Matterhorn on the other, she felt an odd sensation. It was as if the soft wind from the valleys below was caressing her, pulling her downward, compelling her to come closer to the edge and accept its embrace. Instead of fearing the sheer drop, she wanted to rush out at it with the abandon of a lover. Her breath came rapidly and her head swirled with conflicting thoughts. Something locked away for almost ten years was being released. "Papa," she called across the void. Never, even during the worst of her trials, had she felt his presence. But here she did.

The bright blue sky whirled above her and the sun dazzling on the ice broke up into diamond shapes, which spun away in tantalizing fragments. The sky was slipping below the mountain; the mountain was moving closer to her.

"So, you are feeling all right?" Bernie was beside her. "The altitude can have strange effects," he said to the others. "Her lips are quite blue. That is a sign she is not getting enough oxygen. We must watch for that in each other."

Eli looked concerned. "Nicole, take a few deep breaths."

Lily complied.

"Can you sit up now?" Bernie asked.

Sit up? She felt something hard and cold beneath her. She was lying on a stone bench. Bernie rubbed her hands. "You are a very strong girl; you are just not used to this altitude. If you take it a bit slower the first few days, you will be able to go to four thousand meters soon."

Eli asked, "Do you think it's vertigo?"

"Possibly," Bernie replied. "It is something which affects everyone differently." He lowered his voice. "The exposures she was seeing were quite intense for a first experience. There are certain tricks of light and distance that can fool the mind into thinking the body's on steady ground, when in fact it's falling forward, and vice versa. We had better be certain she is escorted in the more open areas, even if the path is wide."

As Lily sat up she could barely make sense of the out-of-focus scene around her.

"Nicole . . ." Charlotte was unwrapping one of her chocolate bars. Without comment, Eli watched Charlotte break off a square and give it to Lily.

"I will make some coffee in the hut and we will have lunch here," Bernie said solicitously. "Afterward, we will commence our descent work." All the while he held Lily's hands to warm them.

A fierce tingling shot up Lily's spine and intensified as Bernie massaged her skin.

"Is that all right, Nicole?" he asked.

"Yes, it is," Lily answered weakly, but she was thinking: Just do not stop rubbing my hands.

CANDIDATE DOSSIER

Volume number:	325590
File name:	Rachel Yariv
File opened:	30 December 1949

I. Personal File

Name:	Lily Jaeger
Age:	23
Residence:	Tel Aviv, Israel
Sex:	Female
Birth date:	14 August 1926
Religion:	Jew
Birthplace:	Amsterdam, Holland
Height:	1.7 meters
Weight:	59 kilos
Eyes:	Gray
Hair:	Blond
Marks:	Strawberry birthmark on back of neck into hairline, whip marks on back, small bullet scar on left thigh

II. Sponsor Eli Katzar

III. Education

Primary:	Montessori Kindergarten
Secondary:	Jewish Secondary, first form only
Advanced:	None
Languages:	Dutch, German, French, English, Hebrew

IV. Financial

Employer:	None

Income: None
Assets: None
Debts: None

V. Marital Status Single

VI. Medical History
Diseases: Typhus, typhoid fever, pneumonia, malnutrition leading to secondary amenorrhea
Injuries: Ribs and arm broken during beating at Bergen-Belsen
Allergies: Sulfa
Defects: Possible psychological and medical repercussions from concentration camps, still undiagnosed

VII. Legal
Driver's License: None

VIII. Military
Haganah: Took the oath in 1948 in Cyprus. Trained in intelligence at Caraolas.
Army: Negev Brigade, 1948–1949
Foreign Ministry: Special services training at Ramat David begun December 1948.

IX. Family History
Father: Jacob Jaeger
Born: Vienna, Austria, 1896
Occupation: Baker
Died: 1942, Auschwitz
Mother: Anna Mayer
Born: Amsterdam, Holland, 1901
Died: 1942, Auschwitz
Siblings: (1) David Jaeger
Born: 14 April 1929
Died: May 1945, two days before liberation of Theresienstadt
(2) Peter Jaeger
Born: 9 May 1931
Died: December 1942, in hiding, from internal bleeding

X. Mission Assignments

Code name: Daisy

Cover: Nicole Schmidt:
                           French Passport No. 761129.
                           Born to an Alsatian family. Father killed by
                           French, who suspected him of being a
                           collaborator. Mother took Nicole to Paris and
                           lived with relatives during occupation. Died of
                           breast cancer. Left small estate to only daughter.

XI. Notes   Admitted to Phase 1 training, 12/49. Extremely
                           observant. Never forgets a face or detail.
                           Uncovered Nazi sympathizer hiding in Cyprus
                           camp. Multilingual and versatile. Non-Jewish
                           appearance an asset. Tragic background. Hidden
                           in Holland for over two years, survived
                           Theresienstadt and Bergen-Belsen; serious
                           illnesses. Physical fitness: exceptional considering
                           background. Excellent attitude in training. Has
                           unlimited potential. (G.T.) Admitted to Phase 2
                           training, 4/50. Pushes herself to excel in all areas.
                           Quiet, difficult to understand at times. Some
                           depressions, as expected. (B.C.) Approved for
                           Phase 3 under Y.R.
                           Orientation: 6/50
                           Departure: 1/7/50

❖   ❖   ❖

Charlotte had locked herself in the bathroom to soak her aching legs. Their third day's hike had finished with a ten-kilometer stretch snaking downhill from Schwarzsee, the black lake at the northeastern side of the Matterhorn. The trek had been the easiest so far. She had almost skipped down the stony path, across the flowery fields toward the fairy-tale village in the cleft below. Along the way Jasmine discovered marmot holes, which they monitored during lunch until they had had a good long look at a few of the shy, sweet rodents. Not until this morning did the stress on the muscles at the back of her thighs and calves become obvious. Getting out of bed, she could barely stand. How could she possibly go on today's hike, which Bernie promised would include their first rope work, feeling this way?

The water in the tub was soothing. As she massaged her legs with soap, she stared at her body. She wished her round, floating breasts were more like Nicole's. Unashamed to show her body in front of her roommates, Lily paraded her small pointed breasts with nipples like pink strawberries, and her slim, almost boyish hips, which looked so sleek in her hiking breeches. Her thinness, instead of appearing unhealthy, suited her long-legged body; and her hair, obviously a natural blond, curled prettily around her authoritative face after only the most gentle of brushings. There were scars on Lily's body. Lacking the courage to ask, Charlotte had turned her eyes away from the raised lines on her back and buttocks. Even these she admired. A man would too. Closing her eyes, Charlotte imagined Eli lying next to Lily, kissing her welts. Charlotte sucked in her breath and forced herself to think of something else.

At least she could be grateful that her body was not as muscular as Jasmine's. Nevertheless, the young Israeli woman's wide, dark, penetrating eyes revealed a passionate spirit. Her features were regularly formed, with a nose that was prominent but not disfiguring; generous lips; and strong cheekbones. With her dark hair brushed back from her high forehead, Aviva resembled a Biblical heroine. At least Aviva, unlike Charlotte, probably had no difficulty with the rigorous physical fitness training Charlotte had undergone. The mandatory desert hikes, the midnight runs, the obstacle courses, had almost defeated Charlotte. While she had come in last in most of these events, she had persisted, which, she later discovered, was all that mattered.

Perhaps Aviva's greatest asset was her skin — the color of a young fawn. Even with the most glorious of suntans, Charlotte could never achieve the warmth and burnish of that incredible flesh tone. Charlotte was certain Aviva had been selected in part because of her Arabic, yet ordinary, looks. It was no advantage for an agent to stand out in a crowd. They were told to be forgettable, taught how to make themselves less interesting. In Charlotte's case, her trainers had endeavored to undo ten years of her mother's work to make her daughter as irresistible as possible.

Charlotte knew that she could never pretend to be anything but what she was: American. Her flat, slightly nasal, educated New York accent was immutable. She could not speak one sentence of a foreign language without immediately betraying her origins. Her body was that of a healthy young woman who had been given unlimited quantities of milk, butter, and beef all through the war. Her teeth were white, square, and straight; her face was unblemished, her posture perfect. She had already proven that border-crossing guards found no reason to detain her. Her credentials were her flawless skin, her tapered fingernails, her matched Halliburton luggage.

When Eli had proposed her for the first few assignments during the UNSCOP meetings, she knew his superiors had resisted using her until he convinced them that her all-American personality was her strength. Charlotte was so obviously who and what she seemed, she would never be suspected of carrying money and messages. And she never had been.

Although she could not hide her origins, Charlotte did have a re-markable facility for transforming her appearance. A mere change of clothing from a frilly summer dress to a tweed suit with padded shoulders affected her whole personality. She could assume a differ-ent walk, repertoire of gestures, even facial expressions, as easily as any well-trained actress. She also had an innate talent with make-up and hair styles and could change them on a whim — or an order.

Her hair, naturally a mousy brown, was a hair colorist's dream, for it readily accepted the full palette from Norwegian blond to Spanish black, with every shade of auburn and chestnut in between. She experimented wildly when at Vassar, returning home for week-ends and holidays a "different daughter" to amaze and confound her parents. For a while, she had stopped her metamorphoses to please Calvin Webster, the Yalie she had been semi-engaged to during her sophomore year. He wanted her to be natural, which was a joke be-cause he had never seen her true hair color. His favorite seemed to be a light chestnut, so that was the one she had gone back to for his sake.

Another asset was Charlotte's oval face, devoid of any peculiari-ties. She had standard, symmetrical features, arranged in such a way that she appeared attractive but undistinguished. The cut of her hair, sometimes fashionable, sometimes girlish, was what someone mentioned first in a description of her, so she had mastered quick changes by keeping her hair shoulder length. The difference between a classic French twist and a dowdy bunch at the nape determined whether she would be considered pretty or ordinary. Even her eyes, a pale hazel, could be called blue, green, gray, or perhaps brown, de-pending on her mood, the weather, or the state of her health. When she was out of breath they turned their best color — sky blue. If she had had a mirror on the mountain yesterday, she was certain she would have seen them at their loveliest — but surely nobody else had noticed, she decided ruefully.

Maybe Eli had, but then, he would not have let on. She knew he liked her, always had from the moment he had seen her at Northolt Aerodrome. That is why he had singled her out for her first assignment — the one she didn't know until much later that she had undertaken. Eli had watched to see if she would be questioned or detained about the crucial box, but her fresh American face passed her through every gate. While she had never found out what was in the bundle, she guessed it could have contained anything from pounds sterling to secret messages to explosives.

Charlotte turned on the hot water tap. Steam filled the bathroom as she reminisced about her first encounter with Eli at Lydda only moments after arriving in Palestine. The trip had been forced on her by her father. Panicked at the idea that his daughter might actually marry Calvin Webster, a New England Protestant with an impeccable pedigree for any family but a Jewish one, he decided that she needed to experience her own culture before she so freely renounced it.

"Let's see if 'my little chameleon' can become a Jew for her next change," he had said, not snidely, but with an unfamiliar passionate inflection.

Harry Green had prospered during the war. He had been one of the first textile manufacturers on Seventh Avenue to put aside florals and damasks for khakis and camouflage. With some of the largest defense contracts for uniform cloth, he had only been enriched by the conflict. Instead of flaunting this wealth, he had hidden it, requesting that his family live more simply. Of course, he would not ask Sarah to scrimp on food for the children, but they gave no parties and purchased no elaborate clothing or gifts.

During the war, Harry Green had never quite believed the stories of camps that exterminated Jews. Nevertheless, he contributed generously to every Jewish appeal. In the summer of 1945, Harry Green was taken to the secret meetings organized by the wealthy Rudolf Sonneborn, where he listened as a disheveled, emotional Ben-Gurion, with his tufts of white hair framing his cherub's face, eloquently explained that a Jewish homeland was a necessity for the hundreds of thousands of displaced Jews in Europe. He was told how the Jewish Agency was getting the survivors out of Europe to Palestine despite British blockades. Meanwhile, they were asking the United Nations to recommend the formation of a Jewish state.

Ben-Gurion finished by predicting that when the British left, the

Arabs would mobilize. "This time the Jews will fight. This time we will win."

Harry Green found personal salvation in the cause. All his guilt for not doing enough for his people during the war could be expiated. His factories became secret repositories for weapons; his banking connections transferred money for arms purchases; his trucks, warehouses, and cubicles in his Forty-fourth Street office were available to the cause.

Thus, it was even more of an impossibility for his daughter to marry a Gentile. Fortunately, this boy friend was in law school and not about to marry until he had gotten his degree, obeying the edict from his own parents, who were paying all his bills. With this in mind, Harry made a shrewd guess about the durability of his daughter's romance. "You go to Hebrew University in Palestine for your junior year, and if you want this Webster fellow when you return, I'll never say another word."

Charlotte acceded reluctantly, but from that moment on, she never returned home except for brief visits. When she was sent to Lake Success to work for Moshe Shertok, her parents never knew about it. Day and night she took messages to the lobbyists who were rounding up votes for the roll call on the Palestine partition resolution. She danced with Ralph Bunche and told the Venezuelans all about the wonders of Jerusalem. She arranged private limousines for Saudi delegates through her "Uncle Jack" in the Bronx and then rode in the surveillance cars that followed the diplomats. With the primitive listening devices "Uncle's" mechanics had installed in the cars of the opposition, they tuned in to their conversations. Tucked in her girdle, were sensitive notes on the backgrounds of delegates to the Jewish Agency staff meetings.

On the twenty-ninth of November, 1947, Charlotte was in the audience at Flushing Meadow, listening for the results of the U.N. decision on the fate of Palestine. The tension leading up to the roll call was breathtaking. On a pad of paper she listed all fifty-six countries that would be casting votes. In one column was the predicted vote, in the other the actual. Even though her South American friends assured her of their support, it was with great relief she heard Bolivia, Brazil, and Ecuador vote in favor of a Jewish state early on. She took Argentina's and Chile's opposition personally until France's surprise move for the Jewish state buoyed her hope. The jubilation following the victorious outcome swept her away. All during that crazy night of celebration, she wished that Eli could have been there instead of on assignment in Cyprus. No matter where in the world he was, she knew his feelings united with hers — and all the Jews of the world.

The next day, Moshe Shertok asked her if she wanted to return to the new state and work with him "to protect us against our enemies." Charlotte had readily agreed, not for lofty reasons of wanting to do her part, but to see Eli again. In the past two years, she had made hardly any progress with him. The early assignments, the training — Charlotte attacked them all with verve and dedication to prove her worthiness. Once she had believed he had singled her out specially, pulling all sorts of strings to get a girl — an American one at that — accepted in the ranks of intelligence professionals. Now it appeared he had a whole platoon of neophyte women spies under his command. And even if there were only the three, surely Lily, with her faraway eyes and sorrowful past, was his favorite.

To Charlotte, Eli was even more attractive in Switzerland. The mountain sun had streaked his hair with golden highlights. His face, particularly his high, polished brow, had tanned. His eyes remained a clear, honest blue, and as they hiked the mountains she continued to admire his sturdy, athletic body with wide shoulders tapering down to the high, taut buttocks of Michelangelo's David. Best of all, she adored the dimples in his chin and cheeks, which deepened when he grinned.

As she thought about Eli, Charlotte became more and more infuriated. Why had he humiliated her the previous evening? The session had begun after dinner at Bernie Petrig's home. His wife, Irma, made the local specialty, raclette, by softening a half wheel of Bagnes cheese beside an open fire and serving it with potatoes boiled in their skins, a crusty peasant bread, pickled spring onions, and gherkins.

"A good kosher meal," Eli joked under his breath.

Irma insisted they drink kirsch to aid digestion. They were exhausted from the day's climb, but the generous glasses of the morello cherry liqueur with its oddly almond flavor helped them forget their aches temporarily.

After the meal, Eli asked the women to come to his room. He began by criticizing each of them for a few minor slips in the behavior of their cover characters. Then his voice had lightened. "Chris, do you like play-acting?"

"All little girls do." Charlotte had smiled lopsidedly because of the kirsch. "It's what our mothers consider preparation for life." She had thought the words clever, but the others did not laugh.

Eli then said, "I remember you once told me about a particular achievement of yours when you were a child." Charlotte looked perplexed, so he continued, "An acting role . . ."

"I was just a little girl and —"

"Forgive me for putting you on the spot, but sometimes it is good to share the fears and accomplishments of our youth. It helps us to better understand the forces within us today." He turned his back on Charlotte and spoke to Aviva. "Perhaps you will tell us about one of your most satisfying moments as a young girl."

Aviva was sitting cross-legged on the floor, wearing a hand-knitted sweater in muted tones of pink, green, and black that flattered the unique cast of her skin. Her heavy-lidded eyes barely opened as she spoke slowly and deliberately. "I was only eight years old when I started to tend the sheep during the lambing season. We could not afford to lose any, so children were stationed all over the hillside to report whenever a birth took place. One afternoon most of the adults were in a kibbutz meeting. I followed a ewe who was behaving as if she was about to give birth. By the time she started to deliver the lamb, I was in a far pasture. She strained for an abnormal length of time, so I assisted by breaking the bulging sac. I dried the newborn lamb with grass and tried to coax it to nurse. But the mother was not interested; she was heaving with pain. Then I saw the second lamb — a twin — emerging, and helped to pull it free. Later they told me I may have saved the mother as well as the twins. The custom was for lambs to be named by the person who first saw them, so I called mine Adam and Eve. They were my special pets and later were saved from slaughter and became part of the breeding stock as a favor to me."

Charlotte was impressed. At the age of eight, she had been mastering jump-rope chants instead of kneeling in a field delivering livestock.

Eli did not register any emotion. He lit a cigarette and offered his pack around. "None of you smoke?"

"I do, sometimes," Charlotte admitted. She took one from his pack.

"It's a good skill to have. Cigarettes can be used for all sorts of diversions and signals. Brand names can be part of your cover. But that's unimportant, isn't it, Nicole?"

"What?" she asked.

"What were you thinking about?"

"How I could not answer your question. I have achieved nothing so far."

"I know otherwise," Eli responded softly. "Why don't you tell us about a life you have saved, any one of the many."

"My own. I saved my own." Her voice was clipped and tense, but Charlotte was taken with her every gesture.

"Nicole . . ." Eli coaxed.

Grim-faced, Lily launched into her tale. "My brother David and I were deported in the last roundup of the Dutch Jews on the eighteenth of August, 1944. My younger brother, Peter, did not even make it to Westerbork, but that is another story. When we began, we were sixteen altogether. Ten did not survive the typhus epidemic in Bergen-Belsen. Then we went on a forced march to Theresienstadt. One little girl, Bette, was taken away by one of the guards. She was very pretty — and smart. Perhaps she survived, if she serviced him well. Then there were five of us."

Aviva began to shiver. Eli pulled the comforter from his bed and tucked it around her shoulders.

Lily continued in the same low voice. "Clara was very weak. Her feet began to swell and she would stumble. We would rush to her and hold her up, but once when David had to relieve himself and I was not watching, she tripped in the road. Before we could get to her, she was killed by an unleashed guard dog who was trained to attack anyone who lingered behind." She paused to take a long breath that ended with a queer panting.

"Then there was Otto." Lily's voice was barely audible. "He had stopped speaking while we were in hiding, but he was so sweet and loving. He slept in my arms every night. It was as if he were my special baby. I adored him so! When he began to falter, David and I made a sling and carried him the rest of the way — it must have been fifty kilometers — for more than a week. Only the three of us made it."

"What happened to Otto?" Aviva asked.

"He died a few days later. Next to me, in the night. I awoke and he was cold."

Charlotte blanched and put her head down for a moment. "David?" she whispered.

"He died two days before liberation. Two days. From the sixteen children, I was the only one who made it . . . unless Bette . . ."

They were silent for less than a minute. "Chris, are you ready to tell us your story now?" Eli asked unemotionally.

Charlotte was appalled at the question.

"Chris." This time it was an order.

" 'The Princess and the Pea,' " she said weakly. "When I was in the fifth grade, our class was putting on a play. I wanted to have the part of the princess, but everyone knew that Dolores Hartman would be picked. Dolores was the prettiest girl in the class. She had golden ringlets her mother said were more natural than Shirley Temple's and big blue eyes. She recited loudest in the class and took ballet lessons to develop what she called 'poise.' I didn't even know what poise meant, but I was determined to get some quickly so I could be the princess."

"What did you do about it?" Eli asked easily, as if this could possibly be discussed in the same context as a guard dog ripping out a child's throat on a railroad siding in Czechoslovakia.

"The only way I knew to get something I wanted from my father, who always said no to a first request, was to keep asking. Not nagging, but asking ever so nicely over and over. I tried the same technique on my teacher, Mrs. Flynn. First, I came right out with my request. 'That's nice, dear,' the teacher said. 'I'm sure every girl in this class wants to be the princess, but we must pick the perfect one for our play, don't you agree?'

"The next day I showed her drawings I'd made of the princess, what she should wear in each scene, with sample dialogue as captions. The teacher put them up on the bulletin board. The following day" — Charlotte spoke as rapidly as possible to get the ridiculous story over with — "I brought a cushion for my seat. When Mrs. Flynn asked about it, I said that I was very sensitive, just like the princess. In all my actions I made it perfectly clear that if I wasn't given the part, my life would be shattered." Charlotte caught her breath. "Dolores Hartman became a lady in waiting."

Mortified to have been forced into telling such an inane reminiscence, Charlotte prayed they would refrain from comment.

It was Lily who spoke first. "You would have managed very well at Theresienstadt. Play-acting is part of survival."

"How true." Eli had put out his cigarette and stood as a signal that the meeting was over. "Shalom," he had said, kissing them each good night on both their cheeks.

The bath water had long since grown cold. Aviva and Lily had been down at breakfast for more than half an hour. If she did not join them, Eli would come after her. Nothing short of complete physical collapse would excuse her. She had gone too far to quit because of hurting legs or wounded pride. Charlotte hurried to dress.

❖ ❖ ❖

Aviva could hardly believe Bernie was taking them on the Gornergrat cog railway instead of expecting them to hike to the three-thousand-meter mark. "You need to experience that altitude, but there is no reason to take all day getting there. By now you should be in shape for the climbing part of the course."

On the train Charlotte sat beside Eli, and Lily shared a seat with their guide. Aviva was by herself in front of Lily.

Lily tapped her shoulder. "Jasmine, are you listening?"

Aviva turned around. "To what?"

"To Bernie's story."

"What story is that?" Aviva asked.

"The conquering of the Matterhorn."

Although Aviva already knew the sketchy facts of the tale, Bernie told it as if he had witnessed the climb himself. In fact, his grandfather had known all the participants, had even led Edward Whymper, the British illustrator, on some of his earlier climbs around Zermatt. Together they had made two first ascents: the Aiguille Verte and the Grandes Jorasses, but Whymper was not going to be satisfied until he had mastered the Matterhorn. He had started several times from Breuil in Italy with his guide Jean-Antoine Carrel, but after a falling-out with Carrel decided to attempt it from the Zermatt side and win the victory for the Swiss.

"My grandfather was not invited on the climb, a fact he had resented at the time," Bernie said, "but later he felt it was God's way of saving him for other work. For even though Whymper's group set foot on the summit of the Matterhorn early in the afternoon of the fourteenth of July, 1865, on the return home the least experienced member of their party slipped, carrying another British climber and a Zermatt guide down twelve hundred meters to their death. Three days later, Carrel reached the summit from the Italian side, only to discover another flag in place." Bernie was quiet for a moment. "Every victory is also a defeat," he finished philosophically.

Aviva was perplexed. "Every victory? Surely every climb does not result in a loss of life?"

"You must not take me so literally," Bernie said. "For instance, each time a new summit or a new route to a peak is conquered, one more goal has been shattered. If a man ever lands on the moon and sees the earth, an additional mystery will be solved. Is that not so?"

"Well put," Eli added. "I remember once reading something George Mallory said about his own climbs. 'What have we conquered? Have we vanquished an enemy? Nought but ourselves.'"

" 'Nought but ourselves,' " Charlotte repeated dreamily. "Whatever happened to him?"

"Mallory?" Bernie sighed. "He never returned from the 1924 Everest expedition. Only he and Irving know if they made a successful assault on the summit. Someday I hope to follow in their footsteps," he concluded as the train pulled into the Gornergrat platform. "So, we are here," he said as if he were relieved to get back to more concrete matters.

They were met by a friend of Bernie's, a younger guide named Emil. Together the six hurried down a rocky path that ended abruptly at a cliff. Bernie and Emil lifted the ropes from their shoulders and began to uncoil them.

"We will need one man and one lady on each rope," Bernie explained.

Aviva felt apprehensive as Bernie called her forward to demonstrate how to tie on their ropes. She did not like being singled out, but she found security in being tied to a companion, especially with the edge of the mountain so close to where she was standing.

"Jasmine will come with me," Bernie announced. "Watch what we do."

Timidly, Aviva followed him. The terrain was fearsome, but she had complete trust in Bernie's ability to manage any climbing situation. Although she was hardly graceful, she negotiated some of the milder pitches and was not unduly frightened by the open vista.

"Exposure is what does in most climbers," Bernie had claimed during their previous hikes when he had them stand on various ledges, ostensibly to enjoy the view. "The exposure factor is measured by how far the drop below your feet is; nevertheless, a fall of two hundred meters will kill you as surely as two thousand."

In less than an hour, all three pairs of climbers had managed the pitches, each pitch — the climbing distance from the leader's initial move to where he stops to bring up the next man — being between thirty and fifty feet. Eli and Charlotte seemed to be having the most difficulty, while Aviva and Bernie had achieved the minor summit first. It seemed almost too easy. And then Bernie said, "Now you go down the other side ahead of me."

Aviva was confused. "Which way?"

"Down!"

She peered over the mountain's side, but saw only a straight drop into the faraway chasm of the Gorner Glacier. Not wanting to appear completely stupid, she asked, "Do I go left or right first?"

"Down!" he repeated firmly.

Aviva did not budge.

"Straight down. *Now!*"

Aviva stared beseechingly at Eli. He came forward and looked over the steep, smooth-sided precipice, opened his mouth as if to also protest, then quickly closed it. Aviva put her fate in Bernie's hardened hands. She went over the side, her eyes riveted to his. The rope burned under her clenched fingers; her feet strained to find their mark.

"Lean away from the rock," Bernie ordered calmly. "That's fine. Now face out when you climb down or sideways. Only face in when it is very steep."

"This *is* steep," Aviva moaned. Bernie did not seem to hear her.

"Take small steps. Put your boots flat on the rock. You are working too hard with your arms."

The fact that her hands and feet were in contact with the mountain meant that she had to be doing something right, but she did not stop to analyze it. The moment she arrived on a solid ledge, she felt she had won a private war. From her relatively safe vantage point, she watched Bernie climb down his own rope effortlessly. Together they waited for the others.

At the top, Lily had begun to sob. For the first time that week, her icy reserve had broken. Emil spoke to her in German. Aviva could barely understand what he was saying, but she recognized the tone as soothing. As if hypnotized, Lily crept toward the edge and dropped over the side. For a second or two it seemed she was under control.

The rope twisted slightly and she screamed one long, unmistakable word: "Mama!" One of her precious handholds gave way and a small shower of rocks pelted her face, blinding her momentarily. Her feet had lost their grip and she dangled wildly on the end of the slim line.

Lily kept on screaming. It was an unbearable, inhuman sound that reverberated off the canyon walls like the shock waves from an explosion at sea crashing to shore.

Aviva clutched Bernie's hand. "Can't you help her?"

"Ai! Ai! Ai —"

Perhaps Emil could have pulled her up, especially if he had enlisted Eli's help, but Bernie was shouting for him to let her recover herself. As Aviva watched, she felt they were being unspeakably cruel. For Lily to have come so far, to have overcome so much, only to be propelled off a cliff in a useless exercise, seemed, after all she had endured, utterly unfair.

Eventually, Lily's swinging feet stopped their wide arcs. Using her arms to control the rope, Lily shifted herself up against the rock wall. On the second try, her foot found a niche on the face of the cliff. More fragments of rock tumbled downward. Bernie protected Aviva with his body until the rocks passed. When they looked up again, Lily was in control. A few moments later, she arrived on their ledge white-faced and trembling.

"I do not know what happened. All at once I saw flashing lights. I was dizzy. I could not control my hands or feet."

"Another touch of vertigo," Bernie said soothingly. "It happens. But you did well. You got yourself down."

Next it was Charlotte's turn. While Charlotte tired easily on their walks, on the rope she was remarkably graceful. "Heights don't bother me," she had said the first day out. "I find them exhilarating. Put me up in the air any day." Her complete absence of fear stood her in good stead on this part of the course. Dropping down to the ledge with a final swift, clean maneuver, Charlotte grinned. "Wasn't that fantastic!" Her perfect white teeth flashed in the sun as she spoke. "Didn't you just love it?"

Aviva caught Lily's eye and both of them laughed at Charlotte's enthusiasm.

After a brief stop for lunch at the Gletscher Couloir, a steep gully with less exposure, Bernie and Emil talked them through their first experience of rappelling down the Skyline Ridge. Bernie coaxed Aviva as she lowered herself down through space to drop beneath a cliff she never could have climbed down.

The rappel, a controlled slide down a doubled rope that is securely fixed to an anchor, such as a rock above, was a thrill — once the technique was learned. But by the end of the day, Aviva's nerves were frayed. She felt as mentally exhausted as she had ever been in her life. It was just what Eli had wanted, for he intended to keep them up the entire night for a different sort of test.

⁘ ⁘ ⁘

"What are you always rubbing in your pocket?" Eli's attention had unexpectedly shifted to Lily.

The queer twisting sensation in Lily's gut was unnerving, but she was determined not to let the group notice. For the last five or six hours Eli had been prodding the other two mercilessly to talk about themselves, questioning their beliefs and assumptions. Charlotte had cried several times; Aviva had been distraught but had behaved stoically. She supposed it was her turn.

She felt in her pocket and pulled out a dinner roll. "I always carry something to eat, an old habit."

"Surely you don't need that here. There's room service, for Christ's sake," Eli said harshly.

Lily shrugged. "It is a habit, I told you."

"Just like Heidi," Charlotte interjected.

"Heidi?" Aviva asked.

"It's a Swiss children's story. Heidi lived in the Alps, but when she went to the city she saved soft white rolls to bring to her friend, a blind woman, because she'd never eaten anything except black bread. One day someone found all the bread she had stashed under her bed . . ."

Lily's eyes closed involuntarily. It was almost four in the morning. When would he let them get some sleep? Usually, Lily prided herself on the ability to do without: food, sleep, warmth — almost anything — for a longer time than most mortals. It was controllable by the mind. Considering all the times she had been tested, she sometimes thought herself invulnerable to the ordinary suffering caused by minor deprivations.

The fortunate little American had never had to learn such tricks. Lily quite liked Charlotte even though the American was overly in awe of her. It was as if her past had bestowed a special status. What Charlotte did not understand was that her own inexperience in the matter of pain and misfortune made her a much more valuable human being. Lily wanted to say that now, to say it aloud.

If any moment was ever appropriate, this was it. Eli had led them through various exercises in truth-telling, and they had each revealed petty secrets about indiscretions and guilt — all terribly in-consequential, but she supposed it was serving the purpose he had in mind for the gibbush: bringing them closer together, binding them as a newly formed family. Was it not a fallacy to believe deprivation, such as the lack of sleep they were now enduring, would strengthen a bond? Eli, of all people, should have known better. He had been in the camps at Cyprus; he had had an opportunity to observe true de-nial. But he had not personally experienced dehumanization. If he had, he would have noticed that the men and women copulating be-hind the flimsiest cloth partitions were fulfilling a sexual hunger, not giving or sharing love. To avoid falling into the trap of fervid, hour-long romances, she had found it best to be unapproachable. In the end, there was far less pain that way. Too much of her life had been taken, spent, and broken against her will for her to give away one drop more than she desired.

The Nazis had understood brilliantly how to break the spirit, of both a person and a people. Their plan in Holland had been master-ful.

"Now we will talk about fear, about what it means to be afraid," Eli was saying. "Nicole, will you begin by telling us the first time you can remember a terrible, overwhelming fear?"

Lily could have picked any number of incidents, but she was thinking about the Germans and their conquest of Holland. The first time . . . It had come quite early, before anything truly tragic had occurred.

From the first moment of "Operation Yellow," the German army's invasion of the Netherlands had been successful. In May 1940, the progressive breaking of the Dutch Jews had begun. Lily's father had kept a calendar of the events, as if by organizing them, he could somehow circumvent them. Stupid! Lily recalled with re-newed anger. If he had put his mind to getting them *out,* they might be together today. She could remember his neat diary entries in his tidy black scratchy script.

July 2, 1940: The *Verordnungsblatt des Reichkomissars für die Besetzten Niederlande* [*Official Gazette of the Reich Commissioner for the Occupied Neth-erlands*] announces the following decree: "All Jews of other than Dutch nationality are required to report at once . . ."

"After the decree, my father, who had been born in Austria, stopped coming home at night," Lily said aloud. "He slept at the homes of Christian business associates, never more than two nights in a row so as not to compromise their safety. Of course, he did not report, for then they would confiscate his business." She wondered if Eli and the women were awake enough to listen. "Then someone in the Dutch Alien Office telephoned a warning to my mother. She became very frightened, but Papa told her to go on as usual. Very early the next morning, I awoke to the sounds of cars in front of the house, a ringing of the doorbell, and the voice of our landlady, Lotte. I drifted off to sleep and then was frightened awake by someone pulling at the covers of my bed. I looked up and saw a blond young man with a boyish face and a death's-head on his cap. He spoke quite softly, apologizing for disturbing me. I was certain they were searching for my father, but for a moment I was more captivated with the soldier's appearance. He wore snug riding breeches and I marveled at his stance with legs wide apart, shiny boots, and nervous fists resting on his hips."

Lily looked over at the sabra. Disgust that she could have been even vaguely attracted to a Nazi was clearly written on Aviva's face. "He left again. He was not looking for Papa at all, but for a Social Democrat deputy who had once lived in our house. We could honestly say we did not know where he lived."

"You did not seem to be terribly afraid," Aviva pointed out.

"The first moment I felt the covers torn away and looked up and saw him was the worst. Then I calmed. Perhaps my brain found him attractive and permitted me to relax enough to size up the situation. If I had not kept my wits, I might have blurted something which would have caused by father harm. Who knows? The point I am making is: After that incident was over, I said to myself, 'So, this is how it will be from now on. I will be frightened, then it will be better.' You cannot live in fear; it is too exhausting. You must somehow find a way to endure beyond it."

She caught Eli's eye. He was not smiling, but he was pleased. "That is what happened on the ropes, isn't it? I saw you struggle, then take control. You cried out, but hung on. There is no possibility of foretelling how every situation will end. In this business you will step off a cliff into an unknown chasm quite frequently. You will have your lifelines in most cases, but you must also grasp onto the rocks yourself — find your handholds, as it were."

Charlotte was nodding. "I always suspected there was a method to your madness, professor."

"Method to your madness?" Aviva grinned. "I love the way Americans speak!"

Eli rubbed the sides of his face with the palms of his hands. "To bed," he announced, and was instantly obeyed.

Lily could not sleep. She listened to the rhythmic breathing of the others in the larger room. She should have told more; she should have gone on listing the other minor fears, which compounded as they mounted. All had been meticulously chronicled in Papa's book, one of her few possessions that survived the war.

October 22, 1940: The *Official Gazette* announces that all commercial firms owned by Jews or having Jewish partners are to be reported.

Papa had signed over the ownership of the bakery, which had been in his wife's family almost one hundred years, to his most trusted employee, Hans de Vries, on a "temporary basis."

November 25, 1940: Dismissal of Jews from all governmental and public offices.

January 9, 1941: The Dutch Association of Theater Managers is instructed to forbid Jews entry into motion picture theaters at all times.

January 10, 1941: All persons of the Jewish religion, or wholly or partly of Jewish blood, are to report. Failure to report will be considered a crime.

February 22, 1941: First roundup of Jews in Amsterdam.

December 5, 1941: All non-Dutch Jews are to report for "voluntary emigration."

April 29, 1942: Introduction of the star for Jews in the Netherlands.

The day the stars came, the day Mama and Aunt Marta sat sewing the black-bordered, six-pointed yellow star, the size of the palm of a hand, bearing the Dutch word "Jood" for Jew in black, Hebraized letters. Mama had been made to stand in line to obtain the stars and forced to surrender one stamp from her cloth-ration card for each member of the family. Every outer garment had to carry the yellow star on the left side. The regulations further specified that Jews were forbidden to appear on the balcony, in the garden, or even by the door or window of their own homes without displaying the star. Lily's younger brothers had defied this edict as frequently as they dared risk Mama's anger, but Lily had worn hers dutifully, so as not to upset the family.

At first many of their Gentile friends, following the example of King Christian X of Denmark, wore stars in sympathetic protest. Eventually, energetic measures against them — including deporting them as Jews — pacified their consciences. One by one their neighbors appeared, downcast but starless.

·:·   ·:·   ·:·

"Nicole?" Charlotte called in a hushed voice.

"Ja?"

"You're still awake?"

"Not much point in sleeping. It is almost morning."

"May I come in?" Charlotte stood in the doorway of the sleeping alcove. Her shoulder-length hair curled prettily among the lacy edges of her long pink nightgown.

Lily patted the bedcovers.

"What were you thinking about?"

"My family."

"I'm ashamed I know so little about what happened in Holland."

"What do you want to know?"

"More about what it was like ... for you."

"Quite soon it becomes ordinary. People disappeared. One day a child would be in the classroom; the next she would be gone. The teacher would not say anything; her name would just be dropped from roll call. We would speculate she had gotten to Switzerland or America, but in our hearts we knew she was on her way to Westerbork."

"What is Westerbork?"

"A work camp. In school we used to cheer each other up by saying it could not be as bad as we imagined. When I was finally there, I decided it the worst place I had ever seen. By comparison to what came later, it was quite luxurious."

"How was your family caught?"

"My parents went first. My father was in a café when the Gestapo came storming in. Papa had time only to take his gold watch and address book from his pocket and toss them under the table, where they were retrieved by one of his friends. Those were returned to Mama that night. Papa was never seen again. Later we found out that he had died at Auschwitz."

Charlotte shuddered and Lily insisted she get under the eiderdown. They both propped themselves up with pillows and pressed together to keep warm as the first edges of daylight beamed into the room.

"The worst moment was when my mother —" Her voice caught.

"You don't have to —"

"One afternoon we were visiting some Gentile friends who had been wonderful to us after Papa disappeared. My brothers were playing a game of ball in the garden down the street while the mothers and daughters had a tea party. Then Lisle, the woman in whose house we were visiting, decided to play the piano. We were all standing around, singing Dutch songs, when the officers came to the door. They had a list. They started reading names we recognized of Jewish friends. Lisle hugged me to her and squeezed my hand. All at once I heard the name 'Anna Meyer Jaeger.' My mother stood. '*I* am Anna Jaeger,' she said nobly. The officer looked around. There were half a dozen girls ranging from five to sixteen years old. 'Which one is your daughter?' he asked. My mother never even turned in my direction. She stared directly at the German. 'She is not here,' she said and walked out the door. Lisle held me down with great force while my mother walked away, denying that I was hers. You cannot imagine the fury I felt. Later, I understood she had shown the most beautiful act of courage."

"Jaeger," Charlotte whispered. "Was that — is that — your real name?"

"I should not have —"

"I won't tell."

"Of course not," Lily said. "That is why Charles has us all here now — to ensure we never will betray each other."

"How could we ever do that?"

"It happened, it *happens* all the time. In the end we only save ourselves."

"Not mothers," Charlotte added solemnly. Silent tears streaked her cheeks.

Lily pulled away to the far side of the bed. She was quiet for a long while. "No, not mothers."

Aviva, who had been standing in the doorway for several minutes, said sadly, "I do not think it is necessary to go over it endlessly. Life goes on. We are all here now; that is what matters."

Charlotte sat up rigidly. "Do you think Nicole can just forget? Isn't she here because of it? More than any of us, she must want vengeance."

"Vengeance?" Aviva hissed. "Is that true?"

Lily's eyes darted back and forth wildly. "I would not have put it in those words myself, yet, there are certain feelings . . ."

"Does Charles know these motives?" Aviva asked.

"Do not put words in my mouth. Speak for yourself. Why are *you* here?"

"For Israel."

"You are very patriotic, Jasmine," Charlotte began. "But how would you feel if the Nazis had killed your family, if —"

"You are speaking foolishly," Aviva shouted. "You know nothing. Maybe you heard of the Mount Scopus massacre? A convoy of patients on their way to Hadassah Hospital was ambushed by Arabs. There were seventy-seven casualties. My mother was incinerated in a burning lorry. And, since we are counting, my brother was hung by the British in '46."

"I didn't know . . ." Charlotte sobbed.

"Do you know why you are crying?" Lily asked sharply. "You are sad for yourself, not for me, not for Jasmine."

Charlotte's tears increased as she nodded in agreement. "In Israel nobody would take me seriously because I was American. All the rest of you had been in the scouts together, then the Haganah or Palmach. You had a reason to fight. I was always an outsider — as I should be. My parents, my sisters, are safe and always have been. What do I know of the world?"

"And what of me?" Lily interjected. "I have spent most of my life in hiding or in a camp. I am terrified by all the choices, all the possibilities. I cannot go into a store the way you do, Chris, and pick out a scarf or pair of boots without great anxiety. Everything worries me. Every new person looks more like an enemy than a friend. You are the strong one. Goodness, not evil, makes for power."

"Truly?" Charlotte took her hand. "You always seem in perfect control."

"It is what I must do, or I would dissolve like a lump of sugar in a cup of tea."

"A lump of sugar!" Charlotte exclaimed nervously.

"We must get some rest," Aviva said gently.

Charlotte crawled out of Lily's bed and followed Aviva back to bed. "I'm sorry," she whispered to Aviva. "I didn't know. I didn't mean to start anything."

"Shhh. Forget it. She will not hold it against you. She is not the type."

"I know but . . ."

"Good night, Nicole," Aviva called.

"Gute Nacht," Lily responded, even though she knew she would remain wide awake.

❖ ❖ ❖

In his room directly above, Eli clicked off the machine. To be certain he had made a good recording, he rewound it for a few seconds and pressed "play."

"I would dissolve like a lump of sugar . . ." was followed by yawns, rustling bedclothes, footsteps, and various good nights.

He pulled his own quilt up to his neck and fell asleep — smiling.

❖ ❖ ❖

The hour-long trip down to Visp provided the young women recruits with a well-deserved rest. Eli had suggested they take a short journey without him, claiming he had some paperwork to complete.

"What about the thermal springs at Leukerbad, just down the mountain?" Charlotte suggested. The others had agreed enthusiastically.

At the station in Zermatt, Charlotte had wondered aloud, "Do you think Eli's *really* working?"

"Maybe he has got a girl friend," Lily teased.

"Perhaps . . ." Charlotte replied slowly, then could not resist a jab. "I wonder what Bernie's doing today . . . with his wife?"

Lily grimaced reflexively.

Charlotte would not let the matter drop. "What do you think, Jasmine?"

"I think . . ." Aviva paused. As much as possible she wanted to set herself apart from the tension between Lily and Charlotte. ". . . if Charles is smart, he will sleep all day!"

Before either Charlotte or Lily had a chance to respond, the bright red train pulled into the station. Aviva adjusted her daypack straps and beckoned the others.

The three young women made themselves comfortable on two seats facing each other. As soon as she was settled in her seat, Aviva tucked her pack behind her head and fell asleep with surprising swiftness.

Aviva woke just as the train was pulling out of Stalden and she started to massage her stiff neck. Lily and Charlotte were sharing the opposite seat. Lily's head rested on the windowpane; Charlotte's was on Lily's wide shoulder. Aviva was pleased the two were not arguing. She had not expected the competition in the group. On a kibbutz there was some, to be sure, but it was much less open than what had occurred in the last few days. And most of it revolved around Eli Katzar.

Only at the kibbutz where he had undergone his Palmach training had she ever sensed his interest in her. Since then he had wrapped his arms around her in friendship, even kissed her cheek in greetings and farewells — nothing more. Foolishly, she had supposed he had selected her for this special assignment above all others, never expecting that there were at least two others who had found similar favor with Eli.

Even if Charlotte was easily the most beautiful of the three, she was also the most inexperienced, and it seemed Eli was doing everything in his power to play on her insecurity. With the most intelligence background of any of the women, Aviva understood his motives. Those who did not perform perfectly would not be sent into the field. Aviva continued to wonder how Charlotte had ever come to be accepted in the first place. Her own Palmach commander had told them the only way to prove bravery was under fire; until then, all courage was just thin air. While Charlotte said she had served in the Haganah during the 1948 conflict, Aviva doubted she had ever been under attack. Charlotte had remained in Jerusalem through the hardships of the blockades, but that hardly qualified her to be in a position where she could harm Israel with an unfortunate slip in diligence.

Lily was another matter. Even among the most militant of the Palmach women, Aviva could not remember one more hardened. True, she had almost failed the climbing test, but who could criticize her for a momentary lapse, dangling in midair thousands of meters over a glacier? The only reason she herself had remained calm was that she had never felt the wild, out-of-control swinging that had unnerved Lily. With the most combat experience, training, and knowledge of Israel and its ways, Aviva felt especially qualified for her Foreign Ministry training before leaving home. Here, with Eli applauding Lily's tales of despair, Aviva was discovering that pain — not practical wisdom — was what mattered. If she had a choice, though, she would rather forget her own sorrows than dwell on them.

She had responded to Eli's questions about fear by describing her participation in the second battle for Latrun. From Biblical times, the hills of Latrun had been of strategic importance. The main road snaking up to Jerusalem through the gorge of Bab el Wad was controlled by the faction holding the high fields above where Joshua had bade the sun stand still to permit him more time to conquer the Canaanites and where a foresighted Richard the Lion-Hearted had built "a vigilant citadel," which was destroyed by Saladin on his march to the Holy City. In 1917, General Allenby had wrested Latrun from the Prussians and the Turks. And so it was not unexpected that Ben-Gurion would demand of Yigal Yadin and his senior officers, "Take Latrun!"

The first battle, on the twenty-fifth of May, had been a bloodbath. Many of the men on the battlefield were new immigrants hurriedly inducted into Zvi Hurewitz's 72nd Battalion. Just three days off the S.S. *Kalanit* from Cyprus, they had been taken from Haifa's docks to Tel Hashomer and welcomed into the ranks of the army of Israel. Next they had been split into platoons, organized by the language they spoke; issued British Lee Enfield rifles; and taught enough rudimentary Hebrew to understand simple battle commands.

Everything possible had gone wrong. First, an Arab lieutenant caught sight of the immigrant soldiers moving in the direction of Bab el Wad — so a surprise attack was impossible. Next, the Arabs' superior position enabled them to sweep devastating fire across the hillsides, mowing down the Jews who vainly attempted to cross the wheat fields. Desperately short of ammunition, the Jews retreated, leaving hundreds of wounded and dead in their wake.

Aviva, who had helped train many immigrant boys, had been overcome by remorse. Seeing them arrive on the shores of the Promised Land with such victorious smiles, watching them volunteer without flinching, she was shocked by how many had become cannon fodder for the Arabs.

"An outrageous necessity," Haim Laskov, her commander, had declared with a sigh.

When it came time to prepare troops for the second battle for Latrun a few days later, Aviva insisted she be permitted to participate. Laskov was reluctant.

"Who better than I?" she argued. "I have had more training than fifty in the last group."

Laskov needed a radio operator in the command half-track. Aviva was one of the best. Disagreements about femininity were a luxury. Haganah and Palmach units had been stressing equality for years; now women were playing an invaluable role.

"Just after midnight on Monday, May thirty-first," Aviva had told her fascinated audience in Eli's cozy room the previous night, "I was in the third half-track, making my way toward Latrun.

"We were divided into three attack groups. The first would draw the forces at the forefront with a concerted attack; the second would seize the village of Latrun; and the center group would attack the former British police station, the Tegart fort, on the hillside.

"Our group was chosen to take the fort because Laskov, during his employ at the Palestine Electric Company, had been inside it and knew his way around the installation. I was communicating directly with him. All along the way I relayed messages like 'The lead half-track is fifty yards from the gate' or 'Flame throwers ready!' We had specially designed flame throwers that could shoot a jet of fire twenty-five yards. While they were very effective in clearing the path ahead, nobody had expected the flames would light up the battle area and give the enemy a perfect view of the tanks. A few minutes later, the force commander left his car to see what was happening in the building. He was killed. The two half-tracks in front of me were engulfed in flames. We decided to abandon our vehicle after the one behind us was hit. While I was running to the rear, my uniform caught fire. Someone pushed me down and rolled me in the grass. I was one of the few from that area to escape."

Lily and Charlotte had listened with amazed expressions on their faces.

Latrun.

The name conjured up defeat. Three hideous conflicts, three downfalls. Even now the hill was in Arab hands and probably would stay that way forevermore. "Every victory is also a defeat," Bernie Petrig had said. Could the reverse also be true? Were all defeats victories as well? Aviva sighed deeply. This week had left her too exhausted to sort out so difficult a philosophical point.

It was only a few kilometers up the Rhône Valley road to the little town of Leuk. Although they probably could have walked the distance, Charlotte suggested they splurge on a taxi. Neither Aviva nor Lily disagreed.

Bright pennants waved invitingly in front of the spa. A few children were splashing in a rushing mountain stream running along the far side of the building. A strange mist swirled from above the water, but the air surrounding it was perfectly clear.

"That is odd," Lily commented.

"That pipe is discharging warm spring water into the stream," Charlotte noted.

In the distance, they could hear the whir of huge pumps.

"What a tremendous amount of water those springs must produce," Lily said. "That pipe is almost a meter wide."

"It is quite lovely; the fog is like dancing spirits," Aviva added.

After paying the entrance fee, each was handed a yellow rubber cap and a locker key, and they were sent downstairs to undress in a pristine, tiled changing room. Signs everywhere insisted they shower completely before entering the huge open-air baths. Other placards extolled the cleanliness of the pools, listing the times each one was completely drained and refilled. Water was not permitted to stand more than six hours without being changed.

Outside, the odor of sulfur spiked the air. At first unpleasant, the smell became more tolerable as they walked around the edges of the various pools deciding which to enter first. Lily wanted the hottest, which was labeled 41°C, while Charlotte suggested working from the coolest, at 28°C, on up. Weary of the discussion, Aviva slipped into the nearest bath, gasping as the steamy water stung every scratch on the surface of her skin. She swam a few tentative strokes.

A voice on a loudspeaker made an unintelligible announcement in German. There was a buzzing sound, then a whirring as water began to pour out of jets below the surface of the pool. The force pummeling her back propelled Aviva forward. Looking around, she noticed the other bathers, wearing vibrant blue or red or yellow or green caps, quickly occupied the area directly in front of the water nozzles. Rising and falling under the force of the water, they looked like cheery-faced beach balls bobbing on the surface. Aviva swam back to her own water jet. After a few minutes of experimentation, she decided she enjoyed the reverberations on the small of her back the best. She relaxed and stared up at the huge jutting cliff across from the pools, marveling at the circumstances that had brought her from an Israeli kibbutz to a Swiss health spa.

"Jasmine." Charlotte was tugging her arm. "Have you seen Nicole?"

"I supposed she was with you."

"She said she was going to try the thermal spring in the cave. I went to join her, but she wasn't there."

Aviva was completely calm. "This place is enormous. Why are you so alarmed?"

"Eli, I mean Charles, wouldn't be thrilled if we lost her here, would he?"

"I am sure she is fine, but I will help you look, if that is what you want." Aviva swam over to the ladder and climbed out. Another bather quickly occupied Aviva's choice spot by a whirlpool pipe.

"Where is the cave?"

"You have to go inside the building. I'll show you the way."

Steam and sweat commingled in the small stone-lined room where the over-40°C pool was located. The skin of most of the pale Swiss bathers was either a mottled pink or a boiled-shellfish red. It looked quite unpleasant, Aviva decided. In any case, Lily's head was definitely not among those floating in that scalding caldron.

Outside, Charlotte took huge breaths of crisp air and asked, "Where could she be?"

"She could have gone anywhere: to the children's pool, the diving rocks, the giant whirlpool, the toilets. There is even a refreshment area."

As they started to approach the farthest pool, they stopped suddenly. A curious crowd encircled the rocky end where children had been diving earlier.

"An accident?" Charlotte asked.

"No," a voice behind them whispered. "Come with me, quickly."

"Nicole —" Aviva gasped. "Where have you been?"

"Sh! Come. *Now!*"

Aviva and Charlotte were both trembling from standing wet in the wind. Lily handed them each a towel. Surprisingly, she was completely dressed, with her rucksack slung over one shoulder. Two uniformed guards rushed past without looking at the trio.

"What is —?" Charlotte's voice sounded gravelly.

Lily was searching for a place they could talk privately, but the whole layout was exposed. The long inner walkways had glass walls to view the pools from both sides; the landscaping was devoted to bright geraniums and low, immaculately trimmed hedges. There were no natural barriers to hide behind. A group of frightened bathers ran past.

Lily herded her friends to the side of the building where nobody else could hear them.

"The cave baths were too hot, so I went off to the far whirlpool, the one they turn on each half hour. The water is so forceful it pushes you around in a serpentine pattern. All the swimmers move about quite fast, people bumping into one another. I did not care for it, so I got out and followed some children who were going to dive into one of the smaller whirlpools. There was one little girl who reminded me of a friend I used to have in school in Amsterdam. I wanted to see if I could hear what she was called. Stupid of me, actually. Magda would have been all grown up by now. She was not Jewish ..." Lily's voice faded away. She bit her lower lip before continuing more rapidly. "Anyway, I watched the children dive off the rocks. There was a space behind it where I was out of the way. Nobody could see me, especially from the other side where two men were arguing very intensely in German. One cursed the other, then groaned. From where I was I could not see what happened, but the conversation had stopped. I looked out in time to see one of the men hurrying away. A few minutes later, I saw him climb over the fence and thought it strange, until I looked down and saw the water at the far end of the diving pool foaming red. I got away as quickly as I could, put my clothes over my suit, and stuffed your shoes and clothes into my bag. We have got to leave right away before we are questioned."

"We all brought our papers. Did you get them from our bags?" Charlotte asked.

"Yes, but do you think they would hold up in a murder investigation? In forty-eight hours they might discover the falsity of at least one of our documents."

"Who would accuse us, three girls from a climbing school?" Aviva asked.

"I was a witness. That is bad enough!"

"Why was he killed?" Charlotte asked shakily. "Do you think he was a Nazi or —?"

"He was probably sleeping with the other man's wife."

"Are you sure?" Charlotte pressed.

"How should I know?" Lily replied furiously.

Aviva spoke rationally. "We cannot let anyone discover our connections to Israel or we will all be considered suspects, no matter how pure we appear."

"We have got to leave," Lily snapped.

"How?" Aviva wondered. "There is only the main entrance through the turnstiles. We would be too conspicuous climbing the fences. The other side is sheer cliff."

Lily handed them their shirts and climbing breeches. "Come, we will try the front door."

They dressed in the corridor. The uncomfortable rubber swim caps had kept their hair fairly dry. In a few seconds, they were almost presentable. As casually as possible, Lily led them down the long glass corridor to the entrance. A long line of similarly inclined bathers had gathered at the doors, which were already locked. A policeman was kindly, yet firmly, explaining they would all be requested to remain while the investigation was under way.

"This could take all night," Charlotte groaned under her breath. "The Swiss are so thorough."

"We have got to get out of here," Lily said tensely. "There must be another way."

"If we hang around, looking as though we're complying, but not volunteering to go first, perhaps it will get dark and then we can try the fences," Charlotte suggested.

"By then they will have policemen guarding the entire perimeter."

"Nicole, since you think you saw the culprit climb the fence earlier, I think you should give that information. At least they wouldn't suspect us then."

"Are you crazy, Chris? I told you I cannot be a witness. My papers would be scrutinized more than anyone else's."

"She's right," Aviva agreed.

"Do *you* have any suggestions?" Charlotte challenged abruptly.

"Yes," Aviva answered because she was cornered. At the moment she did not have a plan, but she knew they had to formulate one — quickly. "First, let us get out of this crowd."

They walked back outside. Other similar groups were milling around, wondering what had happened, and what they were going to do. Mothers were shouting at children; tempers were frayed. Two middle-aged women in modest black bathing suits that could not hide their rounded stomachs strolled nearby, chattering nervously.

Aviva was certain their own worried expressions and quiet conversation did not seem unusual considering the circumstances. One of the most important lessons of their training was always to appear as if you belonged. "For now we must be calm and fit in," she counseled.

Lily nodded, but Charlotte seemed ready to bolt.

"The mind is the most powerful weapon we possess" was a phrase Aviva recalled from her intelligence training manual. She willed herself to think clearly. In her Palmach days she had been complimented on her "tushia," her keen ability to find an ingenious solution under difficult circumstances. The present situation could not have been more perfectly devised had it been a test.

More police streamed onto the grounds. The pool where the man had died was the focus of attention. Lily listened intently as one of the policemen answered the questions of a frightened mother with a baby in her arms. "Der Selbstmord . . ." she heard him say.

"Suicide," Lily translated.

"But the other man?" Charlotte whispered.

"Hush," Aviva warned. "There might be other English-speaking people in the vicinity." She spoke calmly and quietly. "Let us walk slowly, consider every possibility . . . for escape."

Escape.

Once she had been part of an escape mission — the release of immigrant Jews held by the British in the detention camp at Atlit. Aviva had helped by carrying babies up the western slope of Mount Carmel. At the top, trucks waited to take them the rest of the way to Kibbutz Bet Oren. When they heard that British soldiers were approaching the kibbutz, their commander, Yitzhak Rabin, asked her and another boy to creep closer and return with information. They were told to pretend they were lovers if caught. In less than an hour, they came back with the news that the British were covering three sides of the kibbutz. On the fourth side there was only brush, barbed wire, and steep rocks. She told Rabin it was possible to enter that way. Soon the refugees were safely mingling with the rest of the residents and confounding the British, who could not sort out the immigrants from the kibbutzniks.

If only there was a "fourth side" to Leukerbad; if only there was a way out!

An announcement on the loudspeaker requested all visitors to line up at various stations.

"Foreigners to station three," Lily translated.

Aviva's eyes darted between the pools and lobby areas where

makeshift signs were posted. Guards were beginning to process the bathers.

"Witnesses to station five."

Charlotte began to tremble. "What if someone saw Nicole near the pool?"

Recognizing the signs of panic, Aviva struggled for an answer. Just then, a child chased a ball down the sloping path. She watched him pick it up when it came to rest on a slight indentation in the concrete.

Aviva pulled at the rucksack on Lily's shoulder. She unzipped the front pocket, intentionally spilling some loose change, a comb, and cosmetics. As the others kneeled to help gather the items, Aviva said softly, "See where the lipstick disappeared? That grating covers a pipe."

"So . . ." Charlotte said uneasily.

"Look down there. I think it leads to the pipes that empty the pools. Remember the size of the pipe we saw outside earlier, the one with the mist blowing off it? It was about the same diameter as this one. If we crawled out through it, we would be near the parking area."

Charlotte gasped. "Through a pipe?"

There was another curt announcement over the loudspeaker.

"Oh, no! They are calling for a tall woman in a yellow cap and black bathing suit," Lily said. "I think they are looking for *me!*"

Aviva looked around rapidly. Nobody was in the vicinity at the moment. She pulled on the grating and managed to budge it. Lily helped to move it halfway aside. There was more than enough room to slip down into the concrete pipe.

"No —" Charlotte protested, but she was pushed in first. Lily handed the rucksack down next and went in on top of her. Aviva followed. With great effort, she was able to slide the grate over enough so, from a distance at least, it would not appear to have been moved.

"That is good enough," Lily pronounced.

Kneeling inside the dank, dark pipe, each waited for the others to make a move. In the distance there was a hushed pumping sound.

"Which way?" Charlotte asked.

Aviva attempted to get her bearings. "Must be to the right. Just follow me. I can see a light at the end."

Charlotte seemed frozen until Lily pulled her forward. In line, the three women crept through the slippery pipe. The space was too narrow to raise their heads or use their hands so they inched forward on elbows and knees. Lily dragged her knapsack in back of her, but the strap kept getting tangled on Charlotte's arm. "Go faster," Lily suggested.

"Can't. I keep scraping myself."

Aviva led the others. Somehow she could not get the movement right. Her bottom kept hitting the top of the pipe in one position; in the other, her head knocked with each forward thrust.

"Do you see anything?" Lily called ahead.

"More light. It's not too much farther," Aviva answered.

"I hear voices overhead!" Charlotte choked. "Listen . . ."

They stopped moving. A child was crying; a mother was shouting. Lily moaned. "We are going the wrong way!"

The faraway whirring sound changed. A slight rattle reverberated down the pipe. The pool of water in the concave section beneath them began to increase in flow. Suddenly it was obvious which way was out. Aviva lost her grip and flipped onto her back. She pulled her knees toward her chest to prevent them from crashing into the sides. Her nose was pressed to the top of the tube and she was floating, moving faster and faster, her feet leading the way. She opened her mouth to say she knew what was happening, but it filled with water and she began to choke. She fell back into the swiftly running water, protected her face with her arms, and thrust her legs forward. She felt that if she did not breathe her chest would burst. Slowly she exhaled into the water, telling herself that by the time all her air was gone, she would be out. And then she was falling . . . from the fire into the sea. The sound was a sizzle in her ears; the feeling was a splitting pain up her spine. Her mouth opened and water spewed forth. At last she sucked in a dry, cool breath.

Someone was lifting her. She opened her eyes as Charlotte tugged her up a slippery bank. Lily was already sitting on top, her head between her hands. Blood trickled down her fingers.

Aviva pushed Lily's hands away from her face and brushed her hair back to see where the injury was. "Are you all right?" Aviva asked between heaving gasps.

"I am bleeding, but it does not hurt."

Charlotte came close and examined Lily's face. "It's only a small gash above the eyebrow. Face cuts often bleed profusely. I don't think this one's serious." She turned to Aviva. "What happened to your nose? It's raw."

Aviva felt the spot, which had been abraded by the pipe. It was tender, but not bloody. "Do not be concerned with it."

Relieved that no one was seriously harmed, Aviva tried to think what they should do next. Her training in actual battle conditions came into play. She evaluated their position.

They were on the edge of the building, away from the eyes of anyone guarding the entrance. On the other side of the stream was a camping site. Nobody was around. Aviva scrambled over to a caravan and opened the door. "Hello?" she called. No response. She signaled to the others to follow. In a few moments they were drying one another with towels from the bathroom and munching biscuits found on the bedside table. A cloth pressed to Lily's wound had stopped the bleeding.

"We cannot stay here too long," Aviva ordered. "We will have to hike into Visp. By that time it will be dark and we should be almost dry. Is everyone able to do that?"

The others nodded.

"What will Eli think?" Charlotte asked.

"Do you think this was a coincidence?" Lily grinned slyly.

Charlotte was shocked. "He couldn't have —"

"No, certainly not," Aviva said firmly, "but when he hears the whole story he will surely say that we have all graduated."

"Do not be so certain. He might be very cross," Lily said as she untangled her hair.

"I don't see why," Charlotte argued.

Aviva held her hand up for silence. "Listen!" She thought she heard rustling outside.

Lily opened the trailer door a crack. "There is nobody around," she hissed.

Aviva clasped Charlotte's hand, then Lily's. "We must leave. Follow me."

4

The love of justice is simply, in the majority of men, the fear of suffering injustice.

François, Duc de La Rochefoucauld (1613–1680)
Maxim 78

LONDON, ENGLAND: APRIL 1979

The taxi rumbled down St. James's Street and turned swiftly into St. James's Place. "I'll get out here," Eli said to the cabbie, knowing how difficult it was for the wide car to make a turn in the hotel's narrow gaslit courtyard.

"Right, gov'nor."

In the lightly falling rain, the old façade, covered by a softly focused haze, looked like a set for a romantic movie of the thirties. Colin would even have been able to name the one Eli had in mind. Why were today's young men nostalgic for times they never experienced? Eli thought as he entered the flower-bedecked lobby.

At reception, he gave his name as Charles Ivy. The young girl on duty did not know him, but, well trained, went directly to a card file and learned he had stayed there in the past. "I'm afraid I do not have your usual room available, sir. In fact, we are rather full. How long had you planned on being with us?"

"Only one or two nights."

"Suite Two is available, but I would only charge you for your usual single. Would that be satisfactory?"

"Certainly. You are most kind."

"I'll call Harold to help you with your luggage."

"I'm afraid the airline has misplaced my bag. They don't expect it to arrive before morning."

"How inconvenient. We have a 'gentleman's packet' for emergencies. May I send one to your suite?"

Ah, the Dukes, Eli sighed. He felt almost as if he were home. This was his little secret, the place he came between assignments when he wanted to be in London. He would visit with Colin, shop for his parents, even see old friends from his school days. Nobody knew he stayed here — except Lily. He had brought her here a long time ago in what turned out to be a glorious mistake.

Once ensconced in his rooms, Eli showered and shaved to remove the lingering odors of roof tar and smoke. He turned on the televisions in each of the two bedrooms, as well as the one in the parlor, to separate channels, and listened for news of the explosion at Wheeler's.

"One waiter dead, six seriously injured, including an assistant chef who lost a hand and foot . . . Probably originated in the kitchens or possibly a gas leak in the plumbing . . . Under investigation . . ." came from the twin-bedded room. Eli rushed in to see film of an ambulance arriving at a hospital, followed by an interview with patrons who had been showered with debris.

An astonished American with a Southern accent recounted: "A chunk of plaster fell from the ceiling onto the table and demolished the platters. I had just lifted my drink and didn't spill a drop."

". . . Irreplaceable. This is the original Wheeler and Company . . . Been here since 1858. Of course, we shall rebuild," a spokesman for the restaurant was saying on the television in the parlor.

Eli stared at the telephone on the desk, yearning to pick it up and make the necessary calls. The use of hotel phones was absolutely forbidden. Whether he liked it or not, he would have to go out to a phone box. Damn it all!

The doorman asked, "Shall I get you a cab, sir?"

"No, just a stroll. I'll be back shortly."

"It's raining quite hard now, sir. If you need tobacco or a paper we have a supply at the desk."

"No, thank you."

The doorman pressed an open black umbrella into his hand. From experience, Eli knew the nearest phone box was up on Piccadilly between the Ritz and the Green Park tube station.

Eli dialed an emergency number, manned around the clock. The rain poured through the cracked roof of the red box and down his neck. The line rang six times before it was answered. "I've had to leave the tower. I'll phone back in one hour exactly," he said without waiting for a response.

Eli returned to the Dukes. A large bowl of fruit had been placed on the table in his parlor along with a bottle of Beefeater, Schweppes tonic water, and a silver dish with lemon slices. The file card in the office apparently had noted his taste in liquor along with his preference for apples — there were six in the bowl. He cut one into neat slices and ate them very slowly while removing his wet shirt and hanging it on the heated towel rack in the bathroom. He put on the thick terry robe with the Dukes' crest and, with a shaking hand, poured himself a drink.

How had he been located in London so rapidly? he asked himself as he paced the parlor. Conrad had met him at the airport and taken him to the safe house, where they had stayed only briefly. The call to Colin was from a phone box, and nobody else knew about the meeting. That meant he had been followed.

Eli made his way into the larger bedroom and lay down on the crisp down-turned sheet. If *he* were to organize such a surveillance, it would take a team of five or six people to cover a subject from the airport to Wheeler's. And what did it all mean? What sort of offensive had the other side launched? Dr. Ze'evi had been killed. Why? Had they been after *him* then as well as now — or only now? He had been an easy target in Toulon. What were they waiting for? Was the bomb in the loo meant only to frighten him? Or kill him *and* Colin?

My God! Could they have known Colin was his son? No, nobody knew that. Nobody in the Mossad, nobody in London, nobody in the world . . . except Maura.

He laughed bitterly, sat up, and finished the gin. What if Maura were also a secret agent and, Jew-hater that she was, served an Arab secret service, pitting herself against him? A feminist Moriarty . . . his nemesis. I'm losing my grip, he thought. He got up from the bed, clutched the cut-glass tumbler, and fixed himself a refill.

The man with the bomb had stared into their dining room at least twice, and each time, he had actually caught Eli's eye and held it for a second. Why place a bomb in the men's room? There was no certainty he would go there. Maybe the terrorist intended the bomb to wreak more devastation. The restaurant was old, with wooden floors, tinderbox tables and chairs. Even so, why would he want to kill innocents? But that was what terrorists did, wasn't it? If they wanted to kill only him, they could have arranged it far more efficiently. Maybe that was coming next . . . Perhaps it was not known yet if he had been hurt in the explosion at Wheeler's . . . He could be under observation at that very moment. No, the streets had been too deserted. Anyone even entering the Dukes' courtyard would have been challenged. They don't know I'm here — yet.

On the television they were making inane connections between the IRA and Wheeler's. Idiots! And yet, it served his purpose. Let Colin think that they both had merely been in an unfortunate place at an unfortunate time.

"Hello . . ." He was back at the phone box exactly sixty minutes and three cocktails later.

"He is not in," came the reply. "You will have to meet him at the office."

"Tomorrow?"

"No, right away. Can you get to the Royal Albert Hall?"

"I'll be there in about twenty minutes."

The phone clicked off.

Just after midnight, Uri Ben-Yehuda pulled up in a car in front of the Royal Albert Hall and drove the short distance to the Israeli Embassy in Palace Green. Even though Eli was with Ben-Yehuda, there were two rigorous security checks: at the gate, then in the entry hall. In a few moments he was led through the embassy kitchen, outside once again, and into a concrete "garden house." In the first room sat three men wearing earphones and turning dials on monitoring equipment. Ben-Yehuda unlocked a second metal door and ushered Eli into a fortresslike conference room.

Alex Naor turned around. "Eli . . ." He shuffled pages with teleprinter holes down the sides. " 'Jephunneh is home; Ephratah has arrived; Shobal has returned,' " he read. "This means something to you?"

Eli nodded. All were Biblical names relating to Caleb. Lily, Charlotte, and Aviva had reached their destinations safely.

Alex's face remained stern, impassive, just when Eli needed desperately to feel he was among friends.

But Alex could never have been considered a friend. From the very beginning — from the circumstances of his birth and Eli's — the two men who ostensibly were compatriots had joined very different camps. For years Eli had tried to overcome the handicap of his Christian father, the police superintendent. How many times had he proved his devotion to Israel? But there were men like Alex, men whose hatred for the British had never wavered, who looked upon him as a genetically inferior person, someone who could never be entirely trusted. So, that is how it is, Eli told himself with a long inward sigh. The gap has widened into a canyon. We are adversaries.

❖   ❖   ❖

Alex Naor had been born Alexander Rosinsky in 1923, son of a Polish Hebrew scholar and a seamstress. Like many other Jewish youths of their time, Alex and his older brother Nicholas (who, at the age of thirteen, had renamed himself Herzl after the Zionist visionary) had fallen under the spell of Vladimir Jabotinsky's revolutionary proposals: first, a Jewish state; second, something he called Legyon, or military training, for all Jewish youth; third, Giyus, national service in the homeland; fourth — and most essential — Hadar, the transformation of the ghetto Jew from victim to independent proud citizen. By the time he was twelve, Alex was enrolled in Jabotinsky's Betar movement, named after the last fortress to fall in the Bar Kokhba revolt against the Emperor Hadrian's Roman rule in the second century A.D.

"You are directly descended from a great line of Kings and Prophets; you are the heirs of great warriors and judges," Alex was told by his group leader, who was preparing the boys for immigration to Palestine.

He enthusiastically embraced the parades and rituals. He sang with fervor:

> "From the pit of decay and dust
> Through blood and sweat
> A generation will arise to us,
> Proud, generous, and fierce.
> Captured Betar
> Yodefet and Masada
> Will arise in strength and majesty."

Against his parents' wishes — they were opposed to the militaristic approach of the Betarim — seventeen-year-old Herzl Rosinsky ran away from home to attend the Betar naval training station in Civitavecchia, Italy. To defend his brother's actions, Alex quoted from Jabotinsky to his father. "If you do not know how to shoot, you have no hope."

From Italy, Herzl was transferred to Palestine to work without wages, to build as well as to defend, to serve, and to sacrifice. Alex, four years younger and unwilling to break his mother's heart, remained home. It was 1937.

Herzl fell in with many of the most zealous Betarim who, in splitting off from the less militant in the Haganah, adopted the name Irgun Zvai Leumi (National Military Organization). His regional commander in Jerusalem was David Raziel. To Herzl, Raziel was the perfect model of the calm, cerebral military Jew who fought from deep religious convictions. In letters home, he wrote, "Raziel believes that Jewish redemption shall only come by the sword. Already he has written manuals which we have found useful on subjects ranging from the practical (revolvers and their use) to the theoretical (a commentary on Clausewitz). Each morning he puts on his tefillin to pray. While I have been out of that habit myself for some time now, our father might be interested to hear that when I am with Raziel, I follow his lead."

What Herzl could not write was that Raziel's faction had rejected the policy of nonretaliation to Arab violence, which the Jewish Agency had adopted officially. Exactly what Herzl helped to organize or which actions he actually participated in, Alex never discovered fully. Arab quarters in Tel Aviv and Jerusalem were being attacked more and more frequently. Early in July 1938, an "Arab" porter carried milk cans into the Haifa market and disappeared into the crowd. Minutes later, the bomb detonated. The explosion killed twenty-three Arabs and three times that number were wounded. Some said Herzl was responsible; some disagreed. Everyone would come to know, however, where Herzl was the following week. He was pushing a wheelbarrow filled with melons into the Old City of Jerusalem's produce market. During those tense days, the Arabs were especially alerted to strangers and this boy looked unfamiliar. An Arab woman selling pita bread began shouting, "Yahud! Yahud! He's a Jew!" The spice merchant in the next stall ran out and searched the wheelbarrow. Among the melons was a bomb. Herzl ran through the crowded alleys, but the cries followed him relentlessly until an Arab leaned out from a doorway and shot him. He staggered on, bleeding heavily, until he was rescued by disguised members of the Irgun who rushed him to the hospital. After emergency treatment, British security forces moved him to the government hospital, where, as a suspected terrorist, he was guarded round the clock. His condition deteriorated; he began to run a fever, and drifted in and out of delirium. Afraid he might babble information that would lead to the arrest of Raziel or his other comrades, he reached down, reopened his own wounds, and bled to death.

The last letter Alex had from Herzl contained only a quote from a poem by Shlomo Skulsky entitled "Rosh Pinna" and dedicated to Ben-Yosef, who had, like Herzl, come from Poland the year before and crossed the Syrian border into Palestine illegally. After facing the frustration of nightly attacks on his village, Rosh Pinna, he and two other friends had fired at an Arab bus. No one was hit, but Ben-Yosef was hung by the British two months later. Jews around the world would soon hear his last words: "I am proud to be the first Jew to go to the gallows in Palestine . . . Let the world see that Jews are not afraid to face death." A newspaper in Warsaw reported the words he had written on the wall of Acre Prison, "To die or conquer the height."

The line Herzl Rosinsky had quoted from the poem was "The height will not be conquered/If no grave is on the slope."

When the Germans invaded Poland a few months later, Alex tried unsuccessfully to convince his family to escape by joining him at a Betar camp in the countryside in eastern Poland. They remained in Warsaw and eventually died at Auschwitz. After a few months at the training camp, Alex was under Russian jurisdiction and was conscripted into the Red Army, where he served in menial positions until, under the terms of the July 1941 agreement between the exiled Polish government and the USSR, a Free Polish Army was established. Immediately, Alex was recruited and joined General Wladyslaw Anders's division, which left Russia via Iran for the Middle East in March of 1942.

Two months later, he arrived at the banks of the Jordan River. As soon as he was settled in Jerusalem, he attempted to track down his brother's friends. He learned that David Raziel had been killed the year before while helping the British suppress Rashid Ali el-Khilani's pro-Nazi rebellion. His movement, the Irgun, was falling apart. It was not long before Alex fell in with the Palmach and defected from the Polish army. Believing his parents might have survived, he set out to arrange immigration for them and recognized, to his horror, that the British had all but closed the gates to the Promised Land. "I want to help immigrants" was his only request to his Palmach commander.

Alex distinguished himself during training and was assigned to the rescue operations at the northern border of Palestine in the upper Galilee. His group, known as The Unit, was based at Kfar Giladi. After escorting the refugees across the border and into the nearest kibbutzim, Alex would be in charge of moving his assigned groups to population centers while eluding the ever-watchful British authorities. When the Arab guides became increasingly more demanding in their head tax, as well as suspected of being informants to the British police, Alex trained Jewish guides to become familiar enough with the Syrian borderlands to lead without outside assistance. Some of his exploits, with large numbers of frightened refugees over difficult terrain in pitch darkness, won him notoriety as a man of great daring.

The Arab guides, however, resented the loss of revenue resulting from Alex's trainees' ability to work without them and started a campaign of threats at gunpoint to inform the police unless they were paid blackmail for their silence. Alex ordered his men to pay, rather than risk lives, but in one such holdup against his own group, an overzealous Arab stabbed one of Alex's men. Suddenly, the Arab with the knife dropped his weapon and slumped to the ground, unconscious. He had been hit on the head with the butt of a revolver hefted by Hannah, one of the Palmach girls. A year later Hannah and Alex were married.

After the war, Alex joined Palmach intelligence and during the War of Independence was sent behind Egyptian and Jordanian lines to do surveys and report positions at great personal risk.

When Ben-Gurion appointed Boris Guriel head of the Political Department of the Foreign Ministry, he favored those with a European background and a certain arrogant quality. Alex Rosinsky fitted his needs perfectly. He rose rapidly to become a high-ranking member of Guriel's team. In fact, it was Guriel who suggested Alex select the Hebrew name Naor, which means intelligent and fair-minded.

Fair-minded. Hardly! In truth, Eli had always found Alex extraordinarily stubborn on inconsequential points; and, over the years, they had clashed frequently. From the first, Naor tried to influence Guriel against Eli's team of professional women agents. And while they each progressed in the Mossad bureaucracy, they seemed always to be on different sides of the table politically. While Eli had been content to manage his department, Alex had allied himself with the men who became the policymakers. Whatever his "official" title in London, Alex, Eli knew, had great autonomy as head of the Mossad's European Division.

The conference room was lit with fluorescent bulbs. There was an annoying electronic hum in the background. Alex sat at the head of the table, sipping coffee from a chipped china cup. He shuffled the print-outs and skimmed the top page until he found what he wanted. From his breast pocket he took a pen and made slashes on the paper. "Big troubles?" he said in a flat voice. He offered Eli a cigarette, which he declined.

"Uri has briefed you?" Eli asked.

"Up to the point you abandoned the safe house."

Eli explained about Wheeler's, but left out any mention of Colin.

Alex rolled the sheets of teleprinter paper into a tight tube. "Did anyone see you leave?"

"No, I went out over the roof."

"You are not a listed casualty." His voice was flat.

"No."

"This is very serious," he said in a whispery voice. Alex opened his fist, and the rolled papers popped open and scattered in front of him. "I have agreed to work on the problem of the body. We do not think the French authorities know about it yet. There is a chance of getting it back ourselves, thank God. You didn't remove the fingertips, did you?"

"He's on a false passport and not on any Interpol lists."

"You didn't think to do it?" Alex asked with more than a hint of challenge to his voice.

"Lo," Eli answered in Hebrew. "No, I didn't."

"Whom do you suspect?"

"The Iraqis. The body ... There were the usual marks of revenge."

"You will fill out a form detailing everything you saw later, but for now we must look to the ongoing threat. Clearly, your security was breached. One of your operatives must have leaked a tremendous amount of material —"

Eli cut him off. "Impossible."

Alex arched his wide gray eyebrows. "So? Who else knew as much?"

"This wasn't a bunch of amateurs. This was my Ezra team. We've been through three wars, Cherbourg, the MiG plane incident . . ." Eli hated the way he sounded.

"Nobody is immune, not even your precious women." Alex's voice was bitter. "I knew from the start it was a terrible mistake. Would anyone listen to me? No!"

Eli felt his face turning crimson. "You're permitting your prejudices to color your judgment a bit too obviously. There were also six men in that operation and —"

"Not in key positions, not with access to *you*. And *you* were the link to the scientist."

"Who told you that?"

"Tel Aviv."

"The leak could have come from Tel Aviv just as well," Eli stated brusquely.

Alex leaned toward Eli and sniffed like a bad-mannered dog. "Or from you."

Eli slammed back into his chair. What in hell's name was Alex up to?

"Eli, this wouldn't be the first time something like this has happened," Alex said in a conciliatory voice. "An agent is also a person. Over many years their ideas change. We are investigating to see if one of them had financial difficulties: both men *and* women have done less for love. At their ages, however, this is not our major concern. There are other forms of coercion: threats to family members, political persuasion, so many techniques. You yourself could write the handbook . . ."

A few weeks ago Eli believed he had come to the end, to the last job — it was all to be a fitting finale to his career. The time had seemed right. Israel was more stable than it had been in years; he had left his mark on his organization; he would be remembered by the few who knew where he had been and what he had accomplished; and he lived with the special knowledge that his many unrevealed tasks had made a monumental difference. The illusion was shattered now.

Somewhere out there was a person he had schooled in deception who had turned against not only him but their righteous cause. No — certainly not a person on his team. It was someone on the fringes, someone who wanted to implicate him. Someone who was frightfully clever.

I am in a box, Eli decided — a box with a hidden panel. All the obvious sides have been tapped, pushed, pulled, yet it remains tightly closed. There must be a secret way out.

Alex's hands were crossed on the table. His eyes were those of a relentless interrogator.

"Let us say I killed the scientist," Eli began hoarsely.

"No one has suggested that."

"Just follow my reasoning, Alex. You're the logician. See if this makes sense. I come to you with the report. I ask for your help with the body and all the rest. You provide me with a safe house. I go out for a meal. I put a bomb in my pocket and place it in a restaurant's crapper and escape at the last moment. All suspicion is diverted from me. So what if innocent people are maimed or killed? I'm doing it for my cause."

Alex was nodding in a maddening way.

"Let us say that all this is true. What the hell is *my cause*? Why would I do that?"

Alex stood up. "I cannot supply that answer. That is the one piece of work you will have to accomplish on your own."

Eli's eyes blazed, his fists clenched. The room suddenly swirled with colors and the other men's features blurred. If someone was speaking, he could not tell. The only sound in his ears was a distant ringing. He tried to stand but slumped back into his seat and closed his eyes. When they opened, he saw that Alex had walked away from the table and was by the door conferring with Ben-Yehuda.

Alex nodded and walked out.

"Eli . . ." Ben-Yehuda came forward, his lips pursed in concern. He had filled a plastic cup with water and pressed it under Eli's nose. "Have a drink," he offered solicitously.

Eli pushed his hand away. The water formed uneven puddles on the varnished table.

"You did not sleep at the safe house, did you? Come, there's a bed upstairs in the cultural affairs office. Lie down for a few hours. We'll all be able to talk about this more sensibly in the morning."

"Uri —" Eli pushed him away again, then regretted his harshness. "I'm sorry . . . Yes . . . I will lie down. I must sort this out . . . for myself."

5

There will come about an age of small and independent
nations whose first line of defense will be knowledge.

Charles Proteus Steinmetz (1865–1923)

TEL AVIV, ISRAEL: AUGUST 1950

As the plane swooped over the Mediterranean, the great sea appeared as silver on one side, an endless indigo on the other. Then the
land: the roofs of Tel Aviv, spots of green among great expanses of
rocks and dust, the triangular airport markings of Lydda. All of a
sudden, Eli felt a weight lifting. His fingers unclenched — he was
home. Home in the new State of Israel. Passport control was a familiar, almost welcome formality. He recognized several of the clerks on
duty, but did not greet them. Because nobody in his family expected
him, he was not met at the airport. He had some time before the next
sherut, a seven-passenger intercity cab, departed. Waiting inside the
terminal, he speculated idly on the passengers coming through the
lines and wondered which he would have detained if he had been in
charge.

Techniques on how to ascertain, both logically and intuitively, if
someone was suspect, had been drilled into him in preparation for
his Bremen posting. By now he knew all the tricks of border control
work: letting a passport fall open naturally, then checking that page
with an eagle eye, because a doctored page was more likely to have
been opened the longest time; staring at the person rather than the

papers to see if the bearer betrayed himself by the size of his pupils, the tremor of an eyelid, a flicker of the tongue across a dry lip. Eventually, he was able to "smell" which papers, which people, might be problematic, no matter how correct their documents or demeanor appeared.

Although he was due in Tel Aviv for his meeting early the next morning, he wanted to sleep in his own bed that night. He would have to get up early, but being home would be worth it. The trip to Jerusalem in the shared Koppel sherut was far too slow. He was squeezed between two women in the back seat of the DeSoto sedan. Each was overburdened with hand luggage that pressed annoyingly against Eli on every turn along the tedious old road around Latrun. Eli ached to be among his own meager possessions in the one place he called his permanent home.

The small apartment in the Nahalat district of Jerusalem was sparse, but it was his haven, his refuge from the world. During the conflicts with the British, it had been a Haganah safe house. A false wall behind the bed was used as a slik, a cache for guns and ammunition. Built in the 1880s for the families of workers and artisans Moses Montefiore persuaded to come to live outside the walls of the Old City, these buildings were later popular with Kurdish Jews who expanded them, creating a warren of doorways, roofs, alleys leading nowhere, gates and towers, inner and outer staircases, and hidden passages to confound anyone but a long-term resident.

He let himself into the flat and poked around to assure himself that all was well. Eli loved the simple whitewashed walls, the display of antique iron menorahs, the bed with its oiled wood frame and white coverlet. The tile floors were bare. Four metal cups hung on pegs above the kitchen sink, a blue-and-white-striped bathrobe was draped over a hook on the back of the water closet door, and his tattered leather slippers from Cambridge days were placed under the bed. Everything was as he had left it before departing for Switzerland.

He filled the kettle and took out the teapot. There were no soft seats — only three hard kitchen chairs and a table big enough for two. The rest of the living space was given over to glass-fronted bookshelves containing his entire collection of books, from childhood fairy tales to cryptography texts. This was the one place that never changed: not the position of the menorahs, not the softness of the pillow he had had since he was a boy. Even the neighbors remained constant.

Next door, Yoav Gutmann was tending his garden, which could be measured in centimeters, lavishing care on each pepper and tomato plant. He always greeted Eli with a welcoming nod, but never a word or question. Leah Talmi had watered the plants on his patio. All were flourishing. Tomorrow was Friday. She would notice he was home and bring him soup and leave it on the stove. Nothing but the most polite banalities were ever exchanged between them, but she watched out for him.

As he poured his tea, Eli attempted to prepare himself for the next day's meeting. He expected to be questioned mercilessly on the behavior of the girls in Zermatt. He had better be ready or his whole plan could be abandoned. To his superiors, he had to prove he knew his operatives as well as any human being could know another. No matter who they tested, how they probed, a person could, either willfully or inadvertently, turn out differently from one's expectations. Maura, for instance.

After Maura, Eli believed himself a master of the misjudgment of character. She had shown him how easy it was to not see the obvious, to avoid the difficult questions, to miss all the clues. And yet, he had not looked for faults in her, had he? He had loved her, as blindly as the cliché, and that was supposed to have sufficed. Since then, he had become an expert on motivation, testing, stress, sexuality, eye movements, galvanic skin response, identity checking, graphology. Today he would have sensed Maura's antipathy to Jews long before it became an issue between them. He had talked to psychologists, read all the books, dissected personalities, until he was confident no woman would be misjudged by him ever again.

❖   ❖   ❖

"I could not have devised a better practical test myself," Eli said as a finale to his briefing on the progress of his female recruits to the group his chief of staff had assembled.

The four men sat on hard wooden chairs in a makeshift conference room atop the roof of a six-story building in Tel Aviv. The sign on the door read: VETERANS' COUNSELING SERVICE. For several years this unassuming building had been the headquarters of the Shai, the official intelligence arm of the Haganah. Since the birth of the State of Israel they had branched out to other areas of the city, but this room continued to be used for events requiring tight security.

The men opened the files Eli had sent ahead, which contained all his notes on the project up to and including transcriptions from his recordings in Switzerland. The next phase of Eli's plan, if approved, was a costly investment. At least a year would be necessary to firmly establish the young women in their covers. Funds would have to be allocated from the new state's meager treasury to set them up in their foreign locations.

Eli had every confidence he would walk away from this morning's meeting with a final approval. It was unlikely he would have been permitted to go so far with his scheme if others had not seen its merit. This was a formality to answer questions and secure the concept of developing professional women spies equal to men in their background, training, and future assignments. Out of the dozen or more women he had considered, Charlotte, Lily, and Aviva had risen to the top.

At first he had been disappointed by each in turn. Although Charlotte had more outward sophistication than the others, she had not experienced the hardships that contributed to a deep commitment to Israel. Nevertheless, she had come through the training course honorably, even when her instructors had been especially hard on her. Her scores in marksmanship, explosives, radio work, and field assignments had been in the top half of her class. The only area where she had shone was logistical planning.

Given the circumstances of a make-believe operation, Charlotte would select the best personnel methodically — often hitting on an unusual, quite brilliant cover for an operative. Her lists of supplies, transportation, auxiliary help, were remarkably complete. For a while, Eli wondered whether she might be best suited to a desk job in Tel Aviv, rather than as an agent in the field. But her U.S. passport and American demeanor had such long-range potential, he had played his hunch and signed her up for Zermatt. Before the incident at Leukerbad, he had harbored an uncertainty: How would she react under pressure? But she surprised him with her courage during the most stringent Alpine climbs and she had, by all accounts, managed the spa disaster masterfully.

Aviva could hardly be faulted during her training in Israel. She was by far the most expert in radio work, codes, and call-signs. She was able to dismantle and reassemble a radio receiver-transmitter in record time, find a loose connection, and repair it with minimal tools. With uncanny speed and using a variety of mechanical gadgets, she could efficiently reduce to seconds messages that would normally take several minutes to transmit. Another of her specialties was converting harmless-looking, everyday articles like talcum cans or hairbrushes into microfilm containers. But she was neither as inventive nor as thorough in her planning work as Charlotte and was woefully unsophisticated in matters concerning travel and foreign customs. During the time it would take to establish her cover, he hoped she would acquire the necessary polish and perfect her English. He had worried over her file particularly as he waited for the girls to return from their day's journey to Leukerbad. But once he heard that it had been *her* idea to climb into the pipe, he had been reassured. Aviva's experiences in the Palmach had not failed her. She was as solid as anyone could expect a novice to be.

From the beginning, Lily was Eli's prime candidate. He had worked with her in the camps in Cyprus long enough to know her intuitions were brilliant, her memory unfailing. Nobody else had mastered the skill of "scanning" as well. When she walked into any new situation — classroom, restaurant, street scene — her eyes were beacons, picking up details and movements on all sides. Even though every new agent was drilled in this, nothing could replace the years when this ability had been a survival skill for Lily. The instructors had tried to trick her. They would change brands of cigarettes to see if she noticed; tell her to wait for hours at a train depot, then question her about who came and went at the busiest time of day; ask her to describe each of the store windows she passed on a rapid walk through the city. Invariably, Lily impressed them with the depth of her responses. That was why she rarely smiled. It took so much concentration to memorize her new locales, she was never completely relaxed. In fact, teaching her how to *appear* at ease had been written into her personal course of study.

There was a side to Lily's character nobody dared penetrate. Nevertheless, her devotion to the cause could not be doubted. Her commitment was far greater than Charlotte's could ever be, and next to Lily, even Aviva had led a sheltered and charmed life. No, she had not distinguished herself on the cliffs above Zermatt, but her problem with vertigo and heights was not an uncommon one. Most important, she had not disintegrated altogether and, in the end, had accomplished as much as the others in the climbing portion of the course. Then there was Leukerbad — as close a trial as anyone could have devised, and one Lily had managed as well as any master spy.

As he sat facing the committee, Eli felt secure in saying, "I have no reservations about any of my recruits."

Boris Guriel, the man who had tentatively approved Eli's scheme, listened curiously while Eli recapped his program's goals for the future. A slight man with a tractable nature, Guriel did not appear authoritative. Yet all assembled deferred to him as the head of the Political Department of the Foreign Ministry. Sitting on either side of Guriel were Alex Naor and Mike Vered, two division chiefs who had been apprised of Eli's proposal earlier but were there to be brought up to date. Both were well aware of Guriel's philosophy of intelligence and knew his goal was to build a substantial network, with agents planted all over the world.

"Bring me information on a country's politics, its power structure, policies, the personal habits of its leaders. Analyze the psyche of a country. Tell me *why* events are happening. Political intelligence is what I am after," he would emphasize. "At every moment I must understand which way the wind is blowing, who is on the outs, who is up and coming. I need to know where the elite eat, sleep, amuse themselves. My emissaries should mingle with the established leaders along with the bright stars on the horizon. Let the Shin Bet handle domestic affairs; let the military ascertain the location of bases, the technology of the weapons; what I want is to feel certain of the *intent* of our enemies."

Eli believed women would suit Guriel's concept of his newly formed agency perfectly. But Mike and Alex, with their backgrounds in military intelligence, were more traditional. He knew neither well, but had a grudging respect for both because of their accomplishments as leaders in the Shai. Mike had organized the protection organization for Kol Israel, the illegal Voice of Israel broadcasting service of the Jewish resistance movement. For years, he had led the British CID on an elaborate cat-and-mouse game as they searched for the transmitter despite the powerful mobile detection apparatus used by his adversaries. Alex was a member of the Mossad le Aliya-Bet, set up to organize and carry out illegal immigration into Palestine. His section was a network of trustworthy Arabs, particularly on the frontiers with Lebanon and Syria, which brought thousands of Jews to safety. During the War for Independence, he turned his intimate knowledge of these same villages into a tactical advantage.

Both Alex and Mike had participated in brutal actions. They were men of high ideals tempered in the forge of harsh reality. Out of necessity they had both served with women in wartime; nevertheless,

Eli suspected they were brought in on this meeting precisely because they would be the most difficult to convince.

"Professionals . . ." Eli began. "The purpose of my plan is to have a team of women who are as professionally trained as the men. Not just for single assignments, but for the long haul."

"Precisely my objection!" Alex interrupted. "How can you expect a woman to make a career as an agent when she is likely to be preoccupied with a family and babies most of her useful working life?"

"Men do not have families?" Guriel countered.

"Mothers do not leave babies at a moment's notice."

"Don't forget the benefits," Eli countered. "Who would suspect a mother traveling with her children? Who would suspect a woman with a well-established cover of an ordered family life? During both world wars women operatives in Britain were uniquely successful at eluding capture."

"What about Mata Hari?" the dark-eyed, mustached Mike asked.

Eli snapped at the bait. "Surely you are not comparing that grossly overromanticized and extremely inefficient case to this situation? Margaretha Zelle had numerous warnings meted out to her by both Basil Thompson and Sir Reginald Hall. But then, we are not training our operatives to consort with other suspected agents to obtain information, are we? From the start we have removed sexuality as a tool. If men can gather information without screwing their sources, so can women."

"I have seen all three of the ladies in question, Eli" — Alex smiled wryly — "and I think you are naïve."

"I would volunteer to team with any one," Mike added.

"If you would place your life on the line alongside one of my operatives, then I've done my job well," Eli replied smoothly.

Mike grinned. Eli sensed the men in the room were feeling positive about his plans, but they had to formally meet and play the devil's advocates before a proposal as radical as his could become policy. He turned to observe Guriel's reaction.

His superior's wide mouth was pursed tightly, as if he needed to strain to remain silent. "Let us review the advantages, then," Guriel broke in. "Our early studies indicated the women tested out as more dependable, more able to follow directions without altering them. And these three candidates seem exceptional."

Alex stood up and walked across the room. "They will not work out to our advantage," Alex said with surprising firmness.

"Why?" Eli asked as calmly as possible.

Alex sat down again, but shifted uneasily. The tall man, three inches over six feet at least, was clearly uncomfortable on the rickety chair. "Each is too much of an exception for my taste. First, there is the American adventuress. How long do you expect her to endure? It is all well and good to send her on a climbing holiday in Switzerland or offer her the short-term excitement of a war between Jews and Arabs, but she is bound to fall in love with someone and disappear. She has no long-standing ties or loyalties to Israel or anyone but herself."

Eli began to object.

Guriel shook his head. "No, let Alex continue."

"Then there is the little Dutch girl. We are just beginning to understand how people with her background will handle the pressures of day-to-day life. Can you predict how she will react under stress? Of course you cannot! Besides, don't we owe *her,* of all people, some semblance of a normal family life? Isn't it immoral to require her to give anything more because she had the misfortune to be born Jewish when madmen were ruling the world?"

Guriel was nodding. "I see your point, Alex. However, the sabra is not in the same class with the other two, so —"

"No?" Alex cut him off. "Just because she is a whiz at punching a Morse key does not make her material for undercover work. No, Eli, I am sorry, but your scheme is a far-fetched, though I will admit romantic, notion."

"It has nothing to do with romance," Eli retorted. "I have three well-trained potential agents who look as good on paper as any man in the service."

Mike broke in. "I would like to ask you about your relationship, your *personal* relationship, with each of the women in question. The American, for instance. She is a beautiful girl."

"That is hardly your concern."

"But, it is. How can you evaluate her objectively if you love her?"

"I do *not* love her."

"You have never made love to her?" Mike wheedled.

Eli caught Guriel's eye. He nodded for Eli to reply. "I have not. The only Israeli I know she has slept with was a Haganah boy named Teddy. She managed his safe house and comforted him when the CID were hot on his trail. He died shortly afterward, defending an arms slik. The British claimed he was 'escaping normal arrest.'"

"But you wanted her . . ." Mike challenged.

Eli threw up his hands. "I have never taken a vow of chastity."

"Of course not," Mike backed off. "But you must see how this might appear to others. They could say you were a Svengali with the helpless girls under your spell. Even if you have not made love to their bodies, you have manipulated their feelings in order to bring them into the program."

"*If* the girls are doing it because they are infatuated with *me* — which is just a supposition on your part anyway — what the hell is wrong with that? Why are any of us here? Because we love individual people: our mothers, fathers, children, our country, our God . . . whatever motivates, whatever works."

Alex slumped back into his chair. "Women — God bless them — react with their hearts, their feelings, their physical attraction to another human being far more so than men do. My Hannah would agree with me, even after all she contributed, that in dire straits we must use every available resource, but not today when we have more choices."

Guriel took a long breath before he spoke. The features of his face had a distinctive Oriental cast and his high cheekbones gave evidence of Tartar blood in his veins. "I am always wary of putting emotional labels on anyone: man, woman, Jew, Christian, British, French, Egyptian." His voice was muted, but the delivery was clipped and precise. "It is my experience that people cannot be codified, no matter how convenient it would be to do so. You all know my background. When I spent three years as a POW, I saw aspects of human nature under duress that both frightened and impressed me. All of us are subject to irrational hates spoon-fed to us by our parents, our religious leaders, our governments. It takes a truly civilized man to refrain from succumbing to them in moments of crisis — and decision."

All during Guriel's speech Alex had been grinding his jaw and clenching and unclenching his fists. Why so much anger? Eli speculated uneasily. His attempts to catch Alex's eye failed. There was something else here — something personal, something impossible to refute.

Finally, Alex spoke. His voice was low and tense. "Are not most women 'truly civilized' by your definition? What if one decides that a particular Arab enemy agent, for instance, is a good fellow with three young children who should not be reported. Doesn't this civilized person feel more empathy? Isn't that person more emotional than ruthless?"

"Did the women in the Palmach not hold their own? My God, where would *you* be today without Hannah?" Eli's voice was tense but steady.

"I already told you she would side with me on this," he replied through twisted lips.

Eli placed his palms out in appeasement. What else could he say? He had been through these same tedious arguments before when he originally proposed the idea of developing a section of highly skilled women agents. In the past, he had won each round. His recruits had been permitted to undergo the full military training process and he had received approval for the Swiss exercises — but not without enduring massive criticism.

Initially Guriel did not want to approve the trip to Switzerland. "Let them climb Mount Meron!" he argued.

"Since my agents are being trained to be activated outside their own country, I must test them crossing borders and managing in foreign environments," Eli had reasoned. To justify the expense, he had explained his cost-effective methods. "First, I will be conducting final training exercises; second, I will be developing gibbush and simultaneously establishing credible covers; third, the girls will come away with a logical reason for having known one another."

He believed he had successfully accomplished their training, and his elaborate written report and wire recordings had been self-explanatory. At the start of the meeting Eli had been quite secure. By now he had lost considerable ground.

"Well, Alex, Mike?" Guriel asked.

"I have no further objections," Mike replied.

"I do," Alex said curtly. "Let us leave aside the equality of women and all that nonsense for a moment. Let us even remove Eli from the equation. Let us concern ourselves with one fact: if one of the girls was ever captured, we know she would be treated in the most diabolical manner, subjected to torture, rape, disfiguration, severe pain, and —"

"Is it any worse for a woman to be tortured than a man?" Guriel asked.

"To me, yes. If I were to approve this and one of the women was caught, I would feel personally responsible for her."

"And you would not feel responsible for a man?"

"Perhaps I am biased because I am the son of a woman, the husband of another, the father of two young daughters; I cannot help the way I feel."

Guriel was silent.

"If you would prefer, I will eliminate myself from this committee because I sense we will all someday deeply regret an affirmative decision," Alex added.

Eli stared at Alex. "Is that all?"

"What can I say? I am not against *you*, my friend. On the practical side, I do not think they will ever contribute enough information to justify the expense and I do not feel they can truly handle the deprivations of a long-term assignment. If you were proposing one or the other for a special task, if they brought particular skills to a mission, I might consider it. But as it is . . ." He threw up his hands.

Guriel turned to Mike. "Do you have any final comments?"

"The propaganda value of capturing an Israeli woman spy would become a serious problem for us as a nation. In the end, the political repercussions at home and abroad could outweigh any slight surprise advantage a woman operative might have."

"Your objections have been noted, gentlemen." Guriel turned to Eli. "You are authorized to continue this project for one more year. The funds will be adequate, but not extravagant. The girls must be established in tight covers by that time and ready to undertake actual assignments. They will be monitored not only by you but by a committee to which both Alex and Mike will be assigned. Any, and I mean *any*, concerns about one of your operatives must be reported to me immediately. Do you understand?"

"Certainly, Boria," Eli said, using his superior's affectionate nickname.

"I have only one major reserve."

"And that is?"

"All three are terribly young. And unmarried. I do not see this as being so much of a problem for Lily and Charlotte, but Aviva is another story. With her Semitic appearance, we expect to use her in an Arab country eventually. Even with the so-called enlightened upbringing in her cover, I cannot see her moving in circles yielding significant information without a male partner."

"There are many refined women in Arab countries who frequent the higher social circles of men," Mike volunteered.

"And they are accepted because they perform special services for these men," Guriel parried.

Mike winced at the reprimanding tone of voice.

Guriel added, "We are not training high-class whores, *are* we, Eli?"

"No."

"Then you see my point."

"So now I'm to be a shadkhen, a matchmaker, too?" Eli asked.

Guriel shrugged. "Not necessarily. All I am saying is that I want her to have the appearance of a respectable married woman before she is sent on an assignment."

Eli's silence was his only response.

"That is all, then." Guriel turned to leave the room. "Shalom," he said.

"Shalom," the three men chorused.

Eli permitted Alex and Mike to leave during the first two ten-minute intervals. He was in no hurry. Guriel had asked to see him later that afternoon at his office, but Eli was uncertain why. Eli did not dwell on the matter, for he had learned long ago not to attempt to second-guess Boris.

⋅⋅⋅   ⋅⋅⋅   ⋅⋅⋅

At the Café Stern on Dizengoff Street, Eli ordered goulash and a cup of tea. Almost all the stores along the usually bustling street were closed while Israelis took the menuchat tzaharaim, the afternoon rest period.

Eli took a long sip of the cooling tea. He wanted to make plans for his team, yet he could not focus his attention on the many details that had to be attended to. Considering how much he enjoyed being alone, both at moments like this and in his Jerusalem flat, Eli wondered if he would ever wish to share his life with a woman or children. Perhaps he was cut out to be what he had become: a lone operative. He could take risks; he could accept assignments; he could work ceaselessly whenever necessary. He was deep in thought when someone called his name.

"Eli Katzar? How are you?" The accent was straight out of a gentleman's club in London.

For a moment he did not recognize the slender man with the heavy beard.

"Gideon Shashua," he reminded Eli. "I'm calling myself Gideon Tabor now. We've all taken Israeli names."

"Of course. How are you?"

"I don't mean to disturb you . . ."

"Not at all. Would you like to join me?" Eli asked, even though he was reluctant to give up his solitude.

"You're very kind."

"What would you like?"

"I was going to have something to drink."

Eli signaled the waiter and Gideon ordered tea.

"How's your family? I haven't seen your mother since before the war," Eli said.

"Very well, thanks. Mother is living with Aunt Louise and Uncle Yossel at the farm."

Eli remembered how much he had always enjoyed Gideon's family. His mother's side of the family, the Hillmans, were early settlers in Palestine who had pioneered citrus growing in the Rehovot area. Many of Eli's boyhood friends had come from the Hillman clan. But Eli had not known Gideon in Palestine because he had been raised in India. Gideon's father, Maurice Shashua, descended from a long line of distinguished Iraqi Jews who were encouraged to follow the British to India and prospered there. There was an interesting story about how Eleanor Hillman had met Maurice Shashua — something to do with orange trees for Bombay — but Eli could not remember the details.

When Gideon was sent off to school at Clifton College, Eli's mother had written to ask him to contact her friend's son. Dutifully, Eli had met with him several times, but had not seen much of Gideon since. Through the family grapevine, he had heard that Gideon had served under Mordechai Makleff in the Carmeli Brigade in 1948.

"This place brings back memories," Gideon said as he stirred milk into his tea and looked wistfully around the restaurant, which had a reputation for attracting the artistic crowd.

Eli tilted his head politely. "Really?"

"My cousins brought me here. Sigal and Nurit had literary pretensions. They would always get excited if a writer or journalist was sitting nearby. I guess it rubbed off. Sigal's writing a novel about the family's early days in Palestine."

"Sounds fascinating." Eli looked at his watch. It was almost time to meet Guriel.

"I'm sorry. Am I detaining you?"

"I have a few minutes more before I must leave for an appointment. Tell me, what are you doing these days?"

"I was at the London School of Economics, but since my father died . . ."

Eli remembered Maurice Shashua had been killed in a plane crash in the Mediterranean.

". . . I've been expected to tend to the business. Unfortunately, it doesn't interest me."

"You should strike out on your own perhaps?"

"I've considered it, but frankly, I don't know what direction to take. Since the army, I haven't felt I was making a contribution."

Eli stared at Gideon with renewed interest. Gideon had inherited the luxurious black hair and coal-black eyes that ran in the Shashua family. The whole clan of Iraqi origin looked more like Arabs than Jews. Gideon probably fit right in with the sons of sheiks at the school.

"You aren't married?"

"No, I'm not."

"Any prospects?"

Gideon seemed surprised by the turn in the conversation. "No, why?"

"I know of a position that might suit you . . . but it is only available to a single man."

"What does it involve?"

Eli glanced at his watch again. "I'd love to talk to you more, Gideon, but I must rush off."

"But —"

"I'll be in touch." He paid his bill and waved good-bye. As he crossed the street, Gideon's eyes followed him.

❖   ❖   ❖

Eli approached the Kirya, the government compound in the heart of Tel Aviv, until he reached the small brass sign on the barbed-wire-topped wall: MINISTÈRE D'AFFAIRES ETRANGERS. Vivid pink and orange bougainvillea draped the stark doorway of the office building. Eli walked quickly through three small rooms, where civil servant secretaries busily affixed the appropriate government stamps to export and import documents, to the end of a twisting corridor created by the attachment of sheds to the sturdier houses left over from the time the area was a German Templar farm. He opened two locks and stepped inside his own modest work space, where Boris Guriel was already seated at the rickety round table mounded with statistical and scientific papers.

"Shalom," Eli said quickly. There would be no reference to their recent meeting. "I've read all the material you requested."

"Yoffi! Wonderful. I believe you have the technical background to comprehend the data as well as the political experience to weigh the scope of the issues."

"It doesn't take a genius to recognize there are seven to eight hundred thousand Jews in Israel and thirty million Arabs in the surrounding enemy states. Sometimes I feel that if we survive at all, it will be miraculous."

"While you are praying for divine guidance, I am searching for salvation in science. If war is an extension of diplomacy by other means, intelligence and covert acts can function as an intermediary step between the two and thus preserve the peace. The more knowledge we have, the better we shall sleep every night."

Eli gestured to the pile of documents in front of him. "Do you think the government will support an Israeli bomb?"

"Last year Ben-Gurion said it is the only weapon that can tip the balance to our side."

"Boria, what has this to do with me?"

"You know Shlomo Shamir from the Haganah?"

"Of course."

"He is the link between the army and the potash project. The army's scientific corps is supervising the Negev operations with technical assistance provided by the Sieff Research Institute. To support the field work, a chemical laboratory is being set up in Haifa. They will be attempting to extract the impurities from the low-grade uranium. Once this is accomplished, there will be the problem of producing weapons-grade uranium."

"You mean uranium high in the isotope U-235?"

Guriel grinned. "Exactly. The United States is solving the problem with an enormous gaseous diffusion plant in Tennessee, but the capital costs of such a plant, plus its enormous energy demands, are far beyond Israel's means. Our scientists are searching for a more economical method of separating U-235 from U-238 by using an ultracentrifuge. Besides fundamental research here, we need to know the developments in the East as well as the West to aid our scientists. One area we want studied is the work of a Dr. Jesse Beams, who is the world's authority on the ultracentrifuge. Weizmann has one of our most promising scientists studying with him in Virginia. We have other talents in Britain, Switzerland, the Netherlands, and, most important, France, because they have been most gracious in opening their secret nuclear laboratories to Jewish scientists."

"This is all fascinating, but where do I come in?"

"Until now, I have been the liaison for the security of the scientists as well as the movement of the data, both legally secured and derived from intelligence and diplomatic sources. The field is so enormous that I have decided to set up a special desk to coordinate all information on nuclear matters."

"Does that include hydrogen bombs? Other fissionable sources?"

"Anything you might imagine and then some. It seems men have no limits to their imaginations when it comes to plotting their own self-destruction. All recent scientific developments which might help our own scientists in their work and all material regarding similar work by our enemies should come to your attention. You will have your own unit, your own funds, and report directly to me or my successor. You will, however, answer to the Prime Minister whenever asked to do so, and he will be the only other person to know the exact nature of your mission."

As Eli's mind raced with the challenge and responsibility he had just been handed, the discussion of a few hours ago seemed remote.

Guriel was saying, ". . . All weapons-related research and development qualifies. I expect you to establish a separate network to provide intelligence on our most immediate enemies. We will be filtering all related data from our information networks in these countries."

"This is a massive undertaking. I suppose you will be relieving me of my other duties."

"Yes, and we might move you to Rehovot to be near the Weizmann Institute."

"What about the ladies in Europe?"

"I do not see a conflict there."

"If you wish me to continue managing their training on the side, I could do it, but I could turn them over to another operative if you would prefer."

"Why? I expect they will be the core of the Ezra project."

"The Ezra project?"

"I am calling it that because of the references in the Book of Ezra to the 'strange wives.' If the girls prove themselves, they will, in a fashion, be married to us."

"I'm surprised that you would want women in on this type of a job, Boria."

"Ah! So you do not think they are capable?"

"Not at all. When they are fully trained, they will undertake whatever assignment Israel needs them to fulfill."

"I am delighted with your response. There is a man I want you to meet immediately. Are you free to go to Rehovot tomorrow?"

"Certainly. Is it someone at the Weizmann Institute?"

"Yes. Dr. Ze'evi." Guriel did not miss the sparkle in Eli's eyes. "Do you know the name?"

"Asher Ze'evi? He's a cousin, or rather married to a cousin."

Guriel's straight, small teeth glimmered as he smiled. "In this tiny country we are all mishpokhe — we are all family — but this makes it even better."

PART TWO

ESTABLISHMENT OF A COVER

6

And she said, "I will surely go with thee; notwithstanding the journey that thou takest shall not be for thy honor; for the Lord will give Sisera over into the hand of a woman." And Deborah arose, and went with Barak to Kedesh.

Judges 4:9

LONDON, ENGLAND: 1950–1951

Aviva stepped out onto Piccadilly. After her day behind the desk at Thomas Cook and Sons, the air, while cold and damp, felt wonderful. As she walked toward the Green Park tube station, she pulled out the letters she had written to Chris and Nicole and posted one in the red pillar box on the north side of the street. As an extra precaution, she would wait to mail the second envelope until she arrived in South Kensington. After the letter slipped into the slot, she hesitated and scanned the crowd queuing for the bus.

Everything seemed normal. To avoid being followed, she would take a diversion along St. James's Street and turn down Bennet Street. This quiet spot appeared at first to be a cul-de-sac, so someone on her trail might hesitate momentarily. Then, if nobody was in sight, she could turn down Arlington Street, circle back to Piccadilly, and be only a few steps from the station.

Anyone tracking her was testing her, so she kept herself alert, always ready for examination — both practically and emotionally. Whenever she suspected someone had marked her as his object, her pulse beat faster, her mind sharpened, and she forced herself to care as much as if her life depended on it.

"At any moment you might be activated," Eli had warned. "Never believe you are practicing for naught. In fact, what you might perceive as just another test could very well be an actual situation. *Never* relax your guard."

Her work at Cook's was interesting. As a trainee, she was assigned the coach tours most of the time. Customers with a tight budget might request "Spain for under sixty quid" or "châteaux for ninety pounds" and she would help them select something suitable from a huge notebook on her desk. At today's close of business, she satisfied an elderly gentleman who was surprising his wife with the "Continental Combination: France, Italy, and Switzerland for only seventy-seven guineas." It was a wonderful buy, and the sweet man had been thrilled to discover he could even choose their seats in advance.

Once in a while, a "customer" would mention a code name — "Mr. Grant said you would be expecting this" — and hand her an envelope. Later, someone else entirely would come by and give the companion code phrase — "Mrs. Martin's itinerary for the south of France" — and she would turn it over to him or her. These transactions kept her on her toes. She had to extrapolate the phrases by the day of the month and an alphanumeric key that would prove out "Grant," "Martin," and "France" as acceptable code words. A slip could have dire consequences — for her career or, possibly, for someone whose mission depended on her performing a small task perfectly.

Sometimes she pretended the person following her could harm Eli if she let him stay on her trail. Avoiding him became her way of saving Eli. It was a childish notion — she knew that — but it worked to keep her motivated. Building a cover was a tedious business; she had been warned about this, but she had not realized how futile her life would sometimes seem. Ideals were fine; they carried you over the years. The long-range goals were clear in her mind; the security of her homeland was at stake. But here, thousands of miles away from Israel, forbidden to speak her own language, living a false identity, monitoring every word and move, she sometimes began to lose sight of the big picture, especially because her routine work seemed irrelevant. A single face, a single set of eyes to remember, a single voice to prompt her to do her best, was what she required to keep going on cold mornings and dank evenings. So she indulged herself and conjured up Eli's soft mouth, Eli's adorable dimples, Eli's hooded, pale blue eyes, Eli's brows that peaked with sharp upside-down vees,

Eli's lemony scent, Eli's voice with its singsong version of Oxbridge English.

Down the passage leading to the Piccadilly line, Aviva drifted in the sea of pressing commuters. The first train into the station looked packed, but she managed to squeeze in. She had not seen Eli in half a year. The last time was when he had come to Paris and briefed them on their next phase of training. Charlotte confided that she sensed Eli had difficulty in finalizing their active status. After so much time and effort had been expended, not only on their education in Israel but on the trip to Switzerland, Aviva never considered the possibility of being passed over. If she had had doubts about an American having the necessary shrewdness for intelligence operations, she had felt quite differently after their escape from Leukerbad. Lily, on the other hand, was the most perfect example of an operative she had ever met. She had never been to Paris before, yet she acclimated the most rapidly and seemed to blend in effortlessly.

When asked how she did it, Lily explained, "At a café on the Boulevard St.-Germain I found a model to follow. I studied everything about her — from her hair to her shoes. I listened to what she talked about to the boys at the next table. I noticed what she ordered, even the newspaper she was reading. The next day I tried to mimic everything, including the mannerism where she curled her hair around her finger as she spoke. It was awkward at first, but in a few hours I felt as though I was changing. In another day it felt right; it felt a part of me."

Aviva was reminded of something Eli said about establishing a cover. "It helps if the agent can avoid revealing too much about her own preferences or personality," he had explained. "You must force yourself to eat foods you normally do not: chocolate ice cream if you prefer strawberry, rice instead of potatoes. Unimportant details, but the mood of caution remains with you longer if you never relax your guard."

Aviva tried to follow Lily's example. When she drank tea, she continued to wish for coffee. Each time she took a sip, she was a little startled, a little annoyed. But maybe that was what Eli wanted.

In Paris Eli explained that he had received final approval for all of them to develop their covers. He also allowed them to reveal their names to each other for the first time. Aviva much preferred "Charlotte" to "Chris," but felt "Nicole" suited Lily better than her given name. The three had been ordered to keep in touch by mail every few months, the way friends who meet on holiday might. They were to write strictly under their new identities, but could discuss anything — work, boy friends, apartments, fears, hopes and aspirations. Aviva looked forward to receiving and writing her quota of letters, for they were her one link with others sharing a similar baptism. Lily seemed to have a very pleasing new life studying art in Paris; Charlotte had been sent "home" to Ohio for a semester at Antioch College. To Aviva, both situations seemed preferable to her assignment.

At the Gloucester Road station she hurried quickly to the huge lift that took thirty people at a time up to street level. Next, she made a quick stop at the greengrocer for bananas, carrots, and potatoes, and another at the bakery for a loaf of day-old bread. It was almost dark. She posted the second letter at the corner of Cromwell Road and turned into Gledhow Gardens, where her untidy bed-sitter awaited. Mentally, she prepared a simple supper: she would boil the potatoes and carrots together and season them with salt and garlic. There was some leftover cheese, which would be good with the bread. The bananas would do for a bedtime snack. Not a feast, surely, but a filling, warm meal that would be simple to prepare on the hot plate in her room. She pushed open the gate.

Aviva's meditations had caused her to lose her concentration. The hand on her shoulder came as an awful shock.

"Miss, I am sorry, miss . . . I didn't mean to scare you. But don't you work at Cook's?"

The man was only a few inches taller than Aviva. He wore a shabby brown overcoat that was much too long in the sleeves. Although he was in his twenties, his forehead was high and his teeth seemed yellow in the lamplight.

"Yes, I do." To deny she worked at Cook's might place her in more jeopardy. Who was he? Aviva's mind raced with the possibilities. This *could* be a coincidence. She saw so many people every day that this man might be someone she had dealt with. Or, he could have been sent by Eli. She knew she could be expected to be contacted at any time. Worst of all, he might be a British or enemy agent who had discovered her Israeli affiliation.

"I thought so. I was in about a tour to Greece two weeks ago."

"I do not remember . . ."

"You wouldn't — it was the lady at the next desk who helped me out. She wore tortoise-shell glasses and had white hair. I don't recall the name."

"Oh, that would be Mrs. Whitney."

"Yes, that's it. I must admit I looked over your way several times. You were involved with your own customer, so it's no wonder you didn't notice me."

"Yes, well . . . I am certain you will enjoy Greece."

"Have you been?"

"No, I have not."

"That is a pity. I was going to ask you for a drink and some free advice."

"I would be pleased to look up more information at the office if you care to stop by, but I am expected for dinner here and . . ."

"I supposed this was where you lived."

If the man knew she lived here, lying was useless. If not, he was probably harmless. "I do, but my friends in the flat above invited me tonight."

"I see. Well, I'm terribly sorry. I have never done this before, but I wanted to meet you. I live in the other direction, off Old Cromwell Road. My name is Oliver Deacon. What's yours?"

"Jasmine Gregory."

"You're not from here, are you?"

Aviva started to pass through the opened gate. "I'm afraid I must . . ."

Deacon's hand touched the string bag holding her produce. It seemed as if he were reaching to help, but the pressure was stronger than that. He meant to detain her. Aviva was frightened. She knew enough self-defense to hurt him, but he might be armed. To create any disturbance meant she would compromise her cover. Six months of difficult work, language study, not to mention all the corollary paperwork built up around her identity, would be lost, possibly for nothing more than a desperate admirer.

"Couldn't I come in for a few minutes?" The man's grip tightened; his voice changed. It wasn't pleading; it was softer, more secure. "Charles Ivy suggested we meet."

"Ai!" she moaned, with both shock and relief. "Not here."

"Do you know a pub called the Hereford Arms?"

"At the corner of Wetherby Gardens?"

"Right. Could you be there by nine? Would that give you enough time with your friends?"

The dinner was fiction, of course, but Aviva welcomed the interval to gather her thoughts. "I will manage to get away." Without another word, she entered the small front garden and took out her door keys. As she turned the key in the lock, she looked over her shoulder. Mr. Deacon was nowhere in sight.

Who *was* Oliver Deacon? His accent was slightly British yet hinted at someone born outside the country — a colonial upbringing in India perhaps? Or Palestine . . . ? Aviva deliberated as she unpacked her parcels on the rickety counter in the cooking area of the room. She kicked off her shoes and lay down on the bed, too mentally exhausted to begin to prepare a meal. Later she would have to discuss Mr. Deacon's approach with him. He had frightened her badly — without necessity. If she had panicked, it could have destroyed them both. But she was not supposed to panic, was she? She had probably displayed much more jumpiness than she should have or . . . Aviva leapt up and began to pace the cramped bedroom area. She had not done anything wrong. Any girl approached by a stranger on a dark street would be wary. Nor had Mr. Deacon. He had come up to her in a friendly way. Only the touch on her shoulder could have been questioned, but it was a way of stopping her without calling out and attracting attention from inquisitive neighbors. Before revealing himself, he had made a preliminary identification of her by asking her if she worked at Cook's. He postponed their meeting for several hours to give her time to check up on him, and he had picked a neutral spot in the neighborhood. Aviva had no reason to criticize him. The mysterious Mr. Deacon had done it by the book.

Suddenly she felt hungry, but there was not enough time to cook the potatoes, so she made a cold supper of the cheese, bread, and fruit and several cups of tea. She checked her watch anxiously. She was impatient to find out what this was all about. Was she going to be selected for a mission, sent to another country, chosen at last to be useful?

Rummaging through her bureau, she found her best sweater set. The soft pink of the lamb's wool was flattering next to the dark cast of her skin. She matched the sweater set with a plaid skirt, a scarf, and her black pumps. Her long black hair was brushed into neat, thick waves; she pinned one side back with a large shell barrette. Then she applied powder and lipstick. The final glance in the mirror was pleasing.

By nine, the crowd at the Hereford Arms was just warming up. Oliver was standing by the bar when she came in. Even though he seemed to be making light conversation with the landlady about the quality of the house beer, he did not miss the exact second she came into the room.

"Why, hello, Jasmine!" he said quite loudly. "Glad you could come."

He pointed to the half-finished pint of beer in his hand. "I'm having a lager. Would you like the same or prefer something else?"

"Only an orange juice, please."

"How about something a wee bit stronger, just this once?" he teased, as if they had known each other for years, not minutes. "They have excellent cider."

"Got to work tomorrow, you know that. Can't afford one of my headaches."

"Oh well, one orange juice for the lady. We'll be over there."

As he steered Aviva to a table, he placed his arm across her shoulders. She did not flinch. Nor did she resist when, just before seating himself, he leaned over and pecked her on the cheek.

"Have you seen Charles lately?" she asked.

"Actually, I have. He sends you his best regards."

"Anything else?"

"I'm rather enjoying this. Do we have to get right to the point?" He smiled easily. Aviva noticed his teeth were not as unattractive as she had earlier thought.

"When are you going to Greece?"

"That trip might have to wait."

The landlady's daughter brought the orange juice and a fresh pint of lager to the table. Aviva kept up the conversation's flow determinedly. "That is a shame. I know how long you have been looking forward to getting away."

"Do you enjoy working for Cook's?" he asked.

"I like the people. You never know who will come through the door next. The routine work can be a bore, but once in a while I am asked to plan a personalized trip. Just last week, I prepared a fascinating itinerary on the overland route to India."

"How long does it take?"

"If all goes well, only about three weeks. In Kirkuk, you must motor between rail stations, and you can cross the Bosporus by ferry. It is supposed to be less trying than the sea journey, but I cannot say I would prefer it. The gentleman wanted an adventure and I assured him one was in store."

"I've spent some time in India myself."

"Your accent reminded me of someone I once knew who was

brought up there." Aviva stopped herself. Was Oliver's comment based on his cover story or was he revealing something true about his past? Should she draw him out or make it easier by going on to some less personal subject? If only there were an etiquette manual for spies.

Sensing her discomfort, Oliver kept up his end of the discussion. "On one occasion we went there by Imperial Airways. Ever hear of it?"

"Didn't they have the flying boats?"

"Yes. Magnificent planes. Very luxurious. They flew all the way from Southampton to Australia in nine or ten days, landing on water all the way. Each night we would arrive well before sunset and have time for a brief tour before sleeping in a hotel. It would take only three nights to reach Karachi."

"From where?"

"We got on in Palestine . . ." Aviva knew he was wondering if he had given too much away, but the moment passed. "It landed on the Sea of Galilee in Tiberias, then went on to call at Lake Habbaniya outside Baghdad, Bahrein, and finally, Karachi."

"How old were you then?"

"It was 1938. I was thirteen." Oliver grinned. His smile was slightly crooked, but charming.

Aviva felt that he was telling her a true story even though she was certain his name was a cover. "Tell me more about the trip" was all she said. He obliged by rambling on, which was perfectly fine with Aviva, who could not think of how to keep up her side of the conversation.

"It's time, gentlemen," the landlady called.

"I did not realize it was so late," Aviva said.

"I didn't either. This has been very . . . enjoyable." Oliver looked at her half-finished glass and his empty mug. "Do you want another?"

"No, thank you, but go ahead if you wish . . ."

"I'm ready. Can I see you to your door?"

"Yes, thank you."

Although the quickest way home would have been around Hereford Square, Oliver steered Aviva toward Gloucester Road, winding back through Brechin Place.

On the corner of Rosary Gardens and Dove Mews there were no other passersby. Oliver stopped and turned to face Aviva. "Do you think we might get along?"

"Certainly. If Charles wants us to work together . . ."

Oliver swallowed hard. "I'm pleased to hear you say that."

"Can you tell me any more?"

"About what?"

"Is this an assignment or another training session?"

"All I may divulge is . . ." A man walking a Yorkshire terrier rounded the corner. Oliver pulled Aviva to him and gave her a strong kiss on the lips. She did not resist. Posing as lovers was a typical ploy. Neither Oliver's nor her lips parted. How many times had she been warned that romantic involvements made you lose your concentration, which was the ultimate self-protection? But this was play-acting; this was part of the job. By the time the dog had finished its business and he and his master were headed across Old Brompton Road, they had been pressed together for several minutes. Oliver's hand capped her head protectively. A curious sensation stirred in her, but just as she tried to identify it, Oliver broke away.

"Are you free on Sunday?"

"I think so."

"We're supposed to meet again and talk. We're to be seen together. That's all I can say."

"At my office, too?"

"Yes."

"I do not work on Sunday."

Oliver laughed. "We don't have to do this all at once. But, actually, you're right. I need to go to Cook's to pick up my tickets tomorrow. I'll be certain to strike up a conversation with you."

"Fine. On Friday you can return and take me to lunch."

"You're rather forward, aren't you?"

"Just following orders." Aviva started walking up Bina Gardens briskly. Oliver rushed to keep up.

"And Sunday, how about Kew Gardens if the weather is fair. Have you ever been there?"

"No, but it sounds lovely. What time?"

"We can decide that on Friday."

At Aviva's gate Oliver behaved like an exemplary suitor. He stroked her cheek with the back of his hand and stared into her dark eyes so longingly anyone would have believed him thoroughly smitten. Aviva played along. This is not entirely unpleasant, she reflected. Oliver reached over and kissed her on the cheek.

"I'll see you tomorrow. At three-thirty exactly. You'll be at your desk?"

"Yes, certainly."

He closed the gate behind her. "Till tomorrow . . ."

"Good night," she called. At the door she turned back to watch him leave. Oliver remained standing by the gate. Silently he mouthed something. She looked perplexed. He did it again, this time exaggerating the movements of his lips. Aviva nodded she understood and repeated the word "Shalom" under her breath as she opened her front door.

Aviva arrived at Kew Gardens almost an hour early. She was to meet Oliver at the Palm House. Unsure of where to find it, she was determined not to be late. The afternoon after their first meeting he came by her desk as promised, flirted easily, asked her advice on Switzerland — a country for which she routinely wrote tours — and spent enough time to establish a visible interest.

When he departed, Aviva spoke to Adele Whitney. "That man asked me to lunch. Do you think I ought to go?"

"He's well dressed and polite. I've dealt with him several times and see nothing amiss," the older woman advised. "Besides, how much could go wrong at lunch?"

"I've never been asked out by a stranger," Aviva demurred.

"Can't see the harm in it. In fact, I recall he said something about selecting a tour on which he might meet other young ladies, so I don't think he's married, which is the worst sort of mess for a young girl, take my word for it."

"Do you know his profession?"

Mrs. Whitney looked up his file card. "Oliver R. Deacon," she read aloud. "He gives his business address as Ames and Anderson Imports on South Audley Street. Sounds respectable to me."

"Well . . ." Aviva's voice quavered deliberately. "We will go up Piccadilly to Richoux, and if I am not back by two you had better come after me!"

Friday afternoon she reported to Mrs. Whitney that the lunch had gone rather well. The groundwork was set. Oliver and Jasmine had been seen and noticed together. As she paced the paths at Kew Gardens, Aviva felt she was about to discover just what was in store for her next.

The March air was brisk, but the sky was remarkably cloudless. More families than she had expected had braved the chilly morning to stroll the park. Early spring flowers dotted the gardens. From the main gate she walked around the pond to where the vast greenhouse sparkled in the sunshine. Built entirely of iron and glass, the curved roofs seemed from a distance like floating apparitions. Once she was inside, the atmosphere was deliciously hot and moist. Aviva unbuttoned her coat and began to walk the perimeter. Long stalks of bananas were ripening on tall trees with fanlike leaves. Dates and figs seemed remarkably healthy in their manmade environments. In a few minutes she was sweating from the heat and removed her green cloth coat.

"Just as hot as Tiberias in summer!" Oliver said quietly.

Aviva started. Where had he come from? "You are early."

"So are you."

"I was afraid I would not find this place right off. Kew is enormous. Also, I thought the train did not run as often on Sunday."

"You're very prudent. I like that."

Aviva wondered what she should do or say next. "What's that stairway for?"

"Don't know. Let's make a thorough investigation." She followed as Oliver climbed up a winding staircase at the corner of the large central portion of the greenhouse. It led to a narrow metal walkway under the roof. The closer they were to the glass panels, the warmer it felt. Aviva was perspiring, but Oliver seemed surprisingly cool. At the opposite corner he led her down the stairway. "Let's go outside and talk."

Aviva followed Oliver past a sign that pointed right to the Azalea Garden and left to the Rhododendron Dell. He took a smaller, unmarked path past a row of leafing beeches and stopped behind one with a massive trunk. Leaning against it, he seemed remarkably at ease. If his clothes were better tailored, his hair cut in the latest style, his hat less worn, he could be considered almost handsome. Aviva decided she liked the man, if only because he was the first person in England who shared her convictions and circumstances.

He cleared his throat noisily. "The other night you said you believed we could work together. Do you still feel that way?"

"I do not mean to be unfair to you," Aviva began nervously, "but I would work with anyone I am asked to. It is not the people, it is the purpose."

"Well said." Oliver paused. He opened his mouth several times but words did not come. He looked around uneasily. Then he spoke in Hebrew. "Nobody can hear us and I cannot say all I need to in English. Is that all right with you?"

Aviva nodded. Even though his English was far more expert than hers, she understood the strain he was under.

"They want us to stay together . . . What I mean is . . . live together. This assignment calls for a married couple. They selected me to join you. But only if you find me acceptable. They want you to know that nobody will think less of you if you choose not to volunteer. I'm the easier one to replace here."

"Why?"

"There are more men than women in the business."

Aviva was shocked by the whole proposal, but she tried to remain calm. "If I say I do not want you, they will send another man for me to examine?"

"I think so."

She threw back her head and laughed. "It's what every girl dreams about."

"I wouldn't know . . ."

From the tightness of his voice, Aviva understood how inadequate he must be feeling. It was *he* and not she who was under appraisal and might be found wanting. The uniqueness of the situation was at once delicious and frightening. She felt a strange surge of power. She could send him away or accept him. If she accepted him, what would that mean? They would live together day and night as man and wife? Even share the same bed? And what else?

During their last two brief meetings she had cared only about fulfilling her professional obligations to meet him and be seen with him. The feelings she had the first time he held her had been transitory, and here in the glare of the sunshine, she could not recollect what had excited her. His body was not appealing. Nothing about him stirred the slightest romantic interest. If she required too much information before she could make her decision, she would be compromising his cover. But how could anyone expect her to live for several years with a man she did not know anything about?

Oliver had begun to encircle the tree, his eyes to the ground. There was an ordinariness about him that made him the perfect unassuming agent. She wondered how Oliver had sized her up when he had first seen her. Had he also been given an opportunity to get out if he had not liked her? Did his presence mean that he accepted her?

"What do you know about me?" she asked warily.

"I've seen your file. Most of the names and identifying aspects were blanked out, but I discovered you came from a kibbutz. I know about your war record —"

"Not my name."

"Just your file name and current cover name."

"May I know yours as well?"

"Which?"

"Your file name."

Oliver waited several beats. "Barak Har-Even."

"Har-Even . . . Mountain of stone," she translated. "Are you?"

"A mountain of stone? Hardly, but I was flattered to be given it. I've managed a fair amount, so I suppose that's why they chose it."

"Where were you?"

"In '48 I fought in the Galilee with the Carmeli Brigade."

Her eyes widened. Somehow he did not look the part of a battle-hardened soldier.

"I understand you saw some action too."

"I helped with the radio work."

"At Latrun," he said respectfully.

"How much do you know about my brother?"

"Not a great deal."

"Dan was my idol. He was a passionate member of the Irgun. When he was only twenty, he was captured by the British while on his way to attack an installation at Lydda Airport. They sentenced him to death by hanging for having wounded a British soldier as he attempted to run a roadblock."

"He was executed?"

"Yes. Along with two other comrades at Acre Prison. Everyone in the cell block sang 'Hatikvah' as he was led to the gallows." She brushed away a tear. "I am here to finish his work." She stared at him. He did not avert his eyes. "Can you tell me your name?" she asked impulsively. "Just your real first name?"

"I . . ." He hesitated for a second. "Gideon. And yours?"

"You honestly do not know?"

Gideon shook his head.

She sucked in her breath. "Aviva." Saying her own name aloud was tremendously exciting. "Aviva," she repeated. "Do you like it?"

"What difference . . . ?" he started to say, then sighed. "Very much, Aviva, very much."

"What else can you tell me? Where are we to go? What are we to do together?"

"I am not certain. However, I have my guesses. Your cover is half-Egyptian and you speak Arabic. So do I. It would be a waste to keep us in Europe. While I don't know *what* country, I would expect to be sent into deep cover in a hostile situation."

"It will not be Mayfair or Piccadilly? No more British lager?" Aviva grinned.

Gideon rubbed his hands together as if he were trying to stave off a chill. He walked twice around the tree while Aviva followed him, waiting for answers.

"Also"— he coughed —"I am to explain to you that headquarters feels it would be safer if we were married." He threw up his hands as if abdicating responsibility for the decision. "A family isn't as suspect."

"A family? With children and all that?"

Gideon shrugged his shoulders. "We couldn't be expected to come ready-made with children."

Aviva was silent. This was not to be play-acting after all. They would not just be co-conspirators doing an undercover job. They would not only pretend to be married; they *would* be married. The whole megillah! The service was certainly keeping with Jewish tradition. She glanced at Gideon, then turned away. Was this how an Orthodox Jewish bride summed up the results of matchmaking when she first met her intended? She felt the strange stirring once again. She wanted to be closer to Gideon, touch him, discover if she could tolerate his hands on her body, know for certain she would not be repulsed by his smell.

She offered him her hand. "What do we do next?"

He entwined her fingers tightly among his own. "You . . . you are accepting?"

"Are you disappointed?"

"No, but I expected you would want to think it over."

"I have. I am volunteering. It is not a permanent assignment, is it?"

Gideon seemed stunned, but his voice was composed. "I don't think there is such a thing."

"Yoffi." Aviva could tell she was beaming. For the moment she felt special, chosen, selected — by a man, by a profession. He must have had a hand in the decision. No one would ever force him into this position. She was wanted, needed — even desired. Wasn't this how any woman would have felt to be asked by a man to live with him, to be his wife, to bear his children? They had done away with the modern trappings of courtship; they had dispensed with the traditional parental approval. Their commitment was not eternal, yet their purpose was as lofty, as noble, as that of any two young people starting out on a life together. Not for a second did she feel she was being pushed into the alliance. All she wanted was to find a way to affirm her approval, convince everyone — Eli, Gideon, anyone else who would follow her dossier or write notes in the margins — that she was willing.

"So, what happens now?" she said. Her moist, dark eyes gleamed; her lips opened into a broad smile.

"I send my messages tonight. Then we wait for orders."

Gideon released her hand and offered the crook of his arm. She felt honored to walk by his side toward the main gate. Would there be a fresh identity or would Jasmine take Oliver . . . as her husband? Oliver/Gideon. The first name was so tweedy and proper, a bit intellectual, somewhat boyish. She liked it. The syllables rolled off her tongue easily. Ah, but Gideon was a name for the night. Gideon, who received a direct call from God to undertake the task of delivering the land from Midianites and Amalekites. Was this Gideon a man who spoke to God? Was he a balanced person, a kindly one? What were his skills? Why was he committed to Israel? He had spent a privileged youth — some special schooling abroad, travel on Imperial Airways to India. All this indicated wealthy parents. Who were they? Aviva longed for the answers, answers that would come only with time.

A wind was blowing off the Thames. Winter's errant leaves and sticks rushed recklessly across the dry grass. Treetops dipped and sighed uneasily. What must he be thinking? Is he disappointed he will be saddled with me? Maybe he sees it as an assignment, nothing more. If so, why this stuff about babies and families? Surely there are other ready-made alliances for this type of work. She sucked in her lower lip. Tears stung her eyelids. She turned away from him slightly. No, Israel was so young that few women had her depth of training. Gideon was making a brutal sacrifice.

They stopped in front of an outdoor café. "A cup of tea?" Gideon asked gently.

"Yes, thank you," she replied stiffly.

Aviva sat at the tiny white table and tried to compose herself. In a few minutes he returned with a full tray. He removed the cups and saucers and placed one squarely in front of her, the other across the way. His long, tapered fingers were pink with the cold. He poured the tea and offered the milk and sugar gracefully. He is considerate, neat, generous. He will be pleasant to live with.

"Yes?" Oliver cocked his head as if she had asked a question.

"I did not say anything."

"I know, but you want to ask me something. Don't be afraid."

"There is so much I . . ."

"We'll have plenty of time . . ."

"Well, I have a request. I do not know if you will agree and, if you do not, I will not insist."

Oliver's heavy-lidded eyes, slightly reminiscent of Eli's, closed slightly. "I'm listening, Jasmine."

"I would like . . . to do *it* properly. I would not want anything to happen to you — to us — because we were imprudent."

"What do you have in mind?"

"That . . . that we should be married — I mean truly married — under our cover names."

"Our passports are not intended to undergo extreme scrutiny," he pointed out.

"Who would bother . . . for a wedding?"

"It could happen. But I see your point. In fact, I should have thought of it myself. If we do it, will you feel happier about living with me?"

"I think so. We would be so much safer."

"I mean, will you be happier in your heart? You know, of course, nobody can order us to love each other — either spiritually or physically. If it happens, if we *both* want it, nobody would object either."

"I am not a child, Oliver," she blurted awkwardly. What had she meant to say? That she knew all about these matters — when she did not? Was she ashamed to admit her virginity? Or, did he already know? Did the medical section of her dossier have a notation: "Hymen intact"?

"We don't send children to war."

Aviva decided to concentrate on more practical matters. "If we get married as Oliver and Jasmine, it would be a civil ceremony."

"Wouldn't you prefer a rabbi?"

Aviva laughed so hard the tea sloshed out of her cup. "What rabbi would marry Jasmine to Oliver?"

"I was thinking of Gideon to Aviva," he replied seriously. "Isn't that what you would prefer?"

Aviva lowered her eyes to the table so he would not see them filling with tears again. He reached for her hand and stroked her wrist with only one finger. "I'll see if it can be done both ways. It is the least I can do."

7

There are three things which are too wonderful for me,
Yea, four which I know not:
The way of an eagle in the air;
The way of a serpent upon a rock;
The way of a ship in the midst of the sea;
And the way of a man with a maid.

Proverbs 30:18–19

SPRINGFIELD, OHIO: 1950–1951

"Hold those brakes! Tighter! I'll crank her this time, but one of these days you're going to have to do it yourself, sweetheart."

"Ah-ha ..." Charlotte managed to murmur a response as he placed the metal wheel chocks on the ground and set the prop at the angle to get the best compression stroke. Although she had been shown how to do it, the idea of turning a propeller was terrifying. All she could imagine was her hand getting whirled off when the engine caught.

"Prime her," Mitch called.

Charlotte gave the Piper Cub the two required shots; then Mitch pulled the prop nine times to advance the fuel into the cylinders.

"Clear!" he shouted. The first turn did not take. Mitch went back and reset the angle. The second died just as quickly. He reached over into the cockpit and adjusted the throttle. On the third down stroke, the whole plane seemed to lift up on its wheels and vibrate.

Swiftly, he pulled the chock cord to release the wheels and jumped into the rear seat — which was not as easy as it appeared, for he had to jackknife his body back through the horizontally split door while twisting around and swinging a leg over the control stick, making certain his feet were kept off the wing struts. The first few times Charlotte had tried the same maneuver she had found herself facing the wrong way with a leg dangling outside.

Click. Mitch's seat belt was in place. "Give her some juice and let's go!"

As gently as possible, Charlotte eased the power forward and concentrated on steering the Cub with her feet as they taxied away from the fuel pump. For a metal and canvas machine, it had a friendly feel. She had heard that planes had personalities. Some could be ornery, some malleable. The Taylorcraft she had flown in as a passenger in Israel had seemed more balky than the Cub. Maybe it was the smiling bear motif on the fin or the jaunty black lightning streak along the taxi-yellow fuselage that made the Cub seem less threatening. At least she knew the plane, a 1948 model with the new metal spars and a Continental engine, was loved and cared for. It was her instructor's most cherished possession.

"It's a simple machine. I don't worry about a lot of fancy gewgaws falling apart. Just look at the design of this gas gauge." Mitch had pointed to the cork float with a wire-rod level indicator projecting through the filler cap. "When you look out you see just exactly how much gas you have. You don't have to worry if the damn needle is sticking," Mitch bragged. She knew that the cork could become saturated and lose buoyancy, so she had been careful to check the fuel contents visually as part of her pre-flight examination.

Sitting on the runway at the Springfield Municipal Airport, Mitch talked her through the run-up before takeoff. "Rev 'er up to seventeen hundred rpm. Check the left magneto, next the right, then back to normal. Good. Altitude setting is ten fifty-two. Now what?"

"Watch out for traffic."

"How about carb heat?"

"Oh . . ." She reached down and pulled out the red-handled knob by her right thigh. "We lost a hundred rpm. It's okay."

"*Now* check the area for traffic."

She made a 360-degree turn.

"Righto."

Charlotte waited a few beats for further directions. When none came, she turned and looked behind her to where her ruddy-cheeked instructor was smiling broadly. "Shall I take off?" she asked weakly.

"That's what we're here for, sweetheart."

As she pulled back the stick, the dotted line of the narrow runway seemed to curve away in the distance. The noise of the propeller roared in her head. The smell of well-worn seats, the fuel and oil, mingled with Mitch's heavy scent of Old Spice. When she first met him, she had decided he probably sprinkled the cologne instead of bathing, but now she found the pungent aroma as comforting as the sight of his large sun-browned hands on the stick and his well-worn shoes bumping her hips on his set of rudder pedals.

Mitch was waiting. Taking off was not so bad, she consoled herself. It's the landing I have to worry about. Besides, he won't let us both die — this was her last thought as she forced her mind to focus on the mechanics of getting the plane off the ground. She slipped her feet off the narrow brakes, applied pressure to the metal control frames, and gently eased the rudder left and right as the plane glided forward slightly. Down at her right side she noticed that Mitch's familiar battered brown shoe was not on the pedal in the rear. I'm on my own, she decided.

Because she knew Mitch liked her to think aloud, Charlotte began her litany. "Right hand on the stick, left on the throttle, throttle slowly forward to full power." To herself she kept repeating: steer, steer, steer — not with your hands, with your feet. She continued down the runway's middle, making slow little "s" curves to glimpse what might be in front of her because the plane's cockpit was too low to enable her to see directly over the engine. She didn't expect to encounter any other aircraft, but a stray cow or dog was a possibility. The plane wobbled slightly from side to side, but as it picked up speed it became easier to maneuver. She had been warned how important it was to control the plane on taxi to prevent a dreaded loop from pulling a wing into the ground and flipping the plane. She held the joystick well back into her belly so the tail wheel could not lift off. Bravely thrusting the throttle all the way forward, Charlotte glanced at the air speed indicator. "Twenty, thirty, forty, forty-five," she called out. The nose of the plane began to climb at too steep an angle. Almost automatically, she made the correction, bringing the nose to the best angle of attack for getting over the trees without losing air speed.

"Good girl," Mitch shouted. "A little more right rudder. You must be in positive control of the aircraft at all times."

Charlotte jammed her right foot to the floor to curb the natural tendency of the plane to pull to the left during takeoff, but she overcompensated. The Piper was veering off course to the right — a minor matter for the moment. It was more important to watch the air speed and altitude. At four hundred feet above ground level, the plane was traveling the correct sixty miles per hour. She called out, "V-y. I'm going to best rate of climb," and tilted the plane's nose to a lower point on the horizon. As the wind rippled through the plane, a lock of hair blinded her momentarily. Mitch preferred to have the windows left wide open so he could "feel the flight," but Charlotte would have enjoyed the security of being closed into the contraption. Finally, she placed the plane on a due west heading and let out a long sigh of contentment.

❖   ❖   ❖

If only Eli could see me now, she thought. He was the one who had insisted she fly over Israel as part of her training, even though she was uncertain why. Perhaps it was another way to prove her courage and commitment, for the battered Taylorcraft at Tel Aviv's Sede Dov field had not inspired confidence.

From three thousand feet, the two population centers of Tel Aviv had seemed an isolated strip of civilization in the midst of the drab desert. But Jerusalem was a golden glow. For Charlotte, Jerusalem personified Israel. When she was near the city she felt religious yearnings she had never before experienced. Intellectually, the centuries of holy wars seemed senseless to her, but there *was* a magnetic pull to the place. Somewhere deep in her heart she believed it was the mystical center of the earth. The walls of the Old City encircling the spires and domes taunted her with their proximity. Less than three years ago it had been taken forcefully by the Arabs. The memories of the Jewish Quarter aflame, of the first wave of refugees crowding through the Zion Gate with smoke at their heels, were brutally fresh wounds. The fact that she could no longer walk the streets of the Old City was a personal loss.

Never before had the tiny nation appeared so vulnerable as it did from the air. In the small plane it was less than an hour to almost every enemy border. Roads, if perceived as escape routes in case of attack, were pitiful, meandering lanes in the wilderness. Arab villages on the highest slopes commanded the tactically superior positions.

"How frightfully small, close to each other, and indefensible it all is!" she had worried aloud.

"Good. Do not ever forget how easily Tel Aviv could be pushed into the sea or Jerusalem could be surrounded and cut off from supplies again," her pilot had replied adamantly.

As Charlotte stared down through the open doorway at the even squares of Ohio's corn fields, she was struck by the lushness of the land. But there was little time for sightseeing. She concentrated on flying the plane. The first few lessons Mitch had coaxed his set of controls gently enough to make her believe she was actually handling the plane. "You need to feel the consequences of your moves," he had explained during the last critique. "That's the only way you'll ever learn how to make the adjustments. Remember, flying is a long series of small maneuvers and corrections along each of the axes of the plane."

With increasing confidence she was following Mitch's commands to keep the plane at a given altitude and heading without needing him to touch the controls.

"Show me a power-on stall in a climbing turn with full power and the air speed dropping."

Charlotte swallowed hard and obeyed. The air speed disappeared into a region of uncertainty at the bottom of the dial. She held her breath.

"Remember, if you force it on, she may gently shudder into level flight."

The plane recovered beautifully. Once again Charlotte was comforted by the fact that the Cub's stalling characteristics were considered as safe as those of any airplane.

With intense concentration, she followed the course Mitch had set out for her when they were on the ground. He always kept a pair of binoculars for reading street signs in case of emergency, but already she knew the local terrain quite well. The air rushing by in the slipstream was cool and sweet. In the rear seat, Mitch was softly singing "Zip-a-dee-doo-dah."

At first she had been intimidated by the tall, lanky, tough-talking instructor. An Air Force veteran who had fought in Europe, Mitchell Landon was a local hero. When he returned to his hometown of

Springfield, Ohio, he married the first girl he impregnated, took a job as a farm equipment salesman, but felt content only when he was airborne. With thousands of flying hours on his record, he exuded the balance of easy confidence and technical proficiency that put even the most terrified student at ease. It occurred to her that Mitch might have been happier training a pilot in Israel to protect his homeland than a silly college girl supposedly seeking a thrill.

"I've taught a few of you Antioch girls before," he had said when she signed up for lessons. "They come out here and see Virginia Thomas, our local lady ace, fly like a bird and go wild. After two or three lessons, they quit. Never had one go all the way to a ticket. Maybe you'll be the first."

Just to prove she was different from the others, Charlotte wished she could. But she did not dare go through the official FAA paperwork under her cover name. All created identities were to be considered too flimsy to pass scrutiny by government agencies. She was using the birth statistics of a girl who had died in childhood. Her assignment had been to create a trail of legitimate information by establishing a college record at a small Midwestern school for a year. She was getting only average grades, since she was not supposed to distinguish herself in any way. For the same reason, she lived alone in an off-campus apartment outside the town of Yellow Springs, rode a bike so she would not have to register a car officially with the school or state, and kept to herself as much as possible.

She had chosen Antioch because some friends from Scarsdale had gone there and she knew the school's reputation for being liberal and innovative. Eli approved, particularly as Antioch did not have a Middle Eastern studies program and had few foreign students. This was important because it lessened the possibility of her meeting up with a former student later on in her career. Eli had especially liked the cooperative educational plan that required her to leave campus to work at a course-related job to gain practical experience. He had asked her to apply for one of the many library jobs available and had been elated when she received her first-choice placement: the Library of Congress.

Although her duties there as a "deck attendant" were of the most routine clerical nature, she managed to get herself assigned to the "U" and "V" stacks in the Annex, which housed the military warfare collections. An amazing array of government documents was readily accessible and she was able to secretly photograph those of strategic importance. Fortunately, Charlotte's superiors at the library had been understanding about her "chronic colitis attacks" that caused her to spend longer than normal periods in the ladies' room. It was there she took her documents to copy. To cover the time lost, she made certain to work late or arrive early — a diligence that was duly noted on her cooperative work report for the college.

Sitting on the toilet, her panties pulled down around her socks so she looked properly engaged through the bottom of the stalls, Charlotte would take out the latest government report on nuclear research or biological warfare and photograph it with the Minox camera she kept hidden in a pack of cigarettes. The documents led to a trail of other sources — none top secret, or they would not have been accessible to her, but all unavailable to the general public. Soon the Washington contact to whom she delivered the films became alarmed at the sheer quantity of the materials she was duplicating. Eventually, orders came for her to ease up, so she became more selective. Even so, she delivered an astounding number of technical books and scientific surveys.

The three-month job period had been sandwiched between study semesters on campus. Fortunately, Antioch had a loose system of basic requirements. The registrar had not blinked twice when her course load included Mrs. Nevshenko's Russian I, Mr. Federighi's Bacteriology, Mr. Knorr's Electron Theory, and combatives to fulfill her physical education requirement. In the privacy of the stacks she studied Egyptology, weaponry, and nuclear physics. While girls in neighboring carrels were lost in D. H. Lawrence and Thomas Mann, Charlotte was plodding through George Merck's reports in *Chemical and Engineering News* on "Peacetime Implications of Biological Warfare," Ellingson and Kadull's studies on "Cutaneous Anthrax," Bookwalter's "Streptomycin Treatment in Tularemia," as well as her regular survey of recent articles in the *Bulletin of the Atomic Scientists.*

Nobody at the college knew about her flying lessons, which she arranged privately. Eli had only told her, "You should feel confident taking off and landing a small, single-engine plane, charting a course from maps and physical features, plus typical radio communications for amateur flights. Cover your own radio experience — you are supposed to be an amateur. You can say that your uncle, I believe he's called Sanford Albertson or Uncle Sandy in your cover biography, took you up in his crop-dusting plane when you were a child. That will explain your interest."

"Righto!" Mitch shouted. "Take her around and get into the pattern."

Charlotte pushed the stick forward and began her descent to eight hundred feet above ground level. Apparently, she was too slow for Mitch. She felt the stick tugged from her control and the bottom seemed to fall out of the plane. They leveled off at eighteen hundred fifty feet. From the position of the cattle in a nearby field, she determined the wind favored runway five.

"Line up with the faces of the cows," Mitch had taught her as a joke. "But only if they're cooperating. Otherwise, check the wind sock. It's usually more reliable."

The view across the wing strut indicated they were in perfect alignment with the downwind leg of the runway. "Power to fifteen hundred rpm — speed to seventy," she called out.

"Bring her round sharp. Righto!"

Under his breath Mitch finished the chorus of "Zip-a-dee-doo-dah." Then he called, "Line 'er up. That's a girl. We have more of a headwind than last time. Add power. Righto! Good angle of glide. Add power . . ."

All of Charlotte's concentration was focused on keeping the end of the runway at the correct angle of sight. It seemed to be moving farther and farther away, so she continued to add power. At last she was on glide slope.

"I want those mains on the ground first. Your usual three-point landings are fine for babies, but you're ready to do it correctly." Mitch leaned close to her ear so she would be certain to hear him. "Bleed off the power and walk those rudders."

Charlotte pulled back on the stick until it was pressed against her stomach. Outside she could see the right wheel poised above the asphalt. Bump! The main wheels hit first. She inched the power back slightly and held the stick over to the downwind side to keep the aileron up. Bump! The tiny tail wheel touched down neatly.

"Nice! Keep holding that stick into yourself tightly. There's enough wind for us to lift off again at this speed."

She pulled the power back and concentrated on steering to the taxiway. "Shall we go around again?" she asked.

"Nope. You wore me out, girl."

"Was it okay?"

"Sure was. Tomorrow, you solo."

"But —"

"Tomorrow you solo!"

"Righto!" She beamed back. "Righto, Mitch."

⋮ ⋮ ⋮

At two o'clock the next afternoon Mitch Landon pulled up to her two-room apartment above a garage. Charlotte was out on the wooden stairway, looking up at the thundery skies. She did not think Mitch would expect her to solo in this sort of weather, but because visibility was above minimums, he might insist.

He parked the pickup truck. "Don't know about this storm," he called out. "Maybe we'd better wait a bit and see."

"Do you want to come up?"

"Righto."

At first that expression had grated on Charlotte. It seemed an affectation out of character with his flat Midwestern accent. "Where did you learn that?" she had asked.

"From a Brit I flew with during the war. That's the last word I heard him say. He had taken a hit and I'd asked if he was okay. 'Righto,' he radioed, then fell from the sky. Ever since, it just comes out. I'm glad. Helps me remember him: the best damn flyer I ever knew."

From then on Charlotte had been more tolerant.

Mitch stood on the landing outside her door and waited to be invited inside. For a man close to six feet four inches tall, his features were surprisingly soft, almost like a child's head on an oversized body. His wavy reddish-brown hair was cut military short, yet seemed permanently wind-blown. "Will you be disappointed if you can't go up today?" He ducked through the doorway.

"A little. I wasn't looking forward to soloing so much as getting it over with."

"Everyone's the same on that score. You never feel *ready* to solo, you just go do it. I wish you could've gone up today. Kinda breaks the momentum to have to wait another week."

"It might be a nice weekend."

"I've got to go to Cincinnati." He shuffled his feet uneasily. "My wife's cousin is getting married. It's a big family shindig."

"I'm sorry I don't have a phone. It would have saved you the trip out here."

"No trouble." He glanced down at the truck. "Do you think your landlady will mind my parking in front of the garage?"

"I don't think so. She doesn't have a car."

"Is she the kind that watches every young man who comes and goes?"

"There haven't been any."

"C'mon, Christy girl."

Charlotte turned away from Mitch and shrugged. "It's too far off campus." She kept her back to him and walked into the efficiency kitchen. "As long as you're here, do you want something to drink? I've got tea or Ovaltine."

"No coffee?"

"I don't drink it myself, and as I just told you, I don't entertain here."

"Tea will be fine. Lots of milk."

As Charlotte filled the teakettle, Mitch idly picked up a letter on her table. Noticing the stamps, he asked, "Who do *you* know in England? The Queen?"

Charlotte started slightly, but recovered quickly enough to answer smoothly. "A girl I met in Switzerland. She's living in London now. She wrote to say she's getting married. Funny, a few months ago she didn't even mention a boy friend, but ..." She stopped herself. There was so much more about Aviva's situation that she would have liked to share with Mitch.

"But what?"

"I wish I could go."

"We could fly there — the two of us — like the Lindberghs." He laughed uneasily. "Matter of fact, I've already plotted the route I'd take to cross the Atlantic: up through Nova Scotia to Gander, across Greenland, then to Reykjavik, landfall probably in Glasgow before flying on to London."

"Would you really attempt it?"

"In a minute, if I had the time and money. The Piper's not about to get us there. I'd want to modify one of those new Beechcraft Bonanzas with extra fuel tanks, a decent radio, and —"

"I hope you get to do it someday."

"It won't happen. Too much money. It's just a dream."

Charlotte felt her earlier intuitions had been sound. Mitch would have been happier in Israel than here. She brought the tea to the table and served it with some stale Oreo cookies. "It's starting to rain."

Mitch did not look up while she poured the tea. "Alice thinks I'm getting parts for the tractor. She knew the weather wouldn't be good enough for flying. She wanted me to take her to Dayton to shop for the wedding."

Mitch's face was tight. She touched his bronzed hand. He trembled. "I don't love Alice. You know that, don't you?"

Charlotte did not reply. She knew very little about Mitch. All she had done was check his credentials as a pilot. The fact that he kept his lesson plane at a small field near the college was all she cared about. It was important for her to stay away from the military types who flew out of Wright-Patterson Air Force Base. She had heard he was independent, low-key, and dependable. He had proved to be all three.

"When I came back from the war, I was a big shot around here. There were parades, parties, speeches. All the girls stood in line, felt it was their duty or something. The truth is I liked Alice Bridwell the least. She had a fresh mouth and those big bulging eyes — has to do with her thyroid or something and it isn't her fault — but when there's a baby on the way, you don't have any choices so . . ."

Outside, lightning cracked through the sky and the rain began to pound furiously on the side of the garage. "It's getting dark in here. Maybe I should turn on the lights." Charlotte stood up.

"No." He pulled her down on his knee. "Leave it this way. You look beautiful." He stroked her shoulder-length hair, which she had pulled back with a black velvet bow. She did not resist as he bent forward and kissed the cleft of her neck with a sweetness that made her shudder.

She wondered briefly if this was against the rules. Alliances while you lived under a cover were discouraged. They made you difficult to forget to at least one person and you left a trail. But a married man was not about to collect letters, mementos, evidence. On the other hand, even Eli would agree that a person could not live somewhere without making friends. You just had to be prudent and cautious. Who better than Mitch? What could be the harm?

Before she could think out what to do or say, he was kissing her chin, her cheeks, her nose, her eyes. He had not once touched her breasts or thighs. She wondered how experienced he supposed she was.

Her first lover had been Calvin, when she was at Vassar. Cal . . . the reason her father had sent her to Palestine in the first place. She did not even know what had become of him. Next had been Teddy, the Haganah boy who had been wanted by the CID. She had stayed with him at a safe house for several weeks, cooked and shopped for him so he would not have to go out. With nothing else to do, they had spent the time in bed exploring each other. Mostly, he had been pretending she was his girl friend from Haifa — he would call out her name at the most intimate moments. Yet Charlotte had never resented it. In truth, she had been thinking about Eli. Teddy and Eli were of similar height and size. All she had to do was close her eyes.

Except Eli had never been drawn to her. In fact, Eli was the only man she had ever known who seemed not to require intimacy. God knows there had been opportunities for them to get together, but he had always been scrupulously proper. Now she understood why. If she *had* slept with him, there would have been no way he could have chosen her to become a member of the Ezra group. She was more grateful for the opportunity than despondent about Eli. Her work gave meaning to the smallest of matters. Most of the other students at Antioch seemed so purposeless by comparison. They had no understanding of their place in the world and spent their time securing the most transitory of pleasures. And while Charlotte might not know where she would be next year or even next week, she knew she would be in the center of some action directly benefiting her people. Privately, she would admit it was her attraction to Eli that brought her into the service, but she had gone on to distinguish herself without him.

"Oh Lord," Mitch moaned. "Don't you know I'm in love with you, Christy?" He kissed her again before she could reply.

She pulled back and studied his face. His eyes gleamed with expectation.

"Don't you want me?" It was the question of a child expecting to be rejected.

"I think so," she whispered. There had been nobody she had desired since Teddy — except Eli. It mortified her to remember how once she had thrown her arms around Eli, only to be rebuffed — gently, firmly, with a silent warning to never again act so impetuously. The overpowering smell of Mitch's Old Spice drew her back to the present. She bent forward and returned his kiss. He nuzzled her breasts and she willingly unbuttoned her plaid schoolgirl blouse.

It was Eli, however, who occupied her mind. He knew everything about her, from the circumference of her ankles to her blood type, her I.Q., her ability to withstand heat and cold, her scores at target shooting, even her most intimate statistics. She would never have him, she accepted that, but she was devoted to him as well as the cause they shared and tried to prove it daily. But it was Mitch who was here, begging her to hold him, to touch him.

She let him guide her hand to his zipper, open it. He felt warm and throbbing. She wanted him. She wanted to be close to him, to somebody, anybody. She led him to the bed, and coaxed him through the initial clumsy motions.

Mitch was so excited by the sight of her body, he barely touched her before he was satisfied. "Sorry, so sorry, Christy girl," he apologized with kisses. In a surprisingly few moments he was ready again. This time he took infinite care to arouse her. For the longest time he suckled at her breasts while caressing her with slow circular motions along every inch of her groin. When he begged her to climb astride him, she found her body remembered the lessons Calvin and Teddy had taught.

Afterward, while Mitch slept, she felt supremely satisfied. Yet she did not feel she wanted more from Mitch, not then, not in the future.

Next week she would solo, next month she would be away from school . . . and where? Something was about to happen. From Aviva's letter she surmised her fiancé was more than that. She had spoken of moving to another country soon, of not writing so often. Aviva was on *her* way, that was certain. Charlotte's time had to be coming soon. Cautiously, she laid her head in the crook of Mitch's arm. His smell was of salt and sand and wind. Curving her body as close to his as possible, she drifted into a sublime half-sleep as his breath against her cheek felt like the most gentle of summer slipstreams.

8

Silver and gold are not the only coin; virtue too passes current all over the world.

> Euripides (484–406 B.C.E.)
> *Oedipus*, fragment 546

PARIS, FRANCE: 1950–1951

The phone in the Galerie Medina rang at two in the afternoon. Lily waved for her assistant to answer it. "Mademoiselle Schmidt n'est pas là. Elle reviendra après trois heures," Jeanne prevaricated easily. For security's sake, Lily had explained she was "avoiding an old lover," although her most guarded secret was the distinct lack of lovers in her past.

"Qui était-ce?"

"Un Monsieur Ivy. He will be in later this afternoon. Is that all right?"

"D'accord, Jeanne. C'est un ami."

So, Lily reflected, he is coming again. The last time Eli was at the Place des Vosges had been to approve the lease for the Galerie Medina at number twenty-one. It was to feature Middle Eastern antiquities, with the main collection being prime examples of Islamic art. Besides providing Lily with a cover occupation, it was supposed to act as a link to the Arabic community. At first Eli had disapproved of placing the gallery on the oldest square in Paris, but there were so many favorable aspects to the plan, the first being that the lease was owned by an English Jewish industrialist (who knew only that he was helping Israel in some way and never inquired further), that Eli had consented, much to Lily's satisfaction. She had worked for months to make the arrangements in accordance with the service's directives.

The building itself was one of the two-story originals built around the square in the early 1600s. All featured a like symmetry, brick and stone façades, and steeply pitched slate roofs pierced by windowed dormers. The gallery business was owned by a man called Assad Fahmy who traveled widely to acquire pieces for his collections and had homes in many countries. On the infrequent occasions he came into the gallery, he seemed satisfied with her work — though his comments were vague, his manner distant.

Lily had not been told the true identity or affiliation of her employer. Supposedly, he was an Egyptian art collector, but she suspected he was another Israeli agent. In almost a year of dealings, he had never let up on his cover story and she had never dared question him. A slip could have tragic consequences — not only in destroying an elaborate (as well as expensive) cover operation, but it might jeopardize her career.

"Jeanne, do you want to have your lunch now? I might have to go out with Mr. Ivy later."

"Oui, merci. Je passerai à la poste."

Lily nodded. Jeanne was working out wonderfully. Mousy-looking in her loose stockings, shapeless beige skirt, and unraveling sweater, she blended into the background easily and took directions flawlessly. Fond of stray cats and children, the art student had a heart that was too pure and experience too limited to analyze the subtle aspects of the gallery's purpose.

Several hours later, Lily checked the wall clock. It was almost three. Through the glass storefront window stenciled with the reverse of the words "Antiquités, Achats-Ventes, Décor Islamique" she could see him. Eli's back was turned away, but the shape of his silhouette and the streaks in his light brown hair were wonderfully familiar.

A buzzer sounded when he opened the door. She willed her expression to be pleasant, controlled. Her smile was deliberately impersonal. "Mr. Ivy, I heard that you had phoned. I am delighted to see you again." She hoped he was noticing how much her English had improved. "Are you in Paris for long?"

"I'm afraid not. A short trip on business." He looked around the tidy shop and nodded approvingly. "Is it going well?"

"We are specialists, so we do not have crowds to contend with. Mostly we appeal to the odd tourist who happens upon us searching the Place des Vosges for the ghosts of Richelieu, Victor Hugo, or, possibly, Madame de Sévigné. I'm pleased to say we are also building a reputation with the experts in the field because we are concentrating on quality. Would you like to see some of our pieces?"

"Very much." Eli strolled to the far side of the room and began to examine the antiquities displayed on spotless glass shelves. His hand hovered over a piece of pottery. "May I?" he asked before lifting it.

"Certainly. That is a particularly fine example of a loop-handled juglet from Jericho."

"And this?" He pointed to a delicate sculpture of a woman and a swaddled child, labeled "Cypriot Idol." "Cyprus?" he asked.

"Cyprus," she agreed flatly. She could read his mind. He was thinking, as she did whenever she saw the piece, of the mothers and children of Caraolas. She lifted a broken icon. The wood was cracked in several places, but the colors were rich. "This is a seventh-century piece found in a village in Middle Egypt. It is the latest piece we have for sale."

"What's the oldest?"

"It is difficult to say. We are beginning to acquire pieces from early Mesopotamia dating back to over three thousand years before Christ. The most expensive one is this calcite statue showing Gudea, one of the Sumerian kings, holding a vase. Notice how the water pours down his chest and arms with fish flowing out. It is supposedly a divine attribute — he is a lifegiver."

"How old is that one?"

"Approximately, from the year 2150 B.C.E., or more than four thousand years old."

"I'm impressed. Too impressed to even begin to wonder at its cost."

"It probably will wind up in the United States."

"They're the only ones who can afford it." His eyes flickered for a moment. Then he asked, "Can we go somewhere for coffee?"

"I'll just tell Jeanne. Would La Guirlande next door be suitable? It is fairly quiet . . . unless we should just take a walk."

"The café would be fine."

Lily was disappointed he had taken her up on the first suggestion. If he had something exciting to impart, he would have needed a more secure location. Frankly, the routine of days spent at the gallery and evenings at the art school was becoming wearisome. In the last six months she had accomplished very little. Oh, there had been occasional messenger jobs, although she had no way of knowing if she was performing a valuable service or just being tested for reliability.

"Bonjour, Yves," she said to the café's owner, who was always inviting her in for a Pernod after the gallery closed. Yves lived with a boy friend and was unabashedly homosexual, so he made an excellent, undemanding friend in the neighborhood. With the most discreet of glances he asked if her companion was of particular interest. As he pulled out her chair, she replied with a definitive lack of facial enthusiasm.

"I always sit here," Lily said by way of apologizing to Eli for the table beside the kitchen door. "It is the spot nearest the pastries."

Eli's laugh betrayed his nervousness.

"The chef makes the most marvelous cream filling — with a hint of ginger, I think."

Lily sensed Eli's eyes boring into her as she babbled on. Her cheeks pinked under scrutiny. She hoped her costume was pleasing him. She was dressed all in black: a woolen turtleneck, long pleated skirt, utilitarian tights, and scuffed boots. The total effect was supposed to be arty, yet not too outlandish. She did not care so much for the clothes as for the look. From a distance, she was unlikely to be noticed; up close she knew she appealed to customers who admired her svelte figure and delicate facial bones.

The clatter of forks against plates, cups touching saucers, metal chairs scraping against the tile floors, dominated the room. Voices carried well. One could tune into any nearby conversation. "Perhaps we should have gone elsewhere?"

"No, this is lovely, Nicole. It is *good* to see you again. You are looking so . . . healthy."

Lily absentmindedly rubbed a silver circle hanging from a chain around her neck.

"What's that you're wearing? A medallion?"

"A coin, actually. We have a large collection in the safe. It is probably the most profitable part of the business. I got the idea to wear it from an American who came in a few months ago. He looked like a cowboy and wore a big gold watch and a diamond ring the size of a walnut. He wanted to see only gold Greek and Roman coins in two specific sizes. He was very taken with the ones of Brutus represented between two lictors, which are incredibly expensive, and the smaller and even dearer gold stater of the Macedonian period."

Lily paused to order the coffee and pastries. "May I choose for you?" she asked Eli, but did not wait for a reply. "These are the best." She pointed out a cornucopia filled with chocolate and cream and a slice of hazelnut torte. "Trust me." As soon as they were served she resumed her story. "Anyway, the cowboy bought eight coins in all. The total bill was astronomical. He paid right then and there in U.S. dollars. As I was wrapping them, he blurted out, 'Aren't you wondering why I picked these?' To please him, I told him that I was. So he said, 'I'm going to have them made into buttons for my blazer.' "

"What a travesty!"

"At first I *was* shocked, but later I decided that they were as useful on his coat as tucked away in a vault. Too bad he was not curious about their history."

"So, that's when you decided to wear a coin also?"

"Yes. It seemed like good advertising. I had it banded in gold and given a loop so it could be worn without harming the integrity of the coin. The jeweler did not touch the edges, so it remains in perfect condition."

"Is it terribly valuable?"

Lily smiled playfully. "These are fairly common, although this is an especially good example."

"What is it?"

"A tetradrachm of Tyre. It was one of the largest four-drachm pieces ever minted and was widely circulated in the Holy Land." She hoped he had noticed she said "Holy Land" and not Israel or even Palestine.

"What are the symbols?"

"This side, which we call the *obverse,* or heads, carries the principal art design. Here we see a faded rendering of the Phoenician god Melkarth."

Eli suppressed a smile. "You certainly have the patter down."

"The other side, the *reverse,* or tails, was used for statistics to help identify it in terms of monetary value and place of origin. It is the one I prefer to show. Can you see it is an eagle standing on the prow of a vessel with a palm branch over his shoulder? The words translate as 'Tyre the sacred and inviolable sanctuary.' "

"Tyre? In Lebanon? It would be an interesting place to visit one day. There is supposed to be a well-preserved chariot-racing circus." Eli tasted a piece of his torte. "How old is it?"

"The cake?"

Eli grinned. "No, the coin."

Lily rubbed the coin thoughtfully. "From about the time of Christ, give or take a hundred years on either side."

"Aren't you hungry?" Eli noticed she had not touched her pastry.

"Yes, but . . . I guess I am surprised you are here."

"The reason is because I would like you to meet me in England next week. Our mutual friend is going to be married and she wanted us to make the effort, as she has no other family or friends there."

"Jasmine?" Lily was shocked. What did this mean? Was she resigning? If one of them dropped out before completing the training period, she would be wasting an enormous amount of the government's time and money.

"Exactly. She needs two witnesses."

"Does this mean she will be quitting her job?"

"At Cook's? I suppose so. I hear she'll be moving away from England altogether, but her plans aren't definite."

So, Aviva, or rather Jasmine, was being transferred within the service. But what would they do about her husband? Lily yearned to ask a dozen questions. "This is rather sudden. She never mentioned a boy friend in her letters."

"They were introduced by friends quite recently and they got on right away, I'm told. Some romances blossom effortlessly."

Lily was getting the point. Her lips tightened into a line. "That would never happen with me," she muttered.

Eli sipped his coffee and shrugged. "We're all different, aren't we? Do you think you could get away for a few days?"

"I expect so." She fumbled for her cigarettes and lighter in the pocket of her sweater. After three hard clicks the lighter flamed and she puffed her cigarette alight. "Would you care for one?" she offered belatedly.

"No, thank you. I'm cutting down."

Lily felt his eyes boring into her. She ground out her cigarette. "Excuse me for a moment."

In the toilet cubicle, she aligned the seams in her tights but decided not to use the Turkish squat facility. She was there because she needed a break from Eli. Her heart raced ridiculously. What was there to worry about? Eli was safety; Eli was her connection. To calm herself, she primped in front of the clouded mirror. Her hair was swept back into a loose bun, with wisps of pale blond curls falling around her angular face. She pursed her lips and grimaced at her image. She did look especially fine today. And the delicate whiteness of her hands contrasted interestingly with the starkness of her mono-chromatic clothing. Her cheeks were flushed. In the last few months, her flesh had filled out, especially in the arms and bustline, which this sweater definitely flattered. Parisian food, even the simple fare she could afford, had appealed to her far more than food in Israel, where rationing during the tzena, the hardship, had made it difficult to get decent meat or more than one egg a week.

Eli couldn't keep his eyes off her. Even when he was pretending to be interested in the artifacts, she knew he was staring at her body. She should have been flattered; she felt annoyed instead. In the last year, her life had just begun. No matter that it was an invented life, a past created by a Tel Aviv bureaucrat in a back office, it was a life of freedom and promise far different from any she had ever known. And if it grew distasteful to her, she could leave and resume her old identity anywhere she chose. As Lily Jaeger she could flirt with Eli all she wanted, but right now she chose to be Nicole Schmidt, and Nicole Schmidt was definitely not interested.

"Do you want me to show you the square?" she asked when they were outside.

Eli offered his arm. "Are you ready for a change?"

She paused in front of the Pavillon de la Reine. "Does this mean I will be called away too?"

"Not necessarily. We need to get you a radio. We want you to make regular transmissions. Do you see any difficulty in that?"

"No, my location is good. I am on the top floor and the place I would put out my antenna is already obstructed with wash lines. It would never be noticed. I keep to myself, so I am never bothered in the evenings and I never invite anyone home with me."

"It must be very difficult for you," Eli said.

"Actually, I like being by myself. If I did not, I would not be suited to this work, would I?"

They strolled quietly once again. After they had made one cir-cumference of the square, Eli steered her toward the Rue St.-Antoine. "You have done remarkably well. All three of you women have exceeded perhaps not *my* expectations, but those of the depart-ment."

"So, what happens now?"

"After the wedding you are to cease your correspondence with your Swiss holiday friends."

She waited a few beats. "This marriage ... Is it what Jasmine truly wants?"

Eli screwed up his face before he answered. "The marriage was the joint decision of Jasmine and her friend. We only asked them to consider a dual cover for the job we offered. We may have made a better match than we expected. It was *they* who decided on a real marriage under their true identities."

"I do not even know her actual surname, do I?"

"Not yet. But you are hardly a security risk. That is why we would like you to be one of the witnesses required by Jewish law. Other 'friends' will stand up for the groom."

"I am honored. Besides, it will be wonderful to see Jasmine again. For a while she did not seem too happy in London."

"That's all changed."

"So, they'll be married twice: under the real names and under their cover names as well?"

"Yes."

"Will they have the same passports?"

"That's a technical question I'm not at liberty to answer."

They were almost at the Place de la Bastille when Lily looked at her watch. "I have got to get back."

"You will be contacted three times in the next week. The first will have the information on the London trip. She will mention the wedding. The second will set you up with a radio. That person may have access to your flat, after handing you a book about Botticelli. The third . . ."

"Yes?"

"This will be somebody in one of your art classes. Be receptive. He will call himself Gérard."

"You said I wasn't going to have to . . ."

"He's happily married. But you will be spending a great deal of time with him, preferably at his studio. There is a new skill we want you to master."

"What is it?"

"The gentle art of forgery."

For a moment Lily seemed slightly startled. Then she threw up her hands and gave a deep, warbly laugh. "I will try my best." She stared at her watch again.

"You must go," Eli said reluctantly.

She nodded.

He could not take his eyes away from her.

"Will we meet in Paris again?"

"Only in London."

"Oh . . ." She reached over and kissed him hard on both cheeks. Before he had composed himself fully, she was crossing the Rue des Tournelles at an angle, hurrying to get back to the gallery as rapidly as possible.

Maître de la Mure devoted the first hour of his life drawing class at L'Ecole des Beaux-Arts to one-minute poses. Lily found this exercise excruciatingly frustrating. Methodical, minute feature-for-feature drawing was her forte. Rapid impressions of line and proportion eluded her.

In the large, drafty studio she took her usual position in the back of the room. By some never-spoken but inviolate code, one moved forward — or to the right or left — only if a position was vacated by a departing student. Even if someone was absent, it would have been unthinkable to step into his spot. Usually there were several vacant places in the front row, reserved for former students who came for refreshers, as well as established artists and friends of the professor. That evening Lily noticed a new man in the front row. He was shorter than she, with wide shoulders and a stocky, almost square frame. Some of the others gestured greetings when he arrived. A moment later the Eurasian model shuffled out, dressed in a dirty blue flannel robe and furry slippers.

Maître de la Mure clapped his hands. The sound echoed off the hard wooden floor and smudged skylights. "Let us not forget we are working for rapid impressions on the movements. Look for the direction of the figure, the general line; relate to the paper only so long as necessary to find a reference point. Permit your arms to align themselves with your eyes. Move with that line!" He gestured expressively. "Follow the body, not your crayon. Nature will dictate; do not dictate to nature." He jumped forward with his hands outstretched. "Free yourself!" Accustomed to the professor's volatile style, nobody in the front row flinched.

"I have asked Monique to give us very wide variations tonight. Three of your best sketches should be left for me to critique." He clapped his hands. "Mesdemoiselles, mesdames, messieurs — pouvons-nous commencer?"

Lily steadied the leg of her drawing board between her knees and centered the pad of cheap newsprint. From her work apron she pulled out two Conté crayons and a tortillon, a small rolled-paper stump used for rubbing and blending the soft crayons. During the first pose, the model was bent over as though washing her hair in a stream. Momentarily, Lily was transfixed by the pale yellow light reflecting off Monique's naked shoulders and the way her breasts drooped into elongated teardrops. She managed only to sketch in the curve of the back and the angle of the head, and start on the pointed tips of the protruding dark nipples, before the jarring buzzer sounded. She ripped off the top piece of paper and crushed it into a ball.

Holding the board steady with her left hand, the crayon poised in her right, she was alert as the model next arranged herself at the top of a short set of stairs with one leg up, one leg down. The muscles in the hips and buttocks rippled as the legs strained to simulate running. Before Lily put a single line on paper, the African student on her right had completed two versions of the figure.

Maître de la Mure, who was touring the room, had stopped to admire the black pupil's work, saying, "You have captured strength but lost the relationships between the angles. Look at the distance from the ankle to the elbow. Do you see it?"

The student nodded as the buzzer went off.

When the model struck the third pose, Lily was acutely aware of Maître de la Mure hovering behind her. As rapidly as possible, she tried to fix the main points of the figure, to draw lines to relate the head to the legs and the arms to the shoulders. Her Conté crayon curved for the knees and elbows, slashed for the legs. She did not dare to look down at the paper as she worked, since she knew the professor wanted her eyes to be forward.

"Zzzzing!" The buzzer announced the time for that pose had elapsed.

"Votre papier, mademoiselle," Maître de la Mure said severely.

She looked up at him, perplexed.

His hands were outstretched. "This one is quite interesting; I want it for my critique. But I am afraid if I do not take it now, I shall never see it." He gestured to the crushed wads surrounding her.

During the break between the shorter and longer poses, he called her to his easel. "Look at Mademoiselle Schmidt's knee," he said to those gathered nearby.

Lily lifted her skirt and everyone laughed appreciatively. Maître de la Mure, who had a sense of humor, waited patiently, all the while twisting his mustache. "If you can draw the knee, you can draw any part of the human anatomy. With only four lines, this drawing has captured the essence of the knee in movement. However, that is the only part of this picture worth discussing." He handed it back to Lily with a disdainful gesture.

Lily returned to her seat. "At least he liked *something*," the new man in the front row called sympathetically as she passed by.

She stopped and smiled shyly. "I do not mind the criticism."

"You are new here?"

"This is my second semester."

"Then you know le Maître by now. He was complimenting you."

"Yes, that is his fashion. I do better with the longer poses."

"Do not get too involved with the details or you are putting your own preconceived ideas on paper, not what nature is presenting you." The man mimicked the professor with wicked accuracy. "My name is Gérard Cousin, by the way."

"Nicole Schmidt." She shook his hand formally and headed back to her position.

Lily was all the way to her easel before she realized who this was. Gérard!

Only today, Eli had mentioned the name and here he was already.

For the rest of the class she was distracted. From her spot she had a good view of Gérard's drawing board. His figures were brilliantly formed and shaded. Often he did mirror-image studies on the same sheet of paper. How in the world could he manage such a perspective? Fortunately, the professor did not pay much attention to her work for the rest of the evening.

The class ended promptly at ten. Lily gathered her supplies quickly so she could get outside before Gérard and place herself in a position to make inconspicuous contact.

At the doorway to the studio, he caught up to her. "Mademoiselle Schmidt . . ." He touched her arm lightly. "Some of us are going for supper. Will you join us?"

She was supposed to say yes, but something made her want to pull away from him. What was it? A natural reluctance? Yes. She was not in the habit of going out with strangers. "I do not know . . ." she hesitated. "It is late."

"Have you ever been to Les Halles?"

"Only once."

"You *must* come with us. Jacques is an expert on the architecture. Elise and Annette are coming as well. You will be perfectly safe."

"I was not worried."

A fine rain was misting the streets. Elise, a very fat, very talented student, lifted her face to the sky and called out into the night, "The stars are anointing us with grace."

"Come now," Gérard said with mock annoyance, "don't carry on, or our new friend will think she has landed with a bunch of lunatics."

"Well" — Annette grinned mischievously — "hasn't she?"

Gérard put his arm around Lily's shoulders solicitously. "Do not mind them. After some soup and wine they always soften up."

During the ride in the Métro, Gérard asked the usual polite questions, but did not offer any information about himself. At Les Halles, Jacques walked along on one side, Gérard on the other. Down the dark, deserted streets Jacques whistled "C'est Si Bon" with bell-like clarity. As they approached the huge market area, Jacques clasped Lily's hand and rubbed it excitedly. "Les Halles has been on this very site since the year 1110."

"Jacques was an architecture student before the war. He knows facts like this about almost every building in Paris."

"Over there . . . near St.-Eustach" — Jacques pointed to a church — "was the market pillory where they exposed dishonest traders publicly."

"I wish it were in operation today," Annette commented.

"The buildings that exist now were built by the architect Baltard in 1851," Jacques continued in a louder voice. "The plans called for halls of iron girders and glass sides and zinc roofs. All ten of the original buildings remain standing. The most amazing part of the structure is underground, where there is a maze of store-rooms and passageways. Sometime I would like to take you down there."

Lily shuddered involuntarily. Ever since her years in the bakery cellar, she avoided being below street level. Even the Métro was so daunting she would walk a great distance to avoid using it.

Gérard sensed her discomfort. "Jacques was with the resistance. His cell operated out of Les Halles," he said gently.

Elise was leading the group down the gloomy Rue Coquillière to the restaurant. "The hell with iron and glass! You know what Zola said. 'Les Halles is the belly of Paris.' Let's eat!"

The restaurant was called Au Pied de Cochon — Pig's Feet. As Gérard opened the door for Lily, he whispered in her ear, "Hardly kosher, chérie!"

In the bustle of removing coats and hanging them on the brass pegs on the opposite side of the room, he was able to speak to her alone. "After dinner, say you take the Métro from Châtelet. We will talk then."

By the time the soupe à l'oignon, boudin noir poêlé, tarte aux pommes, and two bottles of vin ordinaire were consumed, it was past midnight. The winding streets of the marketplace were only beginning to come alive. Jacques tried to convince Lily to walk the produce stalls with him, but she begged off. "I have to open the gallery tomorrow. My assistant has a morning class."

"Which Métro will you take?" Gérard inquired.

"Châtelet would be best."

"For me, too. I will stay with Nicole. See you all again soon."

Gérard began to walk briskly away from the group. Lily followed him. After turning the first corner, he slowed. "Do you know Eli well?"

"Who?" The use of Eli's real name shocked Lily.

"Should I have said Mr. Ivy?" Gérard laughed heartily. "I am not a cloak-and-dagger type. I just help out when I can."

"What do you do?"

"I am a maître verrier. I repair les vitraux — the stained glass windows in cathedrals. Since the war, the demand is so enormous I can hardly keep up. Someday we would like to work on something for Israel. Perhaps they will build a great synagogue or memorial that will utilize my skills."

We? "You are married?"

"Yes. My wife's name is Hila. It means halo. I named her myself when we took Hebrew names after the war. Mine is Motti Bar-Joseph. When we are alone you must call me Motti."

"But . . ."

"It is all right. Ask Eli when you see him. You are supposed to relax when you are with us. I am to be your teacher . . . your friend too, I hope. Next time you must come to the house and meet Hila. I have been told we three have much in common."

"We do?"

"Hila and I were liberated from Auschwitz. Hila was pulled from a pile of bodies where she had been left for dead. An American soldier saw her foot twitching and rescued her. I met her at the hospital. I had only been there a month. They kept me busy in the crematorium."

"I cannot talk about it as easily as you. I am sorry. Also, I am not free to give you my name or other information. When I have been cleared . . ."

"I understand, although I am different. I would rather get it all out in the beginning. It clears the air."

Lily felt herself pulling away from Gérard or Motti or whoever he was. She did not care to dredge up painful memories. "How shall we proceed?" she asked stiffly.

"I will give you my address at Châtelet; come for Shabbes dinner, day after tomorrow."

"I may have to go out of town."

"No problem. There is a telephone in the hall. Just let us know."

As they approached the corner of the Rue de Rivoli and Boulevard de Sébastopol, Gérard reached into his pocket, pulled out a cigarette pack, and offered her a Gauloise. She took it before she noticed it was his last. "I do not want to take —"

"Please. I will buy another at the café across the street. Wait for me." Quickly, he rushed across the wide street and into a smoke-filled doorway. In the distance, Lily could hear the high-pitched pinging of the flipper machines. In her jacket pocket, she found some matches and lit Gérard's last Gauloise. The rhythmic sound of a police wagon's siren approaching made her jump. It was the same wail of the Gestapo trucks . . . the same piercing shrill of the van that carried her mother off into the night . . . She could not listen to that sound without images of terrified children flooding her mind.

Where was Gérard? He must have stopped for a pee. She would not mind one herself, but the cafés in this area were filthy. She could wait till she got home.

A woman was shouting, "Une rafle! Une rafle!"

What was happening?

There were shrieks from doorways up and down the street.

"Les flics! Attention! Les flics!"

Two black and white police vans converged on the corner where Lily stood waiting for Gérard. Before she understood what was happening, she was lifted on each side by uniformed policemen, carried to the back of the wagon, and handcuffed to the wall. She had the next to last place on the bench. A woman in a pink satin dress with a bristling black wig was shoved beside her. The policeman rapped on the sides of the vehicle with his matraque, or nightstick, and called out, "C'est tout!" Then he closed the mesh grating and locked it in place. As the van rumbled off, Lily saw Gérard running toward her, his hands outstretched in impotent supplication.

It took her only a few moments to recognize she had been caught in a periodic raid of prostitutes. She had read about them, even heard stories about students and tourists getting picked up accidentally. All she would have to do is show her papers and find someone to verify her identity. Sometimes it took several hours. She might be in overnight. Suddenly the enormity of the mistake was clear. Her papers! They would be scrutinized by the police. All the work in establishing her cover would be lost. It was not her fault — or was it? Eli would ask her what she was doing at one in the morning standing alone on a street corner well known to be frequented by whores.

As the police wagon — curiously nicknamed panier à salade, or salad basket — rumbled through the deserted streets, the prostitutes moaned and swore. At the corners and lights, they were tossed around so furiously they fell across one another. Tossed salad, Lily thought to herself. Now I understand the meaning of the word.

A few of the prostitutes made bets on how long it would be before their pimps bailed them out.

"My maq never takes more than an hour!" a buxom girl with torn black net stockings bragged.

"So long? What a cold fish," the girl next to her punned, because "maquereau," the French word for pimp, also means a mackerel. She rubbed her thighs. "I'd get too sore."

"I bet my Carlo will be there even before we are," a girl with voluminous breasts said confidently.

"Va te faire foutre!" the first girl, with bleached white hair, said obscenely. "Your maq's too busy fucking his newest number — the one who's just graduated from candy lollipops to real ones."

"Ta gueule! Shut your mouth!" Carlos's whore said as she attempted to slug her opponent with her free hand. The space between the rows was too far, but on the arc back, the girl's fist slammed Lily in the nose. Blood dripped down her chin.

"Now look what you've done!" a tall black girl shouted. "Salope! Slut!"

The girl who had hit Lily was instantly apologetic. "Sorry, chérie. You don't belong here, do you?"

The blow had weakened Lily's reserve. Tears flowed. "I am an art student. I was waiting for my friend to pee."

"You'll get out. We'll tell the police. We know all the guys. Right?" she called to the girls in the van. "What's your name?"

"Nicole."

"I'm Simone. Stick with me."

The van pulled up to the Commissariat de Police. The officer who had locked them up undid the handcuffs. "Let's go. Allez! Allez!" He prodded Lily forward. When he came to Simone, he helped her down, then goosed her playfully. She giggled and reached for his genitals.

Inside the station, Lily could see the handkerchief over her nose was soaked with blood. Simone marched forward to the officer at the desk. "You guys made a big mistake!" She pointed to Lily.

The police clerk looked up. "Bon Dieu! Poirier! You damaged the merchandise. Can't you be more careful with those matraques?"

"Nobody laid a hand on her!" the officer who arrested Lily said defensively. "She must have bounced around in the truck."

"Is that what happened?" the police clerk asked Lily directly.

She was crying, this time not from fear or pain, but because she decided it was the most sensible way to behave under the circumstances. "I . . . fell into . . . one of the girls . . ." she choked.

"Call the matron and get her cleaned up. When she's ready to talk, bring her to me."

As Lily was taken away, Simone winked. "Don't worry."

In the washroom, Lily was searched and permitted to use one of the open stalls. The matron watched her every move. Lily had to urinate so urgently she could not care less. As she washed her face and checked her nose, she remembered the last time she had injured her face. She had been cut when she fell out of the pipe at Leukerbad. As she trembled at the memory, her nose began to bleed afresh. The matron handed her some shiny toilet paper, which did not absorb at all. Tilting her head back, Lily pinched her nostrils tightly and cursed her luck. Both times she had been unwittingly trapped by circumstances: the murder in the baths and now a routine roundup of prostitutes. Was she jinxed?

One of her instructors in Tel Aviv who was a veteran of hundreds of Haganah exploits had told them stories of just this sort of coincidence. "Traffic accidents, flat tires, sudden storms, airplane delays, unanswered telephones, incorrect addresses — all the stuff that makes for amusing anecdotes in ordinary life can become a matter of the gravest consequence in our profession. Never forget: we are not immune. Every plan must allow for just such contingencies."

Contingency plans. She had none. The authorities were going to require verification, but whom could she call? Eli was in Paris, but had not told her where. Gérard had not had time to give her his address or telephone number. Jeanne lived with her mother in a suburb; to have the police call there would create unnecessary suspicion with her family. Monsieur Famhy was supposed to be out of the country. Of course, she had emergency contacts, but using them would indicate she was in so much trouble she could not handle it on her own. She could imagine the phone call to the Israeli agent manning the lines in case of dire disaster. "This is the police. We need you to identify Nicole Schmidt." Impossible!

Who else was there? She had only a few acquaintances and no true friends in Paris. All she needed was someone who could vouch that she *was* Nicole Schmidt. Her concierge? No. With a transmitter arriving soon, Lily could not afford to have her confidence undermined. A student would be best — someone like Elise or Jacques — but she had no idea how to locate either of them, since she did not know their last names. There had to be some acquaintance from the art school with a listed telephone . . .

When Lily returned from the washroom, she saw Simone's pimp holding the prostitute's hand. Lily could hardly believe he was wearing a shiny black suit with wide lapels, a floppy felt hat, pointed shoes, and a garish silver-and-white-striped tie. He looked as though he had stepped out of a movie.

"Simone said I should pay the fine for you too. Might not be a bad deal . . ." he offered in a slippery voice Lily found disgusting.

"Idiot!" Simone shouted at him. "Don't you know how to be nice to a lady?"

"Only trying to help." He shrugged.

The officer at the desk gestured her forward. He asked for her papers. After scanning her I.D. and student card, he said, "Merde! You are going to take longer to process than an actual putain! If I didn't have you on the manifest, I'd let you walk out of here. Who can you call?"

"I do not know very many people. I am new in Paris."

"Someone where you live?"

"The concierge has a dirty mind. She would throw me out."

"Someone at the school? A friend?"

"I know very few —"

"One of your teachers?"

"There is Maître de la Mure. I was in his class tonight, but I do not wish to awaken him."

"Put her upstairs in the commissaire's office and lock the door," he said to the matron. "I won't awaken your professor until seven. Will that be satisfactory?"

"Oui, merci beaucoup," Lily said weakly as the woman with rough hands led her to the police superintendent's office.

She lay down on the cracked leather couch and closed her eyes. Another siren-blaring vehicle was approaching. The smell of rancid hair oil and old shoes gagged her. She covered her swollen nose with her fingers to block the odor. Her imagination raced on uncontrollably. Who had sat where her head was now? Overweight politicians with shiny rear ends? Young girls bargaining with their bodies for lenient treatment? Tearful lost children? Lily's breath became heavier and slower. Her pulse throbbed between her eyes. Tossing fitfully, she dreamed of other lost children whose tears no longer flowed, of other women spreading their legs for a day's ration, of police truncheons cracking faces into pulp and bone, of evil sirens slicing the silence of the night.

9

The beginnings and endings of all human undertakings are
untidy.

John Galsworthy (1867–1933)
Over the River

TEL AVIV, ISRAEL: APRIL 1979
Less than a week after the explosions at La Seyne, the body of Asher
Ze'evi was laid to rest in Rehovot. The victim of an "unfortunate
automobile accident en route from Basel to Freiburg" was brought
home in a sealed coffin after considerable difficulty with documentation and garbled explanations as to the actual cause of the collision.
At the funeral, some whispered the professor had had a heart attack
and lost control of the vehicle; others shared the rumor that he had
had too many beers with friends at the university where he had been
attending a conference. Esty, his widow, vented her grief by attack-
ing the Israeli authorities, who were tardy in reporting the news of
her husband's death and further frustrated her by making it difficult
to import the body until a seemingly infinite number of official
forms had been processed.

One by one the departing mourners placed a pebble of remembrance on the freshly covered grave. Ruth Short turned to Hugo and
shuddered. "Such a waste, such a tragic waste."

"Yes, I agree." He touched his wife's cap of snow-white hair tenderly. "He leaves a legacy of scientific accomplishments."

"And three fatherless children." Ruth sobbed openly.

"Ruthy, they're all grown, with families of their own."

"Whenever a parent dies, you're orphaned . . . at least in your mind." She wiped her eyes. "I wish Eli could have been here. His office says he's out of the country. All they would do is take a message. But after a week, you would think they could have located him, at least for a family emergency."

"Asher was just a cousin by marriage. They would not have considered him immediate family."

"Stop it!" Ruth swallowed hard. "I hate it when you're so rational. Why did Eli choose such a lonely life? Why didn't he ever . . . ?"

"Ruthy, please . . . not now." Hugo led her to their car and drove back to Jerusalem saying as little as possible. Exhausted by her grief, his wife fell asleep. And Hugo occupied his mind counting the kilometers until he could get home and pour himself a most necessary Scotch.

❖　❖　❖

Eli, who knew full well about the funeral in progress, was only forty kilometers away, staying as a "guest of the government" at a secret debriefing center near Herzliya. Alex Naor had sent Albert Conrad to accompany Eli to Israel and to make a full report to headquarters on everything he said and did.

Initially, Eli had been questioned in a familiar manner designed to efficiently elicit all information about the more successful aspects of the French mission. Indeed, the explosive charges had, for the most part, done the intended job, although it was hinted that more powerful ones could have inflicted greater damage. First reports indicated the damaged parts could be replaced in less than two years, so this hardly constituted a major setback to the Iraqis' becoming a nuclear power. Nevertheless, the final phase of the plan, which involved manipulating world opinion on the explosions, had proceeded better than expected.

On his third day back in Israel, Eli was taken to a briefing, led by the long-term associate whom he had first met in London as Saul and today knew by his Israeli name: Ehud Dani.

Dani stood at a lectern in a tightly secured underground war room. Completely bald except for a silver fringe that contrasted with his leathery-brown neck and shiny bronzed pate, he was wearing loose-fitting khaki slacks and a military-style jacket. When all the visitors were seated, he began his remarks in a hoarse voice that Eli attributed to the more than three packs of harsh Israeli cigarettes he smoked daily. "As you already know, gentlemen, stories began to appear in the popular press the afternoon following the incident. These ranged from accusations that a group was attempting to steal elements from the core to the claim the Iraqi equipment was destroyed in order to — and I quote from a Swedish wire service — 'neutralize dangerous weapons for the sake of the future of the human race.' "

Dani paused to light a cigarette. "Spokesmen for the French DST security forces have issued a statement doubting the guilt of the French ecology group that is claiming responsibility. Of course, the Israelis were mentioned as 'the most professional likelihood,' yet other suspects range from Libya's Colonel Qaddafi to the CIA."

"Could you clarify?" asked a man wearing a general's uniform with the combat intelligence insignia.

"There is an article in *Le Point* suggesting the CIA wanted to avoid nuclear proliferation in a strategic zone. It was the most far-fetched of the editorials."

"What are the links to Israel?" a man in a black T-shirt and tan shorts asked.

"Some highly regarded reports suggest that scientists from the French Nuclear Energy Agency supplied us with assistance because they were concerned about the Iraqis' goals for the reactor. In fact, the *International Herald Tribune* goes a step beyond, hinting that French secret service officials decided it was not in the best interests of France for Arab nations to have this reactor, and the clandestine approach, which, by the way, could be blamed on fanatics, was the best way to control a complicated diplomatic situation without harming French-Iraqi relations. Any further questions, gentlemen?"

The meeting continued for most of the morning. It was decided to promote press coverage on the consequences of an Arab state acquiring the bomb because world interest was currently high on the subject after Toulon.

Finally, Dani asked the general to read the statement that he would deliver at a forthcoming press conference. "If anyone in the world is likely to use atomic weapons pre-emptively, it's Iraq," he began. "The scenario might begin with Iraq getting the bomb first; then the Russians would feel they must give nuclear weapons to Syria because they are frightened of Iraq ..." The general concluded with an impassioned plea: "The civilized world must not be so shortsighted as to deal with the devil in order to keep the oil flowing today."

Before they adjourned, Eli departed by a side door and walked out onto the grounds, which were disguised to look like those of an ordinary military facility. High above a main artery to Tel Aviv, the site had once been a British depot. Its legacy remained in the form of rows of fragrant eucalyptus planted as a windbreak as well as a natural fence, and the long wooden barracks, which had been oiled into burnished brown. Eli strolled past the guard at the gate, who, seeing him coming, straightened up and repositioned his M-16 rifle. At the far end of the compound were fairly recent concrete and glass structures framed by a high electrified fence. On their roofs were a forest of antennae, communications dishes, radar receivers, and other mysterious twentieth-century electronic fortifications. Nearby, three men stood beside a helicopter pad talking among themselves.

It was too hot to remain in the fierce sun any longer, so Eli made his way back to his room in the one-story barracks building that had once housed British officers. A hole in the wall where an air conditioner had once been installed had been rudely covered with plywood. Inside, the room was furnished with a cot, a thin foam mattress, and the usual three olive-green blankets issued to soldiers. Yesterday, one of the women staff members had graciously brought two sheets and a pillow for his comfort. Only women in the Israeli army were permitted the luxury of linens. Must remember to thank her, Eli told himself as he opened the creaking door and went inside. A luncheon tray had been delivered while he was out. He stared despairingly at the soggy salad, pita bread, and container of yogurt. The coffee in the cup was cold and bitter, but it soothed his scratchy throat momentarily.

Above him a chocolate-brown Bell 205 helicopter was coming in for a landing. He stepped outside in time to see a smoke bomb being lighted to give the pilot a fix on the wind direction at ground level. As soon as it was down, it was surrounded by armed soldiers. A blindfolded man was led onto the field. His hands were bound behind him with plastic fasteners for handcuffs. Where had he come from? Lebanon? He must be a fairly big PLO fish to warrant such special attention. This place probably has a high-level interrogation center somewhere on the grounds, Eli decided.

He walked back into his boxlike room and sat down on the bed. The rotors of the helicopter began to whir again. Those huge dron-

ing monsters had always seemed to Eli like modern-day re-creations
of Ezekiel's wheel.

"A noise of a great rushing . . ." Wasn't that what the Bible said
about it?

As Eli recalled the tale, Ezekiel was taken up and away, but he
was not pleased about it. "I went in bitterness, in the heat of my
spirit . . ."

In bitterness . . . Eli recalled as he lay down on his bed and closed
his eyes. Is this what it has come to? He had seen others in the Mossad fall out of favor. He had lived through the great crisis of the
Lavon affair, the German scientist's debacle that resulted in Isser
Harel's defeat, as well as the changes in style the Mossad had undergone with different leaders: from the familial approach of Guriel to
the brilliant but disorganized leadership of Shiloah, to Harel's hu-
manism and Amit's military approach. He had survived them all by
attending to his tasks with great diligence and originality. Already
his Ezra group had become the stuff of legends. Only one of his operatives had ever been caught. Besides that tragic case no other identity had ever been revealed. While Aviva, Lily, and Charlotte had
surely paved the way for other women, they were each acknowledged to be top-flight agents with as many successful and daring
missions to their credit as any man in the Israeli secret service.

Years ago Guriel had warned him, "If you remain with me, you
will never taste glory. Nobody will ever know what you have done
for Israel." He had understood and willingly agreed. Guriel, however, had been wrong — he had *had* the glory as well: there had been
the incredible amount of information the Ezra team had acquired
over the years . . . his assistance in the Mirage blueprint project . . .
the Iraqi MiG . . . All he had to do was recall the planning and brilliant execution of these missions to feel noble and heroic *inside*. He
admitted he had a bit of a Sydney Carton complex. A far, far better
life had been his than the vapid, useless ones of those around him. As
he had told his operatives, "Whatever works for you is fine. For me,
the final results of my work — though intelligence secrets — have
given me more satisfaction and meaning than a thousand public
awards would have."

Eli gritted his teeth anxiously. Without being told, he was aware
that he was not free to leave the government "guest house" facility.
His family did not know where he was, nor could he join them in
mourning Asher, though he silently had said the prayers for the
dead, both morning and night, since he had found the body. Nobody

in the Mossad would suffer Asher's death more than he. He could not be punished further. At least he would have expected some cheering, some sense of victory on the completion of the rest of the mission. Based on the morning's conference, it appeared the political ramifications were turning out even better than predicted, yet nobody had congratulated him — not even with a silent smile, nod of the head, or extra-firm handshake. The mood around him was sour. One look at this pathetic room and meager luncheon tray was evidence enough that he was in disgrace.

He stared out to the distant blue line of the Mediterranean, which had become smudged as the khamsin blew across Israel from Jordan to the east. Already the sky was the color of cement. The air was so dry, moisture was sucked from the skin. Eli remembered his mother rushing around berating him to drink more water when the sandy winds started to howl. Even though the dingy room would become unbearably hot, Eli closed the shutters against the swirling grit that was settling like a nasty blanket on every exposed surface.

A knock on the door startled him. "May I come in?" It was Ehud Dani. Eli graciously offered him the only chair and sat on the bed.

"A bit early for the khamsin, don't you think?" his visitor asked.

"I remember them more in January, but those were from the west and eventually brought rain."

"They've seemed more frequent in recent years. I wonder why," Dani said amiably.

"Perhaps because we're older, less tolerant. After all, khamsin means 'fifty.' "

"Fifty days out of a year. That's about one day out of seven. It doesn't seem we have them that often."

"They're all bunched together. Not spread apart."

"Perhaps in the desert they have fifty full days."

"Maybe," Eli said flatly. He was annoyed by the ridiculousness of the conversation.

Dani took out his customary pack of Broadways and gave a slight shrug, which was supposed to suffice for "Do you mind if I smoke?" The air was so unbearable to begin with, Eli would have preferred to do without the acrid tobacco smell, but he did not object.

"So, this is a long way from a flower shop at Covent Garden." Dani's tone was almost that of a professor talking to a prize pupil — yet not quite. He stood, walked over to the window, opened the shutters, and peered out as a helicopter landed.

"Another prisoner?" Eli asked evenly.

"What do you mean?" Dani turned around sharply.

He thinks I am talking about myself, Eli realized. He gave a wry smile. "The last one delivered a hooded man. Looked like PLO to me."

"Don't know about that. This chopper's for the general. Do you want to look?"

Eli remained where he was. All at once a huge blast of sandy air blew into the room. Dani closed the shutters with a bang. "Sorry!" He choked and coughed as he brushed himself off. Eli's bed was now gray with dirt. He leapt up and shook off the top sheet and pillow.

Dani touched his shoulder. "Listen, we need to talk. I'm assigned to your case."

Case? Eli bristled at the word. Since when had he become a case? "What would you like to know?"

"Sit, sit . . . We should be comfortable. Why don't we commence with the Friday-the-thirteenth matter? It went through your department, did it not?"

"I've made that connection already. I even discussed it with Alex in London before I left. You must have the report."

"Let us examine the facts together — unless you object."

"No, I'm just weary. I've often wondered whether we acted too severely in Paris last year."

"You believe *this* action might be the reprisal?"

"Partially. It's difficult to explain —"

"The explanations will follow the events. Do you want to start or shall I?"

"You might as well." Eli leaned back on the wall and watched Dani light another cigarette.

"Your group had been following the career of Ibrahim El Setouhy for some time. The reports go back to the early 1950s when your operatives discovered him at the University of Alexandria — is that correct?"

Eli nodded. Charlotte's work . . . So meticulous. She had ferreted out many of the German and Arab scientists who had been the core of Egypt's nascent nuclear industry.

"He went on to lead a group at the Egyptian Nuclear Research Center in Einshas until the budget cuts during the late sixties and early seventies were a sign that Egypt had, for the time being, renounced the nuclear option. Then he disappeared for a while, didn't he?"

"I picked up his trail in France." Or rather Lily did. "We had an intermittent surveillance aided by insiders' reports on visiting scientists of special interest. El Setouhy's name appeared in connection with his trips to the French Nuclear Center in Saclay, where, as you know, the French seventy-megawatt nuclear reactor, the model for the Iraqis' Tammuz project, is located."

"When did you begin to suspect his high-level appointment?"

"His travels led us to most of the suppliers: Technicatome, the designer of the building and the reactors; COHSIP, the installer of the electrical and control systems; Bouygues Offshore, which specializes in nuclear plumbing; Société Générale Techniques Nouvelles, the experts at the running in of hot facilities; and, of course, Constructions Navales et Industrielles de la Méditerranée for the metal coating of reactor pools and construction of the cores. Thus we deduced he had been given a supervisory role."

"In your report last June you suggested that Iraq's employment of key scientists such as Ibrahim El Setouhy would advance their nuclear capabilities for both peaceful and military uses significantly. Am I correct?"

"What good does it do to bring all this up now? I made a recommendation. You know I had no responsibility for what followed, nor would I have condoned it if I'd been asked for an opinion, which, I might add, I was not!"

"Suddenly you are crying over one life?"

"The killing of scientists, ours or theirs, is not my idea of a defensible action."

"What were you expecting? Voodoo dolls?"

"In the past, we have dealt with these matters more subtly. Swiss bank accounts are great equalizers."

"How do you know that wasn't attempted? How do you know what truly happened? After all, you had nothing to do with the Friday-the-thirteenth operation, did you?"

"No. I was asked only to suggest someone from my team who could identify El Setouhy."

"The American."

"I don't even know for certain if she —"

"Eli . . ." Dani pressed his cigarette butt into the soiled coffee cup for emphasis. "You knew everything about that operation."

"Not from the inside. On four occasions my group followed him in France. On his last trip, we got wind of the fact that El Setouhy had checked out the shipment of the first twelve-kilogram load of ninety-three percent enriched uranium and had meetings with the Centre d'Etudes et Recherche Baghdad boys in Paris. One of our highly placed (and I presume highly paid) CERBAG informants warned that the Egyptian scientist had completed his assignment in France and would be moving to the Tuwaitha complex. Signs that this was imminent were verified by my staff, who observed him doing extensive shopping for his family: lingerie, toys, wines — that sort of thing. Since he would soon be out of our immediate reach, we passed the intelligence on."

"And two days later . . ."

"I am uncertain what happened. You probably know far more than I do." Eli's blue eyes blazed a challenge.

The details of the case were extremely muddled. He had known little more than what appeared in the press or was discussed semi-officially. Although some were certain the Egyptian scientist's blood was spilled by agents of the Mossad, others argued the Israelis would have finished the job more efficiently.

The facts were these: Ibrahim El Setouhy had returned to his hotel room on the fourth floor of the Royal Monceau on the night of Friday, October 13. Before retiring, he had been approached in the bar by Francine Mayenne, a young woman known to provide special services to male guests. (Mademoiselle Mayenne's report took on additional significance when she was killed in a hit-and-run accident less than a month later.) In her original story to the police, she had accompanied the scientist to his room. At the door he reluctantly rejected her offer but gave her a small tip anyway.

"A sweet little man, he did not want to hurt my feelings," she recounted. "Afterward, I went to the elevator and stopped. I was thinking I should not take his money and started back to return it. When I reached the door, I almost knocked. Maybe he just needed coaxing. You would be surprised how many men are like that. I changed my mind when I heard voices. Maybe a woman was there already? I wondered. But no, it sounded like two men. They were speaking loudly, but not in French. So, it's like that, I decided. He does not prefer women. All of a sudden, I did not mind keeping his money . . . until I heard what happened."

Saturday morning the chambermaid ignored the DO NOT DISTURB sign and walked into the room to find the Egyptian scientist on the floor between the two beds. Blood was spattered everywhere. His head had been beaten into an unrecognizable pulp. After an exhaustive investigation, the French DST could find no one to charge in the murder. The motive was debated as possibly sexual or criminal or romantic or political. Only robbery was excluded, since his wallet contained over twenty-five hundred francs. The sheer brutality tended to rule out the work of a professional.

Eli believed that Francine Mayenne had been hired by the Mossad to place the scientist in a compromising position to prove to the Iraqis he was too much of a security risk to be trusted on the Tammuz project. Similar tactics had already been successful with certain Italian and French scientists. This would leave El Setouhy even more vulnerable to a substantial monetary offer to cease working for Iraq. The man in his room might have been the Mossad agent ready to offer him a deal, and if the scientist had been surprised and had tried to attack the intruder, a murder might have been inevitable.

"I have never understood the mutilation."

"There are two explanations: first, that the intruder was a Syrian photocopying documents in El Setouhy's room to learn how far the Tammuz project had progressed."

"Or?"

"That a certain degree of doublethink was employed by our man, who wanted it to appear the work of the other side. The point is that the facts of that case are too close to Dr. Ze'evi's to be mere coincidence," Dani concluded. "His murder is a double-edged warning: If you try to stop us, we will do the same to you — and, we know who *you* are."

Ehud Dani coughed and reached for his pack of Broadways. It was empty. "Damn. Mind if I step out to get another?"

Eli gestured with his hands that he was free to go.

"I'll be back in ten minutes. You will be here." It was a statement.

The opening of the door caused the sand gathered at the sill to sweep into the room. Annoyed, Eli found a damp bath towel and brushed the unwanted filth outside. Quite close to the door, he noticed the red boots of a soldier who was leaning on the opposite wall. Red boots . . . a paratrooper. Otherwise the soldier was dressed like almost everyone else around the base, in faded cotton fatigues with side pockets. His corporal's insignia was attached with a safety pin to his shirt. He is detailed to watch over me, Eli realized. Deliberately, he walked over and greeted the soldier. If he had known the man's name he would have called him by it. There was no saluting in the Israeli army; everyone — from the lowest recruit to the most decorated general — was on a first-name basis. And this one was a study in casualness. But the Uzi machine gun was close at his side and his darting eyes were more alert than his slouching posture indicated.

All of a sudden, the barbed wire, the barricades, the military presence that had always seemed so comforting, had become — in some
inexplicable way — "the other side." Eli was not actually "under arrest," yet he was "a case." The old feelings from Caraolas surfaced.
He sensed himself beginning to assume the defensive posture of the
interned: monitoring every gesture, word, and decision in light of
what *they* thought it meant. His mind was analyzing how to fool
them, circumvent them, prevail over them . . . Them. And us. No,
not us . . . me. Them against me.

What was going on here? He had expected a formal hearing to unravel the mystery of the professor's murder, not this personal,
chatty — but entirely serious — inquiry by an old friend. No one
was answering *his* questions and this, more than anything, was an
indication that he had lost all authority. Silently, behind some
closed door, he had been stripped of his status. He had gone from
leader to *case* in one stroke of a pen — or transmitter key. Who was
behind this?

Alex.

Alex Naor had been in military intelligence around the same time
as Dani. Both had been brought back into the Mossad when Amit
took over after Harel. It was Alex who had been politically ambitious; Ehud had remained in the background, but not without influence. And it was Alex who had never trusted the Ezra group.

Without a second glance in the soldier's direction, Eli entered the
latrine building at the end of the row of barracks. The smell of disin-
fectant was overpowering, but necessary to cover the stink from the
squat toilets lining one wall. He washed his face with green soap and
rinsed it several times. He combed his hair several times, but fine
sand continued to flake from his scalp. In the mirror his face seemed
ashen and weary. His lower eyelids were lined with dark, hollow
crescents. His mouth sagged. How had it come to this?

Some men find the history of bureaucracies particularly fascinating.
Eli speculated that Alex Naor was of that ilk. While Eli had slogged
away for whatever master was the current memuneh — the appointed one, or Mossad chieftain — Alex aligned himself to better
his own position. At the moment, he was of an age where he was
either considering retirement or — what seemed most likely given
the circumstances — being groomed to lead the organization after
the next change of command. Not that Eli had not been affected by

the trends in intelligence. Every boss had altered significantly the guidelines of Eli's job.

Boris Guriel had correctly assessed that he was an excellent analyst, with the patience to decode lists of numbers for months on end, to find pattern in seeming randomness, to direct events from a base of objective reasoning. He had a set of skills far beyond the routine intelligence operatives Guriel had been training and employing in the early days of the State.

"You have surprised me," Guriel had said when Eli initially outlined the concept of the Ezra group. "I did not think you were especially keen on working with people. We saw you as a desk man."

Guriel had given him his chance — with a hook. The nuclear desk kept him busy digesting all intelligence relating to unusual activities in weaponry and warfare. He was one of the few people in the world with the most accurate statistics on which powers had the raw ores, the most productive reactors, and the best scientists in the field. The numbers became grimmer every decade. During the last five years, he had specialized in data on research reactors where weapons-grade plutonium was being produced at an alarming rate. Besides the huge amounts of plutonium produced by Canada, East Germany, Sweden, and Switzerland, there were half a dozen states, including Brazil, Argentina, Egypt, Spain, and — most worrisome — Pakistan, that would not sign the nonproliferation treaty but already had stockpiled over one hundred fifty kilograms of separable plutonium.

"All it would take is one well-placed bomb somewhere between Jerusalem and Tel Aviv to destroy most of Israel's population in a matter of minutes," he had said a thousand times. Each memuneh in turn would pat him on the back and thank him for his dedication. But nothing changed. The world continued on its course of blind self-destruction at an exponentially increasing rate of speed.

For more than twenty years Eli had watched Mossad leaders fall in and out of favor. Guriel's star had plummeted in the fall of 1951, just as Eli's young women were settling into their complex field assignments, but fortunately he was replaced by Eli's first champion, Reuven Shiloah, an enthusiast for the ground-breaking techniques in espionage he had learned from the CIA.

"Israel must have an independent intelligence agency responsible only to the Prime Minister," Shiloah explained to Ben-Gurion, who agreed it was time to revamp Israel's intelligence organization. Against Guriel's wishes, the Political Department of the Foreign Ministry was disbanded and the Central Institute for Intelligence and Special Missions — to be known simply as the Mossad, after its predecessor in charge of "illegal" immigration in the thirties and forties — was formed.

Guriel's colleagues reacted more strongly to his resignation than anyone expected. Many of his operatives in the field returned immediately to Tel Aviv to resign en masse. Only a few senior men, including Eli, stayed on. Shiloah sought Eli's cooperation in forming a commission to seize the files of the recently dissolved Political Department and telling defecting employees they had but twenty-four hours to return or lose their jobs. It was a task Eli hated at the time and, in retrospect, decided he should have refused. He had no experience at being either a mouthpiece or a hatchet man. Shiloah should have chosen someone with either more diplomatic skill or a thicker skin. And Shiloah should have chosen someone without a British police superintendent for a father.

Alex Naor, one of Guriel's fiercest protectors, departed for a high-level position in Aman, Israel's military intelligence branch, with harsh words to Eli. "It is only what I would expect from a man born with treacherous blood."

Although Shiloah did not last more than a year, he took a personal interest in Eli's projects. Impressed with the quantity of data Eli was amassing, he taught his protégé an unforgettable lesson. "You must listen attentively — all the while trying to distinguish the *voices* from the *noises*. Throughout recent history there are countless situations made worse because a government read the noises as voices and vice versa. The Israeli intelligence community is faced with so many noises we must listen acutely to determine which Arab leader is making just another grandiose boast and which is giving a warning to be heeded. A country like Egypt or Morocco might make one statement for home consumption, another for international attention. Which one is right? Is the determination somewhere in between or something else entirely? What is the true voice?"

Despite the fact he was a brilliant analyst and adviser, with boundless enthusiasm for ideas and principles, Shiloah was hopelessly disorganized. Even Eli had to admit he was a poor administrator. In the end, Shiloah failed to listen to the voices closest to him, and so it came as no surprise when, in September 1952, Prime Minister Ben-Gurion reshuffled the intelligence community, appointing Isser Harel to run the Mossad as well as the Shin Bet.

Eli was one of the few who regretted losing Shiloah, more for sentimental than practical reasons. But his remorse did not last very long. Harel increased the department's budget tenfold and had visions of creating a secret service that would have global reach.

Harel had approved of Eli's assignments. After a briefing on Charlotte's status in Egypt, Aviva's in Iraq, and Lily's in Paris, he had been mightily impressed.

Looking back, Eli saw that the glory days of his career had been under Harel. "I have always liked you, Eli," Harel once began as they shared a small settee in Harel's sparse office. "You are an honest man, doing a scoundrel's job. But if I had scoundrels doing a scoundrel's job, what would happen to Israel?"

Isser Harel permitted Eli autonomy over his department. While he had superiors in areas such as finance, Eli reported directly to the memuneh on all nuclear matters. Harel might not have been as intellectual as Guriel, or as filled with fresh concepts as Shiloah, but he had a way of imparting love and trust — of parenting his men rather than ruling them — that inspired in Eli, as well as many others, a rare intensity of loyalty.

While nobody outside official circles would ever know exactly what Eli had accomplished, the entire world was to be awed by the exploits of Harel's Mossad in case after case, culminating in 1960 in the successful kidnaping of Adolf Eichmann in Argentina and bringing him to justice in Israel. Although Eli could never have predicted what would happen next, the end of the Harel era was close at hand. Soon Eli would unwittingly play a part in Harel's downfall, as well as the subsequent rise of Alex Naor.

Eli never understood why Alex tried so cavalierly to end the Ezra project before it began, and he had distrusted him ever since. Perhaps it was a simple difference of philosophy. But Eli suspected that Alex's dislike for him had far deeper origins.

According to men like Alex there were two types of people: those who had suffered and those who had not. Of the Ezra group, only Lily could have been on Alex's "acceptable" list. Charlotte would have been considered too soft; Aviva had never been beaten, jailed, or martyred enough to suit his lofty tastes. Give Alex a man who had seen his mother raped or murdered, or a woman who had hidden in Siberian forests through two subzero winters, or a soldier who had trekked the Sinai on his hands and knees. *They* were Mossad material. All the rest were lesser mortals who could never "understand what Israel is about."

But even Charlotte, the charming, flighty American girl from an upper-class home in suburban New York, was more acceptable to

Alex than Eli himself — for Eli had committed the worst sin of all: he had been born British.

❖ ❖ ❖

Ehud Dani returned armed with three fresh packs of Broadways, a Thermos of coffee, and a bottle of Maccabi beer.

"Pick your poison, as they say."

Eli reached for the beer, which at least appeared cold. He opened it by wedging the cap under a corner of the table and took a few swallows.

"Good?" Dani's voice was solicitous.

"Yoffi. Todah."

"Now where were we?" He stroked an unlit cigarette absently. "The El Setouhy matter, wasn't it? The point is, since one of your operatives identified the Egyptian scientist before the murder, revenge against your group is suspected as the main reason our scientist was killed. The problem? We think it fits too neatly. A scientist for a scientist. Our enemies are usually more devious."

"Murder is almost always senseless."

Under his breath Dani muttered something.

"What?"

He looked up and stared at Eli with huge dark eyes. "Nothing, just something someone said about you — it fits." With great purpose, he took his time lighting the cigarette.

Eli was incensed. "You are acting like a boy in a schoolyard calling, 'I've got a secret.' "

Dani spoke slowly, licking his lips at the pauses. "It is of little importance. All he said was something to the effect of 'lily white hands' — yes, that's what it was. 'Katzar is so proud of his lily white hands.' "

"Alex."

Dani shrugged and ground out the freshly lit cigarette. "Look, my friend, it is time to put our posturing aside. There has been a terrible screw-up, a breach of faith. Nobody else knew about Dr. Ze'evi's participation in the Caleb operation except you and the memuneh, am I right?"

"He may have cleared it with others. There were certain passports and documents, so someone in that department had to have been informed."

"We have checked out those sections already. They are clean."

"And I am not? That is what this is all about, isn't it? First Alex, and now you are accusing me of complicity in the murder. Or are you suggesting I did it myself? If so, what is your reasoning, for God's sake?"

"We are wondering the same."

Eli shook his head and stared at the ceiling. "There must be a hundred explanations. I could have been followed . . ." Eli hated how shrill and defensive he was sounding. "Their shadows are as professional as ours. Or they could have tailed one of the girls. Each one had direct contact with me at various points in France."

"Ah" — Ehud raised his slim gray eyebrows into twin arches of surprise — "the girls, or should I say 'women'? Working with the press I have had — how do you say it in English? — my 'conscience raised.' "

"You are talking about operatives who have been loyal for thirty years. We only activated them because of their expertise and the sensitivity of the mission. They have been through far worse in their careers. I assume you have seen the files."

"Ken, ken, we have been over all this in staff meetings. And yet there are certain clues — clues I am afraid I cannot divulge to you at this moment in time — which show a similarity to the codes your group used to employ before we became more sophisticated electronically. If someone did not have access to the latest equipment, they might have thought these older systems would suffice for minimal traffic, which, in fact, they did. That is why I do not believe you knew anything about this, Eli. *I'm* on your side in this, as much as I can be. You, of all people, should have been more clever."

"But others see it differently?"

"That's obvious, isn't it?"

"Naor . . ."

"His arguments are convincing in lieu of more substantial evidence that would point to someone else."

"How could he have *evidence*? I have told him the truth from the beginning. He has all the facts at hand. Even if he distorted them, I would not come up a suspect."

"You don't see the gaps, do you?"

"Gaps?"

"Our concern begins with the explosion at the restaurant in London. As we understand it, you were placed in a safe house. A trip out for tobacco or reading matter would not have worried us, but given the critical circumstances . . . At a time before any debriefing had taken place, you went out to dinner with another gentleman — and then you expect us to believe the building is fire-bombed by sheer coincidence. Eli . . ." Dani's voice was condescending. "Eli . . ." He threw his hands in the air. "What could be more suspicious?"

"We . . . I was almost killed!"

"But you were not. If you were a marked target, there had to have been several opportunities to kill you far more cleanly. Isn't it possible you set the explosive as a way of diverting suspicion from yourself?"

"This is beginning to sound like a cheap softcover mystery."

"A melodramatic one as well, Mr. Honesty, Mr. Truth, Mr. Clean Hands!" Dani had raised his voice angrily. Next, it softened for effect. "Eli, we know all about your mysterious dinner companion. There has been a file on your phony society and corporation for a decade, at least. Oh, you told us it was used as a mail drop for personal reasons as well as official business, so nobody worried about it seriously — until now. If all this hadn't happened, your secret would have been safe. Nobody else would have followed up; nobody else would have known about your precious Mr. Stewart. Your . . . son."

Eli bristled at the way Dani had spoken the words "your son" so cruelly.

"You don't think Colin . . ."

"No. We do not. He has been checked out most thoroughly."

"Have you . . . spoken with him?" Eli's voice quavered.

"You are very protective of the boy, aren't you?"

"He does not know . . ."

"What?"

"That I'm . . . his father."

"Come now, Eli. I told you I was on *your* side. Don't make this even more difficult for me to swallow. You have been in touch with Mr. Stewart since his school days and you mean to tell me he does not know your identity? Who does he think you are? Father Christmas? The tooth fairy?"

"He knows me only as Charles Ivy. Now I'm a friend. Originally I was but a member of a 'scholarship committee.' "

Dani was shaking his head with disbelief. "After Toulon, after the murder, when you were so disturbed, you rushed to see him. What comfort could the boy give the so-called scholarship committee? Don't you see you are not making sense? Don't you see why others are concerned about you?"

"He contacted me — weeks earlier, as it turned out. I got the message from Conrad. Colin wanted to see me for important personal reasons of his own. I doubted I would be in London more than a night or two and took the only brief opportunity I had. Even though he does not *know* about me, he *is* terribly important to me." Eli's voice faded. "I have no other family . . ."

"Your parents are alive."

"You know what I mean."

"I am sorry, Eli. But I needed you to see why your word has been doubted. What other secrets have you kept? What other connections, liaisons? That is what they are asking in London and Jerusalem." He put his hands on his lap, palms up. "Here is my problem. I am charged to get to the bottom of the matter. You must help me. I do not know the details of your mission, the members of your organizational team here in Israel and abroad, the local task force — all the operatives."

Eli stared at Dani, hardly believing what he was hearing.

"What you must do for me is to prepare your own investigation. You may have a research staff, anything you require. It can be set up right here at the guest house."

"I am not permitted to leave here?"

"Certainly you are. Go wherever you need — just keep the receipts. You must report your whereabouts to me daily. You are the only one who can bring us the answer — first, because you know the most; second, you have the — how shall I say it? — the greatest motivation. It is the only way to clear your name."

"Aren't you worried I will disappear?"

"Not at all. There's Colin Stewart to consider . . ."

Dani tucked what remained of his cigarette pack into his rear pocket and stood by the door.

An eerie howling wind burst into the room the moment Dani opened the door. The khamsin was so intense they could no longer see the building along the opposite row. The twilight colored the swirling particulate matter an otherworldly coral.

"You will start tomorrow?" Dani managed to choke before he covered his nose and mouth with his arm and shut the door.

But the latch did not hold. A gust of wind blew it in with an ominous clatter. Eli called out into the churning, tempestuous void. "Is there another choice?"

PART THREE

OPERATIONS

10

Ye have seen what I did unto the Egyptians, and how I bore
you on eagles' wings, and brought you unto Myself.

                                                    Exodus 19:4

ALEXANDRIA, EGYPT: 1953–1954

"Saida," Charlotte said to the guard as she left her small cottage behind the Keladas' house at seven in the morning.

"Mâ-assalama." He touched his forehead and replied deferentially.

The heat made the air as visible as a thin sheet of moiré silk.
Charlotte's freshly washed hair drooped in the humid veil and her
nylon panties chafed at her waistline. Everything in Egypt had a
particular physical sensation. One could not exist in one's mind anymore; one was made to suffer the day: its heat, its smells, its noises, its
silences — all reminders that she was living a double life in a hostile
land. As Charlotte sniffed the pungent air, a mixture of blossoms and
sewage and sea, she resigned herself to another brutal scorcher of a
day.

Thank heavens the section where she worked at the United States
Information Agency library was cooled by a wheezing old air conditioner they lovingly called Sammy, short for Smart Aleck Machine,
and doted on it as if it were an elderly relation. If it sputtered, someone would either rush to attend to it, saying, "C'mon old boy, you're
going to make it," or turn it off for a few hours in deference to its age.

It was a leisurely twenty-minute walk to the Thomas Jefferson Library at 93 Rue Fouad if Charlotte took the most direct route, ten minutes longer if she went via the beaches and the quays. Professor Kelada, her landlord, had offered to drop her off on his way to the university each day, but Charlotte explained she enjoyed the walk. When the professor assured her she must not feel she was imposing on him, she had quoted the epigraph to her favorite guidebook to Alexandria, written by E. M. Forster. "As Ibn Dukmak wrote: 'If a man make a pilgrimage round Alexandria in the morning, God will make for him a golden crown, set with pearls, perfumed with musk and camphor, and shining from the East to the West.' " The professor had been charmed and thereafter insisted only when the weather was foul.

Charlotte loved the feel of the Leica swinging from her shoulder. She took her camera along twice a week. The Keladas knew she was working on a portfolio of photos of the city's children.

"I'm captivated by the differences in their skin colors, their eyes, their clothing," she had told Mrs. Kelada.

Daphne Kelada had approved of her project, even volunteered to escort her to neighborhoods where she might not feel comfortable alone. This morning, however, children were not to be Charlotte's subject.

There were dozens of variations on the route she could take: to the west of the Municipal Gardens, up the Rue de La Porte Rosette past the Greco-Roman Museum, or along the seaside Corniche. Each path was premeditated to take her past some sector of interest. She varied her routine to cover the port activities and, twice a week, to meet her associates for hand-offs of letters written in secret inks underneath seemingly harmless messages. Eli had insisted she agree to personal contact for security's sake, even though she had been prepared to communicate with Tel Aviv only by radio. While she seemed so safe in this most cosmopolitan of Egyptian cities — protected by her American nationality and her work for the U.S. government — she had to remind herself continually of her real mission and its dangers. With the enervating heat, the repetitive nature of her cover job, the generally indolent life, maintaining "the edge" was more difficult than she had expected.

What *had* she expected? What crazy, idealistic streak had brought her to this place? It was something she could never express to anyone else in a logical manner, but she felt more at peace with herself in Egypt than ever before. The time when she had felt the most uneasy, the most oppressed, had been the last time she had spent with her family.

Before she was sent to Egypt, Eli had insisted on a six-month hiatus between Ohio and the Egyptian assignment — in Scarsdale. "To be entirely certain you can accept the alienation from your parents, sisters, and friends. We're worried it will be particularly rough in your case since you were reared in a close-knit family."

When Charlotte had objected, he had given a second reason. "Recent political upheavals in Egypt after the overthrow of the monarchy have left us with information to digest. We must rework our research on the areas of concern and brief you properly. This cannot be done overnight."

Reluctantly, she had returned from Israel to a joyful family reunion. A few months earlier, her sister Evelyn had married Marty Berman, whose family owned a chain of movie theaters. As a wedding present, they had given him one of their most profitable theaters in White Plains to manage. Charlotte's mother did not hide her resentment that her eldest daughter had not made it home in time for the wedding, but she was pleased she would be around for the second celebration: the marriage of Charlotte's younger sister, Grace, to Jeff Levy, a dental student.

Charlotte cringed as she attended the bridal showers (there were five), the rehearsal dinner, the luncheon for out-of-town guests, and the ostentatious wedding at the Waldorf-Astoria, which included lavish flowers (white orchids) and caged doves. To Charlotte, the wasteful extravagance was repulsive. She could not help but contrast it to how the Israelis were struggling with food rationing and housing shortages. Not that the family cared. They had come to view her interest in Israel as "an obsession" and did not encourage her to talk about it. To make matters worse, every aunt, uncle, cousin, and friend of the family asked a version of the same question: "Nu? When do we dance at *your* wedding?"

Behind her back they were whispering. Her hair had grown long in Israel and she wore it pulled back in a severe style ("Like a peasant from the Ukraine," chided Aunt Minnie). The once-glamorous fashion-conscious Vassar-girl daughter of Harry Green had been metamorphosed by her struggles in Palestine, but all her kin could see was "a pretty girl who let herself go."

Charlotte's mother, who could barely hide her shame at having a twenty-five-year-old single daughter, hinted broadly about "an important Israeli" whose affections Charlotte had won, but her daughter was "being difficult" about making a decision. "I don't know how I feel about it," she would say in a stage whisper. "Do I really want my grandchildren living thousands of miles away?"

The sting of Charlotte's inability to capture a man was minimized when at the wedding supper itself — right after the bride danced with her father — Evelyn hugged her mother and told her she was expecting. Tears flowed and shouts of "Mazel tov!" rang in the great hall. Champagne corks popped and Charlotte was able to shrink into the background with her Pittsburgh cousins and amaze them with stories of the siege of Jerusalem and the combat she had witnessed firsthand. If they only knew, she said to herself over and over. If they only knew. That private litany kept her sane.

After the wedding had come three agonizing months of supposedly looking for a job and deciding what she would do with her life.

"Finish your education," her father suggested. "I'll gladly pay the bills." The fact that she had never graduated from Vassar irked him. He had made certain Evelyn and Grace both won their "B.A.'s before their M.R.S.'s" from Wellesley and Smith by pointing out their elder sister's breach early — and often.

"How about NYU?" Sarah Green suggested. "You could live in the city. We'd find you a little apartment in the Village."

"Or Stanford," her father added brightly. "The climate's like Tel Aviv; the boys are very smart. You could even go on for a master's if . . ." He stopped himself, but Charlotte knew he had meant to say, "if you don't find anyone special right away."

"I'll probably go back to Israel. I'm needed there" was all she would reply.

"Who is *he*?" Evelyn and Grace each asked their eldest sister privately.

Charlotte decided they might accept her loyalty to Israel more easily if there was a human angle. "Someone I've been working with for several years."

"Is he married?" Evelyn asked nervously.

"No. It's complicated."

They pretended to understand. But they did not. Finally, word came that she was to fly to London. Charlotte told her family that the job she had hoped would come through had become available. She was vague about her assignment and said only that she would be returning to Israel but might also be traveling "in a governmen-

tal capacity." She explained she could not always be reached immediately and mail delivery might be slow, but she would write often.

"Charlotte's an Israeli diplomat!" her parents could finally brag,
along with spreading the news of Evelyn's pregnancy or Grace's husband's offers to join lucrative orthodontic practices.

Eli had arranged for Carla Christopher to be accepted as a librarian by the USIA and assigned to the Alexandria, Egypt, branch. Her
recommendations from her Antioch work experience at the Library
of Congress had been "flawless." When Charlotte arrived in Egypt,
she was taken in by the library director herself. Stella Patterson —
the wife of a cotton exporter, who had lived in Egypt for more than
twenty years — felt she had to translate every nuance of Egyptian
lifestyle and customs to Charlotte, although the librarian was ignorant of everything except the lifestyles and customs of the *American*
community.

Charlotte had been well prepared for her boss's maternalistic behavior. When she was told that "the girls always live together in the
Stanley Bey quarter if their families aren't here," she had been ready
with a reply.

"I'm a horrid roommate. I have strange sleeping habits. I require
only two or three hours and then I'm up. I turn the light on and walk
around, make tea, read or write poems. Then I sleep for a few more
hours before dawn."

Mrs. Patterson had been taken aback. "Oh, hon! That *is* odd!"

"I always had a single room at college so I wouldn't bother anyone."

"Do you think you should drink tea in the middle of the night?"
Charlotte shrugged.

"You're so sweet and an excellent fourth at bridge," Stella Patterson said. "Jasper and I would love to have you continue to stay with
us."

"No, I wouldn't even consider it. My mother believed it was best
to have some distance from an employer, and while I'm certain we'd
get on splendidly, she probably was wise in her recommendation. As
I go on in life, I learn how often she was right and I . . ." She choked
sensitively. (Chris's mother had died from cancer two months before
she applied for this assignment.)

"You're a very wise young woman. I'd be worried about another
girl on her own, but I think you'll manage well. Let's see what I can
arrange."

It was imperative Charlotte find suitable living accommodations quickly. Soon nightly radio transmissions would become a mandatory part of her assignment. Tel Aviv would monitor her radio signal between two and three in the morning, preferably during the first five minutes after the hour. Ideally, she would find a flat on a high floor in an apartment building, but there were few of these in Alexandria. With such close proximity to Israel, this was not essential. Most important was privacy.

Mrs. Patterson located a room with one of her husband's business associates in a grand old house five kilometers out of town.

"The room is beautiful and sunny," she reported to her boss, "but I'm concerned about meeting friends and getting around safely from that area." The main problem was the paper-thin walls in the bedroom, because it was sandwiched between those of the family.

"Quite right. You'd be stranded out there once you got home. Yesterday, Jasper made inquiries at the American Sporting Club. How does this sound?" She handed Charlotte a piece of paper with an address typed on it. "It's a garden cottage behind the villa of a Professor Kelada. Jasper did some checking and learned that the owner is a geology professor at Alexandria University. His Greek wife is a trustee at the Greco-Roman Museum and is also an accomplished tapestry designer. Their children are grown and the cottage originally housed the professor's mother, who died a year ago."

"You're certainly thorough!" Charlotte laughed and agreed to inspect the cottage at once.

To enter the Kelada compound, Charlotte passed through a gate guarded by a man who watched it and five other houses protected by the same contiguous concrete wall. Charlotte liked this feature because Mrs. Patterson would agree that this was a safe location for a single, foreign woman.

The cottage was on the far side of a reflecting pool and separated from the main dwelling by twenty-five yards of high shrubbery. With the two-burner gas cooker, sink, and refrigerator, she could be independent in her meal preparation. The bedroom was small and dark, with only one high window, which made it difficult for anyone to see inside.

"It is cooler that way," Daphne Kelada explained while Charlotte was calculating its security for her transmissions.

It took only a few minutes for Charlotte to decide the situation was perfect.

"The wages of the gardener are included in the rent, but the last tenant paid a bit more for housecleaning and laundry," Mrs. Kelada pointed out.

"I'll try to save on that," Charlotte replied. Even though her Zamir radio transmitter, crystals, secret inks, and papers were well hidden in cleverly devised books, scales, cosmetics, and luggage, it would take a while before she was sent a man to construct even more secure caches, so the fewer people with access to her rooms, the better.

"The laundry is quite difficult. We have no machines. At least the linens —"

"Perhaps those," Charlotte said to avoid seeming argumentative.

The Keladas' house turned out to be a wise choice for another reason: It gave Charlotte access to an intellectual family with ties to the university community. Although she was not specifically interested in geology, the Keladas had connections with other scientific circles closer to her secret specialty. Also, Professor Kelada was a Copt, one of the Christian descendants of the ancient pre-Arab population, and therefore far more tolerant of a single girl's lifestyle than a Moslem might have been. Furthermore, Mrs. Kelada's artistic leanings fit in with the intellectual image Charlotte was fostering for herself.

Charlotte walked quickly, taking a short cut down Rue Prince Moneim behind the Armenian Orthodox Church so she could make a quick tour of the Western Harbor before beginning work. Last night, while Jasper Patterson had driven her home from a bridge game, she had seen some unidentified ships looming under the crescent moon. Naval movements were within the realm of her directives, so this morning she would shoot a roll of film and hand it over to the contact she was scheduled to pass that afternoon. Her step quickened as she became hopeful of finding something of significance.

Charlotte was well aware that she had accomplished little during her first six months in Alexandria. Her nightly radio broadcasts were nothing more than the coded signal indicating she was fine and had nothing to report. Dismayed by her lack of progress, Charlotte also knew there was not much she could do to speed up the process of gathering the data her superiors desired.

"You are a long-term investment," Eli had explained before he saw her off in London. "We schooled you properly, we developed your cover by the book, we are willing to sit back and wait. The more cautiously you proceed, the more you minimize the risks. Always remember, you are protecting *our* investment by being prudent."

There were so many times she had wanted to move ahead more forcefully; it was agonizing to have to restrain herself. The most difficult aspect was making the acquaintance of men powerful enough to have useful information. Meeting people involved following a long chain of social, diplomatic, and professional relationships, and was further complicated by her status as a single American young woman living alone in a Middle Eastern city. The Pattersons had welcomed her into their social set of older American and British women who played cards twice a week and on Sundays attended St. Mark's in the Square, the Anglican church. After a few polite weeks of this, Mrs. Patterson herself suggested Charlotte should find "a younger crowd" and encouraged her to get to know the "boys at the consulate."

Gordon MacDonald, a junior career officer in the foreign service who worked as the first assistant to the commercial attaché at the U.S. consulate, was the first to whom she had been introduced, and he had offered to show her around as a favor to Jasper Patterson. The favor quickly blossomed into a romance — at least on his end. Charlotte quite liked the ruddy-faced, lanky man. Gordo, as she affectionately called him, was the first to laugh at himself, the first to protect a friend. But the man was attracted to Chris, the librarian from Ohio who wanted to see something of the world outside of books before settling down. Gordon saw her as a somewhat shy girl, more knowledgeable about ancient cultures than current hemlines. As kindly as he could, Gordon suggested she consider wearing her skirts a bit shorter, trimming her bangs above her eyebrows, and working to make the most of "your terrific figure." He enlisted Charlotte's colleague Nadine, who had a way with scarves and barrettes, and Leslie, his best friend's wife, who knew all the best shops and dressmakers, to convince Chris to relax her studious image — precisely the one she so recently had cultivated. Charlotte acceded to some suggestions, not to please him but to serve her own purposes — for Gordon, the up-and-coming young diplomat, received invitations to every interesting function in town. Most nights Gordon gave her a choice: cocktails at the French consulate, coffee at the Brazilian delegation, or a musical evening at the German Society. All were places where she could meet people who might be helpful to her, but being a single woman, Charlotte would never have been "insulted" with a personal invitation to these affairs.

The same problem existed within the university community. Unfortunately, the only vaguely interesting people she had met through the Keladas were a professor of mathematics with a brother in the physics department and an Italian woman in the political science department. At the end of the evening, the political scientist said good-bye to Charlotte and added, "It was refreshing to meet an American interested in Egyptian history more recent than King Tut. We will have to talk again."

So there was hope; there would be a next time. Slowly . . . brick by brick . . . they were getting to know her, to trust her, but how long would it take?

By the time she reached the waterfront area behind the Rue Ras el Tin, Charlotte's forehead was covered with perspiration. She pretended to be taking a picture of a mangy dog nursing a surprisingly healthy litter of puppies under a boxcar while concentrating on a French gunboat moored in the center of the harbor. A few French sailors were walking along the quay in front of the lighthouse where, according to her Forster guidebook, the prehistoric harbor had existed before the modern one, the Eunostos, was dredged. Some claimed the ancient harbor was the one alluded to in the *Odyssey*.

" 'There is an island in the surging sea, which they call Pharos, lying off Egypt. It has a harbor with good anchorage, and hence they put out to sea after drawing water,' " she had read aloud to Gordon, who, even after living in Alexandria for almost four years, had not known that. What was thought to be Homer's island was the promontory of Ras el Tin, where more French sailors were congregating presently.

A few fishing boats intermingled with the usual motley group of rusty steamers — including the S.S. *Enotria*, which regularly made the crossing between Bari, Italy, and Alexandria. Last night she thought she had seen the outline of a Soviet-built Skory-class destroyer. She had been told to be on the lookout for two: the *Ibrahim el Awal* and the *Damietta*. Both were of World War II vintage; both were rumored to have been refurbished recently by the Egyptians. Perhaps she had been prematurely enthusiastic or perhaps it had sailed on the early tide. In any case, there was nothing more of interest to photograph. Eleven shots of commercial vessels would be a boring roll of film. What would Eli say when he saw it? Or would he even see it?

Suddenly, she unwound the coil of hair from the back of her neck and let it fall gracefully on her shoulders. She unbuttoned the top three buttons of her round-collared blouse, held her camera out to the full extent of her arms, and smiled flirtatiously. Click! She was still grinning when she spun around to see a tiny boy, his arms like sticks, staring at her with coal-black eyes. A cloud of flies blackened his arms, but he did not seem to have the energy to shoo them away. He will grow up to point a gun at an Israeli, she pondered as she walked rapidly toward the Rue Fouad. The boy followed her all the way to The Square.

She spun around and confronted him. "Awiz eh? What do you want?"

He held his hand out pathetically.

She shook her head. She did not give money to beggars. She did not want them to remember her.

"Gu'ān. I'm hungry," he said in a husky voice. He pointed to a bakery across the street.

She relented and paid the baker the few coins necessary to fill the child's tiny stomach.

"Mutshakreen awwe . . . as-salâm alaikoom," he said with a full mouth, careful not to let a morsel drop out. "Good-bye and peace be with you."

Stopping at a newsstand on the corner of the Rue Nebi Daniel, Charlotte purchased the English daily, the *Egyptian Gazette*. She scanned the headlines, then checked her watch. It was almost seven-thirty. She tried to arrive at her desk as close to eight as possible. This made her presumed walking time consistent. There was time for a cup of coffee at the nearby Cleopatra Café. She took a seat and ordered her coffee "mazboot." The waiter smiled and brought her a plate of the aiysh, or flat bread, he knew she liked along with the nei-ther sickly sweet nor pungently bitter coffee.

"Hi, Chris!" Gordon MacDonald came running across two lanes of traffic, his tie flapping in front of his already damp shirt. "It's going to be another ferocious day. Honestly, I don't see how Washington can expect us to wear suits in this blasted furnace." He hung his double-breasted navy suit jacket on the back of the bentwood chair and smoothed back the mop of reddish-blond hair that covered his right eye. "Ziyada." He ordered his coffee sweet.

Charlotte puckered her lips. "I'll never understand how you can drink that syrup."

"Insulates from the heat."

"Really?" She grinned.

"Listen" — he caught her wrist — "I'm glad I found you. Arnie and Leslie want us to go to the movies with them tonight. It's *Roman Holiday* with Audrey Hepburn."

"I saw it last year in New York with my sister."

"I didn't know you had a sister."

Damn! Charlotte cursed silently. She had been thinking of Grace. They had gone to the movies together the night before Charlotte left for London. Her current dossier did not list any sisters. "I don't. It's my stepsister. You know, the daughter of the man my mother married when she moved to California. I hardly know her, but we were in New York together and it is easier to say 'sister' than have to explain about second marriages, my father dying and all that." She hoped she had covered her momentary lapse.

"Sorry, Chris. Jesus, we've gotten the day off to a rotten start. Would you mind seeing the film again?"

"I guess not, but you know how I feel about seeing American movies all the time. When are we going to an Egyptian one?"

"They're supposed to be awfully childlike and romantic — fairy tales for grown-ups."

"So's *Roman Holiday*."

"If that's what you'd prefer . . ."

Charlotte gulped the last of her coffee and stood up. "Thanks, Gordo, you know how much I want to experience the *real* Egypt. If I don't, I'll turn into a Stella Patterson and —"

"Impossible!"

She glanced at her watch. "I'm late —"

"I'll pick you up at home?"

"Yes. I'll need to change." She started to pay for the coffee, but Gordon handed the coins to the waiter first.

"Eight?" he called as she rounded the corner. But Charlotte did not respond. She was thinking about the little hungry boy . . . about his dark eyes . . . the black swarm of flies . . . and that they were enemies.

❖   ❖   ❖

"Good morning, Mrs. Patterson," she said cheerfully as she passed the director's office on her way to the children's library.

"Mornin', hon."

Nadine Pepper, the Egyptian-born wife of an American military attaché and the assistant children's librarian, was banging on the air conditioner's rusty side panel as Charlotte entered the room. "Sammy's on strike," Nadine complained.

"Sammy," Charlotte coaxed, "it's story circle day. You don't want us to have crying, miserable, hot children, do you?" She turned the dial off, then rapidly twisted it on to the highest setting. The old box shuddered and spit out a puff of blue smoke. "Darn!" She switched it off.

"Shall I call maintenance?"

"I think we'll probably need an undertaker, but let's wait and try again before the children come. I'll plan a shorter program, just in case."

She started pulling books off the shelves and decided on *Madeline, Stone Soup,* and *The Five Chinese Brothers.*

"And, to inspire Sammy, we'll finish with *The Little Engine That Could.*" She and Nadine laughed as they arranged the mats into a circle.

While the children filed into the room, Charlotte studied their bright little faces — a spectrum of shades from the darkest Moroccan nut-browns to the fairest Minnesota-bred blonds. They represented not only the range of Americans transplanted to this, one of the most cosmopolitan crossroads in the world, but all those with English-speaking connections. In the streets of Alexandria one heard fragments of Armenian, Greek, Amharic, English, French, Italian, and a dozen dialects of Arabic; in the faces of these children one saw the result of the intermingling of men and women from many nations brought together on this historic tip of Africa. How right they should come together to learn of little Madeline in Paris or five brothers in China, Charlotte thought as she smiled to herself.

Sometimes, during her first weeks in Egypt when she had been filing in the card catalog, shelving books, or listening to banal comments on the difficulty of importing Campfire marshmallows for the Fourth of July, Charlotte had felt locked out of both the American community and the vibrant city of Alexandria. That was before she discovered "the secret of Alexandria," the jewel of a guidebook E. M. Forster wrote during the First World War when he was stationed in that city as a Red Cross volunteer.

It was Forster who introduced Charlotte to the Mouseion, the great intellectual achievement of the Ptolemaic city. The building was surmised to have been located west of the present Rue Nebi Daniel — quite near the USIA Library — and had contained lecture halls, observatories, and a library with more than half a million volumes. Forster had written that "the post of 'Librarian' was of immense importance and its holder was the chief official in the Mouseion." Charlotte believed the intellectual life that flourished then had created the foundations of modern civilization. More than two thousand years later, here she was: a librarian in Alexandria providing information to protect her tribe. She was a link in a long chain, she decided proudly.

The children were squirming on their mats. She welcomed them in English, French, and Arabic, then picked up *Madeline.* "I'm Miss Christopher and this is our first story for today."

Nadine was turning Sammy's dials.

"Vroom!" It rumbled once and began to churn out waves of slightly smoky cold air.

"Inshallah," Nadine murmured.

Charlotte pointed to the little girl in the straw hat on the book's jacket. "This is Madeline." She opened the book and read the simple words upside down so the children could follow the pictures.

> "In an old house in Paris
> That was covered with vines
> Lived twelve little girls in two straight lines.
> In two straight lines they broke their bread
> And brushed their teeth
> And went to bed.
> They smiled at the good
> And frowned at the bad
> And sometimes they were very sad . . ."

❖   ❖   ❖

The following month Gordon invited Charlotte to attend a horse show at the Nady El-Faroussia — Cairo's Cavalry Club. Arnie and Leslie Showers were going as well. Gordon and Arnie, who was a visa officer, had been invited because of the assistance they had given Abdul al-Hakim, an electronics importer, with documentation and licenses. Leslie was not particularly interested in horses and, frankly, neither was Charlotte, but the word "electronics" was the most promising she had heard in weeks.

Arnie and Gordon sat in the front seat of the sky-blue Buick while she sat in the back, listening with one ear as Leslie chatted on about coloring her hair. "Do you think I should let them peroxide the whole head?" She patted the few streaks of blond in her permed and elaborately coifed hair. "What if I hate it? What if Arnie does?" She babbled on while Charlotte attempted to concentrate on the men's political discussion.

Gordon MacDonald saw all events — both historical and current — in terms of how they would affect *his* career. Charlotte knew he did not agree with the policies of Jefferson Caffery, the American ambassador to Egypt, and wondered whether Gordon could advance further at this post because of it. He graduated from Georgetown University's School of Foreign Service and had gone to work at the State Department. After two years in Washington, his first assignment had been in Marseille. Three years later, he had been posted to Alexandria, and since 1950, had observed the upheavals in postwar Egypt firsthand. For a man of thirty-one, he was on a track that he unabashedly hoped would culminate in an ambassadorship. Charlotte knew Gordon needed a wife at this point in his work. On the surface she had most of the required qualities: intelligence, education, willingness to travel and live in remote regions, the love of children, a solid Christian, Midwestern farm background, and — most significantly — no strong family ties that would pull her back home. She had emphasized these assets to win Gordon's favor, totally aware she was, as the girls at Vassar would have said, "using him."

Leslie was a superb pipeline, transmitting Gordon's confidences to Arnie directly back to Charlotte. "He's more than enthralled," she had reported in her cute Alabama drawl, "he's in *love.*" Charlotte had laughed at the way Leslie dragged out the "luuuv."

"Not with *me,*" she teased.

"Why, he never takes his eyes off you. He's going to propose. I just know it! Christmas is just around the corner."

When Christmas of 1953 had passed without a surprise ring, Charlotte was relieved. She had to restrain Gordon without totally alienating him. She needed his friendship, but she neither wished to hurt him nor become so entangled her duplicity might trip her up. "I came out here for some adventure. I'm not ready to settle down," she had told Leslie in hopes that her friend's communications system worked in the opposite direction.

By the time they reached the halfway point to Cairo, the town of Tanta in the Nile Delta region, Leslie had nodded off to sleep. Arnie and Gordon were arguing about Nasser's land reform programs. Charlotte knew that Gordon was deeply interested in the transitional nature of Egypt's current political situation.

On July 22, 1952, a group of young Egyptian officers had staged a coup overthrowing King Farouk, their obese, extravagant, and degenerate monarch. Among their grievances was Egypt's miserable performance against Israel in the 1948 war. At the time of the military coup, the power appeared to be in the hands of the elder statesman of the group, General Muhammad Naguib, an intelligent liberal. For a brief period there was hope — especially in the United States — that his rule would create a pro-Western regime. Israeli intelligence believed Naguib was a figurehead and the seat of power belonged to Colonel Gamal Abdel Nasser. A Pan-Arabist, Nasser sought a united front against Israel. Charlotte knew the Israelis had long dreaded the day when an Egyptian leader would put Arab primacy ahead of Egyptian cultural pride to launch a holy war against Israel and they were monitoring Nasser's movements closely.

Gordon, who was pro-Israel in most of his opinions, did not like Nasser. "He's a man to fear," he had said to Charlotte only a few weeks earlier, after a party at the Swiss consul's home.

"Why? He's very popular."

"Not with the British. He's making some very unsubtle overtures for them to withdraw their troops from the Suez Canal zone. If they depart, war will break out."

As usual, she found herself playing devil's advocate. "Can you blame them for wanting to rule their own nation?"

"Look, Chris, Nasser hated the British all along. Everyone knows his sympathies were with the Nazis during the war, as were those of that alter ego of his, Anwar el-Sadat. Sadat has a long record of cooperating with the Mufti of Jerusalem, who paid him to hire assassins to liquidate British officers."

"Where do you get your information?"

"You can be so naïve, Chris. Your life revolves around books and parties. If you'd open your eyes, you'd see the scheming and backbiting all around you."

Privately, Charlotte had to agree with Gordon's analysis. Nasser frightened her.

It was a bright and relatively cool March morning as they entered Cairo. Gordon pointed out a spot where two women were washing their linen in a wide, scummy section of river. "That's where it's said Moses was pulled from the bullrushes."

Leslie did not even turn her head. Usually Charlotte was disgusted with the shallow girl's narrow focus, but today she wondered if Leslie might not have the right attitude. It was best not to look at certain parts of the city too closely. The longer view, though, could be glorious.

In a few minutes they were driving onto the island of Gezira and through the ornamental iron gates of the Cavalry Club, conveniently situated next to the racecourse of the Gezira Sporting Club. Crowds were gathering on the immaculately trimmed lawns. Some people, seated in brightly striped lawn chairs, sipped coffee; others rode horses, stopping to chat with one another. In the main riding enclosure, two men were exercising a matched pair of gray Arabian mares. As they strolled over for a closer look, Charlotte and her friends were greeted by their host's wife, Madame Sabina al-Hakim, on the arm of a dark-skinned Egyptian in a trim riding uniform.

"Permit me to introduce General Youssef Rizk, the General of Police and, more importantly" — Madame al-Hakim laughed throatily — "Honorary President of the Cavalry Club."

The general bowed deeply and kissed Leslie's hand, then Charlotte's. "That is my mare in the ring," he announced, pointing proudly. "Do you like horses?" he asked Charlotte directly.

"Very much. Yours is magnificent . . ."

"Yes?" the general asked. "You were going to say something else?"

"A lady mustn't always say what's in her mind, sir."

"Please, I shan't be offended, I promise."

Charlotte had noticed the reins being tugged quite sharply. "It seems the horse is nodding her head, so perhaps she is being choked up too much. Don't you think she'd show better if her movements were less restricted?"

"You are absolutely right. I've spoken to Ali about hanging on her mouth." He offered Charlotte his arm. A bit sulkily, Gordon followed Madame al-Hakim.

During the sporting events, Gordon was kept occupied by his host, Abdul al-Hakim. Leslie had taken refuge in the shade. Arnie was receiving the special attentions of the bosomy and highly perfumed Madame al-Hakim, so it was a simple matter for Charlotte to remain at the side of General Rizk.

The general's uniform was precisely tailored to his slender figure. While his polished manner and authority awed Charlotte, she knew she had to move beyond her fear and make friends with the man. For once she was grateful she had followed Leslie's instructions to wear her best summer dress — a cabbage-rose-splashed chintz with a tight waist, full skirt, and discreetly curved but exquisitely cut neckline.

Eventually, everybody of consequence came up to the general's seat to pay their respects, and he patiently introduced them all to Charlotte. When they were out of hearing, he would whisper a few

pertinent details. It took every ounce of her concentration and mem-
orization skill to retain the crucial information, for almost every introduction brought her a handshake with yet another potential
intelligence source.

"Ah, Wolfgang Zink and Madame Karin. So good to see you
again. I would like you to meet my charming American friend," he
would say graciously. Then in Charlotte's ear: "Always the German
ex-officer. Can you believe he even clicks his heels? He is supposed to
manage a German investment concern here."

Charlotte did not dare ask the general to explain further. She just
remembered: Wolfgang Zink.

"And here come Claudia and Johann Shafer. They own an elegant villa at the Pyramid Gardens. He is supposed to be Viennese,
but there is something odd about his credentials and he lives a bit
too grandly, as well."

"Perhaps I read too many books," Charlotte said, not fully aware
of what she was going to blurt out, "but he sounds like a spy." What
a crazy chance to have taken!

But the general laughed heartily. "Precisely my thoughts, but no
proof. Besides, a few spies liven up the party, don't you agree?"

"He seems very nice . . ."

"Do you think I am nice as well?" The general lowered his head
and played the part of an insecure boy.

Charlotte folded her gloved hands in her lap. "You're one of the
kindest people I've met in Egypt. It's so hard to make friends in a
new country."

"Tell me, Miss Christopher, why did you come to Egypt?"

"Why does anyone travel? It is not to see new sights or meet new
people — that's why they say they do it, but it is not the reason."

General Rizk brushed a lock of wavy hair behind his ears. The top
of his head was bald and it glistened with perspiration. "Yes?"

"I came looking for myself."

"You are a very profound thinker for a —" Charlotte knew he was
about to say "woman" but had stopped himself. "For one so young,"
he finished diplomatically just as Madame al-Hakim stepped
forward to remind him it was time to hand out the trophies.

"I will look after your lovely companion, General. Do not fret, you
will surely see her later at the cocktail party." She turned to Charlotte. "The Shafers are giving one jointly with us this evening. It is in
my garden because my roses are at their prime. Claudia has the better cook, so the food should be divine."

"We have not been invited," Charlotte replied softly. With one eye she watched as the general marched off, his boots glinting in the sunlight.

"Nonsense! Of course you have," she said, steering Charlotte toward the veranda where the ladies were drinking tea. On the far side of the ring the men were being offered whiskey from cut-glass decanters.

"Madame al-Hakim," Charlotte said in a low voice, "may I ask you something?"

"Yes, my dear?"

"Is General Rizk married?"

"Most certainly. His wife is a modest Moslem girl. She would not be seen at a function like this one."

"That's what I guessed."

"Are you concerned with your reputation?"

"No. I just didn't want to hurt Mr. MacDonald's feelings."

Madame al-Hakim raised her artistically penciled eyebrows. "Surely you know that Mr. MacDonald is very taken with you. He told me he was pleased you were able to make friends so easily. And do not worry about the general. With you he will behave most properly."

Madame al-Hakim excused herself after Leslie joined them. Leslie's blue taffeta skirt billowed around her legs as the wind blew in from the riverfront. She tried to hold it down so as not to expose her thighs. "If I'm not careful I'll be giving everybody quite a show." She giggled nervously. "That's some handsome man you latched on to! Gordon's positively green."

"Are you sure?"

"Don't tell me you didn't notice? Aren't you glad you wore *the dress*?"

Charlotte nodded and chatted with Leslie, aware that her friend had not found anyone else to talk to. It was a pity she was too bubble-headed to get beyond the basic pleasantries.

At the al-Hakims' villa, Charlotte was reintroduced to many of the same people she had met that afternoon. Most had come without their wives. All Charlotte had to do was circulate, chat amiably, or, if nothing else, listen intently to ensure her next document in secret ink would make interesting reading. As she sat in a corner talking quietly with Leslie and Arnie, General Rizk handed her a glass of champagne. She took tiny sips because she did not dare lose her concentration. A short time later, they were joined by some others in uniform. Charlotte's ears perked up when General Rizk introduced Squadron Leader Gamal Wahid.

"I'm very pleased to meet you," Charlotte began hesitantly. Then, more boldly, "Are you a pilot?"

"Yes, I am," Squadron Leader Wahid replied.

"Wahid was the personal pilot for General Aziz al-Masri," the general added. "He flew him toward German lines in the Western Desert in 1941."

"My uncle was a pilot. He used to take me up all the time."

"So you like to fly?" Squadron Leader Wahid beamed. A gold tooth glinted from the center of a row of brilliant white teeth. "Would you like to fly with me?"

Thank you, God, Charlotte sighed to herself and said, "Oh, yes! Ever since I've been in Egypt I've longed to see the pyramids from the air — and the Nile — and the desert. But it's not possible, is it?"

General Rizk placed his arms across his broad chest and smiled expectantly. "Well?" he challenged the pilot.

"Not military aircraft, of course, but I am a member of the Aero-Glider Club at Heliopolis. You could be my guest there."

"You are very kind, but I'm afraid I don't live in Cairo."

"What are you charming gentlemen talking about?" Madame al-Hakim asked as she passed by.

The general explained Charlotte's wish.

"Why not come up next weekend and stay with me? I will be your chaperone so everything is proper. Would you like that, my dear?"

"I spoke out of place. I should not have made such a request —"

"Nonsense. This is going to be most enjoyable!"

"The planes only seat two, I'm afraid," Squadron Leader Wahid demurred.

"You would never get *me* up in one of those contraptions, Gamal, but Americans are braver than we, I think." Madame al-Hakim tugged on Charlotte's arm. "Now, come with me. I cannot permit these war heroes to monopolize you." As they passed General Abdel Shawqi, a man who had been giving her sidelong glances all evening, he bowed formally. Then, when she turned to follow her hostess, Charlotte felt him lightly pat her buttocks.

When they were in the hallway Madame al-Hakim said, "Your young man is not looking too well — too many araks and not enough food. I have put him upstairs in the guest room. Your friends have agreed it is best if you all spend the night here. It is far too late to drive back."

"I don't —"

"My dear, it is my pleasure," she said with great sincerity, rolling her "r's" with immense sensuality. "I'll show you to your room."

Sitting on the canopied bed, Charlotte worried about returning to Alexandria in time to make her nightly radio transmission. The previous night she had signaled Tel Aviv she was leaving for Cairo, so they would remain on alert until they learned everything was normal. Since there was nothing that could be accomplished by fretting, Charlotte returned downstairs after recombing her hair. The party ended fairly soon, yet there had been time to chat with General Shawqi, who informed her he was Chief of Security for Armament Bases, and to smile sweetly at the pilot and the general before she retired.

❖   ❖   ❖

A ladder of lemony light spilled across the bed. Charlotte blinked and stared at the partially opened shutters, surprised the sun was already so bright. A soft breeze was whipping panels of silky curtains into the room, but another, sharper movement caught her peripheral vision. Gordon was leaning against her door.

"Morning," he said in a sloppy voice.

"How long have you —?"

"Ten minutes, maybe more. I like watching you sleep. Did you know you stroke your lips with your thumb?"

Charlotte pulled the sheet up around her body. The spaghetti straps of her hostess's voluminous red silk nightgown had slipped from her shoulders, revealing the curve of her breasts. She tugged them into place. "You shouldn't —"

Gordon did not budge. "Are you shy with me?"

"I just don't think —"

He moved more swiftly than Charlotte expected and sat on the edge of the bed. "I have a confession to make," he began in a gravelly voice. "Last night I was frantically jealous of you flirting with every man in sight."

"I was only being sociable," she said contritely. "Besides, they were all married men."

"I know. You didn't do anything wrong. I couldn't help feeling the way I did. I drank too much and . . . What I'm really trying to do is apologize."

Charlotte sighed. Gordon did look miserable. "How are you feeling?"

"A slight headache. It will pass." Suddenly his tone changed. "You did surprise me."

"How?"

"I never expected you would be a social success."

"All I did was listen politely to a bunch of boring men telling how important they were."

"Everybody seemed to interest you — the military types, the businessmen, even the goddamned Germans."

"Gordon, shhh! Someone will hear you."

"I don't give a shit!"

"Well, *I* do! You're in *my* room. What will they think?"

"Madame al-Hakim won't care one whit. She's probably slept with half of Cairo."

"Gordon!"

"I'm sorry, Chris."

"What do you have against Germans anyway? You're not Jewish, are you?"

"Christ, that's the kind of comment I'd expect from Leslie, not you. How can you have such a short memory? Those Nazis make my skin crawl."

"Even *you* know that not all Germans were Nazis." Taking a contrary position was the perfect foil once again, even if her stomach churned as she took a pro-German stance.

"I don't *believe* you! One of those guys worked with Goebbels. Don't you know why they're in Egypt?"

"Not really, and I don't much care." She stared at him as defiantly as she could manage. This was the most difficult charade she had ever played with him. Of course she — or rather Charlotte — knew why the Germans were here.

The contacts between the Arab nations and the Nazi authorities began to take shape in the early 1930s. At the outbreak of the Second World War, the Germans strengthened their connections with the Arab National Movement, especially with Haj Amin el Husseini, the Mufti of Jerusalem, who offered to organize an anti-British rebellion behind Allied lines. At the same time, there had been a strong pro-German movement among the junior Egyptian army officers. After the war, German armaments specialists, who were released from forced labor in Eastern Europe or felt it safe to come out of hiding, found there was no place for them in occupied Germany because, under the peace agreement, their country was forbidden to manufacture or develop weapons and aircraft, so they looked elsewhere to utilize their talents. In King Farouk's Egypt, they had found a congenial atmosphere as well as a regime willing to allow them a free hand in technological development.

Charlotte wanted to sort it out without Gordon's overbearing presence. It was far too early in the day to come up with clever arguments thought up by an altered personality. "I'd like to get up now —"

Gordon grabbed her wrist. Charlotte struggled free. "I need to go into the bathroom and get dressed. We can talk about this later," she snapped.

"First answer my question."

"About what?"

"The Germans."

"Why they are here? How the hell should I know? Because they got kicked out of Europe? Or wanted suntans?" Charlotte pulled the sheet around herself and jumped off the bed. She opened the bathroom door. "I'll see you downstairs," she said stiffly, then turned into the cool confines of the tiled bathroom and locked the door tightly.

Soaping her hair under the faucet, she let her hot tears mingle with the cool splashes of water. Had she gone too far with her remarks? This was getting more complicated by the minute. While she fully expected to feel lonely, to be challenged and frustrated by her long-range tasks, she was surprised how sticky personal relationships had become.

With Mitch, it had been easier. He was married; she knew she would be in Ohio for only a few months. They had shared two interests: flying and each other. After the first sexual encounter, they had eagerly sought out opportunities to be together. In the few hours they could find to be alone, their precious time was not squandered on anything: food, formalities, sweet talk. She had once kidded Mitch that they were setting Olympic records for clothing removal and penetration. But he had been good for her — he had made her feel a loved, desired, sensual woman.

"I'll never forget you," he had said hoarsely when he had taken her to Dayton Airport for her flight to New York. "Think of me — when you fly."

She had promised she would, but she had not flown since.

Egypt was different. There was no time limit on her stay; there were no maps to follow in the uncharted territory of how close a friend one could make, what you should say, which political opinions to espouse. The less she knew a person — like the general — the easier it was to be her false self; but with someone like Gordon, someone who saw her day after day, someone who was beginning to care for her, the charade was becoming a nightmare.

As she came downstairs in her slightly rumpled chintz and her day-old underwear, Charlotte felt even more ill at ease. Madame al-Hakim was sitting on the veranda drinking coffee.

"Good morning, my dear." She clapped her hands and a servant poured Charlotte a cup. "Did you sleep well?"

Charlotte sipped gingerly. Happily, it was not too sweet. "Yes, very." In fact, she had not even awakened at the hour she ordinarily sent her transmissions, something she usually did before her alarm went off.

The servant placed a dish of sliced fruits in front of her along with a bright yellow linen napkin and set of ornate silverware.

"Am I the first one up?" She bit into a giant purple grape. Its blood-red juice stained her fingers.

"I heard some other voices, but you are the only one I have seen. I am an early riser myself." She held out her cup to the servant. "This is my third refill."

"It's very good coffee."

"Do you remember your conversation with Squadron Leader Gamal Wahid?"

Charlotte nodded.

"He came by about an hour ago to say he would like you to be his guest at the Aero-Glider Club later this morning."

"That's fabulous!" For once Charlotte did not have to feign enthusiasm. "But I didn't mean to put him to so much trouble."

"Actually, he is more excited about it than you are." She lit a long pink cigarette. "He tells me you come from a family of famous pilots."

"My uncle was a crop duster. Do you know what that is?"

"The chemicals come down from the sky onto the fields?"

"That's right. He would take me up with him when he went out on a practice run and he taught me to fly as well."

"You can fly?"

"Yes."

"Does Gamal know this?"

"Not yet. Do you think I should tell him?"

Madame al-Hakim laughed. "He would never believe you. Women do not fly in Egypt. You must be very clever."

"It isn't that difficult, once you get over your fears."

Madame al-Hakim's blue-black eyes studied Charlotte intently. "I wonder if you Americans know when to be afraid."

Charlotte swallowed her second mouthful of grapes. "Should I be afraid of Mr. Wahid?"

"Certainly not. He is only trying to be courteous to a foreigner."

"Then it would be proper for me to accept his kind invitation."

"To go to the Aero-Glider Club? But of course! The members are all very fine gentlemen."

Leslie and Arnie came out onto the veranda. Leslie was smiling in an odd, self-satisfied way and her husband was exceptionally cheerful. Charlotte could tell they had just made love. For a moment she was envious of the simplicity of their life together.

"Where's Gordo?" Leslie asked.

"I haven't seen him," Charlotte lied, then bubbled over with the news of her invitation to the Aero-Glider Club.

"May we come too?" Leslie asked their hostess.

"You are all expected. Gamal would not have asked a single American girl to come by herself. He is a very proper sort."

"I don't know about this," Arnie said to Charlotte.

"Don't know about what?" Gordon asked as he came outside. He was the only one in the group who did not appear to be wearing yesterday's clothes. How he had managed not to rumple his shirt or lose the creases in his pants confounded Charlotte.

Arnie relayed the day's plans as the houseboy whispered a message to Madame al-Hakim.

"Squadron Leader Gamal Wahid's car has arrived," she announced. "Gamal will be meeting you at the airfield. He wanted to personally ensure everything would be in order."

"I'm ready," Charlotte responded. "I'll meet the rest of you out front."

A dusty road led to the Heliopolis Aero-Glider Club at the far end of the military airfield. Despite its promising name, the club consisted of one modest building that served as a club room on one side and maintenance hangar on the other. On this weekday afternoon, only one other member, an elderly British gentleman, was seated on the veranda. He squinted out toward the runway as a weary-looking Piper was being fueled.

Wahid made the introductions. "I would like you to meet Miss Carla Christopher of the United States Information Agency. Miss Christopher, this is Wing Commander Alistair Fielding of the Royal Air Force and consultant to the Egyptian Air Force. He is also secretary of the club."

Charlotte shook Fielding's hand firmly, noticing his palm was dry and trembly. Gordon and the others were also presented.

"Are you all going to fly today?" the wing commander asked the pilot.

"Miss Christopher has been wanting to see the pyramids from the air. I have offered her my services. If the others would also like —"

"No, no," Gordon interrupted, "we wouldn't want to put you out further. We'll be delighted just to watch."

"What about you, Mrs. Showers?"

Leslie clutched Arnie's hand. "I don't care for heights."

The wing commander patted his forehead with a neatly folded handkerchief. "I'd take you up myself, Miss Christopher, but I'm afraid my medical has long since expired. You're in good hands with Gamal."

Charlotte flashed her all-American teeth. "Yes, I'm quite certain of that."

"I will see to the plane." Gamal bowed slightly and walked across the airfield.

"Do you mind if we wait in the shade?" Leslie asked Charlotte.

"Not at all."

Arnie pulled out a chair for his wife. The British officer asked if they would like some refreshment as he clapped his hands to alert the servant. Charlotte declined. "Not before I go up. Perhaps later."

"Very wise," the wing commander said with a wink.

"If you'll excuse me, I don't want to keep Squadron Leader Wahid waiting." She started down the path to the runway.

"I'll be right back," Gordon said and ran after Charlotte. When he caught up to her, he tugged at her arm. "I really don't like you doing this. Look at that antique!" He pointed to the ten-year-old Piper Cub, approximately the same vintage as Mitch's training plane. Instead of the taxi-yellow finish, its canvas had been painted a military gray. Even so, the outlines of the bear cub insignia were visible on the tail.

"I'm not worried, but I'll do my own pre-flight."

"What's that?"

"Checking the gas, the oil, the brakes."

"How would you know what to do?"

"My uncle was a pilot. I've told you about him."

"That doesn't mean you understand —"

"Gordo, I could fly this thing from here to Cyprus and back. I'm a trained pilot."

"C'mon Chris, you're not serious!"

"The hell I'm not!" She strutted quickly to where Wahid was standing. "My friend Mr. MacDonald is being a bit overprotective." She smiled winsomely. "I trust you completely — and this little Cub. It's my favorite airplane."

"Why is that?"

"My uncle had one like it. Do you mind if I do a brief walk-around? I think it would make Mr. MacDonald feel easier."

"Certainly."

The pilot followed Charlotte as she checked for tears in the fabric, her hand running over the canvas to test that it was tightly stretched. "This is a pre-1946 model, isn't it?"

"About 1945, I am told. How did you know?"

"After 1946 they went from wood spars to metal ones. How many quarts of oil?"

"Four. Do you wish to look for yourself?"

Five would have been better, but four was an acceptable minimum. It would have been an insult to quibble. "No, that's fine. Would you like me to hold the brakes while you turn the prop?"

"I was going to call the mechanic, but if you know how . . ."

Charlotte hopped into the front seat and gave the engine two shots of prime. The propeller caught on the first try. As Wahid approached the door she asked, "Would you prefer me in the rear?"

"I can fly from either position, but that would be best."

In a few seconds they were taxiing down an unmarked runway. Sand rushed alongside as they picked up speed and blotted the side view. As the plane lifted off smoothly the air cleared considerably. Her heart soared. She was flying, flying over Egypt! She looked below and saw several rows of military aircraft. I could count the planes if I wanted. In fact, I should, she realized, but she had been too excited at the triumph of having come so far and the opportunity passed. The plane turned to the south and began to climb over Cairo. On one side, contours of brown and beige desert undulated in perplexing patterns; on the other, a line of vivid green looked as though a child had drawn across the barren landscape with a smudgy green crayon; ahead, the city of Cairo appeared, the Nile neatly slicing it into two distinct halves. The plane swooped lower.

Right over the largest island in the river Wahid shouted, "There is the Gezira Sporting Club." He tipped the wing to the left. "And the Salah el-din Mosque."

"Is that the Manyal Palace?"

"Yes, and at the tip of the island is the Manisterli Palace. Have you been there?"

"No."

"You must permit me to escort you," he shouted as the plane swooped upward and continued west to Giza, where the pyramids commanded the northeastern margin of the plateau of the Libyan Desert.

From the air, the pyramids seemed rather flat and almost melted into the powdery medicinal yellow of the surrounding sand and rock. When Charlotte had seen them for the first time, she had been awed by their height as well as by the mystical angles as the sun moved across the sky. Approached by land, they loomed with a presence that was entirely missing from the air. From this downward angle, even the Sphinx was but a long mound with a curved end and a slightly flattened top; all mystery of expression in the recumbent lion with the Pharaoh's head was lost. A genuine tourist might have been disappointed, but Charlotte was enthralled as she got her bearings in the air and analyzed how to make the most of the trip. At first she was annoyed she had not brought her camera to Cairo, but now she knew it was for the best. Desiring photographs was one excuse for repeating the journey.

The squadron leader was banking the plane sixty degrees around the peak of the Pyramid of Cheops, the largest in the Giza group. "The turns do not bother you?"

"No. I like the G's!"

"Remarkable," he called as he pulled straight and level. "Is there anything else you might like to see?"

"Could we go back via Abu Roash? I've heard so much about the pyramids there."

Charlotte had been told a visit to the antiquities in that area required traveling by camel, donkey, or jeep over rough terrain and then a thirty-minute climb on foot. Although she was not particularly interested in seeing them, she knew the request was valid and would impress upon her pilot her serious study of all things Egyptian.

"My pleasure," he called over the roar of the engine.

The plane swerved dramatically to the northwest and in a few minutes they were over the Pyramid of Djedefre, the son of Cheops. After a quick air tour of the main pyramid, Wahid turned over the village of Kerdasa. "They make beautiful carpets there. My mother has one in her home. I would like to show it to you sometime."

"I would like very much to meet your mother."

He pointed to the fuel gauge. "I am afraid we must return. We will be approaching Cairo from the west."

On the way back the city was glaring under an almost midday sun. Emerald-green lawns and palm trees gleamed like jewels amongst the burnt ocher of the sand-drenched buildings. Here and there a whitewashed hotel or glass-clad office building sparkled. Along the industrial corridors a haze of pungent smoke hovered. A strong scent of sulfur assaulted Charlotte's nose and her eyes teared.

As Wahid steered the craft, the stick moved between Charlotte's legs. She held it loosely in her right hand and tentatively rested her left hand on the throttle. The memory of flying with Mitch was fresh. She kept her eye on the air speed indicator. Squadron Leader Gamal Wahid was flying by the numbers.

She waited until they cleared the heavily populated center of Cairo and were headed back to Heliopolis and — when the commercial airport was in sight — tapped the pilot on the shoulder. "My turn," she said mischievously.

"What? Is there some difficulty?"

"Not at all. I'm going to fly your airplane — with your permission," she said so timidly her voice was drowned out by the wind.

Charlotte gathered her courage. "Watch!" She grabbed the stick. Expertly, she maneuvered it in concert with the rudder pedals and made a 180-degree turn to the left, then repeated the maneuver to the right. Next, she did a power-off stall and recovered perfectly.

As the pilot turned to watch her, she was afraid he was annoyed. On the contrary. He was beaming. She made two passes over the military airfield: first, to make a rough count of the aircraft on the tarmac; second, to put the plane into the pattern. She lined up for the approach turn. "Shall I land it?"

"Yes," he said in English, then muttered something in Arabic that sounded like "Mashallah."

Eyeing the runway, Charlotte was able to judge her distances quite accurately. By controlling her angle of descent, she kept the plane at the correct seventy miles per hour and, when the runway was made, bled off the power. She could almost hear Mitch's voice reminding her to "walk the rudder" as she let the wheels down by pulling the stick into her chest and maintaining level flight until she was in ground effect. All three wheels hit at the same time. "Damn!" she cursed under her breath. She had wanted to impress Wahid with her technique. As the plane slowed, she felt the pedals moving without her pushing them. Wahid had taken command and taxied to the clubhouse. Leslie and Arnie waved wildly. Wahid turned off the fuel flow and the plane sputtered to a stop. He jumped out to help her down. She took his hand and eased herself over the side.

Gordon was waiting for them at the clubhouse. "Does *he* know that you can fly?" Wahid asked as he offered his arm and escorted Charlotte up the walkway.

"He didn't believe me."

"I wouldn't have either. Who taught you?"

"My uncle."

"He would be very proud."

"No. He would have hated that landing. I'd like to prove I could do a better one."

"That is hardly necessary. There was a bit of a crosswind. Under the circumstances, it was an excellent landing. The approach was superb as well."

"I need more practice."

Wing Commander Fielding was on the stairs, a cold glass of orange juice in his hand. "Practice?" he asked.

Charlotte accepted it gratefully. The servant handed the pilot a beer. "Did you see that landing, Commander?"

"Nothing to brag about, Gamal!" The British officer laughed so hard his glasses slipped down his sweating nose. He pushed them back up and mopped his face with his damp handkerchief.

"For a lady who has not flown in quite some time, it is an achievement."

Fielding looked at Charlotte in amazement. "*You* landed the Cub?"

Wahid related how she had taken over. Gordon, who was listening, was equally stunned. "Chris, you *actually* flew that plane?"

"Yes, Gordon. I told you I've been flying for years. I learned in a plane exactly like that one."

Leslie jumped up and clapped her hands. "Oh, Chris, would you take me up with you?"

"I thought you didn't like heights," her husband reminded.

"Maybe it would be different with Chris," she said defensively.

"What about you, Gordon? Would you go up with me?" Charlotte challenged. The moment she said the words, she regretted them. Gordon's mouth had frozen into a gaping oval. Charlotte tried to recover by telling everyone how wonderful Cairo was from the air. "The pyramids looked like children's toys strewn about. I only regret I didn't have my camera and that the time was so short."

"You must return to Heliopolis soon, Miss Christopher," the Egyptian pilot said.

"You've all been so kind, but I know how busy you are, Squadron Leader Wahid."

"My schedule is sometimes demanding, but it would be my great honor to fly with you again."

"What would you like to see next?" Fielding inquired.

"Oh, Alexandria would be lovely — and Luxor — and I wonder what the canal looks like from the air."

"Following the Nile south is fascinating, with the added benefit that you can't get lost," the British officer chimed in. "I regret I can no longer offer my services. It's my heart, you see — some irregular beats."

"Might I be so bold as to ask if I could fly *you,* sir?"

"Only club members may act as pilot-in-command," he said pompously. Then his jowly face became wreathed in a smile. "However, I do not see why you could not apply for membership. We often extend privileges to diplomats and the like."

The pilot was frowning. "Sir, there are no women members."

"Ah, that is true. But nothing in the rules prohibits it. We accept military flying credentials. Otherwise members must be checked out in the aircraft they intend to fly. How much instruction do you think she would need to be certified in the Cub?"

"Two or three hours. I would volunteer my services —"

"You gentlemen are very sweet, but I live in Alexandria and don't often come to Cairo."

"Well, now we have given you a good excuse to come up, haven't we?" The British officer winked.

It was all Charlotte could do to contain her glee as she thanked the wing commander and pilot profusely. Gordon barely spoke all the way back to Alexandria, which was just as well, for Charlotte's mind was busy plotting where she would fly next and how she could photograph the sites on her list of suspicious installations.

That night she could hardly wait to prepare her message, which first explained her absence, then detailed her flight, with specific mention of the lines of planes at the military airfield. After the message was coded, she removed the transmitter hidden in her bathroom scale and attached the crystals secreted in false-bottomed cans of talcum and stomach powders. All her studies in aerial photography and recognition were finally going to be of use.

Charlotte had spent the last two months before leaving for Egypt in a dingy room near the Kirya, working with an endlessly patient man she knew only as Douglas, who had been an aerial photographer in England. Most of his exercises were based on his photographs of Channel ports and German aircraft. They began with verticals, photos taken vertically from above. She studied both how to take a good photograph and how to analyze what she saw from the air. Gradually, she learned to distinguish between railway lines, with their gentle curves, and roads, which more closely follow the lay of the land.

"Notice that there are always shadows on daytime high-altitude photographs," Douglas pointed out. "If you place them with the shadows falling toward you — as if the sun were shining down on the photograph from beyond the surface you are working on — it is easier to visualize the prints."

His next priority was to teach her about shipping. "Counts must be accurate. Initially, this is done by listing the vessels by size. Afterward you will learn the recognition points to identify the types." Finally, they moved on to aircraft. Charlotte had been looking forward to this, but the first aerial photograph she studied — a busy fighter base in the Pas de Calais — was most perplexing. She knew she was expected to count the aircraft on the field, but even under a magnifying glass the ME 109s were no bigger than pinheads. "I'll never be able to do it," she had groaned when she had not been able to identify them as Messerschmitts.

Douglas had not been daunted. "Try this." He gave her clearer photos of a French airfield near Bordeaux. This time she was able to recognize seven different types of aircraft. When she had given her list to Douglas, she pointed to one in the shadows of some trees. "I can't name this one."

Douglas shook his head. "Neither can I. You have done remarkably well."

In a few weeks, she advanced to stereo prints, which fascinated her because her Grandmother Green had an antique stereopticon and a shoebox filled with yellowing views of the Johnstown flood, Indian Sikhs sleeping on beds of nails, and other oddities of the world that had so fascinated her as a child. Here the same technique was employed for quite a different purpose. She was shown how to take a pair of photographs by moving the camera only a few inches between shots. When developed, they were placed in a simplified stereoscope, which she was taught to make from a pair of spectacles mounted in a single rectangular piece of metal and supported by four metal legs that held it a few inches above the photographs. The two side-by-side prints were edged backward and forward until the still images fused — by some optical illusion — into one. The effect was incredibly three-dimensional: buildings in the foreground seemed to leap off the paper and a remarkable lifelike depth was achieved, permitting details to pop out and be understood more clearly.

Her concluding lessons involved a dizzying array of photographs of the ports and airfields of Egypt, which she was to memorize. "You must know at a glance what is normal. Then you will recognize the abnormal when it occurs. If you are driving down a street and a ball bounces out in front of you, you will assume — quite rightly — that a child is playing nearby, and even if you *never* see the child, your brakes will be on, you will be watchful and slow. That's because you know what's normal as well as the *significance* of what you see when you see it. It's the same with one of these photos."

Douglas showed her Dutch shipyards crowded with barges having their bows cut away. "As soon as we saw this, we knew the importance of what was happening because we had studied the regular routine of those yards. Remember, on some assignments you will be an interpreter, not just a photographer or cataloguer. To the interpreter, the details are all," Douglas insisted.

Douglas was so thorough, he had even given her a final exam. At the last minute she had crammed: memorizing that a merchant vessel is like an oblong box with pointed ends, a naval unit is cigar-shaped; measuring how the wing span of a German airplane differs from an English-built one; combing *Jane's All the World's Aircraft* for markings; checking the calculations to determine a ship's speed from the wave formations. In the end, Douglas had been pleased with her performance.

In Heliopolis, without reference textbooks, Charlotte could only guess at what the military planes had been. One row had been twin-engine aircraft with a shapely line similar to that of the Mosquito. She knew they came in several models, but they looked like the Mosquito Tmk III. The Egyptians' single-engine fighters appeared to be Mustangs well camouflaged in blue-brown paint. She might even have recognized some British-made Vampires and one MiG-15 of Soviet origin. The actual numbers on the field she could only estimate, but the next time up they would be easier to count.

Laboriously, Charlotte coded the transmission, using the Book of Ezra as the key. By transposing the date and making the basic calculation, she began with Chapter 7, Verse 3. "The son of Amariah, the son of Azariah, the son of Meraioth . . ." As she worked, she wondered who would be reading her message and what they would be thinking when they saw it. Would the young radio operator understand the data's significance? Who would see it next? How long before it got to Eli? How long before he would know she was about to prove her worth to him?

.:. .:. .:.

Balance and restraint.

Eli had underlined those words on a blackboard during a final briefing. "Because it may take months or even years to establish oneself, when a target is located or information becomes available, the natural tendency is to pursue with vigor. That is the very moment you must pull back . . . wait . . . proceed with the utmost caution, for success may be the greatest danger. First, because you might be falling into a trap; second, because you may be creating your own trap with blind enthusiasm."

At the time Charlotte had not comprehended what he had meant; now, his cautions seemed to have been constructed for her exact situation. Information was all around her and access was simplicity itself. She had an open invitation to fly over Egypt virtually unfettered. When the friends of the Shafers and al-Hakims learned of the American girl's ability to fly an airplane, her social status soared and she was wanted as a centerpiece for every gathering. Although she could go as the al-Hakims' guest, for Madame al-Hakim had taken her under her wing, it was preferable for her to be escorted by Gordon.

The difficulty was that Gordon disapproved of both her flying and her association with the Germans, so managing Gordon became her primary problem. If she could have broken off with him and retained the status quo, she would have done so immediately, but it was Gordon who held the key to her entrée into the diplomatic circles of Alexandria and Cairo; it was Gordon who made it possible for her to be seen with General Youssef Rizk and Squadron Leader

Gamal Wahid without nasty gossip spreading. Gordon had become even more proprietary toward her since she began to fly, letting everyone know his claim on her. Surprisingly, Charlotte did not resent this as much as she expected. Gordon was charming, amusing, and attentive. He indulged her by driving up to Cairo often and she could not help but be drawn to his bright wit and incisive mind. His kisses were not suffocating. He demonstrated a remarkable sensitivity about not pushing her too far or too quickly. All he seemed to want was her company, and this she could give freely and honestly.

Her guest membership in the Aero-Glider Club was a much talked about accomplishment. After being checked out to solo, she tactfully insisted that Gordon be her first passenger. After his initial reluctance, he had enjoyed the flight over Giza immensely and proudly hugged her after they landed — to the applause of the audience on the veranda. After that, other club members, especially the Egyptian military officers, lined up for the privilege to fly with Charlotte — even offering to pay for the gasoline. Charlotte indulged them all. It gave her an excuse to bring her camera and ask them to hold the controls while she photographed the sights around Cairo.

Balance and restraint.

She took no aerial shots of the military airfield, so as not to raise suspicion. She could memorize enough — curious ships in the harbors, unusual aircraft on the field, military convoys on the roads — to clog the airwaves from Alexandria to Tel Aviv. For the present, she was biding her time until she could take off in the little Cub on her own without anyone thinking much of it. Then she would attach her telephoto lens, set it for infinity, and snap all the photos she wanted, later secreting the exposed film in her false-bottomed containers, and eventually turning them in to her courier on her regular route.

She had sensed Eli's pleasure in the brief tone of the radio replies. Once she had dispatched the names of her recent contacts, including the Shafers, a long list of people to seek out and befriend was transmitted to her frequency. Most were within easy reach. All the names were German.

Tel Aviv was especially interested in Wilhelm Voss. She had been briefed about him before arriving in Egypt. During the war, Voss had been the manager of the Skoda Munitions Works and arrived in Cairo in 1948 as an adviser to King Farouk. It was believed that he had laid the foundations for the establishment of the Egyptian armaments industry.

Another important name on her original roster was that of the retired artillery general Wilhelm Fahrmbacher, who was said to have
brought more than fifty other former Wehrmacht officers to Egypt
with him. There were Leopold Gleim, who had headed the Gestapo
in Warsaw; Willi Brenner, who had helped organize the Mauthau-
sen concentration camp; and SS General Oscar Dirlewanger; all
were known to have altered their identities. There were fifteen German test pilots and technicians who had replaced the British experts
at the De Havilland aircraft assembly factories, which had been set
up by the British in the waning days of King Farouk's reign. Surely,
if she kept up her contacts with Squadron Leader Wahid and his
friends, some of these Nazi advisers would surface.

Charlotte had to remind herself she was not a Nazi-hunter. Her
job was to gather raw data and deliver it to her contacts on the
streets of Alexandria who, in turn, had some way of getting the information to Israel. She knew little about her intermediaries besides
their code names and the procedures for meeting them. In addition,
she had been given one phone number in case of extreme emergency
or if she had "hot" data or film she needed to unload immediately.
So far she had not used it. Martine and Homer had sufficed. She had
been told almost nothing about them — only that they were Egyptian-born Jews and complete professionals.

The Jews of Egypt were a community unto themselves. In the
early 1950s they numbered under a hundred thousand. While the
Jews resided in Egypt, they did not consider themselves Egyptian; in
fact, they were not even permitted citizenship in the country of their
birth and were referred to as "hawagat," or gentlemen, with a mixture of contempt and envy. They kept to their own quarters, attended their own schools, and spoke English (the language of the
government) and French (the language of culture) more fluently
than Arabic. They patronized Jewish hospitals and were buried in
Jewish cemeteries. Most were Zionists who collected money for the
Jewish National Fund, learned Hebrew, visited Palestine, and even
invested money there. Until 1948, when the Egyptian army invaded
Palestine and, simultaneously, the police swooped down on the Jewish communities in Alexandria and Cairo arresting suspected Zionists, they had seen no reason to flee Egypt. By the middle of 1950,
more than half of Egypt's Jewish community departed via a mass
migration aided by the Mossad le Aliya-Bet.

Martine was born in Alexandria in 1928. Her father had fled Bul-
garia on the eve of the First World War to avoid conscription and

married a French woman who bore him three children. Educated in Jewish schools, she joined the Hashomer Hatzair youth movement and dreamed of someday immigrating to either Palestine or America. In the meantime, she was interested in sports and played on the women's basketball team, taught swimming, and was secretly trained to help with the immigration movement before being drafted to work directly for Israel.

Homer, who was born in 1933, was a member of a prosperous family who lived in Alexandria's Cleopatra quarter. His Greek-born father was the director of a chemical import firm; his mother was from a long line of Jaffa rabbis. At school — a religious establishment founded by Alexandria's chief rabbi, Rabbi Ventura — Homer had become active in the Bnei Akiva movement and later had served as an instructor. When one of his closest friends moved to the newly formed State of Israel, they kept in touch. In 1951, his friend returned home to organize a cell working for Aman, Israeli military intelligence.

All Charlotte knew was that she could entrust her precious evidence — the aerial surveys and the more complex letters, written in secret inks, describing the people in her new social circle — to either Homer or Martine.

By May, after Charlotte had flown fifty hours in the Aero-Glider Club's plane, she was no longer a curiosity. The al-Hakims' guest room had become a second home where she kept several gowns purchased at Rivoli's, Cairo's most elegant shop. Madame al-Hakim — who took all the credit for bringing Charlotte "out of her shell" — was now "Aunt Sabina."

As often as possible, Gordon accompanied her to Cairo, but he lodged with the Taylors, American friends connected with the embassy, so as not to compromise Charlotte's reputation — something he was pleased she guarded meticulously. Fortunately for Charlotte, Gordon was required to be in Cairo on weekends frequently, for embassy briefings. In April, as he had predicted astutely, the thirty-six-year-old Nasser was elected Prime Minister and took de facto power from Naguib (who was eventually ousted on the charge he was co-operating with the Moslem Brotherhood, a band of religious zealots who twice attempted to assassinate Nasser). In the fluctuating political climate, the Americans were unsure of their own status, and Gordon was capitalizing on his clever observations to win points with the embassy staff.

While Gordon was engaged in diplomatic meetings, Charlotte would take to the air. Her solo flights had systematically covered strategic grids of the country and had encompassed a huge armor base in the desert just east of Heliopolis. In the course of four brief flights over the strategic area, she had made a series of fine-grained stereo aerial photographs, which she expected Tel Aviv had enlarged a thousand times and was using to count the rivets on the tanks. Sometimes she regretted that she never saw the developed films and hoped that one day she would encounter them again on some intelligence analyst's desk in Israel.

On one occasion, she actually saw the tanks moving out to the north and reported that a unit was going on maneuvers in the direction of the canal. At the same time, she had sent along photographs of an airfield on the road to Medinet el-Faijûm and received a terse reply that they already knew this was a "dummy airfield."

"Bullshit," she coded back.

"Document, please," came the curt response.

To defend her position, she had written a long letter in secret ink and delivered it to Martine. The correspondence asserted they *were* real planes because she had seen several take off when she was in the vicinity and had confirmed her observations by innocently inquiring of a wing commander who frequented the club whether she had "accidently violated restricted airspace."

"What were you doing out there?" the pilot asked excitedly.

"I'd flown over the Pyramids of Dahshûr and was on my way back, following the road instead of the river, when I saw the airfield. I turned back immediately. There was a great deal of activity and I didn't want to embarrass the club by being shot down." She laughed flirtatiously and the officer was charmed.

"It would make a good alternate airfield in case of emergency. That runway is two thousand meters long."

"They must be expecting much larger aircraft than the ones I saw, which were fairly small twin-engine types — I don't know what they were."

The officer lit his long-stemmed pipe and sucked at it loudly. "They must have been our new Vampires. I have flown one myself recently."

While Charlotte longed to engage him further and possibly wangle a close-up look at one of the aircraft, she controlled her impulses. At least she had enough data to satisfy Tel Aviv. A month later headquarters informed her of what they suspected might be under construction in three locations: armament bases in the vicinity of Inshâs el-Raml and south of the Bitter Lakes at el-Shallûfa, and possibly a new Messerschmitt factory close to the airfield north of Bilbeis. Two of the sites were short flights within the recreational range of the Aero-Glider Club. But the flight to el-Shallûfa was a more serious undertaking in terms of time and fuel consumption. The problem was she had never taken such a long cross-country trip before, and in order not to do anything out of character, Charlotte needed to plan some intermediate flights that would indicate she was extending the scope of her air tours gradually. Studying the maps, she realized el-Shallûfa was closer than Alexandria.

"Wouldn't you love to see Alexandria by air?" she asked Gordon one day shortly after receiving the directive.

"Possibly . . ." he wavered. "That's an awfully long time to spend in that cramped cockpit."

"C'mon, it would be only a few hours up and back."

Gordon agreed with some trepidation, but after completing the journey admitted he was glad he had made it.

With that successful trip behind her, Charlotte decided she could arrange another extended cross-country in a few weeks without creating any suspicion — but this time her destination would be quite different.

In the beginning, her trip to el-Shallûfa was to be no more than the briefest aerial survey. There would be no circling the area, just a leisurely cruising altitude above the Bitter Lakes as if on a direct flight from Suez to Ismailia. Then a few unexpected events — no single one particularly meaningful in itself — were to alter her scheme drastically. Together, however, they placed Charlotte on alert.

The first incident was Professor Kelada's illness. In the middle of the night he had been taken ill with violent stomach pains. She had awakened to his screams. The Keladas' servant had run to her door and asked her to come to the big house. Daphne had been frantic, an ambulance had been called, and she had gone along because Daphne had begged Charlotte to stay with her. In the end, the professor's illness was diagnosed as perforated ulcer. After surgery, an uneventful recovery was predicted. Daphne had thanked her for having been there when she needed someone. Charlotte was happy to have helped — except she had missed an important transmission and had been chastised in the next coded reply and warned never to miss a signal again.

Next, Martine and Homer began acting strangely. Instead of her usual fashionable clothing, Martine showed up in a torn smock and sandals. Her expression was downcast, her eyes furtive, and she did not speak. Homer was absent three times in a row. When they finally met, he seemed peculiarly jumpy.

After spending a three-day weekend in Cairo, Charlotte saw neither of her contacts for five days straight. Had they been arrested? Was she being followed? Using every technique she had been taught to ferret out a shadow, she was certain she was in the clear, so she began to wonder if they had been recalled and, if so, why she had not been informed. It was all quite unsettling, so she reported the odd behavior during her next transmission. She was given the signal not to be concerned.

The third worrisome incident was of a romantic nature. Gordon had to drive up to Cairo for a meeting and offered her a ride, knowing full well she would take advantage of the situation and go flying.

"I don't mind if you go the airfield, but I don't want you staying at the al-Hakims' this time."

"Why?"

"I can't be seen associating with them right now."

"Why ever not?"

"All I can say is I'm doing work of a sensitive nature."

"Where do you propose I stay?" she said coyly to cover her curiosity about what he was up to.

"The Taylors said they would be delighted to have you."

"Madame al-Hakim will be insulted if she finds out. She's been so kind to me."

"Please, Chris, just this once." His voice was plaintive. There was no way she could refuse him.

She had flown around the airfield only a few times, then played bridge with Wing Commander Fielding and his wife before Gordon picked her up and took her back to the Taylors to change.

"You look absolutely divine," Donna Taylor commented on Charlotte's new strapless chiffon gown with a beaded waistline and matching handbag. "Won't you do me the honor of wearing my pearls tonight?"

Charlotte was perplexed by her hostess's generosity, but she had to admit the triple-stranded choker with its diamond and ruby clasp was particularly suited to her mauve gown. She accepted graciously.

When Gordon, dressed in an elegant white linen jacket, pulled up to the Al Hatti — one of Cairo's most impressive restaurants — he waited expectantly for her reaction. Dutifully, she admired the crystal chandeliers, gigantic mirrors, and plushly carpeted floor over which the tall, ebony-skinned Sudanese waiters glided silently. An orchestra entertained with a combination of Oriental and popular Western melodies while silver platters of delicacies were served in a choreographed sequence.

By the time the champagne was served, Gordon was acting the part of the young intellectual to whom she had first been drawn instead of the harried diplomat of late. His reddish-gold hair glinted in the candlelight and his face was flushed — not with the usual stressful blotches but with good cheer and glowing happiness.

"You have never looked more beautiful," he began. "No wonder every man in Cairo is jealous of me. Everyone at the consulate is always asking about you."

Everyone at the consulate! Charlotte's stomach churned. Her worst fears of becoming too well known were coming to pass. She would have to be more circumspect.

Eli had warned, "You might be withdrawn from your assignment when everything is going well — even perfectly. There is a sense of timing, which you cannot discern yourself. I am predicting you will feel supremely frustrated when the inevitable summons home is given. This is the one job in the world where you cannot be permitted to make a single mistake — or be *too* successful either."

Had she reached the saturation point already?

Gordon was mumbling something about Persian poets, the tug of the ancients, and other philosophical gibberish that she usually found captivating. He was trying so hard to please her. Oh, Gordon! If I were really Chris I would love you. You are good and kind and forthright. You hate phonies, and Nazis, and can see through fiery speechmakers to their terrible dictatorial cores. You are a true patriot; you would die for your country — my country, too; and if you knew who I really was, you would be proud of everything — except my deception.

"Do you know what Plotinus said?" he was asking.

"What?" She had not been following his train of thought.

"He wrote, 'To any vision must be brought an eye adapted to what is to be seen.' "

"Yes, go on."

"The vision I see is the woman with whom I wish to spend the rest of my life, Chris. I know that now with all my heart."

Her jaw slackened and her eyes blinked back tears. She was utterly appalled by his proposal.

The orchestra was playing "It Takes Two to Tango." The waiter topped off her glass of champagne and served a pastry dripping with honey and rolled in slivered nuts. Gordon was biting his lower lip. Charlotte was thinking this was the worst moment of her life. If she did not genuinely like the man, it would be easier.

But Gordon, gentle Gordon, sensing her discomfort, backed off. "I didn't think this would come as such a surprise. Leslie and Arnie and Donna Taylor — they all expected you'd have guessed by now." He swallowed hard. "How should I know what a woman is thinking about?" he groaned.

"Nasser's mind is easier to read, isn't it?"

"Infinitely!" He sighed with relief that she had broken his somber mood.

Charlotte decided she could hedge. "It's so difficult for me. If my mother were still alive . . . I guess I'm not quite over her and this trip to Egypt was to be a time to avoid, not make, commitments. Do you think you can understand that?"

"I can try."

"It's not that I don't like you, or even love you, it's that I don't know what I want. Give me some time — a few more months is all I ask. If I choose to stay in Egypt, it will be with you."

"There is one difficulty —"

"What's that?"

"I may not be in Egypt that much longer. There's talk of a new assignment."

"Where?"

"I'm not certain. I've been asked to consider Indochina. It would be a move up the ladder. Enough said. I wanted to warn you. It will probably happen at the end of July. And I wanted you to go with me. The idea of . . ." He gulped so hard his throat quivered.

She touched his hand. "Soon, Gordo" was what she said, but she was thinking that Gordon's departure would be a relief.

Until then she had his gentle ultimatum with which to concern herself. She could not avoid him; she could not satisfy him. The whole situation put her on guard. During the day she was on edge; at night she could not sleep more than a few hours. She was waking up to imaginary screams — like the ones Professor Kelada had called into the night, but they twisted into Martine's voice, or seemed to come from Homer's hawkish face. Sometimes she feared she herself might be calling out, and shut her windows tightly, just in case. Nerves were an expected part of the job; breakdowns were not uncommon either. Everything could fall apart at any minute. Suddenly, she sensed her time was almost up.

•ː• •ː• •ː•

The el-Shallûfa flight became an all-consuming project. Not that the scope was so vast; there were just so many details that could not be overlooked. First, she needed an excuse to be in Cairo on a Friday. She promised herself she would not rush out and create a reason — it had to evolve naturally and, preferably, derive from somebody else's need or suggestion. Several weeks passed before she found a logical opportunity.

Leslie Showers had confided to Charlotte that she was pregnant. But after almost a month of feeling sick, she began to have a problem with spot bleeding. When her doctor at the Swiss hospital recommended a specialist in Cairo, it was Charlotte who took the time off from the library and volunteered to drive her the next afternoon — Thursday. Leslie was told to expect to stay at least one night, maybe more, because certain tests were to be performed. As Charlotte had surmised, Leslie was hospitalized and Charlotte went to the al-Hakims' to spend Thursday night.

"There is nothing you can do for her," Aunt Sabina said. "She needs to rest more than anything. Why not go to the Aero-Club tomorrow?"

"I'm terribly worried," Charlotte said dejectedly.

"Many women have a rough month or two in the beginning. My sister went to bed for the first six weeks with each of her children. Afterward, she was strong as an ox."

"The afternoons are so hot this time of year, I'd rather fly in the early morning hours. Then I could spend the rest of the day at Leslie's bedside."

"An excellent idea," Aunt Sabina agreed.

Friday morning, the second of July, Charlotte was up before dawn. Every step she would take had been enacted mentally. She had worked out alternate courses of action and promised herself she would abandon her plan if any element was askew.

In the kitchen, Charlotte helped herself to fruit and bread, leaving crumbs and a soiled plate as evidence that she had taken the time to eat breakfast. In her bag, she had already packed a few cosmetic items, a bottle of mineral water, two oranges, a box of English cream biscuits, a small pita bread, and a chunk of soft white cheese. There was a separate package of biscuits, library books, and fruit readied to take to Leslie later. These she would leave in the trunk of Gordon's car. Inside the pita were two measured pieces of white twine; pressed into the cheese were windings of copper wire. All was ready. She tiptoed out of the house.

In the distance she caught the voice of the muezzin reciting the Ebed. "The perfection of God, the Deserved, the Existing, the Singular, the Supreme . . ." As the sweet prayers wafted through the barely fluttering palms, her determination almost faltered. The words were a potent reminder: You are in a foreign land, you are a stranger, an infidel; our God does not approve of you. ". . . His Perfection be extolled."

She took a deep breath and started the car.

The road to Heliopolis was quiet, even for the early hour, because it was the Moslem Sabbath. Charlotte choked on the foul air. Cairo was blanketed in a mist of beige dust, black soot, and an undefined yellowish chemical haze. This outlying area of the city was a brutal place to live. Here, several million of the unluckiest people on earth subsisted without water, without sewage, without more than the flimsiest tin-and-scrap-board roofs and walls. Many survived on the remains of a more substantial culture by huddling in old cemeteries, in the broken husks of mosques, under tents of rags. Just as their ancestors stripped the polished limestone off the pyramids to build Cairo, so they reused the detritus of a newer civilization to breed yet another.

The road leading to Al-Mazar, Cairo's international airport, was desolate. Charlotte scanned the sky for larger aircraft. Nothing was in sight. As she drove through Heliopolis, she eyed the Helio-Lido Club, where, she had been told, most of the German experts belonged; she regretted that a woman would never receive an invitation to cross that hallowed threshold.

Even the military airfield, which ran alongside the Aero-Glider Club, was unusually silent. The parachute unit often trained in the mornings when the winds were light and the air was cool, but Charlotte had already determined they never jumped on Fridays.

As she expected, only the caretaker was at the Aero-Glider Club so early in the day. "Sabah el-kher," he greeted her and opened the door to the office.

"Allah yisabbe'hkum bilkher." She gave the polite rejoinder. "May God grant you a good morning." From a hook behind the secretary's desk she took the key to the Piper Cub and made the appropriate entries in its log book:

Time off: 7:15 A.M.
Fuel: Full tanks
Destination: Ismailia and return
Expected flight time: 2 hours
Estimated time of return: 11:00 A.M.
Pilot: C. Christopher

By the time she was finished, the caretaker had a cup of coffee poured for her and the table laid with yellow linen. She smiled her appreciation but did not take time to sit down. Instead, standing, she gulped the coffee.

As was her usual custom, she stopped by the rest room before going out to the plane. Washing her hands and face, she could feel herself trembling. For a moment she worried she was going to be sick, but a few more splashes of tepid water eased the nausea.

The plane was tied down on the far end of the field. The tanks were not full, so she signaled the caretaker to help her take two fuel cans out. She carried her small bag, from which the water bottle and pita bread were purposely peeking out to demonstrate she was prepared for a long journey. After fueling the plane, the caretaker untied the wings and tail while she walked around the aircraft, checking it thoroughly. Knowing full well the caretaker would stand there because the prop needed cranking, Charlotte bided her time until she could complete the most important phase of her scheme.

When she started the plane, she underprimed the engine so that the prop would be difficult to turn over. When it finally did, Charlotte leaned out the mixture improperly and it ran rough at first, but she jiggled it before it quit. In a few seconds, the plane seemed to be functioning perfectly.

"Naharak laban!" the caretaker shouted. "May your day be as white as milk!"

"Mutshakreen awwe. Thank you very much."

"Allah yisallimak! May God preserve you in safety."

"Saida." Charlotte taxied on the north-south runway before taking off away from the clubhouse. At four hundred feet, when she would have made the turn out of the pattern and headed on her easterly course, she leaned the fuel mixture once again and the engine ran rough. After slowly counting to ten (the period of time she had allotted for a cautious pilot making a decision about whether to proceed or not), she came around and made a landing on the side of the runway farthest away from the clubhouse. Quickly, she dug into her lunch pack, pulled the wire out of the cheese, and felt inside the bread for the string. In her pocketbook she had stashed cotton dress gloves. These she put on to help prevent electric shock. Next, she tied the string to the copper wire with the knots she had practiced. After securing the brake pedals by attaching a cleverly shaped piece of wood used by pilots to jam the brakes down while turning their own props, she permitted the propeller to run, hopped out of the plane, and chocked the wheels.

She had to work quickly. From the distant clubhouse it should look like she was inspecting the rough-running motor — nothing more. Through the side of the cowling where the cylinders stuck out a bit, she could see the spark plugs. Bending each length of copper wire into the shape of a hook, she slipped the wire around the insulated part of the upper spark plug lead. She attached a second string and wire to the bottom spark plug lead on the same cylinder. She tugged to make certain they were secure, then extended the strings from the cowling and into the cockpit as she simultaneously pulled in the chocks and vaulted into the plane.

If Mitch could only see me, she thought excitedly.

Back inside the plane, Charlotte tied the strings off so they were snug but not too tight. With one long inward breath, she set the throttle to full power and took off again, this time heading across the Eastern Desert on a course to Ismailia.

The only navigational aids she had were her compass, the position of the sun, and the major wadis, or water ditches, which sculpted the swirling sands. "Wadi el-Gafra," she called aloud jubilantly when she crossed her first checkpoint.

Flying into the sun, she was parched and sweaty almost at once. It was too soon for the water, so she only wet her lips and took one swallow.

Since Charlotte did not have a chart of the area, she had memorized the major gebels, or hills, and their altitudes on the route. On this course, two peaks, one right after the other — Gebel Umm Raqm, then Gebel el-Girba — would indicate that the military base she was looking for should be slightly north and due east. The hills came into view sooner than she expected. She was making excellent time, but she would not make the turn north until the waterway was in sight. At this point she had figured she would stay on course better if she followed the old caravan and pilgrim route to Mecca. From this altitude it looked to Charlotte like a scratch on a sleeping giant's back.

In ten more minutes she checked her watch. Even though the horizon was a blur where sky and desert blended in the distance, she knew she was almost at her destination. It was time to eat the pita and the cheese, to open the biscuits and have at least two. She could not afford for any of the food, where she had hidden the string and wires, to be found. The biscuits were an extra touch; girls were supposed to like that sort of sweet. She drank the water sparingly — just enough to digest the food.

It should be soon, she was thinking, just as the narrow vein of waterway joining the Gulf of Suez to the Bitter Lakes came into focus. North of the lake was the southern end of the Suez Canal, which flowed up to Port Said. For the second time a sickening anxiety agitated her stomach. The taste of cookies and cheese filled her mouth as she realized she could cross the canal right there, fly up the western edge of the Sinai, and by curving along the Mediterranean coast to El-Arish, land somewhere on the Israeli side of the border. Would she have enough fuel? she wondered.

The beckoning blue-green waters of the lake calmed her. This was the Biblical Marah of Exodus where "they could not drink of the waters ... And the people murmured against Moses, saying: 'What shall we drink?' " Charlotte reached for the water bottle and took several long gulps.

The shoreline ahead was flat and sandy. She searched for el-Shallûfa. The place she wanted should have been halfway between the railway line and the road. There it was! Her eyes followed a long snaking lane leading off the main highway. It had its own railway spur. There was a tiny roof at one end — probably a guard hut. In the distance was a small complex of buildings, the skeleton of a few more under construction, some long metallic-roofed sheds, and a short — three or four thousand feet at the most — runway. She washed her face with the water and let some drip down her blouse. She moistened her armpits, leaving less than a quarter of the water in the bottle. It was important to look fearful — thus drenched with perspiration — when she landed.

Charlotte figured she was about two miles from the runway and fifteen hundred feet in the air. Her heart beat relentlessly as she reached for the ends of the string. She started to untie them, but her hands hovered in midair. A sound echoed in her head. It was her mother shouting to her: "No!"

She plucked the string as tight as piano wire. Charlotte squeezed her eyes closed, but popped them open when the engine shuddered violently.

"It worked!" she shouted. Grabbing the yoke, she fought the plane for control. With one cylinder shut down, the engine was vibrating so hard her teeth knocked together and the view outside the plane blurred. She aimed the tremulous craft toward the base. As soon as she was certain she could make the runway, she pulled even harder on the string, which was wound around the palm of her right hand. The soft metal hooks straightened and pulled off the spark plug wires. After checking to see that she had all the parts in hand, she tossed the contraption overboard into a desolate stretch of desert before coming over el-Shallûfa and making her "emergency landing."

The plane quivered to a stop. Charlotte placed her head on the yoke and sobbed. Genuine tears of relief at having accomplished so much and tears of terror of what might happen next mingled with the water that already dampened her face.

A soldier was the first to arrive at the plane. He pointed a submachine gun at her and shouted in Arabic something to the effect of "What the hell are you doing here?"

She started to put her hands up, but stopped herself when she noticed she had not yet removed her gloves. Quickly, she peeled them off and tucked them in the pocket of her khaki skirt. As she got out, Charlotte squeezed her lids so more tears soaked her cheeks. "Ana fi'ardak!" she gasped. "I am under your protection!"

"Ismak eh?"

"Ana ma bakallimsh 'arabi," she choked. "I don't speak Arabic. Bitkallam ingleezi? Do you speak English?"

"Eh da?"

Four more soldiers surrounded the plane. One was gesticulating for her to get out. "Iftahi el bâb!" he ordered.

Charlotte had to keep reminding herself this is exactly what she had wanted to happen. A jeep pulled out in front of the airplane and blocked its path while Charlotte jumped onto the tarmac. Immediately, a soldier began to search the airplane. She turned around to protest when he turned her bag upside down. The oranges, biscuits, and almost empty water bottle tumbled out. A second jeep pulled up and this time a senior officer stood up and asked a few questions of the man in the plane.

The officer climbed down from his car with precise movements, the revolver at his hip jutting forward menacingly. "Good morning. Are you British?" he asked Charlotte in flawless English.

"No, American." She looked him squarely in the eye.

"You have had some sort of trouble here?"

"My plane started running rough. It was shaking apart. I had to land."

"Where did you fly from?"

"The Aero-Glider Club in Heliopolis."

"You have come a great distance out of your way."

"I was flying to Ismailia and back."

"To what purpose, may I ask?"

"I fly for the pleasure of it. I've tried various routes out of Cairo, but never this one."

The soldier held up her camera, which he had found tucked under the seat. "Is this yours?" the officer asked.

"Yes."

He took the camera and slung the strap over his shoulder. "What do you photograph?"

"Children, mostly. I am doing a series for the library in Alexandria where I am employed."

"What is on this film?"

"The camera is empty. I have not used it in several days. I was going to a hospital later this afternoon and planned to take some pictures there."

The officer fumbled with the back.

"May I?" Charlotte reached over and pushed the release button. The camera was indeed empty. It was part of the plan.

"If you will come with me . . ." The officer indicated she should get into the back of the jeep.

They drove off the runway. As they passed some deep excavations where concrete had recently been poured, Charlotte reviewed how she should behave. Some advocated belligerent righteousness under these circumstances, but she had settled on the polite, fairly passive behavior of a librarian who had found herself in unexpected difficulties.

In the office, a curious buzz of excited soldiers surrounded her entrance. The officer led the way to a private room and closed the door. "What is your name?" he demanded imperiously.

"Carla Christopher."

"Where are your documents?"

"My passport is in the plane. I should have gotten it . . . I'm sorry I . . ." Her voice cracked naturally. She could cry anytime she wanted, the tension was so great.

"I am Captain Yunis. By now it must have occurred to you that you have landed at a military facility which is not open to foreign guests."

"An emergency — the plane was breaking apart."

"So *you* say." Captain Yunis raised his eyebrows suspiciously. "Tell me what happened."

Charlotte explained that the plane had run rough when she first started it up in Heliopolis and she had landed again and double-checked the magnetos and fuel lines. "I decided it must have been carb ice, because it was fine the second time I took off. There were no problems whatsoever until I was above el-Shallûfa. I don't understand what —"

"Our mechanics will make a full report." He excused himself and sent someone to check the plane and retrieve her passport.

"This is very serious business. Have you any weapons aboard?"

"Weapons? Of course not! Just some snacks and personal supplies. I was returning to Cairo in time to have lunch with my friend in the hospital."

As the officer questioned her further about Leslie and the Aero-Glider Club, she responded confidently. Her story was solid.

After knocking on the door, someone handed her passport to the captain. He checked it thoroughly. After a second knock, he went into the hall to confer with the mechanic. His voice was raised and much harsher than it had been with her — so far.

"How is the plane? Will I be able to fly it home?" she asked when he returned.

"Perhaps. The problem appears fairly simple. Two spark plugs worked loose. My mechanic says it is a routine repair. He can do it himself. So far it seems you have been telling me the truth. But how do we know you are who you say you are?"

"I have many friends in Alexandria and Cairo. You could call the embassy or the consulate and check."

"If you are an American spy that will not help me."

"I have Egyptian friends. You could try General Youssef Rizk; he's the General of Police in Cairo."

"How do you know him?"

"I met him at the Cavalry Club. There's also Squadron Leader

Gamal Wahid, who first took me flying in your beautiful country."

"You have some very important friends. I shall put someone on this right away."

While Captain Yunis was out of the room, coffee was served. What Charlotte wanted more than anything was a trip to the bathroom, but she could not get the man with the cups and coffeepot to understand her. Finally, she made her request to Captain Yunis when he returned. She could see his eyes darting back and forth as he wondered if she might try anything in the toilet. She was grateful that he relented.

"General Youssef Rizk is not available and his office cannot identify you," Captain Yunis announced when she returned. "Your air force friend is also not around. A Friday is a particularly difficult day to get anything done in our country. We may have to detain you overnight — or longer if necessary."

"I must get to the hospital!" She allowed herself to sound slightly frantic.

Captain Yunis shrugged. "This is a pity."

"There are other friends who could identify me. Couldn't you try to locate Lieutenant Colonel Latif al-Din? He's on Nasser's staff at present."

"How do you know someone like that?"

"I stay in Cairo at the home of Abdul al-Hakim, the brother-in-law of the lieutenant colonel. Mr. al-Hakim and his wife are my closest friends."

"We will try the colonel," Captain Yunis said, bowing slightly as he departed once again.

Charlotte sucked in her breath. "Captain Yunis," she called out. He spun around.

"I just remembered someone else."

"Yes?"

She took a gulping breath and plunged in. "There is a very charming gentleman who let me ride his horse, and in gratitude, I took him flying over the pyramids. He has communications in his car as well as his office and home." She paused meaningfully. "His wife told me she can never get him away from the apparatus, so maybe he can be located more easily."

"What is the name?"

"General Abdel Shawqi."

Captain Yunis swallowed so hard his Adam's apple sunk behind his stiff military collar. Charlotte locked her jaw to prevent a triumphant expression from melting her face. Just as she suspected! This was an armament base and her fanny-patting friend was Captain Yunis's boss.

In less than an hour, the captain's whole tone had changed. She knew, without his saying so, that he had received confirmation of her identity. "While we are servicing your plane, Miss Christopher, we would like you to be more comfortable. May I invite you to the officers' mess for luncheon? There, we even have ice for a cold drink — a luxury in these parts. Is there anything else we might do to assist you?"

"If it isn't too much of an inconvenience, I'd like to telephone the Aero-Glider Club and ask permission to fly their plane back. I must also accept full responsibility for any damage to their aircraft or your facility here."

"It will be as you wish."

The captain's jeep rumbled up a steep hill to the highest point on the base. Under a circle of lush palms, a building with a wide veranda was perched to command a view of the entire area. From that shady vantage point, Charlotte could look down on storage bunkers, administration buildings, and, far in the distance, sixteen wide circular areas that were under construction. She sensed this was being readied for the upcoming withdrawal of the British from the canal zone. From similar layouts she had seen in photographs, she guessed the circular pads were to be some sort of launching sites. Eli had briefed her about the dangers that the new rocket technology posed. It was hard to believe that a weapon in this location could be blasted across the Sinai Peninsula all the way to Tel Aviv.

Two long, low hangars were of special interest to her, and she yearned to ask questions about them but did not dare. Instead, Charlotte kept up her end of the conversation by discussing her interest in Alexandria and its history, her photography hobby, and her concerns for Leslie.

After Charlotte and the captain had a delicious meal of grilled lamb and eggplant, the mechanic came to report her plane was repaired and refueled. She asked to reimburse them for the expense, but Captain Yunis appeared insulted by the offer.

"I am concerned for your safety, Miss Christopher."

"I will do a thorough pre-flight and then make several circles of the field. If there are any unusual vibrations, I shall land immediately."

"That sounds sensible."

On the runway, Charlotte began an elaborate inspection of the plane. She noted that her personal belongings had been replaced and two fresh bottles of water were perched on the front seat along with a basket of fruit. "You are very kind," she said to the small cluster of soldiers who were in awe of the woman who could fly. Just before she was ready to take off, she turned to Captain Yunis. "Would you like to come up with me while I test the plane?"

"Why not?" he replied enthusiastically and followed her directions for getting into the plane and buckling up.

After a slow climb-out in the heat of the day, the Cub performed flawlessly. Charlotte concentrated on memorizing as much as she could about the base from the air, since photographs were out of the question. The long, curved roof structures perplexed her. Just as she made her final pass over the field, she was rewarded as the doors of one of the long sheds were flung open. A line of tanks moved slowly out into the courtyard.

She called to the captain, "It looks like a children's battle game from here."

"Yes, that is quite true. Could you fly over them? I want to make certain they are in proper formation."

"Right, sir," Charlotte shouted. She banked the plane steeply and made a lazy circle over them. She recognized a few World War II vintage German Mark IIIs, but most were more recent Soviet-built T34/85s. They kept streaming out in a seemingly endless line. There were dozens of them. What the hell were they doing so close to the canal? She concentrated on counting them in groups of five: ten, fifteen, twenty . . . forty-five tanks from one hangar . . . times two . . . ninety . . . maybe a hundred. Oh, Eli, a *hundred* tanks.

❖   ❖   ❖

That evening Leslie miscarried and required minor surgery. The next morning, when Arnie and Gordon arrived in Cairo, Arnie rushed to comfort his wife while Gordon, who had heard the news of Charlotte's emergency landing, hurried to her side and found the al-Hakim household caught up in the exciting aftermath of the American girl's adventure. Huge bouquets of flowers had been sent to the heroine of the Aero-Glider Club by her many friends in almost every branch of the military, but Charlotte was unable to receive the visitors who clamored to congratulate her in person. She had spent the previous night holding Leslie's hand toward the end of her ordeal. When Charlotte left the hospital, she was exhausted, yet too overwrought to sleep. By midday, she was suffering from a sick head-ache.

Gordon sat beside her on the velvet settee and stroked her hand. A moist towel covered her forehead to soothe the pounding pain.

"I was so fortunate to be near an airfield," she said as she haltingly described what had happened. "What if I'd had to land in the des-ert? It's so hilly in that section, I don't know where I could have brought it down, perhaps on the road . . ."

"My darling, all that matters is that you were not injured."

She sat up and stared into his pale blue-green eyes — the color of the Bitter Lakes, she reflected absently. "Do you think I've been ter-ribly foolish?"

He adjusted the cushion behind her back, lifted the cloth from her head, and dipped it into a pan of cool water. "I can't help wishing you'd be content with your library books, but then you wouldn't be the woman I adore, would you?" He wrung out the towel and patted it in place lovingly. "A woman with your spunk is perfectly suited to become a diplomat's wife." He grinned charmingly. "While you were away I *was* offered the position of chief commercial attaché in Bangkok."

"Oh, Gordo! That's wonderful for you."

"I was hoping you would think it was wonderful for us both."

"Please . . ." She pressed her hands to her temples.

"The idea of leaving you behind —"

"When must you go?"

"The first week in August. I must tell them by the end of next week whether or not I accept the assignment. If you don't want to —"

"You mustn't consider me in this."

"How can I not?"

"Accept the appointment, if that's what you want. Either I go with you or — let's face it, you shouldn't tie yourself down with me."

"Chris . . ."

A knock on the door interrupted them. It was Arnie and Madame al-Hakim. "Come in," Charlotte called, grateful for the interruption.

"How are you feeling, my dear?" her hostess inquired.

"Better. How's Leslie?"

"Sleeping. They did something called a 'D and C' under anesthe-sia," Arnie replied. "She won't be able to go home until the middle of next week. I'll stay here with her. Are you going back?" he asked Gordon.

"I could be called in at any time. After yesterday's —" Gordon caught himself and stared meaningfully at Arnie.

"What's this all about?" Charlotte asked.

Madame al-Hakim ducked out of the room. "I will have your tea sent up."

Gordon looked dubious momentarily, then spoke softly. "There's been a bit of trouble in Alexandria, Chris. A bomb went off in the central post office."

"Was anyone injured?"

"At least one clerk, maybe more. So far there's been nothing in the press about it."

"Why would anyone bomb the post office?"

"That's what we're trying to figure out," Arnie said. "The evacuation agreement for the British army to withdraw from the canal zone is scheduled to be signed on the twenty-seventh of this month. Some are speculating the incident is related to that."

"Frankly, I don't want to leave Egypt at such a critical moment," Gordon added. "Dulles is staking his political future on the Baghdad Pact and has appointed Henry Byroade — a pro-Arabist — to head the Middle East section. You met him once a few months ago. He's a good friend of Ambassador Caffery's."

"I don't remember him," Charlotte lied. She closed her eyes. The bombings . . . the withdrawal from the canal zone . . . the change of U.S. officials . . . the Soviet tanks and the construction for the armament base at el-Shallûfa . . . Were they all pieces of the same puzzle? And, if so, how did Israel fit in? Tel Aviv was expecting Nasser to blockade Israel from the canal zone as soon as the British were out. She was more certain than ever before that her tenure in Egypt was going to be suspended. She needed to transmit her data on el-Shallûfa, along with the information on the bombing, at the first possible opportunity.

"I'd like to go back to Alexandria tonight, Gordon."

"It's a scorcher today. Why don't we stay over and visit with Leslie again? We could go home either Sunday night or early Monday morning. Besides, so many of your friends are anxious to see you. I've told Madame al-Hakim to hold off, but maybe by tomorrow . . ."

"No, Gordo. I must go home tonight."

"But Chris . . ."

"I won't rest until I'm in my own bed. Please . . ."

"All right, Chris." Gordon sighed. "I'll drive you back tonight."

"Thanks, Gordo," she said. Gordon was so thoughtful and kind, he deserved a good wife. She hoped he would find someone more worthy of his affections in his new post.

Back in her cottage that night, she prepared to contact Tel Aviv at the usual time. Their response to her opening message was curt: Do not transmit more than a brief sign of well-being. Repeat: no data.

Frustrated, Charlotte prepared an elaborate secret-ink letter. As a back-up she microfilmed her notes before burning them, tucked the negative under the cap of a L'Heure Bleu perfume bottle, and wrapped it as a gift. The perfume was for Martine, the note for Homer.

Tuesday morning neither showed up at the appointed time. The rest of the week there was no sign of anyone. The following Monday Charlotte was seated at the front desk, relieving the librarian who was usually on duty, when Martine and Homer strolled into the library hand in hand. Homer walked directly into the adult fiction stacks, while Martine examined some magazines on the front stands. When nobody else was around, she came over to the desk and spoke directly to Charlotte. "Do you have *Life* magazine?"

"Yes. What date?"

"Sometime in the fall of 1953. It contains the Churchill biography and the Nobel Prize for Literature."

"Right, the Hemingway issue. I'll show you where to look." Charlotte led the way to the periodicals section, prudently taking her purse along. As soon as they were side by side, she handed the gift-wrapped package to Martine, who took it wordlessly.

"These are the magazines. If you can't find it here, we can look in the periodicals index."

"Thank you very much," Martine replied in a normal voice, then lowered it. "Do not come to work on Wednesday. Do not ask questions. You will never see us again. Good luck."

As Charlotte looked down at Martine's hands, she could see they were trembling. Something was terribly wrong. Charlotte wanted desperately to question her; instead, she allowed Martine to replace the magazine and walk away.

Considering how much time she had lost from work recently, staying away on Wednesday was problematic. What was she supposed to do? Remain at home? Wait to be contacted with further instructions? A mission like the one to el-Shallûfa, which she had controlled, had been exciting; following someone's unexplained orders was maddening. Maybe she was being recalled. If so, she welcomed it. She would no longer have to answer to Gordon, the Ke-

ladas, the al-Hakims, Mrs. Patterson. After her little more than a
year under cover, the pressures were mounting incrementally.

The perfect excuse for Wednesday was offered on a silver platter.
Leslie, who had an appointment to see a local doctor for a check-up,
continued to be weak from her miscarriage. Arnie asked Charlotte if
she would accompany his wife "as a special favor." Even the Mossad
could not have come up with anything better.

"If the doctor says she's well enough, we'll all celebrate tonight at
the Bastille Day party the French attaché is hosting at the new St.
Stephano Hotel," Arnie had added.

Mrs. Patterson had given her the day off graciously. "You can
make up the time later, hon. Do you think Nadine would mind
doing the story hour? You could select the books for her."

Story hour ... the children ... Martine's warning. Charlotte felt
dizzy momentarily. "Trust your instincts first, your thoughts second,
your beliefs last" was Eli's motto.

"Let's not have a regular story hour this week," she replied hurriedly. "Why doesn't Nadine take the children to the Kom el Dik
Fort? It's the site of the ancient Paneum, the Park of Pan. She can
tell them myths while they are there. Don't you agree the children
will welcome the change?"

"What a marvelous idea!" the librarian agreed.

"Thank God!" is what Mrs. Patterson was saying Wednesday evening as she scurried about relating her version of the bombing of the
USIA library to anyone who would listen. "They wouldn't let me
inside. There were floods of water in the street, scorched pages fluttering up and down the Rue Fouad. Dozens of Britannica volumes
were tossed out on the lawn; the microfilm room was a total loss.
Why, if Leslie had not needed Chris, if Chris had not suggested the
children go to the park —" Stella Patterson broke down weeping in
the rose garden of the consulate, where the stunned American community was congregating.

Arnie had rushed to the clinic to claim his wife and Charlotte as
soon as he heard the news and brought them to his own office. He
told them what he knew.

"The fire began in the periodicals room just before lunch. Nobody
was injured."

"Where was Mrs. Patterson?" Charlotte asked.

"Fortunately, she was attending a luncheon fête at the French
consulate."

"And Nadine?"

"On an outing with the children. The rest of the library staff were away from the areas where the incendiary devices went off."

"Arnie, what if Chris had not been with me?" Leslie sobbed.

"Do you know what happened?" Charlotte asked.

"Officially, the press is being told there was a short circuit, but —"

"Yes?" Charlotte and Leslie chorused.

Arnie lowered his voice. "This is not for general circulation, but we've learned that at approximately the same moment the library in Alexandria began to burn, a bomb went off at the USIA library in Cairo. You know the one in the wooden annex to the American Embassy on Sheikh Brakat Street? Again, no one was injured."

Charlotte's shock was genuine. She fell back into Gordon's arms.

"Oh, Chris!" Leslie flung her arms around her friend. "It's been such a horrible month. This impossible weather, my troubles, and now this! I can't believe anyone would do this to Americans. We've always been such good friends of Egypt."

As she rattled on, Charlotte was filling in the blanks mentally. Martine and Homer! When they came to the library they were checking it out. They had warned her to stay away. But why would Israel want to blow up American libraries, for God's sake? It was utter insanity! And worst of all, she was square in the center of it.

"Chris!" Gordon was calling her name. He was shaking her wrists. "Chris!" Her face was cupped in his hands.

"Yes?" Her voice was thin and drifting.

"She's taking it awfully hard. Do you think we need a doctor?" Leslie asked.

"I'm fine. I just can't understand it. First the post office, now this."

"Do you feel up to the party tonight? There are going to be fireworks, Chris," Leslie said childishly.

Charlotte stared at her with disbelief. "No, but you should go if you want. Gordon, please, take me home."

The next week was fairly quiet. Charlotte helped with the depressing tasks of cleaning up the library and salvaging what remained. The library was to be closed the rest of the summer and it was suggested she take her holiday in August. Mrs. Patterson, who probably knew as much about Charlotte's romance as she did, was waiting to be told that Charlotte would be leaving Egypt with Gordon. Meanwhile, Charlotte was expecting a message from Eli with instructions for what to do next. Unless there was a dire emergency, she would wait for her orders.

On the weekend of the twenty-third and twenty-fourth of July, the Egyptians were to celebrate the anniversary of the overthrow of the monarchy. With anti-American sentiment rampant, the American community of Alexandria was warned to avoid public places and large gatherings. Gordon was on duty for the entire weekend, so Charlotte accepted an invitation to spend Saturday evening quietly with the Keladas and their friends from the university. The party turned out to be more interesting than she had expected. Along with the usual group of Daphne's artistic friends, Professor Kelada had invited some members of the science faculty. Immediately, Charlotte's curiosity was aroused by a Dr. Ibrahim El Setouhy, a physicist who, she quickly learned, had diplomas from both American and Russian universities. She engaged him in conversation about Boston and how its climate compared to Moscow's. He was most charming and soon let on that his specialty was "something quite boring to all but a few devotees of the industrial applications of nuclear energy."

Charlotte could barely contain herself. They are falling into my lap faster than I can do anything about it! Feeling she might never see the scientist again, she took the opportunity to learn as much about him as possible.

The sirens began about ten that night, but nobody made more than a few offhand comments about drunks on the road and over-zealous partying. Charlotte was in bed before midnight. The next morning she was awakened by Gordon's pounding at the door.

"What is it?" she called as she struggled to tie her bathrobe before letting him in.

"There have been more bombings. Last night one went off in the Métro theater here in Alexandria and two more were set off in the Rio and Rivoli theaters in Cairo. Several people were killed and many more wounded."

"Oh, no!"

"Look, darling, I can't tell you how I know what I do, but I have reason to be worried about you."

"Why me?"

"Not you especially. We're suggesting all Americans take extra precautions, not travel alone, that sort of thing. You should move in with someone you know."

"Let me at least get dressed."

While Gordon waited in the Keladas' garden, the guard at the gate called to him. A package had been delivered for Charlotte. When she came outside to sit with him, he gave it to her. She held it gingerly.

"Aren't you going to open it?"

"Don't you know what it is?"

"Why should I?"

"It's not from you?"

"A boy brought it while you were dressing."

Charlotte did not believe him. It was small and wrapped in expensive paper. It had to be a ring. She tried to smile warmly, but her mouth drooped with tension. With infinite care she opened the box. Inside was the same Guerlain perfume bottle she had given Martine. A reply had to be under the white seal pressed into the cap.

"Gordon, it's lovely, thank you."

"It's not from me," he repeated stiffly.

Although she knew it was not, Charlotte giggled. "C'mon. Who else would send me perfume?"

"How should I know? One of your flying aces?"

"There's no card or anything."

"A secret admirer."

"I do love secrets."

"But not me," he said petulantly.

"Gordo! There's nobody else. I promise. Let me put this away and we'll go out for a walk."

With that Gordon perked up. Charlotte rushed inside and locked her bathroom door. She opened the bottle of L'Heure Bleu and pulled out the note. "Leave Egypt as soon as possible. Do not contact anyone. Homer has been arrested. The others may fall soon. Save yourself."

Save herself? How? There was no prearranged escape plan. How long could Homer hold out under the inevitable torture? Her rational thoughts faltered. She clasped her head in her hands, groaning. Oh, my God! What should I do?

After a few frantic seconds, something in Charlotte's mind tightened. She would not break down! Could not! Forcing herself to concentrate on how to proceed minute to minute, she began to go into action. First the message was flushed away. Then the Zamir transmitter and supplies had to be destroyed. She poured out all her secret ink vials, which had been labeled as cosmetics, and refilled the bottles with water. The crystals and transmitter would come later, after she had been out with Gordon. She combed her hair and applied her lipstick lavishly. As a final touch, she dabbed some of the L'Heure Bleu behind her ears. How ironic, she mused. The blue hour.

A few minutes later, as Charlotte and Gordon walked hand in hand along the fog-draped Corniche, two feluccas sailed by. Veiled by the mist, they seemed like ghosts from another century. She shuddered and drew closer to Gordon.

As Gordon took her arm protectively, it was all she could do to keep herself from recklessly blurting out her desperation and let come what may. Instead, she mentally girded herself by staring out at the rolling waves of the slate-gray Mediterranean. At that very moment the tide was tugging the same waters across the beaches of Tel Aviv, yet that safe harbor was as good as a million miles away. A soft wind churned the fog off the cresting foam and lifted to the level of the minarets and monuments of Alexandria. So this is how it happens . . . Her turbulent thoughts tumbled together until they coalesced with a shining burst of clarity: this is how a decision is made, how a life plunges off in a new direction . . .

"Gordo," she whispered. "Gordo, my darling."

He wrapped his arms around her and stared longingly into her green-and-golden-bespeckled eyes. She kissed him so forcefully he reeled back with both pleasure and shock. He is a good man, she thought. Perhaps too intense, too competitive, too demanding. But he loves *me*. It might work out. It could . . .

As a streak of sunlight sliced through the clouds, their mist-moistened cheeks shimmered like mirrors. "Chris . . . oh, Chris," Gordon murmured lovingly.

"I'll marry you, darling. I'll marry you tomorrow, if you'll have me."

"Tomorrow?" His voice was high and squeaky. He laughed lightly and cleared his throat. "What made you change your mind?"

"I never changed it; I just didn't know it. And now that I do, I can't see any reason to wait. Can you?"

"Oh, Chris!" He crushed her to him, oblivious to the other Sunday strollers, and kissed her salty eyes, her warm throat, her chilled fingers, and finally — and mostly — her ready mouth.

❖   ❖   ❖

Charlotte remained in Egypt long enough to be terrified by what the news services were calling the "crackdown on a Jewish-Communist spy ring with the subsequent arrest of several members who, so far as it has been established, are responsible for recent outrages of arson and bombings. Investigations are continuing and further arrests are anticipated."

A numbing fear propelled Charlotte through her wedding at the American Embassy in Cairo on the sixth of August. Unrelenting fear stalked her departure just as further arrests were being made. Unbearable, excruciating fear created havoc in her mind and body during the last moments when security police swarmed the airport as she was being cleared through passport control. The result was a breakdown in Gordon's arms as the BOAC plane departed Egyptian airspace. Gordon interpreted her sobs as the normal response of a newlywed about to embark on an unknown adventure, and he was entirely sympathetic. Charlotte allowed him to caress her, to whisper comforting endearments. But they did not assuage her terror as she realized she had avoided incarceration as a spy in an Egyptian prison only by marrying, under false pretenses, a man she did not love.

What would Eli think when he heard? Would he be pleased she had found a safe way out and had not embroiled the Mossad in the disastrous events playing out in Egypt, or would he condemn her for taking a coward's escape? Damn him if he did! He had not contacted her; he had not sent any message other than the one with the L'Heure Bleu bottle. Silence had greeted her last futile transmissions. What had happened to Israel's solemn promise to stand behind its operatives? They were behaving as if she did not exist! At the last moment she had gone to the Marconi Telegraph Company, telling Gordon she was going to send the news of their impending marriage to relatives and friends, and tried to word a telegram to Eli's London front. Her first efforts were so muddled, she gave up entirely. Now he would have to wait until she was out of Egypt. Her safety was far more important than informing him of her intentions.

From Athens and later Bangkok, Gordon was able to follow the Egyptian political scene fairly accurately. Charlotte pretended to have only the remotest curiosity about the Zionist spy news, which was exploited by lurid and sedate periodicals alike. In early autumn, he brought home a week-old item from the *New York Times* with the headline: EGYPT CAPTURES "SPIES": CHARGES RING WAS DIRECTED BY ISRAELI INTELLIGENCE OFFICE.

"CAIRO, Oct. 5 — Egyptian security forces have seized members of an alleged spy network said to be under Israeli direction.

Lieut. Col. Zachariah Mohyeddin, Interior Minister and chief of military intelligence, said today at a press conference that the gang had been engaged in gathering military, economic and political information throughout the Arab world.

It sought to create internal disturbances in Egypt and in this task had the cooperation of "certain societies and organizations hostile to the present Egyptian regime," he said.

Investigation has shown that members of the ring were trained by the Israeli Intelligence Department in the use of firearms, wireless transmitters and codes, the Minister declared. Some also received training from Communists in France.

Within the next few months Charlotte learned more about the fate of her friends from other outdated New York and London papers.

CAIRO, Oct. 12 — Twelve men and two women were accused today of being members of an Israeli spy organization. The charges were made public by the Egyptian Military Prosecutor's office.

The death penalty will be asked . . .

The alleged organizer of the spy organization is Abraham Dar, alias John Darling, identified as an Israeli army officer now living abroad . . .

The trouble was that Charlotte, who had never known the identities of Homer and Martine, could not follow their cases individually. Could Homer be this John Darling who escaped? No, Martine had reported him captured. Then was Darling another name for one of the people to contact in case of emergency who had not been available when she had needed them?

Gordon reported receiving advance word through the embassy that Max Bennett, a twenty-seven-year-old major in Israeli intelligence, had committed suicide, using a rusty nail pried from his prison cell door to puncture his veins. Could Max have been Homer? No, Charlotte decided, her contact was younger than the major. She held out hope for her friend until she learned all the rest were coerced into pleading guilty.

The London *Times* was the first with the verdict.

CAIRO, Jan. 27 — Two Jews, Moussa Marzook, a surgeon, of French nationality, and Samuel Azar, a teacher, were sentenced to death here today . . .

The World Jewish Congress appealed for a reduction of the death sentences, "which can only result in a grave deterioration in the relations between Egypt and the civilized world." — Reuter

They were hanged on the last day of the month. Charlotte was certain that one of the condemned men had to be Homer. Most of the others received life at hard labor, while the two women involved and another accomplice in Cairo were sentenced to fifteen years. Even after the executions, the press kept the matter alive. The Egyptians were continuing a worldwide search for the master spy who had set up the bombing rings. He was described as an operative from Aman, Israel's military intelligence network, who had posed as a German businessman.

The whole affair rocked the Israeli government. What were Israeli operatives trying to accomplish by blowing up post offices, civilian movie theaters, and American libraries? the world asked. It took several years and high-level government resignations — including that of Minister of Defense Pinchas Lavon — before most of the story was divulged.

Gordon, who was considered an expert on Egypt by the others in the Far East, enjoyed expounding on the stupidities of the mission. "The philosophy behind it was absurdly simplistic," he would begin at the slightest provocation. "Israeli military intelligence believed their country's position was strategically weakened by the failure of the American and British policymakers to understand Nasser's true hostile intentions toward the West as well as Israel. According to the plan, British and American property in Egypt were to become targets for ultra-right-wing terrorists, if you can imagine such convoluted reasoning. The Jews believed this would cause Egyptian security forces to crack down on their 'real enemies.' In this scenario, the country would seethe with civil unrest and the Western powers would see Nasser's junta for what it was. The short-term goal was to force the British to remain in the canal zone."

The American ambassador to Thailand was particularly taken with Gordon's astute analysis of events. "He told me I should consider a post in Israel one of these days. Frankly, I wouldn't mind sitting on the other side of that fence. It would give me a unique perspective, don't you think?"

"No!" Charlotte had responded too adamantly. "I've had enough of the Middle East for a while."

"You were the one who didn't want to leave Egypt."

"Well, now I don't want to go back."

"I don't understand you." Gordon shook his head. "If I were given the opportunity, you'd go with me, wouldn't you?"

"You'd consider *my* feelings, wouldn't you?" she challenged.

"Look, Chris, I've never lied to you. My ambitions do not include stamping waybills the rest of my life. I want to be involved in negotiations, in the process of diplomacy — the stuff of history — not commerce."

"From the sound of it, you're more into intelligence," she retorted daringly.

Gordon only laughed at her and said, "Yup. You got it! That's why I'm so good between the sheets."

Wish that were true, Charlotte thought ruefully, but kept it to herself.

From the beginning, she had believed both Arnie and Gordon were far too knowledgeable about behind-the-scenes policies and events to be merely clerks. Even in Bangkok, Gordon was privy to sensitive information about the hysteria in the Israeli government that followed the arrests.

One day, as he was preparing for bed, he chatted on that Israel's Prime Minister Moshe Sharett (Charlotte's boss at Lake Success, who had changed his surname from Shertok) had informed his intelligence chiefs this was a "criminally insane melodrama" and became obsessed with trying to discover who was responsible for launching the Egyptian operation.

"How do you know that?" she had asked in as noncommittal a voice as she could muster.

"Can't say, but it's all terribly fascinating. Besides Lavon, General Benjamin Gibli, chief of military intelligence Moshe Dayan, and the head of operations on the scene are all being blamed for the decision to set the bombs."

"Who's Lavon?"

"Can't you remember anything?" he asked in irritation.

"I get confused."

"Their Minister of Defense. Do you want me to go on?"

"Only if you're not revealing state secrets," she snapped.

"This is in the public domain. The Israeli press loves to launder its linen in public and the Lavon affair is truly dirty. Good old Jewish guilt." He stopped to brush his teeth. Afterward, he sat on the edge of the bed, clipping his toenails. "So anyway, after Lavon resigned, the only person who could soothe the nation during the crisis agreed to accept the position as Sharett's defense minister. Guess who that was?"

"Moses?"

"Close. It's David Ben-Gurion."

"So it's finally over —"

"Hardly. There are too many unanswered questions; too many lies have been told. Our thinking is that unless the truth of this bizarre affair is established once and for all, their intelligence network will be haunted by the specter of false accusations from within and without."

Charlotte rolled over in bed, her back to her husband. Gordon was right . . . It would never be over.

TOKYO, JAPAN: JULY 1955

After her marriage, Charlotte had twice talked to Eli on the telephone. The first time, from the airport in Athens, she let him know she had escaped. His voice had been cool, his responses curt. She knew he could not say anything substantial over the phone, but she had hoped for some warmth, some sign of approval. Nothing. From Bangkok she had phoned to wish him a "Merry Christmas." Holiday calls would not be suspect, even to Israel. This way he would know her whereabouts. Someday he would find her; someday he would rescue her — it was just a matter of time.

But he never showed up in Thailand, never sent a letter, a card, a message with another agent. All right, she told herself, how many Israeli agents ever get to Bangkok? Even so, she was bitterly disappointed. When Gordon was unexpectedly offered the job as vice-consul in Tokyo, because his predecessor was sent home suffering from a severe relapse of malaria contracted on an African post, he did not even ask Charlotte's approval before accepting.

"You haven't been happy here anyway" was his curt response to her resistance to the move.

Bangkok . . . Tokyo . . . the moon . . . What did it matter? She was no closer to extricating herself from the prison of being Mrs. Gordon MacDonald.

After almost a year had passed since she had cleaned out her desk at the Alexandria library, Gordon brought home a letter addressed to her that had been delivered to his office at the consulate.

"In Japan on business and hoped we would get together. Yours very truly, C. Ivy." She had to read it a second and third time before she realized what this meant: Eli had finally come for her!

She phoned his hotel the next morning. "Where shall we meet?" he asked. His voice was as calm as hers was breathless.

"I live outside the city," she explained. "I'll come into Tokyo with Gordon and meet you at the hotel at ten."

Three hours later she was in his room. First she asked about Homer and Martine. She was horrified when Eli told her Homer was indeed one of those executed and that Martine was in prison. "Is there any hope of getting Martine out?"

"Eventually there will be prisoners to trade . . ."

"It could have been me," she gagged. "They told us what would happen if — they made us say that we understood the risks — but we didn't — we couldn't have known. Martine was not prepared. Nobody *could* have been."

Eli waited patiently until she calmed. Sitting on the far side of the room, he was maddeningly aloof. Finally, she asked about Lily and Aviva.

"They're continuing on assignment" was all he could tell her. "Both are well. Aviva is expecting her second child. The first was a girl."

"So am I," Charlotte replied hoarsely.

After a few seconds her words seemed to have been absorbed. "A baby?"

Charlotte nodded glumly.

"How far along?"

"Five months." How could he have missed her shapeless dress and swollen appearance? "Can't you tell?"

"I don't know much about these things. Besides, your face seems thinner. You haven't been well, have you?"

"Thailand didn't agree with me. The humidity — the heat — the smells — I don't know why exactly. In Egypt, my stomach held up long after everyone else's failed, but I felt cramps the minute I set foot in Bangkok and haven't totally recovered yet. Gordon knew how miserable I was; that's partially why we are here."

"Wasn't this new post an excellent opportunity for him?"

"Oh, yes. Gordon would never do *anything* that didn't advance his career. He wouldn't even buy a shirt or order a drink that wouldn't be considered proper."

"You regret it, don't you?"

"What? The marriage? Leaving Egypt? Working for you?"

"All of the above perhaps?"

"Oh, Eli, I was *happy* in Egypt. Another year, or even a few months, and I could have accomplished much more. It's all so unfair! I was not a part of that Aman operation. They were only my links. Jesus! How could they have fucked up so badly?" She sat up straight and smoothed back her hair, which had grown out to a luxurious length. Gordon loved her hair long, but she had never known how Eli felt about such matters.

"Have you been in touch with your family?" he asked.

"Barely. They think I'm on a fact-finding mission for Israel in the Orient. With the baby coming —" She gulped, then rallied and shouted with surprising fierceness, "You're supposed to be the operation's director! What the hell do you think I should do?"

Eli's head tilted like that of a judge hearing a case. He stared at Charlotte with his deep, blue, penetrating eyes. He stood up and walked across the room with his characteristic long, loping strides. His tan, muscular arms were outstretched to her. He sat beside her and touched her cheek, forcing her to confront him directly. "Forgive me, Charlotte." Hearing her own name aloud made her shiver involuntarily.

She placed her hands on his arms and pressed tightly. He allowed his head to lean against her shoulder and soon she was stroking it. "Eli, I can't go on like this."

He looked up. She leaned slightly forward and their lips brushed. Eli's breath caressed her face, drawing her deeper. As she leaned back on the bed to make room for him, he slid beside her and held the length of her in his arms. She wondered if he noticed her swollen abdomen pushing him slightly off. The closeness was almost too much to bear. She moaned.

Eli twisted his hips away to relieve any pressure. "Did I hurt you?"

"No, I just —" She pressed closer once more and clasped him with her slender legs. "I want to be with you."

"You're married," he said pointlessly.

"No, *Chris* is, *I'm* not," she insisted. "I always wanted it to be *you.*"

He mumbled something she didn't quite hear. Later she thought he had said, "I want you," or "I'm here for you." Whatever it was, it was the last utterance, for the rest of the morning was spent in a splendid silence where nothing was spoken — yet everything was said.

❖   ❖   ❖

"Where does your husband think you are?" Eli asked. It was the third morning they had spent entwined in his fifth-floor hotel room while the sounds of commercial Tokyo roared beneath them, as comfortingly repetitive and anonymous and — to them, at least — as romantic as any seaside surf.

"With a friend I met in Switzerland. He's happy I have a diversion." Charlotte sat up in bed and tucked a pillow behind her shoulders. Eli rested his head on her moist thighs and breathed in the sweetness of their mingled aromas. "Next week he's going to a meeting in Taipei. After he's gone, I want you to come to the house."

Eli sat up abruptly. "Do you think that's wise?"

"He suggested it."

"That's because he believes I'm your girl friend, not your lover."

"So?"

He took her hands in his. "Charlotte, darling . . . I cannot do that."

"Why ever not?"

"He'll find out. Someone will tell him. You must have servants or neighbors."

"Both." She directed his hands to her breasts, which were somewhat swollen from her pregnancy. Gordon had said that he found the darkness of the nipples supremely erotic, and she hoped they were having the same effect upon Eli.

"Well?"

"Don't you see . . . ?"

Charlotte noticed he was becoming excited again. She stroked him lovingly.

He pushed her hand aside. "This is an impossible —"

"No, it's the only way." She kissed him, lavishly exploring his mouth with her tongue to prevent any further resistance. She climbed astride him. "This is the only way I can ever be free."

Slowly, Eli was getting the point. He would help her shatter her marriage by the most conventional means: adultery. He never formally acquiesced; he never resisted, either. While he remained as enigmatic as ever, it did not prevent him from cupping her buttocks in his hands and doing what he had come to learn she wanted him to do — had always yearned for him to do, over and over and over again.

❖   ❖   ❖

Knowing that Charlotte would never have been satisfied living in one of the American compounds in Tokyo, Gordon had found them a Japanese-style home in Chigasaki, a town just south of Yokohama on Tokyo Bay. The ocean was visible from the porch of the wooden house set across the street from the beach and in the midst of a small but detail-perfect Oriental garden. Charlotte was delighted to be living outside of town, where she would not be bothered with the American ladies' perpetual luncheons, teas, fashion shows, and reading circles, which — had she lived any closer — would have demanded continual performances by Chris, the rising diplomat's wife. Thus, the MacDonalds chose to remove their shoes before entering their home, eat traditional Japanese foods from a low table, and bathe by washing and rinsing themselves completely while standing on the slatted wooden floor before immersing in the steeping tub. Gordon refused to accept only one Japanese custom — sleeping on futons rolled out in the evening on the straw tatami mats — and ordered an American spring mattress. Charlotte had gone along with him because he suffered from frequent backaches, but now she was happy because she could not imagine sleeping on the floor during her pregnancy.

Eli had been enchanted with the tiny rooms enclosed by translucent paper screens, the gentle simplicity of the fresh flower arrangements that appeared in the ikebana niches every morning, and the glorious shadows that played on the plain walls from the sculptural shrubbery in the gardens. The exotic smells of crackling sesame oil, pine needles, steaming rice; the tastes of soy, sake, ginger; and the salty frosting the sea air formed on their lips all mingled deliciously. Her home, both inside and out, was meant to be a serene haven with everything in balance, but until Eli's arrival, Charlotte had never felt at ease.

Eli flinched when the servants bowed to him. "I can't understand how they can be so respectful when they know damned well I'm fornicating with their mistress."

"Perhaps they think this is what all infidels do." She giggled conspiratorially. "Oh, Eli, I'm so happy and content that I don't care what *anyone* thinks."

Eli cared. Charlotte knew he did and wished she could shake his guilt and make him see that what was happening was all for the best. As they walked along the beach and admired the wind-tortured pines and the arching hills that were capped by clouds, she wanted to admonish him for not abandoning himself to the simple joys of the moment. No matter how much she wanted it to be, she knew this was not going to be simple. In another week, Gordon would return and would have to be told.

Gordon. The American diplomat who did not know he was the husband of an Israeli spy who had married him under false pretenses and was cuckolding him with her boss. It was too crazy to think about in those terms. That is why she had wanted to set it all aside and concentrate on the fact that the man she had always loved was finally by her side, reveling in her lustiness and obvious desire for him.

Step by step, she attempted to analyze why Eli was there, what his expectations were, and whether or not he would be willing to not only help her out of the dilemma she had — *no,* they had both — created, but stay and join his life to hers. What were the obstacles?

Gordon.

And the baby.

From some of his comments, she knew Eli could not but feel the interloper whenever her baby made itself known. Mostly it was quiet, but then it had its tumbling times and he would feel it knocking at the wall between them. Once he said, "It's warning me away." In the night, when she curled against his back, the little taps would awaken him and he slipped away from her grasp. That is what she loved about him. He had a heart, a conscience, a mind. He knew the past and thought of the future. She would show him the present was only a path. Eventually he had to realize, after all they had been through, they could go on better together than separately.

Charlotte planned excursions for them every afternoon. Slightly sore, but hardly sated after their inevitable early coupling, she took him to Kamakura to see the great Buddha, to the temples on Enoshima Island, or into Tokyo to explore the city. What Charlotte had known intuitively took Eli longer to understand, but he came to agree that only he could assist her in winning a divorce from Gordon and was willing to put up with a short period of unpleasantness for her sake.

Their love affair was a curious amalgam of pragmatism and passion. At the same time she was revealing her needs, he let her know why he had come to her. He had been sent by Isser Harel to debrief Charlotte on everything she knew about Martine, Homer, the explosion in the USIA library, and all the events surrounding the incident. While he did not expect her statements to yield anything fresh, there were nuances and details of her experiences in Egypt that would be of immeasurable help to the analysts at the Mossad. Charlotte cooperated fully because she was aware that every piece of in-

formation she divulged would be important to Eli's future — and
hers.

"What do you want to do next?" he had asked.

The question seemed foolish to Charlotte. They had been walking
in the Emperor's Gardens, admiring swans in a lagoon. She laughed
so hard the swans started and swam away. "Motherhood is at the top
of the agenda, whether I like it or not."

"You didn't plan the baby?"

"No. I didn't *not* plan it either. I was so confused. We were moving
to Japan, everything was screwed up, I didn't pay attention to my
dates. When I found out, I became frantic, but Gordon was very sup-
portive."

"Will you remain in Japan?"

She did not understand the question. Had not Eli figured any of
this out or was he just testing her? She played along. "I don't see how
I can. The only people I know are through the embassy, and quite
soon I'll be an embarrassment to everyone there."

"What if Gordon doesn't want to give you up? You've told me he
loves you."

"*Thinks* he loves me, or did love me. From the moment we were
married, everything changed between us. Of course, it was mostly
my doing. I was so upset over the bombings and arrests I could
barely eat or sleep. I went a little crazy: first in Athens, later in
Bangkok — crying all the time. Gordon had never seen me like that.
Before the wedding he used to accuse me of not being emotional
enough, of intellectualizing everything. He once said, 'If you didn't
read it in a book, you wouldn't know it existed.' "

"That doesn't sound like you."

"It was the overlay of my cover: Chris, the librarian. Maybe I did
put it on a bit thick, but it fooled everyone."

"What did Gordon think was wrong with you?"

"He decided I was immature and not ready for marriage. He said
I had been right to resist it and he had been wrong to push me. He
also suggested I had not resolved the death of my mother. He
wanted his parents to come to Thailand so I'd feel a part of a family
again."

"Did they?"

"Yes." Her voice was flat. She walked over to a bench and sat
down dejectedly. "It was terrible. The MacDonalds were so kind to
me, but I wasn't very responsive to them. I had just discovered the

pregnancy and was not able to cope, for — until that moment — I believed I would escape this marriage ultimately. One day we'd simply decide we weren't suited to each other and it would be over." She rubbed her bulging tummy and smiled. "Mrs. MacDonald — Alberta's her name — tried to make me understand that most women feel ambivalent about a pregnancy, especially when you haven't been married very long and are living in a foreign country. She was *so sympathetic* — it made me feel even worse. She didn't deserve all the complications I was going to bring on her family. All Gordon wanted was for me to cheer up while they were there. I couldn't do it. I got worse and worse. He decided it was Thailand; he hoped I'd do better in Japan. How could I tell him —?"

"But you *could* have, you know. You still could. We could go — together, if you wish — and explain everything, or almost everything."

"I can't. He would never forgive me."

"Look, Charlotte, you are going to have his child. He has some rights."

"He'll live in Japan; I'll go home to New York. I won't ask for any support and —"

"Do you think a father forgets a child?" Eli's voice was unexpectedly strident.

"Maybe if he never sees it?"

"No!" Eli shouted. The heads of two Japanese women with toddlers in tow turned momentarily; then they politely looked away. "You would never forgive yourself . . . The child wouldn't either."

"You're right." Charlotte hung her head. "I'll ask Gordon for a divorce. I'll tell him I'm in love with you. Then I'll go home. My parents don't know about him, but I can tell them something about a brief marriage — or maybe it would be easier if I said it's an illegitimate child. My marriage wasn't legal, so there's no difference in the end." She stared at Eli penetratingly. It was time to lay her cards on the table. "Or, I could marry again . . ."

"I can't," he blurted.

"Why?" Her voice was clear.

"It won't solve anything in the long run. One sham is enough."

"But, I love you, I have for years. You must have known —" spilled out. She was not asking for so much — they could always separate later if they did not get on. But it *could* work. It would! She knew she could make him happy. She clutched his arm. "Tell me you don't love me!"

"I have always cared for you. I have admired you and wished for your happiness —"

"But?"

"I —"

"There's someone else?"

"No." He paused. "Yes. There is someone else; I don't know if it will ever work out."

Even though her vision fogged and her speech slurred, she managed to ask "Who is it?"

"Nobody you know."

Why was she certain he was lying? Suddenly, Charlotte sensed Eli's basic problem. "Won't she have you?"

"I'm not certain." He paced in front of the bench. "Even if she won't, I couldn't marry anyone else unless I felt as deeply as I do about her. From your experience with Gordon, you would have to agree . . ."

Tears spilled from Charlotte's eyes; her nose was running. She must have looked desperate — and ugly. "I needed to save myself."

"I'm not saying you weren't justified or that I wouldn't have done the same under the circumstances."

"I need *you* to save me now."

"I'm sorry, Charlotte. We owe you. We'll take care of you, the child, your expenses —"

"*We?*"

"The office."

She recoiled as if she had been slapped, leapt up, and started down the pebbled path. Blinded by her tears, she walked into a lamppost. Eli caught up to her and took her arm. When she was calmer, she begged him to at least help her play out her charade. To this he agreed.

It was easier than either of them had expected. Gordon had become disenchanted with his wife. Her emotional outbursts and inability to handle her position at his side had become a liability. And after she confessed her affair with Charles Ivy, Gordon was able to release his hold on her without remorse.

Charlotte related her last conversation with Gordon to Eli.

" 'I'm glad you didn't hold out until after the baby was born,' Gordon began. 'Another woman might have used a baby to get child support.' "

"That just proves how some men feel about children," Eli replied angrily. "He probably wouldn't have been much of a father anyway. If it were mine —"

"How I wish it were! Sometimes —" She stopped herself, though she wanted to tell him how often she had pretended the baby was theirs. "I said to Gordon, 'You can see the baby whenever you wish.' Gordon answered that since we would be separated by oceans the child would suffer more confusion if he floated in and out of its life."

"He might be right," Eli acknowledged, "but if it were mine, I would have insisted on —" He broke off and switched gears. "What will you tell the child about its father?"

"When I asked him that, Gordon said, 'Whatever you like, just speak well of me. My intentions were always to love you and the child. I'm not going to disappear. I can always be found if you — or the child — want me.' So . . ."

"It's over. Your nightmare is over."

Charlotte knew this was not the end of anything. Eli escorted her back to New York. He waited in the background as she made the painful explanations to her family about a brief, disastrous marriage to a diplomat she had found entirely unsuitable. Eli was pleased to learn the Greens were delighted to accept a grandchild without too many questions. Professional to the end, he had provided a complete set of forged papers documenting Charlotte Green's marriage to Gordon MacDonald — whose name she decided to keep for the child's sake. As compensation, Eli was also able to arrange a modest stipend for Charlotte, which she could say came from her husband's settlement.

Then he was gone.

He was not there to hold her hand when the first labor pangs came or when she lay bleeding on a stretcher in the darkened halls of a maternity ward — she would have died if an orderly had not slipped in the vast pools of blood that spread across the linoleum. He was not there when the infant cried in the night and Charlotte was crazy with lack of sleep. He was not there to tell her how she should spend the rest of her life when she could no longer practice her profession. He had abandoned her. He had run back to Israel or wherever; he had returned to the woman who had usurped her proper place in his heart.

She was not bitter. She would not be bitter. The risks had always been stated. It would be far worse in an Egyptian prison, worse with Gordon, worse in the pink bedroom in Scarsdale or locked in the suburban life that her sisters apparently found so blissful. Most people must look back to the glorious, finer times of their girlhood or boyhood with similar pangs over lost opportunities, lost loves. And so could she. Life was like one of those bell curves. Her peak had come the day she had landed the plane at el-Shallûfa. After that, it had been a fairly rapid slide down the far side.

All she had wanted had been one man — one eminently eligible, suitable, compatible man. His body had merged with hers in perfect harmony. Their careers and interests meshed. Yet somehow she had failed in her ultimate mission. He had rejected her — totally, irrevocably, stupidly. She would not be bitter. That would be self-defeating. She could not permit malign sentiments to corrode her outlook on life. Not when she had a child to guide through the miseries this planet could inflict.

And so, without illusions, without hope, without comfort or purpose, she accepted her loss and settled in to raise her daughter, a bright-eyed, freckled little sprite she named Allison MacDonald.

11

And Moses sent them to spy out the land of Canaan . . . and said unto them: ". . . see the land, what it is; and the people that dwelleth therein, whether they are strong or weak, whether they are few or many."

Numbers 13:17–18

BAGHDAD, IRAQ: 1954–1960

Shortly after Aviva Ben-Zion and Gideon Tabor's marriage in a rabbi's study in Hendon (attended by Lily, Eli, and two of his other hastily recruited friends who could vouch for the bride and groom — a necessity to comply with Jewish law), the couple had returned to Israel to train with their team. Once their indoctrination was complete, they were sent to England to solidify their covers. Now, more than a year later, Eli brought them back to Israel and had them meet him at the Weizmann Institute of Science in Rehovot.

"My father came here in 1934 for the opening ceremonies of the Sieff Research Institute," Gideon told Aviva as they passed through the gates to the campus.

Eli met them in front of the Wix Auditorium and showed them around the elegantly landscaped grounds. "This building houses our Van de Graaff accelerator."

"That's a linear accelerator, isn't it?" Gideon asked.

Aviva was impressed with her husband's knowledge, but Eli seemed to take the comment for granted.

Eli guided them into his office. The sign at the entrance read:

MOLECULAR BIOCHEMISTRY DEPARTMENT. "My office is in the back." He unlocked an unmarked door. A secretary buzzed them through the next barrier. Waiting there for them was a man working on some calculations.

"Shalom, Asher," Eli greeted him. "I'd like you to meet Aviva and Gideon Tabor. This is Dr. Asher Ze'evi — the head of our nuclear science department — and also a member of my family. Unfortunately, one cannot inherit brains by marriage."

"Na'im me'ohd. Pleased to meet you," Aviva murmured.

"How are Esty and the children?" Eli asked the professor.

"Hakol beseder. Everything's fine."

"Gideon will go with you for the briefing. Aviva and I have some paperwork to finish here." The scientist stood and mumbled a few additional courtesies to Aviva before taking Gideon off with him.

"What was that all about?" Aviva asked.

"Dr. Ze'evi has some technical matters to discuss with Gideon while we handle the more practical side of the assignment." He gave Aviva a folder with codes and communications data to study. "It's all fairly routine. No surprises."

After a few minutes of leafing through the papers, she agreed with him.

Eli shifted around in his seat before speaking in a slow, raspy voice. "How goes it?" He arched his eyebrows meaningfully.

Aviva pretended she did not know what Eli meant.

"With the marriage. You don't regret it?"

Aviva was silent for a while. It was too soon for regrets, but the early months had not been without some difficulties. Gideon had been reluctant to consummate the marriage at first, even though Aviva had hinted she was more than willing. At last he confided in her that he had been having a problem ever since a Mossad doctor had suggested — but not insisted on — a minor surgical procedure to strengthen his cover as a British subject born in India.

"The doctor said it was unlikely that I would have been circumcised," Gideon explained. "After an embarrassing examination, he informed me I was one of the 'lucky ones' with enough foreskin remaining so that a repair would hide my religious origins. I was reluctant at first — well, who wouldn't be? — but the idea made sense."

"How would an enemy find out?" Aviva asked. "Unless you were already caught —"

"Men are always pissing next to each other."

"Oh."

"So, I had the surgery."

This confession was a great relief to Aviva, who was afraid that her husband found her utterly undesirable. For almost a month they had shared a bed but barely touched. Now that she understood he was recovering from this painful episode, she could wait as long as necessary. After several more weeks had passed, she awoke in the middle of the night and, without thinking about what she was doing, reached across the six-inch separation they had managed to maintain between each other and stroked Gideon's well-muscled back. He sighed and turned to face her, staring into her eyes for the longest time before kissing her mouth with surprising fervor.

"Have you ever . . . ?" he asked hesitantly.

"No."

"Do you want *me* . . . ?"

Aviva would never forget the way he said "me." Her own innermost question had been whether he could ever desire her — not as an assignment but as a woman. Their fears were mutual. "If you can . . ."

"Yes, I think so — yes . . ."

She pulled him on top of her and guided him. The rest was terribly clumsy, but they managed much as men and women have from the first. Neither seemed especially pleased or satisfied, but it had been a beginning.

At last Aviva addressed Eli. "I have confidence we will be a good team."

"Aviva" — Eli cocked his head to one side —"you don't have to put up a brave front for me."

What could she say to Eli? She had strong feelings of loyalty and attachment to her husband, but she suspected they were not the same emotions an enamored bride would have experienced. How could she tell Eli that Gideon's body did not appeal? It was sleek, smooth — virtually hairless — and slender. Because she herself was broad-shouldered and strong, she was concerned that her husband might have felt himself physically inferior to her, even though he was by far the more beautiful one. Sometimes, he seemed too pretty, too boyish for her. Studying Eli's jutting chin, his wide brow, his penetrating eyes, how could she tell him that when she lay with Gideon she imagined what someone else — someone like him, with substance and grace — would have felt like skin to skin, pelvis to pelvis?

"Gideon is a wonderful companion. He's fluent in more languages than I am; he has read so extensively — I learn something new from him every day. In preparation for Iraq, he has read the Persian poets, the Rubáiyát, the New Testament, and the Koran, along with the mandatory political and historical treatises. For me, he brought home the diaries of Gertrude Bell. Did you ever hear of her?"

"No," Eli responded.

"She was a turn-of-the-century Englishwoman traveler, explorer, archeologist, and administrator of post–World War One Iraq. I found her quite fascinating."

"I'm sure you did," Eli said with a slight smirk as he accepted the fact that Aviva was not going to confide in him. "I just want you to be happy in your work," he said with a sigh just before Gideon returned to the office.

Aviva waited impatiently while Eli sorted some papers. She was anxious to learn if they would soon be on their way. Although they had been ready for some time now, Eli had not permitted them to move to Iraq because of the confused political climate there. When they had returned to England, Gideon began to prepare in earnest for the more prosaic aspects of his cover employment as a sales representative for Grim and Bonner, a British manufacturer of pumps, and had become quite knowledgeable about their use and repair. It was hoped that his cover would give him an excuse to travel throughout Iraq to major industrial and military installations. Gideon and Aviva had been entrusted with a twofold mission: to report on military and commercial build-ups, especially those with nuclear potential; and to assist the dwindling Jewish community in escaping to Israel.

Despite sporadic persecutions, the Jews of Iraq had prospered for several thousand years, ever since their ancestors had been driven out of Jerusalem by the Babylonians. After almost twenty-five hundred years, the most serious threat to their survival had come in 1919, just after the British assumed a mandate over Iraq, which coincided with the rampant Arab nationalism that swept across the Middle East in the wake of the disintegration of the Ottoman Empire. Those who managed to survive the first wave of violence were attacked once again during the pro-Nazi coup in 1941. When — for a brief time — emigration was encouraged, more than a hundred thousand fled to Palestine. Those remaining found their professional lives restricted, their assets under perpetual audit, their community organizations outlawed. On May 15, 1948, at the moment Israel declared itself an independent state, the Jews in Iraq became nationals of an enemy nation and had lived in danger ever since. One of Gideon and Aviva's first priorities was to establish how many Jews remained and what could be done to aid them.

Aviva would have no cover position, other than that of Mrs. Oliver Deacon. While Gideon was expected to travel and bring in a broad range of intelligence findings, she was given the authority to manage their network of operatives and communicate all data to Tel Aviv. As the time drew closer for them to be sent into the field, Gideon surprised her with a suggestion.

"I think we should have a baby," he had ventured unexpectedly.

Aviva's breath caught in her throat. Was he saying this because he wanted a child from her or because it would be good for the assignment if they were parents? She never asked. Within six weeks she was pregnant. Eli decided not to send them into the field until after the baby arrived and so their daughter had been born in London and registered under the name of Sheila Deacon.

"The tiniest spy," Gideon whispered to Aviva to make her laugh during the somewhat complicated recovery period.

Privately, they gave her a Hebrew name, and the birth of Shulamit Tabor was dutifully recorded in Israel by Eli.

At last, in the small office in Rehovot, Eli told them exactly what they expected to hear. They were to depart for Iraq within the week. Aviva looked at Gideon. His eyes were bright with excitement. She turned to Eli. His were dimmed with concern.

⁘　⁘　⁘

Baghdad tilted — or so it seemed to Aviva. From a distance the city appeared as in a drunken dream: minarets and industrial chimneys pierced the sky above the flat horizon, each leaning slightly to one side or the other; dusty palms swayed as though they were riding the sea instead of the desert; the domes of the mosques fragmented the vivid sunlight and sent it shimmering out over the squalid streets and alleys undulating below. Often an acrid pall of smoke hovered above the Tigris and the flat-roofed houses hugging the riverbank haphazardly. If there was romance, mystery, or magic here — as portrayed in films and books and poems — that side of the city was lost on her. To the Arab mind Baghdad might be Paradise itself; to Aviva — brought up on a kibbutz surrounded by flowering fields — it was a purgatory to be suffered on behalf of a greater cause.

During the first few months of setting up a household and managing a cell of operatives, Aviva was constantly tense. Sensing her nervous condition, Sheila became more difficult, waking several times at
night to nurse, spitting up frequently during the day. Aviva's unexpected second pregnancy did not lift her spirits either, despite the
fact that her maternity was a further camouflage.

In Baghdad, the Deacons lived in a small apartment building on
the western side of the Tigris. Despite the fact that their flat was
shabby, with rudimentary plumbing and creaking floors, it was superb from a logistical point of view. There were nine separate units
in the square building. Each L-shaped apartment faced a central
atrium that nurtured three prize date palms. The dates themselves
were leased to others and it was forbidden to pick them. Once in a
while a barefoot boy would come into the courtyard carrying a basket, some wire, and a sharp, curved knife. He arranged the wire and
an attached square of scarf into a climbing device that permitted
him to walk up the trees. When the dates were in bud, he carried the
pollen from the male to the female trees and trimmed any branches
that might interfere with the fruit. Occasionally Gideon could not
help tempting fate by stealing one or two of the ripening dates,
which had turned to a luscious yellow and were within arm's reach
of their inner balcony.

Aviva chided him for taking even the slightest risk that could
bring the authorities around. "What would Eli say if you were arrested for stealing dates?"

The Deacons had the middle apartment on the second level.
When an apartment on the bottom level became available, they arranged for two of their own task force to move in. By employing a
simple system of leaving a door open or hanging out a specified laundry item, they could signal the key members of their group.

One of the first acts of intelligence Aviva performed was getting to
know the habits and background of the others in the building. There
was Majid, the plumber, who received a discount on his rent for his
maintenance work. His wife, Sabha, refused to cook inside their
kitchen and preferred to squat over her Primus and brazier in the
courtyard. Most of the day she tended large pots of pungently spiced
stews while her two little children tumbled about with their foul-
smelling sheep dog.

The third floor housed an extended family of Syriac Catholics
headed by Omar Feili, the family's obese patriarch, who would take
time away from his water pipe only long enough to bark orders to

Marie, the harried daughter-in-law who slaved to please him, her indolent husband, and their five noisy children.

The Deacons' next-door neighbor on the second level was the one they needed to concern themselves with the most, since he might be aware of any comings and goings at odd hours, the sound of the Morse key tapping, their whispered voices. Fortunately, Dr. Khalid Gharbi was a quiet, scholarly man with a busy dental practice on the other side of the river. He rarely came home until after the evening meal, had a few quick araks, then passed out for a long, snore-filled night. As long as the common wall between their bedroom and Dr. Gharbi's vibrated, Aviva and Gideon knew they were safe.

Once, when Gideon was away selling pumps to an oil depot, Aviva awoke to a strange weeping sound that seemed to be emanating from the doctor's side of the wall. She stayed alert for the rest of the night, and just before dawn, the door to the doctor's parlor opened and conversation could be heard on the inner walkway, followed by a softly padded bumping down the stairs. She peered out her shutters in time to see a young boy turn and wave up at the doctor. When Aviva related the incident to Gideon, they decided it was not an immediate problem for them, but they alerted the rest of their staff to the dentist's proclivities — just in case.

The rest of their team consisted of four young men. Two shared rooms across the ground-floor courtyard. Aziz was supposed to have been Indian, for indeed he had grown up in India and had known Gideon's family there; George, a Palestinian by birth who had lived most of his life in Leeds, where his father had taught mathematics, was a British subject. Both were "archeologists," carried the appropriate accreditation from the University of Manchester, and had made connections at Baghdad's ancient Mustansiriya College. Actually, George was the radio technician and Aziz was Gideon's liaison to the Jewish community, where two additional operatives, Ahmad and Karim — Iraqi Jews who had been born in Baghdad and were adolescents when they and their parents immigrated to Palestine during the wartime hostilities — were stationed. Each had participated in the maneuvers that smuggled Jews out in British army trucks. After the war ended and this sort of emigration became more difficult, both went to work for the Jewish Agency. Ahmad was accomplished at dealing with Arab smugglers; Karim had worked behind the scenes on the semilegal airlifts until they came to an abrupt halt on the day Israel became a state.

Over the previous five years many tricks had been employed to get the Jews out. Most had been successful, but only for a brief time. Then the strategy had to be changed. Under Aviva's supervision, Karim and Ahmad were to determine the best method to apply to each individual family's case and provide all the assistance — technical as well as financial — needed to deliver them to freedom.

Fortunately, nobody in the building thought it odd that the Deacons befriended the British students shortly after they moved in. When Aviva went to the clinic to deliver Harold (or Hillel, as he was secretly named), Sabha — who was the eyes and ears of the other tenants — told everyone that it was most kind of the English boys to stay with little Sheila during her mother's absence.

Because Aviva was home at all times, she was available should any member of their group require her. A home-bound life was made even more convenient by the strolling merchants who stopped by the courtyard each day to hawk their wares. In the round trays they carried on their heads they displayed bananas, dates, oils, spices, pickles, manna, cottons, and all manner of fresh vegetables and sweetmeats. If one waited long enough, almost any necessity or curiosity would arrive on one's doorstep: furniture, carpets, strolling singers, Bedouin fortune tellers. Aviva did her shopping in this manner for the convenience, as well as being able to avoid the narrow lanes and fetid smells of the souk.

On the surface at least, the Deacons fit into the tightly controlled Arab society, which prescribed strict roles and rules for both men and women. Only Gideon knew how difficult this life could be for Aviva. Raised on a kibbutz where men and women were treated as equally as anywhere in the world, if not more so, she had had little training in running a household. To her, learning to cook was more difficult than becoming proficient in telecommunications or military matters, and they suffered through many a miserable meal until she felt confident with a few simple dishes. Sabha was delighted to teach her some Persian specialties, including curried smoked fish (Gideon's favorite), brinjol (eggplant), stuffed cucumbers (which came out too oily), and meat pastries (which often burnt).

With supreme grace, however, Aviva supervised most of the missions. It was she who coordinated the myriad details of each smuggling operation, she who assigned the team members their roles, she who knew where everyone was — or should have been — at any given moment. With a babe at the breast, she had a free hand to tap the Morse key or decode a radio transmission. Proudly, Gideon called her the glue that held them all together.

Like a true sabra, Aviva was rarely ruffled. Every problem had a solution. The boys would flock in with their dilemmas and she would sort them out by setting priorities, making lists, suggesting alternatives when initial plans went awry.

In the meantime, Gideon busied himself with his own information-gathering duties. During the initial six months, he found it easier to sell pumps than to make strides in his intelligence work. Because his pumps were used at construction sites, his questions about what was being built where and for what purpose raised no suspicions. Although very little data of interest emerged at first, he persisted, making contacts that led to others that, they hoped, would bring him into the circles of influence where he would be able to pick up signals regarding political and military trends. With Aviva assuming the role of the devoted housewife and Gideon acting the part of an aggressive salesman, their lives rarely meshed. Neither complained. Their goals superseded their personal desires for friendship and comfort.

❖   ❖   ❖

That year the month of the fast of Ramadan came at the height of a hot and languid summer. During daylight hours, the Moslems prayed and rested to quell the hunger and thirst they were forbidden to slake. The streets were unnaturally somber and deserted, but at night they burst into activity.

"Ramadan comes during the ninth month of the Moslem calendar to commemorate Mohammed's receipt of God's revelation," Gideon, who had lived in other Moslem countries, reminded Aviva. "This is what you would see in any city or village in the Islamic world: from Morocco to Afghanistan, from Turkey to India."

Aviva had been waiting for this moment for her first major maneuver, believing the distraction provided by the festivities would make it less dangerous to relocate some very old, frail Jews who — after refusing to depart in earlier, perhaps safer exoduses — had stated their wish to die in Jerusalem. She presented her plan to Gideon for his scrutiny. He praised her thoroughness and agreed it looked workable. For several weeks she trained her operatives. They walked through the scenario over and over again, checking their watches to be certain everyone would function synchronously, sharing their suggestions for improving the efficiency of the delicate operation. For the first few days of the festival of fasting, they only went through the motions. By the end of the week, they were ready to commence.

After each day of enforced abstinence, the city came exuberantly alive moments after sunset. Operation Magic Carpet went into motion when Aviva left home with her children for a stroll through the enchanted streets hung with twinkling lanterns. Shortly thereafter, George and Aziz proceeded to a designated coffee house and sat where they could be seen. Waiters, wearing long striped gowns and sashes and red skullcaps, filled their cups with the rich cardamom-spiked coffee from the traditional beaked coffeepots. When Aviva passed by and gave the signal, they knew the operation was on. They dispersed, going to the areas where the vehicles were waiting.

More and more of the population took to the streets: buying oranges from the greengrocers, tasting the sweetmeats arrayed tantalizingly at every corner, and frequenting the tobacconists who had been closed all the long day. While Baghdad celebrated, Karim and Ahmad prepared the night's travelers for their journey to a new life.

In the midst of the merrymaking, several heavily laden produce trucks did not attract attention. Nor did the plane that taxied to the end of a dimly lit runway and revved up its engines. From her position in a car across from the airport, Aviva watched as the doors of the battered cargo plane were thrown open and some thirty Jewish families were hastily welcomed aboard.

The first night, all went smoothly, too smoothly for Aviva's taste. She worried that the authorities had been on to them and were waiting on the sidelines to pounce and arrest them. Gideon told her there was nothing to be concerned about, and when nothing happened for several days, she felt confident in approving another mission for two nights later. Once again Aviva, with her children in tow, observed the emigrants' progress from a distance. Instead of the signal that they were safely on their way to the Promised Land, a flashing light warned that a hitch had developed. She had to risk herself — and the children — by moving closer to the airfield. George came out to advise her that an old man with chest pains was jeopardizing the mission. Immediately, she decided he should not go on that flight.

The following evening, George signaled again. Aviva lost her patience with George as he explained that a woman had twisted her ankle. "For this you halt the operation?"

"That's the protocol."

"You have the authority to make minor decisions. You have the pills to sedate her, don't you?"

"Yes, but —"

Aviva realized that George had done what he believed was best and she apologized for flaring up. The three subsequent airlifts were trouble-free. Aziz calmed a hysterical child with promises of sweets upon landing. On his own, George located a mechanic to repair a disabled truck at the last minute.

When tension was the highest, Aviva functioned at her prime. Her mind was taut; her instantaneous resolutions were inspired. When she evaluated the dangers that had been present, she quivered in retrospect. Every success was disquieting, for she calculated that the more often she did not get caught, the greater the chances she would be the next time. In a few days, however, a form of amnesia took effect and she would begin to plan the next mission with intrepid optimism.

Gideon complimented her leadership. "Teaching the boys how to make decisions is far more practical than keeping them dependent on you. The time will come when they will have to rely on themselves, and it's best to prepare them as early as possible."

Aviva glowed as he spoke. "They are functioning better than I expected, but —"

"Yes?" Gideon asked.

"The boys accepted this assignment voluntarily — just as we did. But now I am wondering if we have the right to imperil the children."

Gideon did not reply. She knew he shared her fears. She also knew he would back her up if she decided to resign. Not yet. They were saving too many lives.

At the end of the third week of Ramadan, more than two hundred Iraqi Jews had escaped without serious incident. Then, on the night of Id al Fitr, the holiday celebrating the end of Ramadan, came a most unexpected problem.

"Don't you think that George is suffering from staying out so late at night?" Sabha asked Aviva when she came to pick up her children. Trying to seem as normal a neighbor as possible, Aviva exchanged baby-sitting services with Sabha now and then.

"He may be a bit pale," she commented absently.

"He looks worse than that."

Aviva knew Sabha was right and was angry at herself for having

missed the warning signs of impending difficulty. Only a few days
earlier, she had dismissed the tremor in George's hands and the
twitch that had developed around his eyes as normal reactions to exhaustion.

The Deacons invited George for tea and asked him how he was
feeling.

"I just need more rest. You've made me responsible for arrangements during the day and then expect me to transport people half
the night and remain alert for the early morning radio transmissions," he complained.

Even though Aviva's infant, Harold, was nursing at her breast and
Sheila was stumbling around the room demonstrating her prowess at
walking upright, all of Aviva's mental concentration had to be
directed to the operative whose hand quivered so badly he could not
hold the teacup.

"You may be right," Aviva admitted. "Perhaps I should relieve
you from the radio work."

"No! That's *my* job," he whined childishly.

Aviva glanced at her husband. Gideon stepped forward. "What
might we do to assist you?"

"I don't need any of *your* help," he spat out unexpectedly. Then he
tore at his shirt and moaned, "I'll never see my darling Liat again.
Never!" Aviva moved closer to Gideon while George rambled on uncontrollably. "I feel something terrible is about to happen to me —
to us all."

This does not surprise me, Aviva thought to herself. Of all the
boys in the cell, she had liked George the least. From the first he had
been moody; his dark, small eyes hardly ever met hers directly; and
he rarely laughed at the jokes that kept the rest of them cheerful
through the most stressful moments.

Aviva passed him a plate of date-filled cakes. "Do you want to go
home?"

"Yes," George replied diffidently. "Don't you?"

"Our task has only begun."

"It seems senseless."

"Yes?"

George crumbled the pastry in his fingers absently. "All this trouble, all this risk so a few old men can be buried in Israel!" he exploded. "How many lives is that worth? Yours? Those of your
children? Remember that night when the battery went dead on the

truck? You could have been caught. We all could have gone to jail. Your children would never know you."

Aviva spoke with deliberate calmness. "Our work is worth the risks."

"No — nothing —" George began to tremble violently.

Aviva remembered seeing someone shaking like that only once before, when a kibbutz member had suffered a relapse of malaria. "Are you ill? Why did you not say you were sick?" She lay the baby down on the carpet and reached over to touch George's forehead. He seemed to be sweating, but his head was cool and clammy to her touch. "George, drink some tea," she said evenly. She handed him a cup, but he pushed it away and it crashed to the floor. Sheila screamed and the baby awoke. Aviva's eyes narrowed. She was frightened but kept tight control.

"George —" She took him in her arms and pressed him to her bosom.

He reached around her back and held her as tightly as a frightened child might. "They have found me!" he moaned helplessly.

"Who?" she choked.

"The Directorate."

The Iraqi secret service? Aviva felt her gorge rising. "When did you suspect?"

"I was not certain at first. Now I am. In Haifa, I was an assistant to the military commander. We frequented a café where often we were served by a young Arab waiter. He came to know our names, what drinks we usually ordered — that sort of thing. Then one day he was not there anymore. My boss inquired about his health and was told he had moved to Iraq. The commander became suspicious, I do not remember why, and had the waiter's credentials investigated. It was rumored he had gone to work as some sort of police informer in Iraq. That was many years ago and I had almost forgotten about him until —"

George held his head in his hands and coughed. Aviva handed him some water, which he sipped slowly. "About a week ago I came face to face with a man near the Maude Bridge. We stared at each other for a few moments, as if we were both trying to remember why we looked familiar to each other, but neither said a word. We went our separate ways. Since then, I have been searching my mind to discover where I had seen him before. It finally came to me. *He* was the waiter from Haifa!"

Aviva sucked in her breath.

"You do not believe me, do you?"

"Why should I not?"

"You have never trusted me."

"On the contrary," she said tenderly, "our lives are in your hands." She turned her head to indicate her two children. "Let us imagine it *was* the waiter and he *did* recognize you. So what? How could he find you again?"

"They must be searching for me — a Jew, an Israeli who worked with the military commander. Eventually, they will find me. Already I have felt I have been watched."

Gideon signaled for Aviva to leave the room. In the kitchen she refilled the teakettle and he whispered to her, "Best not to argue with him. He is not rational."

"Do you think he *was* recognized?" she asked.

"Frankly, it's doubtful. The boy's under a great deal of tension. Perhaps we have pushed him to make decisions he has not been ready to handle; perhaps it is an old weakness that has only now come to light. Whatever the cause, he has snapped. We have got to watch him. He must not be let out while we follow the emergency procedures to get him out of the country."

Aviva nodded her agreement. She went back to George. "We are going to send you home."

"I want to go tomorrow."

Although she knew his request was impossible, she humored him. "We are making the arrangements now."

Gideon came into the room carrying a second cup of tea. Aviva questioned her husband with her eyes. He nodded surreptitiously and she knew he had mixed it with a sedative.

When George went limp, they helped him back to his flat. After he was settled, Aviva outlined the procedure for George to be relieved of duty safely. Gideon would send a message that would set the wheels in motion. In a few days George would receive a telegram from a sick relative and be called to London.

Everyone in the building was told the young student had the flu and had taken to bed. Aviva brought him soup laced with a tranquilizer twice a day, and Sabha made an Arab cure of honey and pomegranate. It was Sabha who directed the messenger with the telegram to George's flat. Aziz was home and "broke the sad news about his mother's illness." To aid his sick friend, Aziz went to the travel agent and purchased the ticket to London for the next evening.

A few hours before departure time, Aviva hosted a small farewell party to which the neighbors were invited. George was encouraged to drink excessively. Just before the flight, he was bundled into a taxi with Gideon and Aviva and taken to the airport.

After the driver was paid, Gideon whispered in George's ear, "If you say one word, your life isn't worth a shilling. I will personally turn you over to the police."

The poor befuddled man's clothing reeked, and he stumbled so badly they each had to guide him by an elbow. To calm herself, Aviva approached the journey to the airplane as a series of small victories: We are through the front door and past the security police. The tickets are stamped. We have crossed the hall to the departure area. Unfortunately, there was only one flight leaving at that time of night and the lounge areas were almost deserted. George's drunken behavior could not go unnoticed.

In front of passport control, Gideon stopped so abruptly George's knees buckled and he almost knocked Aviva over. "What —?" she started to ask until she followed Gideon's eyes to a tall, broad-shouldered man talking with two mustached guards.

"Say nothing," Gideon muttered between clenched teeth. He waved with his free arm. "Hello!" He unhooked himself from George and left him leaning on Aviva as he stepped forward to greet the man.

"Deacon!" The man clapped him on the back heartily. "Are you flying tonight?"

"No, it's a sad business. A young neighbor of ours received word that his mother is in a bad way — a brain tumor. They want him home immediately. He's been so distraught since he got the news — well, as you can see." He gestured to Aviva, who was having trouble supporting George's floppy weight. "We had a small farewell party and he's had a bit too much Dutch courage, I'm afraid."

"Maybe that is for the best. At least he will sleep during the flight. It is running late as it is."

After two men escorted George to a seat, Gideon introduced his friend as Bassam Shehadeh, head of the Kirkuk Cement Works and a customer for some of his most expensive mud pumps. "The plane's going to be delayed," he said apologetically to his wife.

"Oh, dear. Sabha's looking in on the children, but the baby will wake soon . . ."

Gideon, bless him, caught her meaning precisely. "We'll have to stay until the flight leaves. This poor chap's in no shape to get him-

self settled on board. Frankly, I'm even worried about getting him
through passport control in his condition."

"Look," Shehadeh interjected, "I know everybody around here.
Maybe we can get him cleared and onto the plane so you can get
home sooner. It's a fairly empty flight; they shouldn't mind doing *me*
a favor."

"That is very kind —" Aviva started to say.

Gideon laughed raucously. "Wait a minute! This is going to cost
me my commission on the next order, right?"

Shehadeh clapped him on the back again. "Only half!"

Aviva watched George's progress from the waiting room. The
passport is stamped. They have checked their list; his name is not on
it. He is through the gate. He is on the plane!

Aviva's heart thudded as they said their farewells to Shehadeh
and got into the taxi. In the distance, they heard the beautiful whine
of the airplane taking off sooner than expected. Aviva leaned against
her husband and quivered in silence all the way home.

❖   ❖   ❖

Aviva and Gideon's next five years spent living in deep cover progressed without another serious incident. After few Jews remained in
Iraq, the focus of their mission shifted to military intelligence. Their
children grew, a third (Dorothy Deacon/Dalya Tabor) was born,
and Gideon found his niche in the international business community. It had taken several years before Gideon's contacts led him anywhere.

From the first, Gideon had kept up with Iraqi political events and
scrutinized each development in light of its impact on Israel.
Through the Technical Assistance Program, Iraq had received more
than ten million dollars and the services of more than a hundred
American technicians. He had paperwork that outlined the details of
the Mutual Defense Assistance Understanding, through which the
Americans furnished Iraq with more than seven hundred motor
transport vehicles, rocket ammunition, eighty-five pieces of artillery
and recoilless rifles, and substantial amounts of signal communications and engineering equipment. But eventually his contacts led to
a firsthand perusal of the recently delivered matériel — proving to
Tel Aviv (and himself) that all their efforts were bearing fruit.

On May 2, 1955, King Faisal's birthday — and the second anniversary of his coronation as well as the fourteenth anniversary of the
outbreak of the Rashid Ali revolt, when open warfare between Brit-

ish and Iraqi forces had begun at the Habbaniya Air Base — ceremonies were conducted to transfer the control of the air base from the British to the Iraqis. At the festivities, Gideon was an honored foreign guest who was able to examine the weapons on public display. Eighteen months later, on the occasion of the thirty-sixth anniversary of the founding of the Iraqi army, Gideon was once again a guest-observer as the latest armaments were exhibited at the Mu'askar al-Rashid Camp and could confirm that the Iraqis were proud owners of twelve new Mark VII Centurion tanks, thirty Ferret scout cars, and scores of eight-inch howitzers, all of which the British and Americans had given Iraq.

Over the years the Deacons' staff had changed. They were unwilling to suffer another agent's nervous breakdown, so no young man was given a tour of duty longer than twenty months. As the boys came and went, Aviva studied their personalities to satisfy herself they were mentally balanced. George's collapse was an experience she did not wish to repeat. Some of the assistants were more personable than others. While she enjoyed mothering the boys, privately she preferred the loners who did not require so much of her energy.

One of the most recent recruits, a radio operator cover-named Hani, was an unlikely spy. Conspicuously overweight, he soon developed a reputation as a gregarious café clown. After his late-night carousing, he would return to his flat on the other side of the courtyard and make his nightly transmissions. His indiscreet behavior worried Aviva, but Gideon was unconcerned.

"The somber types can attract attention too. He's a good boy."

Aviva reluctantly agreed with her husband's acceptance of Hani, but Gideon's latest assistant, Larry Hodges, she disliked on sight. The fact that Hodges had an impeccable cover as a graduate of a British engineering school did not help. The two men enjoyed each other's company immensely; they shared books and theories, often talking long after Aviva had fallen into bed exhausted. Larry was too smooth, too polished, too confident.

"I don't understand you," Gideon had argued, "First you complain about the uneducated boys fresh out of the military who don't know anything about the world. Then, when we are given someone with Larry's qualifications, you find fault with him, too."

"I do not trust him," Aviva countered.

"Do you know what I think? You resent the fact I confide in someone besides you."

Aviva felt as if she had been slapped. Maybe Gideon was right.

She wished there was someone she could confide in. But how many female spies were there? She had not seen Lily since her wedding in London, nor Charlotte since the time they had spent in Paris after Switzerland. That was when they had been permitted to learn each other's real identities. On one of their vacations, Eli told her that Charlotte had married briefly, had a young daughter, and was "no longer active" and that Lily was on assignment and "was doing exceptionally well." From Eli's tone, Aviva sensed that Charlotte had been dismissed in disgrace — or maybe she could not handle the additional burden motherhood imposed. God knew her own three children made incredible demands.

The wives of Gideon's business associates were always suggesting she get additional household help. She attempted it, but it was more of a strain than it was worth. A maid had to be watched to be certain she did not dust around the shelves that were caches, or open closets containing parts of the transmitters tucked in shoe boxes and pump crates. An overzealous laundress had started to undress one of the children's dolls, meaning to wash its soiled clothing. Aviva rescued the toy just in time, for its panties covered a repository for radio crystals. When the laundress departed shortly thereafter, Gideon joked they should have traded her in for a cook, since the only dish Aviva ever mastered was Sabha's mutton chop stew with dried apricots, walnuts, chickpeas, raisins, curry, and dried pomegranate seeds. The truth was she abhorred everything about keeping a home and yet that is how she was forced to occupy herself most of the time.

So, instead of their double life in Baghdad becoming easier, it became harder and harder. Aviva knew enough to dread the oppressive summers and the torrential rains that swelled the river dangerously. A ready supply of Flit guns was the only way to keep the insect level bearable; they never disappeared entirely. Nevertheless, a few days in early spring could be quite magical. The buds would poke out on the peach trees and a veil of transparent golden light seemed to cloak the minaret- and dome-fringed city in angelic loveliness. The voice of the muezzin calling the faithful to prayer blended with the musical notes of the mating doves, making life more tolerable for a few short weeks. The second release of the year was their annual holiday in Europe, where they met members of their family and were debriefed by Eli.

Each time they were out of Iraq they were given the opportunity to resign their posts. Aviva's intense longing for Israel grew stronger with each year, but she was able to convince herself her own desires should be subjugated a while longer. Although Gideon agreed that their children should have an Israeli education eventually, he believed he and Aviva could devote several more years to the service of their country.

Their spring 1960 holiday included, for Gideon, a trip to Paris to meet with Israeli air force officials.

"They want us to concentrate on airplanes," Gideon reported to his wife when he rejoined her in London. "The Americans said they were going to supply Iraq with some F85-6-F jets — six initially — which are intended for training purposes; then more will be coming. The Iraqi Prime Minister has convinced the Americans they need them to protect the northern oil fields from possible air attacks from the Soviet Union."

Aviva nodded. That sort of request was nothing extraordinary.

"They also want us to get them a MiG," he slipped in smoothly.

"A Russian plane?" Aviva laughed.

"That's right."

"We are supposed to hand them one on a silver platter?"

"Just about."

"The trouble is we have done our job too well. Last year they reduced our staff to only a radio operator and one assistant; this year they want miracles."

"We'll talk to Eli tomorrow and he will brief us."

In the morning, they left the children with a nursemaid and took the train to Cambridge — the one place they regularly met Eli each year. Since both Gideon and Eli had been to school there, the men enjoyed the nostalgic visits to favorite locales. Aviva always felt the odd one out on these occasions, but never complained.

As they waited for Eli at the train station in Cambridge, he playfully jumped out from behind a post. "Shalom!" he greeted them. "Hi!"

Aviva clasped her heart. "Eli, you must not do that!"

"Just testing your reflexes."

"After so long in the field, they are a hell of a sight better than yours," Gideon joked.

Aviva was furious. She had been up all night with a sick child and her nerves were already frayed. But she said nothing. As they walked past the Fitzwilliam Museum, Eli and Gordon talked animatedly about their school days. At a stop light, Eli grinned apologetically. He took her arm and steered her between him and her husband. Gideon, who had not noticed anything awry, continued to prattle on.

Though temporarily miffed, Aviva quietly compared her marriage to those made by friends and members of the family: she probably had as good a one as any. Gideon was a concerned father. Always soft-spoken, he had a cerebral solution to most every difficulty. He had willingly provided her with three bright, sweet-faced children, but since then had expressed only the most fleeting interest in her sexually. If there was no passion in their bed, she could not fault him, for that was not why they had married. What did she know of passion anyway? The only man who had ever stirred her was Eli, and he had been utterly unreachable from the first.

Beside her, Eli was laughing. His face remained delightfully youthful, probably because of his rounded cheeks and luxurious eyelashes. Her arm was hooked with his; their steps were in unison. She looked up at him. A thick lock of sandy hair covered his right eye. He tossed his head to push it back in a gesture she found ridiculously erotic. She pulled away from him and walked briskly around to Gideon's far side, leaving the two men to themselves as they strolled through King's College.

When they reached the chapel, they found a bench outside it, facing an incredibly lush lawn. Eli waved for Aviva to sit with them, and when she complied, he began to explain his latest directive. "We want one of those new Russian MiG-21s."

Gideon removed his glasses and began to wipe the lenses with meticulous care. "So do the Americans."

Aviva knew that if the Russian claims could be believed, this was the most advanced aircraft in the world in terms of speed, instruments, defensive equipment, armaments, and performance capabilities.

Eli turned to Gideon. "You've made excellent contacts in the Iraqi air force, haven't you?"

"Yes, but there's nobody I can tap on the shoulder and ask to borrow one of their planes. Besides, the Russians are responsible for aircraft security, crew training, and maintenance."

"So? Russians, Iraqis — they both have weaknesses."

Aviva signaled Gideon with her eyes. Eli caught the look. "So, Aviva, you think I'm crazy?"

"No more than usual."

Eli unlocked his briefcase and removed a sealed envelope. He opened it and passed them a photograph taken with a very long lens. "One of our agents managed to take this in Syria. It's the only glimpse of the MiG we've had to date. Military intelligence has been compiling lists of all the known Iraqi MiG pilots and has accumulated impressive dossiers on their backgrounds, home lives, military careers."

"Yoffi," Gideon responded enthusiastically, "but where does that leave us?"

Eli attempted to restrain a smile. "After we whittled down the list of possible defectors to only a dozen candidates, one of them walked into our lap."

Aviva gasped. "I cannot believe it!" The Russians knew the risks they were taking by stationing squadrons outside the Soviet Union. Gideon had reported on their extraordinary security measures, both in protecting the aircraft and in their selection of personnel allowed to fly the planes. "You are talking about the cream of the Iraqi air force."

"That's right, and our man would fit into that category. Five years ago he was selected for training with the U.S. Air Force and afterward was prepared for the MiG in Russia. He's a deputy squadron leader with a reputation for being one of their most competent aviators."

"Why would he do it?" Gideon wondered.

"For a small fortune?" Aviva asked.

"It will cost, but that's not the main reason. As you know, some of our best sources are Christian Arabs."

Aviva nodded. In Iraq there were a quarter of a million Christians who were considered second-class citizens. "Even if you have already found this Christian pilot, aren't you overlooking the fact that the Iraqi Christians are under great stress and scrutiny these days?"

"Yes, that is true. The once-prominent family of this pilot is being squeezed economically, and some of their associates have been imprisoned on trumped-up charges already. They've good reasons to want to get out."

Gideon replaced his glasses firmly. "Are you asking us to make contact with him?"

"Not exactly. He's come to us already. You'll be needed to coordinate the mission's teams. This could be the biggest operation of your careers" — Eli paused meaningfully — "and the last — at least in Iraq."

Eli continued with his rough outline to be certain they understood the implications and risks of the assignment. Then he stood up and strolled casually around the velvet lawns of the ancient college to permit Aviva and Gideon to make their decision privately.

"I like the idea," Aviva said. "It would be a chance to make a significant contribution before we are terminated."

"I'm for it if you are," Gideon responded slowly.

"Yes. I have been feeling time is running out. One final operation will satisfy me. And then?"

Gideon shrugged. "Let's not make any plans."

"Why ever not?"

"It's unlucky." He waved for Eli to return.

Eli had been sure of their positive response and now began their briefing in earnest. "Here's what has happened to date. The pilot's name is Tariq Qawasmi. He has a wife, two young children, a father, two brothers and their families, and an elderly aunt and uncle. We think he's going to want them all to have safe passage out of the country before he'll bring us the MiG."

"So many? It is far too dangerous!" Aviva said excitedly.

Gideon agreed. "What could be more of a red flag?"

"It's a price we're willing to pay."

"How exactly did he come to you?" Aviva asked.

"It's a curious story and important because there are some — although I'm not one of them — who think the whole situation might be a trap."

Eli could not sit still. He stood up and beckoned for them to follow him. As he spoke, he led them over to Clare College, across the Clare Bridge, and down toward Queens Road. It was all Aviva could do to keep up with his anxious pace.

"About six months ago a man arrived at our embassy in Paris and asked to see the military attaché," he continued as he walked. "The attaché wasn't in, but one of our men talked to the visitor. His message was simple: If we wanted a MiG-21 we were to have a woman, preferably an American, call a number in Paris and ask for 'Paul.' "

"Why an American woman?"

"Qawasmi, who had some military training in the United States, had a reputation as a bit of a ladies' man. He supposed it would not be unlikely for one of his conquests to ring him up."

"Sounds like a typical Iraqi male to me." Aviva smirked.

"We continued to be suspicious. It could have been a trap. After all, how often does somebody walk in and offer us a MiG?"

"What happened?" Gideon asked impatiently.

"We sent him someone who trained with your wife."

"Really?" Gideon said.

Aviva opened her mouth, then closed it without speaking the word on her lips: Charlotte. She stared at Eli for confirmation of her guess, but his eyes revealed only the slightest affirmative glimmer.

"This is what has transpired so far: the woman, cover-named Adrienne Sloane, is acting the part of a divorcée making a tour of the world on her settlement money. She went to Paris and met our pilot. In her report she paints a picture of a troubled man. First, he is a Maronite Christian with a family beginning to feel persecutions that they fear will increase. Second, he finds himself in complete disagreement with his government's policies toward the Kurds. Time and again, Qawasmi has been ordered to bomb Kurdish villages.

" 'All my life I've been a patriotic man,' he told Marjorie. 'When my leaders ordered us to hate the Zionists, I hated all the Jews. When they ordered us to destroy the Kurds, I killed as many as I could. Now they are beginning to turn on the Maronites — my own people! What do I do about *that*?" He also confessed to having a secret admiration for the Israelis, who were 'so few against so many Moslems.' "

Gideon's eyes darted back and forth as he listened. "Sounds excellent," he pronounced, "but I'm most concerned about the evacuation of his large family."

Eli nodded his agreement. "That's what makes the operation so complex, but we are approaching it from several angles. About a month ago, the elderly uncle received an exit visa to have surgery at a Swiss clinic. Yesterday, he and his wife arrived on schedule. A substantial down payment for the family awaited him there. In a few days, the uncle will send a message to the pilot indicating we've earned the family's trust. We've also gotten a doctor's report for the pilot's youngest son. He's going to require kidney treatments in London, so the mother and other child will depart at least two weeks before the defection is expected."

"How far in advance will we know the actual date?" Gideon asked.

"The planes are fitted with extended-range fuel tanks only when a long-distance maneuver is planned. Worse, the pilots are given less than twenty-four hours' notice before one of these assignments. That's all the time we'll have to mobilize the eleven remaining members of Qawasmi's family."

As Aviva listened to this most unusual of conversations, her eyes drifted toward the river Cam. Punters, in their traditional straw hats, were floating along the meandering waterway. In the background, the spires of the colleges glinted in the midday sun. She was struck by the absurdity of their discussion in such a refined environment.

Eli noticed her odd expression. "What is it?"

Aviva brought herself back to the matter at hand. "I'm concerned that someone — one of the brothers' wives or one of the children — might let something slip too early."

"Only the pilot's father knows they are moving, but not where or when or why. Next month he'll be taking the rest of the family to their summer home in the foothills of the moutains of Kurdistan. When Qawasmi next receives orders to fly toward Mosul — something he does about eight times a year — he'll have enough fuel for the round trip, or enough for a maximum of eight hundred kilometers. He will then alert our team and we'll get a message to the father."

"What if he is not given the orders for Mosul?" Aviva asked.

"He will be. He hasn't gone in nine weeks; therefore he feels he's overdue."

"How will the family escape Iraq?" Gideon wondered.

"We're going to send a team into Kurdistan where we have some Kurdish allies who will help the pilot's family escape through the mountains. A second team will be stationed in Ahwaz in Persia to assist in the next phase of their evacuation. We've also obtained the cooperation of Washington. They're as anxious for a look at this baby as we are."

"Why do we need them?" Gideon asked.

"A direct flight from Iraq to Israel is over hostile territory all the way. While we don't believe the Jordanians could get anything in the air fast enough to intercept the MiG, there's the problem of fuel. The Russians are well aware of the rewards a defecting pilot might be offered and so they severely limit the fuel reserves. Even on long-range missions they are given the minimum round-trip allowance — nothing extra — and the Russian teams monitor the pumps hourly. However, since Turkey is the Americans' closest friendly base to the western corner of Russia, we've made arrangements with them to refuel the MiG at a secret location in that country. Also, American helicopters will fly the family to Ahwaz."

Aviva was astounded at the scope of the mission, but Gideon was concerned. Every detail seemed flawed. Over and over he reviewed Eli's directives critically.

When they were alone Aviva found herself defending the plan to her husband, until she angrily confronted him. "If you do not like it, let us resign now."

"That won't solve anything. I am merely trying to make it safer, eliminate the weak spots —"

"Gideon, be honest with me. You seem reluctant to return to Baghdad."

"I don't know why," he admitted, "but I have an odd foreboding about this."

Aviva labeled his concerns normal trepidations, and finally, Gideon agreed with her diagnosis and focused his attention on the future. He began to talk of returning to school in Cambridge. Although Aviva had her heart set on a kibbutz in Israel, she entertained his ideas to keep his spirits up.

The young men on their team in Baghdad were told only what was absolutely necessary. Hani managed the routine radio transmissions; Aviva keyed in anything relating to Operation Otzem — which Eli had named after one of David's brothers because it means "strong." Larry Hodges was told to develop some dealings with a firm that supplied Qawasmi's father's business so they would have an excuse if they had to contact the family. Day by day the pieces of the operation were implemented without incident. And then Charlotte arrived.

⋅⁝⋅   ⋅⁝⋅   ⋅⁝⋅

Aviva met her at the Baghdad Hotel. Charlotte, looking amazingly youthful, had her hair pulled back into a simple twist that offset her wide eyes.

"You look fantastic," Charlotte said as the women greeted each other. "That's a gorgeous outfit."

Aviva knew Charlotte was only being kind, although she had taken special care with her black hair, wearing it in a stylish cut befitting the wife of a British executive. But next to Charlotte's graceful slimness and unerring eye for fashion, she felt outclassed.

"You look wonderful, too," Aviva said with conviction.

When they were escorted into the hotel's garden restaurant, there was an awkward moment when they both tried to take the seat with the back toward the wall. Charlotte winked knowingly and permitted Aviva to take the bench, which afforded the safest view of the room.

"Your territory," she whispered after the maître d' departed.

Aviva was pleased that Charlotte recognized her authority in the mission.

"What shall I order?" Charlotte asked as she studied the foreign menu.

"Masgouf is a fish from the Tigris. It is always fresh; they cook it along the riverbank over wood fires. Why don't you try it and I will order the kubba."

"What's that?"

"It is made from bulgur wheat, mixed with meat, flattened, and then filled with nuts, sultanas, spices, parsley, and onions. You can share mine if you like it."

"I'll try anything," Charlotte said in the rich, throaty voice Aviva had always admired.

During the meal they talked about the antiquities and excavations in which Charlotte was feigning an interest for this visit. "I'm especially intrigued by the Akkadian dynasty. I hope to see the monumental art achieved by the sculptors of the Stele of the Vultures and the other military reliefs of that period. I understand the best examples of their metal tools and weapons come from the excavations at Tell Brak. Have you seen them?"

Aviva shook her head, partially in response to Charlotte's obscure question, partially in awe of her comrade's extensive preparation for such a minor aspect of her mission.

After the first course was served, they showed each other photos of their children. Aviva was captivated with Allison's copper curls and myriad freckles. How she longed to ask questions about the child's father. Charlotte listened attentively as she described her own children. Of Gideon, Aviva said practically nothing.

After lunch, they strolled along the muddy riverbank. The late July afternoon was heavy with moisture and unrelenting heat. Every few minutes Charlotte would pause and wipe her face and throat with a handkerchief embroidered with the initials "A.S." Aviva admired the detail and wondered once more why Charolotte had been deactivated for so many years. Or had she? Eli could have had reasons for not revealing Charlotte's true situation.

While Charlotte took advantage of the privacy to describe her meeting with Qawasmi in Paris, Aviva continued to observe her intently. Charlotte seemed more beautiful, more sensual, than she had when they were younger. The bones of her face and shoulders were more prominent, her breasts more voluptuous, her expressions more vibrant. As she listened to the warmth in Charlotte's voice as she described the Iraqi pilot, Aviva suspected Charlotte had slept with him.

They walked on slowly in the broiling heat. No one with any sense went out at this time of day. Before speaking aloud, Aviva looked around to be certain they were alone. A hundred yards away was an old Arab. He was playing a haunting song on his mutbidge, a twin-caned instrument more commonly seen in the countryside. Confident he could not overhear her words, Aviva took the opportunity to tell Charlotte about the safe house that had been set up so she could meet the pilot in order to go over the final arrangements.

After she had briefed her on the most essential facts, Aviva allowed herself to speak honestly. "I must say I was surprised to learn you would be on this assignment."

Charlotte smiled enigmatically. "You weren't told about my special skills?"

Aviva blushed. She had not meant to insult Charlotte by confronting the sexual issue.

"You *truly* don't know about me?"

Aviva was genuinely perplexed. "I guess not."

"Eli didn't tell you that I am a pilot?"

"You can fly an airplane?" Aviva gasped with relief and astonishment.

"I'm the *technical* consultant." She laughed lustily. "If they required flesh to tempt the man, don't you think they would have picked someone ten years younger?" Charlotte reached out and squeezed Aviva's damp hand. "I have the coordinates, the flight plans, the compass headings, and radio frequencies. After the flight is definitely scheduled, I'll be leaving for London." She stopped her rhythmic stroll in mid stride. "You're coming with me."

"To London?"

"Yes."

"No!"

"Orders. During your last holiday in England the doctors diagnosed your son Harold as being cross-eyed, didn't they?"

"Yes."

"His surgery's been scheduled." She reached into her purse and brought out a packet from a London hospital. "Here's all the medical information: date of surgery, physician's name, appointment card, everything."

"I have never left Oliver!"

"Your assignment's being terminated. He'll be following in a week when a 'complication' develops with the child. We expect a fairly extensive sweep when the plane disappears, but your husband shouldn't arouse any immediate suspicion."

"But we were to coordinate the Otzem teams."

"You already have done the bulk of that work. None of this would be happening if it wasn't for your superb groundwork. You will continue to follow through until the last moment. Gideon will direct the operation from here after you've left and you will be in charge in London."

"And you?"

"My responsibilities are limited to organizing the flight itself and —"

"Shhh," Aviva whispered. A man wearing the dress of an un-Westernized city Arab was walking rapidly toward them in a long divided skirt. After he passed, she burst out shrilly, "Some people are bound to connect *you* with the pilot. Then you with *me* here today. Hasn't anyone thought of that?"

"I've seen the pilot only in secret and you and I have been prudent today. We shan't meet again, at least not in this bake oven of a city. Truly, I don't know how you've managed to survive here as long as you have. Aren't you pleased it's finally over?"

"I suppose so." Aviva's legs felt weak, her hands clammy and cold. She stumbled to a date palm and leaned against it. "It's this damned heat. Next time we do something in this God-forsaken country, let's have them schedule it for winter, all right?"

❖   ❖   ❖

The plan to bring the MiG to Israel went into motion the moment Qawasmi received his orders to fly to Mosul. Six hours later, Aviva was on her way to London with the children and was reunited with Charlotte at approximately the moment the pilot was due to take off. The children were settled into a hotel suite with a baby sitter and then Charlotte and Aviva left for the Israeli Embassy, where the news of the mission's progress would be relayed to them.

Everyone at the embassy treated Aviva with great respect. She was offered the chair at the head of the conference table and papers were shown to her first, Charlotte second. Unaccustomed to such deference, she was ill at ease, but as soon as she launched into the briefing of what had transpired in Iraq to this point, she relaxed considerably. After the initial meeting, Charlotte and Aviva went off to the powder room.

"You were superb," Charlotte said as Aviva splashed water on her face to revive herself.

"It is easier being in the background."

"Why? You are so assured when you speak."

"I am trembling the whole time."

"Nobody noticed. Every man in that room is in awe of you."

Aviva looked at Charlotte with disbelief. "They cannot keep their eyes off *you.*"

Charlotte tilted her head and grinned. "If you weren't so modest, you would be unbearable, so I'll permit you the illusion of insecurity."

Aviva combed her hair in the mirror. The woman she saw was one who had slept little in the past few weeks, but whose hair was elegantly coiffed, whose eyes were tired but confident. It was possible that she may have helped pull off one of the great intelligence coups of the decade — *if* the MiG made it safely across the Israeli border. She smiled at herself, tossed back her luxuriant hair, and said, "Come, let us see if there is any firm news yet."

Aviva returned to her seat under the portrait of Sir Moses Montefiore in the conference room. The Montefiore family motto was emblazoned on the bottom of the frame: "Think and Thank."

All Aviva could think of was Gideon, and she prayed she would see him again soon. She hoped he was following the plan to stay out of sight for a few days. He had been away from Baghdad prior to the operation, overseeing a pump installation, and it was hoped this would help remove him from suspicion once the MiG was discovered missing. Until they were reunited, she would find it difficult to be very thankful for anything except that the long, dismal years of exile were finally over.

"Are you certain today is *the* day?" a military attaché named Ron asked.

"Yes," Aviva replied. "Qawasmi had been informed he would have the long-range fuel tanks for a routine run to Mosul and back that was scheduled for oh-seven-hundred this morning."

A clerk came into the room with a sheet ripped from a Teletype machine and handed it to Aviva.

"We have word that the family has been airlifted out," she announced.

World sectional aviation charts were spread out on the polished conference table. Charlotte had drawn lines indicating Qawasmi's route. Aviva asked Charlotte to explain the course to the men in the room.

"He'll be taking off from the base beside Lake Habbaniya — this point here"— she indicated a blue dot next to the Euphrates River —"and follow a heading of three hundred forty degrees to Mosul via Baghdad as per his usual flight plan. This won't arouse any suspicion. In Mosul, instead of turning around, he'll be heading three hundred ten degrees toward Midyat in Turkey. That's when he's supposed to use the afterburners to get him across the border and over the mountains. The maneuver will use a great deal of fuel because he'll have to fly the next leg at fifteen thousand feet. We've calculated the fuel as precisely as possible; however, there is a chance he could run short before Urfa."

Aviva frowned. "Are you suggesting he could crash?"

"It's unlikely," Charlotte responded. "At fifteen thousand feet he can glide on the delta wing for twenty miles."

"What time do you estimate his arrival in Urfa?" Ron asked Charlotte.

"One hour and fifteen minutes after takeoff."

He checked his watch. "If Qawasmi left on schedule, he should be there any time now. Will we hear a report from Urfa?"

"No. We've agreed to radio silence until he's in Israel. We're allowing thirty minutes for refueling — a few minutes more if the Americans want some photographs of the bird."

Gil, a portly man smoking a pungent pipe, asked, "After Urfa?"

Charlotte pointed to the red line on the chart. "That's the easy part. He takes a two-hundred-sixty-three-degree course for exactly two hundred fifty kilometers, which will bring him over the Gulf of Alexandretta. Then it's a straight shot for the next five hundred kilometers at one hundred ninety-five degrees to Israel. There will be a Mirage escort out of Haifa into Ramat David."

"Have you figured in the magnetic deviations?" Ron asked.

"No. These are figured in true course. It's only two degrees and Qawasmi knows the deviations."

"Good," Ron replied. "I'd give anything to see the MiG homing in on our runway."

The silence in the room seconded his wish.

❖   ❖   ❖

The MiG landed safely. Aviva was among the first to see it under canvas drapes in a military hangar when she returned to Israel a few days later. Charlotte had flown directly to New York, presumably home to her daughter. Aviva awaited Gideon's arrival at Kibbutz Negba, but Gideon did not appear on schedule. Nor did she receive a coded message of any sort. Hani and Larry were also unaccounted for.

In the beginning, Eli tried not to let Aviva know the extent of his concern. "He could have gone on with his work for a while, feeling it best not to make a move under the circumstances."

"Do you think the message to come to London because of Harold could have been lost?"

"It's always possible."

"Should we send another?"

"Not right away."

"And why have we not heard from Hani or Larry?"

"Gideon may have believed it unwise to make any transmission during this critical time."

Aviva was not mollified. After two weeks had passed, Eli had further news — none of it comforting. Larry had disappeared entirely, a mystery that led to the belief he had turned in the others and had somehow managed to save his own skin with the betrayal. Aviva seethed at this news. She knew she could not trust Larry! Gideon had been too kind to him, too taken in by his intellectual nonsense to see him for what he was. If only she had followed her intuition!

A few days later, her fears were confirmed when it was learned that Hani and Gideon had been seized in their apartment building. Both were imprisoned, but not yet charged with a crime.

"No official reports have reached the press about either the MiG being missing or anyone responsible being captured," Eli offered as optimistically as he dared.

"Official or otherwise, the link is inevitable," Aviva replied.

"There is always hope."

"For two Jews in an Iraqi jail? It is the end for them both."

"It will be difficult to prove a connection between them and the pilot."

"Eli, you are not talking to a child. Neither Gideon nor Hani will be spared the full range of brutality to elicit information."

"Gideon is courageous."

"Nobody is *that* courageous. Besides . . . there is Hani. He is a sweet man, but self-indulgent and soft."

Eli did not argue. He knew the Iraqis would demand revenge for the great shame the airplane's loss had brought to their country.

At the kibbutz, Aviva volunteered for the heavy work in the kitchens to keep herself occupied. The children were well cared for and she was surrounded by solicitous friends and family. Every Saturday Eli came to visit, but he never had any news to report.

One day she attacked him for his reticence and shouted, "Do not bother coming to see me if you cannot bring some information with you!"

"Do you suspect I'm hiding something from you?"

"Yes, I do. But you are making a mistake. Not knowing is worse than whatever is happening."

"Our sources cannot always be trusted — The intelligence is unreliable — Until we had verification I —"

"Damn your 'verification'! What are you keeping from me?"

Eli placed his arm around Aviva's wide shoulders and steered her to the small, concrete patio. "As you know, we monitor radio broadcasts from Iraq."

"Yes?" she managed as her focus blurred.

"Six days ago the Iraqis announced that two Israeli spies had been caught in connection with the MiG incident."

"It is the worst possible news, isn't it?"

Eli was silent for a moment. "Nothing will happen for a long time. There will be a trial eventually, but the Iraqis are not known for moving swiftly."

Aviva could not help but remember the photographs of the Jews who had been hung in Egypt a few years earlier. She moaned and clutched Eli's hand. "What will happen to us?"

"Aviva, I'll always be here for the children . . . and you," he added sincerely.

As Aviva stared into his steel-blue eyes adoringly, she was confident he meant every word. He could not be blamed for Gideon's peril. She and Gideon both had willingly accepted the hazards of the assignment. And Eli was doing his duty by remaining at her side. But what was he offering? Was he saying that if Gideon never returned, he would marry her? Not exactly, but it *could* come to that.

She forced herself to think of the future sensibly. Despite the Mossad's promise of rescuing its operatives whenever possible, a man locked away in a high-security Baghdad prison was beyond their reach. All she could imagine was a noose around his slender neck, severing all his brightness and goodness with a brutal snap.

Over the next few weeks the reports worsened. Hani died from an infection that festered in untended wounds he had received during beatings.

"The body was hung outside the prison. We confirmed his identity from photographs," Eli said as he held her hand. While Hani's death was hideous, all she could think of at the moment was: Thank God it's not Gideon!

After a while she came to dread Eli's visits. There were times when he had nothing to report. He would play with the children, who had come to adore him. More often he had news of one sort or another and shared not only the facts but the Mossad's internal analysis of each situation. The worst moment was when he told her how every Friday afternoon one of the Islamic mullahs was ending his radio broadcast from Baghdad with the vehement exhortation, "We must hang the Israeli spy!"

"Won't they be satisfied with anything but blood?"

"Human kindness has been known to surface in the most unlikely of places."

In November, an Iraqi headline screamed that the Israeli spy had been moved to the death cell of the Baghdad prison.

"He has not even had a trial," Aviva railed. "What kind of people condemn someone without a hearing?"

Eli remained with Aviva at the kibbutz until word of the execution came. The report was delivered not by telephone, as he had expected, but by a special messenger from Tel Aviv.

"He's alive!" Eli announced jubilantly.

Aviva gasped. "How is that possible?"

"Our source is the rabbi who was brought to the jail to administer the last prayers. Apparently, he was brought face to face with Gideon several hours before he was to be executed. The hangman was already busy in the yard. The rabbi talked to Gideon briefly, then chanted a few of the Psalms of David, 'because they're prayers of hope,' he said."

"Did the rabbi say how Gideon looked?"

"About as you would expect: thin, pale, weakened in body — but not in mind. The rabbi said he seemed very lucid and almost peaceful in his acceptance of his fate. He sent his love to you and the children and asked that you remarry for their sake and 'find the happiness you deserve.' His last request was to have his body returned to the family. The prison authorities said it was possible only if he petitioned the International Red Cross, and they gave him paper and pen to write the petition himself."

Aviva began breathing erratically.

Eli made her sit down and poured water from a pitcher.

"He is still alive?" she asked.

Eli nodded.

"How could —?"

"The rabbi saw him struggle with a ball and chain. He had to climb up wooden steps. It was raining and the stairs were slippery with mud. Gideon stumbled and fell back, but the jailer prodded him with a rifle butt and so Gideon made his way up a second time. They removed the manacles from his hands and strapped them to the sides of his body —" Eli stopped himself.

"No, go on. I must know everything!" Aviva insisted.

"The rest is like a scene from a terrible movie. He refused the hood; the noose was slipped around his neck and tightened. Gideon called out, 'Shema Yisrael, Adonai Eloheinu, Adonai Echad . . . Hear, O Israel: The Lord our God, the Lord is One.' The rabbi closed his eyes. It seemed to him a long time had passed. Except for the noise of the pounding rain on the roof, all else was silent. Thirty minutes later Gideon remained standing on the platform. An official came forward and removed the noose and shouted benevolently, 'Our government is very generous. We are giving you a second chance to tell the truth.' "

"So, it just goes on." She slumped over and held her head in her hands. "Now they will only torture him again and —"

"Don't speak like that. He will endure. Besides . . ."

The glimmer of light in Eli's eye surprised her. "What is it? You have an idea, don't you?"

"It might not work —"

"Tell me!" Aviva demanded imperiously.

"The story I've told you is monstrous, is it not? A man is sentenced to hang; he's forced to endure a mock execution."

Aviva nodded glumly.

"You can imagine the scene vividly, can't you? So would anyone else who heard the tale!"

"What are you saying?" she asked.

"*We* let the word out to the press. World sympathies will force them to keep him alive longer."

"No, I cannot allow you to do it!"

"But why —?"

"For the sake of my children —"

"For the sake of yourself, perhaps?"

"How can you say such a thing?"

"I'm sorry. I've only been thinking of Gideon. I won't do anything you find offensive."

"What does the memuneh say?"

"He doesn't know yet."

"If he agrees, so do I."

Eventually, it was decided that quiet diplomacy would do more to ensure Gideon's safety than the media. There would be no renderings of the Jew with the noose around his neck splashed across the tabloids of the world. A month later an elaborate trial was under way in Baghdad, with selected members of the press in attendance. The subsequent reports explained that the prisoner had been offered the choice of a death sentence, life imprisonment at hard labor, or a relatively mild five-year term. Each was predicated on the degree he cooperated by naming all his comrades, the location and identity of his wife and family, and the training he had received in Israel. He refused all efforts to make him cooperate, so the prosecution demanded the death sentence. While the court usually complied with these requests, the judge gave Gideon a life sentence, saying, "Since this prisoner has been spared the hangman on one occasion, it would be tempting the wrath of Allah to condemn him once again to the same fate."

During the following months and years Aviva received infrequent reports when a petty criminal sold information about Gideon to Israeli sources after his release. This was how Aviva learned that after the trial he was kept in the death cell for over a year.

"It was supposed to be the prison's revenge on the court's verdict," Eli explained, "but the truth is that it is more comfortable than a regular cell. He has a mattress on the bed and the best food in the prison — more than he can eat. Often he uses the excess to bribe the guards or arranges to have it distributed to other needy inmates. His generosity is making him very popular."

"That's my Gideon," Aviva said proudly.

"There's the bad side, too. From the death cell he sees all the executions and must listen to the unpleasant interrogations in the nearby chambers."

Six months later there was another report, this one quite long and detailed. Gideon had become a hero of sorts. Moved into a block with other prisoners, he was teaching some illiterates to read and constantly working to improve sanitary conditions in his quarters.

"The typical method of beating prisoners is on the soles of their feet," Eli explained. "Afterward, they receive no medical attention. In the Arab culture, only homosexuals or women can be expected to tend another man's feet. Gideon has been treating the unfortunate prisoners by bathing the wounds with hot compresses soaked in a solution of salt and baking soda. As you might imagine, the victims are most grateful."

Gideon's kindness was rewarded his third year in prison when one of the men he had healed — not a common criminal, but a wealthy political prisoner — came into power. Through this man's influence, Gideon was transferred to the Nugart Salman Prison, near the Saudi Arabian border. "It's a kibbutz of sorts. There are high walls and a hostile desert all around, but inside the jail is run almost entirely by the inmates. They get exercise, cook their own food, manage their own laundry and school. Gideon is permitted a radio and books in English of a nonpolitical nature. We've shipped more than a hundred already."

"He will be there for a long time," Aviva said with resignation.

"Now that he has friends in high places, we might negotiate a release sooner."

"You are dreaming. It has been almost three years. I cannot hide behind Negba's gates forever."

"What do you want?"

"A useful life, important work —"

"You cannot return to —"

"I know, but I want to move the children to Tel Aviv, work in a business. Will you help me?"

"The children are young; they need their mother at home."

"Their mother *needs* work for other reasons."

"It is not necessary for you to make money. Gideon's salary has been accumulating."

"Money has nothing to do with this. I must be active again. Can't you understand that?"

"How could we send you out in the field after what has happened?"

"Isn't it a shame to waste my experience? There must be something I could do here."

"I'll see what I can arrange," Eli promised.

A few weeks later he came back with an offer. "Jasmine has some skills we would like to utilize," he began. "What would you think about opening a travel agency on Ben-Yehuda Street near the El Al offices?"

Aviva was enthusiastic about the idea, which involved her running a small business while using its resources to help the secret service with covert travel arrangements for its operatives. Eli assisted her in everything — from selecting the utilitarian desks, green plastic chairs, and long marble counters, to having the stationery printed and hiring the personnel.

After the first hectic weeks, Eli stopped popping in every day to see how she was faring. She tried to tell him she missed him acutely. "The children are so attached to you."

"And I to them."

"You will come to see us, have supper with us?"

"Not tonight —"

"When?"

"As often as I can" was all he would say. His promise to take care of them had been hollow. Gideon was never, ever coming home alive; and slowly, but inexorably, Eli was drifting away from her.

Her work consumed her and the agency prospered. But there was no pleasure in her accomplishments. More and more Eli was unavailable, even in the little emergencies like Shulamit's appendectomy, her car's breakdowns, a difficulty with the Ben Yehuda Street lease. Her calls to him went unanswered. His office claimed he was out of the country. And maybe he was. Then again, maybe he was not. Oh, wasn't it terribly convenient to have such a perfect built-in excuse to evade one's duties, to gracefully renege on one's obligations? As she resigned herself to a life devoid of personal happiness, her resentment toward Eli oozed and festered.

To think of what she had done for Eli — for all of them! What did she have to show for it? A husband who was not a husband; a father who might never again touch his children; a lover who had never actually loved her? Why had she permitted Eli to manipulate her for so many years? No longer would she blindly accept his authority to tell her what to do with her life. *His* decisions had led to this muddle. Could *she* do any worse on her own?

On the contrary.

From now on she would be able to distinguish assurances from lies. She would stand up for what she believed was right. She would fight her own battles. She would readopt the Palmach mentality of ein breira — of improvising a solution when backed against the wall and given no choice. It would not be easy. It never had been. Nevertheless, for the sake of the children, she would try to remember to smile.

12

And Joshua the son of Nun sent out of Shittim two spies secretly, saying: "Go view the land, and Jericho." And they
went, and came into the house of a harlot whose name was
Rahab, and lay there.

Joshua 2:1

PARIS, FRANCE: 1965

After her thirteen years in Paris, Eli offered Lily an opportunity for
more intensive field work because he had sensed how useless she was
beginning to feel, even though he had told her she was invaluable in
her position, which had come to include a major executive role in the
Mossad's European theater. She had maintained the gallery on the
Place des Vosges and under her guidance it had prospered. The salary she drew had been hers to keep; she received nothing from the
Mossad because she was self-supporting — in a roundabout sense,
since they, in fact, owned the gallery.

By being extremely frugal, she had saved enough to purchase her
own apartment at number five Quai Voltaire — directly opposite
the Louvre. It was the kind of space any Parisian would have
bragged about, but — by necessity — Lily kept it a guarded secret.
First and foremost, the building was wonderfully secure; access to its
entrance into the stone courtyard was gained only through a locked
gate. Four iron exterior staircases led to the various quadrants of the
building. To reach Lily's flat, one took the northwest flight of stairs
to the first level, unlatched an unmarked door, followed the right-
hand wooden steps to the first landing, and then knocked on a door

marked by the remnants of a stenciled numeral "2." After that, there was a private set of fourteen steep stairs to a landing, which were left uncarpeted so that any unexpected footsteps would sound a warning.

The apartment once belonged to an American sculptress who had used the high ceilings to her advantage by building a loft running along the far wall where she had stored her supplies. This Lily converted to a sleeping area reached by an elegant woven rope ladder. Once in bed, she would roll it up.

"It is very atavistic," she explained to Eli. "I feel as if I am protecting myself from the wild animals and enemies below."

Soon after she moved in, Lily was visited by a Mossad carpenter who, following her suggestions, created a cache under the eaves for her radio transmitter, code books, documents, and those forgery tools that could not be concealed among her other art supplies. On the far side of the slik, a panel could be pushed aside for immediate access to a rooftop between two cupolas, both of which had trap doors down to hidden stairways. Even the bathroom had a window leading out onto a firm, wide ledge that could be used as an alternative exit. In all the years she lived in the flat, there had never been the necessity for an anxious retreat, which made Lily wonder if she had not grown too content and soft in her splendid lair.

Using the ropes and pulleys the sculptress had installed to mount some of her pieces, Lily fashioned swinging furniture and a jungle of hanging plants, which complemented her primitive theme. This left her with vast areas of floor space for her easels and paintings, most of which were impressionistic scenes of snow, mountains, lakes, and skies. Lily was entranced with the infinite variations of sunlight breaking through mists, clouds weaving across pinnacles and peaks, and the seasonal differences in the color and clarity of something as mystical as air. She managed to create luminous, ethereal images in the most delicate of pastels, which evoked sensations of a peace and harmony hardly obtainable on earth.

Lily never entertained at home. Friends and associates not connected with the Mossad were always met elsewhere. But her need for privacy caused little speculation among her few artist friends, most of whom had their own peculiarities. Those unexpected house guests she did have would usually contact her at the gallery, identifying themselves by a simple code using the day of the week and month in French. If it was Wednesday — or Mercredi — the person's first name had to begin with "M." If it was February — or Février — the person's last name had to begin with "F." Thus, if a "Michael Finney" arrived on a Wednesday in February, Lily would show him to her apartment without asking a single question. Over the years, she played hostess for her mysterious visitors for weeks at a time, but she had never known their actual identities or missions. At first she had been curious; eventually she had learned not to care.

The only regular visitors at the Quai Voltaire were Motti and Hila Bar-Joseph. Since their first encounter at the art school, the man who taught her all his secrets of forgery had won renown as a stained glass artist, a skill he had also shared with her. A section of Lily's studio currently was given over to panes of glass, copper foil, soldering tools, and patterns for elaborate panels she hoped to one day find the time to execute.

Motti had finally realized his own artistic dream. In 1960, he received the most important commission of his life: the Chagall windows for the synagogue of the Hadassah–Hebrew University Medical Center in Jerusalem. At the Atelier Jacques Simon in Reims, Motti was able to use the special grisaille process he had recently developed of veneering pigment on glass, permitting Chagall to use as many as three colors on a single uninterrupted pane. With the accolades that followed this achievement, he had retired from his government work and devoted himself wholly to his craft.

"You will do the same someday soon," he told Lily, "for in the end, you will have to make your own life."

She did not understand his meaning then. This was the life she had chosen willingly. She had her art, her gallery, her enviable studio and — most important — her mission. Motti made it sound easy to quit, but she knew he had been able to do so only after his "South American holiday" in 1960. Lily had put certain dates and facts together and had confronted her mentor with her conclusions.

"You were in Buenos Aires?" she asked smoothly after plying Motti with his favorite Beaujolais. "More than anything I would like to be part of a team like that. Most of what I do seems to have no meaning. I fix a passport, I alter a visa, I take a message or send one. Sometimes I run an aspect of an operation, act as a back-up, provide a safe house, but to have done what you did!" She sighed, then dared, "Did you see" — she lowered her voice and whispered the name — "Eichmann?"

Motti nodded affirmatively. "I was the documents specialist on the team. For the most part, I stayed alone until I finally had to confront . . . him. I do not know what I expected: a freak, a monster.

When I first went into the room where he was sitting, I could barely force myself to cross the threshold. After I completed my work very late that night, I could not wait to turn the papers over to Isser. I only thought of getting out, getting away."

Hila spoke for her husband. "It was the most important day of our lives. Now we are free because *we* know why we were saved when so many others . . ."

"Justice," Motti concluded. "Nothing satisfies, nothing finishes like justice. I will die content."

Lily never forgot the words "I will die content," nor the satisfaction in his voice as he said them. Contentment was not something she had ever known. Always she felt unfinished, uncertain, unfulfilled. Somewhere there was something undone, some imperfection that needed to be remedied. Nothing was ever bright enough, clean enough, straight enough, sweet enough, sour enough. All she could do was follow her instructions, and by doing so, preserve her people, protect them in some undefinable — yet fundamental — way.

At last she would be on her own, behind enemy lines. Ever since she was a child in hiding she had hungered to know everything that was happening in the world. No longer would she be aware only of pieces of the puzzle; the whole of it was hers to organize, arrange, decipher. The dangers were greater than any she had known, but maybe she would come away with a modicum of what Motti had felt. Maybe — for the first time in her life — she would feel she had accomplished something.

It had all begun when Eli arrived in Paris unexpectedly. The message had been for Lily to meet him at the Louvre. She knew the spot and made arrangements to take the afternoon off. As always, his visits unnerved her. She was happy to see him, to hear the news from the inside. The trouble was that Eli was always so demanding. He wanted more from her than she could give him. He had admitted he had misread her in Cyprus and ever since had felt an inexplicable need to apologize for his suspicions.

"When I recruited you as my assistant in Cyprus, I feared that you would be too harsh as you interviewed people about their identities," he began the last time they were together. "Your response after exposing Hans de Vries was, under the circumstances, understandable. Yet compassion is an essential asset in debriefing work and I wasn't certain you had any to spare. While some refugees exploded

with their stories, others had to be coaxed through the simplest re-
cital of facts about their lives. I was bewildered that some people —
like you — rose above the most horrendous circumstances, while
others were shattered. Was there what my mother used to call a
'flawed character' or a 'naturally good person'? If not, how could you
explain the ones who had shared their crusts of bread to keep someone else alive a few hours longer? Where did these heroes and hero-
ines come from? Were they born, raised, or developed in defiance of
circumstance?"

"I hope I did not disappoint you."

"You never have," he insisted. "I can even recall the moment I felt
completely vindicated as far as you were concerned. You were sitting
on my cot, eating an orange. I'd never seen anyone eat an orange so
thoroughly. You chewed each section: seeds, pith, and all. You must
have made each slice last ten or more minutes — the whole orange
took more than an hour to devour."

"I cannot believe you can remember so much about one orange."
Lily laughed uncomfortably.

"At the time I was rambling on, in a most one-sided manner,
about my theories on the responses of victims. You chewed and listened without registering much of an opinion. When the last of the
orange's flesh had been consumed, you borrowed my knife and sliced
the peel into delicate long strips. 'Everything you say is very interesting,' you responded. 'You must not forget that everyone you are
meeting is living in a camp. It may not be Theresienstadt or Bergen-
Belsen, but it remains a place where innocent people are interned illegally. There is a camp mentality regarding space, privacy, food,
work. There is a camp morality about possessions, love affairs, deco-
rum. Have you not noticed how aggressive some people can be over
something as ridiculous as a place to sit in the shade? Or how generous with their last piece of fruit? While it might not make sense to
you, it does to me, and all the rest of *us*. An outsider, however, knows
nothing — and that is what *you* will always be.' Your tone wasn't
harsh, just matter-of-factly blunt."

"I would agree with that even today."

"Do you remember what happened next?"

"No."

"Well, after you had accumulated a tidy pile of orange rind strips,
you poured boiling water over them and let them stand. 'The bitterness will come out in two or three soaks,' you said. 'Then I will make
you a delicious tea.' "

"Orange peel tea . . . It has been so long, yet I can almost taste it," Lily replied.

" 'The bitterness will come out' — that is what I remembered, though you had not meant it philosophically. To you, situations were either black or white. Nuance was what you lacked, what you needed to learn in your work, yet your senses of what was good and right, bad and evil, were so highly tuned, I had come to respect you mightily." He paused. "I have ever since."

Sometimes Lily wished Eli was not so easily pleased by every little thing she said or did.

At the Louvre, Eli was sitting in their usual meeting place in front of Antoine Caron's *Massacre de Triumvirs*. She came up behind him and softly said, "Bonjour."

He reached out and kissed both her cheeks. "Nicole, it has been a long time."

"Almost a year to the day." She smiled.

He turned back to the painting. "Why do we always rendezvous here? Whose idea was it?"

She looked around. It was a fairly central yet quiet part of the museum. "Mine, why?"

"Of all the beauty and glory in this place, you have chosen to meet by a painting that seems to catalogue civilization's calamities with an obscene grace and devotion."

"So? Is it not the perfect metaphor?" she said perhaps a bit too silkily. She pivoted around and pointed to another huge canvas across the room. "Is that more pleasing an image?"

Here was a luscious Diana the Huntress staring at them provocatively. "Or perhaps you would prefer the Ingres." She steered him into the next room where a flurry of languid nudes illuminated *The Turkish Bath*.

Eli laughed. The light caressing the back of the woman in the turban made her seem the most desirable of the group, even though the least of her body was revealed. He grinned shyly. "Oh, to paint beautiful women — what a life!"

"The men in my drawing class claim there is little difference between an ass and an apple. It is only a matter of texture, light, form."

Eli smiled. "I'm glad I'm not an artist, then." He took her arm and they slowly strolled through the galleries. She listened intently while he spoke.

"In January of last year we followed Nasser's involvement in the Jordan waters disputes. You know about that issue?"

Lily nodded. Ever since the birth of the state, Israel's scientists and engineers had tried to solve the problem of reviving the arid land. Hydrologists had long argued that the Jordan River could be harnessed to irrigate both Jordan and Israel, but in 1955, Jordan rejected the design on political grounds. While diplomats endeavored to convince Jordan to relent, Israel — pressed by growing needs — decided to build a national water carrier, taking from the Sea of Galilee the portion of the river waters that would have been allocated to Israel under the original plan. A furious Nasser invited all the Arab potentates to a meeting at the Nile Hilton in January 1964 to discuss deterring Israel from completing the project.

"We monitored this conference and the ones that followed in Alexandria in September and, two months ago, in Casablanca. For the first time, we saw the Arabs developing considerable organizational abilities, and one event — which drew relatively little outside attention — has come to light. The leaders established a committee they are calling the Palestine Liberation Organization to act as an umbrella for uniting all the groups that serve or represent the Palestinian Arabs."

"What is their purpose?"

"For foreign consumption, their line is that they advocate a secular democratic state in which Jews, Christians, and Moslems would live together peacefully. Their internal premise is that they must fight to regain their homeland and that only Arabs have the right of self-determination within Palestine. In other words, they wish to destroy the State of Israel."

"How effective might they be?"

"They are raising a conventional army from the refugees in Gaza, Jordan, and Syria, but right now we are more concerned with a guerrilla movement called al-Fatah, led by Yasir Arafat. He is the man behind the New Year's Eve raid on the water carrier." Eli opened a piece of paper titled "Military Communiqué No. 1" and showed it to Lily. "This was written before the raid."

She read it to herself:

Depending on God, believing in the right of our people to struggle to regain their usurped homeland, believing in the duty of Jihad, believing in the revolutionary Arab from the Atlantic Ocean to the Gulf and believing in the support of the world's free and honest men, units of our strike forces moved on the night of Friday, 31 December 1964, to carry out all their assigned operations inside the occupied land, then returned safely to base. We warn the enemy against taking measures against Arab civilians, wherever they may be, because our forces will reply to their attacks with similar attacks and will consider such actions as war crimes. We also warn all countries against interfering on the side of the enemy in any way, because our forces will riposte by clearing the way to the destruction of the interests of these states, wherever they are. Long live the unity of our people and their struggle to regain their dignity and homeland! Signed: the General Command of al-Asifa Forces.

"What is 'al-Asifa'?"

"It means 'the storm.' It is the military wing of al-Fatah — the Haarakat Tahir Falastin — Movement for the Liberation of Palestine."

Lily sat down on a bench across from Millet's *Gleaners*. "I think I know the names of some of their leaders," Lily said. "There is Salah Khalaf, Khalid al-Hassan, Khalil al-Wazir, and a lawyer named Ahmed al-Shuqairy. Am I correct?"

"I'll give you a full list later."

"Which one is emerging as the strongest leader?"

"Today it is Ahmed al-Shuqairy. Eventually, I believe, it will be Arafat."

"Who is he?"

"The man claims to have been born in Jerusalem, although some of our sources suggest he was actually born in Cairo, where he served in the Palestinian unit of the Egyptian army and passed an officers' course in sabotage. He vehemently fought against the creation of Israel in '48. Later, he became the leader of the Palestinian students in Egypt, then lived for several years in Kuwait, where, employed as a public works engineer, he was fortunate to be supported by wealthy Palestinian oil workers. While he has been able to hide much of his past, we believe he was one of the band of saboteurs who attacked the British in the Suez Canal zone in 1953. In the 1956 Suez war, he was a second lieutenant. More than Shuqairy, he seems to appeal to the younger and more militant Palestinians, another reason we are watching him closely."

"Where is he now?"

"Damascus — the last we heard. Since his release, there have been twenty-eight raids from Jordan alone, more from Syria, Lebanon, and Gaza. They are getting widespread cooperation among the refugees along the West Bank. New fedayeen camps are being established at Qalqilya and Jenin; those near Jericho are becoming more militant."

"These new camps are almost on the border."

"That is why we are going to have to take action. Another priority is to acquire intelligence from inside the refugee camps, where the leadership is unknown to us."

Lily swallowed the saliva that had started to accumulate in her throat. Something was about to happen to change her life. She stood up and walked away from the bench to clear her head. Refugee camps . . . Palestinian guerrillas . . . How could she — with her fair hair and pink skin, her European languages and manner — possibly be of use?

Eli followed Lily through the nineteenth-century galleries around the Cour Carrée. She halted in front of a painting and moved closer to read the inscription: *Esther at Her Toilet,* Théodore Chassériau (1842).

He touched her shoulder. "Are you thinking what I am?"

"What?" she asked, startled.

"How much Esther looks like you." His voice was matter-of-fact, but also affectionate.

She stared at the picture. Two handmaidens, one probably Nubian, one probably Persian, framed the sides, while the regal Esther, naked above the thighs, was sweeping her long golden hair up and around her head. The breasts were small and high, much like her own, with rosy, protuberant nipples. Esther's abdomen was curved slightly inward with a deep cleft for a navel below a slim rib cage and waist. The arms were stronger than one would expect and ringed in gold bands; the nose was long and squarish, but proportioned to set off a delicate, if determined, chin. It could be she — with a bit more flesh on her bones.

Lily turned to Eli. For years she had known about his attraction to her and had done everything within her power to discourage him. Only that one time in England had she succumbed to his urgent need for her — a weakness she had always regretted. This time she would not permit him to ensnare her with convincing words or gentle gestures. A first lapse is an excusable accident; a second, a stupid mistake.

"Eli, she is much too plump!"

"I was thinking of the eyes," he said uneasily.

"Tell me what you have in mind," she replied, changing the subject.

He turned from the distracting portrait. "I'm asking you to do this only as a volunteer. No one will think less of you if you do not accept."

"When have I ever turned you down?" she responded.

"These refugee camps are nastier than you might imagi——" He corrected himself: "— remember."

"Why me?"

"It must be someone who can pass for a member of a United Nations relief organization, someone with your background, and political savvy."

"My cover?"

"Not completely decided. We would prefer to use Nicole Schmidt. Possibly as a nurse or something clerical."

"A nurse is more likely to hear secrets, inspire trust."

"Exactly, but a nurse's work would be much harder on you."

"I accept."

"You don't have any further questions?"

"No. You have selected the right person for the job. We both know that."

"But —"

"You do not think I should agree?"

"It's not that . . ."

Lily tapped her foot impatiently. She knew Eli was concerned about her safety, but his attachment to her was hindering his judgment. "Eli —" She kissed his cheek with sisterly aplomb. "Eli, do not worry. I will be just fine."

JERICHO, JORDAN: 1966–1967

Jericho is the lowest city in the world. And — with walls dating back more than nine thousand years and evidence of habitation for more than ten thousand years — one of the oldest. Eight hundred twenty feet below sea level the air is compressed enough to be palpable. Lily, who had returned to Switzerland many times since her first trip to Zermatt, had acclimated herself to high altitudes and minimal oxygen; here she felt the density of the air acutely. Each breath could be savored languorously. Physical work, at least when it was not scorchingly hot, was easier. Supposedly, aches and pains were minimized and her tendency toward joint pains did seem relieved. The thousands of refugees in the camps near Jericho, however, were not about to have their hardship alleviated by something as intangible as a change of atmospheric pressure.

Eli had sent Lily into the heart of Palestinian wretchedness. Since 1948, hundreds, then thousands, fleeing the newly created State of Israel crammed their way into the hastily constructed villages along the borders with Egypt, Jordan, Lebanon, and Syria. Of those who had swarmed east from Jerusalem to Amman, thirty thousand or more had chosen not to cross the Jordan River. They made their last stand at Jericho's verdant oasis in the futile hope that they would be displaced for a brief period of time. With so much Arab might pressing down on the Zionists, their leaders promised it would be only a matter of months before the Jews were pushed into the sea and the Palestinian Arabs could return to a cleansed land and an even more prosperous life.

Seventeen years later, their "temporary" camps had spread like a virulent rash. Those sons who lacked their fathers' visionary belief that they would recapture their Palestinian villages fled to the Gulf states where jobs were more plentiful. A few of the elderly died; a multitude of babies had been born and raised amidst the twisting lanes and open sewers. For thousands of others, their lives had frozen the day they were chased, frightened, or coerced from their homes, by Jew and Arab alike. Their first primitive campsites had evolved into tents, then crude mud huts that melted with the rains, later more substantial structures with corrugated roofs and minor improvements. As the dream of the Palestinians faded, an organized attempt was made to relieve the basic suffering of these unwitting pawns of history.

Nicole Schmidt found no difficulty obtaining employment with the United Nations Relief and Works Agency for Palestine Refugees in the Near East. So happy were they for a skilled volunteer, they did not check her credentials very thoroughly.

Eli had decided her cover rationale for leaving the gallery and Parisian art scene should be a love affair that had soured. "That way nobody will ask too many painful questions. The fact that you wish to do some noble service for a downtrodden people is evidence enough of your goodness."

To prepare for the assignment, Lily spent three months in Israel training as a nursing assistant at Hadassah Hospital. At Bahad-18, an intelligence training base, she was given a refresher course and attended political briefings to acquaint her with the latest in fedayeen and other guerrilla activities. Photographs of Palestinian leaders in their various guises were studied until she could recognize them from blurred images. Estimates as to the group's armed strength were made; the identification of recent weapons, mostly of Russian manufacture, was taught, along with the latest in communications and self-defense tactics. Lily had never been a natural with a gun and had not been able to practice much on her Parisian post, so she was put through a rigorous retraining program with the soft-retorting .22 Beretta. She had not forgotten the rules: Never pull out a gun unless you intend to shoot; never leave a safety on; always fire twice in succession, so that if the first bullet does not find a prime target, the second has a chance to do the necessary damage. She was even treated to a refinement in Mossad training she had never before experienced, let alone recognized when it occurred.

One night she was awakened in her room in the nursing students' dormitory at the hospital. A hand was over her mouth. "Say nothing. Get dressed. We are going for a ride." She recognized the voice as that of one of her instructors in the refresher course and was not unduly alarmed.

"Where are we going?" she asked.

"You will find out soon enough."

She dozed until they were just at the outskirts of a hilly city she recognized as Haifa. "If I did not know better, I would think you were taking me to Damon Jail."

The instructor grimaced. "You had best keep your mouth shut for the present."

His gruffness was surprising; he had been most charming and complimentary at the training center. Lily shivered involuntarily. What had she done wrong? At Hadassah Hospital she had been friendly, but quietly reserved. Not once had she even hinted at anything remotely connected with her work. She had not even alluded to all her years in France. Suddenly it came to her: She had been in the synagogue admiring the Chagall windows and mentioned she had known one of the craftsmen who helped construct the work of art — though she had never said Motti's name, nor how she had known him. Could so small an infraction have landed her in so much trouble? What could they do to her? She was an Israeli citizen; she had worked for the government for most of her life. Somehow she would contact Eli. He would make them understand . . .

The man beside her drew out a pack of Europa cigarettes and offered her one. She accepted gladly. He lit her cigarette. "Won't you have one too?" she asked as he replaced the pack in his jacket pocket.

"No, sore throat."

After a few puffs, she gathered her nerve. "What is the purpose of this expedition, gentlemen?"

The driver's head snapped around. His eyes warned his companion not to reveal anything. The man beside her patted her thigh surreptitiously. "It is better you do not know ahead of time." His words were useless, but the touch was reassuring. She exhaled a puff of smoke. The streetlights dimmed and blacked out.

Lily awoke in a room with a bright light shining overhead. She blinked her eyes repeatedly because the image of the room with four blank whitewashed walls and a narrow doorway kept breaking apart into fragments. Her lips felt rubbery, her head throbbed painfully, and her stomach twisted with a nauseating pressure. To her left there was a pitcher. As she reached for it, somebody kicked it and it spilled across the floor.

"Good morning, Mademoiselle Schmidt," a cruel voice said.

"What am —?"

"Allow me to ask the questions." The voice reverberated off the harsh walls.

"You have been brought here by the counterintelligence department. We would like simple answers to simple questions. All you need to do is tell us who you are, for whom you are working, and what you were doing in Jerusalem."

So, this was some sort of examination. She smiled, or tried to, but her mouth was so dry her lips cracked. She winced. "May I have a drink first?"

"Don't play smart with us, Nicole."

"What exactly do you wish to know?"

"Why were you sent to Jerusalem?"

They wanted her to play their game, but what game was it? Was she to use Eli's name? "I am a nursing student."

"At your age?"

"I was unhappy with my life. I wanted a change. People do it every day."

The interrogator stepped forward so she could see his face. He was young and bearded; his eyes were cold and black. He showed her a passport — it was Nicole's. "What's this?"

"My passport."

"How did you get it?"

"I have used it for more than ten years."

"Why?"

"It is my identity."

"Do you know a woman named Lily Jaeger?"

"Yes."

"Who is she?"

"My name, before it was changed during the war."

He seemed satisfied for the moment. He opened the door and came back with a glass of water. As she drank, she wondered if the test was over.

"Now, are you feeling better?" he asked solicitously.

"Yes, thank you."

"Where did you get this passport?" he bellowed.

"It is mine. I told you it is mine!" she shrieked, then regretted her outburst.

"You're a lying whore! You got it from somebody who told you to check out the hospital and other areas around Jerusalem, right?"

"No!"

"We'll soon see about that."

He opened the door and two burly men burst into the room. They each grabbed one of Lily's arms and dragged her into an adjacent chamber.

The senseless questions continued. Lily became so exhausted she vomited and cried, but did not reveal any information other than her names and her reasons for studying nursing in Israel. Nor did they change their line of questioning. Countless hours passed. At last she was given an injection in her arm and transported back to Jerusalem. She awoke in a strange apartment. A note was taped to her pillow which read, "Contact me tomorrow at my office." It was signed "Yoel," Eli's file name in Israel.

"Damn you!" she screamed at Eli when she located him. "How dare you permit them to do such a thing to me!"

Eli disavowed any knowledge of what had occurred.

"You had to have been partially responsible."

"From your description of the events, you got off rather lightly. I've heard accounts of ice baths and other . . . indignities. I suppose they spared you because of your sex and long-term employment."

"For this I should be grateful?"

His only apology was to say "Look, where you are going is not exactly Paris."

He had been right. Jericho was not Paris.

While it was said Marc Antony gave Jericho to Cleopatra as a gift and Herod built a holiday retreat among its glorious palms and heated pools, the present-day Jericho was more reminiscent of King David's valley of the shadow of death in the Twenty-third Psalm. The first of the refugee camps to be built was Aqabat Jabar, just outside the town of Jericho. A few miles nearer the ancient Spring of Elisha was the Ein el-Sultan camp, after the Arabic name of the well — the Sultan's Spring. Even farther out were the smaller encampments of Nu'eima and El Uja.

Some of the workers from the United Nations Relief and Works Agency for Palestine Refugees in the Near East had found lodgings in the better villas in the town. Most, including the more recently arrived nurses like Lily, commuted every day from East Jerusalem. Lily had an inexpensive room at the Gloria, a small hotel inside the Jaffa Gate. There was an indefinable satisfaction in coming home every evening to look down onto the domed and flat roofs of the Old City from within. If she peered out her window in one direction, she could see the Holy Sepulcher and the Dome of the Rock. Lily felt it a special privilege to be one of the few — perhaps the only — Jews who slept inside the sacred walls each night. Inside these sturdy ramparts, she was an outsider — an experience that was not unfamiliar to her. What a curious feeling it must be to feel a part of a cohesive group, to be known by name and parentage, to be told you belonged and to believe it as well.

Her alienation was less acute if she made a slight turn to the west. This brought a different prospect, that of West Jerusalem: the stark windows of the King David Hotel, the onion domes of the Russian Church, the towers and roofs of Mount Zion, the absurd silhouette of the Montefiore windmill. And on the street were Jews: the Orthodox with their covered heads, beards, long earlocks; their women modestly dressed with hair discreetly covered by bandanas; the modern Israelis in shorts and European dress; the children laughing and playing; the Jewish soldiers guarding their segment of the center of the world.

In Eli's office was a framed reproduction of a sixteenth-century map of the earth. The continents of Africa, Asia, and Europa were designated like petals of a flower, the center of which was a bright circle labeled Jerusalem. A floating island north of Europa was called Anglica, and far off in the corner was a section of land marked America Terra Nova. From the window of the Gloria, the map made perfect sense to Lily — except the center of the world had been sundered into two repelling halves.

Lily despised the partitioned city. She saw her present mission as abetting a series of events that would unite Jerusalem once and for all. Yet the Jordanian soldiers patrolling the ramparts and the occasional sniper fire across the walls were continual reminders of how remote her dream was.

Each morning Lily dressed before dawn and took a breakfast of coffee and pita in her room overlooking David's Tower. Eli had told her his father once had been posted there when he was a police superintendent. These days that same fortress was manned by the Jordanian army. As the sun rose across the Valley of Kidron, taking the path of the proverbial Messiah toward the Golden Gate, Lily could forget about strife and dissension momentarily. The bright glow beating down on the Dome of the Rock reminded her that the small, blue and white UNRWA bus was waiting at the Damascus Gate.

As the Old City stirred, Lily was on the road, nodding pleasantly to the other passengers but rarely talking as they descended the white chalk hills of the Wilderness of Judah in arching spirals.

Jerusalem itself was in the lowest part of the Judean mountains and followed the ancient path of pilgrimages and conquering and retreating armies alike. As they approached the road sign announcing SEA LEVEL, she had the curious sensation of going down into the depths of the ocean. Perhaps most others did not notice it, but Lily could feel the texture of the air actually changing from thin to thick.

The UNRWA workers became a bit more talkative by the time they reached the Inn of the Good Samaritan. Lily was continually enchanted by her first daily view of the Dead Sea looming far down in the valley to the right, its waters a blend of translucent pinks, greens, and blues. Farther off to the south were the Mountains of Moab in Jordan, and on a clear morning, she could catch a glimpse of Mount Nebo, the place from which Moses viewed the Promised Land, where the aromatic balsam tree grew and gave the area along the West Bank its name, for Jericho in Hebrew means "fragrant."

Several thousand people living without running water or toilet facilities belied that name now. Half the health problems in the camps could have been solved with a vigorous sanitation program, but any major improvements were considered a concession on the part of the refugees, who refused to admit their status might be permanent. The only relief they would accept was of either a transitory or emergency nature.

In 1950, UNRWA began by providing tents. These were replaced by mud-brick shelters and, finally, more substantial buildings of concrete blocks. The typical dwelling had two rooms surrounded by a compound wall for privacy. The largest houses or family groups shared a latrine, while others made do with public facilities. Water was available by truck delivery. Only the health clinics, community centers, and a few other larger buildings had the luxury of their own taps.

While UNRWA provided some necessities, the Jericho refugees were under the control of the Hashemite Kingdom of Jordan and that government was responsible for the maintenance of law and order. Theoretically, the residents were free to move in and out at will.

The UNRWA volunteers — who came from Denmark, Belgium, and Canada, among other countries — accepted Lily's commitment immediately and understood her unwillingness to discuss the details of her distressing "love affair." Most of them spoke English as well as some French and German. Only Lily understood any Arabic, which she claimed she had studied in preparation for the job. She fumbled with the language more often than necessary and pretended to follow conversations far less precisely than she actually did.

The most experienced UNRWA nurse was Constance Sommer, a white-haired, chubby Belgian woman who always carried with her a Bible, matches, aspirin, a bag of dried figs, a Thermos of tea, and a packet of syringes — something for every emergency. A Red Cross nurse during the Second World War, she had married a war hero and raised eight children. After her children had grown and her husband died, she had dedicated the rest of her life to the service of the downtrodden. When Lily arrived, Constance Sommer had been in Aqabat Jabar for a record two years and had won the largest room in the best villa in town as her reward.

The others on staff were relatively new. Robin and Pamela Watts were Canadians. He was medical director for the entire region; she was the midwife in charge. Karin Orda was a red-cheeked Danish girl with huge breasts that won her the affection of every passing Arab man, many of whom developed medical problems they swore required her special attentions. The entire section was under the jurisdiction of the local UNRWA director, a dignified Swede named Thorsten Osbeck, who was billeted in Amman.

Within a few weeks of her arrival, Lily understood why Eli had chosen her for the assignment. What would have seemed an impenetrable warren to an outsider was a familiar sociological structure to her. From her fairly invisible role as a low-echelon nursing assistant at the maternal-child health clinic in Aqabat Jabar, Lily observed the structure of the camp and quickly zeroed in on the Palestinian leaders who thwarted Israel. Just as an entomologist could slice an anthill and, after getting his bearings, point out the food gatherers, the queen's attendants, even those responsible for removing the bodies of the dead, so could Lily focus on the refugee camp's power bases, the hierarchy among the women as well as the men, the families that required the most assistance, the troublemakers who had to be monitored.

Pamela Watts, Lily's immediate superior, put Lily in charge of preventive maternal and child health care. Complications were to be referred to one of the senior nurses. Only the most severe, life-threatening cases could be seen by a physician. There were four well-child stations scattered throughout the camps so no mother would have to walk a long distance to receive help. Regular health supervision was provided for children up to three years of age. Immunizations were supposed to be the keystone of the prevention program, but there was rarely enough serum to go around.

Only a week earlier, the inoculations were finished before noon. More than a hundred barefoot children dressed in rags and suffering from a myriad of minor or serious infections were waiting when the vaccine ran out.

Lily's assistant, Randa Hamid, sent the children home, but many remained in line. Their mothers had ordered them to get the treatment and they feared punishment if they did not comply. Patiently, the Palestinian aide explained the situation again until the bright, expectant eyes dimmed and the children moved slowly away.

"With the rains comes the cough," Randa said dejectedly. "We always lose the weakest ones."

"Maybe we will get the next shipment soon," Lily had suggested lamely, although she knew it would be weeks before additional serum was sent and, even so, there would never be enough to go around. After a few months in the refugee camp, she had already learned the futility of planning.

Pamela impressed upon Lily the importance of making certain the children of the mukhtars, or village leaders, received priority for food and medications. "This will encourage the others to come in, but more importantly, we cannot do anything to insult the balance of this fragile society. In these camps, people cluster around their impotent leaders, looking to them for guidance in all matters, just as they did in their villages. We must remember, we are their guests and thus must play by their rules."

"Do they not complain about the fairness of our actions?" Lily asked naïvely.

"Fairness — as we see it — plays no part in their system. One more thing," Pamela added rather hesitantly, "boys will always be given preference over girls. Treat the boys first, the girls second, even if a girl seems sicker than a boy." She noticed Lily's horrified expression. "Remember, before we came these women rarely had *any* medical care. We are making a difference in their lives, no matter whether it is minimal by *our* standards."

Lily had not argued with Pamela. Her "job" was to be a public health nurse, not a rabble-rousing administrator. Likewise if she wanted to move mountains to save the lives of a few children, she could not permit herself to become well known or it would interfere with her assignment: to report on the Palestinian leaders in the camps — their politics, their personalities, and the degree of danger each presented Israel. Besides, she knew Pamela was right. Just getting the mothers to accept any help had been an immense undertaking. Horrid sanitation conditions from the open sewers, pit latrines, community water wells, and piles of rotting garbage combined with the virulent pests and debilitating heat to turn minor stomach complaints into diseases that killed many children during the first year of life. If Lily had been in charge, she would have diverted health funds to deal with the poor sanitation first; otherwise the problems could only be held at bay but never cured. But Lily was not in charge.

Lily would give the mother on a prenatal visit a week's ration of iron tablets. The most difficult part of this job was convincing the woman to take them and then, once she was convinced of their necessity, explaining that she was not to swallow seven tablets at the same time. If a woman was having difficulty in breastfeeding and requested supplemental bottles, Lily would painstakingly demonstrate how to prepare formula and how to keep the bottles clean, only to have the baby return with signs of having lost weight due to receiving diluted concentrations of milk or infections from filthy nipples or contaminated water. All these cases Lily found she could handle with equanimity. The ones that infuriated her dealt with the

Arab culture's insane distrust of women, which began the moment a female was born.

At the first birth Lily attended as Pamela's assistant, a baby girl was delivered. When the mother and daughter were ready to receive the man of the family, Lily and Pamela waited outside. The father stepped into the sleeping room and yelled insults at his wife for daring to give him a third daughter. Lily heard the sound of two loud slaps as the man punished his wife for her stupidity.

"I doubt the child will survive," Pamela predicted.

Lily was aghast. "Might she kill her daughter?"

"Not purposely. He'll insult his wife into neglecting the baby."

Pamela had been accurate in her assessment. The baby lasted less than forty days, and when the mother appeared at the clinic, she reported the death of the baby was Allah's way of permitting her to "have peace and give peace."

Next, Lily had to contend with the childhood circumcision of girls. Pamela had warned her to be on the alert for girls around the age of six or seven who seemed to be in pain or bleeding. "There is less of it, but some of the more traditional families cannot be convinced to give up the barbaric operation," she explained.

"What do they do?"

"The daya — or midwife — comes in the middle of the night. Two or three women in the girl's family grasp the child's thighs and pull them apart to expose the external genital organs and to prevent her from struggling. With a sharp razor, the daya excises the clitoris."

Lily blanched. "Is that legal?"

Pamela shrugged. "Anything they do to a woman is legal. She has no rights at all."

"Can't we do anything about it?"

"We're trying. One of the most ignorant dayas believed in cutting deeply to radically amputate all parts of the sexually sensitive organ. Severe hemorrhages often resulted, and after two children died, we put pressure on her to retire. Lately, we are seeing only minimal mutilations, but even so . . ."

Lily discovered the dayas had little notion of antisepsis, so inflammatory conditions as a result of the operation were common. Even after their bleeding and urinary complications subsided, Lily was obsessed with the psychological shock this procedure inflicted on the little girls and wondered what wells of hate and fear were a lifelong result. In the first few months, Lily found herself becoming so involved with the women and children, she was neglecting the business of collecting information for Eli.

"It will take time. Don't rush it," he had cautioned. "First they must come to trust you. When you have freedom of movement without suspicion, when you are invited into their homes as a guest, when their children confide in you, then you can make considerable progress. Until that point, you must melt into your cover."

While she had followed his instructions explicitly, she was beginning to feel it would take years to reach any level of acceptance in this closed society. Then came an unexpected breakthrough.

The Salim clan lived in the Beersheba section of Aqabat Jabar. An elderly uncle, Haj Zaid Salim, was the titular head of the clan, but he had been withdrawn and ineffectual for years. When he met Lily he introduced himself by saying, "I am seventy-three years old. I left Palestine in 1948 when I was fifty-five, but I am no older now than I was then. My life ceased at that moment."

Haj Salim's two brothers had been killed in the conflict in 1948. His brothers had sired a total of fourteen children, six of whom remained at Aqabat Jabar. His eldest brother's eldest son was called Rashid. Although Lily had never met the man, from the respectful way his name was said she suspected he was a powerful member of one of the militant men's groups. A younger nephew of the Haj had a position teaching at the UNRWA school. Except for some of the grandchildren, the rest of his charges were "unfortunately" girls.

Arranging marriages was difficult in the camps. For the first years of refugee life, many families held off making alliances until they could reclaim their land and property in Palestine. Eventually, they had seen the folly of trying to keep fertile young men and women apart and matches were more freely negotiated.

Haj Salim had contracted a marriage for a niece with a prominent family from the Jaffa clan. The boy was uneducated and not considered especially useful, but an association between the families was desirable. Haj Salim's pretty niece had brought honor to her uncle by producing a healthy son the first year of the marriage. When the Jaffa family suggested a cousin for Zeinab, another of Zaid's nieces, the Salims were most pleased.

The morning after the wedding, Nawal, the daya, came to the clinic looking for Pamela.

"Mrs. Watts is spending the day in East Jerusalem with her husband," Lily explained.

"Please, I need someone to examine the bride. They will not take my word for it."

"For what?" Lily asked.

"They are saying little Zeinab has lost her membrane of honor, but it is not so. You must see for yourself and convince them I am right."

Lily found their culture's obsession with virginity nauseating. Every female Arab child was brought up to believe her hymen was the most essential part of her body. No visible stream of bright red blood upon the consummation of a marriage was technically punishable not only by physical death, for — although a scandalous divorce could follow any question as to the nature of her virginity — the most common way for the shame to be lifted from a girl's family was to have her dishonor "wiped out in blood."

Pamela had meticulously schooled all her nurses in the physiology of the hymen. "Few people understand that the membrane varies in texture, size, and consistency from one girl to another, in the same way the male organ differs from man to man. A girl with an extremely elastic hymen might marry a man with a smaller than average penis. If finger defloration is not done by the man or the midwife, no bleeding is likely to occur, and so the girl will be blamed for not being a virgin. As disgusting as it sounds, I'm in favor of finger defloration by the dayas, which is ritually performed by some of the tribes. If the hymen doesn't bleed profusely, the daya is not beyond a few tricks such as nicking the vaginal wall to bring forth enough blood to stain a white towel for the father to wave proudly to all the assembled guests."

"Might not the daya cause some damage?"

"Yes, infections frequently result. But, what is more terrible: a dead bride or a sore one?"

Pamela had taken out a gynecological text and read the statistics in a clipped, professional voice. "Eleven point two percent of girls are born with an elastic hymen, sixteen point one six percent with one so fine that it is easily torn and often does not survive an active childhood, twenty-one point three two percent with a hymen so thick that it may need to be perforated manually, and only forty-one point three two percent with what may be considered a 'normal' hymen. You must explain this whenever these questions arise — and you will be appalled by their frequency."

Once Lily had been called in by a panicking mother who wanted to know whether a scalding had any effect on the membrane of honor. Her five-year-old daughter had fallen into a tub of boiling water and the mother was more concerned with the burnt child's virginity than her life-threatening condition.

Lily left for the Salim compound armed with a little book of statistics and diagrams. After a brief examination of the frightened young bride, Lily was relieved to discover this was simply a case of an elastic hymen. She went to see the young husband and asked a few questions in the presence of the daya, several male relations from both sides of the family, and Haj Zaid Salim himself.

"Did you attempt penetration?"

"Yes," the groom responded shyly.

"Did Zeinab cry out in pain?"

"Yes."

"Did you persist despite her cries?"

"Only for a few tries. She begged me to stop. I did not wish to harm her."

"Did you gain entrance?"

"I believed I did."

Lily wanted to question him as to the size of his penis and the hardness of his erection but knew she would never get honest answers. Probably the boy, who could not have been older than seventeen, had been too terrified to have exerted the necessary pressure under such tense circumstances.

"Would you be surprised if I told you that your wife is a woman of great honor? It would have taken a very large and perhaps cruel man to have broken through. You have shown great wisdom and kindness in your actions. You are blessed with a good woman and she with a gentle man."

"I told you she was above reproach!" Haj Salim shouted. "One of my nieces would never bring shame upon our family!"

The joyful shouts from the men in the front of the house brought calls of release and delight from the women secluded in the back. After everyone settled down, Lily suggested that she and the midwife remedy the situation. "After we assist medically, permit Zeinab to rest for two days in seclusion, and then the husband may take her to his bed."

Haj Salim nodded his approval.

After insisting the girl take a bath, Lily used a local anesthetic and performed the minor surgical cut. The daya carried the blood-stained towel out to the assembled family as the banner of proof. Lily was pleased that this case was easy. At least she did not have to lie — something she would have done to save the girl from either everlasting shame or certain death.

As Lily walked back to the clinic, she felt she was being followed. When she stopped and turned around, nobody was in sight; the moment she picked up her pace, the sensation of footsteps could be felt. Curious to discover her shadow, she stopped, turned down an alley, lit a cigarette, and caught the man off guard. It was the young man who had been seated at Haj Salim's right. She questioned him with her eyes. He came forward.

"I wish to thank you," he said in excellent English.

"You are very welcome."

"You saved the life of my sister."

"Literally?"

"Possibly. In our family we do not take action without proof. That is why you were called. Once, when I was a child, a daya informed my family that an aunt of mine was not a virgin. My aunt screamed and protested, but she was murdered by her cousin that night. Later her body was examined by a doctor who told us the daya had been incorrect. Nowadays we try to be more careful. Even if she had lost her honor, we would have inquired to see whose fault it was. Life in these camps has many dangers. If she had been technically innocent —"

"What if she had taken a lover of her own free will?"

The man's palms went out. He tilted his head. "It is Allah's will . . ."

Lily ground out her cigarette on the dusty ground. There was no point arguing with savages.

"You do not hide your contempt for our traditions very well," he said in a soft, throaty voice.

"You mistake my sympathies for the difficulties of a young girl for something quite different."

He was silent for a moment. "Then we are actually in agreement."

"Is such a thing possible?"

"I do not understand."

"Can you permit yourself to be in agreement with a woman?"

He stared at her; she returned it without flinching. Thick black curls set off his strong, angular face. "My uncle and the others only know the ways they have been taught. I myself am a great admirer of intelligent women. Mohammed himself had a young wife, Aisha, who wielded a powerful mind. She fought in several battles and was brilliant in medicine, poetry, and theology. She even challenged the great Prophet of Allah about some of the Koranic verses which descended upon him from Heaven."

"Few Arab women have followed in her tradition," Lily commented dryly.

"Perhaps that is true, yet there are some who inherited Aisha's mind. My own wife was such a woman." His eyes, a soft charcoal color, clouded momentarily. "Forgive me. I have not properly introduced myself. I am Rashid Salim, the oldest nephew of Haj Zaid Salim of Beersheba."

"And I am Nicole Schmidt."

"Where are you from, Nurse Schmidt?"

"Paris."

"Why ever would you leave Paris for this?" His hand swept across the ocher-colored mud huts burning under the midday sun.

"I find I can be of some use here."

"Were you sent by your God?"

"Excuse me?"

"I hope I did not give offense. Many of the women who have come in the past have been members of religious groups."

"I am not one of those."

"What are you, then?"

"An artist. I worked in a gallery and painted. Both were terribly selfish ways to spend one's time. I required a change."

Rashid laughed a bit too loudly. "You have certainly found that here."

"I must return to my clinic."

"Forgive me for detaining you. I wanted to ask one more question."

"Yes?"

"I wish to be of some service to you, as a way of thanking you. I love my sister very much."

"I do not know what —"

"Perhaps there is something the clinic needs?"

"Well" — she paused — "it would take many men."

"Whatever. Just tell me."

"The sewers in our section are clogged with stones and debris. They need to be shoveled out. But I do not want what is removed dumped on the side; the muck must be carted away from the houses."

"Anything else?"

"When we wash up I would prefer the water to flow downhill all the way to the river, instead of forming stagnant pools nearby."

"That is weeks of work!"

"You asked."

"Allah yehannik! May God grant it pleases you. It will be done, Madame Schmidt."

"Mademoiselle Schmidt," she corrected. "Kattar Allah kherak. May God increase your good deeds."

.:. .:. .:.

Rashid Salim kept his word. In a few days, a work crew of young boys began to scrape and dig out the gutters in the front of the clinic. Three-wheeled carts were filled with decomposing garbage and hauled to a dump on the far northern side of the camps by young boys who should have been in school. Rashid had appointed himself foreman. If he had any questions he came to the clinic for Lily's opinion.

"Would you agree to covering the old latrines and moving them uphill?" he asked. "That way the wind will blow the smell away from the clinic." Or, "Shall we wash out the mud before or after the mothers arrive with the babies?"

After a few days, he stopped making excuses to speak with her and hung around, lifting children off and on the examining table, carrying crates of dried milk out from the storerooms, and monopolizing the beaked coffeepot in the outer hallway.

Lily's assistant, Randa Hamid, objected. "The women do not feel comfortable with a man around. Already they are leaving instead of waiting for their appointments."

"I'll try to dissuade him," Lily replied, but she did not want to offend Rashid. She was learning much from their association.

Lily suspected he was a direct link to the central Palestinian committee that secretly governed the internal politics of the camps. His exact position was unclear, but from the speed with which he was able to mobilize and carry out the sewer project, Lily guessed he was extremely influential. Intuitively, she knew she must develop the friendship he proffered.

Rashid began to bring her, and the other nurses, packages of fresh bread for the noonday meals. "For generations the ovens of the Salims have produced the finest pita in Palestine," he bragged. From a small paper sack he produced a dusty green spice called zarta, which he showed Lily how to sprinkle on the bread. At first it looked like a sickly mold, but the taste was wonderfully fresh and satisfying. For some reason it reduced one's desire to drink while one ate. Rashid explained that was why it was popular among desert peoples. During their lunches, to which she contributed cold mint tea and the cheeses she brought from Jerusalem, he would talk to her about his family and their life "before the Zionists stole our birthright."

"I can tell where a Palestinian has come from by the look of defeat in his eyes," Rashid explained in a muted yet impassioned tone. At first Lily had been annoyed with his slow, almost tedious, manner of speaking; soon she found herself caught up with the lilting way he expressed himself. She could follow his soft and precise Palestinian dialect of Arabic very well, so he would often speak in his own language. His technique of pausing frequently — so that others had to hang on to his words — could have been studied or the natural talent of a born charismatic leader. As she listened, Lily found herself not entirely unsympathetic to his cause — as long as he stayed within the realm of truth. When he strayed into areas of historical inaccuracy, she longed to confront him, yet curtailed her urge to correct him.

"Look at my uncle! He used to own hundreds of dunums of land near Beersheba and we were a happy and prosperous clan. We raised cattle and ran flocks of sheep. In our orchards we grew lemons and olives. Our home was large enough for all the sons to bring their wives and have their own rooms; today, my uncle lives in a space four meters square — a little larger than most, I admit — but hot and miserable. He has resigned himself to die without ever seeing his home again."

"Have *you*?"

"No! I dedicate my life to finding justice for my people. Just like the Zionists . . ." He paused for effect.

"What do you mean?"

"Look at me. I am the victim of the victims of the Nazis. Fate has decreed that I also pay the price of the Holocaust."

"I do not follow your reasoning," she said, although she actually did.

Without Hitler, the United Nations would never have voted to partition Palestine into Arab and Jewish states and either the British would have remained in control or the Arab majority would have taken over. If Lily had permitted herself to argue with Rashid, she would have asked what the Arabs would have then done with the native Jewish population of Palestine. She did not question or criticize. Everything he said was an indication of how the militant Palestinians perceived Israel — and what they were planning to do about it.

Sometimes Rashid brought his ten-year-old son, Jalil, with him. He was chubby — with overstuffed cheeks and a pathetic little scowl.

"Everyone feels sorry for the motherless boy. They overfeed him," Rashid explained.

Jalil followed his father like a shadow. Whenever he stopped to talk with Lily, the boy would kick stones until Rashid slapped him to be quiet. Once, when Rashid was supervising the sewer project, Jalil yelled for Lily to bring him a drink. When she did not respond, he stormed into the clinic and kicked her, then demanded the water again.

Lily shouted at the boy. "You may *never* touch me or talk that way to me again!" She grabbed his wrists and held him down. He bit her and ran away. Furious, Lily started after him.

Randa deterred her. "Let him go. He does not know any better. At this age, a boy stays with the women who encourage him to behave like a man who will be the master of his home someday. They would approve of his behavior with you."

Lily was dismayed, but did not pursue the matter. Fortunately, the petulant boy appeared with Rashid infrequently.

If they were alone at the clinic, Rashid and Lily took their meal outside the doorway in the shade of the roof overhang, so anyone passing would see all was proper. On one peculiarly windy afternoon, they were forced inside by the blowing grit.

"Shall I leave?" Rashid offered gallantly.

"That is not necessary."

"You are not concerned about the talk?"

"Just so they know I am here to help them."

"They do." Rashid was silent for a long while.

"How old were you when you left your home?" Lily asked him.

"Sixteen. My father bought me a rifle and sent me to join the Arab Legion. I served under Glubb Pasha. At the time I was betrothed to a girl I had had my eye on for several years. She was the daughter of the wealthiest man in the valley. The ceremonies were put off until the Jews were pushed into the sea."

"Did you marry her?"

"No. I went into the military and my family took the eastern route to Jericho; hers chose the western one to Gaza."

"You married eventually."

"Not her, and not until '53. My father was very ill and wished to see me wed before he died. I obeyed him and took his best friend's daughter as my wife. The family was penniless, but the girl was a gem — even without a dowry. Her name was Latifa. She had been permitted to attend school in the camp when she was eleven and later taught the younger girls."

"Would she have been educated in your village?"

"Probably not. It was a simpler way of life, a simpler world in those days. When she was fourteen she won a scholarship to study in Amman. Her father was sensible and did not permit her to go."

"Why do you contradict yourself?" Lily asked. "First you are proud of her accomplishments, then you wish to limit her."

"What good is a university degree in a place like this?"

"You do not have to remain here. You could be in Amman or one of the Gulf states and building a fine life for your family. There are no bars, no barbed wires holding you here."

"I would never desert my people. Here we must stay until we can go *home*. To leave would be to admit defeat."

It was an emotional stance that could not be countered with sensible arguments.

"Besides," he continued in that steady, modulated voice he had cultivated to great effect, "most of us live in a prison of our own making. For example, you are imprisoned behind walls of glass." Rashid's heavy-lidded eyes closed to narrow slits.

Lily stared at him attentively.

"Do you not know you can break through with a firm pressure from your hand or the tap of a rock? Your walls will shatter and splinter; the sound will be but a soft tinkling and then you will be free. Until that moment, you are as confined as you would be behind bars of iron."

Lily had clutched the teacup in her hand so tightly the liquid trembled. She replaced it shakily on its saucer and stared into Rashid's smoldering eyes.

"Am I wrong? Is that not why you are here? It is your way of attempting to break the glass, is it not?"

"That might be one way of expressing it," Lily responded uneasily.

"Why are you afraid of me?"

"But I am not afraid of you. I am curious. I have never met anyone quite like you. I cannot imagine why you continue in poverty voluntarily. I could understand why the Palestinians remained in the camps the first few years. They were confused; they were led to believe they would soon return to their homes. By now it must be obvious that the Zionists only get stronger. Even if a miracle were to occur and all the Arab states formed a united federation to conquer Israel, do you think they would return the land to the Palestinians? Egypt would carve out a slice from Gaza north to Tel Aviv; Lebanon would take the south and would form a boundary line with Syria somewhere west of the Sea of Galilee. Jordan would be in the best position to grab Jerusalem and whatever part of the Negev Egypt had not occupied already. What would be left for you? The very old and the very young are trapped here in the camps for the present, but why are the men of your generation not finding them land in another part of the Arab world?"

"I see you are a Zionist after all!"

Lily's breath caught in her throat. She should have held her tongue. "A realist," she offered as firmly as possible.

"Your reality is not my reality."

"That is always the case between peoples from different lands," Lily replied smoothly. It was almost three o'clock. Mothers and babies were already lining up. There would be no more time for political discussions that afternoon.

The next morning, when Rashid did not appear with his warm pitas, Lily was more relieved than disappointed. Their closeness had not yielded significant amounts of information. All she had learned was that he had leisure time on his hands — at least during the day. He could summon a crew to clean gutters swiftly but was not expected to lift a shovel himself. The young boys respected him mightily. He did not appear to spend time at the small coffee shops where the village elders played backgammon and smoked their water pipes; in fact, he was rarely seen in most of the familiar meeting places for adults or youths. Where he went and what he did was as much a secret as it had been before they had met.

Randa was the first to mention Rashid's absence. "Do you wish me to bring some pitas tomorrow?"

"That is not necessary. I'm finding good bread in Jerusalem."

"Perhaps he discovered everything he wanted to know . . ." Randa suggested deftly.

"I do not understand," Lily replied.

"Don't you know why he visited you?"

"To supervise the sewer cleaning."

"That was finished in two weeks."

"So?"

"I think he was spying on you."

"Why would he —?"

"They never trust the UNRWA workers. It took a long time before the Wattses were accepted."

"Why are you telling me this?"

"You should know where you stand."

"Where is that?"

"Rashid has decided you are not a threat."

"The last time we had lunch he was very angry with me. He called me a Zionist."

"He was testing you."

"I see. And you, Randa, what do *you* think of me?"

"You are a very kind but very lonely woman. It would be easier for you if you had someone like Dr. Watts. Here you will never find happiness."

"Perhaps not, but contentment is possible. Every time a sick baby gains weight, a mother has a healthy baby, I feel I have been of use."

"Only for a while. These are not your people; this can never be your cause. One of these days you will leave; Rashid and I will still be here."

"I cannot disagree with you. Thank you for your honesty; it is the true gift of friendship."

As Randa's face beamed a wide smile, Lily felt a painful grinding in her stomach. For a brief second, she acutely felt the effects of being split into two people and ached to be wholly herself.

❖   ❖   ❖

Lily went down to Jericho six days a week. Once a month she took a three-day holiday and remained in Jerusalem. Fridays the Moslems flocked to worship at the El-Aqsa Mosque; Saturdays she could watch the Jews strolling the area around Mount Zion and King David's Tomb on the other side of the Old City walls; Sundays the activity increased in the Christian quarter. The three Sabbaths were yet another poignant reminder of the sanctity of Jerusalem to so many and the fact that the holiest of cities was open to so few.

On these long weekends Lily would take the time to compose her report, written in secret ink. She would either mail it via drops in Europe or — if the message was urgent — hand it to a courier, most often an Armenian priest who, like other members of the clergy, diplomats, and some U.N. personnel, had a pass permitting him access to both parts of Jerusalem, crossing through the Mandelbaum Gate. If Lily needed to make contact with a courier, she would go to the American Colony Hotel — originally the palace of a pasha — and sit at a certain table in the center courtyard surrounded by huge baskets dripping with plump fuchsias, lush bougainvilleas, and fragrant lemon trees planted in copper urns. The hotel, one of the first in Jerusalem to cater to travelers who did not want to camp in tents, almost breathed its history. Lily loved to imagine T. E. Lawrence or General Allenby strolling by. She ordered English tea and waited no more than an hour when the signal, a door opening on the second-floor balcony, was given. Paying her bill, she proceeded upstairs past the glass cases of antiquities to a hall with a wooden ceiling painted a celestial blue and studded with gold stars. She took a seat on a leather sofa beside an inlaid Damascus table, which had a drawer. She pretended to read a magazine. Her papers, usually concealed in a current periodical, would be deposited in the drawer when no one was present. The moment an Armenian priest entered, she stood up and started down the staircase.

So far she had confirmed that Rashid Salim was probably one of the leaders of the fedayeen movement within the refugee camp and named some of his associates as men to be watched. One in particular, Fahd Qazza, had been away for several weeks and she heard rumors that he had gone to Damascus, where the Fatah core group was said to be residing. His pregnant wife came to the clinic regularly, so it was not difficult to inquire politely about the health of her husband and learn when — or if — he returned.

After coding the messages she would be sending one weekend in April, Lily deciphered her communiqués (which were passed on to her in an exchange of market baskets once a week) giving her the latest news, informing her of the movements of suspects, and asking the questions she was supposed to attempt to answer. Earlier that month, an Israeli force crossed into Jordan and destroyed portions of the fedayeen staging camps in reprisal for a series of nine attacks from Jordanian territory. She had heard little about this in Jericho, although pictures of some of the martyred guerrillas had sprung up in the coffee houses. The latest bulletins asked her to be on the alert for information on people traveling between Jericho and Syria, because it was believed a sabotage training school had recently been established on the Syrian side of the Sea of Galilee. After studying the most recent data, she burned the pages in an ashtray and flushed the ashes down the toilet in her hotel room.

Feeling unusually agitated by that week's information, she decided to indulge herself by opening the bottle of Cointreau she saved for special occasions and beginning a new book she had ordered from France. Rising, she closed the shutters to the damp night air. There was no place on earth where one could feel quite so chilled as in Jerusalem, she decided. There was something sinister about the way the stone buildings and walls retained moisture, transferring it into the joints and bones of the unwary. For her own room she had purchased woolen rugs in an attempt to insulate the glacial terra cotta floors, but only under covers did her extremities warm.

She sipped the liqueur slowly. Ah, two mornings to sleep late, two more days to herself. The prospect itself was enough to ease the tightness in her forehead and stiffness in her lower back.

Compared to life in Paris, Jericho was brutally hard. Every day she walked miles, suffered from the heat and cold alike, lifted heavy water buckets, and carried sick children in her arms. Fortunately, she had kept her body in shape with her rigorous hiking vacations in Switzerland and her preference for walking in Paris rather than taking the Métro. Even so, she knew she was under a terrible strain. She pulled back the sheets. They were changed on Thursday nights, so they were fresh and crisp. She plumped the pillows and climbed under the covers. After she had drained her second glass of Cointreau, François Mauriac's *De Gaulle* felt leaden in her hands. She put the book and glass on the nightstand and was about to switch off the light when she heard a soft rapping at the door.

Lily was not alarmed. It could be one of the other UNRWA workers with some sort of question or medical problem.

"Yes?" she asked without opening the door.

"It is Rashid Salim. I need to talk to you."

"Rashid!"

She opened the door swiftly. He slipped into the room and locked the door before she could get to the bolt.

In the weak light from the reading lamp, she hardly recognized him. He was dressed in the cloaklike abayah and head wrappings of the Palestinian Arab. Only his piercing eyes and slender, slightly hawkish nose were revealed. Standing beside him in her long flannel nightgown, she was about his height. They both stood by the door and did not move until Lily, aware she was not dressed, reached for her robe at the foot of the bed.

"How did you find me?"

"I believe you once mentioned where you stayed in Jerusalem."

That was not true.

While the UNRWA staff knew her whereabouts, she was certain she had never discussed her accommodations with Rashid. She decided not to confront him on the matter.

"What do you want?"

"I must ask your protection for a few hours."

"I do not understand."

"Let me just say that certain Jordanian authorities did not care for the reason I was in the city this afternoon."

"Why were you here?"

"I came to pray at the mosque. I try to do so once each month. I have told you I am a very devout Moslem, have I not?"

He had not.

"Are you in some sort of trouble?"

"Not exactly. I was meeting some friends and they were detained. You will have to trust me on this. I cannot divulge anything further."

"As you wish, but you cannot remain here."

"Why not?"

"You have always taken care to protect my reputation in Aqabat Jabar."

"That is a very small place. The destination of every pita bread is known to the baker by morning. Nobody saw me come up here; I will depart discreetly."

"Rashid, I cannot permit you to stay with me."

"I ask your protection."

"I am not a Bedouin sheik."

"They are looking for me. If you send me out to the streets —"

Lily did not actually care whether he remained or left. More important was her formal protest that he could not stay. Then if he did, he would be in her debt — a situation on which she might capitalize in the future.

"Would you like a drink or are you so devout you do not take alcoholic beverages?"

"Under special circumstances . . ."

"I would consider this unique, would you not?"

"Nicole, do not be angry with me."

Lily brushed back her hair and sat on the side of the bed. "You must understand the work in the clinic is extremely tiring. I was about to go to sleep."

"I will sit over in that chair. I will not disturb you." Rashid started for the chair, then stopped and listened at the window. "What does this look out on?"

"See for yourself."

Rashid reached over and turned out the light, then opened the shutters and peered down toward the Jaffa Gate. The streets appeared to be deserted. He slumped in the armchair with the bruised velvet upholstery.

Lily remained seated on the edge of her bed. "You are in some sort of trouble with the Jordanian authorities because of your work in Fatah, am I right?" she dared. Most of what she knew was not a secret and he had to suspect she was not completely ignorant of the political life in the camp.

"You are a very intelligent nurse."

"What are you trying to accomplish?" She did not expect him to respond. Lily already knew that a Fatah group was said to be responsible for the bombing of a house, the derailment of a train, and several mines found along major roadways in Israel. The Israelis had retaliated with strikes at the small southern town of Samu, four miles from the Jordanian border, where, a few days earlier, two Israelis had been killed by a bomb. Their prime objective was to destroy the buildings, but a company of Jordanian soldiers ran into the assaulting force and sixteen Arab soldiers had been killed. Thus Jordan had reason to be unhappy with the result of the guerrilla actions and was probably rounding up the leaders. Rashid in hiding confirmed her suspicions that he was a key figure in the underground war.

"There is so much I cannot say." Rashid's silky voice seemed crisper in the dark.

Lily remained silent. She sensed his short rapid breaths slicing through the distance between them. If she were patient, he might continue.

"My wife was named Latifa. You knew that?"

"Yes."

"You know our son."

"Yes."

"Jalil was in her arms when it happened. She was killed by the Zionists."

Lily sucked in her breath audibly. For the first time, she was afraid of Rashid. If he knew about her . . . She forced herself to remain calm. "How?"

"We were living in Jericho and I was making my monthly pilgrimage to the mosque. Latifa had not been to Jerusalem in two years — not since the boy was born. It was the week before Ramadan began and I brought her to shop in the souk. While she went to the market, I left to visit friends. She was walking not far from here — down the street leading to the Armenian quarter — when it happened. A sniper from Mount Zion fired directly at her. She was carrying Jalil. She fell on the boy as the bullet tore into her skull."

Lily remained perfectly quiet.

"Before that moment, I had a job as a teacher of mathematics in the UNRWA school. Afterward, I decided it was futile to do anything but fight the enemy with whatever tactics we could muster: propaganda, terrorism, warfare — all brought me one step closer to revenge."

"Surely she was not killed on purpose. Usually the Jordanians shoot a volley or two, the Israelis return it. Their policy is supposed to be bullets for bullets, bombs for bombs. I cannot believe they were aiming for an innocent woman with a child."

"Kus——" he started to swear in Arabic but, realizing he was in a woman's presence, controlled himself. The "s" melted into a slow hissing sound under his breath. "How the hell do *you* know what they were aiming at? It was a direct hit. Nobody else was around! No soldier was walking beside her. You and the rest of the UNRWA bunch are the worst Jew-lovers I have ever seen. Let us be honest with each other. Who contributes the most money to your organization? The very states which support the Zionists. It is another underhanded effort to phase out the distasteful 'refugee problem.' I have read that damned Clapp Mission report, the same document which provided the blueprint for UNRWA. It wants the burden of supporting the refugees to be passed on to the host governments as quickly as possible and to aid the integration of Palestinians into other Arab lands. Well, what do you think of the way our Jordanian *hosts* have treated us? Seventeen years in a filthy, stinking camp! They do not want Palestinians any more than the Zionists do. That is why we have resisted permanent resettlement. The world cannot forget us!"

He stood and paced the room.

"At first I cooperated. I wanted to work. As soon as I took a job at the school, they took away my ration card, then the cards of my family. I finally got smart and quit. Only by living in poverty are we still refugees. Only by living as animals do we remain refugees. And only as refugees will we retain the right to reclaim our land. We may be oppressed; but we will be vindicated someday!"

Never before had he spoken with such passion. His tone was mesmerizing, but Lily knew how skewed his logic was. Someone with less information might have been taken in.

"What if you cannot reclaim your land?" she asked gently. "I regret to remind you that history does not favor your point of view. After all, how many times have the vanquished returned to their territories?"

"You understand nothing."

"I have been trying —"

He interrupted her sharply. "What do you know of blood revenge?"

"It is a way of regaining honor after a family has been shamed."

"Very good. Let me educate you a bit further. You may think that we are barbarians, but some of our ancient customs are practical forms of justice. Most Arab clans are fairly small. Let us say an average tribe consists of fifty people. Amongst the group would be women, children, older people. In the end, you might have ten or fifteen strong men who could act as soldiers to protect the tribe, so the balance of power — which might prevent a war — is very delicate. That is why, if a member of my family is killed by a member of your family, my family is disgraced in the eyes of Allah until the murder is avenged."

"A life for a life?"

"We say, 'Damm butlub damm,' blood demands blood. Yet we also have other — you might consider them more humane — ways of settling a feud.

"First is the ransom. Let us say a member of my family accidentally kills a member of your family — recognizing, of course, the difference between accident and purpose might be fairly slender in some instances. The murderer will run away to another family or tribe and will ask to be under that sheik's protection. The sheik must grant protection under those circumstances. He becomes the mediator and calls for a three-month cease-fire. During that time, revenge may not be taken and a price for the dead person is determined by negotiation. If the victim was, say, an old man, obviously the price would be less than that of a young man in his prime. A young woman of childbearing age would command a higher price than an infertile elderly woman. A woman who has given birth to males is worth more than a woman who has given birth to females. If a price can be settled upon, a date is set for the sulha, or forgiveness ceremony. At the feast, the mediating sheik holds up a handkerchief with three knots on it — one knot for each of the warring parties, one knot for him. Each side holds his knot, forming a canopy. Money changes hands and the account has been settled.

"The second method of settling a blood revenge is with a virgin. The nearest male relative, usually a brother or the father of the victim, is offered a young virgin as a concubine for the purpose of bringing forth a replacement to the injured tribe. This becomes complicated, however. If the victim was a man and the concubine gives birth to three girls, does this replace the victim? The family can decide if three girls are equal to one boy or reject her and request another virgin. Even if she gives birth to a male, it is not enough. She must stay in the home of the family for another eight years until they see that the boy is healthy and normal."

"What happens to the concubine after that?"

"Sometimes she is returned to her father — who sells her out as a bride at a fraction of her original worth."

"Isn't she dishonored for life?"

"No, there is no shame in the way she lost her virginity. Often she is bought for the reduced bride price and stays with the father of her child. But it is the third system of revenge that is the one most often used, because sometimes only blood revenge will suffice to bring the family out of disgrace from the eyes of Allah."

"The murderer is found and killed?"

"No. It does not have to be the person who committed the original crime. Any member of the guilty party's khameesa — the descent group linked through the father, including five male links on either side — is within the area of responsibility. Also, it is said that a revenge after a hundred years is a revenge too soon. Do you understand the meaning?"

"The longer the revenge is drawn out, the sweeter it is?"

"Ah, yes!" Rashid rested on the edge of the armchair and sighed. "For years all the eligible members of the guilty family's khameesa must go to sleep with one eye open. Eventually, it is decided that the time has come. A close male relative of the victim is selected to exact the revenge and a target in the perpetrator's tribe is selected. According to the law of the desert, you cannot take revenge against someone who is asleep or does not know what is going on. A bomb planted in his car, a throat slashed in the night, does not count. He must be made aware that he is the victim of the blood revenge before he is killed."

Rashid came to stand at the end of Lily's bed. His voice rose dramatically as he continued. "So let us say I have crawled into a tent. I have chosen the object of my revenge. I have awoken him and told him what is about to happen and I slit his throat with my saber. What happens to me? His children and wife are awake. They are screaming. The brothers and fathers come running. Will I be killed? No, not if I untie the keffiyeh from around my head, dip it in the victim's blood, wrap it around my saber, and walk out of the tent carrying it like a banner. Nobody will touch me. In the eyes of Allah I have just accomplished a great deed, so if they harm me, they are killing a man in a state of grace. More practically, every man in that khameesa is saying to himself, 'It is *over!* It is not *me.*' After twenty years the fear is past. If they harm him, they will only reopen the old wound."

"Would you be arrested by the authorities?"

"In most Arab states blood revenge is not considered a crime."

"How is revenge like jihad, holy war?"

"Not at all the same. Do you know the five pillars of Islam?"

"No." For a moment Lily wondered why she had not been expected to study more about the Moslem faith. If she had, perhaps she would have understood her enemy better.

"It is very simple. All Moslems must try to observe five obligatory actions. The first is shahadah, or witness — the giving of testimony that there is no other god but Allah and accepting that Mohammed is his messenger. Anyone — even you — who says these words is a Moslem. Anyone who denies Mohammed as a prophet or associates anyone else with Allah is an apostate and can be punished by death. Second, there is salat, or worship, which reminds us of our relationship with God and takes our minds off worldly matters. When Moslems hear the muezzin call five times a day, we stop to wash our hands, arms, feet, and faces, turn toward Mecca and pray. Third is sawm, or fasting, during the month of Ramadan when, during the hours of the sun, we do not eat, drink, smoke, or perform sexual acts. The devout study the Koran diligently; the lax rest up for an evening of merrymaking."

"What is the reason for a fast over so many days?"

"The shared discomfort creates common bonds between all members of the faith, rich and poor alike. Zakat, or tithing, is the fourth pillar. We are a generous people, or always have been until now. My uncle has never understood why the other Arab nations have been so unkind to the Palestinian refugees."

"You have mentioned four points. What is the fifth?"

"The haj, or pilgrimage to Mecca, which should be made during the twelfth month of the year at least once in a lifetime."

"Have you made the haj?"

"No, but my uncle has. That is why he places 'Haj' in front of his name."

"There is nothing of revenge in what you have said."

"You are correct. Jihad is sometimes called the 'sixth pillar' and means 'the struggle in the way of Allah.' The Koran commands us to 'fight those who do not believe in God or the Judgment Day, who permit what God and His messenger have forbidden, and who refuse allegiance to the true faith.' "

"That means fighting Christian and Jew alike?"

"No. While pagans must be despised, Islam has decreed tolerance toward the older monotheistic faiths."

"Why are most Moslems so militant, then?"

"Those who agree to live at peace and pay tribute are entitled to Islam's protection; those who resist or rebel against our rule must be crushed. Still more important is that we strive at all times to protect our ummah, our community. The Zionists have violated our ummah; thus a jihad to return us to our homeland must be fought."

Lily's eyes were closed, yet instead of feeling exhausted after hours of talk, she was invigorated by Rashid's explanations. The room was charged by his presence.

"Your wife . . . Do you feel you must avenge her death?"

"I did until I decided to honor her memory, the memory of my parents, of all my ancestors, by bringing our people back from their tortured ghurba — their exile — to their rightful lands. I will bring shame upon myself and my family if I do not devote all my strength to this cause." His voice trembled.

Lily wanted to reach out to him, but restrained herself. "What can one man do?"

"It takes men, one by one, to make a revolution."

"What do you mean?"

"You are not blind, Nurse Schmidt, yet you sometimes pretend you are. I suppose that is what being neutral is about."

"I know about the fedayeen, the raids, but what are these accomplishing?"

"For the first time the Palestinian cause is attracting attention. Soon we shall have the money to arm against the enemy properly and will be in a position to bring our case to the forefront of world opinion even more successfully. Some of our people have gone into

Saudi Arabia, into Kuwait and the other Gulf states. Black gold rushes from the ground into our pockets. For now, we must not permit anyone to forget our plight. In the camps, we have been forced to learn a terrible lesson: patience. Ten, twenty, even a hundred years, is but a short period of time. Eventually the Moslems will unite to rout the Zionists."

Lily slipped out of bed and went into the bathroom. She urinated, washed her face, and brushed her tangled hair. When she returned, Rashid was peering out the shutter again. A pale light sifted into the room.

"I must go soon."

"They change the guard at David's Tower station at six. Until then the street is quiet."

"Thank you." He pointed toward the bathroom. "May I?"

She nodded.

When he returned, he came and sat beside her on the bed. For a second she worried he was going to reach for her and pull her into his arms. He remained motionless. "Four thousand years ago Abraham, the father of Ismail and Isaac, separated the brothers when he sent away Ismail and his mother. From Ismail's tribes sprung my people — the Arabs; from Isaac's yours — the Jews."

Lily's head snapped back. "But I am not —"

"Jesus was a Jew . . ."

"Of course," she conceded. How stupid she had been to startle at what seemed an accusation. She was tired; otherwise she would not have been so touchy.

"What a tragedy. We might have been one family."

Unexpectedly, he did touch her — just her hand. His fingers, the color of bronze, were as warm and soft as melting wax.

"What if someone sees you leave the hotel?"

"The owners are cousins. They saw me come in."

"They know you are with me?" she responded shrilly. "You said nobody saw you —"

"You are a European. It will not matter what they think."

"About you. Or me?"

"Either. We're friends, are we not?"

"I hope so."

"I will see you at the clinic on Monday."

"Are you going back to Jericho today?"

"If possible. The roads are few; it may not be safe." He stood and checked the window again.

"Rashid . . ."

"Aywah?"

"Mâ-assalama."

"Allah yisallimak."

After Rashid had gone, Lily lay back on the bed in a daze. His smell, delightfully pungent, permeated the room. She touched the warm spot on the blanket where he had sat. Why was she so drawn to him? Because they were so alike? His parents had died in a war; he had lost a beloved wife to random bullets. He had lived half his life in camps — not that they could be compared to Theresienstadt or even Cyprus. No, it was something more than the surface similarities. Even when he was quiet she had felt she knew what he was thinking.

There was another polite knock on the door.

Lily opened it warily. It was merely her usual tray of coffee and bread waiting on the small table beside the door. She carried it inside and poured a cup of the cardamom-laced brew. The bread was warm, but there was none of Rashid's zarta to sprinkle on for flavor. She leaned back in the chair where Rashid had talked away the night and closed her heavy eyelids. Sleep descended like a curtain.

The jabberings of the Saturday souk at its most crowded woke Lily with a start. The closed-up room was unbearably hot. Her nightgown was plastered to her body. After a quick bath in cool water, she donned a beige dress decorated with Indian embroidery. She needed to walk, to think everything through calmly.

Outside the Gloria, the streets were crowded with merchants and shoppers. Three soldiers guarded David's Tower while more strutted across the ramparts. Lily abhorred their guns pointing into the no man's land that stretched across Potter's Field into Jewish Jerusalem and was home to squatters who lived like pioneers, oblivious to the frequent snipings. All the symbols of division were revolting, from the ugly checkposts to the concrete dividing walls.

Standing outside the Jaffa Gate, Lily wished the stones beneath her could talk. Right here, in 1899, the rampart had been demolished and the moat filled in to prepare for the triumphal entrance of the carriage of the German kaiser, Wilhelm II — with his entourage on horseback — into the Old City as the guest of the Turkish sultan. At the Citadel of David, the fortress had been constructed on the site where Herod the Great had located his palace at the turn of the first century before Christ walked these streets. The three towers Herod built were named Phasael, for his brother; Mariamne, for his wife (whom he subsequently murdered after she was falsely accused by her sister Salome); and Hippicus, for his most faithful friend. At the time of the Jewish revolt against Rome, the Citadel was one of the main fortifications guarding the city. Its fall in the year 70 marked the end of Jewish independence in the Holy Land in ancient times. Would Jews ever again walk these streets freely? Eli, the eternal optimist, had claimed they would.

"You and I will stand by the Western Wall together someday," he vowed before she left for Jericho.

She had agreed with him aloud; inside, she had doubted that day would come to pass.

Lily blinked in a slash of sunlight illuminating the center of the street. The light in Jerusalem was a blend of contrasts. The sun blazed off the surrounding mountaintops, then spilled across the harsh surface of the stone structures to color them every shade from pink to gold as the day progressed. Nowhere else had Lily seen such morbid darks between buildings and starkly ominous shadows formed by the looming hills. Here, in the Old City, one could be assaulted by the glare of the glittering light at one moment, then turn a corner and be plunged into the bleakest gloom the next. If only she had time to paint the skies, capture the light, Lily mused as she walked on.

From the dim alleys, the dank smells of pack animals, rotting hay, spoiled meat, and overripe tomatoes mingled with the scents of fresh bread, flowers, and smoke from narghilehs and Turkish cigarettes. Not far from here was one of the places Lily could meet with a courier delivering notes to her. But no drop was scheduled today. Without that particular concern, Lily continued through the main passageways, gingerly stepping over the slippery garbage, avoiding darting children, her mind focused on her visitor the previous night.

Something tugged at her skirt. She brushed it off. It happened again. She turned around.

A one-armed boy was begging, his remaining hand outstretched. Lily had heard rumors that children were sometimes mutilated by their parents or at least that their natural afflictions were exacerbated to garner more sympathy.

"Please lady, lady with the coin," he called in Arabic. Some of the children in Jericho had used the same name for her, except there she was the "nurse with the coin."

Lily touched the necklace she had worn for the last fifteen years, her tetradrachm of Tyre. Usually, she left it tucked into her blouse so as not to call attention to it; however, the piece of silver had swung loose today and was outside her clothing. She found some almost worthless change and handed it to the boy.

"Kattar kherak," he called after her. "Much obliged."

She hurried along to visit her favorite stalls where she purchased fruit, cheese, and supplies for the week. "Mishmish, teen, fustuk, barkuk . . ." She pointed out what she desired. The Arab shopkeeper obligingly wrapped apricots, figs, pistachios, and plums in paper cones. After her string bag was filled, Lily went to a dairy store that carried the smooth goat cheese she liked. There was one more stop she wished to make: a bookstore carrying foreign newspapers and periodicals. The Sundays she was off duty were devoted to reading and her stock of fresh material was low. She walked out of the Old City onto Nablus Road, passed the area where the moneylenders plied their trade in diminutive storefronts, and crossed over to the bookstore.

As she was reading the headlines in French and English, she felt someone's breath close to her neck.

"Do not turn around," said the familiar mellifluous voice. "Meet me in one hour at El Marrakesh. Do you know where it is?"

Lily nodded her head slightly. She counted to ten before looking behind her. Rashid was gone.

The restaurant was entered by descending a flight of stairs from the street level. The smoky, cavernous room had arched ceilings and niches hung with Oriental rugs. Round hammered-metal tables were surrounded by Moroccan leather seats with embroidered pillows scattered about. The manager, wearing a bright red tarboosh on his head, bowed and led her to a table set for two, then passed through a beaded curtain into a semiprivate room at the far side of the restaurant. It seemed to Lily that she was waiting for a very long time. Two men at the next table eyed her openly while sharing their water pipe. Keeping the narghileh alight, by placing small pieces of charcoal on top of it yet not burning the tobacco too rapidly, was a delicate operation. Out of the corner of her eye, Lily observed the ritualistic manner in which the men passed the mouthpiece.

At last, Rashid emerged, his face wreathed in a smile. He was no longer wearing his abayah, but was dressed in a well-cut creamy linen suit with a blue-and-beige-striped tie. In Jericho, he favored loose workman's clothing. For the first time Lily was aware of the slenderness of his hips and the high, muscular line of his buttocks. "I am honored you could join me."

"I thought you were returning to Jericho today."

"I had to attend to another matter."

She shot a glance at the shadowy figures behind the beaded curtain. A group of four or five Arabs were drinking Turkish coffee. Their voices could not be heard because the music from a radio was playing loudly.

"I hope I am not keeping you from your friends," she said.

"I prefer to be with you." He tilted his head provocatively. "It was fortunate to have met today, was it not?"

Lily's head bobbed in agreement, even though she was not certain their encounter at the bookseller's had been entirely unplanned on his part. If she had been followed, the job had been done by an expert.

"Have you been to this restaurant before?" he asked politely.

"No, but Pamela Watts has. She recommended the couscous."

"So you know couscous."

"It is popular in Paris."

"Ah, yes."

The waiter set out a dozen small dishes of mezzahs, or appetizers. Rashid explained each one. "These are stuffed 'pastels,' stuffed 'cigars,' marrows, artichokes, marinated sardines, eggplant in two sauces. Of course you know the salads, olives, and hummus."

"A feast!"

"I hope you enjoy it. It is my way of thanking you for your recent courtesies."

"Rashid, this is not necessary."

"For me it is. It helps me remember the hospitality my father extended to visitors in my youth. He always kept a khan, a furnished room for travelers. Someday I hope to serve you in my own home."

Lily tasted each dish, but had hardly made a dent before stuffed pigeons, beef tongue with olives, and shashliks of lamb were arranged in front of them.

Rashid ate tranquilly for a few minutes. The only sound was the bubbling of the water pipe at the next table and the crackle of the radio in the far room. Then he put down his fork and began to speak. "How long will you stay on this assignment?"

"In Jericho?"

Rashid nodded.

"We are asked to commit to a year. Ideally, more women like

Randa will be trained and UNRWA will need fewer foreigners like me."

"You have been here six months. Have they been very difficult for you?"

"Not the work as much as the climate. The heat has bothered me. Frankly, I am looking forward to the rains."

"The roof at the clinic leaks."

"Maybe your boys could fix it."

"Possibly. Do you get a holiday?"

"Yes, three a year."

"Where do you go? To Paris?"

"There is nothing for me there."

"Many of the nurses go to Athens."

"I might go there with the Wattses next month."

"If you do, would you let me know?"

"Why are you interested?"

"I have a good friend outside Athens. I would like you to meet him," he said in a syrupy-smooth tone.

If Lily was not completely mistaken, Rashid was recruiting her as some sort of courier. Wouldn't Eli love this! She chewed a tough piece of the lamb while she contemplated her reply. "I have come to care about your people."

Her words seemed to set Rashid on fire. His honey-colored cheeks reddened. "What do you know about my people? You come into the camp for a few hours, then rush back to the safety of your luxury hotel room!"

While the Gloria could not be considered very grand, Lily did not refute him. "You are right about that."

"Some of our people get sick at hours other than when the clinic is open, babies are born at night, old men die in the early hours of the morning. Where are you then?"

"There is a doctor in Jericho."

"But he will not come into the camp at night."

"Have you called him?"

Rashid dropped his cutlery on the table with a clatter. "There is nothing he can do for us. There are no hospitals nearby for emergencies. When Mrs. Watts had appendicitis she was carried on a stretcher through the Mandelbaum Gate and treated by the Jews. Do you think they would take in my sister if she was having a difficult birth or my uncle if he was dying?"

Lily did not respond.

"Last night I judged you were sympathetic to my people. I believed your feelings were sincere. If you want to act on them, quit returning to your soft mattresses and hot baths and remain with us, live with us, work with us," he finished passionately.

"How can I live at Aqabat Jabar?"

"I do."

"I mean, *where* could I live? You have a family, a house . . ."

"My cousins moved to Kuwait a few months ago. Their dwelling is near the clinic. There are three rooms. Perhaps Randa and her daughter could join you. They have lived in very crowded conditions ever since Randa's husband disappeared."

"Where did he go? She never told me."

"Over the border."

"To Israel?"

"To the occupied territories. He died a martyr to the cause."

"A suicide mission?"

"Perhaps . . ."

"Would you do something like that?"

"If it were asked of me, but I doubt that it will be. I have been given other tasks."

"By those men in there?"

"They are my friends."

From her vantage point, she could see three of the men in silhouette. One had a distinctively long, hooked nose; the other had a high forehead and a mustache; the third had a short grizzly beard and wore an army cap. From photographs Lily had studied she believed them to be core Fatah members: probably Farouq Qaddoumi, Muhammad Yusef, and Yasir Arafat. If that was who they were, Rashid was in with a very distinguished crowd indeed.

As the Moroccan tea and honey cakes were served, Lily contemplated Rashid's offer. If she moved into Aqabat Jabar, she would be right at the center of fedayeen activities, most of which occurred at night. If she made herself available to Rashid as a courier, Eli would have early intelligence on Fatah plans. On the other hand, she could not rule out the possibility that all this was a trap.

"I would need permission from Dr. Watts and the UNRWA director, Mr. Thorsten Osbeck."

Rashid's black eyes sparkled in the flickering light of the candles rimming a ledge beside them. "What do you think they will say?"

"I am not certain. My reason will be to provide maternity services at night. If Randa lives with me, they should feel assured of my safety." Randa's father, a former mukhtar, or village chieftain, remained one of the most influential men in the camp.

Rashid excused himself momentarily. Out of the corner of her eye, Lily could see him pass through the beaded curtain. She sipped her tea. Move into Aqabat Jabar . . . Be in the midst of everything . . . The prospect was thrilling. She would require permission all right, and not only from the Canadian medical director and the Swedish administrator. *They* would be easy to convince, but what would Eli say? He could forbid it. They would need to talk it over . . . The solution was Greece.

．ⵑ．　．ⵑ．　．ⵑ．

As expected, Eli opposed the idea. He had taken Lily outside Athens to see the superb mosaics in the eleventh-century monastery of Daphni. In the car on the road to Eleusis, he argued incessantly about the dangers involved. She listened respectfully, then handed him the papers Rashid had given her to bring to a man named Stelios at the Kanaris, a fish restaurant along the Mikrolimano yacht harbor in Piraeus.

He studied the envelope's seals. "You have to deliver this tomorrow? We'll need an expert to break and repair these."

"Eli, what do you think Motti taught me in Paris? Safecracking?"

"Do you have the tools? Is there enough time?"

Lily laughed. "Why do you think I brought my paints and easel along? After all, this is an artist's holiday, is it not?"

She had him pull off the road and set up a work area. By the end of the afternoon they had a loosely coded copy of what appeared to be the plan to start a group called the Heroes of the Return, whose first task was to undermine the Israeli railroads. Detailed maps of freight routes and timetables were included with strike points marked.

Although Eli was properly appreciative, he argued with her about living in the camp. "I cannot condone it. If anything happened, we would have a hell of a time getting you out. A radio would be too risky, so there's not even the possibility of daily communication."

"There was not any before."

"You were closer . . . I could —"

"What?"

"Sometimes I would go to Mount Zion in the evenings. With binoculars I could see your window at the Gloria. Once in a while I would even see you, or the shadow of you."

Lily knew he could never be objective with her. It was a pity, for in all their time together — even when she had slept in his arms — she had never felt the spark that had ignited when Rashid had touched her hand.

"Eli, you must agree it is worth it . . . All these new fedayeen groups, Rashid's ties to Arafat and the others . . . I would be perfectly positioned. It is what the mission's all about." She paused to see if he was absorbing her argument.

"Yes, but —"

She interrupted before he could voice additional objections. "You yourself said Tel Aviv is especially concerned that the PLO is acquiring Communist Chinese arms through Damascus and Russian weapons via Egypt. Maybe I could learn more about their network."

Reluctantly, Eli agreed to a trial period of one month. "You'll return to Jerusalem at least once a week. There, a courier will be available in case you need to make contact. We'll arrange back-ups as well. Also" — he handed her a medicine bottle with a French label — "I've brought you some vitamins."

"What for?"

"In case of emergency."

"Cyanide?"

"No. You've been reading too many novels. Let us call it your parachute."

Lily became annoyed. "You are talking in riddles."

"These pills are something one of our talented doctors cooked up especially for you." He opened the bottle. "Each tablet is numbered. See?" He showed her the pharmaceutical company's logo and the number 346, which indicated some sort of tablet code. "There are thirty pills in here. Five are marked three sixty-four instead of three forty-six. Twenty-five are a harmless vitamin with iron, what a woman your age would typically take. The others are a potent form of sulfa used to fight urinary tract infections."

"I am allergic to sulfa —"

"We know that. You had some in cough syrup once. Your hives were so severe you had to be hospitalized. I remember your eyes swelled shut, you had respiratory difficulties —"

"My God, it is brilliant!"

"One tablet should create a mild rash within twenty-four hours; two will result in giant wheals and severe itching in less than twelve hours; a full-scale serum sickness would appear quite rapidly after three doses. Four could be fatal. Nobody will know you are reacting to sulfa. The allergic reaction could be to another drug, a plant, a food, something you handled in the clinic. It is your pass through the Mandelbaum Gate. Do not hesitate to take it at any time you feel you might be suspect or need to contact us rapidly."

"Once I use it, I could never go back to Jericho again."

"No. It is a one-way ticket. If Nicole Schmidt registers at any hospital in Jerusalem, I'll be notified immediately."

When Lily returned to Jerusalem, Rashid appeared in her room at the Gloria as planned. He wore his long abayah, which complemented his disheveled black curls and falcon eyes far better than a constricting European suit.

"You had a good journey?" he asked curtly.

"Very relaxing," she said as she handed him a bottle of ouzo, a gift from the man in the fish restaurant. She was certain it contained a reply, probably under the cap or label, but had not tampered with it.

He took the gift wordlessly.

"Next week I will be moving down to Jericho," she announced flatly.

Rashid did not seem as pleased as she had expected.

"What is wrong?"

"I should not have asked that of you."

"Babies are born at night . . ."

"My uncle was furious when I took over my cousin's house. We cleaned it for you, found a bed, some carpets. He thought I wanted you for . . . for myself."

"We have never —"

"He knows I meet you here. He claims I have brought dishonor to you already." Rashid clutched the folds of his garment and twisted them. His face was tormented. He could not look at her.

"Rashid . . ." she whispered.

He lifted only his eyes; his head remained bowed. Lily touched his hand. With his other arm he cupped the back of her head and pulled her toward him. "I wanted my uncle's words to be true. I resisted you that night I stayed here. They were the most difficult hours of my life. The distance from that chair to your bed was so short and so vast —"

"Rashid . . ."

He unbuttoned the first two buttons on her blouse and kissed the

hollow of her neck. His lips left wet marks that burned as his breath
skirted it. His tongue licked slightly lower. Lily felt her legs melting. If he had not been holding her so tightly, she would have fallen
away. He fingered the coin on its slender gold chain; then his hand
slid over her breast to her nipple and circled it until it hardened.

"Rashid . . ."

He carried her to the bed. She watched as he unwrapped the
ropelike belt that bound his abayah and lifted yards of fabric over
his head.

Transfixed by the splendor of his lean body, Lily did not move.
Never before had she seen a more beautiful man — from his sculptural shoulders to the feline pattern of hair that led her eyes down to
his elegant erection. He hovered above her, waiting. His muscles
glistened in the fine patina of moisture that covered his smooth skin.
In a trance she peeled off her clothing. He waited, caressing her with
his eyes. Her milky skin flushed under the heat of his gaze.

"Tell me what you like," he requested in a husky voice.

She moistened her lips, but could not speak. Her limited experience with men was impossible to explain.

"I wish to please you," he said plaintively.

"Oh, I . . ." Her legs shivered in anticipation.

With one swift movement he lowered himself onto her and she
opened to greet him. His mouth groped for hers. No lips had ever felt
so velvety, so sweet — not strange, more like a memory come alive
even though there was no similar pleasure in her past. There had
never been sharp bones pressing her pelvis so cunningly. Her fingers
tangled in the thick blackness of his hair, tugging him downward,
forward, inward. Never again would she be surprised by the pathetic
hold a man had on a woman, for she could not imagine not craving
the slip of his belly against hers, the tautness of his buttocks in her
hands, the scent of the inside of the folds of his ear. Her arms and
legs locked him. She was astonished by the enormity of her need for
him — and his patience with it. Every place he touched awakened a
new sensation. Gasping, she tried to stay ahead of the rushing
tide — to move away, beyond, past whatever it was — before it
drowned her. He was unremitting. For a second he would make it
better, then worse, then impossible to stop falling, tumbling away,
forward, downward until — when the end came — all they could do
was tremble . . . together.

They slept. They awoke. They soaked in the large footed tub and
washed each other's hair. They ate apricots and drank some of the

ouzo. From the way he opened the bottle, Lily was certain the message was under the cap.

Rashid spoke very little. At last he found his voice. "You must not live in Jericho because of this. If you come, it must be for my people, not for me."

"I am a nurse . . ."

"You are a sorceress."

"Can we be together?"

"In Aqabat Jabar?"

"Yes."

"If we are very cautious . . ." He kissed her eyes.

And they were.

Not even Randa knew. He came to her when Randa was taking a meal with her family; he always left well before she returned. Rashid stopped by the clinic only when he had business, no longer for lunch. Twice, Lily was invited to eat at Haj Salim's house as a friend of the family. Little Jalil had become very polite to her lately. The rudeness he had exhibited around the clinic had vanished mysteriously. The boy would sit near her at the table and run and fetch hot tea or water for her. Soon Lily began to warm to the motherless boy. When she heard he had been asked to enroll at the UNRWA school, but had not yet attended, she gave him a book satchel to encourage him.

When Rashid was away, she asked Jalil where his father was. "Jerusalem," the boy replied guilelessly. The next time Rashid disappeared without a word to her, Jalil told her he had gone to Amman. A third time Jalil reported his father was in Beirut with his brother-in-law.

"Beirut? Are you certain? That is a very long way off."

"Yes, Beirut. He showed me the place on my school map." Jalil pulled the textbook from his book bag. Some clever cartographer had drawn a map of the Middle East and managed to leave out Israel entirely. Beirut was circled.

"It is on the sea," Jalil said wistfully. "Have you ever seen the sea?"

"Yes, Jalil."

"Would you take me there someday?"

"I will try, Jalil."

On his return, Rashid brought Lily an unexpected present. It was a raincoat. He insisted she try it on. The fit was unflattering, but she tried to be gracious.

"It is only a sample," he said as he apologized for the flaws in its construction. He pointed to the "Newberry" label. "It is a copy of a British design. Look, we are even using the same plaid fabric for the lining. We are setting up a factory in Ein el-Sultan where we can produce these at one-tenth the price they can in England. We have too much idle labor and too little money. It is about time we developed some industries here." Rashid crossed his arms proudly and waited for Lily to compliment him.

"That is very interesting. I hope you will be very successful" was all she said, even though she was taken aback by this new development. Previously, Rashid had argued against efforts to help the refugees prosper beyond the most meager standard of living. He never wanted the Palestinians to accept their status as anything but temporary. What had changed his mind?

Less than a month later she had her horrific answer. In the middle of the night there was an explosion at the raincoat factory. Lily and Randa were called out of bed and driven to the clinic in Ein el-Sultan to attend to the victims.

"Why would so many people be at the factory in the middle of the night?" Lily asked Pamela Watts, who was riding beside her.

"I do not know any more than you do," the nurse replied.

"Perhaps it is cooler to work in the evenings?" Randa offered limply.

From the terror in her assistant's eyes, Lily suspected Randa knew more than she was letting on.

Bodies were piled outside the clinic. Those inside who were supposedly alive did not appear much better off. People with massive burns and missing limbs screamed in agony. A few of the most fortunate were blessedly unconscious. Family members swarmed among the victims, wailing and prostrating themselves on the floor, making it almost impossible for the medics to work. Lily assigned herself the task of calming those who were unhurt, while the experienced doctors and nurses generously dosed the most seriously wounded with morphine and attempted to salvage the few they could.

After the pandemonium had passed, Pamela Watts reviewed the grim statistics. Ten men and women had been killed outright and dozens more were critically injured. More deaths were expected to ensue.

At a staff conference late the following afternoon, Dr. Watts pieced together what he knew about the tragedy. "At first I figured this raincoat factory was nothing more than a way to disguise an explosives operation, but the story is even more incredible than that. The fact is they *were* making raincoats — exploding raincoats!"

"That's . . . that's diabolical!" Constance Sommer choked.

"Apparently they were using the coats as explosive devices, which could be left in cloakrooms or on the back of a chair in, say, a restaurant or movie theater. Who knows, they may have successfully planted a number of these already. They had hundreds of coats in various stages of completion."

"Who ever would have designed anything so vile?" his wife asked.

"My informant tells me they borrowed the idea from the Israelis who used the technique against the British during the difficult days of the postwar Mandate."

"How could they hide a heavy bomb in a raincoat?" Lily wondered aloud.

"I'm afraid the secret has died with the tailors who perished. Or, I should say, thank God the secret is lost." Dr. Watts shuddered before urging his exhausted staff back to work.

Lily had known that Rashid was not in the camp the night of the explosion. The immensity of her gratitude that he had been spared surprised her. She welcomed him back with much affection before returning her coat and asking him to destroy it for her. "If the authorities should come to question me, I do not want to have any evidence."

Rashid had understood at once.

"I cannot believe explosives could be hidden in a coat," she began warily.

He took the garment from her and turned it inside out. "The shoulder pads are an important feature. These are stuffed with layers of blasting gelatin. Then the rest of the coat is lined with thin layers of more gelatin and about ten fingers of dynamite. A small pocket inside one of the shoulder pads is readied for inserting a timer at the last moment. Then, two wires connect that pocket to the electric firing device. The other shoulder pad contained four small batteries joined together, which were also connected by wire to the firing device. Electric detonators were inserted into the explosives and wrapped with a primer to augment the explosion."

He went on with a manic description of how the firing system was hooked up and how all the components fit together. "Before hiding the bomb mechanism, we attached it to a switch concealed in a matchbox, which enabled us to turn it off if something went wrong.

The tailoring in the finished coats was perfect. The only opening was in the timer pocket, so that it could be withdrawn and set at the last moment. There were no telltale bulges, no hint at what it was."

Lily forced herself not to react violently or begin a diatribe about all the innocent people who would be harmed. All she asked was "Were you successful?"

"You know I cannot tell you that," he said slyly. "For your own protection, of course."

"Of course," she responded calmly, amazed he did not notice she was seething inside.

The next day she volunteered to accompany several victims as they were transported to a hospital in Jerusalem and made the most of the opportunity by getting a report on the raincoats to Eli. Over the next few months, Israeli sappers defused five of the deadly garments in public establishments in Jerusalem and Tel Aviv.

After that incident, Lily's spirits plummeted. The break that her rest periods in Jerusalem had offered had been more important than she had understood. To protect her cover, Lily labored harder than anyone else. Even cranky and fastidious Nurse Sommer was impressed with the fact that she had moved into the camps. The UNRWA executives praised her dedication. They hinted that she might be approached for an appointment on a higher level when the Watts family and Nurse Sommer left in July. Pamela asked if she would like to move into their villa in Jericho when it was vacated. While she said she would consider it, Lily doubted she would be remaining at her post much longer because the political situation was heating up considerably. Terrorist attacks by Syria on Israeli civilian installations had been increasing. In an air battle, Israel shot down six Syrian, Soviet-made MiGs over the Golan Heights and chased others in hot pursuit almost to Damascus. If the climate became more volatile, she expected Eli would demand her return. Until that moment, she was determined to make the most of her hard-won contacts and began to take more risks to acquire data.

Since the trip to Athens, Rashid seemed only to trust her more. After the raincoat disaster, he had become slightly wary, then gradually leaked more and more useful information under the guise of educating her to his cause. She suspected she was being groomed to handle even more assignments and so she continued to play the role of his willing convert.

In bed with Rashid she could not help but wonder who was using whom. Was he cementing her loyalty with lovemaking or did he

have any feelings for her? Of this she was uncertain. It did not matter, for when he was with her, he was as loving, as attentive, as she
would wish any man to be, but would *she* have slept with him if she
did not require intelligence from him?

Yes, she admitted. Yes.

After the explosions, her ardor diminished — but only for a short
time. Rashid's physical attraction was so overwhelming that this was
one area where she did not have to pretend. Besides, what difference
did it make if she did or did not dissemble? If he loved her or did
not? The data Eli had decoded from the Athens trip had led to arrests of six terrorists, and countless Israelis had been protected by the
raincoat discovery. Then, in early May, a fedayeen boy who had
grown up at the nearby camp in Ein el-Sultan was captured by Israeli forces while carrying explosives. Lily had alerted Eli that there
was rabid talk of a reprisal on the fifteenth of May — Israel's Independence Day — and increased security measures were taken.

So far Lily had never placed herself in jeopardy. But she did have
to be vigilant. She kept her vitamins in her pocketbook. She even
swallowed one of the harmless tablets in Rashid's presence and offered him one.

"Women's nonsense!" he responded.

Since the explosions he had become extremely touchy. He rarely
laughed. Lily suspected this was because of the dangers that he and
his men were facing.

She desired him. She wanted to have him to herself every night.
Sometimes she wondered how she could have such passionate feelings for the man yet be using any scrap of information he unwittingly fed her. Was there a contradiction?

No.

A peaceful solution to the Palestinian problem would benefit
them all; the holy war he wished to perpetrate against her people
would mean certain destruction of both sides. The sooner he accepted that the Palestinians would never regain control of Israel the
better. Eventually, a solution would be found. For the present, she
hoped only to save as many lives as possible by combating senseless
terrorism. For the present, she would content herself with one more
night with Rashid . . . or two . . . or as many as were left.

In the pre-dawn hours of the fifth of June in the year nineteen hundred and sixty-seven, Rashid visited Lily's room. He lit a candle and

placed it on the milk crate that was her bedside table. He had come in a side door because Randa and her daughter were sleeping in the front room. He kissed Lily awake. She blinked her eyes and smiled sleepily, her lips barely parting. "You are back again."

"Yes. I will be home for a while now. Great days will soon be coming."

Lily sucked in her breath. She had known for weeks that something was happening, from Eli's reports of troop movements and the news on the local radio. Sensing an impending war, he had told her to be ready for a recall at any time. Lily had not taken this too seriously, but she had been following President Nasser's actions closely. Two weeks earlier, he had closed the Straits of Tiran to Israeli shipping and, a few days later, had told the Arab Trade Union Congress that the time had come to annihilate the Zionists. Lily suspected that, at this point, Nasser was merely posturing — waging a war of propaganda instead of staging a wasteful confrontation.

Rashid crawled under the blanket.

"Randa . . ." Lily whispered.

"I know." He took her hands in his. "I needed to see you."

Lily ran her fingers through his thick curls and pulled his face toward hers. He kissed her softly, then moved away slightly. Her fingertips pressed him down and he nuzzled her neck.

"Oh, Rashid . . ."

"I cannot stay —"

"Just a few minutes —"

"Not with Randa here. Her child might awaken . . ."

While Lily wanted to argue with him, she knew he was right. "Thursday she goes to her father's home."

"Thursday . . ." He kissed her cheeks, her chin, her throat, and the coin that was perpetually warmed by her flesh. Then he slipped off the bed, brought the rough blanket up over her shoulders, and tiptoed out the door. Lily was sound asleep almost immediately.

Randa woke her at six. Using the buckets of water they had brought in the night before, they scrubbed with washcloths and the Ivory soap that the Wattses had somehow requisitioned. Lily dipped her head in the bowl and rinsed the ubiquitous reddish dust from her hair. If she had known it was the last cleansing she would have for more than a week, she might have been more thorough, but as it was, there was no time for a full shampoo, which required a complicated setup of buckets and pitchers.

Randa brewed Bedouin coffee with cardamom and spices and laid out some lebneh cheese, chopped cucumbers, two boiled eggs, and pita. By eight, Lily was at the clinic. It was Monday, the day supplemental foods were distributed to pregnant women, nursing mothers, and young children. Those eligible submitted ration cards, but this was a tricky business. UNRWA knew there were far more registered refugees than lived in the camps, but saw no fair way of reorganizing the system. Because there was not enough food for every ration card Lily was handed, she had been told to make her own determination of how much to distribute. By now she and Randa knew most of the families in her district, so there were few squabbles.

Just before eleven, the lines were diminishing. Randa handed Lily a cup of coffee and both of them rested for a few minutes. Suddenly, thunder crackled through the Jordan Valley — not once, but over and over and over. Great booms reverberated from the ancient hillsides.

Children shrieked and called, "Yamma, Yamma!" The clinic emptied as the mothers ran for safety.

A flock of students shouted, "Israel has attacked Egypt."

Men poured into the streets. "Allahu akbar! The holy war has broken out!" echoed up and down the narrow passageways. "God is great!"

Rashid pulled up in a jeep. Lily jumped in beside him. Rapidly, he drove up a narrow hillside road that led to one of the highest points in the area. They stopped at a qasir, a round stone tower used to store olives. Rashid reached for his binoculars and scanned the northern horizon as a flock of jet planes streaked out of Amman toward Netanya. Silhouetted against the sky with his long hair blowing in the wind, he looked like an ancient warrior.

"It has begun," Rashid said with great feeling. "This will be the end of the Zionists."

"How can we find out what is happening?" Lily asked, her mind swirling with conflicting emotions.

"We will go into Jericho. I must organize my men." But he did not move.

Lily took a cue from his extraordinary stability and remained quietly by his side, even though her every nerve was agitated by the abruptness of the events.

"Tomorrow we will awaken into a different world. The borders will fall open and the Palestinians will commence their long march home. Look now and remember the land at peace before the blood-shed commences." His arms embraced the ancient panorama as if it belonged to him.

"Why would Jordan enter into the conflict between Israel and Egypt?" she asked with false innocence.

"The brotherhood of Arab nations will unite for the common benefit. In a few weeks we will triumph! The cost of a few lives will be well worth the redemption of my people."

Lifting her eyes to the parched and brown hills, she reflected on Israel's future. What was happening there now? Were her friends safe? Was Eli?

And what was about to happen to her?

In the dazzling midday light, the Jordan River was but a golden thread weaving in the distance. Behind her the stony, mysterious hills seemed a stark backdrop for the lushness of Jericho — the first city to be captured by the tribes of Israel. What must it have looked like when it was approached from the Jordan by Joshua and the priests who bore trumpets of rams' horns and blew them before the ark of the Lord? Or to Moses, who saw the Promised Land from Mount Nebo on the other side but never set foot on it? And tomor-row, who would stand guard on these hillocks — the Jews, the Arabs, an international body?

Lily felt the heavy air compressing her body painfully. Her breath caught in her throat as the sky quivered with sound waves from an-other flock of fighter jets. She could not determine if they were going east or west.

"The years of preparing and waiting will finally pay off," Rashid was saying. Tears streamed down his upraised cheeks. He was un-ashamed. "Our long hijira, our dispersion from our homeland, our days of dark exile, have served their purpose. The Arab League, so-lidified by the plight of the refugees, has banded together for this very moment! The Egyptians are one of the best-equipped military machines in the world today and, for superiority of numbers, the Syrians cannot be beaten." He clasped Lily to him. "Do you know where I was last week?"

Lily was too overcome to respond.

"In Amman. On the thirtieth of May, King Hussein flew to Cairo to conclude an agreement with Nasser over a joint Arab military command. For weeks we have had intelligence that the Zionists have been massing troops on the Syrian border. The Soviets have prom-ised to back the Syrians. Nasser's forces are stationed in Sinai, and only two weeks ago, he ordered the United Nations Emergency Force withdrawn and U Thant obeyed. Do you know what that means?"

Lily hardly recognized her lover. His manic glee sickened her. She could imagine him murdering her with his bare hands to vindicate his shame at consorting with a "Zionist spy."

He had not bothered to wait for her response. "Two weeks ago, when Nasser closed the Straits of Tiran to Zionist traffic and the Gulf of Aqaba to all shipping to and from Eilat, Algeria and Kuwait sent contigents to reclaim our occupied territories. In '48 our efforts were diffused, uncoordinated, riddled with inefficiency, but today we are united. Shuqairy, who was with me in Amman, has called upon everyone in our group to support our King in Amman."

Our King in Amman! Lily could not believe what she was hearing. Rashid had always been a bitter antagonist of Hussein; and Shuqairy, currently one of the most influential PLO officials, had been opposed by both Hussein and Nasser.

"Today you will see our Arab front attack from every side. With our modern planes and tanks, the Jews will find no place to hide. By tomorrow, Jewish Jerusalem will fall!" Rashid called triumphantly. "We will go home once again!"

I must get to Jerusalem, Lily decided. Whatever happens, I cannot stay here. If the Israelis move in, my life is endangered; if Jerusalem falls, where can I go?

A chasm had finally cracked the fragile ground where they briefly had stood hand in hand. As she stared at Rashid, she understood with blinding clarity how vast the distance had always been. Their encounter as simply man and woman had been doomed from the first. For a few poignant moments she had dared — out of stupidity and desire — to believe otherwise.

"Rashid, let us get back. We will be missed ... or needed." She stumbled to the jeep.

"You have never known war, have you?"

"I was only a child ..." she offered weakly.

Rashid's eyes gleamed with histrionic fervor. "Then you are in for a glorious adventure."

Rashid's intelligence was far more accurate than Lily's, whose reports from Tel Aviv were weeks out of date. She did not know that only four days earlier, Moshe Dayan, the popular chief of staff in the

1956 Sinai Campaign, had been appointed Minister of Defense.
After analyzing the developing crisis, the Israeli leaders had been
faced with the nightmare envisaged in the monumental preparations
for a pre-emptive action against their enemies. With more than a
hundred thousand Egyptian troops organized into seven divisions
and backed by an estimated one thousand tanks deployed within
striking distance of the Israeli frontier, they had been forced to respond with a partial mobilization into the Negev. When Nasser —
buoyed by the positive wave of Pan-Arabism, which had been absent
for over a decade — closed the Straits of Tiran, Levi Eshkol, the Israeli Prime Minister, had attempted to bring international pressure
to defuse the situation. Unfortunately, the Americans were embroiled in Vietnam; the French, surprisingly noncommittal. The
Israelis could not take the chance that Nasser was posturing
or bluffing. Facing economic strangulation and the imminence of
war on three borders, Israel knew she could survive only if she struck
first.

While Lily had been sponging herself from the buckets of well
water, Israeli Mystères and Mirages swept down out of a clear
sky and headed for Egyptian airfields in the Sinai. There they found
the cream of the Egyptian air force lined up in neat rows on the
runways. Each Israeli pilot had fuel for exactly ten minutes over
his target, time enough to make three or four passes. Dropping
bombs — including rocket-assisted concrete-dibbers designed to
penetrate thick runways — they battered the enemy airfields. By the
time the first wave returned home, a second arrived, to be followed
by others at ten-minute intervals until the area was decimated. Similar attacks were made on the airfields in Egypt with devastating results. At the end of the day, the Israelis had wiped out the largest
and potentially most dangerous air force in the Middle East.

The sounds that had stirred the refugees at Aqabat Jabar had
been Hussein's British-built Hawker Hunters on their way to assault
Israeli targets. The war with Jordan came on Israel unexpectedly.
That morning, a message from Prime Minister Eshkol had been sent
to King Hussein via the United Nations' chief observer, General
Odd Bull, assuring the king that if his country kept out of the fighting, Israel would not initiate hostilities. Confident of victory because
of the united alliances throughout the Arab world, Hussein had already appointed Egypt's General Riadh as the commander in chief
of his own forces. Before Hussein sent his planes into the air, Nasser
confirmed that scores of Israeli aircraft had been downed and that

Egyptian armored forces were pushing across the Negev in a maneuver to join up with Jordanian troops in the Hebron Hills. At that moment, even Nasser had not known his air force was smoldering in ruins.

When Lily and Rashid reached the marketplace at Jericho, Israeli Mirages had already attacked the Jordanian airfields at Mafraq and Amman and poured cannon fire into the Hunters as they were refueled. All that the refugees saw of the battle was the astonishing number of planes sweeping so menacingly low that their vibrations rattled the walls of the camps' flimsy dwellings. It would be days before they would learn that the Royal Jordanian Air Force had ceased to exist after a brief twenty-minute battle, yet the Israeli fire dragons continued to return again and again, dropping their bombs on the west as well as the east bank of the Jordan River.

Early radio reports from the Arab countries stirred the patriotism of those gathered around every available receiver in Jericho.

"Arise!" Radio Cairo called out in Arabic. "Go forth into battle! The hour of glory is upon us!"

The dial spun to the right and the Israeli announcer was saying in Hebrew, "Be calm. We are asking all Israelis to be calm. There has been an Egyptian land and air attack."

"The Zionists are in defeat!" a listener brandishing his knife and fork over his head shouted wildly. "Otherwise they would broadcast their victories."

The frequency was switched to Damascus Radio. "The time has come to silence the enemy once and for all. We will destroy him. Palestine will be liberated forever!"

Then it was turned back to the middle of the dial. "This is Kol Israel broadcasting from Jerusalem. The military spokesman reports the Egyptians' armored forces have begun advancing toward the Negev. Israeli forces have gone into action to repel them."

"For twenty years our people have been readying for this triumphant moment," reported Radio Cairo. "The armies of the Arab nations are having their victorious rendezvous in Israel."

"Kill the Jews!" blared Radio Baghdad.

"The jihad, the holy war, has commenced with brilliant results," announced the Syrian broadcasters. "Arise, brother soldiers. Your artillery has already shot down twenty-six enemy aircraft. Defeat is imminent!"

Again Kol Israel was tuned in. "Two Egyptian MiG-21s have shot down each other by mistake," the announcer shouted in Arabic. The jeers of those in the Jericho café indicated they would not be taken in by such ludicrous Zionist propaganda.

For her part, Lily believed none of the media.

Rashid spent the afternoon of the first day mobilizing the several hundred boys under his jurisdiction and commandeering trucks to defend the West Bank.

As second-in-command when Thorsten Osbeck was not in the area, Dr. Watts rounded up all his UNRWA staff at the office in the main school building of Aqabat Jabar.

"All services are to be suspended, except for those of an emergency nature. Apparently, we are in a war zone. This school will be designated a center for information; the clinics will be readied to receive casualties. If the roads to Amman or Jerusalem are cut off, there will be panic and hysteria. All food and supplies shall remain under lock and key to prevent looting."

Lily was impressed with the doctor's quick thinking, yet she was unable to give her full attention to his directives. The instinct to protect herself and flee to safety, which had almost overcome her on the hill with Rashid, returned with a vengeance. The only solution was her pills. If she became sick enough before all hell broke loose, she had a good chance of being taken to Jerusalem and carried through the Mandelbaum Gate to freedom.

"Already we're getting offers of blood donations. Nurse Sommer will coordinate that effort. There are six refrigerators in Jericho at our disposal. We must look for others, as we expect the need for transfusions may be enormous. Any questions?"

As soon as Dr. Watts finished his formal speech, Lily excused herself and swallowed one of the vitamins she carried in her purse. After gulping a glass of water, she realized she had not checked the number on the pill. What if she had taken one of the ordinary vitamins instead of the sulfa? She opened the container and counted the tablets marked 364 that remained. She *had* taken one, but took a second to be certain a rash appeared. She was confident there was time to get out of the country. Even if a war *was* beginning, it was bound to last for weeks or months. No conflict had ever ended in a matter of hours or days. Until then, she would do what she could to help the victims.

❖   ❖   ❖

In Jerusalem, the Jordanian army had launched a barrage of artillery fire from positions around the city. They even occupied the

United Nations observers' headquarters, supposedly a demilitarized zone. The Israeli commander, Major-General Uzi Narkiss, ordered his artillery to reply to the bombardment and a force of the 16th Jerusalem Brigade was sent to oust the Jordanians from the U.N. post. After successfully relieving the U.N. personnel, they continued to the village of Zur Baher along the main Hebron–Jerusalem road. This cut the Jordanians in the Hebron Hills off from the city and the rest of the West Bank and made it impossible for those inside Jerusalem to link up with the Egyptian forces advancing across the Negev.

Other Israeli units made considerable progress around the city. As part of the plan to isolate Jerusalem from the main thrust of the Jordanian army in the north, Colonel Uri Ben-Ari's Harel Brigade was ordered to seize the mountain ridge overlooking the descent to Jericho, which controlled the direct approach from the West Bank to the city as well as the road connecting Jerusalem with the West Bank town Ramallah. This strategy was the key to commanding the Judean Hills and Jerusalem — a maneuver also employed by Joshua in ancient times and the British in the First World War.

With the Jordanian and Egyptian air forces wiped out, Israeli fighter planes concentrated on giving ground support. Their strikes were directed toward the Jordanian reserves in the Jordan Valley and the interception of troops moving along the Jericho–Jerusalem road to reinforce units in Jerusalem. Rashid's pathetic "popular resistance" team of six hundred inexperienced and poorly armed soldiers had barely joined up with the 60th Brigade on the war's second day when Israeli air attacks wiped out their tanks and trucks. A disheartened Rashid directed his boys to put down their arms. As the Jordanians withdrew to the East Bank of the river, the wounded were brought to the makeshift UNRWA hospitals in Jericho.

By the time the first casualties arrived, Lily's sulfa-induced rash had formed bright crimson blossoms on her abdomen and was spreading rapidly. The itching was intense. When she showed her predicament to Pamela Watts, the nurse diagnosed her as suffering from a reaction to stress. Even as Lily argued that it had to be more of an allergic reaction, she recognized nobody had the time to deal with her minor malady in the midst of the groans and shrieks of the seriously injured. A few hours later, when reports of the road to Jerusalem being closed filtered down to the camps, Lily resigned herself to remaining in Jericho. Most of her personal fears subsided when she decided that nobody — Arab and Jew alike — would be suspicious of an UNRWA nurse under these cataclysmic circumstances. Discreetly, she took a few antihistamine tablets as an antidote and went back to work.

The radio reports varied widely from station to station.

"Israeli paratroopers have landed at Sharm al-Sheikh and the Egyptian army is being subjected to fierce air assaults throughout the Sinai," said Kol Israel matter-of-factly. The UNRWA receiver remained tuned to that station. "In Jerusalem, violent fighting has been continuous. In the past sixteen hours Mystères and Mirages carrying rockets and napalm have caused extensive damage in the Jordan Valley. The occupation of both Nablus and Jerusalem may be complete by early tomorrow."

Nobody slept that night. The valley echoed with volleys of cannon fire. Under the glare of Israeli searchlights the fighting continued hard and furious — especially for Ammunition Hill, on Jerusalem's left flank. After four hours of brutal fighting, the Jordanian Arab Legion troops, unsupported by forces from Jericho, began to withdraw. Colonel Mordechai Gur, commanding the 55th Paratroop Brigade, pushed through Sheikh Jarrach toward the Rockefeller Museum, thus clearing the area immediately to the north of the Old City. Contact was made with the Mount Scopus defenders while, farther north, Colonel Ben-Ari advanced to cut the road from Ramallah and isolate Jordanian forces in Samaria. The next logical step was for the Israelis to attack the Old City, but partially because of the United Nations' pressure for a cease-fire and partly because nobody was willing to risk damaging the holy shrines, they waited another day.

On the morning of June 7, Gur was authorized to continue his advance but not to use artillery or tank fire within the confines of the Old City wall. His initial move was to capture the Augusta Victoria Hill with the support of heavy air strikes and artillery. The road to Jericho was finally severed and the Jordanians withdrew. The Old City was virtually undefended as Colonel Gur led the way through the Lion's Gate and, by ten in the morning, stood in front of the holiest of Jewish shrines: the Western Wall.

All that day the planes continued to slice through the skies above Jericho, their fearful reverberations terrorizing the population. Many took refuge in the fields, believing their homes would be bombed momentarily. Foundations did tremble; windows did shatter. The cries of the children were a ceaseless chorus of agony. Every family formed its own strategy for survival: Some chose to cling to-

gether in large tribal groups, not making a move without their
leader's approval; others responded to the more primitive urge to
flee across the Jordan before the enemy trapped them behind the
advancing lines. The more cerebral — and perhaps courageous —
believed they could hold out with a well-organized people's resistance. Rashid was their leader.

Similar victories to those around Jerusalem were achieved by
Major-General Peled in the northern mountainous terrain of Samaria, Colonel Bar-Kochva around Kabatiya, and Colonel Ram in
the vicinity of Nablus — the key to road communications in the
area. When Colonel Ben-Ari's brigade, advancing north from Ramallah, linked up with Colonel Ram's, they forged eastward to the
Jordan River together. The Jordanian defenses fell apart. On June
7, their 40th Armored Brigade — facing encirclement between
Nablus and Kabatiya — attempted to fight its way to the Damya
Bridge, but, pursued by Bar-Kochva, harassed by the Israeli air
force, and ambushed by Ram's and Ben-Ari's brigades, the Jordanians finally abandoned their tanks and escaped on foot.

Along the road to Jericho, the fleeing military forces and the civilian population were strafed by Israeli aircraft attempting to crush
the Jordanians before they could regroup. One military bus took a
direct hit and burst into flames on the outskirts of the Biblical oasis.
The UNRWA staff of overworked nurses and hastily trained assistants was suddenly confronted with hideous burn cases they had neither the competence nor the supplies to manage.

Over the radio, turned up to drown out the groans of the wounded
soldiers, Lily heard King Hussein's weary plea for his nation to
"fight to the last breath and to the last drop of blood." But by ten in
the evening of the seventh of June, King Hussein accepted a cease-
fire, effectively handing over the West Bank to the Israelis. His army,
having suffered an estimated six thousand casualties and the loss of
nearly all its equipment, had ceased to be a viable force. By contrast,
the Israelis had lost five hundred fifty men and suffered about
twenty-five hundred wounded. They had gained not only the strategically important West Bank but the control of the symbolic city of
Jerusalem.

Violent arguments broke out among the leaders of Aqabat Jabar.
Hussein was called a traitor by some, while others berated Nasser for
misleading the Jordanians during the early hours of the war. Rashid
was a vocal detractor of both the Syrians, who had promised a brigade that never materialized, and the Iraqis, who, while stationed in

Jordan, refused to enter the conflict. By the time the United Nations–imposed cease-fire took effect at 6:30 Saturday evening the
tenth of June — the war's sixth and final day — Israel had secured
the Sinai Peninsula, the West Bank, and the Golan Heights.

The agitation increased throughout Jericho. Retreating soldiers
told tales of horror. "The Zionists will not be content until every
Arab has departed. They wish to wash Palestine clean. The streets
will run with blood. Even those who did not leave in '48 are preparing to depart."

Hysteria reigned. The anguished sobs of the children were replaced by the excruciating wails of the charred soldiers. Worse, fires
began to devour the city of Jericho as, in the final hours of the war,
the Israeli planes and approaching artillery scored direct hits on the
army quarters, as well as the tinder-dry fields and orchards where so
many civilians had made temporary camp.

Lily observed Rashid change from gentle persuader to passionate
orator. Outside the ruins of Jericho's town hall, he stood before an
assembly of mukhtars, soldiers, and his young troop of fedayeen
trainees. A steady wind was blowing smoke from the smoldering
Army Camp 88, on the outskirts of the city, across the rim of the
square, blackening the sky with premature darkness. For two days,
the volunteer firefighters had battled the blaze, but water was inef-
fective. They did not know why. Never before had they seen the hellish results of modern napalm warfare.

On the fringes of the crowd Lily stood with Pamela and Robin
Watts and Constance Sommer, transfixed by the swiftness with
which history had changed its course. Her rash had subsided. The
itching had eased.

Rashid called the assembled to attention from atop a makeshift
platform. Standing behind him, with worshipful eyes focused on his
father, was ten-year-old Jalil. Never before had Lily seen such un-
critical adoration on a child's face.

Rashid clenched his upraised fists. "We shall continue to rebel
against this illegal Zionist occupation of yet more of our precious territory until that final great victory in which the righteous shall triumph."

The crowd hooted their approval. He bowed his head and waited
for them to quiet. "A man without a country is without dignity." He
paused for emphasis. "And our dignity is more important to us even
than our lives. We will regain it or we will not survive!" His voice
modulated to manipulate his audience. "This conflict has taught us

Palestinians a crucial lesson. No longer can we expect our rights to be upheld by proxy armies and states. We are not Jordanians! We are not Syrians, Egyptians, or Lebanese!"

Each of Rashid's pronouncements was greeted with cheers. His tone became increasingly loud, his words more forceful. "The Zionists have proven to the world they will stop at nothing until they have conquered the whole of the Middle East. Today it is the Sinai and the Golan Heights; tomorrow it will be Cairo and Damascus! While we are gathered here, secret resistance cells are forming on every street, in every village. Until now, our brothers who have joined Fatah and diligently worked to undermine the Zionists have been abused by the leaders throughout the Arab world. Yesterday we were downtrodden and despised refugees; tomorrow it will be said that we are the only ones who dared challenge the expansionist enemy who stole our birthright!"

As if on cue, a squadron of Israeli aircraft flew overhead. At first there were shrieks of terror as the crowd attempted to disperse. With outstretched arms, Rashid struggled to calm them. Then one plane passed so low it seemed like a plow about to furrow a field. Looking up at its belly, Lily was able to count the rivets on the wings while everyone in the assemblage threw themselves to the ground in a unified reflex. Instead of bombs, leaflets fluttered out like giant snowflakes and blanketed the backs of the prostrate people.

Rashid, who was perhaps the only person besides Lily remaining on his feet, lifted one and read aloud: "Surrender and be safe." Another: "The Israeli Defense Forces are stronger than all the Arab armies united." He ripped the pages dramatically and ground them under his foot.

The crowd rose in a frenzied acclamation. The women wailed by trilling their tongues in the traditional tribal war cry.

Rashid stood back magnanimously as Ramzi Habash, a respected warrior, came forward, his head bowed until the area was silenced.

He began with only two words, mouthed slowly and deliberately. "Deir Yassin."

Just the name of the martyred Palestinian village seared the soul of every Arab present.

Lily knew all about Deir Yassin, the small village a few kilometers west of Jerusalem that the Irgun attacked less than six weeks before Israel became a state. In the course of the fighting, more than two hundred of the Arab villagers had been killed. Chilling descriptions had been circulated by the British investigator and a Red Cross official, shocking the world because never before had Jews been accused of such appalling atrocities against women and children. While Lily had no doubt many of the stories held some degree of truth, there had been numerous conflicting reports about the events, and the most outrageous tales had become weapons in the hands of the Arabs to justify their own savagery. Yet while the error that may have been committed at Deir Yassin was constantly thrown at the Israelis, the world would forget that the Jews had suffered a hundred, no, a thousand, Deir Yassins at the hands of not only the Arab world but throughout history. How many children had she herself seen dragged away from their mothers, burnt in furnaces, killed by dogs, beaten senseless, maimed physically and mentally? In her lifetime, there would not be enough hours to make such a list.

She had not been listening to the speaker's brutal story, a lavish re-creation of the massacre with no detail of molestations and butcherings spared. It was her own memories that choked her. She gasped for breath.

"Nicole?" Pamela pulled her to the edge of the crowd.

The speaker raged on. "Twenty years ago, one of my sons was killed in Palestine; last week a grandson was taken in Jerusalem." Habash wept openly. "But I say this to you: the caravan of martyrs will continue to grow until the last drop of the blood in our bodies has been spilled. We can *never* forget and we will *never* give up!"

Pamela fanned Lily's face. Someone urged her to drink some black coffee. She spit out the cloying liquid as, in the distance, there rose screams for blood and revenge.

"I am . . . better . . ."

"You haven't slept in days," Pamela said.

"Neither have you."

"Tonight should be easier. The worst cases are on their way to Amman. You must go home to rest." She indicated the crowd. "This will go on all night."

"What is going to happen?"

Pamela looked over at her husband.

"They're talking about evacuating," he answered.

"Who is?"

The doctor gestured to the crowd.

"To where?" Lily asked incredulously.

"Across the river. They're afraid they'll all be killed if they remain on the West Bank."

"That is ridiculous. The bombs have stopped."

"I hope so," Pamela said wearily.

"We're having a staff meeting at eight in the morning. I'm working on a plan for all the UNRWA workers," Robin began. "Until then, let's get you home."

⁘ ⁘ ⁘

"They're lining up at the Allenby Bridge," Dr. Watts reported to the assembled UNRWA workers. "Several thousand crossed yesterday. At this rate they will clear Aqabat Jabar in less than a week."

"Where do they expect to go?" Lily asked.

"To Amman."

"Amman cannot absorb a hundred thousand people. That's what it will come to if the entire West Bank moves across the river, not to mention the refugees from East Jerusalem and wherever else in Israel."

"We know that. I've been in communication with Director Osbeck. Tent cities are already forming on the other side that will make the conditions here seem like paradise."

"Can't we warn them? Can't we stop them?" asked Karin, the Danish nurse.

"They don't believe what we tell them." Dr. Watts sighed. "Listen to this communiqué General Dayan issued. It's unbelievable, even to me. It says that Arabs are to be allowed into Israel at all times. He's opened the border to the Gaza Strip and all the bridges are to permit free transit both ways. 'There will be no barriers, no checkposts, no deterrence to the free passage of anyone wishing to depart or enter Israel.'"

Lily was genuinely shocked. "How can he do that? Refugees will return to their old lands and see their homes inhabited by Israelis and want revenge. Every terrorist will carry a bomb in his market basket!"

"I think it's a very clever policy," Pamela answered slowly. "It should defuse some of the anger immediately and it will swing world opinion around to the Jews. Remember, they were the aggressors in this war and they are facing censorship from the U.N. and the major powers. There will be pressure to give back some of the occupied territory. But if they can demonstrate that they will rule a united Jerusalem and the new lands benevolently, they have a better chance of holding the territory — thus ensuring their own security."

Lily was impressed with Pamela's political acumen, but all she said was, "Even if that's so, where does it leave us?"

"Pamela and I will stay at Aqabat Jabar because there are many too old and sick to make the journey, especially under these panicked conditions. Five other nurses and service personnel will remain with us until relief crews become available. Oxfam is on its way and we expect the International Red Cross as well. Nicole, Constance, and Karin, along with any Palestinian assistants who choose to depart, will cross at the Allenby Bridge over the next few days and head for Amman. I have several bulletins on camp setup, minimum health standards, latrine positioning, water rationing, and epidemic control for you to study. We will have at least two support vehicles available on the other side because the bridge has been too severely damaged to permit our vehicles here to cross. You will be met by Director Osbeck and his team in Amman who will be coordinating relief efforts there."

Lily listened carefully. She was being sent to Amman. What could she do but comply? She had tried her sulfa pills once and failed; to use them again would be foolish. After the initial exodus, some semblance of order would be brought to the refugee camp. At that time she could ask to be relieved, fly to Greece, to Paris, then from there back to Israel. If she attempted to return to Jerusalem when she was needed here, she would be suspect. No, the best solution was to continue playing her role and pray for the curtain to fall as soon as possible.

As she helped select food and medical supplies to be carried by hand across the bridge and loaded into the few vehicles sent for them, long lines of refugees marched to the east, fleeing the conquering Israelis. Behind them the squalid huts that had been their homes in exile for nearly twenty years bore resentful witness to their final estrangement from the land they had continued to call Palestine. Ahead of them was Jordan, their host for two decades, but still an alien ruler.

Watching the shabby lines of desperate people lunging across the Jordan, Lily became more and more indignant at their plight. In the back of her mind, she had always believed a compromise to the Palestinian problem was possible if only the powers would talk it over. The difficulty had been the Arabs' refusal to acknowledge Israel's existence. With the recent conclusive victory as evidence, perhaps the Arabs would come to the bargaining table. The refugees who were leaving of their own free will might be giving up their rights to their land forever. It was too soon after the war for the Israelis to have begun to solve the myriad problems that arose at every hour of the day. Already much was being said about their callous indifference, the inhumanity of "forcing" the refugees to trek on foot. Yet, if the Israeli government supplied transport, surely they would be accused of systematic eviction. Or, if they forbade departures and used military force to control the Arabs' flight, they would be labeled tyrants. Israel could neither explain nor apologize. Pamela had been right. Dayan had the only reasonable solution: Open the gates and let the people choose for themselves. But, from her own experience, Lily knew that powerless victims could not make choices.

The trek to the outskirts of Amman during the middle of June was grueling. Military convoys took precedence at the river crossings, so the swarm of refugees would part to permit the disheartened Jordanian soldiers to pass in front of them. The UNRWA team trudged through dust so thick it covered their legs with a grainy powder. A group of Arab UNRWA workers ferried supplies in bundles and baskets until the solitary vehicle to arrive was overloaded.

When they were finally under way, Constance and Karin collapsed on some grain sacks and slept for a while, but Lily was ever alert to the chaos around her. Several times she asked the driver to stop so she could check a walking child who appeared too weak to continue. She handed out water freely, but there was not nearly enough considering the scorching heat and choking grit that swirled under the wheels of the cars and trucks — most of them commandeered by the fleeing Jordanian army. The downtrodden refugees were veiled in a ghostly camouflage.

So many of the old men and women had made a similar flight before. Hadn't they learned the senselessness of fleeing? Lily was certain they would have been better off if they had waited a few months. With the frontiers opened, there was a chance many could have returned to Haifa or Jaffa or Beersheba, or at least found new homes within the recently expanded borders. And while she felt great compassion for the elderly, it was for the children that her heart ached.

Out of a puff of reddish dust came three of them: a thin girl and a tall boy who were carrying a smaller boy in a sling. There was something wrong with his left leg — it seemed twisted at an odd angle. The girl was barely keeping up with the taller boy. She stumbled. The child between them clung to the shoulder of the taller boy to keep from slipping. They stopped and attempted to reposition him. The exhausted girl barely cooperated. The boy became angry and slapped her. The child between them whimpered.

Something in Lily's mind snapped. She was no longer burning with the heat of fierce Middle Eastern sun but shivering in the chill of an East European winter night. The UNRWA truck had slowed slightly. She seized the opportunity and jumped off.

"Nicole!" Karin shouted. "Where are you going?"

Lily ran to the trio of tiny travelers, lifted the lame child into her arms, and called him by a long-forgotten name. "Otto!" she sobbed.

The Arab children were terribly confused. Other refugees gathered around, chattering and gesturing. Constance Sommer and the UNRWA driver pushed their way into the circle.

"I am taking Otto with me," Lily said firmly.

"You know what Dr. Watts —" Nurse Sommer began. Dr. Watts had forbidden any passengers.

"I am not going without Otto."

A lone airplane swooped along the road like a predatory bird. Heaving the packs from their heads and backs, the terrorized refugees, including the older children who had accompanied the lame boy, dispersed and took scanty cover among tall, frail weeds in the field. The boy remained clasped in Lily's arms. Constance Sommer pulled them both behind the truck where the UNRWA staff was huddled. The droning plane headed for the largest clump of human forms in the field and dropped a gleaming object that looked like a barrel. When it hit, the explosion was a brilliant flash that instantly sucked up all the air. Lily's throat seared; her eyelids squeezed to block the intensity of the blast. The ground beneath her buckled. She attempted to reopen her eyes, but the scene was too blinding to be withstood. Several minutes later, it appeared as if a section of the sun had fallen to earth and turned the field into a celestial inferno of the whitest, purest heat.

Lily felt herself being half pushed, half carried onto the truckbed. Otto remained in her arms. They they were moving swiftly away from the flaming Hades. "We should go back —" she managed to groan.

"No use . . ." Nurse Sommer replied in a voice so bland, she seemed a long way off. Her eyes were grossly dilated, giving her an otherworldly appearance. "It cannot be — napalm —"

"What is napalm?" Karin asked.

"A gasoline bomb. The fire cannot be put out, like ones in Jericho. They also use it in Vietnam."

"Not the Israelis — they would not — these are *civilians*!" Lily protested.

The nurse was deathly pale. Her twitching hands were stroking the tattered Bible in her purse. "This is a war, isn't it? There are military all around us. How can they tell who is who?"

Lily gagged at the smell that pursued the truck. Burning flesh . . . My God, she knew it well! Amazing how scents were such accurate triggers of memory — more so than words or pictures. She buried her face in Otto's oily hair and inhaled his slippery essence in an attempt to mask the ghastly memories that clutched at her relentlessly. In the receding dust, Lily saw spectral images of Otto's brother and sister — if that is who the other children had been — but the faces that hovered in the air were those of another brother and sister struggling with their exhausted companion. They were the young David and Lily on the road to Theresienstadt with their little companion, Otto. If a truck had stopped on that long-ago march . . . if Otto had been picked up and nurtured . . . he might have survived. Not David. His death had not been related to the march. Not Lily. That little girl had died long before. Perhaps in the baker's cellar . . . perhaps the hour her mother denied she was hers . . .

The road dipped slightly. The wavering forms of David and Lily vanished forever. Lily turned her attention to this new Otto.

Karin poured water into a tin cup and handed it over. Lily watched tenderly as the boy took his first grateful sips. "Bil-hana, Otto," Lily murmured. "May you enjoy it."

"Surely he's not called Otto," Karin said. "Ismak eh?" she asked the child in Arabic. "What is your name?"

"Ismi Raouf."

"You see, his name is Raouf, not Otto. I think I had an Uncle Otto from Odense. He was very jolly, just like the name, but not like this poor child. I wonder what happened to his leg? A birth defect, do you think?" she prattled on nervously.

"Karin," Nurse Sommer called over the noise of the engine. When she had the younger woman's attention, she indicated Lily with a nod of the head.

Lily knew they were staring at her, but she did not care. She stroked Otto's thick, greasy hair. Minuscule translucent nits clung tenaciously to almost every strand. As soon as they were settled, she would delouse him. She stroked his withered leg. The muscles were strong until below the knee. With a proper prosthesis he might walk almost normally. His teeth were yellow, his fingernails bumpy. She examined his lower eyelids. Pale and anemic. He would need meat, figs, dates, fresh milk. She shifted him from the floor of the truck into her lap. Sighing, he lay back in her arms and tentatively touched the soft sunlit curls that framed her face, his olive-black eyes shining with wonderment.

While the distance from the Allenby Bridge was but fifty kilometers, not much farther than Jerusalem, only a narrow lane remained of the highway; the rest was given over to refugees on foot, carts pulled by animals, and an inevitable line of stranded vehicles. Fortunately, the dependable UNRWA truck made it to an encampment in Suwaili, on the outskirts of Amman, before nightfall. A ragged squatters' city had already sprung up.

"Reminds me of the early days of Aqabat Jabar," Lily overheard one of the Arab elders saying.

The UNRWA driver went to work setting up three emergency tents, which, though torn and mildewed, offered some protection from the sun, if not the rain.

While they were arranging makeshift sleeping accommodations, four dirt-streaked boys came into the compound. "Nurse Schmidt," one called in a hoarse whisper.

"Jalil! How long have you been here?"

"Since this morning. Father asked me to find you and offer my assistance. My friends and I are at your service."

Lily pushed back her sweaty hair and stared at her lover's son. "Where is he now?"

"In Amman. He is preparing to leave for Damascus."

"Where will you be sleeping?"

"My father has friends with a house nearby. There are many rooms."

After Jalil and the other boys helped unload the truck, Lily sent them back to their families.

"Tell your father I am grateful for your help" was all she said to the boy.

By midnight, their section was readied with camp cots and a washing and cooking area. They had eaten only bread and cheese for supper. Karin vowed to locate a Primus and make coffee in the morning.

When Lily tucked Otto in next to her, Constance hovered nearby. "He's quite dehydrated. I'm concerned about him," the nurse said.

"He's already drunk two liters of water," Lily replied defensively.

Constance pressed the child's arm with her thumb. "Look, the indentation remains. If he doesn't make progress by tomorrow, we'll start an IV."

"I was told they were for emergencies only."

"I believe this is a special case."

"Thank you," Lily replied.

"I hope we can locate his parents," Nurse Sommer said gently.

"He has none."

"How can you know that?"

"It is in his eyes."

"We will have to question him . . . later."

Lily wrapped her arms around the trembling child. She had nothing more to say.

❖   ❖   ❖

Karin managed to brew a pot of tasty coffee in the morning and the ever-resourceful Constance produced three hard-boiled eggs from her nursing bag. Lily gave hers to Otto, who seemed slightly more alert. Just as they were finishing their breakfast, the UNRWA driver came in to announce that a third of their foodstuffs had disappeared during the night.

"Let's hope it gets distributed, not hoarded," Constance said with resignation.

Lily organized what supplies remained. After an hour, she checked on Otto. He had fallen back to sleep on the cot. A slick of sweat formed across his face. She felt his forehead. A fever? She took his temperature by placing a thermometer under his armpit. Her fears were confirmed. All the nurses were occupied. There was no time to start an IV. Later she would get Constance to assist her.

Crisis followed crisis. Karin delivered a baby. Constance tended a man with a knife wound. After spoon-feeding a broth made of chicken bouillon and powdered milk to Otto, Lily dozed off at the child's side.

"Nicole?" The voice was directly against her ear.

She started. "Rashid!" He was wearing a khaki army shirt and brown trousers.

"Thank you for coming to the aid of my people once again," he said.

"That is not necessary, but —"

"Yes?"

"Are you staying here?"

"No."

"You are going to Damascus?"

"How did you know?"

"Jalil told me. Will he go as well?"

"I want him with me. He is all I have."

"When will you return?"

"I doubt that I will. Jordan is not my home."

"You will live in Damascus?"

"I will live only for my cause, wherever it takes me." His tone was far more subdued than when he spoke to the crowd, but passion underscored every word. "I am a Palestinian. We are all Palestinians. Soon the world will know what that means."

"I will not see you again?"

"That is doubtful."

Otto turned over and sighed. Rashid asked, "Who is that?"

"A sick child."

He tousled Otto's hair. "Some of your food is missing?"

"Yes," she said while concentrating on Otto's twitching mouth. "How did you know?"

"I have eyes and ears. It will be returned."

"Mâ-assalama," Lily said as she turned back to Rashid, but he had disappeared as quickly as he had come.

She held Otto's hand. "He is all I have," Rashid had said of Jalil. Funny, she already felt the same about Otto, whom she had known less than a day. The boy's body was much cooler. His eyes had lost their glassiness. He asked for bread. There were some hard crackers packed away with her clothing. She went to find them. Thinking about Rashid muddled her mind; caring for Otto cleared it.

After nightfall, Lily stirred some beans over Karin's Primus stove. Otto, who had been watching all the bustle outside the UNRWA enclave, came to find his adopted mother. "There is a man . . ." He pointed to the headlights of a Rover.

Lily supposed this was Rashid returning the missing rations. She steeled herself for a final farewell. Otto tagged along, curious. The Land Rover was marked "Oxfam," for the Oxford Committee for Famine Relief, a British organization. The rear door opened.

"Nicole."

She jumped back in fright.

"Get inside the truck. Immediately!"

It was Eli. She clasped Otto to her.

"For God's sake, Nicole, I need to talk to you."

She crept closer tentatively. "What are you doing here?"

"We've been chasing you on both sides of the Jordan. Why the hell did you go with the refugees?"

"I was needed," she hissed.

"Get *in!*"

Reluctantly, she put one foot up on the rear bumper. Eli grasped her arm and yanked her inside. Otto fell back and whimpered. Lily reached for the boy's pitifully outstretched arms.

"What in heaven's name is that?"

"Otto —"

"Who?"

"A sick child. He stays with *me!*"

Eli swooped the boy up. When they were all inside he tapped on the metal side three times. The vehicle lurched away with a jerk.

"What are you doing? I thought you wanted to talk with me."

"Not here."

"The child —"

"He'll have to come along. We don't have time to locate his mother."

"I do not even know if he has one."

"So much the better."

"How did you find me?"

"We went down to Jericho and spoke with Dr. Watts. He told us where you'd be. He was quite appreciative that Oxfam was on its way to help the refugees. He said he expected conditions to be wretched on the other side. He was right."

"All the bridges were destroyed. How could you cross the river?"

"It's barely a trickle at Um Zuz. We could ford it in four-wheel drive."

"Where are we going?"

"To safety."

"I need to go back. Let me out!"

"We cannot, Lily. It's too dangerous for you."

"My cover has not been compromised. I am perfectly safe here."

"Are you mad? There's been a war. You are behind enemy lines."

"Nobody has *ever* suspected me. These heroics are unnecessary — a waste of resources. In a few weeks I planned to leave Amman for Athens, then return to Tel Aviv."

Eli did not respond. He held her tightly until they had driven a few miles from the encampment. The truck pulled over. The driver came around to the back, climbed in, and closed the door.

"Charlotte!" Lily gasped.

Charlotte clasped Lily's hand. "For now I'm June Pratt and Eli is

Martin Ainley of Oxfam." She turned and spoke briskly to Eli. "This is the place?" She pointed to a yellowed chart.

Eli nodded and checked his watch. "Fifteen more minutes. If Levi and Ezer aren't here, we can assume their first plan is under way."

Charlotte held a flashlight while Eli traced a route on the disintegrating map with his finger.

Lily listened intently. They had not come just to rescue her. Something else was happening. They spoke in code, talking about places by numbers instead of names. Otto coughed as he slept fitfully in her arms. She smoothed back his hair. The planes of his face were elegantly formed, more so than those of the other Otto, who had been hollow-cheeked with a pointed chin and haunting eyes. The boy's breath caressed her hand. Warm living air expelled from expanding lungs beside a beating heart. Life: so tenacious, so fragile . . . Otto on the death march — his skin barely warm beside her as they fell asleep, cold and congealed in the morning. Not this time — no — never again!

Charlotte and Eli continued to whisper. They seemed pleased that their associates had not turned up. For a moment Lily felt compelled to take Otto in her arms and start back to the makeshift UNRWA camp — as if that were where she belonged. She had to force herself to remember that Eli was here to keep the promise that the Mossad, unlike any other secret service in the world, would do anything possible to retrieve an operative. For whatever reason, Eli had decided she needed to be rescued.

Charlotte remained in back with Lily and the boy while Eli took the driver's seat and headed in a direction Lily surmised was west. She surveyed the few sacks and boxes in the Rover. Most appeared empty. "Wouldn't an Oxfam truck have come loaded with supplies?" Lily asked.

"Oh, we were. We had no difficulty finding takers once we reached the first encampment. We looked for you there but they told us that the UNRWA health unit was farther on," Charlotte replied.

Studying Charlotte's face, Lily was surprised at how youthful the American seemed. Her hair was pulled back from her face and fastened into a bun, but it made her appear refined rather than prim. She wore tight jeans, a blue striped blouse with soiled cuffs, and an apron with Oxfam's growing-plant logo.

"What happened to the boy's leg?" Charlotte asked.

"I do not know. I only found him yesterday. He was forced to march across the river."

"Forced to march? Nobody coerced the refugees into leaving."

"They were afraid of being massacred."

"My God! How could they think such a thing? They always bring up Deir Yassin, don't they? Soon they will discover we're not the villains their leaders have made us out to be."

"Oh, no? What do you know about napalm?"

"What do you mean?"

"Otto's family was killed by napalm yesterday."

"That's ridiculous."

"I saw it *myself*! Most were annihilated in seconds. A few survivors were taken into Amman. You have never seen such appalling disfigurations!"

"You'll have to ask Eli. I don't know about such . . ."

As the Rover rumbled through a dark, eerie landscape, Lily wondered what Charlotte was doing there. "I thought you lived in New York."

"I do. I came over to help."

"It is not what you expected?"

"Who could imagine this? Or that Jerusalem is finally a united city."

"You were there?"

"Yes. With Eli. We walked through the Jaffa Gate. Into the Old City —" Her voice was breaking with emotion. "Past the hotel where you stayed, Lily. We saw them removing the fencing, dismantling the checkposts, even blowing up the concrete walls that closed off Jaffa Road and Suleiman Street. In the Moghrabi quarter, they were tearing down the hovels opposite the Western Wall and streams of people were pouring into the Old City. It's the strangest experience. Everybody acts as if this were completely normal! Only two days ago I saw an Arab family — a man with two wives and three little children — walking up King George Street, going inside the stores, looking around at the boxes and bottles with great interest. They seemed so *calm,* so *unafraid.* Isn't that remarkable?"

Lily listened, but did not react. Wasn't that what Eli had predicted? A united Jerusalem! Isn't that what all this was for? And yet, was it worth the price? Even if it were not, what was the alternative? Ein breira — no alternative. Where could they flee? There were no friendly borders to cross. On one side, the Mediterranean waited to drown them; everywhere else, guns were trained to mow them down. The rest of the world had proved its refusal to harbor and protect the persecuted Jews. All they had was their sliver of embattled land.

And all *she* had as well.

Charlotte's hand touched hers and held it. Just then a flare burst across the eastern horizon and was followed by a series of explosive booms.

"What was that?" Lily cried.

Eli stopped the truck. They all got out and stared in the direction of Amman.

"Right on schedule," Eli announced.

"*You* bombed the camp?" Lily asked incredulously.

"Yes," he confirmed flatly. "*We* bombed the camp."

"What about the children — the women there! I thought the war was over."

"Would that it were," he replied sadly. "It may have lasted six days, but there is no rest on the seventh. Our enemy has seen to that."

"Was it *my* camp?"

"Possibly."

"So that is why you rescued me."

"You know as well as anybody there were dangerous terrorists inciting the population."

Rashid! A dangerous terrorist? Of course, that was what her lover had been. Her own reports had labeled him as such. He had staged more than one raid across the border personally, had been the ringleader in the raincoat fiasco, and was certainly on his way to becoming a major PLO policymaker. Her breath came in short little bursts. The consequences of her actions were just beginning to dawn on her. Her heart pounded uncontrollably.

"You have killed Rashid?" she asked in a voice she willed not to betray her.

"Perhaps. I don't know for certain. I only knew you were endangered if you remained there."

"What about the innocent victims? He had a son!" Little Jalil was now orphaned — or dead. She turned to Otto, who was sleeping on some bundles. "He is all I have . . ." Blessedly, the disturbance had not fazed the child, the one she had saved twice already.

"How many innocents was Salim responsible for?"

Lily felt as if her brain were splitting into two halves. Rashid of the refined voice, the delicate hands, the lover who took infinite care with her body. She knew he was a member of Fatah. Yet he was also a moderate man, a man of reason — at least that was the side he had shown to her. The raincoat bombs may not have been his idea, but he had overseen the project. Every one of his policies was vehemently anti-Zionist. What was happening to her? She was even thinking like him, using the word "Zionist" in place of "Israeli." He never recognized the Jewish state — never would have either. And if he had known her true identity, what would he have done? Her mind wandered. She could not focus on his wrath. She could not imagine him turning against her. Theoretically, he could have killed her with his bare hands. But would he have? The question was irrelevant as she recognized that it was *her* reports that had singled him out, set him up for execution. She reeled against the Rover.

"We've got to keep going." Eli gestured for Charlotte to assist him. Together they steered Lily back into the Rover.

As they bumped along the back roads, Lily cradled Otto in her lap and wished she could weep — for the homeless child, for Rashid and Jalil and her other friends. But her face had turned to stone.

Trying to break the morbid mood, Charlotte chattered on. She continued with news of Israeli victories during the war and her own firsthand experiences as Eli's aide. Eli turned the wheel sharply and Lily and Charlotte were thrown together in the back of the truck. Otto opened his eyes for a second, but closed them when he saw Lily was nearby.

Charlotte explained, "We're taking back roads."

In less than an hour the truck jerked to a stop. The road was blocked.

"An ambush?" Charlotte whispered. With a knife hidden in her clothing, Charlotte slit open a grain bag and pulled out two Uzi machine guns. Eli had slipped from the driver's seat and come around the side. Suddenly, there was a burst of machine gun fire. Eli responded instantly. Charlotte covered him. They heard two men scream in the bushes. Then all was silent.

Eli investigated and found two Jordanian soldiers who had been guarding the area. He dragged their bodies out and took their weapons.

Eli was quiet for a moment. How many other times had he killed at such close range? Lily wondered.

"This means they've closed off the road to Um Zuz," was all he said when he finally spoke.

"Shall we go south and try for that spot near the Allenby?" Charlotte queried.

"Too risky. It's the major thoroughfare."

"The Abdullah Bridge?" Charlotte suggested halfheartedly.

"The same difficulty."

"Overland, avoiding the main roads?"

"We can't chance it at night."

"What's the nearest town?" Charlotte asked.

"El-Salt. Why?"

"Ten kilometers back, right?"

"About that."

"Let's return there."

"Why? They'd shoot before asking questions."

"Eli, I saw a sign for an airfield . . ."

Lily thought both of them had lost their minds, but said nothing. Charlotte went to sit up front with Eli. Good. She was tired of hearing her voice.

When Lily was alone she contemplated finding a way back to Amman but, before she could sort her muddled thoughts, the Rover screeched to a halt, backed up, and made a turn down a narrow roadway. In the predawn hours, a half moon was low in the sky. Its light spilled off a metallic structure in the distance. Charlotte's door opened and she went running across a field in a crouched position. In a few seconds she came hurrying back.

"There are six planes. Most are junkers, but there's at least one decent Taylorcraft!"

Lily stood beside Eli. "What's this? Are you going to fly us to Israel?"

"Not me. I cannot fly. Charlotte can."

"Charlotte?"

Charlotte had taken a flashlight from the car and returned to the airplanes. She signaled the others to join her. Eli watched as she aimed her light at the dipstick. "There's a quarter of a tank of oil, maybe a little less."

"Is that enough?" Eli asked.

"Not enough to be safe. Let's check the gas tanks." She climbed onto the wing and banged on a rusty cap. Eli handed her the light. "It's about an eighth full."

"Is that enough?"

"No."

"This is ridiculous!" Lily shouted.

"Look, if there's an eighth here, there might be as much in some of the other tanks. All we have to do is get over the border and find a safe place to land. I'd feel comfortable with fifteen, but I'd fly it with ten gallons."

"Lily, there's a water bottle in the truck behind where the boy is sleeping," Charlotte said. "See if you can find it."

Lily obeyed. Otto was sitting up, looking perplexed. She scooped him into her arms and carried him with her when she took the bottle to Charlotte.

Charlotte loosened the gas cap on the wing of a Piper Cherokee that had a broken landing gear. Using the top of the bottle, she pressed it into the fuel sump — the place where a few drops of fuel are usually drained and checked for water or impurities. Gas trickled slowly into the bottle.

"Jesus! This will take all night! Eli, can you find a small tool — a pair of pliers, even some wire? I have to remove this sump valve."

Eli found an adjustable wrench and twisted out the valve fitting. They were rewarded by a rush of fragrant fuel. In a few seconds the bottle was filled to overflowing. Charlotte stoppered the flow with her finger while Eli ran to the Taylorcraft and poured the gas into its tank.

"This will take hours," Lily commented morosely.

"Find another container for the gas!" Charlotte retorted crossly.

Lily remembered leaning on some cans of dried milk in the Oxfam vehicle. She ran and retrieved two, pried off the lids, and poured the precious powder onto the ground. Soon they had three containers filling with gas. Much of the liquid was lost in trying to pour from the wide-mouthed cans, but they were making progress.

When the Piper was drained, Charlotte assessed the situation. "I think we can get out of here — *if* this damn thing will fly."

"Where's the airfield?" Eli asked.

"I'm going to take off on that grass strip over there." She pointed toward a tattered wind sock. "The only trouble is the wind's mostly from the south — a direct crosswind."

Lily peered into the cockpit. "There are only two seats in this plane."

"There's a large baggage area. You and the child should fit there nicely. Go and get some blankets from the Rover and the basket with the emergency supplies — the one with the pomelos on top."

In a few minutes, Lily arranged a little nest in the plane. Otto sat on her lap and sucked a juicy pomelo, a grapefruitlike citrus fruit, which was the pride of the Jericho region.

Charlotte crawled around with a flashlight, checking the tires, the struts, every surface of the plane. She manipulated the rudder and

ailerons, examined the nicks on the prop, even blew in crevices to remove dust and insect droppings.

"Do you know how to turn a prop?" Charlotte asked Eli.

"No. Can't you do it?"

"I think so." For the first time since they arrived at the airfield,
Lily noticed Charlotte's determination waver. "I've always been terrified of doing it . . ." Her voice was high and thin. "Hold the light
for me," she ordered more firmly, then crawled into the cockpit, dis-
connected the wires from the ignition switch, allowing them to swing
freely in the air.

"What if the battery's dead?" Eli asked.

"We have a magneto. When I pull the propeller through, it should
start." She showed Eli how to hold the brakes down with his feet,
then set the throttle and went out to face the propeller.

From behind the seat, Lily could see Charlotte's fearful expression
as she placed her hands on the blades. In the moonlight, she seemed
a goddess carved in alabaster. Charlotte bit her lip and pushed as
hard as she could. Nothing happened. Once again Charlotte turned
the leading edge of the prop forward slowly until she felt the increasing resistance of compression, then stepped back, steadied herself, and pulled the prop as forcefully as possible through the
compression stroke. She leapt backward in anticipation of its starting. The engine did not fire. Reaching inside the cockpit, Charlotte
fiddled with the mixture knob. While Lily was ignorant of what was
necessary to start the plane, she could see that Charlotte's anxiety
about being so close to what could become a whirring propeller with
the force to chop off an arm was causing her weakness as she thrust
the prop around. She slipped out of the plane.

Eli called, "Lily! Get back in!"

She did not respond to Eli. "You set it up. I will pull it."

"But —" Charlotte quavered for a second, then reset the prop
once more.

With one decisive swoop, Lily grabbed the blade and tugged it
downward. As the cylinder fired, the wind sucked her toward the
propeller. She jumped backward and rushed around to the door. Eli
slammed it behind her.

Otto whimpered. Lily snuggled him close. The child smelled of
citrus rind. Her hair stank from oil and gasoline. The tinny cabin
shook violently as the plane taxied between the strip of vintage aircraft. Charlotte jerked it to a halt and creaked the stick back and
forth. As Lily listened to the scrape of metal, the whine of the engine,

she felt no confidence that it could fly. The aircraft rattled down the
bumpy airstrip, then lifted off with a shudder.

"Yoffi!" Eli shouted enthusiastically.

In front of them, the sky was turning the palest coral; behind them
lay the blackness of the Biblical lands where the Moabites once
roamed. The peak of Mount Nebo caught the first light and reflected it back toward Israel.

"The Dead Sea!" Charlotte called.

Lily got up on her knees and craned forward. Down below, the
fetus-shaped body of water seemed a giant pool of oil in the midst of
the camel-colored desert.

Eli pulled out the map and was suggesting various routes. "We
cannot risk the radar in the Jerusalem corridor."

"As soon as we cross the Dead Sea. I'm going to stay under five
hundred feet wherever possible. I've flown over the northern route
often enough to be wary about the hills. What does it look like in the
south?"

Eli showed her the map. "I'm familiar with the area around Dimona. We'll have to stay clear of that whole sector because of the nuclear center. The best route would be south to Sodom, then west to
Beersheba. Do we have enough fuel?"

Charlotte measured the distance on the map with her fingers. "It
will be tight. Do you think you could help me locate the Sodom–
Beersheba road? I seem to remember it's wide enough to land a
plane on."

The Dead Sea was directly below them. In the spreading light, it
shimmered with a violet-tinged silver. All around it, the rock-strewn
hills were as barren as those of the moon. The plane swooped down
so close to the surface Lily could see crusts of white salt forming
small iceberglike islands.

"Remember this," Charlotte shouted over the drone of the motor,
"you are flying below sea level! My Israeli flight instructor would
have said you are officially members of 'The Thousand-Below
Club'!"

Otto squirmed beside Lily. He pointed to his penis. Lily understood he had to urinate. In the basket, she found the bottle that had
been used to transfer the gasoline and she helped the child use it.
With some of the pomelo peel she fashioned a cork. Otto giggled at
her handiwork.

Lily began to comprehend the enormity of the problem the child
presented. What would she do with him? Even if she wanted to

adopt him, she would be deterred because the boy spoke only Arabic. Sometime in the vast history of the Semitic people her ancestors had sprung from Isaac's seed; Otto had sprung from his half-brother Ismail's. There could be no intermingling. If she tried to keep him, she would be accused of stealing an Arab baby. First, she would find him a family of Israeli Arabs . . .

Her thoughts were interrupted by Eli tapping on the fuel gauge. "Do you think this is correct?"

Lily craned her head. It was reading almost empty.

"Who knows?" Charlotte said calmly. "By my calculations we should have another half hour at least, maybe more. I'm worried about how much oil we're burning. Anyway, we can glide into Israel from here if we have to."

When the Dead Sea disappeared behind the tail of the plane, Charlotte clapped her hands. "We're safe!"

A few minutes later Eli called out, "This course might be too close to Dimona already. We don't want to have fighters on our tail."

"Right," Charlotte agreed. The plane swooped to the north.

"That's safer. We once shot down our own man for violating that airspace."

As the sun rose and illuminated the landscape, Charlotte headed in the direction of the wide ravines of the Wilderness of Judah. All at once the plane started to shake and sputter. "The rpms are dropping," Charlotte muttered.

"What is happening?" Lily's voice was inaudible because of the din. She felt Otto's hand slip into hers.

"Look for the road," Charlotte ordered.

"Over there!" Eli pointed a few miles north.

"Best rate of glide — shit! Who knows what it is in this plane?" Charlotte was talking to herself as the engine missed again and again before it shuddered to a stop. In the silence, the propeller blades continued to windmill. "What's that ahead of us?"

"Tents. Probably an encampment of Huzeil Bedouins — they're usually friendly."

"I certainly hope so!" Charlotte quipped while she centered the dropping aircraft over the roadbed. With amazing control, she regulated the speed by dropping or raising the nose until she had the plane aligned correctly. The highway seemed to extend to a limitless horizon. There was no traffic in view. For a few excruciatingly long seconds the plane hovered in the air; then the wheels bumped the ground. The plane drifted to a stop.

An hour later they were picked up by a truck leaving the Dead Sea potash works and were brought to the Desert Inn on the outskirts of Beersheba. Immediately, they were taken to the Israeli army's southern headquarters command post in the hotel's basement shelter. While the military officials contacted Meir Amit — the man Eli insisted they speak with first — officers brought them grilled shashliks from the Bulgarian restaurant. Lily was too exhausted to eat; Otto only picked at the rice.

She was ushered upstairs to a room overlooking the pool. She bathed Otto, gently sponging his crippled leg, more aggressively shampooing his hair and scrubbing the layers of grime that had darkened his skin considerably. From room service she ordered chicken soup, bread, and ice cream, a meal the child thoroughly enjoyed. Awestruck, he stroked the clean sheets and punched the foam pillow. Lily tucked him in. He slipped his thumb into his mouth and sucked his way to sleep.

Lying down on her own bed, Lily closed her eyes. Her mind tumbled with a vision of Rashid: his smooth body glowing momentarily in the fiery heat of an explosive blast; his dark, fervent eyes illuminated by pain, his complex brain and simple heart bursting apart in fleshy shards. Her body shook violently. As she began to cry out for him, the word that fell from her lips astonished her.

"Jalil!"

PART FOUR

BETRAYAL AND REVENGE

13

It is a commonplace of counterespionage work that success comes and spies are caught not through the exercise of genius or even through the detective's flair for obscure clues, but by means of the patient and laborious study of records.

J. C. Masterman
The Double-Cross System in the War of 1939 to 1945

TEL AVIV, ISRAEL: APRIL 1979

The desolation and urge to flee Israel that Eli felt moments before he was escorted from the army installation began to dissolve when he was given the illusion of freedom in the quest for his betrayer. Ehud Dani offered him the apartment of a "businessman living abroad for a few months" in a fairly new building — one of Tel Aviv's first high-rises — on Shaul Hamelech Boulevard. Built above a series of cafés, restaurants, and the London Mini-Shops, it was most convenient. All his more prosaic needs could be met with one elevator ride downstairs; therefore, he could devote his waking hours to his tedious task.

Time could not be wasted. No matter how gentlemanly Dani had tried to act, Eli knew that he and Alex Naor — and all the others concerned with his case — would be circling and sniffing until he satisfied their desire for a victim and a resolution. He would have to go through the motions of vetting every operative involved in Toulon. One of the men was in Paris; the others were in Haifa and kibbutzim in the Galilee; Aviva was close by in Tel Aviv, Lily was in

Paris, and Charlotte had returned to New York. The most efficient plan would be to complete all the Israeli business first, then proceed to Europe, and end up in New York. That way they could not accuse him of squandering the Mossad's precious funds.

Eli began his investigation by reviewing his papers locked in the Mossad's archives. The secret service allocated him a tiny office only a few blocks down Shaul Hamelech Boulevard in the direction of the Haifa Road. Every morning at seven he strolled down the boulevard past the Municipal Library, the Tel Aviv Museum, the Dafna and Koor buildings, the Asia and America houses, looking as innocuous as any other businessman. Entering a bland glass-fronted structure, he took the red escalator from the street to the lobby, proceeding to the "D" quadrant, where an elevator would take him to the fourth floor. The fifth floor, where his temporary office was located, was locked. He had not been given a key to open the elevator door, a slight that bothered him each time he walked up the double flight of stairs. The Mossad's suite was marked "Margolis Trade and Investments" on one side and "K. Rimon, Engineering Consultants" on the other. Both doors were electronically bolted. The bearded receptionist stared out through a bulletproof window and asked three simple questions. Only the correct answers to each guaranteed one would be buzzed through. After undergoing this procedure each morning, Eli felt mortified. Never before had security checks offended him — they were the necessary baggage of his profession and the protection he had installed and required in his own operations. But all had changed dramatically in the last weeks.

Eli spent the rest of each day closed off in his drab chamber with only a pad, a pencil, and the boxes of material — most of which he himself had accumulated. The notes, dating from before Zermatt, were poignant to read in retrospect. His critical assessments of the applicants, his suppositions about their near-tragic encounter at the baths of Leukerbad, his analysis of their test assignments as they established their covers, stirred him with feelings of wonderment that the entire Ezra project had ever been approved.

Ezra.

The note left on Dr. Ze'evi's mutilated body had quoted from that small but pivotal book of the Bible:

So that the people could not discern the noise of the shout of joy from the noise of the weeping of the people . . . and the noise was heard afar off.

It had been so frighteningly apt. The work of a tidy mind linking Israel's joy at having destroyed Iraq's reactor with the sadness of the victim. And the reference to the noise — to the explosions that had not yet occurred at the time of the professor's murder — was further evidence that the killer knew precisely what the Israeli scientist was doing in France and what event had been about to take place. If Eli stretched this line of thinking further, he came to his mentor's exhortation about discerning between "noises" and "voices" in intelligence work, a theme on which he later schooled his own operatives. Could Reuven Shiloah's lecture have come back to haunt him in such a nasty fashion? Or was his tangled mind taking him too far afield? How had something so inherently successful turned into such pathetic disorder?

As he focused on Aviva, Lily, and Charlotte, remembering them eagerly scrambling across the hills around Zermatt trying to prove their mettle, another voice reverberated in his mind. This time it was Bernie Petrig, their climbing instructor: "Every victory is also a defeat."

Never had that phrase been more apt.

Acutely feeling defeat in the face of triumph, Eli turned back to the documents stacked on his desk. His proud complacency had been smashed, but his bruised ego enabled him to comprehend why Dani was so suspicious of his team, why he himself was considered a possible suspect. Eli knew he was not completely blameless. By failing to protect Dr. Ze'evi he was guilty of inattention, if nothing else. Thus, he would begin where they wanted him to begin. He would follow every path, search out every clue, until he could clear the names of each of his associates. After that? He could not plan that far. He had to remain hopeful that something or someone or some unfathomed motive would be unearthed along the way.

Eli thought of himself as one of the most paranoid men in the world. He had good reason. He knew too much. While the rest of the world fretted about New York, Moscow, and Peking as the most likely targets, Eli believed that the first nuclear war would begin in Israel. All it would take would be one Arab fanatic with the right connections.

Eli kept spread sheets that attempted to account for the fifty thousand nuclear warheads worldwide, more than twenty-five thousand warheads for the United States alone. He organized these weapons in twenty-four categories, from the nine-megaton W53 mounted on the Titan missile to the SADM (Special Atomic Demolition Munition). While his counterparts in the Kremlin and the Pentagon contemplated strategic offensive Titans, Minutemen, Poseidons, and Tridents, Eli's dread revolved around the SADM — with the quaint American nickname of Davy Crockett. Whenever he heard that epithet he was reminded of Charlotte's daughter, Allison, in her coonskin cap. She would sit in his lap and sing the theme song from the popular television show and he would join along in the chorus. Unfortunately, that sweet memory was blotted by the thought of the ghastly potential of the weapon. Weighing less than sixty pounds, only thirty-one inches in length including the fins, and packed into its own tidy case, this twenty-six-kilogram nuclear land mine was one-fiftieth as potent as the Little Boy warhead that wreaked havoc on Hiroshima. But the SADM's delivery system — the backpack of a single soldier — was a terrorist's dream. If the Arab SADMs were not in existence yet, they were certainly on drawing boards in Libya and Pakistan. That is why the mission at Toulon had been so significant. Terrorists could build a nuclear bomb with only eleven kilograms of enriched uranium and the proper equipment. Every hour they were able to keep the raw material out of enemy hands they were safe.

If only for one more day.

In the planning stages were missions to send Israeli operatives into Libya's Tajura Nuclear Research Center — an attractive university-style complex forty miles east of Tripoli — to monitor their menacing projects. Already Eli had planted a highly trained consultant in Belgium's Belgonucléaire, a firm that was negotiating to provide assistance to Colonel Qaddafi. The next step would be to move the operative closer to Libya's TM4-A Tokamak Nuclear Fusion Facility's ten-megawatt research reactor to discover if there was any chance of the Libyans diverting fuel under the eyes of their Russian watchdogs. For the moment, that mission would be on hold, because while Eli knew that Israel feared a nuclear-armed Qaddafi, his paranoia had to be channeled into a much narrower microcosm — his own "family." Now all questions were reduced to one: How had he, a man who had observed the world scene with so much diligence, found himself in such a predicament?

As anxious as he was to abandon the debriefing center, Eli stayed on long enough to study the files on Toulon. Dani delivered each file personally and logged in its return. For the most part, the evidence against his operatives was contradictory, but a few of the notations were staggering. Most alarming were decoded transcriptions of intercepted transmissions that were simplistic variations on the same theme: the Ezra codes he helped devise in the early 1950s. To his mind, this eliminated the other minor operatives who had been involved in Toulon and their back-ups in Europe and Israel. Did this indicate the traitor could only be one of the three people in whom he had placed his trust over the past thirty years? No, it was *not* possible.

Or was it?

Filing the tired charts on Mk-12A re-entry vehicles and air-launched cruise missiles, Eli began three new lists. With his knife-sharpened pencil he wrote headings for the crisp folders he requisitioned: "Aviva," "Lily," "Charlotte."

He underlined them.

Lily.

Charlotte.

Aviva.

His stomach contracted with the queerest apprehension. An acrid taste filled his mouth. Was it possible that Dani, Naor — all of them — might not have been so very wrong to point a finger in their direction? Dread descended like an invisible cloak of ice.

Eli was determined to analyze each operative's movements and motives logically. His mathematical mind graphed the critical changes in the lives of his agents. He translated the results to numbers, so they could be codified, quantified, reduced to essential elements of scientific truth. He started at the beginning, delving into the distressing aftermaths of each of his operatives' return from their assignments behind enemy lines, giving numerical values equivalent to the results of their experiences. Each, in her own way, had been forced to suffer the consequences of that period of service. Eli guessed that like most other Mossad veterans, they would have felt that it was worth it. After all, they had come back with their lives and physical health intact.

At the end of the Six-Day War, when feelings of patriotism had never been firmer and Jewish unity swelled worldwide, the sacrifices of his group should have been placed in perspective. Charlotte's assistance in Lily's rescue had been, in her own words, "the finest hour of my life." Aviva's husband had won his release from the bowels of the Iraqi prison in a prisoner exchange and been reunited with his family. Even Lily had remained in Israel for almost a year because of the child she had rescued. Before returning to Paris, she had comforted Otto through two surgeries on his deformed leg and found him a home with an Arab doctor's family in Jaffa. All three women had gone to inactive status. Each had continued with a business of her own — Charlotte's boutique in New York, Aviva's travel agency in Tel Aviv, and Lily's gallery in Paris. All had prospered. With their quick minds and extensive espionage preparations, they found the world of commerce easy enough to tame. Each of these factors was given a statistical value in Eli's calculations.

Eli put down his charts.

Why had Charlotte never remarried? When he asked her, she had explained insightfully that "no man could equal the thrill of the past."

He wondered if that was Lily's excuse as well. Lily, who never warmed to him and had probably never had a serious lover. After all those years in Paris, not one name had ever surfaced in connection with her. Had the rigors of her job, the necessities of living under a cover name, made it impossible for her to make a life for herself? The tragic results of Charlotte's attempt to reconcile a personal relationship with her professional one had set new standards in the Mossad and was one reason single women were recruited less frequently.

The solution of having Aviva and Gideon marry — one that he had agonized over at the time — had, in the end, been the most satisfactory method of managing the issue. Both had weathered their trials with great stoicism and courage. In fact, the story of Gideon's confinement was now the stuff of legends. Today he was living a productive life as a counselor to victims of torture. Their children were doing wonderfully. Shulamit was married to a professor of physics and was expecting Aviva's first grandchild. Hillel had finished his army service and was attending courses at Hebrew University. Their youngest, Dalya, who had learned computer science during her period of military service, was employed by IBM in Tel Aviv. As hard as he tried, Eli could find no reason for Aviva to have wanted to harm Israel or him, no matter how disaffected she had felt after returning from Iraq seventeen years earlier.

More than the others, Lily had kept involved. After a few months of painting full time, she had admitted she was itching to "get back in the swim" and had returned to managing the gallery. When many of the objects she had selected when the market for Islamic antiquities was less volatile sold for astronomic sums, she insisted that the bulk of the profit be turned over to the government. This was seen as a signal of her ongoing dedication to the cause. A few months later, she was given supervisory status over Israeli operatives who used France as a base.

There was another consideration: the children of the Ezra group — Aviva's three and Charlotte's daughter, Allison. How would they be affected by the events in Toulon? To all four Eli had been close, but he retained a special affection for Allison. Lily, by choice, had remained childless. And then there was Colin, whose life had already been endangered by his father . . .

Eli set his calculator aside. There were far too many emotional issues that did not convert to numbers. It had been a futile exercise to attempt to place people in a coherent context. It was a battle he had been fighting — and losing — for quite some time.

One by one Eli broke the seals on the files. Diligently, he read every entry, searching for the most minute clues. By the end of the first week, Eli was discouraged. While he had sifted through hundreds of documents, no fresh information emerged. All was as he had remembered; there were no surprises.

On his second Sunday at his desk, he was convinced he was making no progress. An unsteady desk fan, one he had bought, whirred atop the splintery desktop. A jug of lukewarm tea was at his elbow. He was almost through the 1960s. After Cherbourg, the paperwork thinned.

Cherbourg.

All four of them had worked together masterfully on that mission. Any resentments from their undercover operations had to have been set aside by then or that complex, world-shattering deed could never have come off so splendidly.

Cherbourg.

He strained to convince himself the answer might be found there. Even if it seemed the most unlikely place of all.

CHERBOURG, FRANCE: DECEMBER 1969
Before his country's blitzkrieg victories of the Six-Day War, Eli had been concerned about the greatest weakness in the Israeli Defense Force — its World War II surplus navy. After Mossad agents supplied intelligence that the Arabs were acquiring sleek Russian-built Komar and Ossa gunboats armed with surface-to-surface missiles with ranges of up to thirty miles, Eli wrote a report stating that Israel

had no tactical response to this potential danger to its coastal cities.

"Our best defense against these ships is to obtain similar craft as soon as feasible, while overcoming the weaknesses inherent in them." He explained that while the Russian boats were equipped with missiles with huge warheads, the Israelis required a more self-contained ship with greater range and the ability to defend it from submarines and aircraft alike. Furthermore, he suggested it should be outfitted with the most modern electronic detection and control equipment. The paper was circulated widely at Aman.

During the early sixties, when Alex Naor was in military intelligence, he had made a secret trip into West Germany before it had established diplomatic relations with Israel. There he found what Israel was searching for — a rapid-response gunboat that had the capability of countering the Soviet threat by being able to respond quickly to an emergency. Under battle conditions the Jaguar could move at an astounding seventy kilometers per hour. Despite their differences, Alex Naor and Eli Katzar had managed to cooperate on matters relating to national security. Both had a hand in the development of the missile boat project and communication flowed freely between their offices. Privately, Eli had always been grateful that Naor was not close enough to breathe down his neck. At their separate agencies, they were on an equal, noncompetitive footing. Unfortunately, that was to change.

In the wake of the Lavon affair — when Meir Amit, Naor's boss at Aman, replaced Isser Harel as the head of the Mossad — Alex moved as well, once again proving his loyalty to a superior. Eli appraised Naor's motivations more dispassionately than some. Sterling opportunities for personal advancement appeared whenever there were changes within the structure of an organization, especially at the top. Alex's initial move to Aman (when his mentor, Boris Guriel, had fallen out of favor at the Mossad) had brought him front and center in the hierarchy of military intelligence, but, for whatever quirks of fate or personality, he had never been offered one of the top slots. His career would have stagnated there. So when the next occasion presented itself, he was quick to seize the chance to switch.

Alex's timing had been brilliant. Meir Amit was given charge of an intelligence agency without long-term directions. Nobody disagreed that Harel's teams had executed magnificent operations with limited manpower and funds, but his organization had been less successful in predicting political outcomes or analyzing the significance of the intelligence they gathered in terms of Israel's future. Loyal associates of Harel resigned within forty-eight hours of Amit's arrival.

Eli, who had always been an advocate of soothing bruised egos, confronted Amit with a novel proposition. "Why don't you consider recalling a senior Mossad station chief and making him your deputy to prove that the army isn't planning a takeover?"

Responding positively to the proposal, Amit summoned Pierre, Harel's top-ranking operative, from Paris (effectively promoting Lily to that post) and placed Pierre, at least nominally, in the role that Alex had coveted for himself — a slight Alex was to hold against Eli. Despite the fact this achieved an uneasy truce in the Mossad's ranks, Amit did not confide in or listen to this deputy, choosing instead to rely on his more tried and true advisers. So actually, Pierre became a figurehead and Alex's influence was in no way diminished.

Finally, Alex Naor was rewarded for his persistence and dedication by being given carte blanche to run his own missions as well as oversee foreign espionage affairs. During his first week on the job, Alex marshaled all the department heads, Eli included, and advised them that they each were to adhere more closely to their individual areas of specialization.

"At first, you may think that we are limiting your scope," Alex began one of his early briefings. "Eventually, you will notice your horizons will widen under this new system." He further delineated stringent regulations regarding analysis and paperwork. "Yes, you must back all your assumptions, but we are willing to give you access to Aman's research staff. After digesting the data, you will be expected to provide reports with a *philosophic* basis, as well as a technical one."

This order had surprised and delighted Eli, who always approached problems from both points of view, perhaps because his first mentor had been Shiloah. So, for the most part, his years under Amit continued to be fruitful ones and the statistics his department amassed were considered invaluable.

Amit, who had overcome some of Harel's squeamishness about the use of women in the field, had approved Lily's mission to the camps in Jericho and had been kept apprised of the bulletins on terrorist activities that had come from this impressive field operative.

"If a man in my position would be permitted favorites, Lily would be the certain winner," he once confided to Eli after receiving news of Rashid's connection with the PLO leader Ahmed al-Shuqairy.

Although Charlotte was inactive for the most part, her work in Egypt had been the backbone of information relating to the German

scientists who had become even more visible in recent years. Her aerial reconnaissance photos were considered the basis for subsequent
investigation into Egypt's defense build-ups. While at Aman, Amit
had been involved in all aspects of the MiG theft, and he had personally worked on Gideon Tabor's tragic situation.

By the time the Six-Day War was fought, some military analysts
would credit the combined efforts of the Mossad and Aman for Israel's decisive victory. "All I can say," commended Moshe Dayan,
"is that the role of intelligence was as important as that of the air
force or the armored corps."

The accolades in the aftermath of the war bolstered everyone in
the Israeli secret services. A period of spirited cooperation reigned
domestically, while on the international front, crucial alliances
soured. When an Israeli commando unit staged a raid on Beirut's
airport to retaliate for the Arab destruction of an El Al plane in
Athens, and thirteen aircraft, two of them French, were destroyed,
de Gaulle (who was under considerable pressure to appease the oil-
controlling Arab states) imposed an embargo on the shipment of armaments to Israel, including the fleet of Jaguar missile boats under
construction at the Cherbourg shipyard of Felix Amiot.

An emergency intelligence meeting was called. Ten men, including Eli Katzar and Alex Naor, gathered in a conference room in a
Tel Aviv office building near the Ministry of Defense headquarters.

Alex, even when seated, towered above the group. He pointed to
folders in front of each of the division chiefs. "These contain the dossier on the history of the project from the Lurssen architectural plans
to the German engine designs. Pay attention to the background information on Felix Amiot, the French industrialist who accepted the
project under the direction of Admiral Mordechai Limon." He
paused. Everyone present was familiar with the illustrious man who,
by the age of twenty-six, had become the commander in chief of the
Israeli navy. Limon now lived in France, where he was in charge of
military purchasing.

Alex beckoned a man in a rumpled khaki shirt to step forward.
"Misha Yuval will update us on the most recent events."

The stocky operative, who had once been known as Pierre, addressed the group. "As you know, five of our gunboats were safely in
Haifa before de Gaulle's embargo was contemplated. I am authorized to announce that the sixth boat cleared Cherbourg Harbor this
morning. This was after de Gaulle gave his order, but before it took
effect legally."

A spontaneous clapping commenced in the room but was quickly stilled by one wave of Misha's broad hand. "Captain Moshe Tabak, our senior officer at the Cherbourg project, and a skeleton crew sailed out with the seventh boat unimpeded the next morning, despite the fact the impoundment was officially implemented by that date." This unexpected news was met by an even louder burst of applause.

Misha Yuval held up his hand again. "Our friend de Gaulle is helping in spite of himself. Yesterday, he informed the Ministry of Defense that the remaining boats would no longer be welcome at the French naval station once they were launched. The only place they can be fitted out appears to be the old ferryboat dock at the commercial pier. This removes them from a high-security environment. Furthermore, after next week, the Israeli sailors may no longer live in the barracks. This will free them of the tight military surveillance which has hampered their movements."

Eli began to make rapid notes on the tablet in front of him as charts of the Cherbourg area were being set out in the room. After filling up several pages with lists of questions and possible courses of action, he went back to the first page of his pad and printed out a title: "Operation Noah's Ark." Underneath, he made a list of talent to call to the fore. Lily was already involved because of her association with Admiral Limon, and nobody except Misha Yuval had a better grasp of how to maneuver in France. In a controlled French seaport — one where nuclear submarines were currently under construction — Eli wanted his most reliable, most experienced, most *invisible* operatives in place. The necessity for skilled manpower outweighed any petty prejudices or personality conflicts and so Alex did not veto the resurrection of the Ezra team.

Following Eli's original concept, the groups were named after the members of Noah's family. Misha Yuval's Shem group was entrusted to study the design specifications of the boats and make recommendations on how they could be altered to hasten their completion. Mossad agents in a dozen European cities were asked to pretend to be owners of tankers crippled in distant harbors requiring crucial parts. Thus, piece by piece, ancillary equipment was delivered to the Cherbourg area and stored in a warehouse rented under a name not associated with the Israelis.

The Ham group, led by Naor, was to satisfy Dayan's orders that the boats not depart France illegally. Aided by the Jewish president of a fruit transportation company, they contacted Ole Martin Siem, a Norwegian shipping magnate. Siem was persuaded to purchase the missile boats for shuttling equipment to his North Sea oil-drilling rigs. No matter that these swift, expensive boats would be as ridiculously out of place as a Ferrari employed as a milk truck; the Norwegian could always claim he found it impossible to resist a bargain. On the fifth of November, the "Starboat Shipping and Oil Drilling Company" was hastily registered in Panama to purchase the ships. If the French authorities failed to see through the ruse, surely Amiot, the builder, was not deceived. What did he care? Wasn't this the best way of finishing the project and getting paid? Even after the paperwork was completed, the Israelis felt they had to move swiftly before somebody recognized the irregularities that riddled the entire transaction.

Eli's Japheth group, composed of the original Ezra team, was to coordinate the ships' departure from France. Being together again — from the initial planning stages through the entire mission — gave them a sense of camaraderie they had not experienced in a long time. In Israel, Aviva began the recruitment proceedings. Minimal crews had been berthed in Cherbourg to test the boats since construction had begun, but five times that number were required to sail the boats to Israel. And since they were working for Siem, they had to appear to be Nordic seamen. The raw recruits, as blond and fair a group as could be found, had to be hastily trained in basic intelligence procedures and conduct, as well as the rudiments of seamanship and Norwegian.

With a December target date for departure, Aviva made all the travel arrangements. Eli's directives specified that no more than two sailors could journey together. Some were to arrive in Marseille by ship and then travel to Cherbourg by train via Paris. Others were originally ticketed by air to Italy and then to Cherbourg by rail, but had to be rerouted at the last minute because of an Italian railway strike. Because Aviva was not dealing with highly trained Mossad agents, she had given each a slip of paper with two contacts: the emergency phone number of an officer at the Israeli Minister of Defense's purchasing mission in Paris and the address where they would be met in Cherbourg.

Alex Naor objected vociferously. "What if one, just one of the sixty, is questioned by a French authority — even for a traffic violation?"

"They understand the need to be extra cautious," Eli explained. "All will be using public transportation for that reason."

"We have never sent an agent out into the field with a typed itinerary before. It is as bizarre as giving a rabbi a ham sandwich for a picnic!"

"Come now, Alex, wouldn't it be more likely for one of these unsophisticated Israelis to get lost or confused? All we've given them is a telephone number so they won't have to seek assistance from a stranger, and their final destination, something most travelers write down routinely."

Alex had not appeared to be mollified, but he did not thwart the plan either.

By the first of December, Charlotte had taken up residence at the Sofitel Hotel in Cherbourg. Her cover was that of an employee of the Norwegian shipping firm in charge of accounting and payroll. This enabled her to organize the provisioning of the boats.

During her final visit to the ferryboat docks on the twenty-third of December, she delivered a gift tied with red and green ribbons to each ship. Inside each package was a detail that was quintessentially Charlotte — she had located five Panamanian flags, which were to be hoisted as the missile boats set sail.

Eli worked on the logistics of getting the boats out of the port. By a set of complex calculations, he had figured out how to obtain a quarter of a million liters of petrol. Because sea trials were conducted routinely on all the vessels, a specific amount — not enough to cause suspicion, but more than was necessary — had been requisitioned each time until every ship had a sufficient, if not abundant, supply. Refueling once under way would still be required.

For several weeks, Lily coordinated the observations made in and around the naval base to discover the nature of the water traffic at night. Cherbourg Harbor, a wide, welcoming curve at the tip of a Normandy peninsula jutting out into the English Channel, was one of the busiest in Europe. Passenger ferries served Weymouth, Southampton, and Portsmouth in England; French naval operations regularly churned the waterways and kept the town's economy alive.

Lily met Eli at a hotel room more than a hundred kilometers away in Caen, which was considered far safer than being seen together in Cherbourg, to brief him about the difficulties in moving the ships out of the harbor. She unfurled the Stanford chart to explain the possibilities.

His finger pointed to a spot above St.-Pierre-Eglise. "Cap Lévy!" He chuckled. "I see our boys have been on the scene longer than I expected!"

"I have wondered about that myself." Lily grinned momentarily. "See these lines here?" She began his briefing in earnest. "This is a two-mile-long sea wall which protects the harbor from the open sea to the north. There are three passages through the wall: the Passe Cabart Danneville at the southeast corner, but it is not advised due to tidal streams and rocks near the channel; the Passe de l'Est, where one must beware of rocks off the Ile Pelée as well as strong currents; and finally, the Passe de l'Ouest, which is the easiest, even though one must remain clear of the right sector near the lighthouse. I have made runs in a small craft on four occasions with a depth sounder to double-check the situation in each of the channels. The western channel is the one most ships prefer. The trouble is that the jetty beside it is a part of the military base."

"Do you think they'd open fire on us?"

"It is an unlikely eventuality, but one we cannot ignore."

"Does anyone ever take the eastern route?"

"A few small craft during calm weather. Not many captains would take the chance to save only a short distance to the open sea. Nevertheless, my soundings have convinced me that the gunboats, with their shallow draft, could make it."

Eli's major concern was the weather. A portable meteorological station and radio center were set up in a building near the wharf. They were manned by an expert, but the reports were analyzed by Aviva. Every weather forecast in English, French, and Spanish was monitored and charted. Tendencies of cold fronts to either linger or pass through rapidly were calculated daily. Eli doubted whether any of the figures would enable them to anticipate conditions on the departure day.

All was in readiness for the optimum moment of departure: 20:30 hours Christmas Eve, when everyone in Cherbourg would be sitting down to their holiday meals. For two days Aviva had been worried over a developing storm pattern, but Eli chose to be optimistic. Unfortunately, the reports the morning of the twenty-fourth were most unfavorable. The VHF radio broadcasts on channel 11, updated at twenty and fifty past the hour, spoke of storm clouds rolling in from the west. The sky lowered into a gunmetal dome and Eli could see the heavy sea pounding the breakwater when he strolled by at noon; even so, he refused to delay the operation. After lunch he stopped by "the gloom room," as he had begun to refer to radio headquarters, only to hear for himself the dire report broadcast by BBC Radio 4.

"The shipping forecast for home waters," the announcer began crisply. "A strong south-southeast wind is gusting at forty knots along the entire Bay of Biscay." Aviva spun the dial to 2691 kHz for the St.-Malo frequency. "Gale warnings are in effect from fourteen hundred —" Angrily, Eli turned to 1694 kHz for France-Inter's bulletins out of Boulogne. "Rafales à force sept."

Silently, Aviva handed Eli a copy of the Beaufort scale. Under "Force Seven" he read aloud: "*Wind speed:* twenty-eight to thirty-three knots, near gale conditions. *State of sea:* sea heaps up, white foam streaks begin blowing from crests. *Probable wave height:* five point five meters." He tossed the paper down with disgust. "Could not be worse."

Aviva shook her head sadly.

"Bloody hell!"

Quite soon a fine rain began to blow inland and by midafternoon a downpour pummeled the town. By seven that evening, the boats were still on standby to sail, but the weather deteriorated even further. Force-eight winds were gusting at forty knots.

At 22:30, the second scheduled departure time, the winds had only increased. Coup de vent, or full gale-force winds, were pounding the French coast. All the crews remained at their stations, ready to pull out on a moment's notice. Eli had Aviva tune in the secret frequencies to Tel Aviv. In code, Alex was commanding the boats to depart! Eli replied that he refused to implement the order. Alex backed off reluctantly. An hour later the forecast for France's zones one to eleven, which included Cherbourg, reported the winds dropping to force six. Eli's optimism returned.

Lily and Charlotte joined them at the command post just after midnight. "The wind's going to change," Charlotte predicted cheerfully.

"How can you tell?" Eli asked.

"When I walked the streets I felt as if a great weight had been lifted from my heart. I know it sounds crazy, but it was a very palpable sensation — like a change in the pressure."

Eli seemed skeptical, but the meteorological expert's enthusiasm was roused. "I know that very feeling. Let me look outside." He glanced far off into the hazy night sky. "Do you see that small patch of stars in the distance?"

Eli noticed only the tiniest hole of clear sky. "Yes, but —"

"That's the front moving closer."

At 02:15 on Christmas morning, BBC Radio 4 announced, "Winds along the coast have shifted to the north."

"That will be fine once the boats reach the channel and proceed along the coast of Brittany," Lily commented.

"They are supposed to be dropping to twenty knots with gusts to thirty possible," Aviva pointed out.

Eli caught her eye and then Lily's. He took the microphone from Aviva's hands as she turned the dial to the frequency that would be picked up in the radio room of each ship. "O-two-thirty," he announced in a firm voice.

At that time precisely — so there would be one chorus of engines instead of five separate roars — twenty motors (four for each boat), with a combined sixty-five thousand horsepower, revved up. Within minutes, all five cast off and headed for the open sea. The lead boat was the *Soufa*, which, appropriately, means "Tempest" in Hebrew — however, this name had been hastily covered with a sign designating it *Starboat One*.

The Israeli intelligence agents in the vicinity were filled with apprehension. Would the weather cooperate? Would their guesses as to the navigability of the narrower, shallower channel be vindicated?

A few minutes after the boats chugged out of the harbor in a single line, all eyes were directed to the sea. While the French government may not have known what was going on (or had chosen not to act on its knowledge), apparently the harbor community had not been as fooled as Eli's team had believed, for, one by one, lights blinked on in the houses that encircled the waterfront. From a few windows, people waved out into the night. These shipbuilders, who had put so much craftsmanship into the boats and had worked side by side with the Israelis for so many years, could not but wish them well on their journey to their rightful home.

By the time radio transmissions acknowledged the fleet was out in the English Channel and heading for the Atlantic Ocean with no difficulties to report, the Israeli operatives had left Cherbourg. By the time the boats were refueled along the route, they had left France as well.

In less than a week, from a cliff above Haifa, the reunited Ezra team watched as Israeli jets swooped out of the sky to welcome the five boats; in France, an irate President Pompidou addressed his cabinet. "We have been made to look complete fools because of the incredible casualness and intellectual complicity of our civil servants."

Four years later, during the Yom Kippur War, these twelve missile boats had to prove whether their advanced design would perform under fire. By then, two more Israeli-built boats had joined the fleet. Outfitted with the Israeli-designed Gabriel missiles, forty-millimeter anti-aircraft guns, depth charges, and other conventional light weapons, they were controlled by advanced electronic gear for tracking and disrupting enemy ships and aircraft. The Israeli navy had managed to concentrate maximum firepower in the smallest vessel possible.

When an assault along the Mediterranean coast was suspected, the missile fleet proceeded toward the Syrian port of Latakia. This fast, highly maneuverable armada — consisting of four of the Cherbourg vessels and one of the newer Israeli-built versions — appeared with lightning speed and took the Syrian warships by surprise. Every Gabriel missile, with its enemy-seeking guidance system, found its target, and three Arab ships went down; none of the Syrian Styx missiles, whose radar guidance systems were jammed by the Israelis to throw them off course, found their mark. Not a single Israeli vessel was sunk, despite the fact that some fifty-two missiles were fired at Israeli targets. Confirmed enemy losses were nineteen vessels, including ten Arab missile boats.

No longer would Israel's enemies boast they controlled the sea lanes or had the power to blockade Israel's ports.

TEL AVIV, ISRAEL: APRIL 1979

As late as 1973 Eli and his cohorts continued to bask in their glorious success at Cherbourg. Until Toulon, it was the last mission all four would share. After the world's press had fêted the arrival of the ships in Haifa, Eli's team dissolved and went back to their lives of studied ordinariness. The part the Ezra group had played in the French seaport had been workmanlike. There had been moments of excitement, highlighted by the thrilling departure of the boats from the storm-tossed harbor, but mostly it had been the unglamorous stuff of coordinating thousands of petty details. The only praise they had received was from within the upper echelons of the Mossad. If Alex Naor had worried about Charlotte and Aviva being taken out of retirement and retrained with only a few weeks' updating on current methods, he had to have been impressed with the competence and professionalism Eli's old-timers demonstrated.

Eli closed the file on Cherbourg. Nothing in those thick volumes hinted at dissension in the ranks. All three women had performed

expertly. Not a single leak had been detected among any of the professional and amateur recruits. Afterward, Eli had heard each of his
women speak of the incident with a twinge of longing. Perhaps that
was why he had included them in Toulon. Ten years after Cherbourg he had offered them one final fling, one last chance to make a
mark. How presumptuous he had been to think *he* was doing *them* a
favor by involving them in the plan. He had fallen into the well-documented trap of believing it was all a grand game instead of a
deadly serious business.

The time had come to confront the issue. The explanation was not
lurking among the outdated government documents. He would have
to face them one by one. First Aviva. Then Lily. And Charlotte.

Yes.

At last Eli felt he was joining the real world. What had taken him
so long?

Years ago, while he worked under Isser Harel, he had drafted a
paper on this very pitfall. Eventually, his theories had been incor-
porated into the Mossad curriculum and he himself had lectured on
the subject to recruits who had progressed from the stage of being
wary and cautious to the cocky phase where they were beginning to
feel the slightest bit infallible. He had labeled his concept konenut
matmedet — the necessity for living constantly on the edge of fear.
The first hours, days, even weeks of living with exquisite vigilance
gave one a superior level of alertness. Smells were more pungent,
food had a more vivid taste, sensuality increased, orgasms intensified.

"Our little reward." He chuckled to ease the tension among his
students. "But to be fair I would have to mention that some report
the opposite effect. What happens is that these profound sensations
are muted after a time. Why? Because no one can sustain a height-
ened level of circumspection twenty-four hours a day. So what is the
result? Relaxation occurs. Not at once. It happens so slowly, so inexorably, that the agent is unaware of the change. One cannot live on
the edge forever. It strains one's mental and physical resources. I
have no scientific proof, but I would expect that the body has only a
limited supply of adrenaline to pump into the blood stream. At some
point, the chemical secretions begin to subside. Whatever the physio-
logical responses may be, the edge dulls and a potentially dangerous
sense of well-being takes over."

Eli gave many examples of how to recognize this pattern of behavior in oneself and others, illustrating the talk with tales of tragedies

and near misses caused by laxness. "How can we battle this insidious syndrome which takes the extraordinary and reduces it to the habitual?" he asked, then went on to give practical advice on varying one's diet, sleeping patterns, and routines.

Nobody had fallen further than Eli. He had been suspended between the true and the false for far too long. By the time he had organized Toulon, he had broken every rule he had ever followed — or made. At last the paralysis was lifting.

The dingy walls of Eli's Tel Aviv office seemed to close in on him. He could not tolerate another day of stale air and unyielding bureaucratic minutiae. He tapped the papers into a tidy stack and replaced them in their folders. He lined up the color-coded packets by date and layered them into the padlocked transfer satchel. Eli went out into the hall, handed the satchel to the guard, and demanded to be buzzed out.

The midafternoon sun was a flash of white after the grimy bleakness of the building. The heat scorched the thinning spot on his scalp, but with determined strides he kept heading along Dizengoff Street, turned on Mendeli Street, and, several blocks later, was standing in front of the Dan Travel Agency. With but a moment's hesitation, he opened the plate glass door.

❖   ❖   ❖

From her desk in the middle of the room, Aviva kept one eye on the door. She noticed Eli's entrance at once. All the agents were busy with customers and she was cradling a phone on her shoulder while taking notes. Thrusting her pen downward, she gestured for Eli to sit. He took a seat on the green plastic sofa he had helped her select when she opened the business. Absently, he thumbed through a cruise brochure.

Aviva's management style was to remain front and center. There were no walls in her agency. The seven agents' desks formed a horseshoe around her own so queries could be passed back to her with the stretch of an arm. When Aviva was away from the office, her second in command, who had also received intelligence training, moved to Aviva's desk and performed the same trouble-shooting functions. The Dan Agency booked trips at the lowest possible fares while giving personalized service to its clientele, so the furniture was utilitarian and the decorations were standard travel posters and large racks of brochures.

Aviva had called the business after her brother, Dan, although most people supposed it had some connection with the nearby Dan Hotel. The unwitting association had been useful to Aviva. From the first it had been successful enough to support her and the children. During Gideon's imprisonment, she had invested her considerable energies in building its reputation. After Gideon's release, she had hoped he would take an interest in the firm, but the opposite had been true.

The world of commerce seemed coldly remote from the survival questions Gideon's skills addressed, so he channeled his energies toward aiding men who had been through the experience of captivity and torture. If Aviva was disappointed in having to manage the business alone, she had never confided these feelings to Eli. Instead, he had come to believe that separate interests were useful in the sustenance of their relationship. Aviva traveled alone two or three times a year to check out itineraries, carriers, and services. Gideon lectured all over Israel, was a consultant on Iraqi affairs to several branches of the government, and was writing a book on prison reform from his unique perspective.

Eli looked up. Aviva was replacing the telephone receiver. She came forward to greet him. She was smiling.

"Shalom, Eli." They kissed each other on the cheeks. "Did you have a good trip? When did you get back?"

He replied with the usual vague politenesses.

"You've added another desk, haven't you?"

"Two. A smaller agency closed and I got some of their best people."

"Mazel tov. I know you don't usually go out at noon, but might you make a special exception today?"

"Why not?" she replied.

When they were on the street, he said, "I must ask you to come back to the apartment where I am staying." He waved down a taxi before she could reply. "Monit!"

From a shop on the ground floor of his building, he purchased pita, falafel, salads, and pastries. "I do not take more than a cup of coffee in the middle of the day," Aviva protested.

"I would rather not eat alone."

Upstairs he laid out plates and cups, and brewed a pot of American-style coffee. Aviva walked to the large picture window overlooking Tel Aviv and the Mediterranean before joining him in the kitchen. "You have one of the best views in the city. Do you like it here?"

"Not especially. It's very drafty and the elevators are always breaking down."

She stared out the kitchen window and pointed to the Ministry of Defense rooftops that were studded with a forest of telecommunications equipment. "The first bomb will land right there."

"You're even more pessimistic than I am."

"Is that possible?" She grinned. "Have you ever been in 'the pit'? " she asked unexpectedly.

Eli was not surprised she knew that the heart of Israel's technologically astounding defense control system was located nearby in a subterranean maze, but he did not respond to her question.

For a few minutes they busied themselves slicing tomatoes and cucumbers, stirring hummus, placing olives in a dish and poppy seed cakes on a platter. Eli carried the meal into the dining room. They sat in mahogany chairs with intricately carved backs and gazed at each other. Recently, Aviva had taken to touching up the flecks of silver in her dark hair, and her face, which had seemed so strong when she was younger, had aged more gracefully than most. The prominent bones were softened by the fullness of her cheeks and chin, and she had learned how to make the most of her imperfect figure by dressing in tailored silk suits of the most flattering color and cut. Her hammered gold jewelry, which might have seemed heavy or excessive on a slighter woman, added to her substantial appearance without seeming gaudy and complemented her unusual skin tone. Eli could honestly say she had probably never looked more handsome in her life.

Without the slightest idea of how to embark on what had to be considered an interrogation, he began with pleasantries about her family. Aviva gave a few brief replies, then called his bluff. "Eli, I have left a busy office to come here. Is there another assignment coming up? Is that what this is all about?"

"Why, would you welcome one?"

Aviva moistened her lips and gave the idea some consideration. "No, I think not. I had settled in my mind that Toulon was the final one. I will not lie to you, it *was* a strain. I am at a point in life where I like my comforts more than ever before."

"What about the agency? Will you give it up?"

"No. Even if I wanted to, I could not. We are dependent on the income. Gideon —"

Eli gestured that explanations were unnecessary. In the silence, he considered how to make the conversation more productive. He wanted to know about her disappointments, her regrets, her reasons for betraying them all — if that was in fact what she had done. It seemed unbelievable, unthinkable — but it *had* happened and he could no longer luxuriate in the romantic delusion that she, or either of the others, was immune. As he tried to phrase the next question, a fresh approach formed in his mind.

"I have my own regrets," he began. Aviva put down her pita bread.

"Are you admitting you are human after all?"

"Yes. Enough to be jealous of you and Gideon."

"That is ridiculous. You know very well our marriage — "

"Not that so much as the children."

"Having Hillel stationed on the Golan Heights in '73 was the worst moment of my life. At least without children you have been spared those worries."

"Not entirely —"

"Why, Eli, don't tell me you have finally found someone. For a man, it is never too late. I know three, maybe four, men who became fathers in their late fifties."

"I have a son," he said evenly.

Aviva gasped. "You — a child?"

"Hardly a child. He's over thirty and expecting a baby of his own quite shortly."

"Why have you never —?"

He cut her off. "A wartime romance . . . The girl did not want to marry me . . . It was not the sort of thing one talked about in those days."

"You have kept in touch with the boy?"

"Yes. It's all very complicated."

Aviva took a sip of coffee before she spoke again. "You have quite overwhelmed me. All these years . . . Why do you tell me now?"

"Perhaps it is a part of a summing up, finishing the business I started so many years ago when I recruited you. So many secrets, they become a burden after a while. I suppose I want to unload the ones I can before . . ."

"Yes?"

". . . before retiring."

"Have you been asked to?"

"No, but it's coming."

"Why? Toulon was a great success."

"Partially."

"The explosions — the reactor parts — everything was destroyed and nobody injured."

"We lost an operative."

"No!" Aviva replaced her cup in the saucer and went to the picture window. Down on the street a bomb squad vehicle wailed by. "That is why we have not seen you since," she said with her back to him. "You have been investigating the case."

"That's partly it." He stared at her with an icy expression. "Someone was after me as well."

Aviva spun around. "Eli, are you certain?"

"I believe so." He responded as blandly as possible because he did not want her to hear the relief he felt at the genuineness of her shock. Aviva was the unlikeliest suspect of them all, but he had to continue his questioning to satisfy his superiors.

"Do you need my help? I could take another leave of absence . . ."

"No, Aviva, that's not necessary. If you can think back and tell me of anything unusual that happened before, during, or after Toulon. The smallest detail might give me a clue. You worked with the two boys, André and Michel. Could they have been compromised?"

"They behaved perfectly."

"Anything else? Anyone contact you? Anyone with access to your files, your radio codes?"

"Impossible. I had total control over everything at all times." As Aviva paced the room, her high heels clicked an unnerving rhythm on the tile floor. "Can you tell me the details of the crime?"

"Not at present."

"I did not expect you could. But you want my help. That is why you came for me. Am I right?"

"In a way."

Aviva walked over to Eli and stroked his shoulder sympathetically. "I have never seen you so confused except . . ."

"Yes?"

". . . when Gideon was captured."

"You went to Iraq under my authority. I often wonder if I had the right —"

"I know you have always held that belief, dear, but you must remember I was a Palmachnik long before I ever laid eyes on you, Eli Katzar. You also tend to forget who trained whom. After '48 I wanted nothing more than to continue to serve Israel; I was looking for any opportunity. The Political Department was exactly what *I* wanted. Nobody twisted my arm."

She took his hand in hers. With a gentle firmness she began to massage his fingers. "I know what you are thinking. You want me to berate you for sending me Gideon. All right, for a time I *was* resentful. There was another in my life, but once I discovered he was unattainable, I decided Gideon would suit as well as any other. Have I ever told you about that other man?"

Eli was confused. Here he was supposed to be running the conversation, but she had taken over the control. He shook his head in response to her question.

"We both had our little secrets. You had your son, I have had my love affairs."

Eli could not imagine her having a string of attentive suitors. All the years Gideon had been away, he had felt sorry for her having to raise her family single-handedly but had not concerned himself with the deficit in her love life. Of all the women, Aviva had seemed the least sexual.

She laughed aloud at his obvious shock. "I cannot help but wonder at a man with your astuteness being so blind. Eli, it is *you* I loved. From the earliest days at Kibbutz Hazorea, I wanted you to notice me. When I was called to the Foreign Ministry, I was certain your hand was in it. It always surprised me when you did not take me in your arms and carry me away." To break the tension, she returned to the dining room and poured them each a second cup of coffee. She placed the cups on the living room table and sat down opposite Eli. "You do not appear shocked."

"I suppose I knew. However, I would have denied it if someone else had suggested it. I also felt a pull toward you at the kibbutz, but at the time I was much too — I was going to say dedicated, but the correct word is ambitious. Yes. I was too ambitious to tie myself to a woman."

"Then you sent Gideon to me."

"Don't forget it was *you* who wanted to *marry* him. We never made that a condition. We never would have."

"I know. It seemed so sensible at the time. I liked Gideon, and he me. From the first there were some very genuine feelings between us. Now the only interest we share is the children and even with them Gideon is somewhat detached. I think that may be because he was away from them during so many critical years. You and I can never imagine the suffering he carries with him. Perhaps that is why he devotes so much time to his work with the other victims. He can relate to them better than to us."

She went on for a while. Eli was not so much interested in what she was saying as her manner. There was no long-standing acrimony.

He tried to bring the point back to himself. "I didn't keep my promises to you."

"Most of them."

"When you started the agency, I left you on your own. I should have looked in more. I'd promised to help."

"No. I was becoming too dependent on you. For a while I even permitted myself to imagine us together . . ."

"I will admit that I encouraged your fantasies. There was a time I had decided to marry you if the worst happened. I assumed we could be great friends and —"

"No, Eli. It would have compounded the mistake. I married Gideon for the sake of safety — not only the security inherent in the legal paperwork of being officially wed but also knowing that no matter what happened, I would not be alone. And look how alone I have been. There is no protection from loneliness. I cannot say that I did not desire you. I did. As I remember it, you reacted to my need by withdrawing. My initial fury eventually diminished to a more manageable resentment. Then, I knew that I had to keep my distance from you to prevent your guilt and my longings from ruining our friendship. Truthfully, we would have been *awful* together."

She took a sip of coffee and smiled shyly. "Then a curious thing happened. Because I felt rejected by you, I needed to prove to myself that there was nothing wrong with *me*. That is when I discovered I was a desirable woman. I had many lovers."

Aviva's frankness was startling. "The other men ... Did they know about your career?"

"Absolutely not. Why? Are you suspecting the leak came through me?"

"*I'm* not, but others may require clarification."

"You are in trouble, aren't you?" Aviva stared so harshly, Eli had to force himself not to avert his gaze.

"The same trouble I would be in if you or any other agent under my jurisdiction was killed. I am required to furnish answers to some difficult questions. I must follow every lead. Since I have never been privileged with the knowledge of your lovers, I must eliminate any possibility of —"

"Quite reasonable, Eli. I am not angry with you for asking. Let me assure you that the complete, scintillating details are yours if you need them. I am afraid you will not find anyone too glamorous or controversial on my list. You knew two of them from your school days; a few I met abroad and were of no consequence."

"I would need to know more about the foreigners."

"If you like. One was a furrier from Boston, another" — she laughed — "a pickle merchant. Really! Then there was a violinist with the New York Philharmonic. I seem to appeal to balding, American Jews who find a sabra quite glamorous. Oh, there was a Japanese journalist about ten years ago and —"

Eli stopped her confessions. "That's irrelevant. What I need to know is if there was anyone more recent, anyone prior to Toulon?"

Aviva's mouth curved downward, her eyelids closed, she folded her hands neatly in her lap. "Nobody for two years now. The last one — the violinist — died from cancer. Since then I have lost interest."

"I am sorry, Aviva."

"I wish I could help you."

As Eli stood up and began to gather their plates and cups, he felt utterly relieved. Aviva's romantic revelations had been shocking for the moment, but in perspective they diminished the responsibility he felt for her happiness and eliminated her main motive for disaffection.

"Do you need to go back to the office?" he asked. If she did not, he was going to propose they see a movie and have a late dinner together. He was tired of eating alone.

She looked at her watch. "I am afraid I have some paperwork to complete." She walked toward the door. "Eli, you need someone. I know some lovely ladies I would like you to meet." She opened the door. "Call me when you get back from France," she urged as she moved to the elevator and pressed the button. It opened immediately.

"Yes, I will," he answered as the elevator door closed. "L'hitra'ot," he called. "Until we meet again —" His voice caught in his throat. How had Aviva known his next stop would be Paris? He stared out into the dim hallway, dumbfounded.

❖ ❖ ❖

Aviva had had the last word. This had never been her manner with him, and the switch, like that of her clothes and the revelation of sexual liaisons, was irksome indeed. Somewhere along the line he had lost track of what kind of a person she was. In his early role as a case officer, Eli borrowed from J. C. Masterman's postwar theories on spycraft and could quote verbatim from his stratagems. The one he had held most dear stated, "It cannot be too strongly insisted that the most profitable cases were those in which the case officer had introduced himself most completely into the skin of the agent." Believing that he had done just that with his agents, he now recognized that while such closeness may have been possible in the beginning, it could not be sustained over so many years.

In fact, he had always underestimated Aviva. From the first, he had seen her as a unique Israeli resource — as malleable as native clay — who would do anything for her country. She had the attachment to her people and land that no outsider would ever comprehend. The central force of the sturdy sabra's childhood had been the defense of her kibbutz. The murders of her mother and brother had been the catalysts for her militancy. She had been an ideal intelligence candidate.

Eli remained perplexed. He had given Aviva every opportunity to show her hand, yet nothing surfaced. If she had something to hide, she would have been more circumspect. Nevertheless, she had not skirted his questions and had volunteered information about her private life. All these thoughts spun around in Eli's mind as he cleaned up after lunch.

His analysis took another turn: Aviva was so proficient in masquerading she might have fooled him entirely. Maybe he had dropped his suspicions of her too rapidly. Maybe he would have to find a way to interrogate her more aggressively.

With a dishtowel Eli wiped down the red granite counter until it glowed. Had he been the victim of Mossad doublethink this afternoon? Let us say Aviva had something to hide and knew what he was after. The best way to convince him that he was on the wrong track was to be so guileless and candid that all mistrust melted. With this in mind, Eli reviewed the afternoon's conversation for hesitations, deceptions, loopholes . . .

How had she known about Paris?

Bloody hell!

He made his way to the bedroom, mentally flogging himself for his idiocy. He pulled out a large Hebrew-English dictionary and removed the folder behind it. Inside was his ticket to France and the States. In the upper right-hand corner, in the box for date and place of issue, he read: IATA 979008, the Dan Agency's number for airline reimbursement. The agency was listed as Global Ltd., a more generalized corporate title that used a Rome address to disguise the Israeli origin of the ticket. At the bottom were two sets of initials, for the person who booked the ticket and the one who wrote it. His read: TY/LS. While these did not stand for anyone he knew, Aviva probably used codes of her own. For years, she had personally handled the most sensitive ticketing — for undercover agents and government officials. His stupidity in the matter was acutely embarrassing.

He would have to look elsewhere for his betrayer. All in all, Aviva was a woman to be admired. If Gideon had not returned, he might well have married her, and despite her protestations, she would have succumbed to him. But Gideon had been released and become a national hero. Eli could not help but compare his years of unsung service with Gideon's one long sacrifice. Gideon had suffered greatly, that went without question, but Eli had produced more — and nobody would ever know it.

As much as Eli hated envy in others, he despised it most in himself.

14

Does not he to whom you betray another, to whom you were as welcome as to himself, know that you will at another time do as much for him?

Michel de Montaigne (1533–1592)
Of Profit and Honesty

TEL AVIV, ISRAEL: MAY 1979

The flight from Tel Aviv to Paris departed at nine in the morning. Eli arrived at Ben-Gurion Airport an hour early and passed through the security entrance. As he waited, he watched the regular passengers going through the stringent clearance procedures.

"Did you purchase anything in Gaza or the West Bank?" the guards, all military-trained in the psychological profiles of terrorists, asked each traveler.

"Where? What shop?"

"Please open your luggage."

"What's packed in here?"

The guards observed eye movements and gestures. They were particularly interested in young women from European countries, people with Arabic features, men traveling alone. Babies' diapers, groceries, camera equipment, bottles, book bags, and purses were all hand-searched.

"Did anyone give you anything to carry?"

"How long did you stay in Israel?"

"What is your destination?"

Reassured that the young men and women were doing a thorough job, Eli made his way to the departure lounge and was among the first to board the aircraft. He stowed his briefcase and closed his eyes.

Whenever he had visited Lily in the past, he had looked forward to it immensely. They had an easy manner with each other, and despite the fact that their sole intimate encounter had been baffling, their reunions were always pleasurable. Obviously, this was going to be a more stressful encounter than most, but he sensed it would be less arduous than the one he had just had with Aviva or the one that would follow with Charlotte.

The stewardess presented her safety lecture to the passengers. The jet engines rumbled. The great metal tube sped forward into the sky. He watched as the airplane banked over the Mediterranean, then closed his eyes once more and thought about Aviva. Was he confident he could seal her file? No, not yet. Charlotte or Lily might reveal something that would rekindle his suspicion.

All his life Eli had trusted nothing and no one. Everyone was a suspect. No mailman, waiter, or steward was entirely written off as benign at first glance. Or so he had tried to convince himself. Had he ignored the corollary to this system of thought? If he trusted no one, did that mean he placed his confidence in everyone equally?

A gentle "ping" indicated the seat belt sign had been turned off. "Passengers are now free to move about the cabin." Eli stood up in the aisle and allowed his seatmates — an elderly couple with New York accents — to make their way to the rest rooms in the rear. He willed himself to order his speculations. He knew where he had to begin. He closed his eyes and recalled his glorious mistake at the Dukes.

LONDON, ENGLAND: AUGUST 1956

The Dukes Hotel looked much the same then as it had only a few weeks earlier when, in his desperation, he had rushed there after the explosion at Wheeler's. The choice of a haven had not been random. To him, the Dukes represented solidity, permanence, refinement — the antithesis of the chaotic world of murder and destruction. Twenty-three years ago, the flower arrangements may not have been as glamorous and the furnishings had been dowdier, but the ambiance was every bit as discreet and cordial.

It was the ideal locale for a seduction. When he had asked Lily to join him there, he had made certain she understood that this was not to be a business trip. No ruse would lure her to London. With Lily, one had to be honorable, for she would withdraw at any hint of deception. Besides, Eli had had his fill of manipulating romance as a means to another end. Although his brief affair with Charlotte had not been unpleasant, he retained regrets about the ethical aspects of what had transpired. Nevertheless, if it had not been for his final confrontation with Charlotte in Tokyo, where he had to admit to her (as well as himself) the existence of another woman in his life, he might never have gathered the courage to declare himself to Lily.

Less than a year earlier he had been sent to search out Charlotte by Isser Harel, who had been after information that might lead to a final resolution of the Lavon affair — a goal that proved elusive in the end. If he had never loved Lily, he probably would have succumbed to Charlotte's considerable efforts to claim him, for Charlotte's skin was the softest, most sensual he had ever touched and her body was wonderfully proportioned. Her delight in sex with him had thrilled him. No other woman — before or since — had so complimented him on his lovemaking prowess. No other woman had been so eager to please him. Charlotte was witty, curious, and thoroughly appealing. But with Charlotte he always held his most vulnerable emotions in check, the crux of his secret self in reserve. And Charlotte had known it.

Charlotte required far more than he could give. Even in bed her needs were never satisfied as quickly as his own. She had a way of pushing her demands, and when she did, he felt himself recoil. At first he had not known why; then he accepted the fact he desired someone else. It was as simple as that. He wanted Lily. From the time she went to work for him on Cyprus, he had been in love with her.

After Eli helped Charlotte get settled in New York, his urge to win Lily led him in the next six months to travel to Paris as frequently as could be justified. He accepted the fact he could not *push* Lily to respond to him. After her horrendous experiences with the baker, her distrust of men was understandable. He commenced his campaign slowly. He spent long hours in her apartment on the Quai Voltaire discussing her operations. Already she had been given decision-making jurisdiction on certain matters and he had been impressed with her rapidly developing forgery skills.

After a few months, Lily warmed considerably and soon admitted she was eager for him to visit more often. They had walked hand in hand, kissed tenderly, and gazed into one another's eyes as if some cosmic secret might be revealed therein. It had been an old-fash-

ioned courtship. Even in as large a city as Paris, they were concerned
that their continued association could lead to Lily's cover being
weakened, and they were therefore uncomfortable in public. Neither
were they at ease in Lily's apartment when it was obvious she was
not ready for a more intense relationship. They began spending considerable hours at the cinema. Caressing in the anonymous darkness
like so many lovers in a similar predicament, they explored Ingmar
Bergman's *Smiles of a Summer Night,* René Clair's *Les Grandes Manoeu-
vres,* and Jules Dassin's *Rififi.* While Eli had been pleased just to be
with Lily, she became enthralled with the medium and talked about
films endlessly.

Because Lily had seen so few movies in her lifetime, Eli took it
upon himself to educate her in the art form and searched out the
classics as well as the popular releases of the day. After sitting
through two showings of *It Happened One Night,* Lily was anxious to
see every other Frank Capra film. She wept over Garbo's performance in *Anna Karenina,* then plunged into a Russian period after seeing Eisenstein's *Alexander Nevsky.* Once they had exhausted the
choices in Paris, Eli had the perfect excuse to invite her to London.

"Join me there for a long weekend," he proposed. "There's going
to be a Hitchcock festival, leading off with *Strangers on a Train.* We'll
see two films a day and catch up on all the recent releases in
English."

"Where shall I stay?" Lily asked in her most practical voice.

"With me."

"In a hotel?"

"Would you mind terribly?"

"No, I think not," she replied with an uncharacteristically shy
smile.

Eli arrived in London two days ahead of time. In the interim, he
bought new clothes, organized their round of filmgoing, purchased
brandy and flowers, and tormented himself about how to make their
time alone together perfect.

Lily arrived in the rain. Even though it was August, the afternoon
was cold and she was soaking wet. "The airport bus dropped me off
at the other end of Piccadilly. Cabs were impossible so I decided
to walk," she said as she stood shivering in the hotel's reception
area.

He took her one small bag and escorted her to the rooms on the
second floor. She did not seem to notice the bouquet of lilies on the
table. He hung up her drenched coat and handed her a thick bath

towel. She wrapped her dripping hair in a turban and eagerly accepted the Courvoisier he poured.

She was trembling. As Eli embraced her, her back stiffened. He rubbed her protectively, but she remained rigid and unyielding. Fortunately, he had splurged on a small suite.

"Why don't you change?" He gestured to the bedroom and made it clear he would remain in the sitting room.

"I will do that," she said diffidently and closed the door between them.

All Eli's hopes of breaking through the barrier between them were dissolving. He understood why. Over the eight years he had known Lily, she had never been linked with a man. After hearing so many gruesome stories of how young girls had been molested by Nazis, Eli could well imagine what she must have suffered. Besides the baker, there could have been many brutal sexual encounters in Lily's past — more than enough to turn her against sex for the rest of her life. Had he been kidding himself by believing that he was the one man whose tenderness and adoration would both soothe and awaken her?

The bedroom door opened. Lily appeared in an extraordinary garment. She was wearing lingerie appropriate for a stage farce. The flaming pink outer robe was trimmed with ghastly ruffles. Underneath was a concoction held together with tiny bows that made her appear to have bulges in the most unnatural places. Lily saw the appalled expression on his face immediately. She stepped backward and closed the bedroom door once more.

Instantly ashamed of his reaction, Eli rushed to reopen it. Fortunately, the door was not latched. Lily was sitting on the edge of one of the twin beds looking like the forlorn bride in an American comedy. He sat across from her on the other bed, regretting that the hotel did not have a room available with a double bed.

"It is awful, is it not?"

"Well, Lily . . ."

"I usually sleep in an old smock, so, at the last minute, I ran out and bought this. I did not even try it on."

Eli slipped beside her on the bed. As he stroked her face, he had to push back a ruffle that was tickling his neck. The fabric was strangely slippery. He pulled his hand away. "What's this made of?"

She scratched her neck. "I am not certain, but it itches." She giggled uneasily.

Eli shook his head and joined in the laughter. "If you must know, I went out and purchased new pajamas." He grinned boyishly. "The only ones I found have stripes. I was hoping to wear them in the dark . . . if at all."

Seeing his discomfort, Lily relaxed slightly. "Oh, *Eli*!" She laid her head on his shoulder. "I feel ridiculous . . ."

The touch of her soft curls against his cheek stirred him. He took her face in his hands and studied her thin line of a mouth. He kissed her chastely. She parted her lips and kissed him as firmly as she ever had. Unexpectedly she drew back. Eli blinked as he opened his eyes. She was untying the peignoir's straps. It slid to the floor. Her shoulders were a pale peach color with a gentle dappling of freckles. He kissed one side, then the other. Lily threw back her head as he moved to the deep cleft in her neck and dared a lick of her fragile skin. She did not resist. Her face was flushed. Her breasts, which were barely concealed by the scoop of the lowered gown, rose and fell rhythmically. It was all he could do to keep himself from flinging her down and ripping off the rest of the flimsy wrapping.

She reached across to him and traced the line of his jaw with her fingertips. "I do not know . . ."

"What?"

"If we should —"

"After all this time? Lily, my darling, don't you know there hasn't been anyone else since I met you?"

"Eli, that cannot be true."

"Nobody I've wanted as much. For years I didn't dare believe . . ."

"I do not know what to do. I expected it would be simple . . ."

"It never is."

"You do not understand —"

"I think I do, or at least I *want* to understand. I want to do what's right for you beyond anything else. That's why I've waited for so long. I wanted it to be right for you. Lily —" His voice caught. "Don't you want me at all?"

"I . . . I . . . do not know what it is to *want* someone. I have liked you, maybe loved you, for years. I have trusted you entirely. I have worked for you. *For you.* Do you understand? It is far easier to do something for a person than for a cause. Besides, I was never one for causes. I go from one event to the other, like a blind person following a wall. My only link has been you."

The fabric around her midriff had loosened sufficiently to bare one of her breasts. She had not even noticed, but the sight of it was irresistible to Eli. His fingers cupped it protectively. "Lily," he gasped. "Lily, I love you so much."

The next few minutes would have been comic if he had not been so earnest. The nightgown, which must have been designed by a sadistic monk, was a most complicated impediment. Finally, he left her to unravel its mysteries and removed everything but his own undershorts. With all the gentleness he could summon he kissed her eyes, her chin, the cleft between her breasts, the indentation between her ribs, and the rising curve just below her waistline. By then his hands had begun caressing her thighs. Soon he was rewarded with the slightest parting of her legs and a sweet little moan: "Eli . . . Eli, I —"

"Shhh . . ." He silenced her mouth with a deep thrust of his tongue. Then he raised himself on his elbows and perched over her. He let her feel his body's need of her with the lightest brushings of his pelvis against her legs. How he wished she would embrace him and urge him onward. But her hands remained at her sides. She squirmed with discomfort.

"Darling, may I?" he asked as his fingers probed between her legs.

"Eli, please . . . I must —"

"You are so warm . . . I love you . . ."

Her hand covered his and pushed it farther in than he had intended to go. "Do you feel me?" she asked.

"Yes, oh, yes!"

"Do you want to try it now?"

"Yes . . ." He was almost sobbing.

Somehow she was taking control of the act. His shorts were being pulled past his knees, her hand was guiding his buttocks. He did not want to be too forceful, but his gentle approach was failing. The next seconds were horribly clumsy. While she was wet and yielding, he could not seem to penetrate. He tried to maneuver her legs into a wider angle, but that did not help; then he reached for a pillow and pushed it under her hips.

"Better?" he mumbled while nuzzling her throat.

"I do not know if —" she replied just as he glided forward a few crucial inches. "Ahhhh!" Her cry came from deep in her throat, and though she attempted to stifle it, he could feel her whole body quiver and recoil. He pulled out at once.

"What's the matter?" He saw tears filling her eyes. "I've hurt you!"

"It is fine now . . . Let us not stop . . . I expected it . . ." With the back of her hand she wiped the tears away.

His erection melted before his mind grasped the reality that confronted him. Easing himself down alongside her, he was overcome with confusion. "Lily, this is the first time?"

She nodded mutely.

Lies!

All these years she lied to him. Could that baker have been innocent of the charges against him? Could Lily have fooled everyone? Had his original assessment of her as a counterfeit Jew been the truth after all?

"How is that possible?" he managed. "I always believed . . . That man in Cyprus. You said . . ."

Lily sat up so quickly her head hit the headboard. "I never said any such thing!"

"The children in the basement . . . He forced you all to have sex with him . . ." Eli faced her squarely. "You lied to us then?"

"*Never* have I lied to you."

Eli stared into her agonized face. Gripping a pillow to cover her breasts, she looked like a distressed waif.

"Then I don't understand."

"No, I do not suppose you could. Hans de Vries was a pedophile. Do you know what that means? It means he liked to have sex with children. *Children.* By the time my parents were taken away I was almost fourteen — too old for his tastes. I had little breasts; I had pubic hair; I had begun to bleed each month. Once, in the first weeks, he ordered me to take off my clothes. He looked me over, felt me everywhere, then said he found me disgusting. While I was undressed, he called for my brothers and made me watch while he examined them. Oh, *God!*" She covered her face with her hands. "That was the worst . . . the first time he touched them.

"He spoke to them kindly and told them how lovely they were. He would bring grease from the kitchen and force me to put it on them . . . to get them ready for him. Afterward, he would leave me to clean them up, comfort them as best I could. Eventually, he went through all the children in the cellar, boys and girls alike. I think he favored the boys mostly, but the little girls could be used both ways and he liked one of them especially . . . he would give her more food than the others . . . and we all learned to cooperate with him or else —"

"Lily, you don't have to —"

"No, no . . . I want you to know everything. Then maybe you will understand why I . . ."

"I *do* understand. I supposed you had been hurt by men when you were little. How exactly doesn't matter."

"Ah, that is where you are very wrong. It *does* matter to me. Can you not imagine how I felt? *I* was as evil as he. *I* had to be the one to prepare the children. Night after night *I* taped their mouths shut so they would not scream and betray us. He made *me* select the one he would be using, so the children came to hate me — even fear me — almost as much as him. I would bribe them, cajole them. Sometimes . . ." She coughed, but despite Eli's insistence she need not go on, sputtered the rest. "Sometimes, I would force them, hold them down, whatever was necessary. I pleaded with de Vries, 'Take me instead.' He laughed at me. Several times he beat me, but he had to do *it* with a child. I was his partner. The worst happened to *them*, not me, and the other children knew it — my brothers knew it. They blamed me as much as him. And they were right!"

"You kept them alive."

"Even if that is true, what did I keep them alive *for*? Was it better they lived longer and were brutalized or would it have been better if they had died sooner . . . and without the agony?"

"One of your brothers held out until the very last days of the war and you survived. I cannot imagine how you remained unscathed, but you — " The moment he said his last sentence, Eli was filled with regrets. He should never have let on that he had believed she was raped by the Nazis. Of course, he had known that she was captured very late in the war and had been under the protection of a Danish boy at Theresienstadt. Not every girl had been attacked; sheer numbers had been in her favor. It was more surprising that she hadn't become intimate with the Dane. But then Lily had a way of putting imaginary walls around herself with her steely manner, her acid stares. These skills had been honed by necessity and had obviously served her well.

Lily was very quiet for a few minutes. "I should have died with my family," she whispered. "I should never have lived. A night does not pass when I do not remember the children. I see their faces on the streets of Paris, in Tel Aviv, wherever I go. The world is unkind to children, even in peacetime. I could never have a child of my own. I could not create anything and watch it suffer. I would never have your child, Eli," she snapped with unexpected vehemence.

He reached for his undershorts, which were crumpled at the foot of the bed. She turned away as he slipped them on. He looked at his watch. "It's almost dinnertime. Where would you care to eat?"

In the dim room, relieved only by a light from the hallway, Lily looked so pale next to the sheets that she seemed to blend into the bedding. The usual vibrancy in her gray eyes had faded. "I am not especially hungry."

"Let's get dressed," Eli urged. "We'll find some place in this neighborhood."

Sharing an umbrella, they walked up Piccadilly. Lily had rejected the Dukes' dining room as too intimate and the Ritz's as too grand. Without a word, they strolled past Fortnum and Mason, St. James's Church, Simpson's. Pausing for a traffic light at the circus, Eli stared up at the dripping statue of Eros and thought how eloquently the image suited his present state of mind. A few blocks up the Haymarket they settled on a small Italian restaurant called Mario's. After walking down a few steps, they were escorted to a table decorated with a red-and-white-checked tablecloth and the requisite Chianti bottle corked with a grimy candle. The prices on the uninspired menu indicated they had found themselves in a tourist trap. Eli was too fatigued to suggest something else.

Lily ordered a broth with noodles and he chose a minestrone. Both politely agreed that warm soup was the perfect choice given the dampness of the evening. They chattered aimlessly, grasping at any focal point: the poster of Naples on the wall, the fashions on the girls around Piccadilly, whether or not to add more Parmesan to the soup. This is like a trite television drama of a honeymoon gone sour, Eli mused — from the negligee to their failure at consummation to the tough veal with the far too sweet tomato sauce. By the time the espresso was served, they had lapsed into a wary silence.

On the way back to the hotel they took the opposite side of the street. They paused and stared down the gated Burlington Arcade.

"Aviva once worked a few blocks from here," Eli said to break the silence.

"I do not suppose you could tell me where she is now?"

"No."

"She is with Gideon, I mean Oliver Deacon?"

"Yes, they are together."

"Remember their wedding? And that funny little rabbi you were able to get at the last minute?"

Eli laughed. He had found someone at the Anglo-Palestine Club near the Windmill Theatre who had agreed to marry them quietly. Rabbi Goren, who was only five feet tall and extremely rotund, had been a chaplain in the British army during the war and had undertaken missions to the refugee camps afterward. Eli had heard he was sympathetic to special problems, the exact nature of which Eli did not divulge entirely. It had not mattered to the liberal clergyman. He found a home in Hendon where the ceremony could take place, and considering the circumstances, the whole affair had gone off rather nicely. Lily had been marvelous to Aviva, treating her as a cherished sister, because the bride had no family present. The women had not seen each other since.

"Is their assignment very dangerous?"

"Possibly."

"More so than Paris?"

"What do you think?"

"I think that I am sick and tired of being treated like a fragile flower."

"You have been invaluable in your present position."

"All I am asking is that if something more challenging comes up you will consider using me. I am growing stale. Sometimes I think you have kept me in Paris as a personal convenience."

Eli resented her tone. Up until the last few months, he had not courted her, had not expressed his feelings for her openly. While she must have sensed his caring long ago, he did not expect she would accuse him of allowing this to affect decisions regarding her professional assignments. But perhaps she did have a point and it would be better to concede it than argue and spoil what little warmth remained between them.

"You yourself know how difficult it would be to establish a new cover and, up to now, there hasn't been anything suitable for Nicole. However . . ."

"Yes?"

"Your name has come up in regard to a slightly more risky venture. Nothing's been decided formally but —"

"What is it?"

Passing the turnoff for their hotel, they had ended up at the bottom of St. James's Street and were facing St. James's Palace. A somber guard poked his chin out from under his bearskin hat into the drizzling rain. Eli steered Lily away from his earshot and spoke in Hebrew.

"Couriers are needed to transfer funds in and out of Geneva. It could be a regular job, but your base would remain Paris. We're looking for a reason for you to travel often — a gallery connection there or —"

"Sounds wonderful." Even in the pale lamplight Eli could see Lily's face glowing for the first time that evening. Her step quickened the rest of the way back to the hotel.

As if Lily and Eli were college roommates they undressed perfunctorily. At that moment Eli was grateful the room was outfitted with twin beds.

Lily came out of the bathroom wearing cotton panties that covered her from crotch to waist and the blue oxford cloth shirt she had worn under her traveling suit. While she had not meant to look appealing, he found the effect more sensual than the frills of the Parisian peekaboo creation. He kept his shorts and undershirt on and was winding his watch before setting it out on the night table between the two chastely turned down beds.

Lily sat opposite him and asked to see the watch. It was the Omega his father had given to him before the war. Noticing how the catch had been poorly repaired and that the crystal was scratched, she said, "You need a new one," as perfunctorily as a sister — or wife.

"I've been meaning to buy one but . . ."

"It is best to get one as a gift; otherwise the decision is too impossible — there are too many choices. Maybe if I get to Geneva . . ." She laughed with a wonderful lightness that gave Eli hope that they might remain friends.

He reached across to flick off the lamp, but her hand caught his wrist. "Eli, we are being ridiculous." In one graceful movement she slipped into his bed. "Let us finish what we have begun. I want it to finally be over."

Her choice of words was unfortunate. The stirrings he felt as she had come across the room subsided instantly. She seemed to regard him as a business transaction that had to be completed, but with surprising wisdom, she did not discuss the matter further. Her lips searched for his and when they made contact she clasped the back of his head and pushed him toward her with increasing firmness. Her lips were apart and her tongue explored his with quick, fiery bursts. As soon as he began to participate, her hands reached down and tugged at the elastic at his waist. Somehow she managed to remove not only his shorts but his shirt and her clothing. Their arms and legs tangled as they positioned themselves on the bed, with the end result of Lily astride him. He blinked up at her serious face and was transfixed by the blush that crept across the delicious drape of her breasts. Reaching up, he grasped the raspberry tip of each nipple between his fingers. As she sensed his awakening, Lily raised her hips and moved from side to side.

"Help me," she asked matter-of-factly.

He entwined his arms around her arching back and hugged her down to him. He cupped her buttocks lovingly for a few seconds, then allowed his fingers to explore her virginal lips.

She poised herself above him for a long moment. "Like this?" she asked as she impaled herself with one hard thrust.

He moved tentatively.

She did not complain. He kissed her mouth, her neck, her shoulders while slowly — as excruciatingly slowly as he could manage — moving up and down, round and round.

She caught the gist of his rhythmic movements and when he felt her body rising and falling, twisting and plunging, he lost all sense of where he was and what had happened and what would happen the next minute or hour and let the seconds pulsate past until containment was impossible.

"Is it over?" she asked in a tiny voice.

"Yes, my darling. How are you?"

"I am fine. I am glad."

Glad . . . not happy . . . Why should she be? She had been far too tense to have found the experience enjoyable. Nevertheless, he was amazed she had taken control of the situation. If it had been up to him . . . what would he have done? Just gone to sleep, he supposed.

Lily went into the bathroom and closed the door. The water ran for the longest time. He straightened the covers in anticipation of her return.

When she came back, she turned off the lamp, but the bed she crawled into was her own. "Laila tov . . . Good night, Eli," she said.

"Laila tov," he responded, dumbfounded that she chose to sleep apart from him.

There was laughter in the hallway as other guests returned from their evening out. In the silence that followed their cheery calls to each other and the slamming of their doors, Lily spoke again. "Todah rabah," she thanked him formally. "It was better than I expected."

"B'vakasha." He told her she was welcome, trying to restrain the pain in his voice.

In the dark, he hear her rustlings and turnings, then the rhythmic breathing of sleep. He remained wide awake, trying to fathom what had gone wrong.

The Lily he had wanted was a woman who would passionately desire *him*. Maybe not the first time, but soon he would overcome her reticence; he would have taught her the glories of her own sensuality and, with infinite patience, would have wakened the nascent sexuality that others had choked — but not destroyed. Eventually, he would come to understand her and she him. They would unite as one.

What lunacy! She had never given him a hint or a sign. Finally, he had to embark on this crusade solo and her early enthusiasm had spurred him on with illusory expectations. The result was nothing short of a disaster.

"Todah rabah," she had said. Thank you! The truth was she was a woman over the age of thirty who had decided it was high time she lost her virginity. Despite the pathetic revelations about her guilty participation in the baker's perversions, she was merely interested in putting herself through an experience. So, why not choose him? A good friend. A discreet associate. As Nicole, she probably had not dared become involved with a man; as Lily, she had had few opportunities. So good old Eli was called in for the sport.

Lily's "It was better than I expected" sounded like one of her ratings of the latest Bergman movie. As the night wore on, his anger subsided. Would he send her to Geneva now? He could not allow his private feelings to influence his professional decisions. He had to think more clearly . . . but a numbness overcame him and this dissolved into a blank, narcoticlike sleep.

The dream ebbed and flowed from light to dark. A great weight was pressing down on him. A heavy breath filled his ear. With every ounce of will he tried to turn over and away from the interference. The pressure moved simultaneously and pulled him onward. He opened his eyes to find it was not a dream at all. Lily was in his bed. He was nude. She was too. She caressed him. The sudden warmth that enveloped him was all-consuming.

They barely kissed. Lily was making all the moves. Her back was arched away from him, her neck snapped back so far he could not have reached up to kiss her face if he had wanted to. Only her breasts were accessible and these he stroked mildly at first, then suckled ferociously. Lily leaned into him to make this easier. In a few seconds she was clutching at him like a drowning victim. Her face grimaced; her legs became rigid; her spine was taut, then limp. Her buttocks rippled and she raised herself as high as possible and impaled herself over and over and over. Losing all control, Eli shuddered and gasped.

He lay back disoriented and exhausted.

He touched her shoulder. It was cool. She kept her hands clasped across her chest. Since they had separated, she had not reached to hold him, kiss him, touch him.

Lily spoke matter-of-factly. "That was better, no? I think that is more how it is supposed to be."

He did not reply with words. He lifted himself and kissed her mouth. Her lips were dry, closed.

He pulled away, wondering what had diminished the flood of tender feelings that had welled during their lovemaking. She turned her head and observed him quietly. He felt awkward, exposed. He slipped out of the bed and went to the bathroom. This time it was he who closed the door.

In the shower his heartbeat raced faster. As he luxuriated in the great volume of hot water that coursed down his back, the taut muscles in his neck slowly softened. By the time he wrapped himself in the hotel's thick terry robe, he came to a decision. Since he had booked two nights at the Dukes, he would give her *two* nights. But that evening *he* would take charge. If she wanted to know about sex, he would damn well *teach* her.

He wanted to see her underneath him with legs spread wide. He wanted her to see him in daylight; to feel him in the vast darkness. To smell him. To taste him. And he her. He would be the first in everything. Ah! The first! His mind swirled with the succulent possibilities. He imagined her on her back, on her stomach, on the floor on all fours. In the shower. In the bath. Pressed against the mirrored door. On the sitting room sofa. He would do it all. Tonight. Tomorrow. And then it would be over. Finally. At last. Over.

❖   ❖   ❖

He had not done it all, but if she had any complaints, he had not heard them. What had occurred was far removed from lovemaking.

Lily had been curiously satisfied by it, and if she had wondered at his mood, she had not bothered to question it.

She was assigned the Geneva run, and her performance at manipulating currencies had been as splendid as he had expected. She had remained in that capacity until she was given the position of chief of European operations when Pierre was recalled to Tel Aviv. Lily had seemed so satisfied that Eli had not wanted to offer her the Jericho assignment until he reminded himself that he had promised not to coddle her. She was qualified for Jericho; she had the right cover, was the right type. It was up to her to decide whether or not to accept the risks. She had welcomed the danger.

Once Eli had accepted the fact that Lily could not reciprocate his love, he was able to let go of his fantasy that they would marry. He began, once more, to think of other women and went on a spree — making love to all who would have him. There were two simultaneous affairs with Israeli women — one was married, one was not — but neither lasted more than a year. Eli was not meant to be a husband; he was married to his work. He promised himself not to get emotionally involved again. The promise had been easy to keep.

PARIS, FRANCE: MAY 1979

The flight was landing in Paris but Eli had not even touched the anemic-looking sandwiches on his tray. Normally, Eli would have taken an airport bus, for he was still on the Mossad payroll and had those infernal bookkeepers to satisfy. If he required a helicopter, three dozen men in Bentleys, or a suite at the Ritz, he could have them — *if* he could justify the expense and *if* he kept the receipts. Damn it all! Hadn't Dani told him that time was of the essence? He splurged on a taxi.

By the time he reached the Périphérique, he had settled back and was sorting out the effects of his grand passion. At the end of the weekend at the Dukes, his mind had been muddled, his body drained.

As they parted, Lily had spoken candidly. "I am not suited to marriage, Eli. The problem is that I would not care enough about my partner. The one person I do care about is me. What I *am* suited for is precisely what I do. I am very cautious; I am always alert. Maybe too alert. I cannot relax my guard. You are more ... more human, more sensitive than I could ever be. With me everything is mechanical. I like it that way. It helps me function in my job."

Even if he had wanted to argue with her, he would not have known how to dispute her sentiments. He could not despise or even dislike her. In fact, he had returned to Jerusalem from the Dukes with a renewed admiration for her directness. Lily was a person with whom he had survived a strenuous encounter. From then on they were more like war buddies than former lovers.

Eli asked the taxi driver to stop at the Gare d'Orsay, where he paused a few minutes to be certain he had not been followed. The explosion at Wheeler's was all the reminder he needed about following procedures to the letter. He rechecked his watch. Five minutes had passed. Staring at the unscratched crystal, he remembered when Lily had given it to him. They had met in Athens. She was carrying half a million Swiss francs to finance an Algerian operation. Although he did not know much about the value of watches, he had suspected this Baume et Mercier with its gold and stainless case was an extremely fine watch. The style was elegant and well suited to him. Ten minutes. Nobody in sight. He turned toward the Quai Voltaire.

A strong wind was at his back as he walked down the Quai Anatole France toward the Pont du Carrousel. He had resisted confronting Aviva. He was not looking forward to seeing Charlotte. Lily was another story indeed. Just the idea that he would be in her company momentarily buoyed him. And the fact that he was far away from Tel Aviv and the likes of Ehud Dani and Alex Naor and all the rest of his nameless nemeses was further cause for rejoicing. A gust of air swirled a discarded newspaper around his feet and it seemed to propel him even faster. Less than a minute later he was climbing the stairs to Lily's atelier.

She was home. Somehow he expected she would be, even though he had his own key.

"Hello, Nicole," he said, grinning on her doorstep.

"Charles!" She kissed him warmly. "Come in. I am not alone," she added cautiously.

Two men in coveralls were crating paintings. The entire living area was covered with rough boards, rolls of brown paper, spools of coarse twine, and sawdust.

"As you can see, I am putting my pictures in storage." She continued speaking in English. "I have found a customer to buy the flat."

"I didn't know . . ."

"But you must remember that the gallery was sold over a year ago when the building at the Place des Vosges was bought from our 'friend' by an 'uncontrolled party.' "

"Yes but —"

"Well, after that I did not see why I should remain in Paris. You cannot imagine how these places along the river have appreciated over the years. I would be a fool not to sell at the top of the market."

"Where will you go?"

"I am hoping to find a ground-floor studio to create my stained glass panels."

"In Paris?"

"No, Paris is too expensive."

"There's your pension."

"That will not get me far in this city and I cannot expect to live off the proceeds from my craft, so I'll need to keep my expenses down."

"Why not go home?"

She looked at him quizzically. "Where is that?" she asked rhetorically, since she did not expect Eli to say "Israel" with strangers around. "Besides, *home* does not exist for me."

One of the workmen was waiting patiently to ask Lily a question. She turned away from Eli and handled his problem in too rapid a French for Eli to follow. He watched Lily's lithe movements as she climbed up to her sleeping loft and handed down three paintings — all studies of the same face. It was a child, the one she had brought out of the refugee camp near Amman twelve years earlier and called Otto.

Eli recalled that the boy had been placed with an Arab family in Jaffa, but he had never learned what had become of him. He summoned a few hazy memories of the boy huddled against Lily during the escape, then swathed in a cast after surgery. The huge black eyes and impish lips had been masterfully captured in the paintings. The boy would be almost eighteen now. Lily's attachment to him had always puzzled Eli.

The rescue outside Amman . . . He had to admit that retrieving Lily was as much a personal crusade as it was Mossad policy. He had not been entirely honest when he told her it had been necessary to rescue her because they were going in after PLO leaders. He could have postponed the bombing if Lily had been in jeopardy. In the end, they had failed to neutralize as many PLO members as they had hoped. Only Rashid Salim, the most dangerous of the terrorists, and two of his underlings had definitely been killed. Salim's death had been welcome news in Tel Aviv.

While the workmen followed Lily down the stairs to the bedroom where so many Mossad transients had been boarded safely over the years, Eli paced the studio area, cautioning himself to not permit his feelings to interfere with his investigation. Dozens of crates had already been closed. Two battered trunks were locked, with the shipping labels attached. Stepping over the carpenters' debris, he stooped for a closer look at one of the tags. It read: Waldhotel Fletschhorn, Saas-Fee.

Hearing footsteps, he returned to the place he had been standing.

"Sorry, Charles, this will only take another moment." She turned and gave the movers a few final instructions.

As the workmen gathered their tools, Lily brushed off a table and laid out two wine glasses.

After they had left, he summoned the words to begin. "I need your assistance."

"You said Toulon was the last of it." She sighed dramatically and took the seat opposite him. "I made plans on that assumption."

"It's not another assignment. There are some loose ends from the previous one."

"That is a relief." She reached into her apron pocket and pulled out a pack of cigarettes. "Would you care for one?"

"No, thank you." He had renounced his fairly casual smoking habit almost five years earlier.

"You were smart to have quit," she said as she lit her cigarette. "Do you remember when I learned to smoke? It was part of our training. I hope you are not ruining the health of young recruits any longer."

"I think not."

"I bet Charlotte was able to break the habit. She had an iron will, even stronger than mine." Lily took a long drag on her cigarette and exhaled elegantly. The next phrase slipped out seamlessly. "I saw her in Toulon, you know. We were not supposed to meet, but it is such a small city, at least the part around the arsenals."

"Where did you see her?"

"The Place de la Liberté, right off the Boulevard de Strasbourg. You remember where that was?"

Eli nodded.

"She did not notice me. She was occupied talking to some men I did not recognize, but then, you probably know who they were."

Without being aware of it, Lily was feeding him precisely the information he needed. "Must have been the two Israeli boys who worked under her," he responded nonchalantly. "I believe you've seen them in the past."

"Cherbourg?"

"Why, yes, they were two of the 'Norwegian sailors.'"

"No, these men were not the right type. One was very tall and dark, the other bald and quite a bit shorter. I dared not linger, so I did not notice much else."

The hell you didn't, Eli swore to himself. Nobody had better recall than Lily. His interrogator's mind went on full alert. He decided not to press the matter. Since she was to have had no official contact with Charlotte on the mission, she must have seen her accidentally. Discreet, as always, she had not revealed herself to Charlotte. His skepticism waned. How well she knew the rule: The less you know about the other operatives, the better.

But if the system were foolproof, Dr. Ze'evi might yet be alive.

"You were right not to bring attention to yourself," he said, closing the matter for the moment. He would have to find another way to resurrect it.

Lily noted the glasses she had forgotten to fill. "I must be more tired than I realized. Will you have some wine?"

"A small glass, thank you."

She went to the kitchen and returned with a dusty bottle of Chablis. Using her apron, she wiped it thoroughly before opening and pouring it. Then her hand indicated the total disarray of the room. "Chaos!" she exclaimed. "I have never tolerated messes. I suppose that is because when the mind is under stress — like during the war — it helps if your own small area is orderly."

Eli smiled sympathetically. "Can I help you in any way?"

Lily drained her glass. "No, I would like to sweep up the worst of it before dinner."

Eli shrugged his indifference. "I noticed those portraits of Otto. What ever happened to him?" he asked to change the subject.

"He is at the agricultural school in Rehovot," she responded as she walked back into the kitchen.

"Do you stay in touch with him?" Eli called into the other room.

"He writes to 'Nurse Nicole' from time to time, but I do not think he remembers me." She returned with a broom and dustpan and began to sweep up the sawdust and wood scraps.

"Do you regret never having had children of your own?"

"Never." She stopped and gripped the broom tensely. "I would have been a terrible mother."

"Why are you so critical of yourself?"

"I am merely honest. People with my background either smother their offspring with affection and refuse to permit them to develop on their own or — as I suspect the case would have been with me — they are too harsh and demanding. Besides, what do I know of mothering? My own mother abandoned me, denying I was hers. Oh yes, I know as well as you that she did it to save me, but a child's deepest feelings at a moment like that are never, *ever* rational. It is a hideous black wave of anger that is renewed every time the memory reappears. No matter how much you try to dispel it with logic, it washes over you again and again. The past is a relentless master."

Eli was silent. He had always admired Lily's accurate self-assessments and yet was puzzled by them as well. If she *understood* herself so thoroughly, why couldn't she free herself of her miseries?

"There is an element of truth in what you say — not that you would have been such a bad mother, but about people being chained to their experiences."

"Eli . . ." Her voice was slippery smooth. "Who knows me more intimately than you? If I had normal feelings of love, I might have been able to give you what you wanted." Her head was turned away so he could not see the expression in her eyes.

"Truthfully . . ." His voice was much too thin. He cleared his throat. "I always felt one day we —"

"Because I never took a husband?"

"Was there ever anyone you wanted to marry?"

"No," she snapped. "It would have been impossible."

"Impossible with me?"

Lily finished extricating some wood shavings that had lodged under the floor molding before facing him. "You or anyone else. Look what happened to poor Charlotte in Egypt."

"Paris isn't Egypt. Something could have been worked out."

"I suppose so. I had a story prepared. Something about how, after the war, lots of names and passports were changed, mine included. I might have found a man who would have accepted my elaborate tale. The point is I did not want anyone to love Nicole . . . only Lily." Lily's voice diminished to a whisper. "And Lily was hidden from view."

"Lily . . ." The name rolled seductively off his tongue. "You were always *Lily* with me."

"Yes. I was. Now I will tell you something that may upset you, so I ask forgiveness in advance." She stood in front of him. "One reason I permitted myself to have that . . . that fling with you was because I wanted my first such encounter to be Lily's. Nicole had to be circumspect. Lily could say and do what she wanted." She was observing him intently to see the effect her words were having. "You are angry."

"Never." His voice seemed to come from a faraway place. He clasped the wine glass and eased it to his lips. A long swallow remained. He spoke calmly. "I guess I loved you because you were the most enigmatic woman I had ever met. At heart I'm a mathematician and my mind craves a complex challenge. I suppose the reason I have stayed in this bloody business is because it is so perplexing. I would have hated a simple life, and yet I cannot help but wonder what it would have been like if I had persuaded you to marry me, if we had had children. Maybe we would have surprised ourselves — and each other."

"I have remained in your service because I admire dreamers. And my God, Eli, you have never woken up, have you? You have some noble vision of the world. You cannot see that it is filled with such despicable hate, so much violence, so many horrendous ways to murder and torture, that a permanent peace is impossible. Sometimes I have wondered whether we should not stop our efforts at conciliation. In the end, what good have we done?"

"We have saved countless lives."

"That is what we say to justify our existence. Why should we not? After all, we are an industry . . . we provide jobs."

"Is that how you truly feel?"

Lily gave a lopsided grin. "Some days. But we *will* be ineffectual in the long run. Not because we have built so many bombs, but because we have destroyed so many children. How many millions more are there like me? How many other men and women lost so much in wartime that they can never reach out beyond themselves to love another generation unequivocally? How many other wounded children are born each year? Believe me, I know that it takes self-restraint not to propagate. If I had been less conscientious, I surely would have brought some pathetic baby into the world to suffer anew."

"And now? Have you no regrets?"

"Only a few," she finished cryptically. "What about you? Don't you wish you had children?"

He was reminded of his same discussion with Aviva in Tel Aviv as he responded, "I have a son."

Lily tilted her head slightly, as if trying to hear more acutely. "I suppose I should be surprised. Why, then, am I not?"

"Had you guessed?"

"No. I wondered why you had never married. In fact, when I first met you in Cyprus I assumed you *were* married. So, I *was* right after all."

"I never married."

"Oh, I see. That is not so unusual either. Maybe that is why you did not settle down with any woman just to have babies. I always suspected you would have made an excellent father, but since you already had a child, you never felt the same need pulsating in your blood. If I had known — " She shook her head and sawdust rained down from her hair. "I must shower before we go out. You are having dinner with me, no?"

"Yes, but Lily, finish what you were about to say. If you had known about my son . . . ?"

"I am not certain, it *might* have changed my attitude toward you. I was under the impression that you wanted me to have your child if I stayed with you, but I promised myself I would never have one — I was starved for so long, I had diseases, I did not think a child of mine could have been healthy. I refused to bring a deformed baby into the world."

"Most survivors have had beautiful children."

"I am not *most*!" she shouted.

"I know that, Lily," he responded softly. "Where would you like to have dinner?"

"There is a new café nearby with an excellent ris de veau toulousaine. You have always liked sweetbreads."

"How well you remember."

"Help yourself to more wine. I shall not be very long."

She was gone more than an hour. As Eli waited, his impatience mounted. He was puzzled that Lily had not questioned him about Colin. He expected she would be curious about his age, who his mother was, whether Eli was involved in his life.

When Lily emerged into the disarray of the studio, she looked beautiful in a slim white cotton dress that might have made most women her age appear too jejune.

At the café, Lily seemed determined to be charming. She chatted about her plans. "And what about you?" she asked as she scraped the caramel off the bottom of a custard dish.

He gave vague responses about retiring in a year or two. She asked a few polite questions, but Eli sensed she was not terribly curious. Lily was far more interested in her own side of the story than anyone else's. A very human trait, Eli reminded himself, but he was miffed. He had always wanted more from her than she could ever give.

As they drank their coffee, he searched for a smooth way to mention Charlotte again. Lily's indication that she had seen Charlotte in Toulon was the first clue linking one of his operatives to unknown contacts.

Charlotte.

Alex Naor had liked her the least. Isser Harel had suspected her motives. Eli had stood by Charlotte. The intelligence she had gathered, especially at el-Shallûfa, had been priceless.

"Where do you go from here?" Lily was asking.

"After another day or two in Paris, I need to return to the south of France for some unfinished business," he lied.

"Where? Since I have spent so much time in the region in recent months I know a few —" His look stopped her. For only a second he saw her fingers flutter nervously in front of her face, then descend to be clasped together in her lap. "How foolish! You know that area as well as I do."

Eli sipped his coffee so he did not have to respond instantly. Was she worried about his poking around in Toulon? He replaced his cup in its saucer. "After that, I'm on my own for a few weeks. Maybe London, maybe even New York."

"Charlotte is there, right?"

"Yes."

"That is who you should have married. She would have jumped at the chance."

"No. I am too set in my ways. My work is all-consuming, and even satisfying at times . . ."

"I am glad you put it that way. In the end you and I have accomplished far more separately than most couples jointly."

"A few minutes ago you were complaining about the futility of it all."

"If you search for a grand design or ultimate meaning to life, you will be disappointed. Let us take your son. I know nothing of him.

He could be a drunkard, an artist, a dope fiend, a doctor. But tell me the truth, does he give your own life more significance?"

"That relationship is more complicated than most."

"Even so, you will concede I have a point."

Lily stood and pushed back her chair. Eli counted out the right number of francs and left them on the table. Outside on the pavement, Lily said, "If you see Charlotte, tell her that when I saw her in Toulon she looked lovely, as usual. And slim. She will be pleased I noticed she has lost weight. She always resented the fact I never needed to diet." Lily started back in the direction of the river briskly, then slowed slightly. "I wonder who those gentlemen were . . ."

Eli did not respond.

They walked two more blocks before Lily spoke again. "From what I have been reading in the French press, the mission was a great success."

"Only partially."

She stopped moving. "Oh?"

"One of my men was killed."

"No!" Her shock seemed authentic. "How?"

"Can't say yet."

"Might it have been accidental?"

"No."

"Eli, this must be difficult for you." The coldness in her moody gray eyes had vanished. "What can I do?" She took his hand in hers and squeezed it warmly.

"Nothing for the moment . . ."

What was her game? Did she know about Dr. Ze'evi?

"Eli, when this is over, come to me." Her eyes were moist. "Don't think I do not know how foolish I have been. We both should have given in long ago."

"I don't understand . . ."

"You wanted something conventional; I did not. A compromise might have suited us both." Her laugh was throaty and erotic. For a flickering moment happiness did not seem so elusive.

Lily steered him across the Pont du Carrousel and led him along the Quai des Tuileries. As they walked she kept stroking the back of his hand and asking him the questions he had been yearning to answer. It took an hour to tell her all about Colin. Soon she understood about Maura, about Wheeler's, about everything.

Lily suggested he stay the night.

His suspicions diminished considerably as he held her close. "No. I've an early meeting." He declined with slightly more than a modest kiss. He needed to think everything through. There would be time to come back to Lily later. Right now he had to retain what modicum of objectivity remained.

They kissed. She smelled of wood chips and newly mown meadows. The river mist rose and bathed his face in a cool gloss, but his lips throbbed with her warmth for several long minutes. He stared at her, enchanted by her silvery eyes, her wistful expression. When all this is over, he promised himself before descending into the harshness of the real world once more.

Lily did not press him. "Let me know when you change your mind," she said as they made their way across the Pont Royal and back in the direction of Lily's home.

Not if, but *when,* you change your mind, she had said.

"You will let me know your whereabouts through the usual channels?"

"As always," she responded. She unlocked her courtyard gate. "Are you certain?" she asked before shutting it.

"No, I'm not." He attempted a light laugh, but the sound was obviously forced. "Good night —" He turned away quickly.

"Bonne nuit," she called melodically into the Parisian night.

15

Nature never deceives us; it is always we who deceive ourselves.
Jean Jacques Rousseau (1712–1778)
Emile

Manhattan was steamier than Eli expected. While he wanted to see Charlotte as soon as possible, he realized he needed a shower. At four in the afternoon he checked into the Stanhope — using Elliot Short's passport for the first time in years — freshened up, changed his clothes in record time, and, by sprinting down Madison Avenue from Eighty-first Street, was able to reach Charlotte's business before it closed at six.

After Eli brought Charlotte back to New York from Tokyo in 1955, she had lived briefly with her parents in Scarsdale until the baby was born. At the first opportunity, she had moved to lower Manhattan. Using the Mossad's small stipend, she opened a boutique on St. Mark's Place. Called "Liaison," as a private play on her daughter's name and her former profession, it specialized in classic designs executed in unusual fabrics and trimmed with antique lace collars and cuffs. After ten years of increasing success, she raised her prices, branched out into more sophisticated styles, and moved uptown to Madison and Sixty-fifth.

Eli paused to catch his breath outside her Madison Avenue shop.

The humid May afternoon had not deterred the long-legged women who strolled the streets and wielded their drooping shopping bags as purposefully as rifles. Strutting with necks craned forward, feet slapping the concrete quickly, they hardly took time to peruse the glittering window displays vying for their attention. The door to Liaison opened and closed half a dozen times. Almost every departing customer carried the shop's distinctive shiny black bag with the yellow tape measure logo. In the window, Lucite mannequins modeled skimpy dresses made from woven ribbons. When the last customer had departed, Eli opened the heavy plate glass door.

"How may I help you, sir?" asked a British salesgirl.

He matched her Oxbridge accent effortlessly. "I'm looking for Mrs. MacDonald."

"She's in a meeting. Were you expected?"

"No. This is a bit of a surprise."

"Who shall I say is here?"

"Ah . . . Mr. Ivy."

The girl pressed a button on what appeared to be a sterling silver telephone. "A Mr. Ivy is downstairs." She paused. "Yes, I'll inquire." She turned to Eli. "Could you wait thirty minutes or so?"

He nodded.

She asked him if he would like to make himself comfortable on the black velvet settee outside the dressing room. Eli sunk into the spongy cushions and stared out the display window at the crowd hurrying home carrying bundles.

A month ago he would have vouched for Charlotte completely, but at the moment she seemed a suspect by default, as well as by the implication of Lily's remarks about seeing Charlotte in Toulon.

Eli recalled Reuven Shiloah's directives on how to approach an intelligence puzzle. "First you step close to examine the tiniest detail; next you move back to view the widest picture," his mentor had instructed. "All the while your mind must be freed to think abstractly while your feet must be planted firmly on the ground."

The details . . . So far they did not add up.

There was nothing to tie Charlotte with the brutal murder except two mysterious men.

Most defectors were bought, but Charlotte had never needed money. Today, more than ever before, she was well established in her own right. Gordon MacDonald, who was killed in a helicopter crash in Cambodia in 1972, had named Allison his beneficiary on a generous insurance policy that had funded her education. And four years earlier, Charlotte's wealthy father had died, leaving her a substantial bequest. Her business seemed to be prospering. Besides, Charlotte had never had a venal nature, so the usual explanations for treachery did not apply. There had to be a motive — a reason for betraying not only him but Israel.

Don't forget . . . someone wanted to kill you . . . Someone almost succeeded . . .

He forced himself to face the ultimate possibility: Charlotte *had* a reason to betray him. But what? Without coercion, she had accepted a variety of difficult assignments. She had gone to Egypt voluntarily. She had married Gordon in her panicky need to escape the country. The marriage had been *her* solution — not the Mossad's. They would have found a way to get her out. There had been no direct link to her and her cover had been considered secure. In the first days after the arrests, the secret service had decided it was more dangerous to maintain contact with her than to leave her in limbo temporarily. Her own actions, however, had pre-empted any plan they might have devised.

Initially, Eli had been infuriated with Charlotte's decision to marry Gordon. When she had advised him of the marriage, she had led him to believe she was in love with the man. She had not asked for his help, so she had to accept the consequences. She had suffered from the deception, but considering what might have happened . . . He glanced around her elegant shop. Compared to Lily or Aviva, Charlotte had won the contest.

The salesgirl was locking the front door. "We're closed for business now. Mrs. MacDonald will be down as soon as she's finished with the buyer from Neiman-Marcus."

Eli leaned his head back and closed his eyes. How much more comfortable this was than that cramped seat on the transatlantic flight. He sighed as he recalled flying to locate Charlotte in Bangkok, then continuing on to track her down in Japan. He struggled with the conflicting images of their lovemaking and her confusion over where to go, what to do after he had rejected her. Could that have been when she had begun to hate him?

TOKYO, JAPAN: JULY 1955
The first Eli heard of Charlotte's marriage to Gordon MacDonald had been her telephone call from Athens to his office. He was so overjoyed to hear her voice coming from a safe country, the shock of her news was secondary. Only later did he comprehend the compli-

cations that could arise from her actually having married a man using her cover identity. Several security experts had studied the implications of her actions, and considering the other ramifications of the bungled Egyptian operations, no one was pleased with the additional headache. In the end, the Mossad's determination was that the government could not interfere in a marriage she had contracted voluntarily. So, for the time being, she would have to handle the repercussions of her commitment to Gordon.

Privately, the memuneh told Eli that while Charlotte's marriage to an American diplomat had been a dazzling feat, she had trapped herself. "I hope she is with him more out of choice than necessity," he said.

"How can she have a marriage under those circumstances?" Eli replied in an agitated voice. "She cannot live under a cover name for the rest of her life. There could be children . . ."

Harel had thrown up his hands in despair. "What can *I* do for her?"

Six months passed before Eli was called to the memuneh's office to discuss Charlotte's situation again. Harel removed his glasses and pointed them in the direction of his settee. Eli watched the man's formidable dark eyebrows arch as he began talking about the remaining difficulties of the Lavon affair. "I need you to study every loose end with a microscope."

"Isn't that what half the government has been doing for six months?"

"Not all sources have been tapped."

"What do you mean?"

Harel replaced his glasses with great deliberation. "I want you to interrogate your American friend."

"Charlotte?" he stammered. "I thought you had washed your hands of her."

"Only while the cyclone was raging. The time has come to get her side of the story. She knew Martine and Homer and —"

"What are you suggesting?"

"It is not impossible she could have implicated them."

"Never!"

"Eli," he said in his most placating tone, "her last reports from Egypt were, well, nothing short of brilliant."

"So?"

"Maybe too brilliant for so young a woman? She went much further than either ordered or expected. Flying onto military airfields, counting tanks, and meeting influential German munitions experts in her spare time."

Until now Eli had been filled with pride at Charlotte's accomplishments, but seeing them in this light he was unnerved.

"Are you suggesting that Charlotte was a double agent?"

"I'm concerned that we could be criticized for never debriefing her. She was in Egypt, in Alexandria; she knew the principals. Don't you think she could shed some light in a few dark corners?"

"Hasn't she earned the right to some peace? At first, everyone was applauding her successful escape from the clutches of the Egyptian security police. You and I know they spent weeks searching for a mysterious female contact of Homer's. All that time, her cover was never blown. So why are you going after her now?"

"Don't you see this is the best way to clear her name?"

Once it became known that Charlotte was not coming back into the Mossad, her status had turned from heroic to disgraced. "I've seen the memos from military intelligence," Eli spat bitterly, "and I know who's behind them!"

Alex Naor should have been front and center during the debacle at military intelligence, since it was *their* people who were captured. But he had protected himself deftly by being on assignment in Europe during the whole of the Lavon affair, returning in time to head up Aman's internal investigations. He must have been privy to the first interagency communications mentioning Charlotte's file name, for he quickly pointed out the waste of effort and money that had gone into Charlotte. Eli resented the fact that Alex had never acknowledged the significant information she had provided during the fairly short time she was living in Egypt. Naor had gone so far as to question the whereabouts and loyalty of the other members of the Ezra team, suggesting that Aviva and Lily be recalled from their posts at the first opportunity.

"As you well know, I am not about to take any advice from that team at Aman," Harel replied stiffly.

Eli accepted that the best way to clear Charlotte was to abide by Harel's orders. Time and again the memuneh had proven to have an amazing insight that stretched far beyond the logical, even scientific approach that Eli applied to a problem. A joke among Harel's staff was "If you showed Isser one side of a match folder, he could tell you — without looking — what is printed on the other." Unless Harel's suspicions were put to rest, the issue would never die. Even so, Eli knew it was unrealistic to believe the Lavon mess would ever be disentangled completely. Any new revelations concerning Israel's disastrous involvement in the bombing of American installations in Egypt could shatter more political careers. But this had not been his concern as he left for Bangkok.

After months of arrests, executions, forged documents, accusations, false testimonies, turmoil, resignations, and vindictive reprisals, Eli was more concerned with how Charlotte had weathered the strains of her continuing deception and whether she was in good hands. At the embassy in Bangkok he was informed the MacDonalds had moved to a new post in Japan. On the flight to Tokyo, Eli had worried about how to contact her without creating a problem with her husband. He had already decided it would be acceptable for Charles Ivy to look up an old friend without creating trouble, but should he do it by walking into the consul's office and introducing himself to her husband and becoming a "friend of the family" or by employing the clandestine techniques with which he and Charlotte were more familiar? In the end, he opted for a combination. He sent a card from the Tokyo Hotel addressed to Chris in care of her husband.

If you had asked him the moment he had landed in Japan what was going to occur next, he would not have had a ready answer, but in retrospect the little drama among Charlotte, her husband, and him had been played out as predictably as if he had picked up a script to a melodrama.

There was the initial period of elation when they reunited, followed by his rapid outline of events since she had left Egypt. Then her buoyancy diminished; her mood soured.

"I'm haunted by Homer's death and thinking about Martine in prison. Why should they be punished when I escaped so easily?" Charlotte asked.

"Isn't your marriage punishment enough?" he replied half-seriously. She had not smiled.

"By now Gordon knows what a horrid mistake he's made with me," she confessed. "He wanted *Chris* — the conservative librarian who would be an accessory to his career — not *me,* not a single aspect of my true personality. And, believe me, Eli, nobody — not even you — could carry off so intimate a masquerade twenty-four hours a day."

When Charlotte made it clear that she intended to leave Gordon, he agreed to help her. Considering there was the baby on the way, Gordon's family, and complications with the U.S. State Department, she had managed wonderfully up to that point. Eli remained at her side — whatever Harel concluded about his extended trip and additional expenses be damned — and helped her extricate herself from the diplomat with a minimum of trauma.

Only six weeks after he returned to Israel, she gave birth to a daughter, a child he had enjoyed watching grow — first into a charming child, more recently into a talented young scholar.

NEW YORK, NEW YORK: MAY 1979

A buzzing sound startled Eli. He sat upright. The salesgirl was on the phone. She placed the receiver down. "I'll be leaving, but Mrs. MacDonald said she'll be five more minutes at the most. Good evening, sir," she said as she set an alarm system.

Once she was gone, Eli felt at liberty to stroll around the store, idly fingering the merchandise. One rack featured skirts and slacks in vivid purples, reds, and blacks. Wide zippers in contrasting colors ran the length of each side seam. "Extraordinary!" Eli said under his breath. Matching sweaters were also constructed with oddly placed zippers which, if undone, would dissect the garment horizontally. He checked the price tags. Two hundred thirty dollars for a skirt that was more zipper than anything else! Who would spend that amount of money on such outlandish clothing?

Charlotte descended the spiral staircase that led to her offices. He was relieved to see she was dressed in tailored beige linen slacks, a matching jacket banded with wide black braid, and a black-and-beige-striped silk blouse. Her dark brown hair, which had been peppered with gray in Toulon, had been transformed.

"Mr. Ivy!" She extended her hand formally. "If you'll excuse me for one moment?" She turned to the reedlike waif of a girl who followed behind her carrying a briefcase under her arm. "I'll let you out, Alicia."

After some elaborate unlocking of the doors, she returned to Eli and stared at him sternly. "Eli, why have you come?"

"I needed to talk with you."

She went behind the black lacquered desk and began to file credit card receipts. "Look, Eli, when I went to France for you, I told you it was absolutely the last time."

"There's no other assignment."

"Oh?" Her fingers stopped shuffling papers.

"There are a few loose ends."

"Who sent you?"

"Nobody in particular."

"Just the way nobody in particular sent you to Japan to find out what I knew about the Lavon affair." Charlotte opened the narrow drawer in the center of her desk and removed a suede pouch. "I need to put this in the safe." She walked across the room and turned out the overhead fluorescent lamps and switched on some dim blue spotlights in the show windows.

Eli was right behind her. "Are you free for dinner?"

"Not exactly."

"You are meeting someone?"

"I'd planned to take some sushi home."

She was realizing she could not get rid of him, so she asked, "Do you want to try some?"

"I'd like that very much."

They were out on Madison Avenue. It was much cooler now that the sun was down behind the highest buildings. "Shall we walk? It's about a mile downtown, then across to Sixth Avenue."

"I can use the stretch. I only crossed this morning."

"From where? Israel?"

"No, Paris."

"Lily?" she asked in a slightly nasty tone.

"Yes, I saw Lily. She's giving up her studio. Apparently it's worth quite a sum."

"By now she probably has a small fortune socked away in Switzerland."

"On her salary?"

"Eli, she was wheeling and dealing in antiquities for years. Some of those coins alone have appreciated a thousand percent."

They paused at the corner of Fifty-seventh Street. "I don't begrudge her a comfortable retirement."

"Are you saying *I* do?"

Eli took her arm and steered her toward Fifth Avenue. "Charlotte. What's upsetting you?"

She waited a few beats before responding. "Toulon took more out of me than I expected."

"It was difficult for me as well," he replied between clenched teeth.

"That's why you're here, isn't it?"

"Partially." They passed Rockefeller Center at a furious pace. Pedestrians going uptown had to divert to let them by. They hesitated as a light changed red, but seeing the traffic hopelessly snarled, threaded their way to the other side.

Charlotte seethed as he guided her to the curb. "When will you ever tell me the truth?" She stumbled forward when she noticed they were attracting attention and did not say another word until they reached Forty-seventh Street. Three Orthodox Jewish jewelers from the Diamond Exchange walked by.

"Did you know we have operatives on this street?" Eli said to break the tension.

Charlotte glared at him. "You don't think of anything else, do you? Once I read a quote by one of the heads of military intelligence — I think it was Aharon Yariv. Anyway, it made me think of you. He said, 'Intelligence is like opium. One can become addicted to it if one loses sight of the aim.' And that's what's happened to you. There's nothing else in your life: no woman, no family, nothing. I used to think that I could help you put it in perspective. Maybe I could have, if you'd given me the chance. On the other hand, maybe I was fooling myself."

Eli wanted to remind her of another intelligence motto: "The first mistake is also the last." He held his tongue.

At Sixth Avenue they crossed the street and walked up the grimy stairs of one of the few buildings in the neighborhood that had not been razed for a monumental office tower. On the second floor, she opened a door to a restaurant identified only by a modest sign that read: TAKESUSHI.

A waitress in a kimono bowed. "Sushi bar or table?"

"Table." Charlotte pointed to one in a remote corner by a window overlooking Forty-fifth Street.

Eli was amused that she took the safe position: with her back to the wall and a view of the entire restaurant.

The waitress poured pale green Japanese tea into pottery cups and handed them warm rolled towels. Eli wiped his hands gratefully. Promptly, the waitress passed a basket to collect the soiled linen and asked if they were ready to order.

Charlotte put down her menu. "Shall I select for you?"

"You're the expert."

"Two miso soups, two deluxe sushi, one California roll, one yellowtail hand roll, two uni, two Kirin beer."

"I'm impressed," he said sincerely.

The soup was served. Charlotte snapped apart her chopsticks and began lifting out the slippery white squares of bean curd while waiting for the broth to cool. "All this has something to do with what happened when you went to the Concorde apartment house. Am I right?"

"Yes," he replied cautiously.

"You were supposed to pick someone up. I waited in the car. That's when it all fell apart."

There was no use denying it to Charlotte. She had been there; she had witnessed his uncharacteristic reactions. "You're right. I could not discuss it then."

"Why? Didn't you trust me?"

"I had to protect you. Ignorance was safety."

"Eli, for God's sake!" She lowered her voice considerably. "There was blood on your shoes. After I took over the driving, you wiped them with your handkerchief."

"One of our operatives was killed."

"By whom?"

"You know as much as I do."

"I might have known a hell of a lot more if I had been told something. What a waste to have employed me so superficially. I was at my prime when *I* was making my decisions, planning my moves."

"You *never* screwed up?"

He picked up the soup bowl and sipped in the Japanese manner. The warm liquid was instantly soothing. Out of the corner of his eye he could see Charlotte's fingers twisting her paper chopsticks case nervously.

Eli was finding her aggression curious. For the first time in all his interrogations, he found himself able to contemplate that one of his operatives could be the culprit. But the basic question was unanswered: Why, bloody why?

She lunged on. "So someone was killed. It happens all the time in this business. You could not expect everything to go perfectly forever. Oh, I know you like to think of yourself as having clean hands. Who doesn't? Truthfully, I've been kidding myself too. Remember the ambush on the east bank of the Jordan?"

"Why don't you ask yourself how many Israeli lives you saved?"

"I've used that self-deception too."

"You have regrets?"

"I fucking well do!" She lowered her voice again when the waitress approached with two large lacquer dishes containing an elegant assortment of raw fish arranged with rice and seaweed. "Any normal human being would."

Charlotte's foul language did not shock Eli. She had been fond of peppering her speech with such words since they had first met — a sign of rebellion she had never outgrown. Funny, though; Chris rarely cursed.

Eli concentrated on the sushi.

Charlotte poured soy sauce into the tiny saucers by each dish. Then she lifted a small pile of green wasabi, the Japanese horseradish, from her plate and stirred some into each of the sauces. "I'll make yours fairly mild. Add more if you wish."

He lifted his chopsticks and reached for a slice of raw tuna surrounded by rice and wrapped in seaweed.

Charlotte tapped his hand. "Use your fingers."

"Truly?"

"That's how they eat it in Japan. Watch me. First you pick up the sushi with your thumb and middle finger — like this — and let your index finger rest at the end of the piece. Then, turn it over gently while moving your fingers to the end of the tané — that's the fish or whatever's on it. See? The tané's on the underside."

Eli tried to mimic her movements without destroying the whole delicate assembly.

"Got it? Good. This is when you dip the tané into the shoyu — that's the sauce."

Eli did as he was told and took a bite.

"Not bad, but you shouldn't get any shoyu on the rice portion and you must position it so that the tané lands on your tongue." She demonstrated the maneuver daintily.

Eli shifted in his seat. "I can't see how eating the fish upside down affects the flavor."

"That's not the point. Let's say a foreigner ordered a Whopper and put the ketchup and pickles on top of the bun. It tastes the same with the condiments on the outside of the roll as on the inside, but wouldn't you agree that the experience is somehow altered?"

"Excellent analogy, my dear. Any other sushi tips?"

"Sweet toppings, such as rolled egg and conger eel, should be eaten without the dipping sauce and, if the smell of the fish or the sweetness of egg remains in your mouth so you cannot savor the vinegared rice, you crunch a piece of pickled ginger to freshen your palate."

As he listened, he was reminded how much Charlotte liked to run a show. Her organizational skills were exceptional, but she had never worked at the center. Only in Egypt had she been given the freedom to control her own day-to-day operations, yet even there she had managed within a range of prescribed limitations. For the most part, she had functioned admirably. Only her hasty marriage had jeopardized her standing. To her critics — like Alex Naor — Eli had defended her actions by asking what they would have done under similar circumstances. As she herself insisted, the bottom line of that mission was that she had escaped Egypt without hurting any other operatives. She had redeemed herself completely with the Iraqi MiG coup. Nevertheless, in locations such as Cherbourg and Toulon, Charlotte had been warned to follow orders precisely. Perhaps Eli had underestimated her resentment at being treated like an underling. Even if that was true, was that enough of a motive to have . . . to have what? To have had someone murdered . . . ? To have almost killed him . . . and Colin? He glanced over at Charlotte. She was eyeing him warily.

"Try the uni," Charlotte insisted, and then in a fast, nervous monologue recited the glories of sea urchin roe.

He swallowed the uni in one gulp, probably missing the subtleties of taste that Charlotte was extolling, and continued with his analysis of what had gone wrong. "Those regrets, what might they be?"

"The list is too long to enumerate."

"I have plenty of time."

"To begin with, we have been taking the wrong tack politically. I heard 'Fatti' Harkabi, one of our esteemed directors of military intelligence, speak when I was in Israel for the El-Ad trial. He said that we 'cannot have good intelligence in a society of fools.' He warned us not to forget to 'filter the gloom and jubilation within the confines of our tiny country, before deciding on policy and its effects.' "

Eli brushed back an unruly lock of hair that covered his left eye. "Yes?"

"These cat-and-mouse games are the most primitive stopgap measures. Christ! It is 1979, not 1948. Thirty years and no sign of peace on the horizon. We have got to make some major concessions if we are ever going to live without fear."

Eli leaned back in his chair. He would let her hang herself. "What might those concessions be?" he asked deferentially.

"How many people are living on the West Bank?"

"About three quarters of a million."

"The vast majority is Arab, right? What the hell good does it do for Israel to govern a land where so many residents are enemies. Forget all the polemics for a moment. The fact is that the West Bank's Arab population isn't going to pick up and move again." She waited for his reaction.

"What do you suggest?"

"Israel would lose all sympathies that it, as the underdog, has garnered from the rest of the world if it forced any Arabs out. And we can't go on with the pipe dream that the Palestinians will be absorbed by Jordan. Actually, it is more likely that the Palestinians will absorb Jordan. So that leaves two choices: annex the West Bank once and for all and grant full citizenship rights to the Arab population — which will screw up the balance of power in the Knesset — or give the West Bank back, but with assurances that it remains a demilitarized zone."

"Do you think that is a *practical* solution?"

"Do *you* think this eternal conflict is practical?"

"It is under control."

"Bullshit! Since '67, we have become disgustingly cocky; we think we cannot lose. Well, we learned a few lessons in the Yom Kippur War, but they don't seem to have stuck. Every time something like the Entebbe raid comes along, we become convinced we are invincible again. We have to remember we are fragile, we are small, we are poor, and we are surrounded by fervent enemies. It is people like *you* who keep stoking the fires, aggravating the situation."

"What do you say to all those Jews who feel the West Bank — or, as they would say, Judea and Samaria — contains the very heart of Eretz Israel where their prophets prophesied, their kings ruled?"

"We cannot continue to make twentieth-century political decisions based on two-thousand-year-old artifacts. But even if we could, that line of reasoning suggests we should give back the coastal regions — which were not inherently Jewish in Biblical times — to the Philistines who became the Palestinians." She gave a deep-throated laugh. "Do you think Israel would trade Tel Aviv for Jericho or the Mediterranean for the Dead Sea?"

Eli was not surprised to hear these sentiments. Similar views were being voiced by many respected Israelis who, after the Yom Kippur War, had formed a movement called Shalom Achchav — Peace Now. Their membership included senior army officers, artists, intellectuals, workers from every walk of life. It was Charlotte's vehemence that was shocking.

"So, you think we should give back the West Bank and call it the Palestinian state?"

"Yes."

"And what is the precedence in history for the conquering army returning territory?"

"Peace doesn't require a precedent. The United Nations Resolution 242 states that it is forbidden to acquire land by war."

"That is as ridiculous as asking the United States to give back California or New Mexico."

"I don't agree."

"Well then, let us assume we call in the Palestinian leaders, sit down with them, and pull out the maps. We say, 'Show us what is Palestine and we will return it to you.' Do you know what they will demand? They will claim the borders of Palestine include the State of Israel, the West Bank, the Gaza Strip, the Hashemite Kingdom of Jordan, south Lebanon, Syria up to Damascus, and northern Sinai. All right, perhaps they will agree they cannot have the whole pie and suggest we divide the land by population. Now we ask them, 'How many Palestinian people are there?' They say, 'Three and a half million.' We say, 'There are three and a half million Israelis also. So, let us partition the territory in half.' But how? Crosswise? Lengthwise?"

"Let me ask you how Jews, without a homeland for centuries, can sanction uprooting another Semitic population?"

"Who is uprooting whom? I was *born* in Palestine. So was my mother."

"How do we justify our prosperity at their expense?"

"I have no patience with that point of view," he said bitterly. "Once, I sat next to some French tourists on a flight from Tel Aviv to London. They said to me, 'We can understand why the Arabs are angry. The greedy Jews grabbed the best land — everything green.' If we had been given Transjordan under the Mandate, we would have made *it* the Garden of Eden and the western areas would still be uninhabitable." He clenched his fists under the table. "There are no simplistic solutions. I'm sorry."

Charlotte was consoling. "I shouldn't have dumped all that on you so suddenly. I've been contributing to Shalom Achchav for several years — along with some of Israel's top generals, I might add."

"I know some of the movement's leaders myself and I believe that if a war began today they would fight to the death for Israel with the same fervor they demonstrate while searching for peace on other fronts. It is my personal view, however, that their perspective is misguided."

"I knew that's how you would feel; that is why I haven't been forthcoming with you — although I don't think anything I've ever said or done has been detrimental to our country or cause," she added hastily.

"I didn't suggest it has," he replied cautiously as he struggled to fathom the nuances of her confession.

"I expected to shock you." Charlotte forced a tranquil smile. "I know you prefer the docile Mrs. Roland Woodrow in Toulon who did your bidding without question. For too long I've been in turmoil on the inside — especially in your presence — but masked it with a veneer of obedience and order. No longer." She paused and lifted her glass of beer. She studied the amber liquid briefly, then replaced it and sipped instead from the lukewarm cup of Japanese tea.

Charlotte moistened her lips. Eli waited expectantly for what she would say next.

"There is a region in Switzerland called the Engadine. Do you know where that is?" she began unexpectedly.

"Around St.-Moritz, I believe."

"Yes, in the Grisons. Allison and I have gone skiing there several times. I was always fascinated by their peculiar style of architecture: they decorate the buildings with a process called sgraffito — that's where graffiti comes from, I believe. Anyway, it's a lovely method of scraping the surface with scrolls and rosettes and . . ."

Eli was becoming impatient with this ridiculous diversion, but he saw no way to interrupt.

". . . The point is . . ."

Finally.

". . . They have the most unusual windows: small, irregularly placed in asymmetrical patterns, and widening outward. At first my sensibilities were offended by the crazy patterns until I went inside the homes and discovered the reason. Each window is constructed to suit the room. Consideration is given to furniture placement, morning or afternoon sunlight requirements: They serve the *needs* of the inhabitants rather than the aesthetic requirements of the world at large."

She poured them each another cup of tea. "What does this mean, at least to me?" she asked without stopping for his response. "For too long I have attempted to master the exterior. In your service, I was determined to have the most ironclad cover. As Allison's mother, I vowed to give her every advantage. In business, I refused to compromise on quality or service. While I was successful most of the time, I never found contentment. Ever since I first went to St.-Moritz, I've had dreams about the delightful Engadine houses, sketched them, even considered owning one someday. When I was in Toulon, I became aware of why they were so much on my mind and concluded that I did not have to *own* one, I could *be* one. To hell with the exterior! From now on all decisions will be made on the basis of what is best for the living quarters." Charlotte tossed her head back and grinned, immensely pleased with herself. "You could apply the same lesson to yourself, my dear Eli — or to Israel."

"I cannot say I have followed your line of reasoning entirely, but you have made some interesting points," he replied. "You would not repeat any of it again?"

"Idiot that I am, I probably would fall into the same traps."

Eli was very still.

Charlotte sipped her tea thoughtfully. "The hotel in Toulon. Sharing the room with you. You'd think a woman my age would have herself under control. Well, damn it, Eli, I don't. I've always tried to remain high-minded about my work with you, but I've finally faced the truth. I am a very single-minded person and I always believed that . . . Shit!" She blinked back some tears and reached for her beer. She finished the glass in two gulps. "When I married Gordon I knew it was a ruse so it didn't count. The only complication was conceiving Allison, but that worked out in the end. She's always been a terrific kid. When you came to Tokyo . . . oh, God, I was so certain everything was about to progress according to my plan . . . but that was almost twenty-five years ago. Twenty-five years. How could I have been so stupid for so long?"

"You're saying that I have been your motivation, your *only* motivation?"

"You cannot pretend to be shocked."

"Frankly, I don't buy it."

She stopped eating. Her greenish-gold eyes bored into his relentlessly. Prying his eyes away, he searched the room for the waitress to order some more beer, ask for tea, anything to avoid confronting the ugly side of her obsession. No reprieve was in sight. The restaurant had filled to capacity and he could not catch anyone's attention.

There was no use skirting the issue any longer. "Did you by any chance see Lily in Toulon?"

"No."

"She was there."

"That doesn't surprise me."

"She said she saw you one afternoon but didn't call attention to herself."

"Of course, she wouldn't. Not that most perfect of persons. What I always wondered was why the hell she wouldn't have you. Is it true she preferred women?"

Eli did not respond.

Charlotte went on. "I didn't see her in Toulon and I doubt she recognized me."

"Lily was quite positive she saw you talking to two men."

"Where?"

"The Place de la Liberté, on the side near the Boulevard de Strasbourg."

"I know where it is, but I've never walked around that area and I certainly did not meet two men there. She was mistaken."

Eli was freezing this denial in his mind: every word, every fluctuation of her voice. He observed that her gaze was shifting, there was a perceptible twitch at the right side of her mouth, and her hands were gripping the chopsticks so hard he expected they might snap.

Eli backed off. "Yes, Lily might have been confused."

Charlotte almost managed to conceal the sigh she emitted.

Eli lifted the salmon roe to his mouth. The slippery orange eggs burst as he chewed. The taste was salty and pungent. He swallowed hard. Charlotte was lying about Toulon and her political opinions were aberrant — at least from any she had espoused in the past.

Boris Guriel used to say that everyone was vulnerable to the enemy, that everyone had a point where they would do the unthinkable. A few could be turned for money; most could be turned for love. Eli remembered disagreeing vehemently until Guriel, with a sly smile, had clarified his meaning.

"You concluded I meant romantic love, didn't you? I am thinking of our natural instincts to protect our children, our families and — in a larger sense — our tribe. If someone threatened to harm your loved one, would you sacrifice him rather than capitulate?"

Eli had been uncertain.

"You are only being truthful with yourself. *Nobody* is immune. *Nobody* can predict his response under duress."

Could Charlotte have succumbed to a twisted variation of this concept in which her unrequited love gave birth to some intense emotions that had gone awry? It seemed far-fetched, but not entirely implausible.

He required more proof, but he did not think he could squeeze any more information from Charlotte. In fact, it would be self-defeating to antagonize her. He needed to ease off, turn to more social matters before she became suspicious. This had to be handed over to the professional interrogators who had the training to extract the truth. Where would they do it? It would be best to get her to Israel, but he doubted if they would be able to make those arrangements. Of course, there were many safe houses in New York . . . Then what? After she confessed . . . after they had the names, the facts, the proof . . . the motive . . . His gut heaved.

He excused himself and went to the men's room. When he returned, he half expected she would have vanished, but Charlotte was sipping tea calmly. Was she play-acting or was she that naïve?

As he was about to take his seat opposite her, she gestured to a cluster of people waiting by the entryway. "They're clamoring for our table. I've paid the check. Shall we go?"

"I was taking *you* to dinner."

"It was my offer, don't you remember?" For the first time that evening her voice was actually sweet.

They walked downstairs and out onto Forty-fifth Street. "Where are you staying?" Charlotte asked.

"The Hilton," Eli lied.

"I'll walk you up Sixth Avenue."

"How's Allison?"

"Very well. She's finishing her master's thesis this summer."

"Is she living with you?"

"No, she's rooming with three girls in the East Village, not far from where my first shop was."

"Is it closed?"

"For almost five years. Didn't you know that?"

"No. I haven't kept track very well, have I?"

"Do you want to call her?"

"Yes, I'd like to." Eli knew he needed to see Allison before turning her mother in. At least Allison should know he was there for her. "May I have the number?"

Charlotte reached into her pocketbook and pulled out a slender pad of notepaper. The pages were pre-creased into thirds. She ripped off the bottom third and began to write out her daughter's work number. Eli could not help but notice what she was doing. "It is difficult to break an old habit, isn't it?"

Charlotte looked perplexed momentarily. "Oh, the paper! Only you would have caught that." Agents were trained to write any crucial numbers, directions, or codes on the smallest piece of paper possible. At the first sign of trouble, the slips were to be retrieved, buried, destroyed — even swallowed if necessary. Charlotte ripped off the second third from the sheet of paper and brought it to her lips. "It meets all the criteria: thin, chewable — this taste isn't even bad. My favorite is rice paper. It dissolves in the mouth." She handed him the number. "Allison's usually at the clinic from eleven to seven or eight in the evening."

"Such late hours."

"She works on her thesis in the mornings. She's very dedicated. You'd be proud of her."

They'd reached the circular drive of the Hilton, a hotel often favored by the Mossad because of its vast lobbies and numerous elevators and stairways. He knew the back areas intimately.

Charlotte stopped by the taxi stand. She stared out in the distance for a moment, then began what sounded like a rehearsed speech. "After Toulon, I did some serious thinking and had decided to sever all ties with my former profession, with Israel, and mostly with you. *All ties.* I want an uncomplicated life." She faced him directly. "I deserve one."

"In Toulon we got on splendidly."

"That's how you may have felt; I was miserable."

"I don't understand —"

"I didn't expect to find it so difficult to be in the same room with you again. But I did. You will have to find another make-believe wife when the next job requires one."

"We aren't training as many women as before."

"That's probably wise."

"Why do you say that?"

"I would have denied this years ago, but after all is said and done, we respond too emotionally."

"What about the women of the Palmach?"

"Those were unique circumstances. The Palmachniks were raised under such violent conditions, certain rules ceased to apply — at least temporarily."

Eli nodded gravely. "I too have so many regrets . . ." He took her hand. It was as cold as ice.

She withdrew it rapidly. "Please agree not to bother me again."

A taxi honk startled him. He drew back against the hotel's façade. "I'm looking forward to seeing Allison" was all he answered. "You know how much I've cared for her —"

"Cut the crap!" she cursed under her breath. "You've fed me that line for years. When we needed you, you were not interested in us. If you choose to contact Allison, do it, but I don't want to know about it from either her or you."

"But —" He was seeming to protest, even though this was a relief. She was making what he had to do far more simple.

"Will you agree?"

"Not to see you again?"

"I want your promise."

"I will not agree to anything so melodramatic. All I will say is that I am sorry that it turned out so disastrously. Good-bye."

He followed a plump woman through the revolving door. When he was inside, he glanced back to the taxi stand. Charlotte was getting into a cab.

He turned in to the Mirage bar and ordered a large, very dry Beefeater martini.

❖　❖　❖

The pay phones in the Hilton's crowded downstairs lobby were all in use. Eli took the escalator up to the convention floor where screenings for the American Film Festival were in progress. A contingent from a company drumming up interest in mountaineering films was strolling around in full climbing regalia. Their T-shirts read, "Pinnacle Productions: Always on Top." Colin would like one of those, Eli mused as he walked into a phone booth down the farthest end of the corridor.

He dialed "0." "International operator, please."

"For what country?" The voice was Brooklyn nasal.

"Israel."

"One moment, please."

Eli studied his watch. It was the middle of the night in Tel Aviv. He vacillated. Waking Ehud Dani would signal urgency. Charlotte was not going anywhere. Even if she suspected he was on to her, where could she disappear? Had she guessed what he was after? He thought not. If she had been concerned, she would have kept her anger in check. What if he waited until tomorrow to place his call? Dani would ask him how long he had known. If he told the truth,

Dani would have faulted him for not informing him immediately.

"What's the number in Israel?"

Eli gave the one Dani insisted he memorize. After only two rings, the phone was answered. "Hello." The voice was wide awake.

"Hello, this is Mickey." Dani had devised a ludicrous Disney-based code.

"Where are you, Mickey?"

"The Magic Kingdom."

"Right. What can I do for you?"

"It's Wendy."

"Are you certain?"

"I can't confirm the details, but there are possible motives at best and some serious discrepancies at worst. Your boys will have to take it from here."

"Is she worried?"

"I don't think so."

"What about Snow White and Minnie?"

"They are clean."

"You are positive?"

Eli was silent.

"Hello?"

"Yes, I am here."

"Are you all right?"

"It has been difficult."

"I can imagine it has. Listen, take a break. I will come over to-morrow."

"You?"

"That is the plan."

"What shall I do?"

"Nothing. I will take it from here."

"Right."

"And Mickey . . ."

"Yes?"

"Thank you."

The phone went dead.

Eli made his way to the street. He walked across Sixth Avenue and up to the park. With forceful strides he made his way toward the Stanhope, thirty blocks uptown. With every step, his agitation increased. What had he just done to Charlotte? To himself?

His head pounded with unanswered questions. How had Charlotte been approached? Who had turned her, and when? How many years had she been feeding information to the other side? And for what remuneration? Just the satisfaction of ruining his career or for monetary gain? Charlotte's store was lavish. The rents must be astronomical. Fashion was a ruthless business. Maybe she had gotten herself in some sort of a bind and needed money.

No, not money — hate. All the pro-Palestinian rhetoric was a justification for what she herself could not face.

She had despised him.

She had wanted revenge.

The bomb in London had been meant to kill him, not scare him. That is why she must have been shocked to see him. She had expected him to be dead but had tried to cover her surprise with her bitchy behavior.

It was all falling into place — or was it?

While Eli could now imagine Charlotte wanting to destroy him, he could not extend her treachery to all of Israel. How she had loved Israel. She had fought for the state, counted each precious vote at Lake Success, committed herself to the service with her heart and mind and body. After thirty years, after Egypt, and the MiG, and Cherbourg — no. It was too much to comprehend.

Eli had reached the Metropolitan Museum of Art. Its façade was bathed in lemony lights. He sat on one of the bottom steps and gazed dully at the off-duty taxis streaking down Fifth Avenue.

By now Ehud would have called London and informed Alex. Eventually, Eli would have to confront Naor himself and admit he had been right to distrust Charlotte all these years. Considering what Charlotte would be facing, however, his ordeal did not seem so grave. The Mossad would never permit her to go free, but they would not get rid of her until they were satisfied she had delivered a full account of her actions and sources. Charlotte was not stubborn. She would see the wisdom in cooperating. Also, Charlotte was softer than the others — always had been. Lily would never have rushed off to marry MacDonald; Aviva would have found another way out. But nobody else had quite Charlotte's flair either. Who else would have had the chutzpah to land at el-Shallûfa? When the dust settled, he wondered what the final tally would be. Would they decide Charlotte's work for Israel outweighed her betrayal? Or were such equations impossible to complete?

His forehead throbbed painfully. Two policemen were patrolling the area. He did not want to seem to loiter, so he crossed the street and entered the friendly lobby of his hotel. The clerk greeted him with a smile as he asked for his key. He said good night and hurried to the elevator.

In his room, Eli stripped and turned the shower on full blast. Even as he lathered his body, he felt unclean. Filthy. Defiled. Was it because of what Charlotte had done to him — or he to her? While he had lived on the fringes of a dirty business, he had been an idea man, a paper pusher, an organizer of the war of minds. All his bombs were on paper. None was ever fired — at least not by him. From the beginning he had located people who had then been turned over to others for "handling." There had been half a dozen in Bremen whom the British had taken away, but these had only been deported or denied exit visas. Then there was Cyprus. Several dozen fakers had been rooted out, although he doubted any had been dealt with as harshly as Hans de Vries. De Vries, the bastard who had ruined Lily's life. On that score he had no regrets. Nor the times when he had killed in self-defense. The massaging shower head pummeled his back. Soapy water swirled at his feet. He turned the hot water off and blasted himself with one long burst from the cold tap, then dried himself vigorously.

He reflected on the major victims of his lifelong battle against the enemies of his people: de Vries . . . El Setouhy, the Egyptian scientist . . . Dr. Ze'evi . . . and how many others before finishing with Charlotte Green MacDonald?

Charlotte.

When he lay down on the bed and closed his eyes he recalled how he first had seen her: lying on the bench at the airport with the book *Hiroshima* tucked under her head . . . the crooked seams in her stockings . . . her slender ankles . . . her shiny pageboy hairdo . . . Her face had been so smooth, her fingers so delicate, and when Sadie Goldfarb had asked the favor she had agreed so readily.

If only he had passed her by.

❖   ❖   ❖

The next morning, Eli ordered coffee in his room and watched the *Today* show. At nine o'clock he pulled out the piece of paper from his wallet and dialed Allison's work number.

"Windsor Clinic."

"Allison MacDonald, please."

"Ms. McDonald isn't in until eleven today. Would you like to leave a message?"

He had forgotten her late schedule. "No, thank you." He hung up the phone. "Damn!" He tried to think of a way to occupy the next two hours. The museum was not open yet and he did not want to walk the bright streets. He switched on the television and watched a talk show and two game shows. At five minutes past eleven he placed the call again.

"Allison MacDonald," the cheery voice identified herself.

"It's Uncle Eli, Allison. I'm in New York."

"Oh, that's marvelous. Have you seen Mother?"

"We had dinner last night. I was hoping to see you before I left town. How about today? Lunch?"

"I get in so late I don't take off for lunch. I have a staff meeting next and, afterward, a group therapy session from one to two. Then I see clients."

"Dinner?"

"When are you leaving?"

"Tomorrow."

"Oh, gosh." She paused. "It's not a good night because I take a class, but I could miss it."

"I wouldn't want you to —"

"No, it's okay. I'd like to see you. It's been how long? A year?"

"About that."

"I'm never quite certain when my last appointment is over because not everyone arrives on time and we still try to give them their fifty minutes. Could you meet me here?"

"Certainly, Allison."

"It's on Twenty-third Street between Madison and Third. Come up to the second-floor reception area. All right?"

"What time would suit your schedule?"

"The earliest I'd be free would be five."

"I'll be there then."

"You won't mind if I'm running late?"

"Not at all."

Eli faced a day with nothing to do. The Metropolitan Museum was the closest option. He crossed Fifth Avenue and absently followed a mother and four- or five-year-old daughter who preceded him up the grand exterior staircase, through the admissions area, and all the way to the Temple of Dendur. The inquisitive child reminded him of Allison at the same age. He had not known Charlotte's daughter until then. Charlotte had agreed to return to Israel for the trial of Avri El-Ad, the military intelligence agent who had headed the Israeli sabotage operations in Egypt under the alias Paul Frank.

He had managed to escape at the time Martine, Homer, and the others were arrested, and was accused of treason. Charlotte had had no contact with him, of course, but her knowledge of the situation was valuable in the preparation of documents for the case prosecuting El-Ad for high crimes against the state. It was hoped that the results of this trial would once and forever put an end to the political crisis of the Lavon affair.

Eli remembered when Charlotte had difficulty with the first baby sitter she found for Allison in Israel and needed an emergency replacement after she discovered welts on the child's buttocks. Allison claimed she was hit for spilling her soup; the baby sitter said it was because the child had kicked her. Charlotte was outraged. Eli's solution was to call his mother. Ruth Short had been delighted to take on Allison during the day, and since she spoke perfect English, Allison took to her immediately. Even Hugo was soon enchanted with the spirited, talkative child with a bouquet of freckles dappling her cheeks.

After a few weeks, Eli's mother had become fast friends with Charlotte. What high hopes both women must have had during that period. Perhaps Charlotte expected his mother and Charlotte's charming daughter would work the magic spell that she had failed to weave. The combination had been as dynamic — and frightening — as a battering ram. To avoid being crushed, he had maneuvered himself as far away from Charlotte as possible. If they had not been so obvious, he might very well have succumbed. His affair with Lily had been over for several years. He adored little Allison. Charlotte was as beautiful as ever. But nothing clicked. Once again Charlotte failed to strike the responsive chord — the one only Maura and Lily had managed to elicit.

Maura and Lily.

An analyst might have had a field day comparing his obsessions with these two thoroughly desirable yet unattainable women, each of whom had rejected him before he could turn against them, while he then rejected the women who declared their interest in him.

While Eli had resisted Charlotte's enchantments, he had not been immune to her daughter's. Perhaps because of Allison's unfortunate experience with the baby sitter, perhaps because of her age or her personality, she began to label every thing, person, or action as either good or bad, right or wrong.

"Tell me a story," she would say when she climbed up onto "Uncle Eli's" lap.

"What sort of story?"

"About a parrot. A good parrot and a bad parrot."

Then it would be Eli's task to invent an amusing tale as rapidly as possible. The beasts varied; the theme remained constant. The bad animal attempted to harm the good animal with some devious trick. In the end, however, the good animal would triumph through cleverness and virtuous deeds. Eli's lead characters were birds, cats, dogs, tigers, horses, aardvarks, even unicorns, before Allison requested a tale about a good camel and a bad camel. After that, she always asked for new variations on the camels. When she was older she reminded him of her favorite stories and could repeat to him ones he had long since forgotten.

In the museum, Eli followed the loquacious little girl and her mother into the Fountain Restaurant. He selected a cup of coffee and a Danish and took a seat on the same side of the courtyard pool so he could overhear mother and daughter discussing what it must have been like to have been a knight who wore a heavy suit of armor. The mother was looking in his direction. Self-consciously, he stirred his coffee and hoped she had not sensed he had been near them for some time lest she might think he was some sort of pervert.

Good camel, bad camel.

Why in the world had Allison been so concerned with morality and ethics at such an early age? Had the issues of the El-Ad trial somehow filtered into her child's mind and required sorting out in a more orderly way? Survival in civilization was dependent on learning what a given society considered acceptable behavior. Growing up involved gradually revising simplistic labels of evil and righteousness.

The Danish was far too sweet. Eli took only one bite and washed it down with the blessedly bitter coffee. The little girl was sipping chocolate milk from a carton and chattering nonstop. Her mother was nodding absently and looking around the room. As Eli stood up to leave, a man wearing white slacks and a kelly green golf shirt came forward to greet the mother. The child did not seem to recognize the man. They were being introduced. The man had slipped his arm around her mother's waist and was giving her bottom a familiar squeeze. The mother was beaming. The man was ignoring the child while openly adoring the woman.

Eli turned away from the little drama and walked out of the dining room. Good camel, bad camel. Good mother, bad mother. Was she divorced? Was she cheating on her husband? He found his way to the front of the museum. Good mother, bad mother. Was that the story he was going to have to tell Allison this afternoon? There were no explanations for what was about to happen. All he could do was offer his help, his friendship, his ... He would call her. He would cancel the appointment. Eli was at the bottom of the museum steps, squinting in the sunlight. No, he had to see Allison again. He owed her that. But what was he going to say?

❖ ❖ ❖

The rest of the afternoon had to be lived out. Eli walked until he found a movie theater. The film was *Coming Home* with Jane Fonda and Jon Voight. Not that he cared. He only wanted a soft seat and darkness and a mindless diversion. He stopped and checked the times. It was ten minutes until the next performance. Two hours later, he knew he had been so caught up in his own turmoil he had not followed the story of the film about Vietnam veterans. All he recalled was Sally in various stages of erotic undress and Luke smashing up a hospital corridor with his cane. As the lights came on, he began to wonder what the movie had been about. With plenty of time before he could meet Allison, he decided it was easiest to remain in his seat.

The second time through, the story began to make more sense, and by the time it was over, he was grateful to have forgotten his own problems for a few hours.

It was five minutes to five when he walked into the Windsor Clinic. The reception room was far shabbier than he had expected. Cigarette butts littered the gritty linoleum floor; cushions were missing from several of the orange plastic sofas.

The receptionist was on the phone, trying to settle an argument. "Tell Timothy it'll just have to wait until I get home." She noticed Eli standing there. "Gotta go now." She slammed down the receiver. "Yes?"

"Allison MacDonald, please."

"She's expecting you?"

"Yes, at five."

"Your name?"

"Just say her uncle's here."

The receptionist shrugged. "Have a seat. I can't interrupt her until her session's over."

Eli pretended to be fascinated with a year-old issue of *Sports Illustrated* while observing the odd characters in the waiting room: a bald man with an earring in his left ear, a black woman — who looked like a fashion model — with an obese daughter, two teenage boys who were holding hands, and a young girl who was so skinny she looked like a concentration camp victim. How could little Allison help these disturbed people? In Toulon, Charlotte had told him that Allison was already doing marriage counseling. At twenty-four! How in the world did she have enough experience? And what couple would trust her to intervene in their lives?

"Uncle Eli!"

Eli stood and almost kissed Allison, but stopped himself when he guessed she might not want to be treated familiarly in this setting. He held out his hand.

Determined to seem professional, Allison was dressed in a slim blue skirt and matching suit jacket. Her blouse was a man-tailored stripe with a brooch at the collar instead of a tie. Her tawny ringlets drooped naturally to her shoulders. Despite the care she had taken to look mature, she could not hide her round freckled face or petite figure that made her seem far too young for the responsibilities she had undertaken.

"Are you ready?"

"No, Uncle Eli. I'm terribly sorry. There was a crisis about an hour ago, so I'm running thirty minutes late. What shall we do? I know you've been waiting already and —"

"I'm in no rush. Take your time."

"Listen, there's a vacant office next to mine. You'll be more comfortable there."

Eli followed Allison back through a warren of cubicles and offices. In one larger room, chairs were set in a circle and a group of pregnant young girls were taking their seats. They stopped at a small pantry with a refrigerator.

"What would you like to drink? A Coke?"

"Thank you."

They continued to a cluttered office. "Here we are. Now, what can I get you to read?" She waved to a stack of professional journals. "These aren't very exciting but" — she opened her briefcase and took out a thick treatise — "would you like to take a look at my thesis?"

"Absolutely."

"I hoped you would say yes. Let me know what you think. I have to defend it in two weeks and I'm scared to death! I'll be back in less than an hour. Promise."

She closed the door gently and left him alone.

The soda can was slippery with condensation. He took a sip and pressed the icy metal to his throbbing forehead. He realized he had eaten hardly anything for twenty-four hours and wondered where he might take Allison to dinner. He hoped she was not another sushi fanatic. What he wanted most was a hot pastrami sandwich.

He stared at the daunting manuscript. He read the title: "Sexual Dysfunction as Sequelae to Post-Traumatic Stress Disorder: Vietnam War Veterans."

Allison had taken up psychology against her mother's advice. Charlotte had told him she felt her daughter would not find long-term satisfaction helping confused people and had argued that the profession was overstaffed and underpaid already.

"Can't you remember your own noble causes?" Eli had asked.

"Why do you think I'm trying to dissuade her from following that path? If only I could tell her the truth about me."

Eli had assured Charlotte that in a few more years partial revelations would be sanctioned. After thirty years, the Mossad was willing to relinquish its hold on certain secrets. That had not satisfied Charlotte. "It's too late. There were too many lies."

He wondered what Allison knew; the less the better, considering what was about to happen to her mother. Disturbed by those worries, he turned back to the thesis.

Allison was more like her mother than she knew. Somehow she had managed to select a hot topic that was receiving media attention. Charlotte's intuitive trend-spotting in fashion had led to her own financial success. But what could bouncy little Allison know about such a convoluted subject? Curious, Eli began to read.

He skipped a long discussion about how her forty-five subjects were selected, controlling for socioeconomic status, age, and race, and her rationale for wanting to learn whether similar symptoms were present in subjects from different backgrounds. The statistical analyses and other charts were incomprehensible. Pages and pages were devoted to her development of a structured clinical interview as well as data on her men, including aspects of their military records. Thoroughly befuddled by all the jargon, he went back to the introduction and reread her explanation of the basic difficulty.

The essential feature of Post-Traumatic Stress Disorder (PTSD), either chronic or delayed, is the development of characteristic symptoms following an occurrence that is generally not within the range of common human experience. These symptoms include re-experiencing the traumatic event and a lessened involvement with the outside world.

The part about the re-experiencing of a traumatic event recalled the movie he had seen that afternoon. One of the characters referred to having "flashbacks to when I got fucked up." So, those flashbacks were not just a scriptwriter's contrivance.

He read on:

> The stressor producing PTSD is usually outside the range of common distressing experiences that many or most people experience over a lifetime, including serious illness, bereavement, financial difficulties, and family conflicts. The trauma may be experienced alone (as in the case of assault or rape) or in a group situation (military combat). Disasters, both manmade and natural, may be stressors.

Eli put down the paper and rubbed his eyes. All along he had supposed this problem was brought on only in combat situations where nice, ordinary young men were forced to cross the ethical boundaries of their upbringing in order to kill other human beings. It was apparently far more complex a disorder than he had imagined.

Gideon's specialty was working with torture victims. Eli wondered if he knew of this research. He studied the next explanations attentively.

> The most severe and longest lasting cases of PTSD seem to appear when the stressor was of deliberate human design (terrorist bombings, torture, death camps).

Death camps. Israel was filled with concentration camp survivors.

The next section, labeled "Dissociativelike States," went on to describe the manner in which painful recollections haunted the subjects in the form of nightmares during sleep stages or hallucinations during the waking hours when the individual seemed to be reliving the event. Was this what was meant by a flashback?

Under the section titled "Emotional Anesthesia" he studied the descriptions of how the subjects felt.

> "I feel detached from everyone, even my wife and children. I don't enjoy anything anymore. Not even my favorite foods," reported Jon G.

Allison summarized this section by writing:

Most men reported the ability to feel strong emotions was seriously diminished, especially those associated with tenderness, intimacy, and sexuality.

"Sometimes I think I *should* want to make love to my wife, so I do, but I don't *feel* much. I'm like a machine," said Pete W.

. . . Like a machine . . . Should want to make love . . . Detached from everyone . . .

Eli turned the pages, swiftly re-reading the descriptions of symptoms. ". . . Exaggerated startle response, hyperalertness, insomnia . . . recurrent nightmares . . . emotional lability, headache, and vertigo."

Vertigo. Lily had suffered vertigo in Zermatt. And insomnia. Lily had terrible cases of insomnia, particularly on assignments away from home.

Headaches: Most women seemed to have them.

Emotional lability: What was that?

Hyperalertness: That must mean being on the alert, being watchful. All Mossad members were trained in this, but Lily's hearing was acute, her visual memory outstanding.

Death camps . . . Stressors of human design . . .

In the next section, "Survivor Guilt," Eli jumped from paragraph to paragraph.

In traumas shared with others where not all victims survived, subjects related painful guilt feelings . . .

"Why was I the only one in my unit to escape?" Marvin T. asked. "Why me? So many of the others deserved to live more than I did. I wanted to die too."

Cases where, in order to survive, subjects were forced to do things that were abhorrent to them in a normal cultural context seemed to have the most severe reactions to PTSD.

The most severe . . . Lily?

To discover if she fit the criteria, he went back to the beginning of the section and read more slowly:

Age at onset: Any age . . . including childhood.

Course and subtypes: . . . Symptoms may emerge after a latency period of months or years . . .

Impairment: ... May affect nearly every aspect of life. Psychic numbing may interfere with marriage or family life. Guilt may result in self-defeating behavior ... suicidal actions ... substance use disorders ... avoidance of situations that may arouse recollections of the painful event.

"My parents moved to Florida but after I visited them there once, I vowed I'd never go back. It's so hot and humid it reminds me of Vietnam. I hate it there. I would rather be in New York any day," Cary L. explained.

What did Lily avoid? Tunnels ... subways ... cellars. Could Allison be describing her?

In a previous section, Allison had listed her diagnostic criteria for selecting men for her study. Eli mouthed the words as he read them.

A. There had to have been a recognizable stressor that evoked symptoms of PTSD.

Eli supposed Lily's stressor was Hans de Vries as well as the death camps.

B. The subject had to demonstrate re-experiencing the trauma by at least one of the following actions:
(1) recurrent recollections of the event
(2) recurrent dreams of the event
(3) sudden acting or feeling as if the traumatic event were happening again, usually because of an association with an ideational or environmental stimulus.

While it was true that Lily avoided basements and subways, dark rooms and small places, he had never seen her lose her composure when faced with the necessity of entering them briefly. No, this was not Lily. At least not by Allison's criteria. This paper was talking about people who lost their grip on reality, who suddenly thought they were back in Vietnam and started shooting up their neighborhoods, guys who heard a car backfire and ducked for cover, pathetic men who woke screaming in the night.

Eli's head felt light, but that was probably because he should have eaten lunch. He hoped Allison would be free soon. He read on to keep from remembering how hungry he was.

C. At least two of the following symptoms had to occur after the trauma:

(1) exaggerated startle response
(2) hyperalertness
(3) memory impairment
(4) difficulty concentrating
(5) avoidance of activities that arouse recollection of the event
(6) sleep disturbance
(7) guilt about surviving or behavior required to survive
(8) intensification of symptoms by exposure to events which trigger remembrance of trauma.

At least two . . . Eli counted four that pertained to Lily. Eli wiped his brow. He was covered in sweat. There was still some soda in the can. He finished it in two long swallows. He removed his jacket and loosened his collar. Down on the street he heard a child crying. A woman was scolding in a harsh voice. The child cried louder. To Eli the sound was profoundly irritating. He looked at his watch. It was almost six. How much longer would Allison be detained?

He picked up the thesis where he had left off, but the print blurred as he tried to read the concluding criteria.

D. Diminished involvement with the external world as shown by at least one of the following:

(1) decreased interest in previously important activities
(2) detachment from others
(3) constricted effect.

Eli did not know what the last one meant, but Lily was certainly the most detached woman he had ever met. In thirty years, she never formed a bond of friendship or love with any other human being: not him, not any man, not any other woman or — or child, he was about to say to himself, but that was not exactly true. She had formed a swift and desperate attachment to that child she had insisted on calling Otto during the last moments of the Six-Day War.

Otto.

He had objected to taking Otto. Under those hazardous circumstances he could not risk a child's life and he could not let the child endanger theirs. But there had been no arguing with Lily. Later, when they were back in Israel and trying to decide what to do with the Arab orphan, she told them that incredible story about why she had rescued the child.

Years later he could recall her halting, dramatic words. "I was riding in the UNRWA truck when I saw them. The Arab girl was very thin, the boy beside her quite tall. I do not know how I knew it, but I was certain they were brother and sister. They were carrying the little one in a sling. The girl could not manage very well and was tripping. Her brother slapped her to keep her going. And when he did, it was as if I felt his hand burn across my own face. When we were on the march from Bergen-Belsen to Theresienstadt, my brother, David, hit *my* cheeks and arms to keep *me* moving. Only then it was not broiling hot. We were freezing in the snow. He did it to keep my blood circulating. I was numb, I barely knew where we were, but somehow we kept moving forward.

"Otto had been with us in the cellar. We carried him in a sling when he could not walk. Out of all the children in our group only the three of us survived the walk, but poor Otto died only a few days after we arrived at Theresienstadt. I slept with him to warm him, and in the morning, he was cold and stiff beside me. He died in the night. You see, in my sleep I had taken the thin blanket and wound it around myself — he could not keep warm enough. Selfishly, I had saved myself, and he had died. I had done it in my sleep, not on purpose. Nevertheless his death haunted me. So when I saw Otto again — the same black curls and scrawny legs — it was my second chance. Then the plane dropped the bombs and the older children were burnt, so I kept him with me. The UNRWA people said it was against policy; they thought I had lost my mind. So what? I wanted *Otto,* do *you* understand?" she had screamed at him.

Eli never had understood, but he arranged the surgeries that followed. Lily selected the adoptive family herself and told Eli she was pleased with the match.

"They had four daughters before the wife discovered she could not have another child. Otto will be the son they always wanted."

Eli believed that the new Otto had eased Lily's irrational guilt. Now he wondered if the situation with Otto was what Allison meant in her thesis by saying "the subject had to demonstrate re-experiencing the trauma." Was the new Otto the only time it happened to Lily? He doubted it. Lily probably had had similar episodes that he had never heard about. Knowing her, she would have kept anything she perceived as a weakness private.

"Eli, I'm terribly sorry," Allison said as she dashed into the office. "Oh, you're actually reading it. What do you think?"

"I am fascinated."

"Really?"

"Yes, I'm most impressed. I saw *Coming Home* this afternoon. Isn't that a coincidence?"

Allison frowned. "I'm afraid a lot of people are making that connection, but I started on this project a full year before the film."

"It can only help you. You're obviously ahead of the trends." Like your mother, he almost said, but caught himself.

"Eli, I have a complication. One of my clients is coming in at seven for an emergency session. I could be a few minutes late, but his problem is fairly serious and —" She stopped as she noticed the ashen color of his skin. "You're not feeling well. What's wrong?"

"Nothing. I just didn't have lunch."

She glanced at her watch. "I have almost an hour. Would you be insulted if we just had a sandwich? There's a deli —"

"Hot pastrami?"

"The best!" She took the thesis from his hands.

"No. Let's bring it along. I have some questions I want to ask you."

The rye bread was fresh and soft, the pastrami warm and spicy, the mustard thick and brown. The unsweetened iced tea soothed his throat. There was a crock of pickles on the table. Eli crunched on his third spear. "Whom are you seeing tonight? One of the men from your study?"

"No. It's a boy I've been working with for almost a year. He was sexually abused by his uncle. His mother called to tell us he was very depressed and talking of suicide. I decided I should see him at once."

"Could he have the same problems as the veterans?"

"Why do you ask?"

"You'd mentioned something about the seriousness of post-traumatic stress in victims who were abused, stressed, by other humans . . . I don't quite recall how you phrased it."

"When the stressor is of human design."

"Yes, that's what I meant. You also said it could happen to children."

"That's true. But not everyone who is raped or goes to war suffers from the disorder, just as not everyone gets the measles when it's going around. Some researchers believe that there may be certain predisposing factors that make some people more susceptible. Also, we have to be careful not to lump every vet or rape victim into this category just because it's current or convenient. I spent a great deal of time working out how to differentiate the diagnosis. Unless the stressor is of a most extreme nature, we usually find the prime symptom — that is, re-experiencing the traumatic event — is absent. If so, we can look to anxiety or depression as the root of the problem. My client this evening suffers mainly from bouts with depression."

"That means your thesis is about a fairly rare condition?"

"The data are too incomplete to make that judgment," she replied deliberately.

"What about a group that shared the same horrible experience — like a plane crash or a concentration camp?"

"The studies are showing they might have some form of PTSD, but, in the case of the death camps, it's been many years since these people experienced the event, so it's hard to tell. I'm surprised you're so interested in my work. My mother throws up her hands and says it's too technical for her."

"I cannot pretend I understand the jargon, but I have a friend in Israel who volunteers his time to work with the victims of torture. He would be very interested in this."

"He's probably aware of the research."

"Perhaps, but he's not a professional. He works with them because of his own experiences."

Allison raised her delicately plucked eyebrows. "Have I ever met him?"

Charlotte had taken Allison to Israel on many occasions as she was growing up. "Yes, he's the husband of an old friend of your mother's."

"Aviva Tabor's husband?"

"How did you guess?"

"He had unusual, sad eyes. I once asked Mother about him and she said he had been in an Arab jail. I've always wondered . . ."

"Yes?"

"About victims of tragedies. Maybe that's why I chose this profession. All my cases are victims of one sort or another."

"Can they be cured?"

"In what way?"

"Lead normal lives, find personal happiness, I suppose."

"I think it's far more complex than that, Uncle Eli. Right now, I see it as a series of minor adjustments, like the fine tunings of an engine. I try to show my clients that while perfection is an illusion, contentment can be won by the smallest of victories."

As Allison spoke, her pale skin glowing, her green eyes shining, Eli could see how she could have a calming effect on the distraught souls who came searching for someone to ease their pain. Pain. What effect did it have on a person's mind?

"Allison . . ." he began hesitantly.

Disturbed by the lowered pitch of his voice, Allison put down her sandwich and gave Eli her full attention.

"The men . . . with this disorder, do they act weird, go crazy, shoot up their neighborhoods thinking the enemy is lurking behind the trash cans?"

"That's pretty much a myth. Not to say there haven't been a few isolated cases and some clever lawyers using it as a defense but —"

He cut her off. "Let me express it differently. Could their normal reactions to situations be altered as a result of their problems?"

"What do you mean?"

"Could their ethical standards break down? Might they rob or steal or . . . betray a friend?"

"I cannot say it couldn't happen, but mostly their pain is locked inside. It's not something they want to take out on other people. Of course, there are the few who want revenge."

"Revenge on the ones who hurt them or revenge in general?"

"Both are possibilities."

"Could it turn a good camel into a bad camel?"

Allison laughed. "It's been so long since I recalled any of those stories. I did pester you so to make them up!" Seeing his solemn face, she became more serious. "There's no question pain can alter a personality, but nobody can predict how. Some are crushed by it; others are transformed for the better." She shifted in her seat and glanced up at the clock above the cash register. "I'm late already. You haven't even finished your sandwich! Would you mind terribly if I left you here?"

Eli finally found his voice. "Of course not. I am honored to have seen you for even a brief time at such short notice. Forgive me for expecting you to bend to my ludicrous schedule."

"When are you going to retire and relax?"

"My load should lighten quite soon."

"Excellent. Then Mother and I will expect you to indulge us with a long, leisurely stay."

Allison stood up and stuffed the manuscript into her briefcase. She pulled out an elegantly tooled leather wallet, something Charlotte must have selected, and fumbled for some bills. He placed his hand over hers. "That may be fashionable, dear Allison, but a man my age does not permit a lady to pay for her dinner."

"I wanted to treat you. You must let me. I've made such a muddle of the evening and —"

"Not this time." He had only a few more seconds and he had not even begun to launch into the reason he had come to see her. He wanted to tell her how he would be there for her if she needed him . . . but Allison was reaching over to kiss him on the cheek. She smelled like carnations. She was closing her briefcase with one hand and slipping the check out from under the pickle crock with the other. With a wink she was at the cash register paying the bill, then out the door with a final wave.

Eli stared through the smudged windows as she ran across the street. She had paid for dinner, just like her mother.

A sickening sensation washed over him. He closed his eyes and rubbed his forehead.

Charlotte. She had no motive. She did not truly hate him any more than he could ever hate her. Why, this had nothing to do with Charlotte. He blinked. The room was in perfect focus. In fact, this betrayal had nothing to do with *him*.

How egotistical of him to think that one of his operatives had held so massive a grudge as to betray a nation because he had scorned her.

This was the work of an aberrant mind.

A sickness.

A rot.

No, a disorder, which could not be controlled. This was the work of someone whose loyalties had been twisted by malevolent events beyond her control. While he did not quite comprehend how it could have happened, he had multiple hints, markers, suggestions, all pointing in one direct line — to Lily.

Lily, who had always told him how detached she had felt from everyone. Lily, who thought she could never feel strongly about anything, who refused to have a child because she could never love one properly. Lily, who could never love him — or herself — or, it seemed, Israel.

He was staring at the deli's clock. It was almost twenty hours since he had spoken to Ehud Dani, twenty hours since he had set the forces in motion to move against Charlotte. His cheeks were burning.

He leapt up and hurried from the restaurant, as if to escape encroaching flames.

Three blocks uptown he found a pay phone that worked. The noise of a passing truck almost drowned out his request for the international operator. After an interminable wait, he got the Israeli connection. Ehud Dani's line rang and rang and rang, the bells echoing with the queer reverberations that sometimes mar overseas calls. Eventually, the operator came back on the line and asked if there was another number he would like to try.

"Yes, in London."

"I'm sorry, I can't help you with that country, sir. You'll have to place the call again."

"Bloody fucking hell!" he screamed into the receiver. He calmed long enough to attempt another call, giving the operator Alex Naor's home number because it was after midnight in England.

"Hello," came Alex's cross voice.

He spoke in Hebrew. "Where is Dani?"

"On his way to see your friend."

"I must reach him!"

"Why? What is going on?"

"We must stop him. There has been a change."

"What do you mean?" Alex's voice was calmer than Eli expected.

"A new development. I do not want to make a move in that direction yet."

"Have you forgotten what is at stake here?"

"That's the point. She is not the one. I am certain —"

"Yesterday you were convinced she was. What changed your mind?"

"Substantial new information."

"You are not at a secured phone?"

"There is no time for that. I must get to Europe. This could be settled in a day or so. Can you get hold of Dani? Ask him to wait in New York? He can keep her under surveillance. She's not going anywhere. She's not suspicious. She wouldn't be. She hasn't done anything wrong."

"Just a moment." Alex put down the receiver.

On his side of the Atlantic, Eli clutched the phone cord.

Alex returned. "Hello, are you there?"

"Ken, ken . . . Yes."

"He arrived at JFK at sixteen-thirty this afternoon."

"Are you positive?"

"There has been a confirmation of his arrival."

"Where is he? I must talk to him immediately."

"I can have him contact you."

"I'm at the Stanhope. Not at this moment, but I can be there in fifteen minutes."

"He will be in touch. Stay in your room."

"Todah rabah!"

"Eli . . ." He spoke his name as a father to his favorite son. "Take care of yourself."

A taxi had paused at a light. He jumped in and almost shouted, "Eighty-first and Fifth."

The events of the last few hours tumbled in his mind. What if he had not gone to see Allison? Or what if she had been on time? What if she had not asked him to look at her thesis? What if he had not understood what it meant? He could have blundered on, with tragic consequences.

Eli checked his watch in the lamplight and wondered if there would be time to fly to Europe that evening. Almost all transatlantic flights departed at night, but if he had to wait for Dani, he would never make it.

The elegant Baume et Mercier glittered on his wrist. He was transfixed by the dial of his watch. After all these years the fine crystal had never scratched. It was far too good a watch for him.

Had Lily's motive been money? She had always lived frugally, but her tastes were expensive. She had once said she would rather go without something than settle for a replacement of poor quality or design. He had taken it as an artistic sentiment, not an avaricious one. She needed money. She had as much as said so herself when she was packing up her paintings, but she was not a mercenary. There had to be something else: this sickness, which had distorted her mind.

He read his watch in the pale, glacial light of the streetlamps. Dani could not have confronted Charlotte yet. He would intercept him. He would come out victorious in this minor battle with the connivances of fortune.

But he had lost the war.

16

And, to end thy cruel mocks,
Annihilate thee on the rocks,
And another form create
To be subservient to my fate . . .
And throughout all Eternity
I forgive you, you forgive me.

William Blake (1757–1827)
Poems from MSS.

SAAS-FEE, SWITZERLAND: MAY 1979

Less than an hour after Eli's phone call to London, Ehud Dani arrived at his hotel room. Patiently, he listened to Eli's not totally coherent explanation of why he suspected Charlotte at first and what he was going to do next.

"I am going to Paris," Eli finished curtly.

"Shall I accompany you?" Dani asked.

"No."

"Is that wise?"

"When I bring her to Israel, I will turn her over to you."

"And if you cannot deliver the goods?"

"It's my ass that was almost blown away in London — not yours."

"Eli, that is why I am here."

Dani refused to back off until Eli saw a way to occupy him. "Do not call off your interrogation entirely — postpone it. Keep Charlotte under surveillance. I would not want to be accused of making the same mistake twice."

"For how long?"

"Give me a few days."

"Can't you be more specific?"

"Thirty-six hours."

Dani had not argued. As soon as he left, Eli was on the phone, trying to find the swiftest way to Paris. He settled on the next Air France flight, but it did not depart until one the following afternoon.

When Eli checked in at the airport, he was handed an elegant beige and brown leather folder, which contained his ticket. Absently, Eli ran his hand over it.

"Flight zero zero two will depart in one hour," he was told. "The first-class lounge will be available for your comfort."

Perplexed, he stared at the Air France receptionist momentarily, then back at the handsome ticket folder. He reached into his pocket and pulled out the American Express receipt he had stuffed there without checking the final tally. He reeled at the price. "This is in dollars, not francs?" he asked weakly.

"That is correct, sir." Suddenly, Eli understood that he had inadvertently reserved a seat on the Concorde. He studied the bottom line on his American Express receipt for a full minute before reviewing the airline's schedule to determine if there were any alternative flights that would get him to Paris that evening, but the others would not arrive until the next morning and he sensed he could not afford to lose more crucial time. The Concorde supersonic jet . . . the Concorde apartment building in Toulon . . . all pieces of the same puzzle melding as the solution to his infernal riddle became evident. Eli confronted the American Express receipt one last time. The cost was astounding — but who cared? His days as an employee of the Mossad were numbered. He decided impetuously: the hell with the bookkeepers! He crushed the stiff paper in his fist, jammed it back into his pocket, and gave the Air France employee a triumphant smile.

"Have a good flight, sir," she said far too mechanically.

Three hours and forty-five supersonic minutes later he was in Paris. It was almost midnight when he arrived at the Quai Voltaire. Only a few jumbled days of transatlantic travel and sleepless nights had passed since he had stood at this very place, but it seemed like a decade. Using his own set of keys, he unlatched the gate to the court-yard of Lily's apartment house. His fury was taking precedence over fear.

A light went on in the concierge's window. A grumbling voice called out, "Qui cherchez-vous?"

"Mademoiselle Schmidt."

"Elle n'est plus là. Elle est partie il y a quelques jours."

"Several days ago? That's not possible!" He ran up the exterior staircase and unlocked the door. He groped for the light at the bottom of her private flight of stairs and stumbled into the atelier.

The entire apartment had been swept clean. All the crates, boxes, trunks were missing. A few cables, which had supported her plants and sculptures, dangled listlessly from their fastenings in the ceiling. In the light of the bare bulb, they appeared as eerie wormlike shapes crisscrossing the room. The refrigerator door was propped open. The built-in loft bed had been stripped. Fastidious Lily had eliminated all traces of herself and vanished. The only sound was the drip in the kitchen sink. Eli ran down the stairs without shutting the door behind him.

"Où est-elle allée? Avez-vous une adresse?"

"Non, monsieur."

"Merci, madame. Excusez-moi pour le dérangement," he called as he rushed out onto the quay and looked desperately for another taxi.

Where could she have moved so swiftly? No. She had not moved. Her artwork had gone into storage. Eli was recalling walking around her studio while she talked with the movers. There had been a trunk. And a label, part of which remained imprinted in his mind: a hotel . . . in . . . Where?

Saas-Fee.

Where the hell was Saas-Fee?

It sounded Swiss. But was it nearer to Geneva or Zürich? He could not find a taxi until he had walked all the way to the Boulevard St.-Germain. He jumped in. "Charles de Gaulle," he said with great weariness in his voice, but he heard only groans in response to having demanded the airport at that time of night. Eli did not budge, so the car lurched forward. Six blocks later, Eli recognized it was far too late to get a flight to Switzerland. For a moment, he vacillated about where to spend the night. Finally, he decided he might as well find a room as close to the airport as possible.

While the Air France agent on the phone took ten minutes to figure out where Saas-Fee was located, he had time to contemplate how very much he was at the mercy of airline schedules.

She came back on the line. "Saas-Fee is quite near Zermatt," the clerk announced.

"That's about equidistant from either Geneva or Zürich, right?"

"Yes, sir."

"Which can I get to first?"

"Geneva. There is a flight at seven-fifteen in the morning. From there you can take the train or rent a car. I would suggest a car, since the train will take you only as far as Visp. From there you would need to get a postal bus."

By nine the next morning Eli was winding his way from Geneva to Lausanne and Montreux. It rained intermittently, and when it was not pouring, a tenacious fog masked any view of the mountains or Lake Léman. As he turned south on the winding road to Martigny, the sky had brightened slightly, but Eli hardly noticed any aspect of the passing scene. Only when he became aware that his hands were trembling on the steering wheel did he pause for a breakfast of Gruyère cheese, fresh rolls, and hot chocolate.

Between Martigny and Sion, the straight stretches of road paralleling the Rhône River were far easier to negotiate. After eating, Eli was calm enough to admire the graceful poplar trees lining the road; by some peculiar quirk of memory, he recalled that it had been built by Napoleon's engineers. He drove straight through Sion, hardly pausing to admire the commanding fortresses built on two rocky peaks opposite each other. Pressing onward, he was at Visp in less than half an hour.

Eli had never driven farther than Visp before. One always took the train to Zermatt, but the tracks did not run to Saas-Fee. That is probably why Lily was there, Eli decided. Lily preferred obscure, out-of-the-way places for her holidays. But this was not a holiday. This was a deliberate escape. She had attempted to flee to a place no one would find her. Ruefully, Eli realized she had almost succeeded.

When had Lily begun coming to Saas-Fee? Had it been when she had become a courier to Geneva? Or more recently? The last time he had been in the region had been for the gibbush — the unification exercises he had put the young women through. He had never taken the time for a vacation in Switzerland since, though his fondest wish had been to climb as he had as a youth. He felt almost as fit as ever and wondered if someday he might be able to attempt it again — if not actual rope climbing, at least some aggressive Alpine hikes. Perhaps Colin would accompany him. Now, there was a cheering thought. He allowed himself to imagine what a trip with

Colin might be like: the two of them roped up together, tramping across a snow field, following a hearty guide up a scree slope, rappelling down a cliff, belaying each other on taut lines, pausing to enjoy a bottle of Valaisanne wine and a chunk of perfectly ripened cheese. Ridiculous! Why would Colin agree to join him on such an occasion?

What had Ehud Dani called Eli? "The scholarship committee!" Sadly, he had to accept that was all he would ever be to the boy. He was kidding himself if he believed their relationship meant anything deeply personal to Colin. Oh, Colin had always expressed gratitude and courteous solicitude, he may even have enjoyed some of those meals at Wheeler's, but the intimate feelings Eli bestowed upon his son would never be reciprocated. His silence in the matter — which had been essential for the boy's own protection — had sealed them into roles that were not inherently emotional. Climbing the mountains, sailing the seas, flying off into the sunset — all were nothing more than the idiotic dreams of a man in his dotage.

At last, Eli's rented Renault was climbing into the mountains, winding up past the Vispa River, greatly swollen with the overflow of melting glaciers. After bridging a gorge at the village of Stalden, the road split dramatically at the Killerhof Hotel. The right fork followed the valley south to the fabled village of Zermatt. He turned left to Saas-Fee.

Signs directed Eli to a car park on the outskirts of the town. Only small electric carts and horse-drawn vehicles were permitted beyond the main road. He left his suitcase in the trunk and made his way by foot to the village square. Across the way, a large sign announced, ZIMMERNACHWEIS. He went into the tourist office and asked for a list of hotels: Alphubel . . . Beau-Site . . . Eden . . . Europa . . . Fletschhorn . . . Fletschhorn. *That* was the name on Lily's trunk. He asked which direction to take and was shown a route to the right of the tourist office.

For almost ten minutes he wound his way up a path strewn with pine needles, past several guest houses and restaurants. At the small village of Wildi he paused, wondering if he had somehow missed his destination because all evidence of habitation had ceased. Then, on a tree, he spied a hand-carved wooden sign: ZUM IDYLLISCHEN RESTAURANT FLETSCHHORN, FRANZÖSISCHE KÜCHE, 10 MIN. The idyllic Fletschhorn Restaurant. The sign had indicated French cuisine. It seemed precisely the sort of place Lily would have discovered.

The only sounds were the calling of birds and his own respiration, which was becoming more and more labored the longer and faster he climbed. He hurried onward, thinking that if he hadn't so much on his mind, he would have felt this fragrant forest, which kept opening out on one view more astonishing than the next, was perhaps the most splendid place on earth.

He rounded a last, steep turn that revealed a charming inn perched on the first rung of paradise. The whitewashed building was dotted with planters overflowing with red geraniums. On one side, it was nestled into a verdant grove; on the other, the cliff gave way to the plunging panorama. Below were the valley villages of Saas-Almagell, Unter den Bodmen, Saas-Grund, and Tamatten, and across were the glistening slopes of the Triftgletscher, which arched up to the perpetual snow peak of the Weissmies.

Eli took a seat under a blue and white umbrella and drew in a few deep breaths of an air so startlingly pure, he felt as if he were breathing a magical medicine that would cleanse the impurities from his body as well as his mind.

Immediately, a waiter, wearing a traditional Swiss shirt embroidered with wildflowers, came out. "Kann ich Ihnen helfen?"

"Mademoiselle Nicole Schmidt. Is she here?"

"Sorry, there is nobody by that name."

For a moment Eli supposed the waiter was lying. "Would her friend, Lily Jaeger, be here?" he corrected himself smoothly.

"Mademoiselle Jaeger? Why certainly. But I am afraid you missed her by a very few minutes."

"Where could I find her?"

"Let me ask Herr Lindt."

So, he thought, here Lily plays herself.

A man Eli presumed to be the innkeeper came out of the kitchen door. "You are looking for Mademoiselle Jaeger?"

"Yes. She was not expecting me. It was to be a surprise."

"Forgive me for not introducing myself. I am Walter Lindt. My wife, Anna, and I are your hosts."

"My name is . . ." Eli paused ever so slightly. The time had not yet come to play *himself*. ". . . Charles Ivy."

"I am pleased to meet you, Mr. Ivy. Mademoiselle Jaeger will be delighted to see you. You are old friends, no?"

"You are very astute, Herr Lindt."

"As I guessed! Lily's always come here alone in the past, but Anna and I believed she would be happier with a companion. At last, she has taken our advice." He pulled up a chair to the table and leaned toward Eli. "Pardon my intrusion, but I must tell you Anna and I both agree that we have never seen Lily looking so poorly. Lily claims she has been under some stress with her work during the last few months, but has at last given it up and is taking a long rest. For that she has come to the perfect place. As have you, sir. Today she listened to Anna and slept late. Then, Anna prepared for her a lunch and sent her on a long walk to put some color in her cheeks." He paused and looked out across the terrace to the mountains. "It is a perfect afternoon for a long hike." He turned back to Eli. "Will you be our guest as well?"

"Do you have a free room?"

"Yes, a very nice one." He pointed to a dormer window. "Would you care to see it?"

"Yes, but later. Do you think I could catch up with Lily?"

"Do you know your way around these hills?"

"No, I have never been to Saas-Fee before, but I have been to Zermatt."

"A climber, yes? You have the build for it."

"You are very flattering. I have never done anything more strenuous than the Breithorn and that was more years ago than I would like to admit."

"A few days of Anna's cooking and our Alpine air and you will be ready to hire one of our fine guides and try one of our less technical climbs."

"I would like that very much, but — Lily — which direction did she take?"

Walter Lindt went inside the hotel and came back with a map of the local trails. He pointed to a red line. "Lily said she had always wanted to do the route to Schönegg. Here it is numbered 'five' all the way. If you go back through the village and take the ski lift to Hannig you will save an hour's walking." He glanced at Eli's tweed jacket and leather shoes and shook his head disapprovingly. "You will be requiring boots and some proper clothing. The route is quite rocky. There are several shops down in the village where you can buy anything you need."

"I hope I'll find her."

"You will. By the time you have made your purchases, I expect she will only be arriving at Hannig. Because it is her first day out, she should be taking it easy."

Eli thanked the genial host, who said he looked forward to seeing him that evening.

"We will prepare our specialties for you both. Do you like Trock-enfleisch, our region's air-dried meat?"

"Very much."

"Excellent. We will do a platter of that along with Lily's favorite, Zweifarbiges Fischparfait, a two-colored seafood parfait with a green sauce, to begin, and then —"

Eli was anxious to get on his way. "I will leave the menu to you, Herr Lindt. It should come as a welcome surprise to both Lily and me."

"It will be our pleasure."

The downhill trek to the village went much more quickly than the climb up to the inn. Along the main street — where only pedestrians were permitted — half a dozen stores sold mountaineering gear. Eli picked one at random and rapidly purchased a pair of thick woolen knee socks, some corduroy breeches, a plaid shirt, and the least expensive pair of hiking shoes he could find. At the last moment, he added a nylon rucksack, into which he stuffed his city clothes before setting out.

At the base of the ski lift, he pulled out the climbing map and attempted to plan his route.

"Where are you going?" asked a friendly man speaking English with a flat, American accent. He was dressed in full climbing regalia with ice pick, crampons, and ropes tied to his backpack.

Eli showed him the path the innkeeper had marked.

"I'm going that way too. Are you hiking all the way to the Mi-schabelhütte?" he asked as the gondola swung around to where they were standing. They stepped in. The attendant locked the door.

"Possibly," Eli replied, not wanting to seem like a timid tourist out for a stroll.

"Wonderful! It's a fantastic spot. Just be cautious in the area before the cables. This early in the season one should expect it to be covered with a layer of slippery verglas in patches, and since you don't have crampons —"

"Thanks. I will watch for it."

As the gondola was pulled higher and higher above the valley, Eli attempted to get his bearings by glancing out the window and then down at his map.

"Also . . ."

"Yes?"

The much younger climber with a fiery red beard was eyeing Eli warily. "You have been in this area before?"

"Yes, many times." He stretched the question to include Zermatt. "Why?"

"You're not bothered by exposure?"

"No, not especially."

"That's good, because there is a particularly nasty place above the gorge to the Hohbalmgletscher. I took a group up there last year and had to talk a fairly experienced man down. He almost went into shock. I have heard stories about people who have walked right off that path into the void. I don't know why, but their perceptions get confused. Thank God that's not my problem." He chuckled as he looked down from the swaying ski lift. "Damn, but I love these mountains! Nothing like this where I come from."

"Where is that?"

"Indianapolis."

As the gondola rocked toward the summit, Eli could not help but admire the view, which stretched three-quarters of the way around the compass.

"Do you know what peak that is?" he asked his knowledgeable seatmate.

"The Weisshorn. It's about forty-five hundred meters high. And over there to the north lies the massive range of the Bernese Oberland. Some days you can see all the way to the Aletsch Glacier, the longest in Switzerland. If you have time, you could drive up the valley toward Gletsch and take the cable car to the Eggishorn . . ." He droned on in his self-appointed role as Swiss mountain guide.

Eli regretted he had asked.

The gondola was easing into the station. "Do you want to follow me? I'm meeting a group that preceded me up, but we've got to get to the hut tonight, so we'll be keeping up our speed."

"No. I'll be fine. I am also meeting a friend."

"That's super. Well, then . . ." He turned to see two men waving at him. "There are my charges. Have a good hike."

Eli decided he was pleased to be rid of the man as he walked around the noisy lift machinery and up the first path he found.

The umbrellas of the Café Alpenblick beckoned from across the rocky terrace. Eli's breathing was short already. He checked his map. He was at only two thousand meters, but, as an Israeli, he was unaccustomed to an altitude more than a few hundred feet above sea level. Also, it was past noon and he had not eaten since Martigny. He decided to have a snack. In the cafeteria other climbers were heaping plates with sausages, rösti potatoes, cabbage, and salad. Eli saw no reason to do otherwise. To his tray he added a bottle of water for his knapsack and two large bottles of the local apple juice. After paying the cashier, he stepped out of the gloomy building and found a seat in the brilliant sunshine.

At first he did not see her because of the glare. He had eaten half his wurst and finished one of the bottles of the Apfelsaft, looking straight down at his plate. When he lifted his eyes, the world was rimmed with shimmering light reflecting off the glaciers, the snow slopes, the white metal tables, the goggles of the expert climbers. All the while she must have seen him, been waiting for him to notice her. Thus, when he did, she probed him with a riveting gaze.

He stood. He lifted his tray. He walked across the dazzling terrace with long, feline strides. Every breath of thin mountain air was searing his throat. The wind churning up from the valley was roaring in his ears. He had to sit down quickly or his legs would have buckled.

He could not — would not — look at her directly. Just behind her, whipping in the wind, were the distinctive flags of five of the Swiss cantons. Five flags. One with red and white stars, one with a bear, one with a nose-ringed bull, one with a key, and one with blue and white horizontal stripes. He counted them again. Five bright flags. Slap. Slap. Slap.

He could not speak.

But Lily did.

"In a better world I would have been born Swiss." Her voice was slow and steady and direct. "I would have lived in a small, clean house with my mother and my father and my brothers. I would have gone to school. I would have learned to ski. There would have been holidays in the country. Visits to the city. I would have worked in an office or managed a restaurant. I would have stayed at home with my children. I would have bleached the curtains and polished the silver. My husband would have held me the night long. I would have painted pictures of the mountains in all the seasons and knitted thick sweaters in bright designs. I would have eaten as much chocolate as I wanted. And just by now, I would have grandchildren who would come to my house in the mountains for holidays. But no. I was born a Jew. In Holland. The wrong place, the wrong century. My father wanted to bring me to Switzerland. He told me stories about the pure white of the Alps during those long, dark nights. I never forgot them. Even in the cellar. The mountains . . . This is the only place where I am at peace."

Eli did not reply. He observed Lily as if she were a laboratory specimen. In the glare of the Alpine midday sun, deep lines etched her face. Her chin sagged. Her once-creamy neck was mottled with liver spots. And her hands! Why had he never before noticed the bulging veins, the bony knuckles?

"I am not coming back," Lily said tautly. "I have arranged a residency in Switzerland."

She was waiting for a reply. He had none. He gazed earnestly at the flag with the key. The banner's lower half was white, but the bow of the key was in red; the upper part was red, with the blade in white. Red and white. Glancing back at Lily, he was drawn to her skin. White with red blotches. Dr. Ze'evi's waxen body drenched in his blood. Eli dared to look directly into Lily's eyes. The veins in the white eyeballs were an angry red.

Back to the flags . . .

He contemplated the bear on one of them.

Eli's reticence was having the desired effect. The power of silence was astonishing. Allison could have told him that. He imagined Allison's freckled face and saw those sweet, contemplative lips set in a position of deliberate repose as she listened to some neurotic break through the barrier of silence. A neurotic, a patient, someone who needed professional psychiatric help — yes, it was best to think of Lily as a victim of an illness. Otherwise, he would be sick with rage. He would want to lash out, crush, destroy the evil force that had tried to annihilate him. There was not so much fury now. No. He could feel it subsiding. He was calming. There was some compassion . left — but not much.

Lily's hands, which she had occupied by folding up the polished paper that had wrapped her lunch, began to quiver. One hand lifted her cup of coffee, the other reached to fondle the trinket at the end of the thick gold chain around her neck. Her thumb and forefinger massaged the silver circle for almost a minute before Eli focused on what she was wearing.

He found his voice. "The old coin from the gallery, isn't it?"

Lily seemed surprised that he had noticed. "Oh, this? My silver shekel. It was the first coin I made into a piece of jewelry. They became very popular items. Did I ever tell you about the Texan and his blazer buttons?" Her tone had a phony lightness.

"Yes. A long time ago."

"He spent over five thousand dollars. My finest gold coins. Blazer buttons!"

"I have forgotten how old you said your coin was."

"Two thousand years, give or take a hundred. It is from Tyre. The silver tetradrachm of Tyre."

Eli concentrated on his half-eaten sausage. It had turned cold and rubbery. The greasy potatoes were already churning in his stomach. He pushed his plate away and finished his apple drink in one swallow. He could not think in these oppressive surroundings. "I am walking in the direction of the Mischabelhütte. Do you care to join me?"

"As you very well know, I also am going that way, but perhaps not that far. The hut is a good three hours from here."

He stood. She did the same. He placed his bread and bottle of water in his rucksack and slung the strap over one shoulder. She wore only a zippered pouch at her waist, which she rearranged on her hips before leading the way to the path marked SCHÖNEGG.

Lily set out briskly. Eli followed only paces behind. Every few minutes, a friendly hiker would pass them coming down and give the traditional mountain greeting: "Grüss Gott."

"Grüss Gott," Lily replied.

"Grüss Gott," Eli echoed.

As they passed a picturesque larch forest that had sprung up in a field of boulders, Eli moved alongside her. "*You* will tell me *why*," he demanded imperiously.

Lily's face hardened. "There is not an answer to every question."

Eli wished for five flags to divert his attention here. He looked around for something else to stare at to prevent the flames of wrath fomenting within from flaring out and incinerating them both. He saw only the nape of her slender neck bowed away from him. How easy it would be to grasp it and crush the breath from her body. "You will tell me. You owe me that." He shoved his hands into his pockets forcefully.

"I owe you *nothing*."

"You bloody fucking well do! My son and I were almost *killed* because of you. My cousin, my dear friend, was *butchered*. An entire operation was compromised. And God only knows how many others have been exposed by your treachery."

Lily had stopped walking. Her back remained turned away from Eli. He grabbed her roughly and spun her around.

"It is not possible. They promised not to touch you — and your *son*? How could they have known about *him*?"

"Who promised not to harm me? Who the hell have you sold out to?"

"I sold nothing. I repaid a debt."

"Lily." Eli's voice was seething. "Who turned you?"

"Jalil."

"Who the hell is Jalil?"

"Grüss Gott," called a stocky Swiss gentleman who waved his walking stick in their direction.

Neither Lily nor Eli responded. The man frowned at their bad manners and moved quickly by them on the narrow path.

"Jalil Salim. The son of Rashid Salim, the Palestinian you — or shall I say *we*?— killed in the refugee camp outside Amman. Perhaps you do not keep track of *your* victims, but *I* do mine."

"Rashid Salim was responsible for the deaths of at least fifty Israelis that I know of. You yourself provided the crucial information that implicated him."

Lily's eyes were downcast. Her shoulders drooped.

"Were you a double agent in Jericho?"

"No."

"In Cherbourg?"

"No."

"I suppose I should feel immensely relieved. For a few minutes I wondered if you had ever been loyal to Israel."

"Loyalty has never been an issue with me. I am not patriotic. I do not believe in any cause in particular."

"How is that possible after all you have — we have — been through?"

"I have had a nice steady government job that utilized my capabilities and served my purposes. I was fond of the gallery and Paris. I liked my painting. Even the excitement now and then was pleasing to me. I did not do it for love, not of any state, or any individual. I did it all for *me*. For *me*! All my life has been a struggle to protect myself. How does that saying go? 'If I am not for myself, who will be for me?' " she finished defiantly.

"Ah, but Lily, you have forgotten the second half of Hillel's quote. Remember the next line: 'And if I am only for myself, what am I? And —' "

Lily had not waited to hear his final words. She turned toward the trail. It switchbacked sharply to climb a steeper section of the slope. Eli allowed her to go ahead. His mind was throbbing with the last, unspoken part of the famous phrase. He whispered it to the wind. ". . . And if not now — when?"

·:·   ·:·   ·:·

Why did they go forward, higher and closer to the Alpine sky? He should have turned around, forced her down, yet they trekked upward, with Lily setting the pace. Relentlessly, she plodded on. Relentlessly, Eli questioned her. Slowly, the story began to emerge.

"I believed that Jalil was killed with his father, Rashid, because they had been together only hours before you came into the camp. To tell you the truth, I mourned the child more than the father — which was odd, since he had been a difficult boy and rather rude to me at times."

"Why would you mourn a PLO leader?" Eli asked.

"Why do you think? He was my lover," she snapped back cruelly. "Are you shocked?"

"We never asked you to get information on that basis."

"I did not sleep with him for *your* sake," she spat.

"You loved him? Is that what this is about?"

"He was my friend. I have not known many men, but he was, in some ways, the most special."

Knowing she was cornered and was lashing out as her only means of self-defense, Eli let the slur against him slide. Not that it did not wound him.

"Right. Jalil found you again. When?"

"About six months ago. He came to me in Paris. At first, he said he was keeping a promise he made to his father. 'My father told me that if anything were to happen to him, I was to watch out for you,' he told me. So, after his father was murdered, he came looking for me at the UNRWA tents. Of course, I was gone by then." She shuddered.

Sucking in her breath, she continued with her recollections. "When I saw the bombs from the road that night, I was certain the whole camp had been destroyed and that all my friends had been killed or wounded. Jalil told me it was only the house where his father and some relatives were staying that was demolished. If he had not been in the latrine, he would have been killed too. Right away he ran to my tent. Nobody had been hurt at UNRWA, but I was missing. Apparently my love affair with Rashid was not as secret as I had hoped, and one of my nursing friends had told the rescue workers to search for my body alongside his. All they ever found were pieces of bone and flesh. No parts of a woman were ever identified. Jalil said the UNRWA people were convinced I had been killed and that Rashid's people were hiding something from them. Of course, Jalil knew differently. He had seen his father ten minutes before the blast. He knew I could not have been there and began to think I might have had something to do with his father's death, so he continued to make inquiries about me. The UNRWA people told him of the little boy who had run away when I disappeared. They asked Jalil to look for Otto. He never found either of us. You do remember Otto?"

"Yes, quite well."

"That was not the child's name, of course. I never knew his real last name, but his first had been Raouf. All through his hospitalizations he was called Otto and it stuck. Even after he was adopted, Otto remained his nickname."

Eli was becoming impatient with her ramblings. "What does Otto have to do with all this?"

"Everything. You see, Jalil never forgot about me. Over the years he became more and more convinced I had murdered his father. He wanted revenge. A year and a half ago, when Jalil was in Jaffa, he heard some teenagers calling a friend 'Otto.' He asked Otto where he lived, and when Jalil told the doctor I had been friends with Otto's family in Jericho, the doctor was happy to oblige with Nicole's whereabouts."

"Then what?"

"Jalil, through his father's friends, is very well connected. Upperechelon PLO. Before he even came to me, he had completed a dossier on me. He knew about my preliminary trips to the Toulon area. He guessed we were after the reactor parts. He could have killed me. Or had me killed. But no, all he wanted was one favor. He was convincing. 'Why should the Zionists have nuclear energy to run their machines and produce their energy and we should not?' he asked. Then he went on to explain about the Iraqi reactor being for peaceful purposes only and that it was a means to raise the standard of living for Arab children. He asked me to remember his downtrodden life in the refugee camps. He talked about the diaspora of the Palestinians and their fervent hope that someday their ghurba — as he referred to their exile — would end. He wondered how the Jews, with whom the Palestinians had so much in common, could oppress them so viciously."

"You fell for that rubbish?" Eli muttered.

"Jalil told me about his life since his father died. His mother had been killed by Israeli snipers when he was a baby. When he was orphaned, he had returned to live with the one remaining family member who had not left for Jordan: an elderly uncle who moved from Jericho to the outskirts of Ramallah. His was a childhood of running barefoot in streets littered with the remains of burning tires, of fleeing from soldiers. He would climb the hills and look to the west over the lands which had once belonged to his family and dream of returning to his homeland."

"Jalil was born on the West Bank, not in Israel."

"Palestine was his spiritual home, just as mine is Amsterdam."

"That's different, you —"

"No. All homeless people are the same." Lily went on mingling Palestinian rhetoric with her own pathetic experiences. A week ago Eli would have been utterly confused, but remembering words from Allison's paper, he understood that he was not talking to a rational person. This was someone with a syndrome, a sickness. Ordinary reasoning, judgment, and punishment did not apply. After all, not guilty by reason of insanity was an accepted defense in courts of law.

This was not a court. He was neither judge nor jury. And yet, in one sense, he was both. Lily was a murderer. She was directly responsible for the death of a friend. She had almost killed him and Colin. When Ehud Dani and Alex Naor and the current memuneh heard his story, they would have to eliminate Lily — after they had finished interrogating her — because she was dangerous. At least few lives would be touched by her disappearance. No husband. No child. Not many friends even. In the end, Lily had been right about having children.

They had walked far past the timberline and were making their way across rocky scree slopes. At several points the trail narrowed dramatically and the exposures increased. Facing the steep rock wall, Lily maneuvered skillfully with her hands and feet to avoid either looking down or tripping over the loose rocks. For more than thirty minutes they had not seen anyone coming in either direction. By this time of day most serious climbers had reached the hut and were planning to spend the night in preparation for an early morning assault on one of the nearby peaks. He checked his watch. There was not time to get back down before dark. The Hannig ski lift would be closed, so there would be the additional walk back through the village. Eli's new boots had rubbed several raw spots on his ankles. Physical exhaustion permeated his bones. Mental exhaustion plagued him as he tried to absorb the story that Lily was unfolding.

He stopped to catch his breath. Lily turned and waited for him. He moved up to where she was standing and was suddenly unable to tolerate her passive, smug face. "After Toulon I went to London," he said without controlling the menace in his voice. "How the hell did you know where I would be?"

"I did not."

"Don't give me that shit! You told Jalil who I was, didn't you?"

"Possibly."

Eli lunged for Lily and grabbed her shoulders fiercely. "They followed me from Toulon to Marseille. They must have signaled someone in London. I was tailed through the city. One man could not have done it; they would have needed a team to mark me as accurately as they did."

"Mark you? What are you saying?"

"*I* am asking the questions. Jalil wanted to revenge his father's death by killing me, right?"

Lily pressed her lips closed. For a moment Eli supposed she would not reply and he swung her around so she could face the vast, falling-away edge of the cliff. The gesture was more of a threat than all his words.

"No, he only wanted to stop what you were doing. There were others working with Jalil. Maybe they wanted to get even with you or warn you off or —"

Eli shook her once more. "Who is Jalil aligned with?"

She sputtered out, "A cell based in Europe."

Eli could easily have hurled her down onto the rocks. "Where?"

"They would not tell me anything like that." Her stare was a challenge.

He softened his voice. "Why not? You work for them."

"No," she whispered hoarsely. "I have finished. I have earned my rest."

"While you rest, while you contemplate the ruthless murder of a gentle scientist, will you think sometimes of me having dinner with my son in London and a bomb being placed nearby, killing and maiming innocent people who were not quite so wary, or so fortunate, as we were?"

"I told you!" she screamed. "He promised to use you only as a lead."

"What does Jalil look like? Is he fairly short, even darker-complected than the usual Arab, with black curly hair cut close to his head?"

"That would describe him, I suppose, but others —"

"*That* was the man I saw in Wheeler's, the man with the bomb. Apparently, his blood revenge *did* extend to me. So you see what his promises to you were worth?" Eli's fingers fell from her shoulders. His mouth tightened into a long, defiant line. He clenched his fist and stamped the mud off his boots. He pushed past and hurtled upward onto a slightly wider ledge.

Once they were away from the plunging exposures across the Hohbalmgletscher and had reached a rocky plateau looking out toward the Spielboden ridge, Eli took out his map and showed it to Lily, who was following docilely at his heels. "I think we're about here." He pointed to a spot below a small snow field. "In another twenty minutes or so we should be at the hut. Considering the time, we ought to spend the night."

"I want to go down tonight."

"There are some tricky spots and, frankly, I am too tired to attempt it."

"Then I shall go back on my own."

"After dark? You are being foolish. You are staying with me."

Eli waited for her to argue further, but she fell silent. Once they arrived at the hut there would be no privacy. "Why did you tell me you saw Charlotte in Toulon when you had not?"

"For obvious reasons — to put you off my trail. I knew she had been there. Jalil showed me photos of her, Aviva, most of the other agents in the area. I identified them for his people. They promised not to touch them — or you."

"And you believed them?"

"I did because, well, I admit I knew Jalil was interested in a blood revenge — but not for his father. He explained why the scientist was perfect: first, because you took one of their scientists fairly recently; second, because it pointed up the fact that the war was to be fought on a technological front in the future."

"Did you know Asher Ze'evi was my cousin?"

"No. They did not tell me who they were going after. I did not discover it until later. I made them prove to me they had not harmed you, that they had kept their word."

"What sort of proof did they offer?"

"A photograph."

"When? In Toulon?"

Lily nodded.

"They didn't agree not to harm the rest of us at another time, did they?"

"I did not know!" Lily protested.

"Of course they would not tell you about the revenge for Rashid Salim. They would not have trusted you with that knowledge."

Lily's breath came in long, heaving spasms.

Eli pressed on. "So you falsified the story of Charlotte and two anonymous men to divert my suspicions from you. That was fairly clever. I almost fell for it, and another innocent would have been harmed."

Lily did not respond.

The only sound was the rattle of the gravel beneath their boots until they came around the far side of a ledge where Eli saw an area that, even in May, remained covered with snow. Because the day was warm, the top layer had melted, and now that the afternoon air had cooled, it was potentially quite slippery. Cautiously, he took small steps across the transitional slope from the rocks to the verglas. The incline was fairly gradual, so he had no trouble negotiating the random slick patches. Lily followed closely behind him and he gave her his hand over the worst spots. When they were standing on firmer ground, Eli took stock of their position.

The drop to the glacier was as sheer and steep as any he had ever seen without being on ropes.

Lily follow his gaze. "Oh, my God!" She closed her eyes and fell back against him. Sweat broke out on her forehead. He took her hands in his. They were cold and damp. "I cannot go on."

"Yes, you can. Look! There are cables bolted into the rocks. Take a few steps forward and grab them. That's it. Now hold on tightly and look at *me,* not down. You will make it."

She was petrified. "No, no . . . I am going back."

"Lily, in a very short distance you will be away from the edge."

He looked across the rugged cleft in the earth. In the fading sunlight it was streaked with long blue shadows. The rocky outcroppings were various hues of purple and brown. High above, the summits and spires of the Alphubel and Lenzspitze and Nadelhorn winked hot white for the last time that day. The buttresses of crystalline rock stood out against the sky with sharply defined, austere edges. The clouds were shot with silver.

"I am going to fall . . . I feel . . ." Lily sank to her knees to keep from tumbling away. "It is pulling me . . . Oh, my God . . ."

Eli could see the horror written into her contorted face. Her skin blanched before taking on a greenish tinge. Amidst the jumbled sensations that her revelations had stirred in him during the last hours, pity was predominant.

"Lily . . . I am here. I am with you. The path is quite wide. You are not about to fall. There is more than enough space for you to get by safely. Just rest for a while. Do not move."

For the moment Lily was safely hunched over, her knees bent into the sheer face of the ledge, her cheek resting on a rounded curve of exposed rock. She seemed like a fragile child trying to find comfort against a great granite bosom. The fierce, defiant woman had vanished. In her place was the mere husk of a person so inconsequential an errant breeze could whisk her away. Eli breathed as slowly and as quietly as possible. He did not dare make any loud sounds or quick movements.

Beyond her the mountains extended toward the valley in all their varied forms: névés, or basins in which snow accumulates and turns to ice, succeeded by glacial tongues traversed by tight networks of crevasses to act as the overflows. Great unstable masses of ice séracs gave the appearance of petrified waterfalls. And below the frozen areas, the vast moraines of rocky debris soiled the purity of the slopes. Farther down the gorge, naked brown hills loomed like bony shoulder blades above the tree line, which appeared as the welcoming green carpet that preceded civilization.

The splendor that invigorated him had infused her with terror. Vertigo!

How odd that it should have been listed as one of the symptoms in Allison's paper. This was not the first time he had seen her prostrated in a reaction to heights. She had suffered a similar episode on their gibbush in Zermatt. But she had returned to the hills over and over again, and this is where she had chosen to escape. Why?

"Lily, listen to me . . ." She did not move a muscle. He kept talking. "As I recall, you loved hiking."

"I do . . ." Her voice quavered. " . . . but I always avoid places like this."

"Remember Zermatt? There were areas just as exposed as this one. Do you remember Bernie Petrig?"

"Yes . . ."

"Have you seen him since Zermatt?"

"Twice. He died in a car accident five years ago . . . A mountain road . . . Nobody knows what happened. He was training for the Himalayas."

"Oh," Eli replied and wondered if he should go on about Bernie at a time she did not need to be reminded of a death in these mountains.

Lily spoke again first. "Remember his tales about climbing? The stories of the famous climbers?"

"Very well," Eli replied. "And remember how he helped you with your first fears of heights? Remember how you conquered them?"

"No, I never did. I have never been on ropes again."

"Lily, you managed then, and this is not anywhere near as difficult a situation. There is plenty of room to walk without getting near the edge. Please, if you will only reach up and take the cables in your hands. Yes, that's it. Hold them. Right. Good. Now, take one step toward me. Just one step."

She did. Her hand slid up on the cables. He reached for her and put his left arm around her waist. He held her so closely he could smell the grassy sweetness of her hair, and as he did, tears stung his eyes. He swallowed hard and eased her up the slope another few inches.

"What else do you remember about Bernie?"

Lily's eyes were opening. She blinked and looked at Eli steadily. "Yes . . . Bernie . . . His lofty philosophies, about every victory being a defeat . . ."

Victory. Defeat. He remembered it well. "That's right." He coaxed her on. "Let's go on a bit farther."

"No, I cannot."

Eli clasped her waist even more tightly while gripping the cables with his right hand. "Yes, you can. You *must*. Keep holding the cables with both hands."

She made steady progress for another several steps with him tugging her toward him. "Let me rest for a moment," she panted.

"All right. Take a few deep breaths."

She did as she was told. A pinkness returned to her cheeks, but her lips remained an icy blue. "You believed you were so damn victorious in Toulon. All that time and money and effort to blow up a few crates in a seaside warehouse. A few crates of worthless junk!" Her eyes blazed with renewed energy.

"What are you saying?"

"I was not interested in helping Jalil with his blood revenge. I wanted to help him help the children. They needed that reactor for fuel, not weapons. The children of the Third World require electricity and water and food like the rest of us. Why should they be deprived because of Israel's paranoia? Jalil's group outsmarted you by substituting the crates. The essential parts were in Iraq for a month before you arrived in Toulon and staged your ridiculous vendetta. You see? While you celebrated your victory, they celebrated your defeat — and vice versa."

"Why, then —?"

"The scientist?"

"Yes."

"A token . . . I do not know . . . I am too tired . . ." She closed her eyes.

It took a supreme effort to push this latest blow out of his mind and move onward. The sky had taken on a crimson — almost bloody — tinge. Soon it would be dark. They had to get to the hut. The full weight of her tale could not be absorbed. The only burden he could accept was how to progress the next few critical meters.

Eli pulled her along by sliding her hands on the cables for her. As they rounded a slight curve in the path, something bumped his ankle. He looked down. A small outcropping of rock blocked a portion of the trail. He would need both his hands on the cables to climb over it safely. He relaxed his grip on Lily for a second and peered over his right shoulder. Less than three meters of the treacherous drop remained before they would be on a much wider section of the path that hooked away from the edge.

"Yoffi," he said, slipping into Hebrew unexpectedly. "Ken, ken . . . Lily. You are doing much better, aren't you?"

"Yes," she gasped, "I think I shall be all right." She crept closer to him.

His fingers were barely brushing her belt. They slid away from her back. "I am going to have to hold on with two hands here and then I will help you over this hump when I am past it."

"What hump?" As Lily looked down at where Eli was standing, her eyes were riveted on the vast emptiness in back of him.

"Don't look there!" He repositioned his feet so he could let go with his left hand and reach for her.

But she did not grant him the essential second.

"Eli —" Her right hand jerked free of the cables and extended out to grab onto him.

He saw that he was too far away for her to clutch with her grasping fingers. He stretched his left arm across to her. She was holding on with her free hand, but she had lost balance with her feet. He heard the scraping of gravel and looked down to see her swinging over the edge — away from the trail — then back toward the wall one final time. His arm remained out, a stiff, expectant anchor for her to clasp as she came back around on the inner arc of her oscillation. Her eyes were closed. She could not see him.

Ah, but Eli's eyes were open. Yes, open. And wide and waiting. And watching — like an observer from a faraway point in space.

He saw that her hand did not make the connection.

He did not seem to comprehend he could have moved toward her, he could have made the connection for her.

His free hand fell to his side.

His other hand's hold on the cables tightened. All the while, her ultimate grip loosened: finger . . . by finger . . . by finger . . .

Her eyes flew open and bore into him with a gaze of laserlike clarity in the last millisecond before she slipped inexorably away.

Another falling climber might have called up in the long seconds of twirling and tumbling in the wild free air.

Another falling climber might have protested with loud, shrill, sky-renting screams.

Not Lily.

She fell as she had lived.

In silence.

❖   ❖   ❖

The walk to the hut was effected by simply following the narrow path up and up and up. One step, another step, then another, and another — up and up and up into the cold, slicing air of the night.

The high Alpine peaks loomed as his only witnesses.

He was fine. He was lucid. He knew where he was and where he was going and what he was doing. He moved along vigorously. His breath warming his cool lips told him he was alive and well and walking onward and upward.

All Eli could hear was the eternal hush of oblivion.

Despite the fact that the hut was draped in a light mist, he saw the glow from a long way off. Sometimes it seemed to be floating, a hovering specter, an ethereal presence. As he moved closer it was more of a steady beacon, a greeting of warmth. He opened the heavy timbered door. Heads gathered around a long plank table looked up as if they were attached to the same beast. He spoke very slowly. The climbers quieted in unison. They listened. He was absolutely, perfectly fine.

They gave him soup and brandy and tea, but nothing remained in his stomach. Someone tall and burly and smelling of sweet pipe tobacco held him while he heaved out onto the rocky slopes, ever watchful that he did not stumble or hurt himself. Someone touched his hand all through the night in the coughing, whispering, fire-crackling room. In the morning, even before sunrise, three climbers from the Mischabelhütte escorted Eli down to Saas-Fee, where the rescue team treated him for shock before they set out to search for Lily's body.

Walter Lindt, the innkeeper, came to Eli's room with the news that Lily had been found. He told about the helicopter that went in for her. He described the massive injuries. He repeated over and over how she had not suffered.

But Eli knew better. He had seen her eyes: wide and expectant and fully cognizant of where she was and was not, what he had done — and had not.

And she had fallen a very long way. Perhaps a mathematician could calculate how much time she had actually had to comprehend, digest, store, recall . . . But who could interpret the impact on her brain cells that may have reduced the absorption into minuscule particles, which it then could process faster — like some futuristic computer — so the full import of her last moments could be assimilated before the great inevitable blackness of the end?

The innkeeper was holding an envelope containing something heavy. "These are the valuables she was wearing. We decided you should have them for safekeeping until her family can be contacted."

Eli undid the envelope's clasp and peered inside. There was a brand-new watch, a Baume et Mercier design, a feminine version of his own, and the silver coin on the gold chain. He touched the raised wings of the eagle holding a palm branch on the coin's reverse side and tried to remember its significance.

Herr Lindt kept on speaking. "After the body is examined, arrangements should be made. Do you know where any next of kin might be located?"

"Yes, I mean, no. She has nobody."

"Who will make the decisions regarding burial or transport?"

"I will."

"Forgive me for saying this, but I knew at once you had been close to Lily. She told us this was her hideaway, the place she came to escape the rest of the world. She would not have confided her secret unless she wanted your company."

Eli nodded morosely. Herr Lindt placed his hand on Eli's shoulder solicitously and allowed him to contemplate Lily's jewelry in peace for a few minutes. The coin winked in his hand. It was as cold as ice, as cold as the glacier that had crushed the life from the poor, tortured body. "My silver shekel," she had said at the Café Alpenblick. He asked its age and she had replied, "Two thousand years, give or take a hundred. It is from Tyre. The silver tetradrachm of Tyre."

The silver shekel! All these years, he had never comprehended what she was wearing; perhaps even she had missed the symbolism. Or had she worn it to mock them all?

The silver tetradrachm of Tyre. Two thousand years old, give or take a hundred years — the piece of silver, or thirty pieces of silver . . .

"How may I help?" Herr Lindt was speaking again. "I could contact the French Embassy. They have assisted in the past with other mishaps in the mountains, which, I am sorry to say, are not as infrequent as we might like."

"Pardon me." He had to pretend he was following the conversation. "Why the embassy?"

"Surely she would have wanted to be buried in France."

"Yes, France . . ." He touched the coin again. This time it burnt his palm. He dropped the coin on the table.

The coin spoke.

What would Allison have thought of so blatant a symbol? She might have said it was a Freudian clue. It was Lily announcing that she wanted to be caught and stopped. She had tried to tell the world. Always she had tried. Just as she had made that effort to love him. She had failed because she could not love anything or anyone. The coin had swung at her neck as a punishment. Yes, she had been punishing herself for what she had done to the children in the cellar — or failed to do for them — and her mother, her father, her brothers, little Otto on the death march. She saw herself as a Judas, a betrayer, a survivor!

Judas . . . Eli was attempting to summon his fuzzy recollection of the New Testament while the innkeeper was going on about the logistical problems concerning the disposition of Lily's body.

He saw Eli's ashen face and said, "Shall I come back later?"

"Yes, I think . . . that is for the best . . ."

"I understand entirely. May I bring you something? Coffee? Sandwiches?"

"I do not think I could eat."

"You must. I shall ask the kitchen to prepare some soup and —"

"Could you . . . ?"

"Yes? What would you prefer to eat?"

"Not food. I have another request. Would you have a Bible — in English?"

Ten minutes later the chambermaid knocked on the door. She served him a large bowl of creamy potato soup, slices of air-dried beef, a basket of buttered rolls, and a pot of steaming coffee. On the tray was a Bible.

She tiptoed out.

He leafed through the unfamiliar passages until he found the references to the pieces of silver and Judas in Matthew: "He cast down the pieces of silver in the temple, and departed, and went and hanged himself." The pieces of silver were taken by the priests who said it was not lawful to put them into the treasury because they were the price of blood, so they "bought with them the potter's field, to bury strangers in." Eli knew the location outside the Jaffa Gate, just south of Mount Zion. He had played there as a child.

He finished his reading and the entire contents of the tray before Walter Lindt returned. "Ah, very good," he proclaimed when he saw the empty soup bowl and bread basket. "Now, how may I assist you?"

"I will have to make some calls," Eli said, fully aware that he would again be asking Alex Naor to make complicated arrangements for getting another body to Israel.

"May I help you with the operators? The lines can be difficult sometimes."

"No, thank you. But wait —"

What was it Lily had said when he met her at the café at Hannig? "In a better world I would have been born Swiss . . ."

If she could not be born in Switzerland, she could, at least, be buried there.

"Herr Lindt, you say you have known Lily for many years?"

"That is true."

"Then you know how much she loved this region. Once, years ago, I was with her in Zermatt, and she told me how much she admired its charming graveyard where so many famous climbers are buried. You know the one?"

"But of course.'"

"I believe Lily would have chosen to be buried in a similar place. You must have a cemetery in Saas-Fee."

"Yes, a beautiful one by the church."

The church. Could Eli permit it? To be buried without family, friends. He closed his eyes and reflected on her anger at being Jewish, an anger she had never resolved. But among strangers? He tried to imagine her grave on the Mount of Olives overlooking the Valley of Kidron — the place so many devout Jews yearned to make their final resting place. A traitor facing the Golden Gate? No! That was an obscene idea. Someplace else in Israel? But where would Lily have wanted to be? She was not religious. The bones of her mother and her father and her brothers were strewn in mass graveyards from Amsterdam to Auschwitz to Theresienstadt. No monuments of remembrance marked their final resting places, yet he could imagine Lily's stone carved with only her name and her dates. It would be surrounded by wildflowers in summer, blanketed by pure white snows in winter, caressed by the sweet, pure glacial zephyrs. Ah, Lily . . . so fastidious . . . always trying to clean up the filthy, imperfect places she could not escape. Israel had been far too chaotic for her tidy mind. She had never known peace there. She had said it was not her home. For her, Switzerland was a haven of order. With everything she had said and done, she had rejected Israel and all her friends. She had turned elsewhere. She had come here.

Eli tucked the piece of silver into the breast pocket of his suit jacket. Switzerland, not Israel, is where she had chosen to spend the rest of her days.

And so she would.

THE BENEDICTION

In tragic life, God wot,
No villain need be! Passions spin the plot:
We are betrayed by what is false within.

George Meredith (1828–1909)
Modern Love

LONDON, ENGLAND: MAY 1979

The day after Lily's burial, Eli arrived back in London. The quiet service had been attended by him, the Lindts, a few of the climbers from the Mischabelhütte, and the rescue team, including the American guide who, in the face of tragedy, had lost his obnoxiousness and become a sympathetic friend who arranged both an ecumenical service and great bouquets of wildflowers.

Only one month and one day had passed since Eli had left Colin dazed and bewildered after the blast at Wheeler's. It seemed like an eternity. Eli ached to assure himself that Colin trusted him still. He owed his son an explanation, but he had not contrived a suitable one as he phoned the BBC studios from the airport.

"Television Centre."

"Colin Stewart, please."

"Who shall I say is calling?"

"Charles Ivy."

"Just a moment, please."

"Charles!" Colin's voice gushed. "Where are you?"

"Back in London."

"I suspected you were away again. I've been trying to reach you."

He was stammering. "Great news — you see, we've had the baby."

"Maz——" He stopped himself from saying mazel tov. "Congratulations, Colin. Is it a girl or a boy?"

"Oh, sorry. It's — I mean he's — a boy."

Eli found Colin's bumbling excitement rather charming. It reminded him of the much younger insecure child he had first begun to love. "When was it?"

"Just on Friday, the fourth."

The day after Lily was killed.

"That is marvelous."

"Listen, Charles, I would love for you to see him. He's quite a splendid chap." Colin rushed on. "In fact, ah . . . I'm leaving to go and see Emily shortly. Could you meet me at University College Hospital?"

"Yes, I don't see why not."

"The maternity division. It's between Gower Street and Tottenham Court Road. Do you know where that is?"

"Approximately. What time?"

"Would an hour be too soon?"

"No, that would be fine."

"And Charles . . ."

"Yes?"

"I'm awfully glad to hear from you. I've been rather concerned — since the last time —"

"And I about you, Colin. See you soon."

"Right, and thank you."

Eli leaned against the wall and took a few long breaths. His son had had a baby. He was a grandfather! He wanted to buy the child some lavish, useless gift like a giant blue rabbit, but he could not. It would have been out of character. Charles Ivy had never once given Colin a personal gift. He went out to find a cab.

When he arrived, Colin was already in the waiting room. Bluish-gray rings framed his eyes. He must have lost several nights' sleep during Emily's confinement. Eli longed to ask for the details, but again, he was not a member of the family and his questions might be considered too intimate.

"Hello, Charles. So good of you to come." As Colin shook Eli's hand, Eli was surprised to find it so moist.

"Wonderful to see you, Colin, but I must say you are looking awfully tired."

"It has been a rough week. Emily went through a night or two of what they call false labor — sort of a rehearsal for the big moment — but we couldn't tell the difference. We came to be checked by the midwife three times before they let us stay. In the end, it went swiftly enough."

"She's well?"

"Oh, quite. This natural childbirth business worked out wonderfully, for us at least. The midwife was amazingly kind and I tried to play my part, even if I did look ridiculous in the bright green gown with a big red cross on the front. Afterward, when Emily was holding him, the midwife brought in biscuits and coffee and we had a little celebration. I could not believe it. One moment there were the two of us, the next we were a family. And the baby! He has the most fantastic big blue eyes and he looked at me right off. I don't know about this nonsense that babies cannot see. *My* son stared at *me* as if I was the most incredible sight on the planet and, well, excuse me for rambling on — I guess I haven't come down off my high yet." Colin paused to catch his breath. His eyes darted back and forth as if he could not quite decide where to go or what to say next. He cleared his throat and began in a slow, raspy voice, "Listen, you have got to see him for yourself. I'll take you upstairs, all right?"

Eli nodded agreeably. He could not wait to see what his grandson looked like.

"Ah, I did not call to warn Emily you were coming" — he looked away from Eli as if searching for someone else in the room — "but she should be presentable. Mum's up with her now." Colin turned back and gave Eli his full attention.

"Her mother?"

"No . . . mine." His eyes blinked with recognition. "That's right, you've never met my parents, have you?"

Eli glanced at his watch. "I might not have time after all. I need to get to the City by . . . "

"Charles . . ." Colin was steering him to a far side of the waiting room. Colin took a seat on a plastic sofa and gestured for him to do the same. "Forgive me for lying to you."

"What?"

"I had not planned to do this today . . . but . . . I have been thinking of how to approach you for the longest time. The last time we were together I had just about got up my courage. I was going to say something after we left Wheeler's — but then, you know what happened. I promised myself the next time I saw you —" Colin's face had purpled. "I was so worried after the explosion — I was frightened I had almost lost my chance — that it was possible that I might never get to see you again." He pulled out a handkerchief and patted his forehead. "Gosh, I didn't expect this would be so difficult. Listen, Charles . . . My mother is not upstairs. Neither is Emily. She and the baby went home yesterday. I lied to you. I wanted to see how you would react if you were about to meet my mother. I had to discover whether . . . I am fairly certain that . . . well, the truth: that you are my . . . my father . . ."

Eli blanched. How could he have discovered his secret? He gazed at Colin. The man was trembling. Eli was at a loss as to what to say, how to help.

Then, Colin's arms were outstretched. Eli reached out to him. The two men locked in a tearful embrace. In any other public place they might have felt acute embarrassment, but here, in the waiting room of a hospital, it was perfectly natural for intense emotions to burst out of their conventional confinements. Nobody paid them the least attention.

After a moment, the two men parted slightly, but clasped each other's hands. "How did you find me out?" Eli choked.

"I have been working on the problem for years. I was not absolutely confident until a few minutes ago when you tried to avoid meeting up with my mother. It all began when Mum told me that tale about my father being Jewish. I tied that in with her earlier remark about my father having gone to Perse and wasted quite some time trying to locate a Jewish Perse boy who had also died in the war. Nobody fit the description. I know Mother said she could have been wrong about Perse, but you see, my mother is not the kind who ever forgets anything, let alone something so significant. Surely she would have remembered the school my father attended, don't you think?"

Eli was nodding to confirm Colin's analysis while thinking: He's more like me than I ever expected.

"Thus, I preferred to believe my father was alive. Of course, I kept my thoughts to myself because I knew it might be a childish fantasy — like my dreams of becoming a race car driver or a famous film director. Funnily enough, the more I considered it, the more plausible it seemed. One reason it made sense to me was because of my mother's reluctance to tell me his name. If my father had been *dead,* it would not have mattered; if he was *alive,* she would be protecting him, or me — I was not sure which.

"I made so many Jewish friends, my mother started to complain.

Isn't that curious, I mean, when she herself had a Jewish lover? Instead of deterring me, her worries spurred me on. Well, most children react the same, I've been told. But in my case I felt more comfortable with my Jewish pals than with the others. Can you understand that? When I met Emily I knew what I wanted."

Eli was too speechless to fill in the long pause, so Colin plunged bravely onward. "I would have supposed an obsession with my mystery dad would have faded with the love and stability Emily brought into my life, but the opposite happened. After I was married, it became even more important to know who I was. I decided our child would be Jewish because of Emily and to honor my father — whoever he might be. When I explained this to Mum, she warned I would be doing the child a gross injustice, but Mum can be quite fanatical sometimes. Emily told me that might be my clue, even though I did not see what she had meant."

Eli nodded. "Yes, go on . . ."

"Did you know a woman named Jocelyn Loughlin? Or rather Jocelyn . . . what was her maiden name?"

"Sedgewick."

"Right. Well, Jocelyn remained a good friend of my mother's. She had two gorgeous daughters by this guy from Aberdeen. He was the headmaster of a school there, but she couldn't tolerate either him or Scotland and eventually divorced him. Today she lives not far from Mum and Dad. Anyway, when she moved to London I asked her about you, but she wouldn't breathe a word. Not your name, or what you were like, or where you were from. Finally, I asked if you had actually died in the war. She refused to reply. Since I was merely asking for confirmation of my mother's story, it would have been a simple matter for her to corroborate it, but she would not. So, I deduced she did not want to lie to me. That meant you *were* alive."

"How did you know it was me? After all, 'Ivy' isn't the most Jewish of names." He laughed nervously.

"I didn't have any way of *knowing*. I *wanted* it to be you. I admired you so much as a boy and appreciated your interest in me. When Randy was tough on me, I'd think of you coming to my rescue. Then when you stayed in touch after Perse, after university — all these years — it seemed what a *father* would do. Besides, I did lots of checking up over the years. I used to volunteer to sweep the records office at Perse and once searched their scholarship files for references to the Threadneedle Street Society, but never found a clue any-where, which I thought curious. A few years later, I even had a jour-nalist friend teach me how to track down the background of your London office, but all I found were dead ends. Russell and Sutton Limited is a front, isn't it? You never wanted me to find out, did you?"

"No. I wanted to protect you."

"And yourself?"

"Believe me, Colin, there is nothing I would rather have done than declare myself to you. But how could I have? As a child, you would have been confused and hurt and it would have interfered with your relationship with your parents. After that, it was too late. How could I tell you that everything I had ever said to you was an untruth?"

"No, I meant quite literally that you needed to protect yourself. You're in some sort of dangerous business. Charles Ivy isn't your true name. That bomb in Wheeler's, it was meant to harm you."

Eli was very quiet. "What do you want to know?" he asked finally.

"Everything."

"There is so much. Where should I begin?"

"With my mother and you during the war perhaps?"

"All right. I loved your mother and wanted nothing more than to marry her. She would not have me because of my background, so she went to look for someone who would accept her and the baby. She made short work of the project when she found your father in hospi-tal."

"I know most of that part."

"I did not abandon her. That is what I have wanted you to know. Whether or not we could have had a good life together, well, that's another question. I suspect we'd have made a muddle of it in the end."

"Who are you really? What's your name?"

Eli grinned. "I am the son of a British superintendent of police named Hugo Short who served under Allenby in the Middle East. There he met a wonderful woman named Ruth Epstein and they lived their own version of happily ever after in Palestine. They had one son, a boy they named Elliot. I was christened Elliot Short."

"You were christened? Aren't you Jewish?"

"They had their own confusions over the matter of religion. I even had two names. In Palestine, I was called Eli, Eli Katzar. Later it was decided I would be raised Jewish in Palestine, Christian in

England, and that I would make my own decision when the time came."

"What did you decide?"

"My sympathies were always with my mother's people. I grew up to consider myself a Jew."

"So you aren't Elliot any longer? I should call you Eli?"

"Yes, why not?"

"I would like to call you Father, but that would not be fair to Randy. He's a sweet old fellow who has tried to do his best by me."

"You are very considerate to put it that way."

"Eli . . ."

"Yes?"

"I was just trying it out." He beamed. "You're not who you said you were — you do something quite unusual, right?"

"I work for the Israeli government."

"And you cannot say anything more."

"Not here, not today, but someday soon I hope I can tell you a great deal more. The best apology I can offer you would be the truth."

Colin looked up at the large clock on the waiting room wall. "I have a screening this afternoon. But before I go, I must tell you another reason I was so anxious to see you. I — Emily and I — would very much like you to be present at the brit . . . to hold the baby and all that. I have never been to one, so I am not certain what's involved but —"

"Colin, I am honored, but you must see that it's impossible."

"Why? Now that everything is out in the open —"

"You are forgetting your mother."

"I can handle her."

Eli's eyebrows arched dramatically. "I am certain you know her far better than I do, but she's bound to be upset if you drag in your long-lost father at such an important moment for your entire family. She cannot feel particularly proud of her past and she certainly would not want it flaunted in front of all your friends and relations."

"Nobody besides Mother and Emily need be told exactly who you are. Anyway, lots of people know about my scholarships."

"I hardly think your mother would want me there."

"I'm not worried about *her*. I think she has suspected the truth about you. I have made it a point to tell her about our continuing association over the years. She has made it a point not to question me further, and believe me, that is out of character for a woman who thrives on knowing exactly who is doing what with whom every minute of the day and night. No. I'm positive she suspected you came into my life from the moment I was accepted by Perse."

"Randolph Stewart, won't he be upset?"

"I'll let Mother decide what to tell him. But I will not press you. I would like to have you there as a link in a chain that has been broken for far too long. But if you cannot see your way to do it, I will also understand." Colin stood up and smoothed his jacket.

"Colin, you may have been planning all this for some time, but I am quite shaken by the suddenness. Not that I am displeased. On the contrary, I am overjoyed to be able to tell you . . . to finally . . . to say . . . that I love you. I always have."

Colin's eyes glistened. "I know that; otherwise you would not have . . . all these years . . . ." He sniffed and swallowed. "Won't you at least think it over?"

"Yes, I will. When is the brit?"

"On the eighth day; that would be Friday, the day after tomorrow. It will be at our flat. Very small. Only the immediate family and a few friends."

Eli also rose to his feet. "I will ring you tomorrow."

Outside the hospital Colin was more composed than Eli. "Which way are you going?" he asked.

"Kensington."

"Didn't you say the City?"

"It's an old habit to say the opposite; forgive me."

"You don't have to explain. We will have to take separate cabs then, that's all."

A taxi was discharging its passengers at the hospital entrance. "Why don't you take it? You're more in a rush than I am," Eli suggested.

"Thanks, I will." Colin headed for the curb.

"Wait!" Eli dashed after him. "The baby — what is his name to be?"

"Oh, I almost forgot —" Colin reached for the open door of the taxi to claim it. "He's to be called Charles. I wanted to name him after you — no matter how it turned out. He is Charles Isaac — unless you mind."

Eli was so startled he could not respond. Tears streamed down his face. The taxi door closed and Colin drove away.

❖   ❖   ❖

Eli's cab turned into Palace Green and pulled directly up to the Israeli Embassy. Normally, Eli would have taken a more circumspect route. Form no longer mattered. Eli paid the fare and strolled up to the gate. A television camera recorded every movement.

"Shalom," he said into the microphone. In Hebrew he gave his name and a code number, and asked for Alex Naor. There was a two-minute pause before the gate buzzed open. At the front door another camera monitored him. All this security was mandatory. A letter bomb had killed the agricultural attaché several years earlier and other attempts were frequent reminders of the necessity for perpetual vigilance. Weary at the idea of this endless cycle of senseless destruction, Eli leaned on the door and waited. The knob had an electrical switch that eventually was pressed to allow his entry to the antechamber.

As in so many similar installations, a guard sat behind a bullet-proof glass. Idly, Eli wondered how many schools could be built, orchestras endowed, children fed, with the payroll of Israel's security forces alone. More questions in Hebrew. He was being photographed. Eli handed his Israeli passport through the slot.

This time the door to the great hall of the embassy was opened by a human being. "Shalom, Eli," said Ehud Dani. "Come this way."

They walked through the conference room with the Montefiore portrait into the ambassador's private office. Alex Naor was standing at attention. "Eli . . ." He held out his hand.

Eli remained motionless. Alex took two large strides toward him and placed his hands on Eli's shoulders warmly. He spoke solicitously. "Eli, it is good to have you back."

Eli felt a knife twisting in his gut. A vile taste filled his mouth. He backed away from Alex.

Dani moved beside him. "You are looking so much better than the last time I saw you, in New York. It must come as a great relief —"

"Charlotte. What did you —?"

Dani's arm was around Eli's shoulder. He led him to the sofa. He sat down beside him. "No. I never saw Charlotte. There was no point in creating a problem where none existed."

Alex stood by a table and shuffled some decoded reports. Eli was certain they were the brief notes he had transmitted with the news of Lily's accidental death. Alex held up his hands — palms out. "Ein breira," he said sadly. "You took the only alternative."

"It was not like that . . ."

"You need not explain. We are convinced you handled the situation as — shall we say — economically as possible. Of course, we do not question your judgment as to her guilt."

Eli was sickened by Alex's uncharacteristic obsequiousness. "You always knew it was Lily?"

"Frankly, we were not positive," Dani interjected. "Some clues led to Aviva, some to Lily; a few did not add up at all."

"That is why we had to involve you," Alex added. "I am sorry we were so rough on you, but unless you felt cornered, we did not think you would ever begin to believe it could be a member of your team. That is quite understandable. It is human nature to protect our own. We hope you can now view the predicament from our perspective. How were we to break down your stubborn resistance to facing reality without backing you into a corner, putting you on the spot, as they say?"

Eli stared at Alex. The man's jaw was tightly set, with his lips thinned to a mean line. The only perceptible movement was a muscular spasm in front of his ears betraying the fact that he was clenching his teeth as he anticipated Eli's response. Eli glared back contemptuously.

"There are two parts to forgiveness," Eli's mother once said after there had been a terrible fight between him and his father. Displeased by Eli's refusal to instantly obey some order, Hugo had taken a precious toy drum and hurled it across the room, smashing it. Eli had never forgotten his anger of the moment. It had exploded inside his head; his eyes had seen crimson, then black. He had pummeled his father's chest with impotent fists and had been half dragged, half carried to his room, where he had sobbed himself into an aching state of semiconsciousness.

Later, his mother had come in with a glass of juice. After one sip, he gagged.

His mother rubbed his back and spoke in a voice as smooth as treacle. "The first part is the most difficult. You must throw away the black feeling." How had she defined it so precisely? "Give it away. Refuse to allow it to remain in your life. It is like doing surgery on yourself — a painful, yet necessary, step."

"I don't think I . . ." he moaned.

"You have great strength. Call on it now. You will surprise yourself."

"Have *you* ever done it?"

"Forgiven someone?"

"Yes."

"Many times."

"Your own papa?"

"Yes."

"What did he do?"

"That is not important." Her eyes had stared off in the distance. "Living with someone is a constant series of small reprieves. Most are inconsequential."

"My drum was *not* inconsequential!"

"No, I understand that." She was very quiet.

Finally, he whispered, "What is the second part?"

"The hardest, actually. You must help the person who hurt you overcome his own feelings of culpability."

"What do you mean?"

"Your father needs you to tell him not to feel so upset with himself."

"I don't want to do that."

"That is why it is so difficult. If you do not do anything about it, the discord is not over, and unless it is finished, unless the circle is closed, the problem will linger. Both parties will continue to suffer. You are the only one with the power to put an end to it."

"But how?"

"By accepting your part in the blame."

"I did not throw the drum!"

"No, but you provoked your father."

Eli had seen her point. She had left him alone to sort it out, and it was not until the afternoon of the next day that he had found the words — and the courage — to tell his father he was no longer angry.

At this moment, Alex was not as formidable as his father, but Eli's feelings of revulsion were far more intense.

The right words began to form on Eli's lips. Even though one part of him wanted to restrain them, the other side — the part his mother had nurtured — permitted them to spill out. "I would have done the same if I had been in your position, Alex. You also had no choice."

Alex's jaw slackened. "That's very gracious of you, Eli."

"Not at all." The pressure in his own chest diminished slightly. He *was* giving it up — not totally, never fully, but for the present, the relief was immense.

"Why, Eli? That is what I keep asking myself." Dani's voice was hoarse with emotion. "I cannot discern a motive."

"She never had one."

"It had nothing to do with you?" Alex asked.

"No, not really. The explanation is very complex, but I will embark on it if you wish." He slid down into the softness of the red leather sofa and rubbed his eyes with the back of his hand.

"Not now," Alex said kindly. "We can see you are exhausted."

"Why wait? I need to be done with this."

"As you wish, Eli; it shall be as you wish."

Two hours later, he had begun to sort out the effects of what he believed was Lily's acute form of post-traumatic stress disorder on her behavior over the years, with emphasis on her reactions since Jericho. Alex and Ehud seemed to follow his theories, but they were reluctant to accept the part little Otto had played in her derangement.

"It does not matter what her problem was, does it?" Alex summarized. "She confessed, she was guilty, and you have efficiently dispatched the problem."

"You have done us a great service," Dani agreed. He stood and excused himself.

Eli bristled at the perfunctory, businesslike finale.

Alex opened the door for Dani. "I need to talk with you alone briefly; then Ehud will take you to a suite at a nearby hotel. A meal has been ordered. I hope you will not mind an enormous steak dinner."

Eli nodded numbly.

"Take a few days off; then come in and we will assist you with the reports. I have Ehud working on them already, so they should not be too much of a strain. After that . . ." His tone was that of a mother tempting her child with a special treat. ". . . there is a new project I would like to talk to you about."

"New project?"

"Well, well . . . you *are* curious? All right, I will give you the highlights; then you must go and have your meal." He unrolled a chart on the ambassador's desk.

Slowly, Eli stood and made his way across the room. He peered down. It was a map of Iraq. Alex was pointing to a spot southeast of Baghdad marked Tuwaitha. It was the site where Iraq's seventy-five-megawatt nuclear reactor was being built. Eli had not yet informed Alex that the crates that their group had destroyed had not contained the pressure vessel for the atomic fuel rods and other crucial reactor parts.

"Operation Babylon," Alex announced excitedly. "We are not going to attack this monster piecemeal any longer. We are going after the beast itself! Not tomorrow, of course. A year or two from now, when it is virtually complete — but before it is fueled — we will make a pre-emptive strike by air and blast it back into fragments of sand. A five-minute blitzkrieg will demolish Osiraq once and for all!"

"A commandolike raid — get in and out fast, right?"

Alex nodded confidently.

"You're crazy! You cannot send commandos almost eighteen hundred kilometers round trip and not expect to be detected by enemy radar numerous times along the route."

"The planes would be very fast; they would fly extremely low."

"How low? At less than fifty meters above ground level across one of the most inhospitable deserts of the world for at least an hour in each direction with no place to either land or hide safely?" Eli's voice rose to an almost hysterical pitch.

"Eli, calm yourself. We are in the earliest planning stages. Do not forget how many times we have pulled off the impossible — in Entebbe and —"

"Entebbe!" Eli shouted, then paused as he remembered Charlotte's diatribe on how exploits like that one made Israelis feel falsely invincible. "Surprise was the key element there. We cannot expect to pull off the same trick twice."

"We are welcoming your input. Surely you are aware that this mission is one *you* should be heading — when you are rested, of course."

"I will not be running any more missions. In fact, I will not be working for our government any longer. I plan to tender my resignation tomorrow."

"Eli, you cannot! You are needed. Only you have the background, the ability, to handle Operation Babylon. We need you."

"I have nothing more to offer. You will have to find someone else." Eli stretched his arms behind his back. Every bone in his body ached. Since his ordeal on the mountain, he could not walk without a severe pain shooting down his left leg. Yes, he needed to rest, but not for a few hours or days. He was finished with the likes of Dani and Naor — and the rest. He had worked long past his prime; otherwise none of this would have gotten so far out of hand. He was tired. He was dispirited. His career should have ended on a more exultant note. But it could not have. As long as he was sliding by, he would have continued onward, never believing he could be fallible.

Today he knew he was.

He was accountable for the life of Asher Ze'evi. He had misjudged Charlotte. The Toulon operation was a mockery. And he had lost Lily — not a few days ago, but years and years earlier — and had been too self-absorbed to have caught any of the myriad clues. He slipped his hand into his trousers pocket. He touched the silver shekel. He would carry it always — lest he forget.

Alex was babbling on with patriotic slogans about peace and protection and the future of the Jewish nation.

Eli turned his back on Alex.

It was far easier walking out of the embassy than walking in.

Forgiveness. His mother's lecture had been prominent in his mind after his affair with Maura. Resenting Maura had drained him at first, but in a year or two, the dark, choking sensations had faded significantly. An acceptance had been possible, yet without a confrontation, he had never been able to take the second step his mother had advocated. And while it had been a relief not to have had to face her, he regretted that the final chapter had never been written so the book could have been closed forever. What had helped him was the fresh knowledge about his parents' marriage, which had placed his disappointment with Maura in perspective.

Forgiveness.

His mother had surrounded the word with shimmering importance. His child's mind had supposed a mother's own experience in granting absolution would have been about matters as petty as his drum. After Maura, Eli knew — without being told — that his mother had forgiven his father for much, much more: for drinking excessively, for some of his other obnoxious habits, and, most especially, for having slept with other women. That had to be the reason behind her remote glances and long sighs. It explained so many other conciliations: why Hugo had remained in Jerusalem when he had always expected to retire to England, and maybe even why they had only had the one child.

After Maura, Eli had known that there was always a woman. Or women, he mused wryly. The mysterious women who had clutched his father's heart as Maura had gripped his. And while he had believed he had assimilated that lesson viscerally, he had just discovered that when it had come to Lily, he had forgotten everything he had ever learned.

❖   ❖   ❖

Eli guessed which apartment Colin lived in from the sounds of laughter emanating from it when he stepped out of the elevator. A baby's cry was further proof. The door was partially open. He let himself in. From the foyer, he scanned the room. He recognized the single braid down Emily's back. She was wearing a long blue skirt and a checkered blouse. She did not notice him.

In the dining room on the left two women were setting out the final touches for a buffet luncheon; a third was lighting candles in preparation for the ceremony. Colin came out of the bedroom followed by a bearded man carrying some towels, a pillow, and a medical kit. Eli knew this must be the mohel, the man who would perform the ritual circumcision.

Colin noticed Eli standing by the door. "Charles! I am so glad you could come."

Eli was pleased they had decided not to introduce "Eli" publicly quite yet. Only Eli, Colin, Emily, and Maura would share the secret that day.

"Rabbi Weinstein, I would like you to meet my . . . my friend, Charles Ivy. He will be the baby's godfather."

Eli greeted the mohel. The two men shook hands.

"So you are the sandek," Rabbi Weinstein said, his bright blue eyes flashing merrily. "Good. Have you ever done this before?"

"No, but I am familiar with the procedures."

"Excellent. I will be with you shortly." He tried to walk away, but Eli's hand had locked on his so tightly the mohel had to extricate himself. "I need to find a chair for the prophet Elijah. Pardon me."

Eli had not heard him. His eyes had fixed on a familiar profile.

Maura's auburn hair had long since turned to a pure silver. Her hips had widened and her face was lined with more than her share of harsh wrinkles. She saw Eli staring at her from across the room and gave him a shy smile.

Slowly, she came toward Eli. Her movements had remained graceful. She extended her hand and he reached his out to meet hers. "So glad you could join us, Elliot," she said with genuine affability. "Colin could not be happier."

"I am glad to be here . . . for him," he managed to say in what anyone might consider a normal voice, "but, remember, we decided it would be simpler if I remained Charles Ivy for this occasion."

Maura was flustered. "Sorry . . ." Her mouth twisted tensely.

Emily passed by, carrying a bundle wrapped in a white blanket. "Oh, you are here at last!" She beamed. "Have you seen our darling Charles?" She unwrapped the fuzzy folds to reveal the baby's round, squirming face. Eli was awed by the sight of the precious child. "I'm going to give Charles a quick feed. Don't you think that's best?" she queried her mother-in-law.

"That sounds sensible to me, dear."

"No, no," another woman interjected, "his stomach should be empty, so when they give him some wine to calm him, it will take effect quickly."

"Oh, Mum, I hadn't thought of that." Emily remembered that Eli did not know her mother. "I would like you to meet my mother, Selma Applebaum. Mum, this is Colin's friend Charles Ivy."

"A pleasure to meet you. If you will excuse me, I am going to have to get some water for your grandmother, Emily; she has become very demanding all of a sudden."

"Shall I help you change the baby?" Maura asked.

"That's not necessary. I have his clothing all laid out."

Eli touched the infant's surprisingly thick hair with his fingertips before Emily whisked him away.

"What a gorgeous baby we have!" Maura announced matter-of-factly.

We have! *Our* baby, our grandson. Eli's eyes brimmed.

Maura led him into the dining room and poured him a glass of wine. "I think the adults need this more than the baby."

"You are right about that."

"I have never been to one of these ceremonies before, so I am going to remain in the bedroom with Emily and her mother. I could not endure watching the baby being cut."

"I will be holding him."

"So Colin told me. I am glad of that. The baby should be held by someone who loves him — not a stranger."

Eli gazed into Maura's green eyes and caught her emotions tumbling together: her mistake, her guilt, and her bid for redemption. The second step. He could finally complete the task, close the circle.

Oh, Maura, I do forgive you.

He hoped he was conveying as much meaning with his own expressions as she was with hers, for — at that moment — he could not find the words to say more than "I will be with him, I promise."

"What are your plans?" She broke the spell with her sensible voice. "Will you be staying in London? Colin has not caught me up completely, but I understand you travel a great deal."

"No longer. I am planning to retire — actually, I suppose I have retired."

"That is wonderful for you. Where will you be living?"

Eli realized he had not thought further than this very moment. Ever since he had walked out of the Israeli Embassy, the next hurdle had been the brit. There was no time to invent a response. The mohel was asking for the baby. Colin was going into the bedroom. The visitors were being organized by a bald man Eli presumed was Emily's father — the other grandfather.

Where will you be living?

Maura's lingering question had demanded an answer, but Maura was excusing herself and Colin's hand was on his shoulder. "Charles, we are ready for you."

"Yes, I will be right there . . ."

Maura was staring up at him. Her emerald eyes were large and luminous and compassionate. "We will talk later," she said as she drifted off.

The mohel took charge. He spoke first to Emily. "Give the boy to his maternal grandmother."

Emily handed Charles to her mother, then walked hesitantly from the room.

"Mrs. Applebaum, would you please hand the baby to your husband." Charles did not flinch as he was lifted by another set of arms.

"Now, Mr. Applebaum, place the baby in the chair of Elijah, the prophet who is called the angel of the covenant and who protects little children." The mohel's tone switched from the pragmatic to the lofty. "This chair is set aside in honor of the prophet Elijah, may his remembrance be for the good," he said first in Hebrew, then in English. The grandfather gently lowered the baby onto a pillow on the chair. He stepped back. The mohel touched Eli's shoulder.

Eli lifted the pillow and baby in one sweeping motion. Everyone present stood and joined the mohel in saying, "Baruch ha-ha. May he who cometh be blessed."

Gently, Eli eased himself onto the table where he was supposed to sit with the baby. Mr. Applebaum placed some heavy books under Eli's feet to support them. Once Eli was situated, the baby was at a good height for the mohel to perform his duties. The blanket was un-wrapped.

"The Holy One, praised be He, said to our father Abraham: 'Walk thou before Me and be thou perfect.' " The mohel continued exultantly, "Praised be Thou, O Lord our God, King of the Universe, who has sanctified us with Thy commandments, and commanded us concerning the rite of circumcision."

Eli stared down at the baby. He was sleeping. His tiny eyeballs twitched behind their translucent lids. Eli bent over and kissed a spot behind his delicate ear. The sweet smell filled him with an immense longing.

A hush descended on the room.

Eli eased the child's thighs apart with one hand. With the other he drew Charles as close to his own body as possible. Then he repeated after the mohel, "Praised be Thou, O Lord our God, King of the Universe, who has sanctified us by Thy commandments, and has bidden us to make him enter into the covenant of Abraham our father."

The other men in the room responded over the cries of the startled infant, "As he has been entered into the convenant, so may he be introduced to the study of the Torah, to the chupah, and to good deeds."

The mohel continued with the blessing of the wine and the naming of the child. "Our God and God of our fathers, preserve this child to his father and to his mother, and let his name be called in Israel: Chaim Yitzhak ben Avraham."

The baby squirmed and screamed lustily. The mohel raised his voice. "Yea, I said: 'In thy blood thou shalt live.' "

Emily's father stepped forward with a piece of gauze that had been dipped in a mild solution of wine and water. The baby took a few long sucks.

Eli looked down at Charles, his baby grandson . . . his bloodline. Rabbi Weinstein's prayers faded and the great roaring in his ears was all-encompassing. The room turned cold. For a second he was gripped by the same tingling sensation he had felt as Lily disappeared into the abyss. He was back on the ledge, holding tightly onto the cables. The lights dimmed.

"And it is said: 'He hath remembered His covenant forever, the word which He commanded to a thousand generations . . .' Hodu l'Adonai kee tov, kee l'olam chasdo. O give thanks unto the Lord; for He is good; for His loving kindness endureth forever."

The blackness lifted. The roar subsided. The baby's crying ceased. "Let us say Amen."

"Amen," chorused the witnesses.

Eli kissed the infant Charles once again before Mrs. Applebaum returned and reached for the bundle proprietarily. Eli stepped out of the center of the group and grappled with how he would respond to Maura's question.

Emily's relatives and some of her friends spontaneously broke into song and chanted "Siman tov, u-mazel tov" over and over. Eli joined in mindlessly, and as he did, he suddenly knew what he would say when someone asked him politely where he was going next. The answer had always been there; he just hadn't stopped long enough to absorb it.

With tears in her eyes, Emily took her baby from her mother. She was surrounded by guests admiring the child. Then Emily's parents paused to speak with him. Eventually, Maura, accompanied by her husband and daughters, joined the group that had moved into the dining room. Maura did not have a chance to repeat her question, but Emily did.

They were drinking wine and tasting the delicacies. Emily was only being polite — the way Maura had been — yet when she asked him where he was going, what he would be doing next, Eli was more than ready with his answer.

His expression was joyful, his voice firm. "I am going to live in New York," he said.

POSTSCRIPT

On the seventh of June 1981, Israeli aircraft attacked and destroyed the Iraqi Osiraq nuclear reactor at Tuwaitha.

―――――――

FROM THE STATEMENT BY
THE REVOLUTIONARY COMMAND COUNCIL OF IRAQ

Baghdad: 8 June 1981

In the name of god, the merciful, the compassionate . . .

Compatriots, today we declare that the Zionist enemy planes yesterday carried out an air raid on Baghdad . . .

O brothers, sons of Iraq and sons of the Arab nation . . .

They will not shake this giant revolution from its determination to be one with the masses and to express hopes and aspirations. The men who have been able through their loyalty to their people and nation, their faith in their cause and their minds and efforts, to bring Iraq's nuclear potential up to the standard which created this amount of rancor and blatant aggression by the Zionist and Persian enemies make us confident that they are also capable of continuing this trend no matter what our enemies can achieve in their attempts to do direct or indirect harm.

The road Iraq has taken in its victorious revolution — the road of freedom, independence and progress, the road of cohesion between the leadership and the masses — will not be abandoned. This road will remain wide open.

God willing, victory to our heroic people and glory to our Arab nation.

FROM THE STATEMENT BY THE ISRAELI GOVERNMENT

Jerusalem: 8 June 1981

The Israeli Air Force yesterday attacked and destroyed the Osiraq nuclear reactor, which is near Baghdad. All our planes returned home safely.

The government finds itself obligated to explain to enlighten public opinion why it decided on this special operation.

For a long time, we have followed with grave concern the construction of the Osiraq nuclear reactor. Sources of unquestioned reliability told us that it was intended, despite statements to the contrary, for the production of atomic bombs.

The goal for these bombs was Israel . . .

Within a short time, the Iraqi reactor would have been in operation and hot. In such conditions, no Israeli government could have decided to blow it up. This would have caused a huge wave of radioactivity over the city of Baghdad and its innocent citizens would have been harmed.

We were, therefore, forced to defend ourselves against the construction of an atomic bomb in Iraq, which itself would not have hesitated to use it against Israel and its population centers.

Therefore, the Israeli government decided to act without further delay to ensure the safety of our people.

The planning was precise. The operation was set for Sunday on an assumption that the 100 to 150 foreign experts who were active on the reactor would not be there on the Christian day of rest. The assumption proved correct. No foreign expert was hurt.

Two European governments were helping the Iraqi dictator in return for oil to manufacture nuclear weapons. Once again we call on them to desist from this terrible and inhuman act.

On no account shall we permit an enemy to develop weapons of mass destruction against the people of Israel.